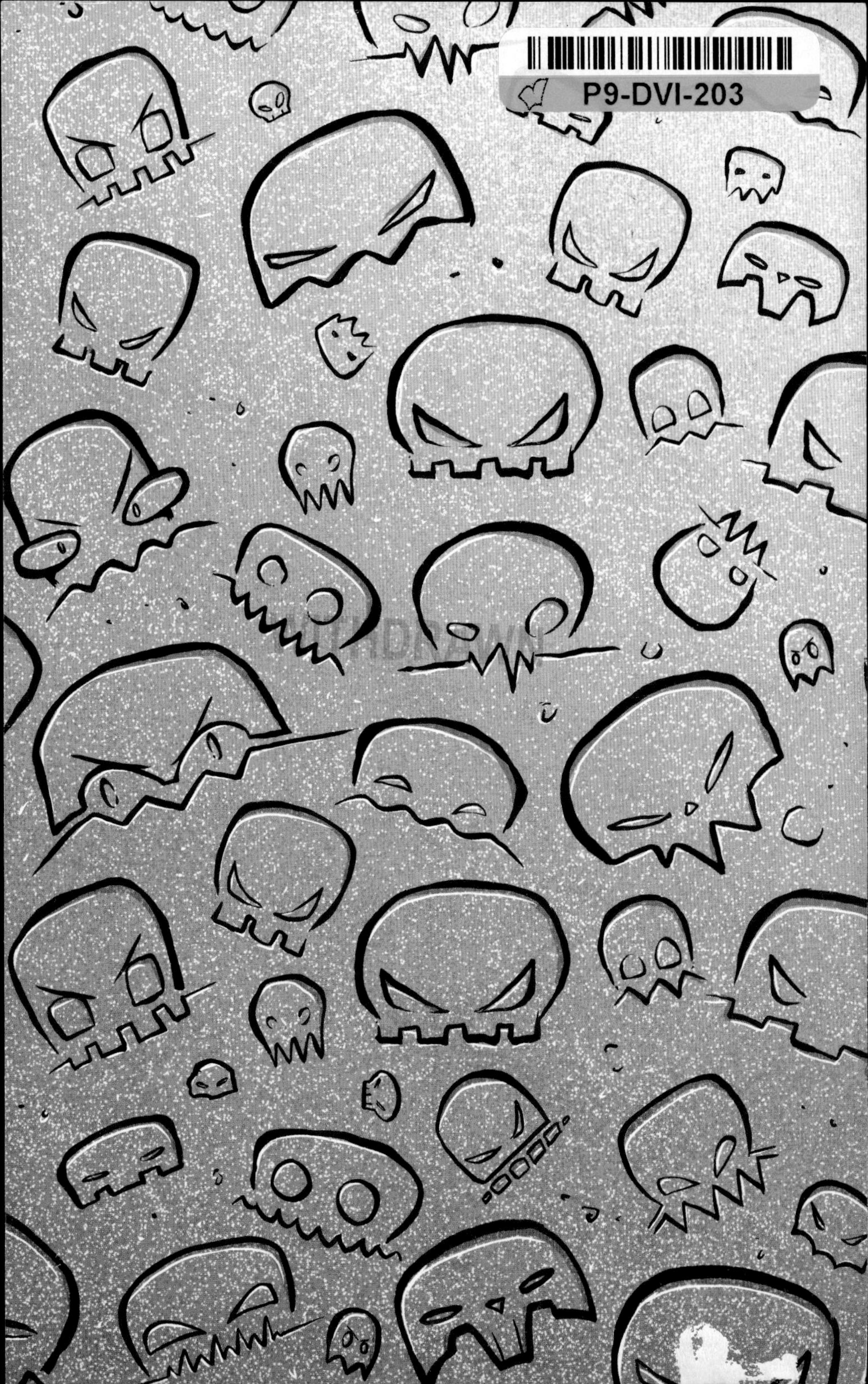

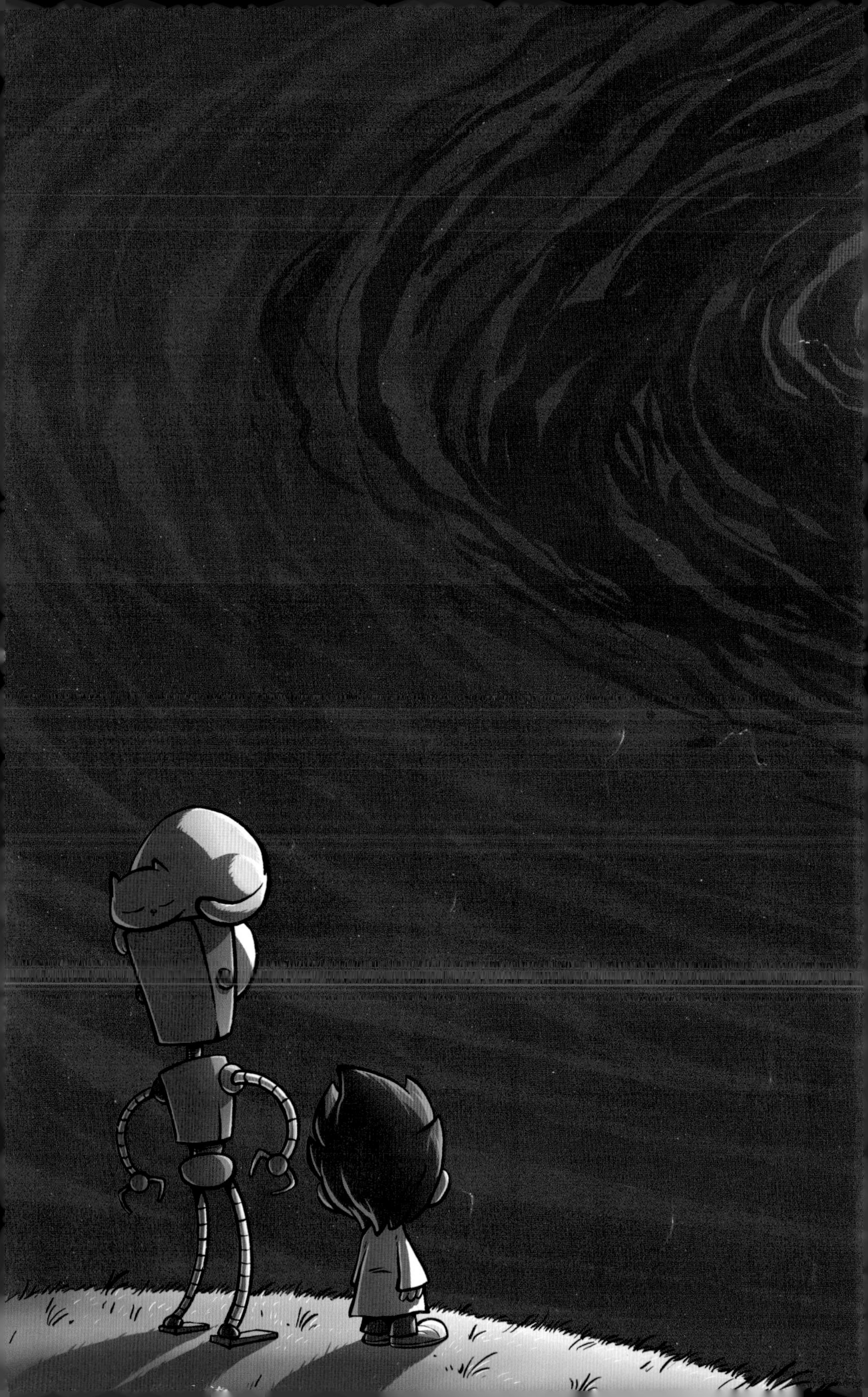

STEVE L. McEVIL

Lucas Turnbloom

Color by Marc Lapierre

CROWN
BOOKS FOR YOUNG READERS

NEW YORK

Copyright © 2022 by Lucas Turnbloom

All rights reserved. Published in the United States by Crown Books for Young Readers, an imprint of Random House Children's Books, a division of Penguin Random House LLC, New York.

Crown and the colophon are registered trademarks of Penguin Random House LLC.

RH Graphic with the book design is a trademark of Penguin Random House LLC.

Visit us on the Web! rhcbooks.com

Educators and librarians, for a variety of teaching tools, visit us at RHTeachersLibrarians.com

Library of Congress Cataloging-in-Publication Data
Names: Turnbloom, Lucas P., author, illustrator.
Title: Steve L. McEvil / Lucas Turnbloom.
Description: New York: Crown Books for Young Readers, [2022]
Audience: Ages 8-12 | Audience: Grades 4-6
Summary: "Steve has plans to take over his middle school, but when a nefarious villain beats him to the punch, Steve will have to consider doing the most horrific thing of them all: teaming up with good guy Vic Turry to save his school and maybe the entire town!"—Provided by publisher.
Identifiers: LCCN 2021038021 (print) | LCCN 2021038022 (ebook) | ISBN 978-0-593-30143-2 (hardcover)
ISBN 978-0-593-30144-9 (lib. bdg.) | ISBN 978-0-593-30145-6 (ebook)
Subjects: CYAC: Graphic novels. | Supervillains—Fiction. | Middle schools—Fiction.
Schools—Fiction. | Humorous stories. | LCGFT: Superhero comics. | Humorous comics.
Classification: LCC PZ7.7.T89 St 2022 (print) | LCC PZ7.7.T89 (ebook) | DDC 741.5/973—dc23

Interior design by Bob Bianchini

MANUFACTURED IN CHINA

10 9 8 7 6 5 4 3 2 1

First Edition

FOR SUZANNE,
MY FOREVER PARTNER IN CRIME

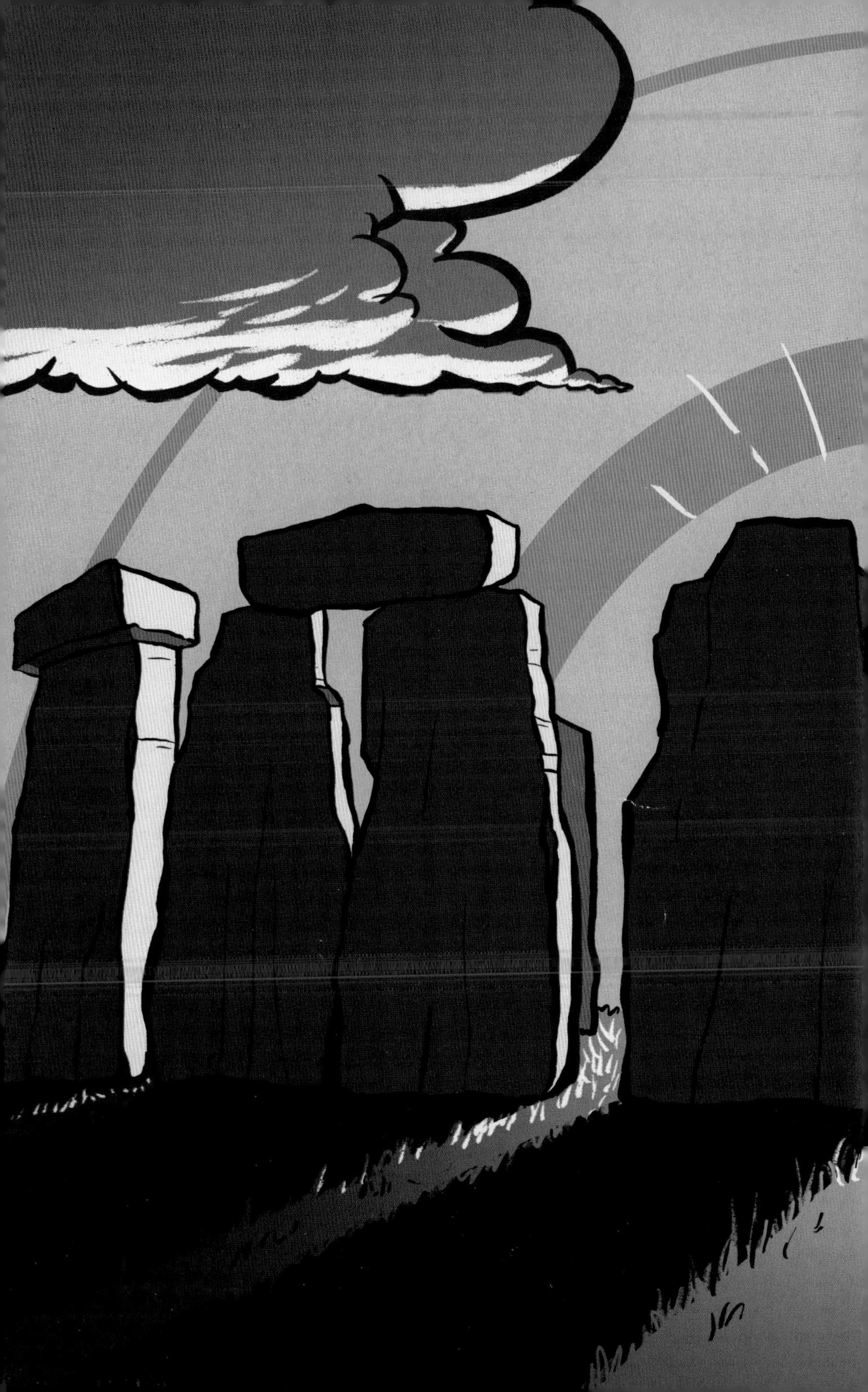

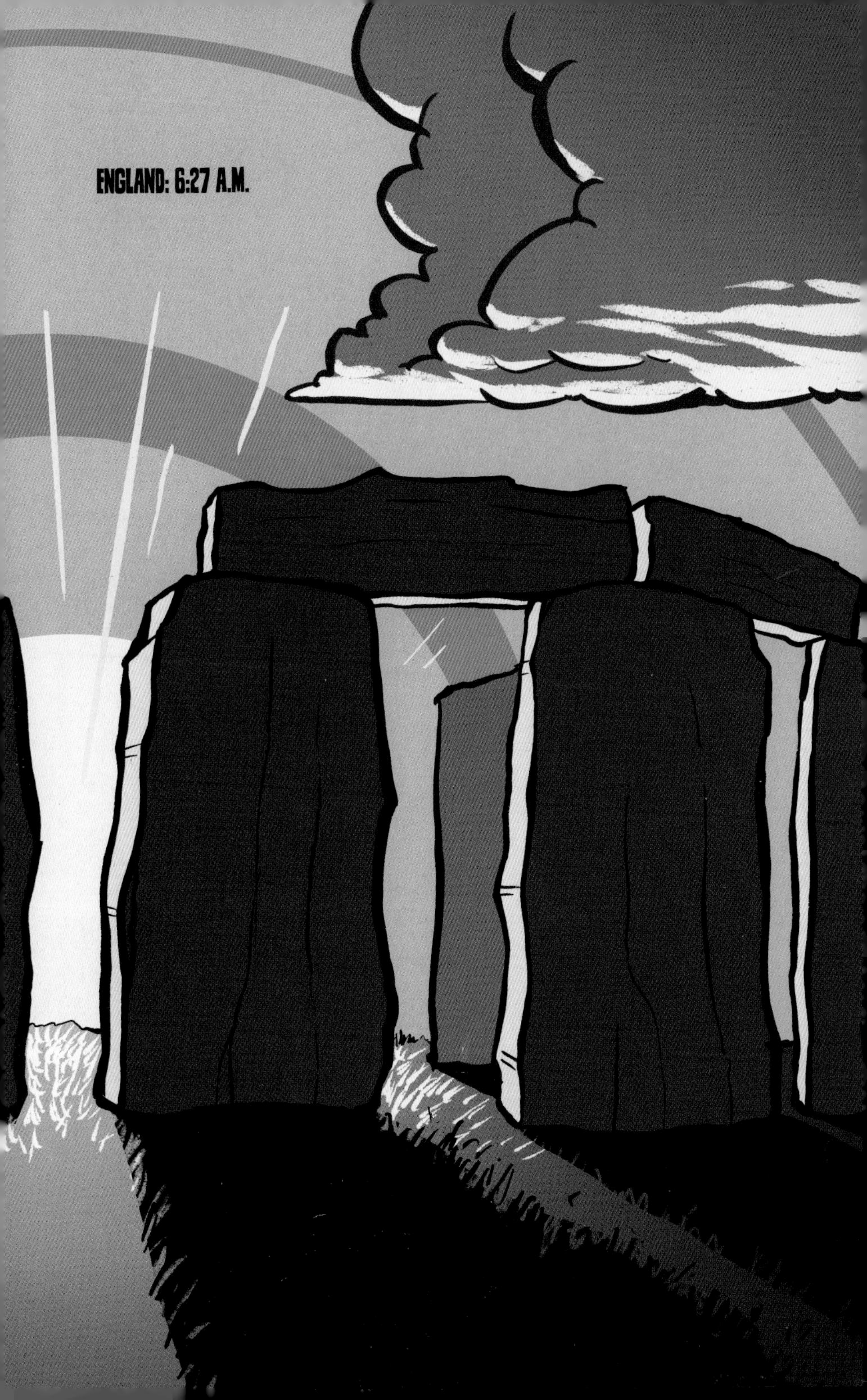
ENGLAND: 6:27 A.M.

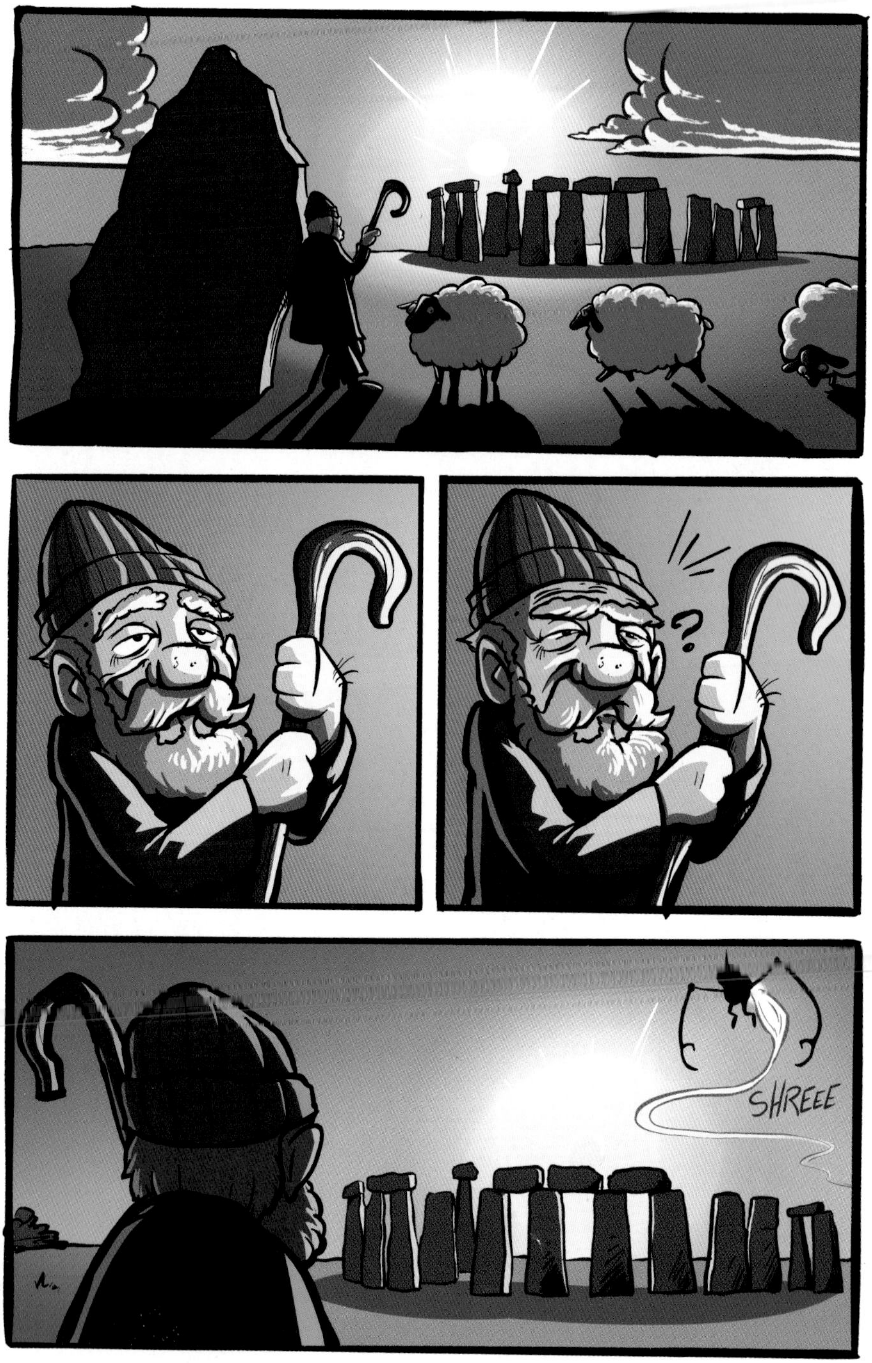
?
SHREEE

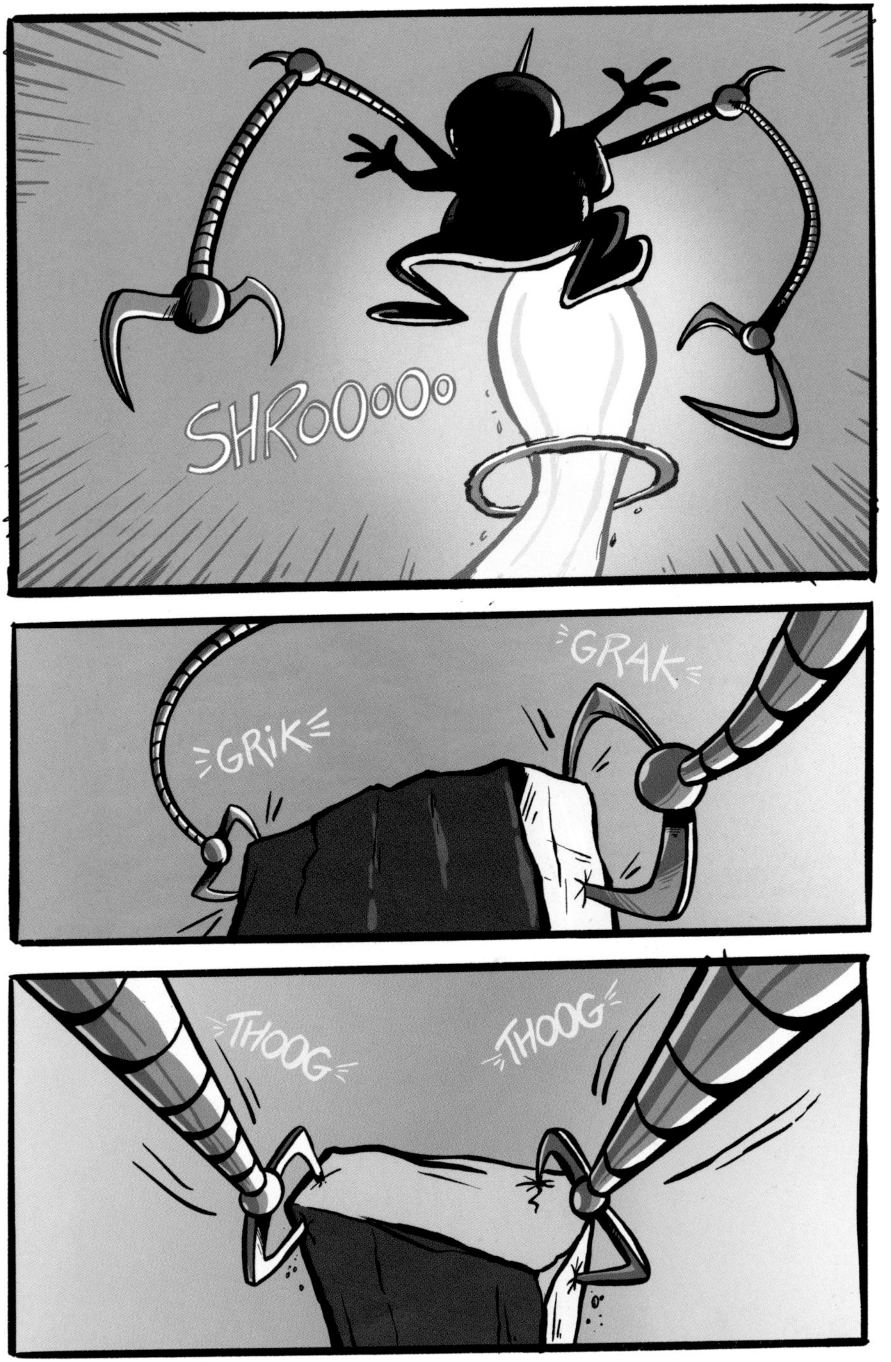
SHROOOOO
GRAK
GRIK
THOOG
THOOG

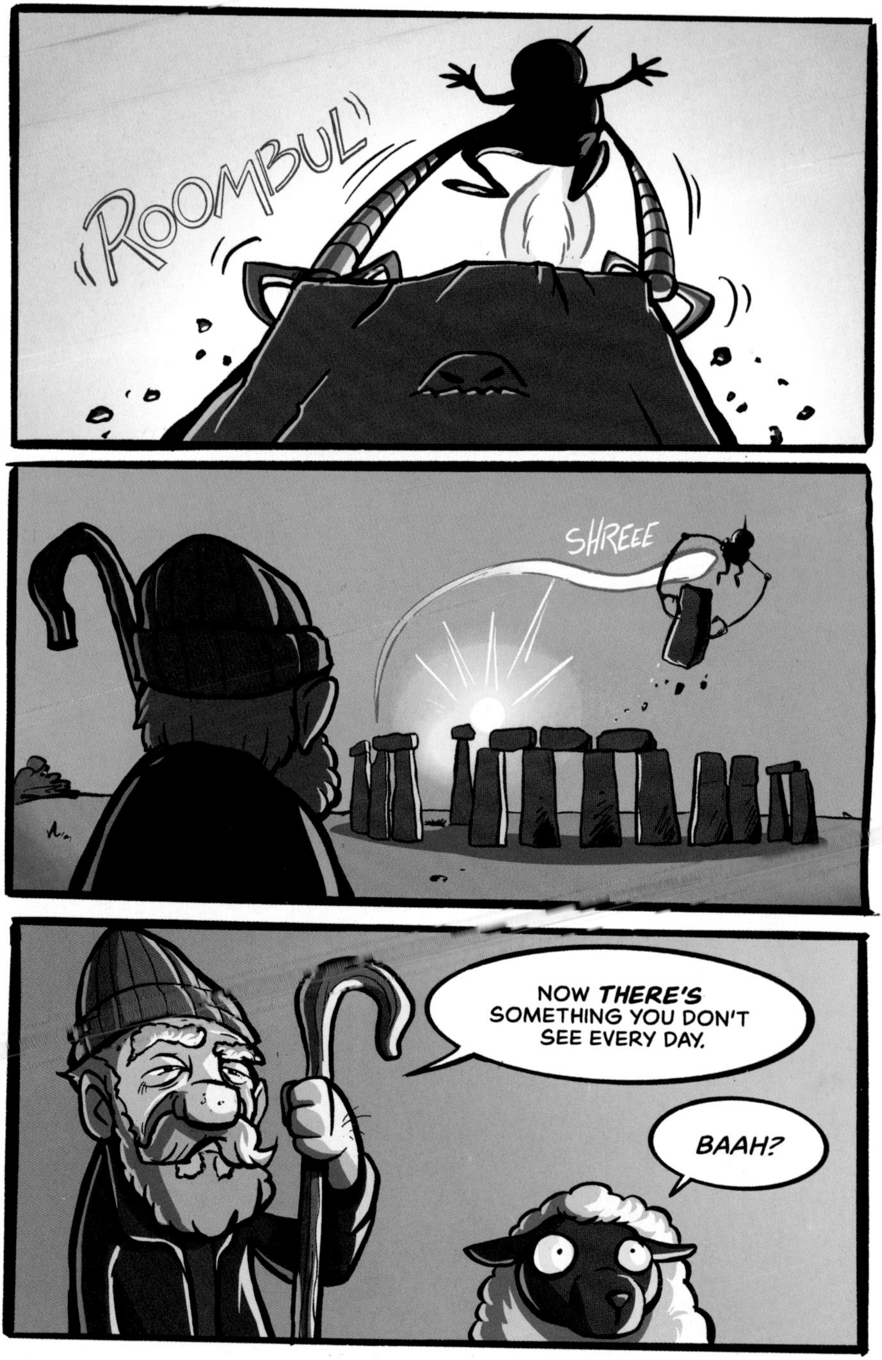
ROOMBUL
SHREEE
NOW THERE'S SOMETHING YOU DON'T SEE EVERY DAY.
BAAH?

CHAPTER 1

Enter the Villain

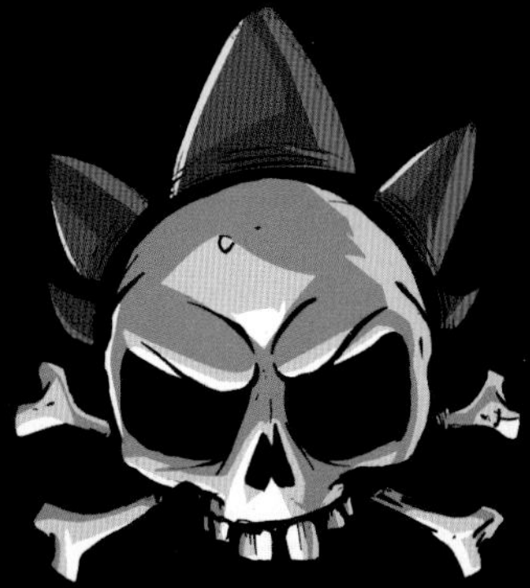

McEVIL HOUSEHOLD: 6:54 A.M.

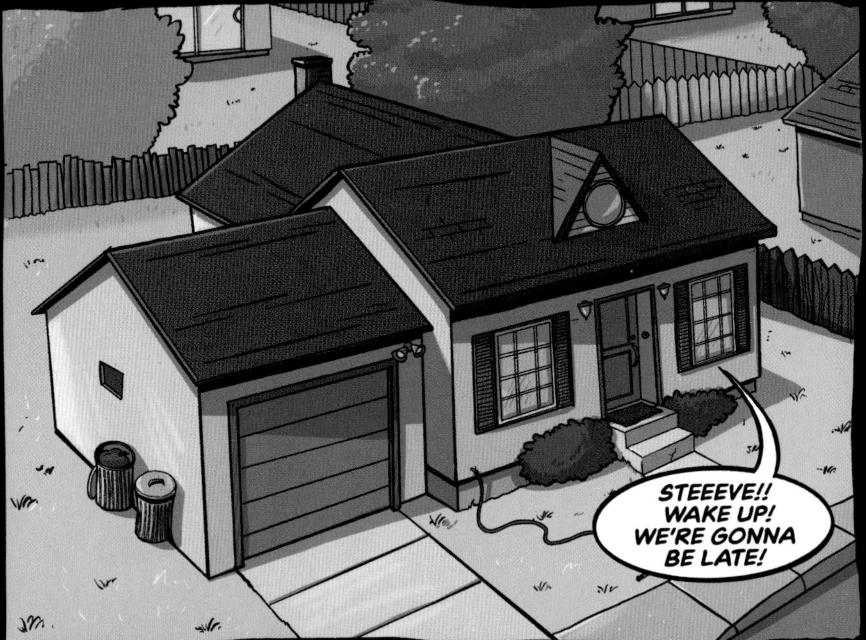
STEEEVE!! WAKE UP! WE'RE GONNA BE LATE!

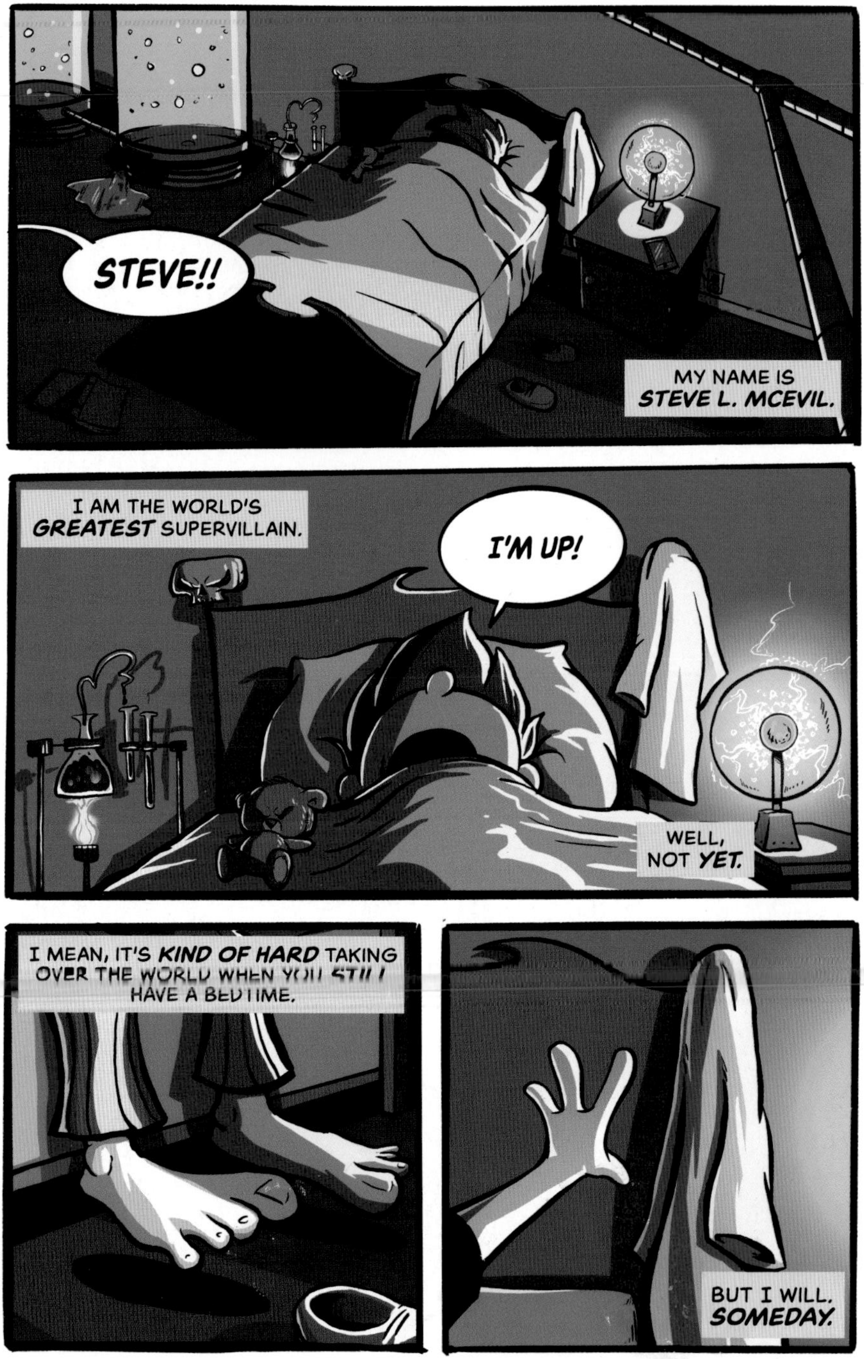
STEVE!!
MY NAME IS STEVE L. MCEVIL.
I AM THE WORLD'S GREATEST SUPERVILLAIN.
I'M UP!
WELL, NOT YET.
I MEAN, IT'S KIND OF HARD TAKING OVER THE WORLD WHEN YOU STILL HAVE A BEDTIME.
BUT I WILL. SOMEDAY.

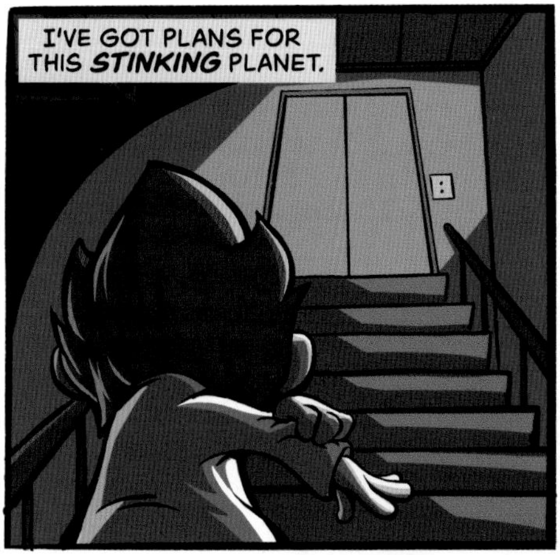
I'VE GOT PLANS FOR THIS STINKING PLANET.

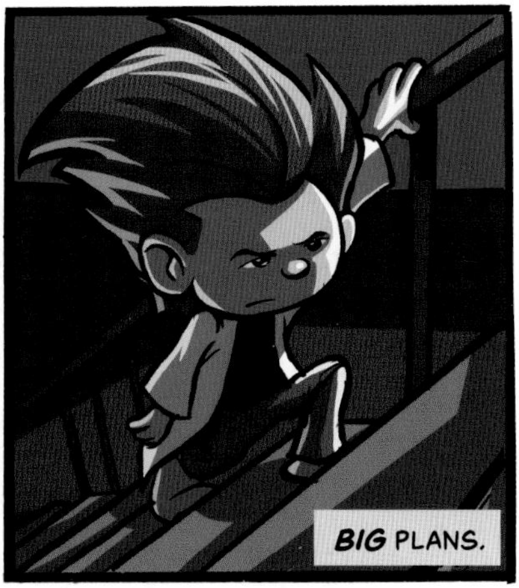
BIG PLANS.

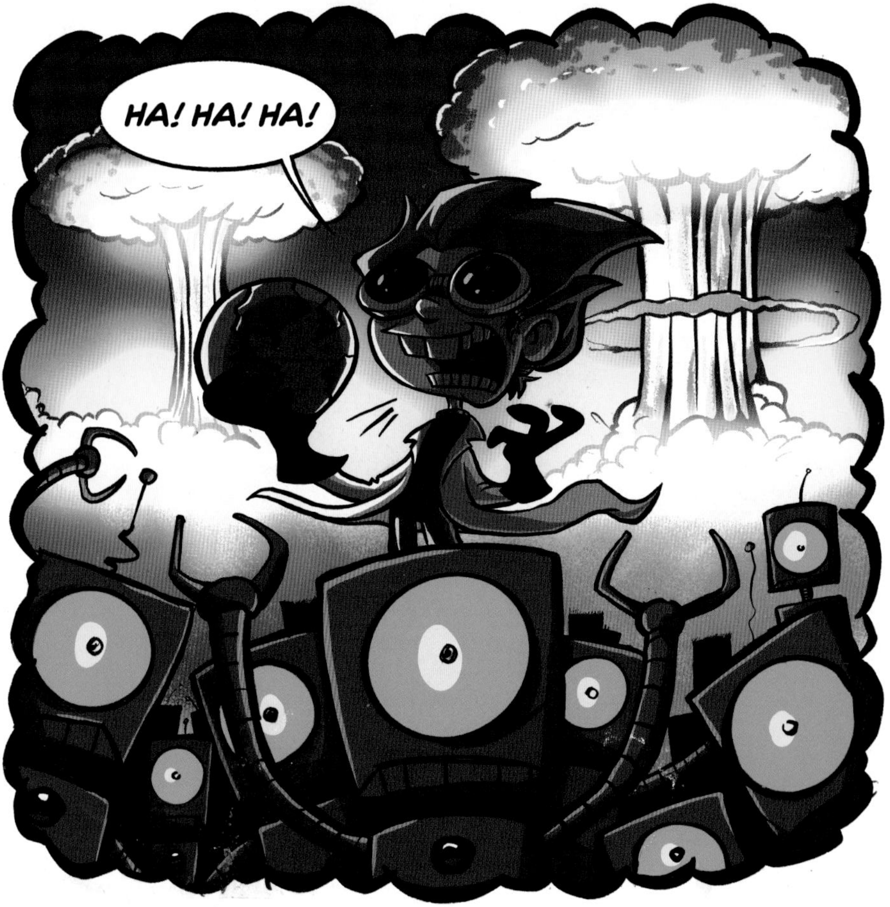
HA! HA! HA!

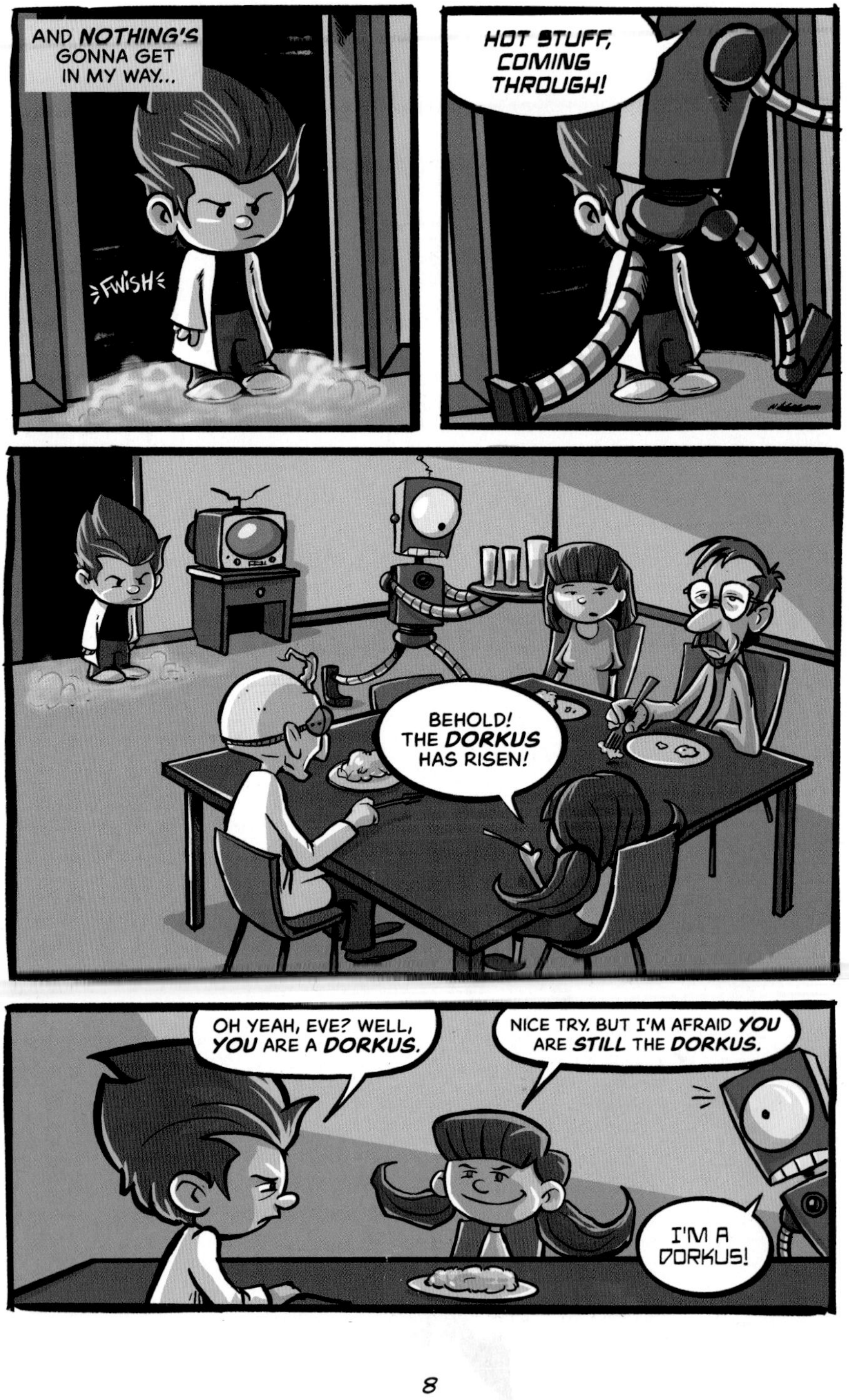
AND NOTHING'S GONNA GET IN MY WAY...
FWISH
HOT STUFF, COMING THROUGH!
BEHOLD! THE DORKUS HAS RISEN!
OH YEAH, EVE? WELL, YOU ARE A DORKUS.
NICE TRY. BUT I'M AFRAID YOU ARE STILL THE DORKUS.
I'M A DORKUS!

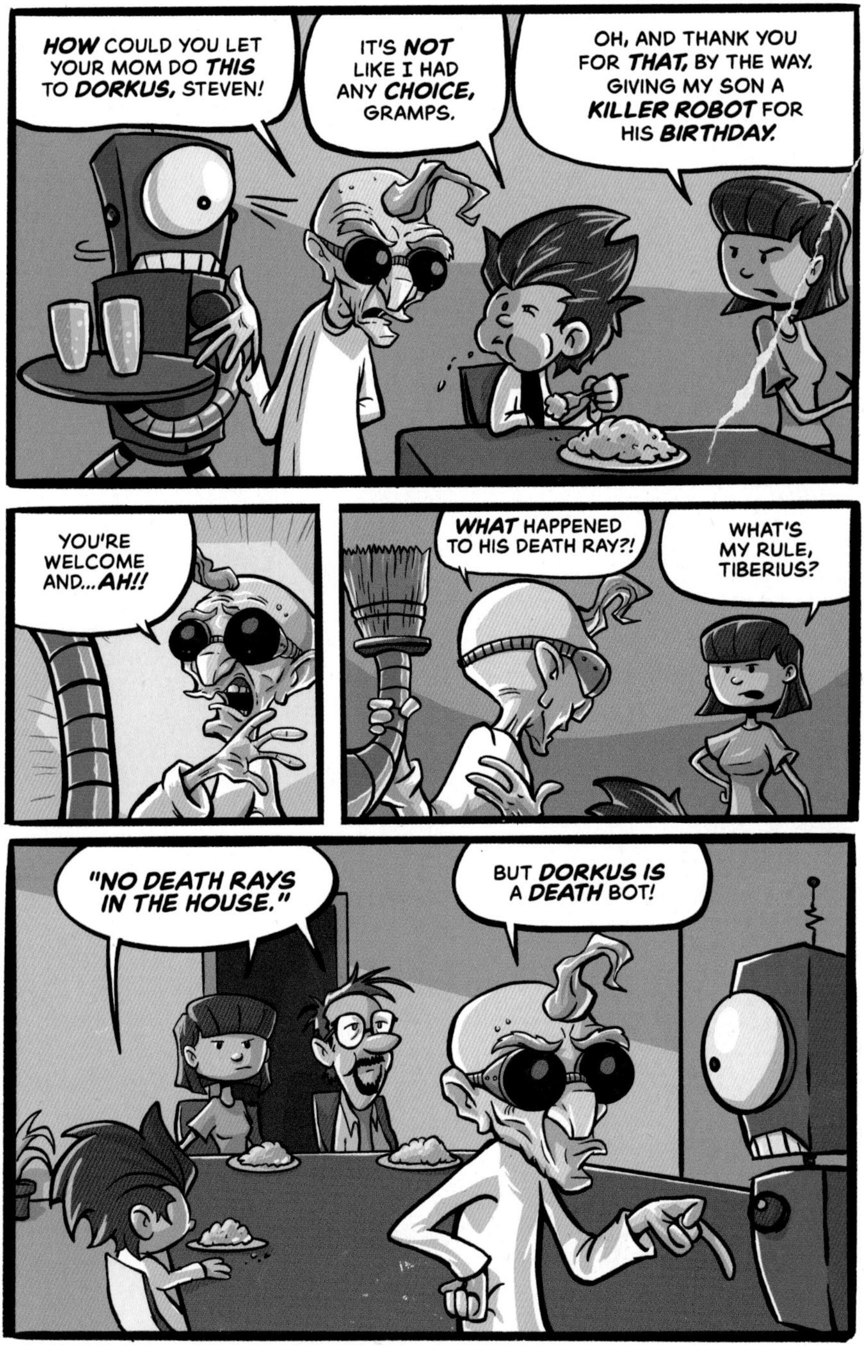
HOW COULD YOU LET YOUR MOM DO THIS TO DORKUS, STEVEN!
IT'S NOT LIKE I HAD ANY CHOICE, GRAMPS.
OH, AND THANK YOU FOR THAT, BY THE WAY. GIVING MY SON A KILLER ROBOT FOR HIS BIRTHDAY.
YOU'RE WELCOME AND...AH!!
WHAT HAPPENED TO HIS DEATH RAY?!
WHAT'S MY RULE, TIBERIUS?
"NO DEATH RAYS IN THE HOUSE."
BUT DORKUS IS A DEATH BOT!

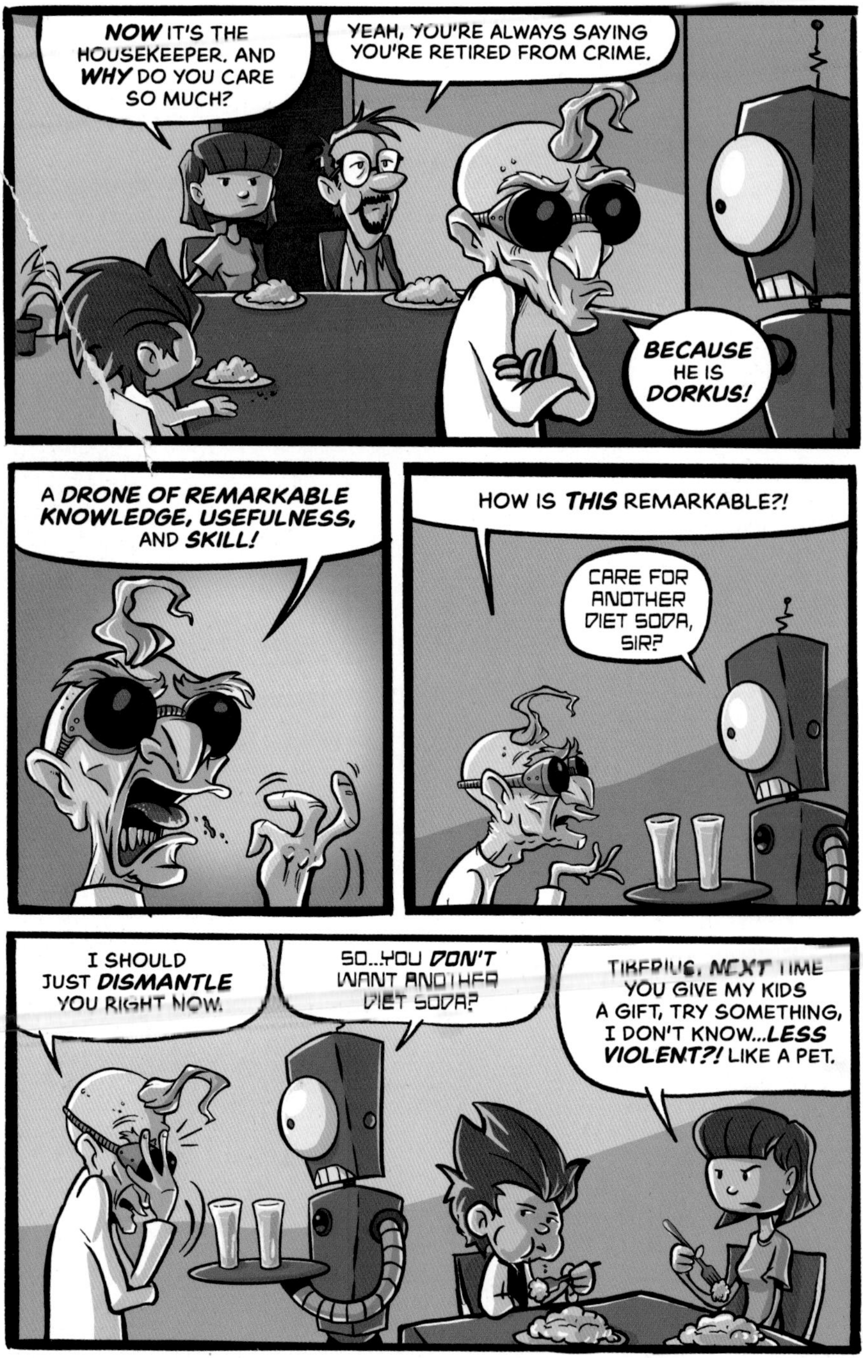
NOW IT'S THE HOUSEKEEPER. AND WHY DO YOU CARE SO MUCH?
YEAH, YOU'RE ALWAYS SAYING YOU'RE RETIRED FROM CRIME.
BECAUSE HE IS DORKUS!
A DRONE OF REMARKABLE KNOWLEDGE, USEFULNESS, AND SKILL!
HOW IS THIS REMARKABLE?!
CARE FOR ANOTHER DIET SODA, SIR?
I SHOULD JUST DISMANTLE YOU RIGHT NOW.
SO...YOU DON'T WANT ANOTHER DIET SODA?
TIBERIUS, NEXT TIME YOU GIVE MY KIDS A GIFT, TRY SOMETHING, I DON'T KNOW...LESS VIOLENT?! LIKE A PET.

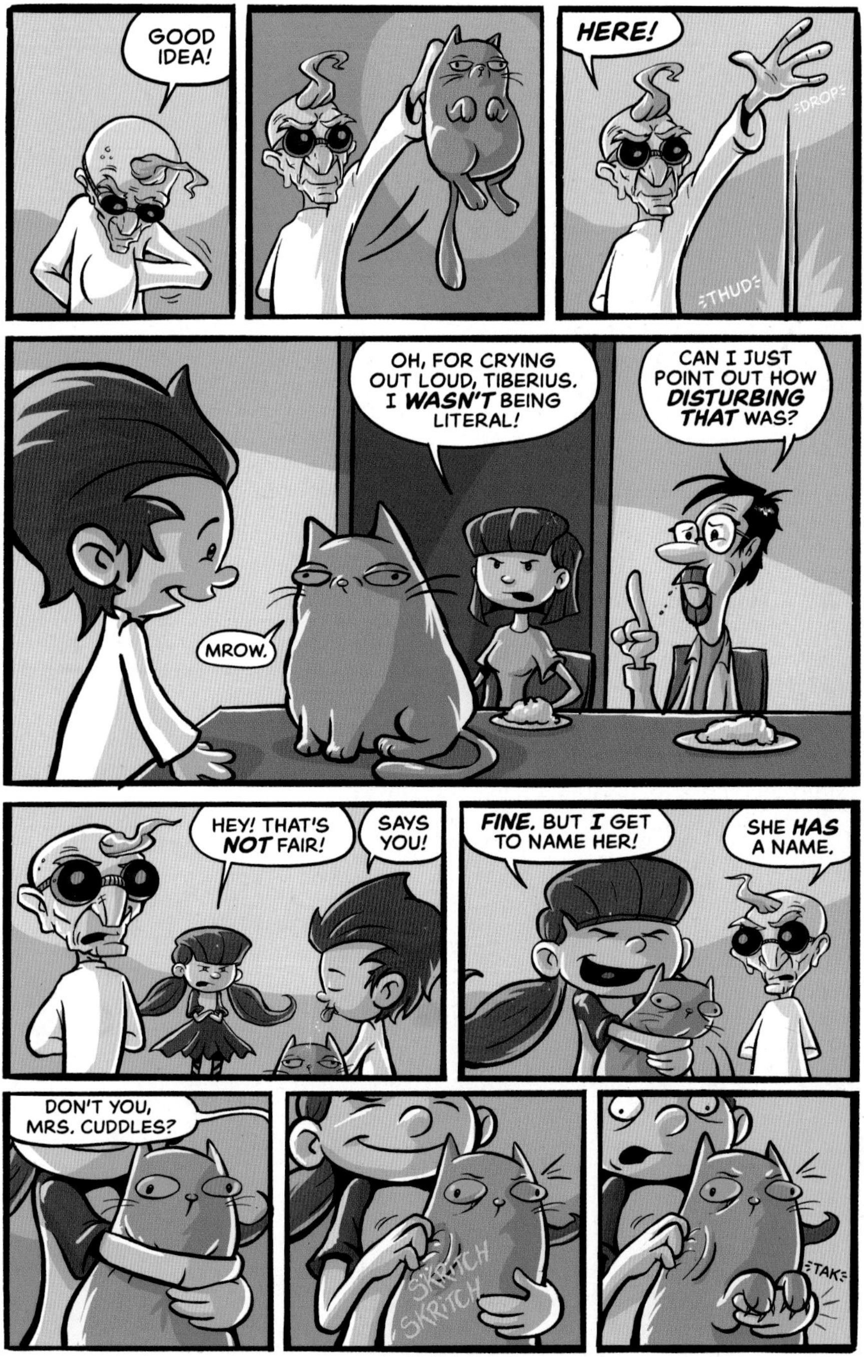
GOOD IDEA!
HERE!
DROP
THUD
OH, FOR CRYING OUT LOUD, TIBERIUS. I *WASN'T* BEING LITERAL!
CAN I JUST POINT OUT HOW *DISTURBING THAT* WAS?
MROW.
HEY! THAT'S *NOT* FAIR!
SAYS YOU!
FINE. BUT *I* GET TO NAME HER!
SHE *HAS* A NAME.
DON'T YOU, MRS. CUDDLES?
SKRITCH SKRITCH
TAK

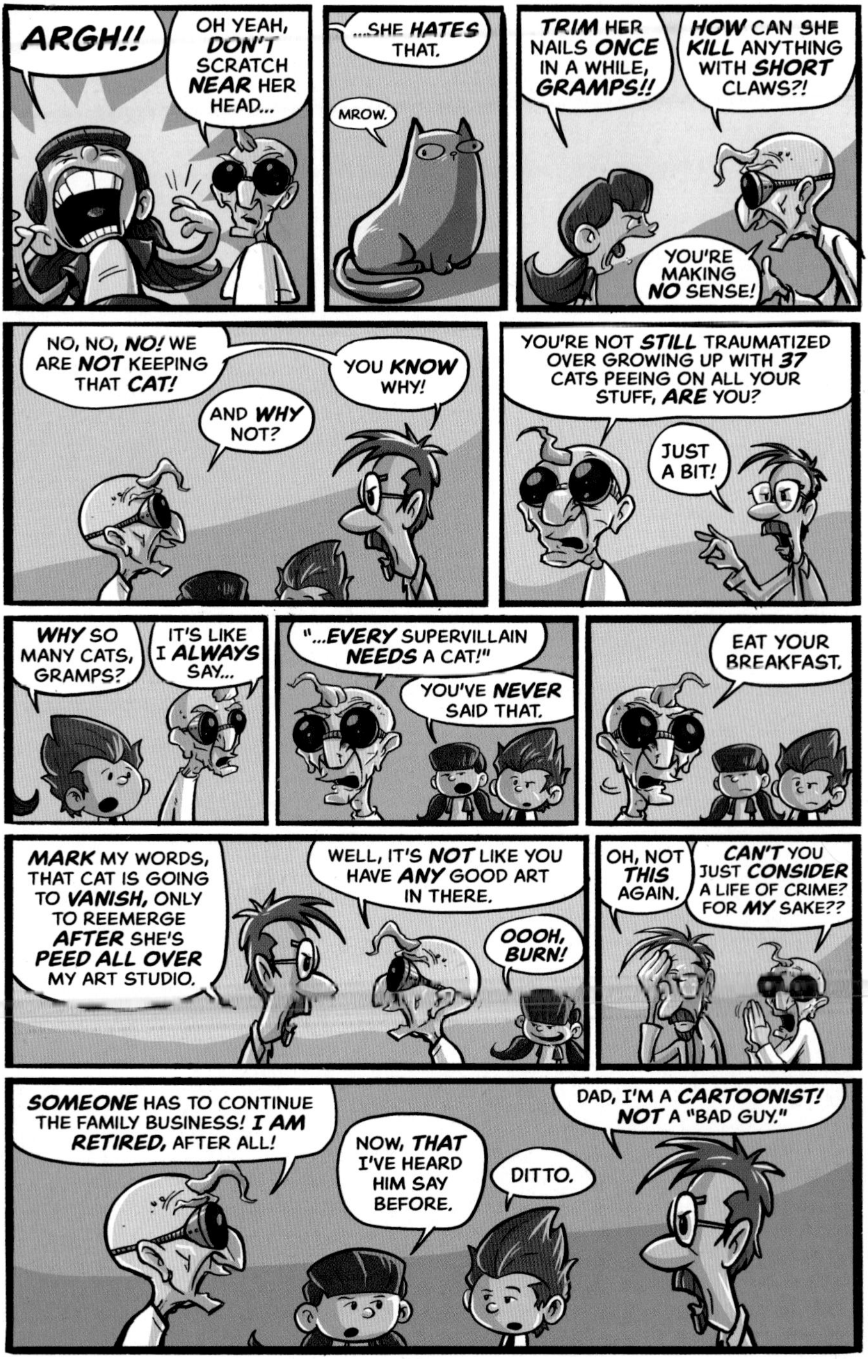
ARGH!!
OH YEAH, DON'T SCRATCH NEAR HER HEAD...
...SHE HATES THAT.
MROW.
TRIM HER NAILS ONCE IN A WHILE, GRAMPS!!
HOW CAN SHE KILL ANYTHING WITH SHORT CLAWS?!
YOU'RE MAKING NO SENSE!
NO, NO, NO! WE ARE NOT KEEPING THAT CAT!
AND WHY NOT?
YOU KNOW WHY!
YOU'RE NOT STILL TRAUMATIZED OVER GROWING UP WITH 37 CATS PEEING ON ALL YOUR STUFF, ARE YOU?
JUST A BIT!
WHY SO MANY CATS, GRAMPS?
IT'S LIKE I ALWAYS SAY...
"...EVERY SUPERVILLAIN NEEDS A CAT!"
YOU'VE NEVER SAID THAT.
EAT YOUR BREAKFAST.
MARK MY WORDS, THAT CAT IS GOING TO VANISH, ONLY TO REEMERGE AFTER SHE'S PEED ALL OVER MY ART STUDIO.
WELL, IT'S NOT LIKE YOU HAVE ANY GOOD ART IN THERE.
OOOH, BURN!
OH, NOT THIS AGAIN.
CAN'T YOU JUST CONSIDER A LIFE OF CRIME? FOR MY SAKE??
SOMEONE HAS TO CONTINUE THE FAMILY BUSINESS! I AM RETIRED, AFTER ALL!
NOW, THAT I'VE HEARD HIM SAY BEFORE.
DITTO.
DAD, I'M A CARTOONIST! NOT A "BAD GUY."

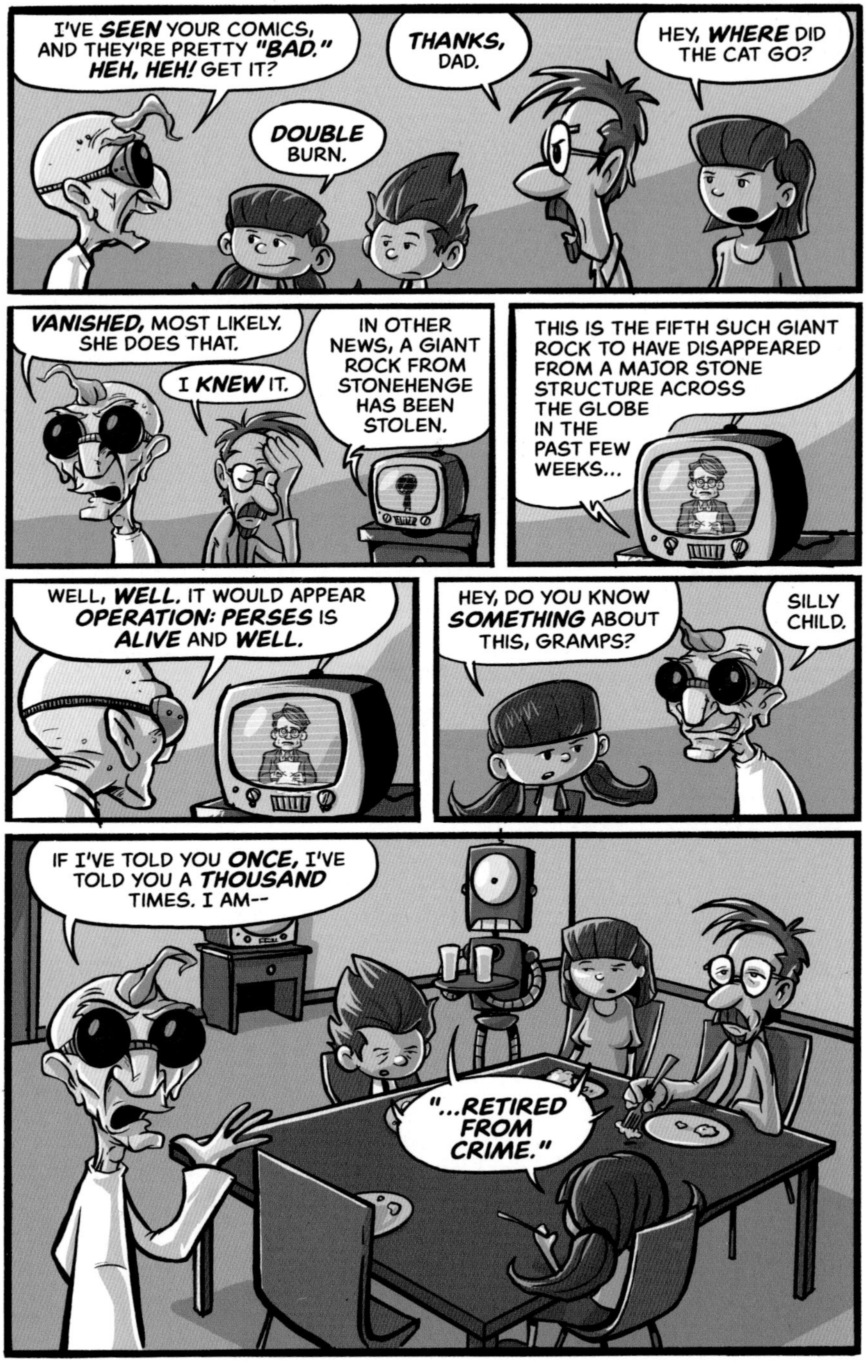
I'VE SEEN YOUR COMICS, AND THEY'RE PRETTY "BAD." HEH, HEH! GET IT?
DOUBLE BURN.
THANKS, DAD.
HEY, WHERE DID THE CAT GO?
VANISHED, MOST LIKELY. SHE DOES THAT.
I KNEW IT.
IN OTHER NEWS, A GIANT ROCK FROM STONEHENGE HAS BEEN STOLEN.
THIS IS THE FIFTH SUCH GIANT ROCK TO HAVE DISAPPEARED FROM A MAJOR STONE STRUCTURE ACROSS THE GLOBE IN THE PAST FEW WEEKS...
WELL, WELL. IT WOULD APPEAR OPERATION: PERSES IS ALIVE AND WELL.
HEY, DO YOU KNOW SOMETHING ABOUT THIS, GRAMPS?
SILLY CHILD.
IF I'VE TOLD YOU ONCE, I'VE TOLD YOU A THOUSAND TIMES. I AM--
"...RETIRED FROM CRIME."

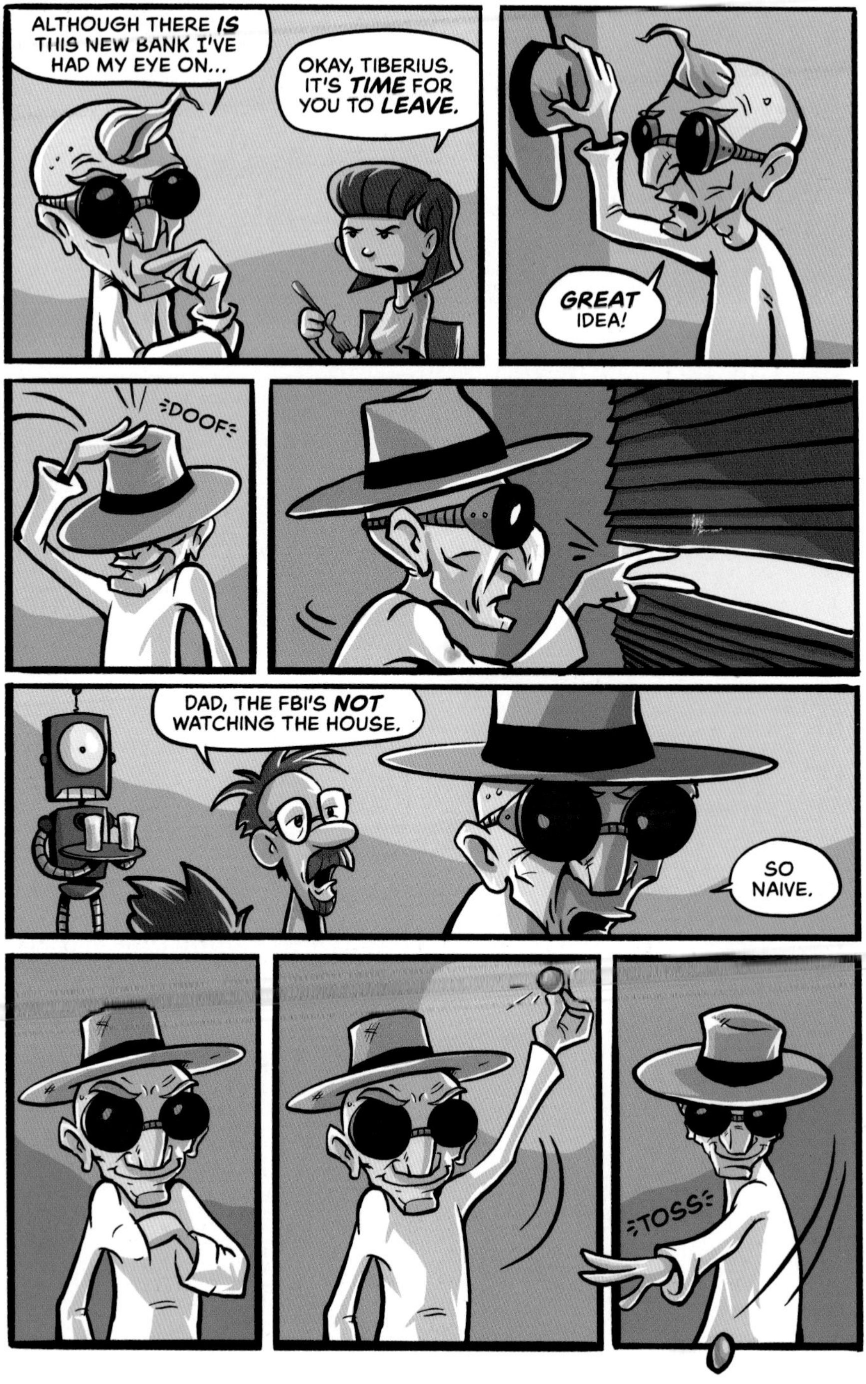
ALTHOUGH THERE IS THIS NEW BANK I'VE HAD MY EYE ON...
OKAY, TIBERIUS. IT'S TIME FOR YOU TO LEAVE.
GREAT IDEA!
DOOF
DAD, THE FBI'S NOT WATCHING THE HOUSE.
SO NAIVE.
TOSS

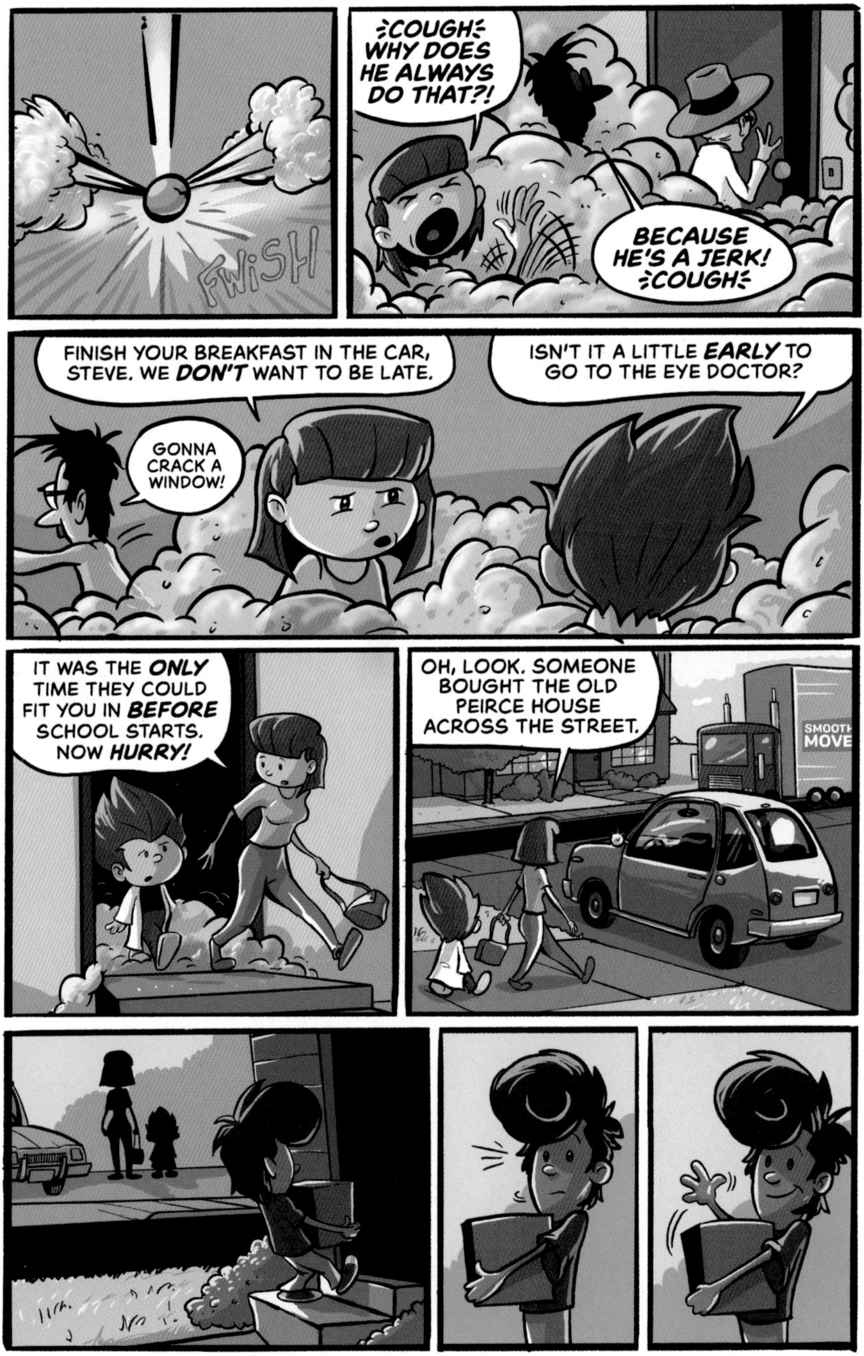
FWISH
¡COUGH¡ WHY DOES HE ALWAYS DO THAT?!
BECAUSE HE'S A JERK! ¡COUGH¡
FINISH YOUR BREAKFAST IN THE CAR, STEVE. WE DON'T WANT TO BE LATE.
GONNA CRACK A WINDOW!
ISN'T IT A LITTLE EARLY TO GO TO THE EYE DOCTOR?
IT WAS THE ONLY TIME THEY COULD FIT YOU IN BEFORE SCHOOL STARTS. NOW HURRY!
OH, LOOK. SOMEONE BOUGHT THE OLD PEIRCE HOUSE ACROSS THE STREET.
SMOOTH MOVE

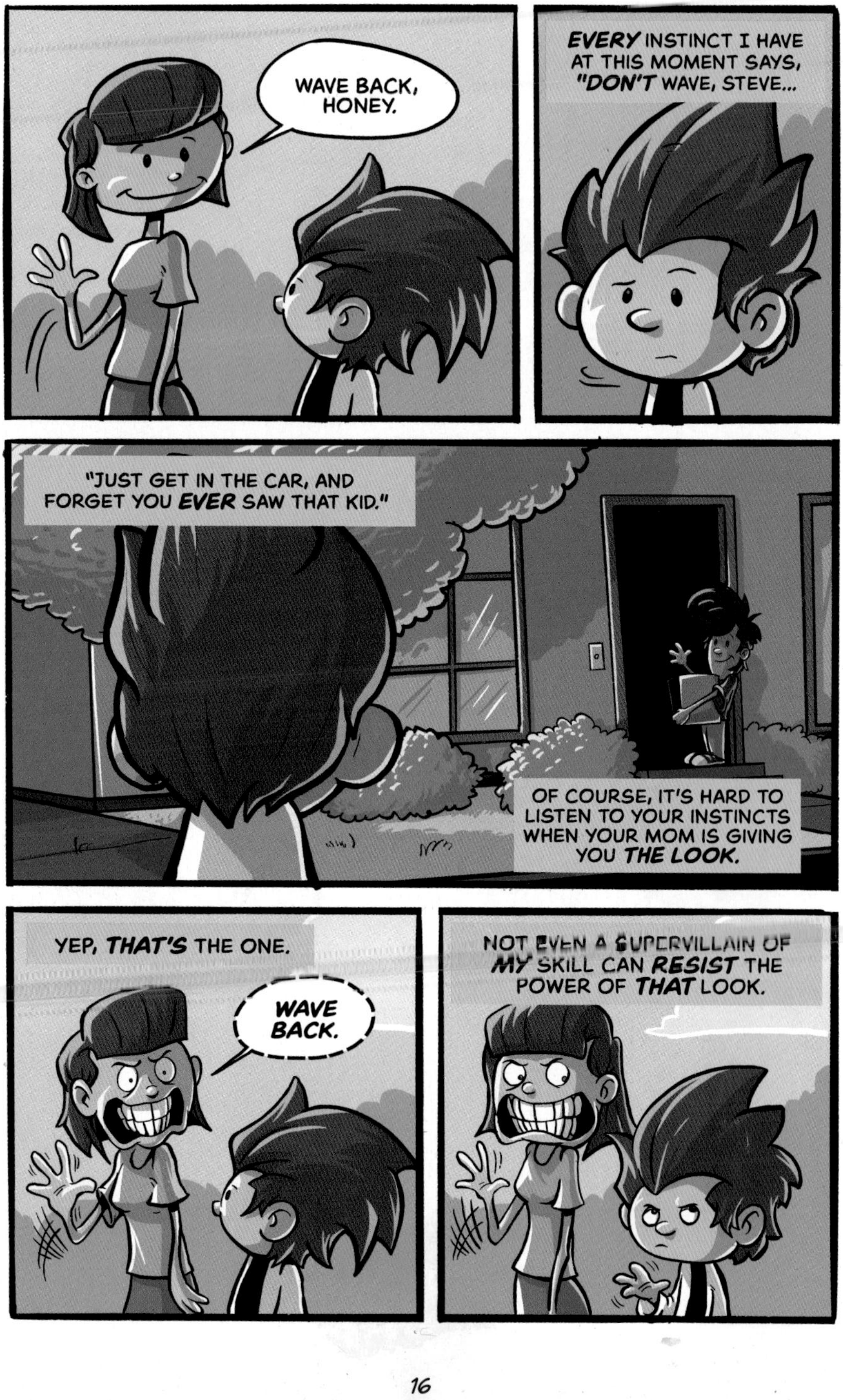
WAVE BACK, HONEY.
EVERY INSTINCT I HAVE AT THIS MOMENT SAYS, "DON'T WAVE, STEVE...
"JUST GET IN THE CAR, AND FORGET YOU EVER SAW THAT KID."
OF COURSE, IT'S HARD TO LISTEN TO YOUR INSTINCTS WHEN YOUR MOM IS GIVING YOU THE LOOK.
YEP, THAT'S THE ONE.
WAVE BACK.
NOT EVEN A SUPERVILLAIN OF MY SKILL CAN RESIST THE POWER OF THAT LOOK.

CHAPTER 2

The Lies of Dr. Eckleberg

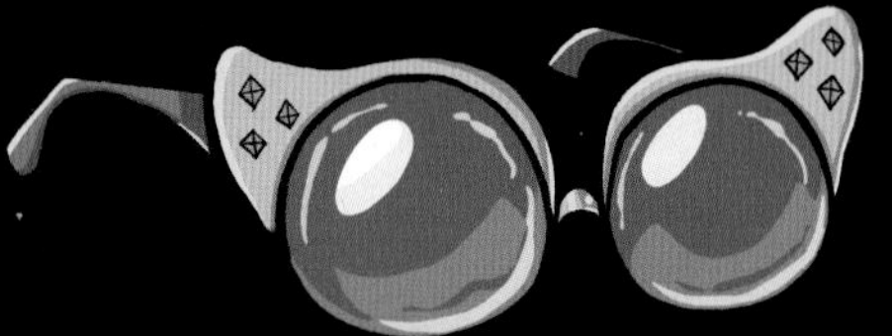

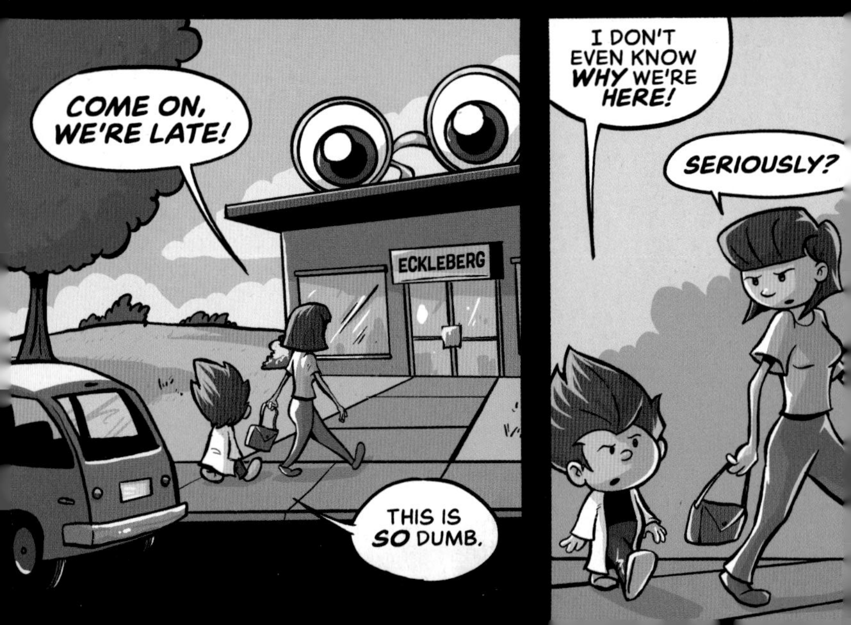
COME ON, WE'RE LATE!
ECKLEBERG
THIS IS SO DUMB.
I DON'T EVEN KNOW WHY WE'RE HERE!
SERIOUSLY?

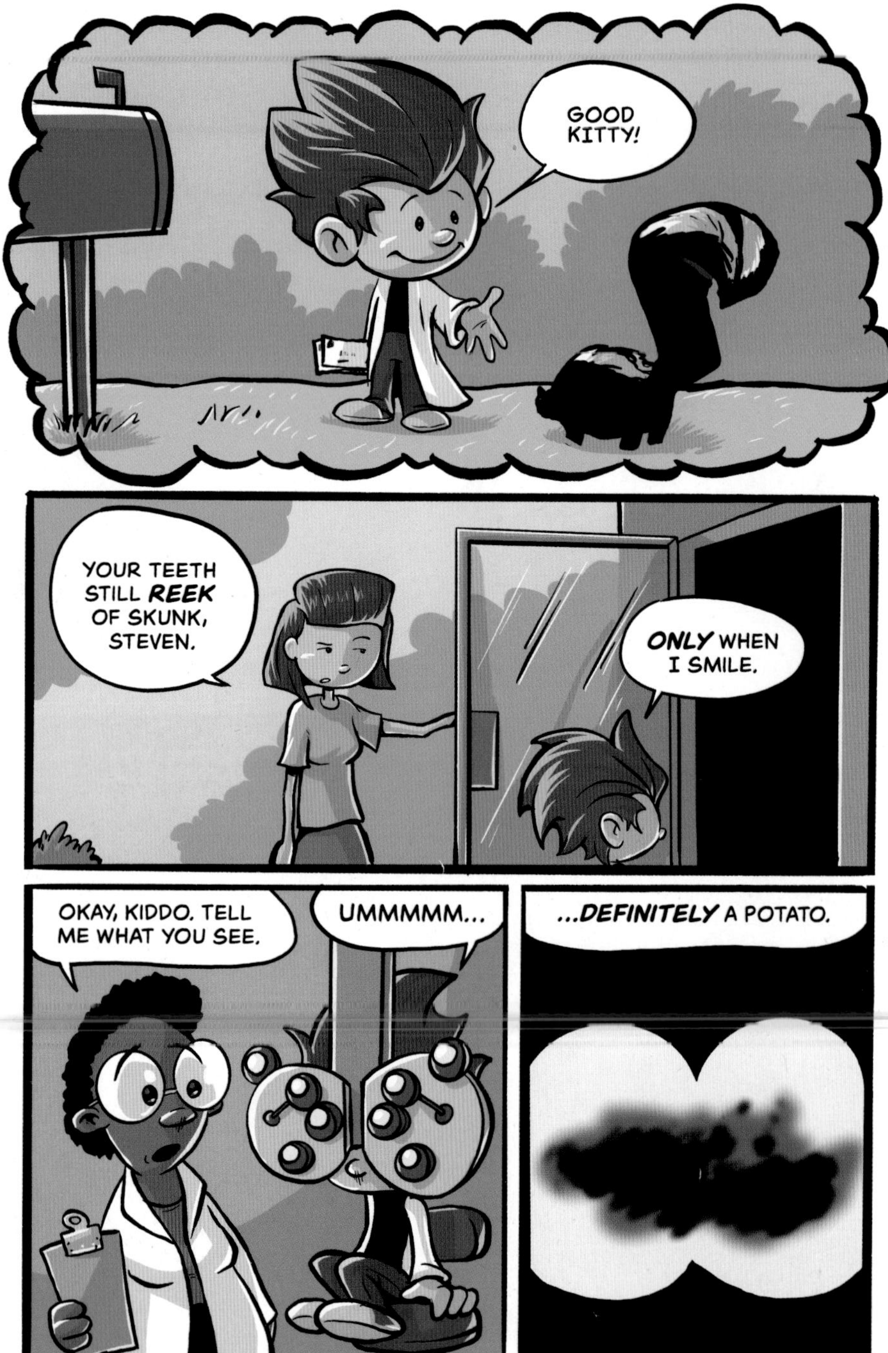
GOOD KITTY!
YOUR TEETH STILL **REEK** OF SKUNK, STEVEN.
ONLY WHEN I SMILE.
OKAY, KIDDO. TELL ME WHAT YOU SEE.
UMMMMM...
...**DEFINITELY** A POTATO.

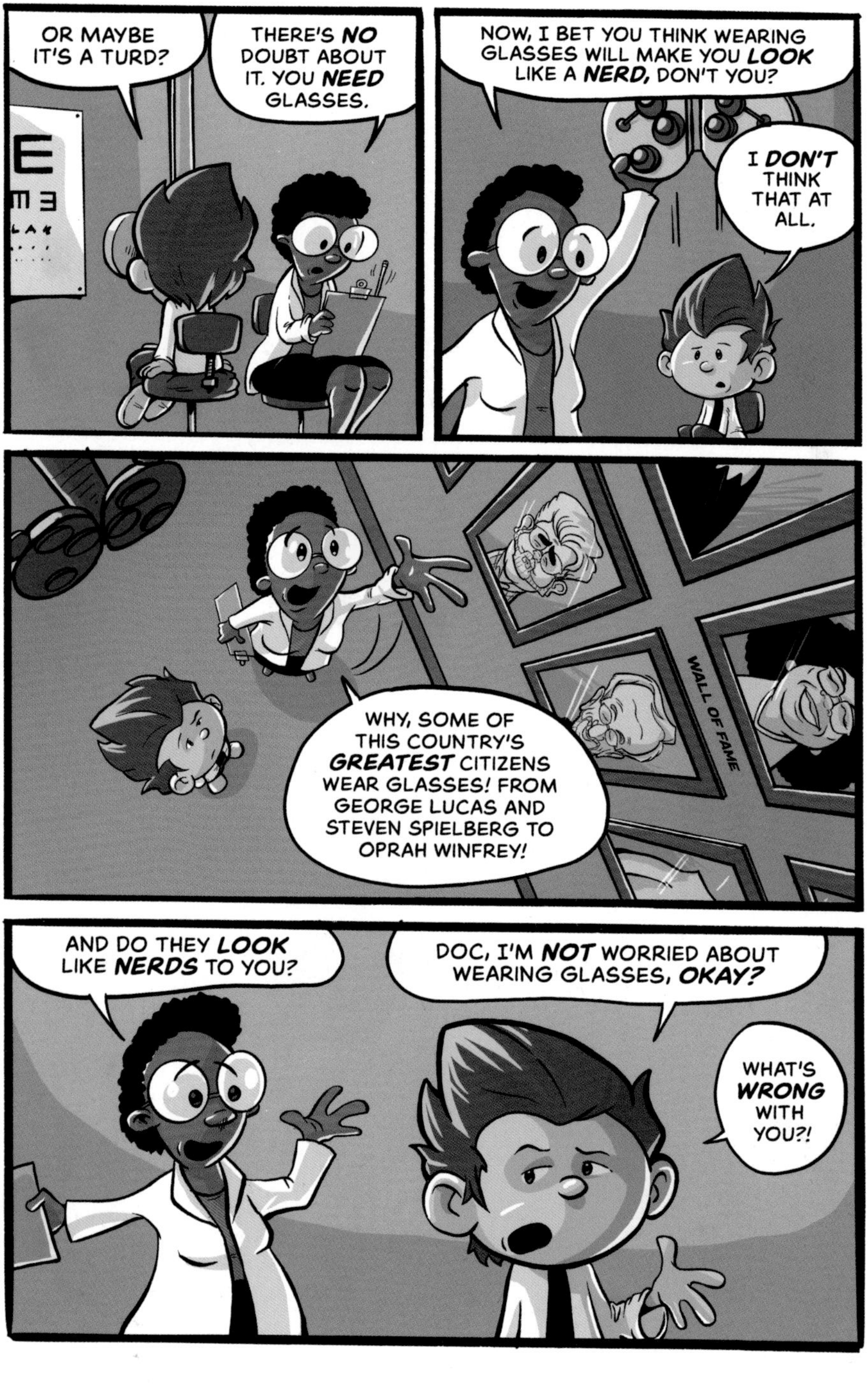
OR MAYBE IT'S A TURD?
THERE'S NO DOUBT ABOUT IT. YOU NEED GLASSES.
NOW, I BET YOU THINK WEARING GLASSES WILL MAKE YOU LOOK LIKE A NERD, DON'T YOU?
I DON'T THINK THAT AT ALL.
WALL OF FAME
WHY, SOME OF THIS COUNTRY'S GREATEST CITIZENS WEAR GLASSES! FROM GEORGE LUCAS AND STEVEN SPIELBERG TO OPRAH WINFREY!
AND DO THEY LOOK LIKE NERDS TO YOU?
DOC, I'M NOT WORRIED ABOUT WEARING GLASSES, OKAY?
WHAT'S WRONG WITH YOU?!

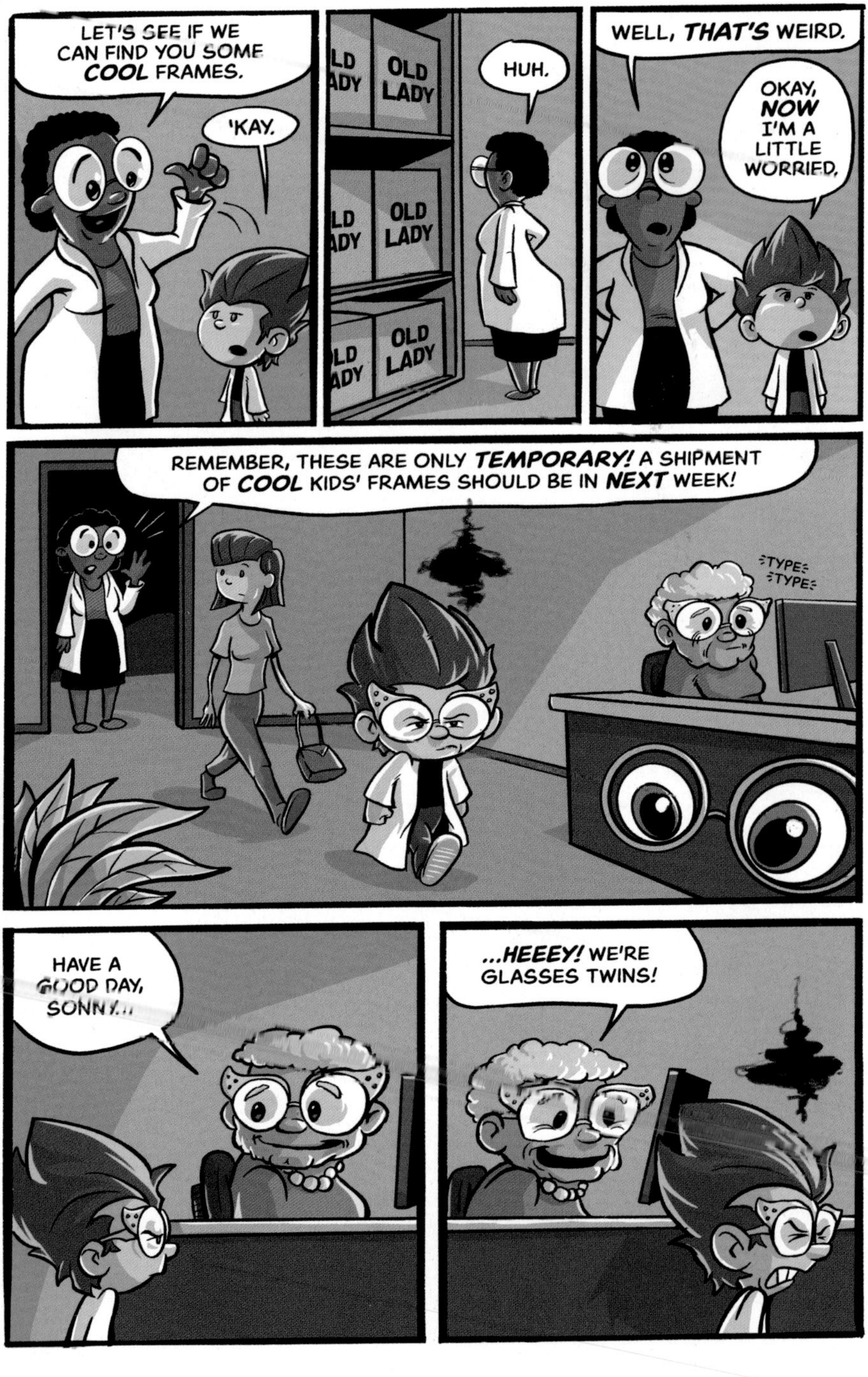
LET'S SEE IF WE CAN FIND YOU SOME COOL FRAMES.
'KAY.
OLD LADY
OLD LADY
OLD LADY
HUH.
WELL, THAT'S WEIRD.
OKAY, NOW I'M A LITTLE WORRIED.
REMEMBER, THESE ARE ONLY TEMPORARY! A SHIPMENT OF COOL KIDS' FRAMES SHOULD BE IN NEXT WEEK!
TYPE TYPE
HAVE A GOOD DAY, SONNY...!
...HEEEY! WE'RE GLASSES TWINS!

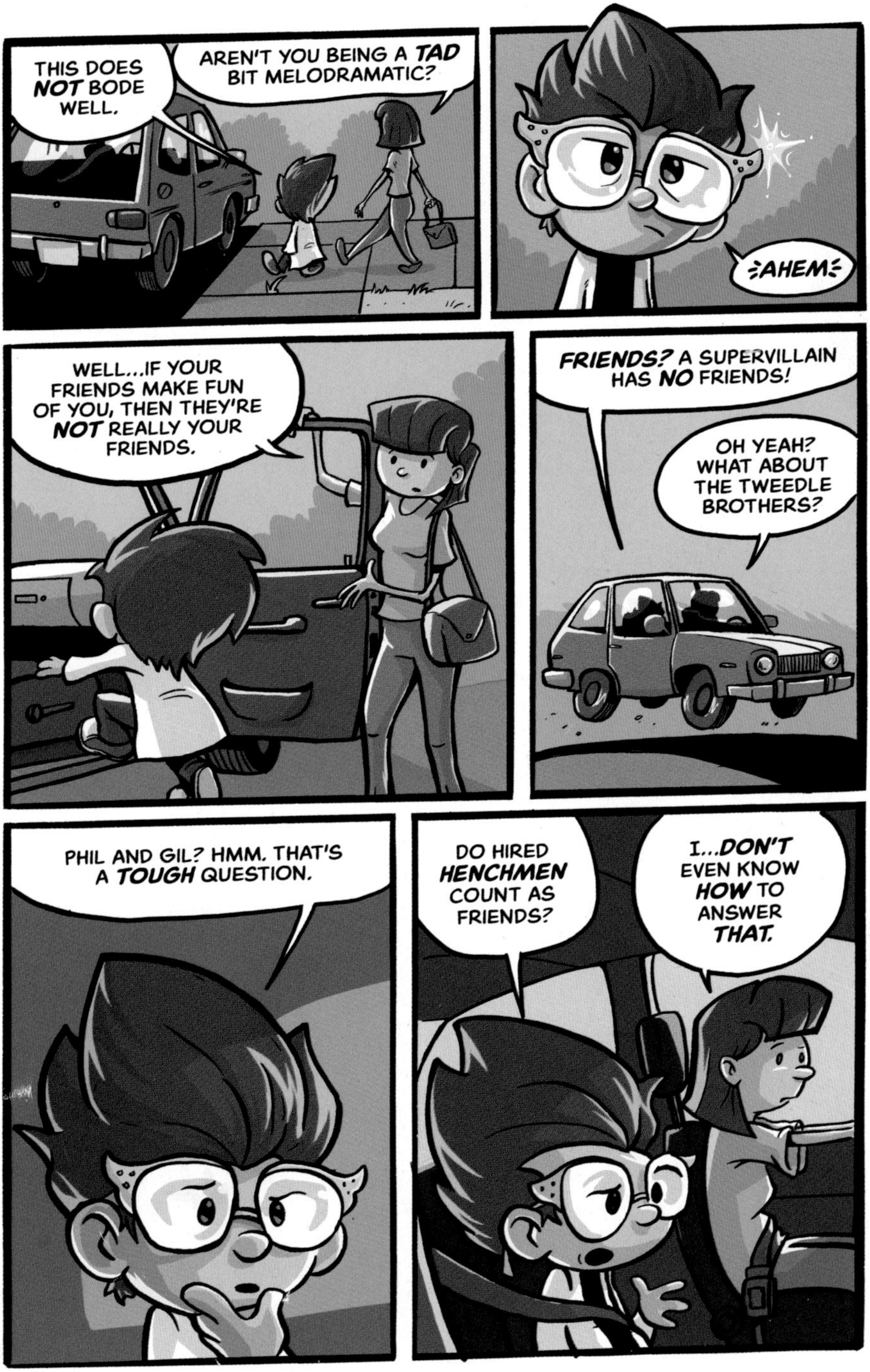
THIS DOES NOT BODE WELL.
AREN'T YOU BEING A TAD BIT MELODRAMATIC?
AHEM
WELL...IF YOUR FRIENDS MAKE FUN OF YOU, THEN THEY'RE NOT REALLY YOUR FRIENDS.
FRIENDS? A SUPERVILLAIN HAS NO FRIENDS!
OH YEAH? WHAT ABOUT THE TWEEDLE BROTHERS?
PHIL AND GIL? HMM. THAT'S A TOUGH QUESTION.
DO HIRED HENCHMEN COUNT AS FRIENDS?
I...DON'T EVEN KNOW HOW TO ANSWER THAT.

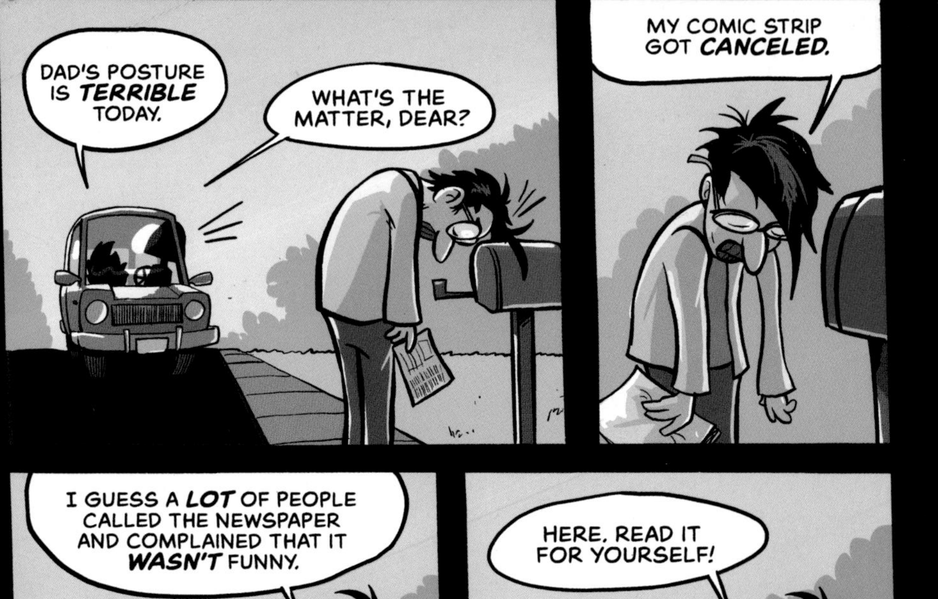
DAD'S POSTURE IS TERRIBLE TODAY.
WHAT'S THE MATTER, DEAR?
MY COMIC STRIP GOT CANCELED.
I GUESS A LOT OF PEOPLE CALLED THE NEWSPAPER AND COMPLAINED THAT IT WASN'T FUNNY.
HERE. READ IT FOR YOURSELF!

Pun in a Million

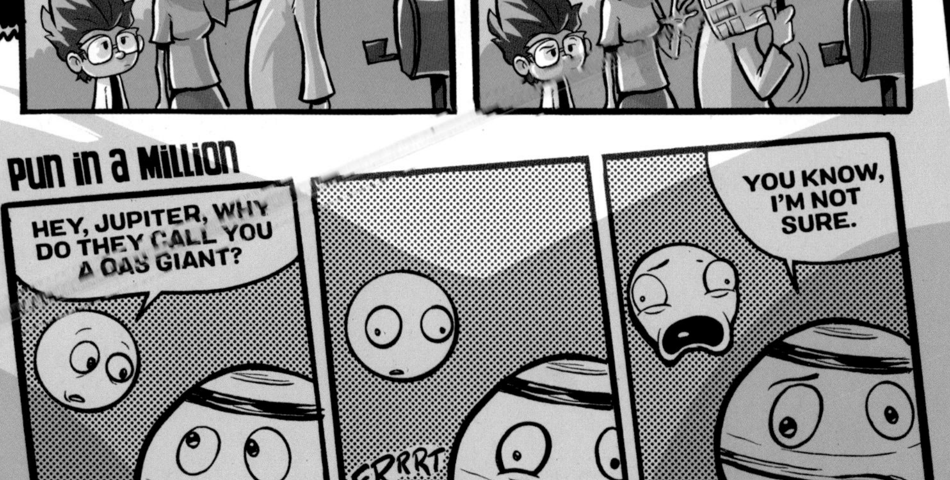
HEY, JUPITER, WHY DO THEY CALL YOU A GAS GIANT?
FRRRT.
YOU KNOW, I'M NOT SURE.

Imagine This

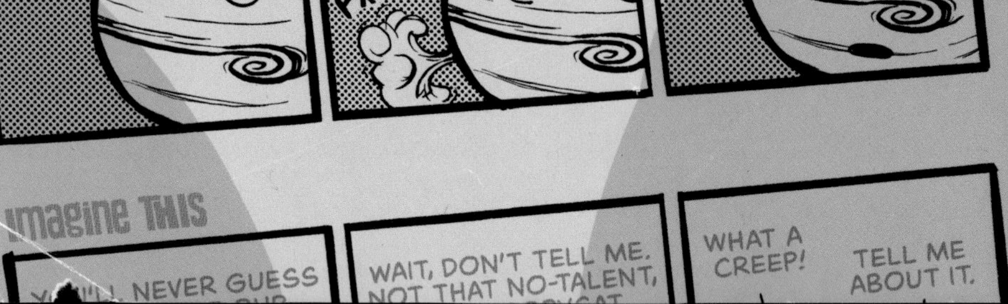
NEVER GUESS
WAIT, DON'T TELL ME. NOT THAT NO-TALENT,
WHAT A CREEP!
TELL ME ABOUT IT.

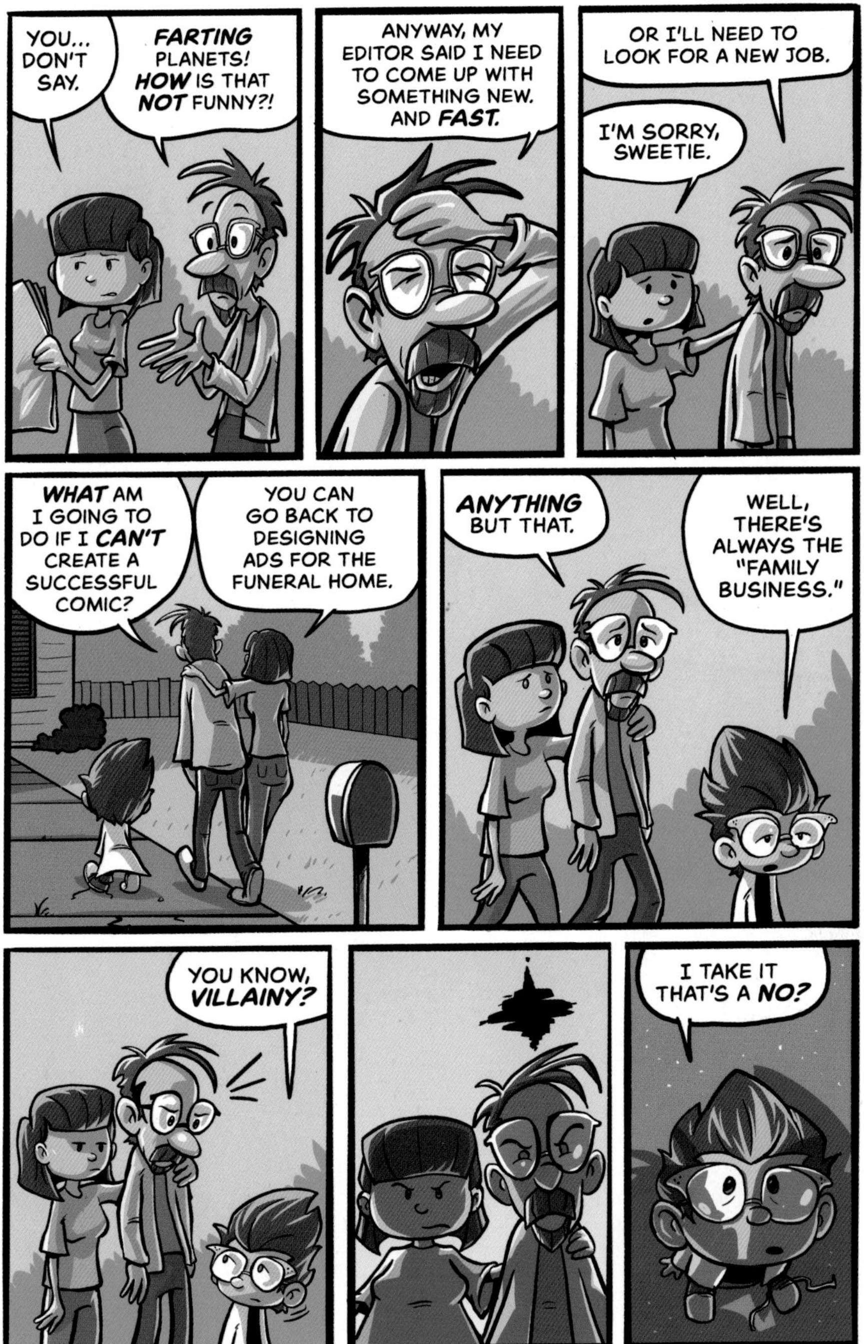
YOU... DON'T SAY.
FARTING PLANETS! HOW IS THAT NOT FUNNY?!
ANYWAY, MY EDITOR SAID I NEED TO COME UP WITH SOMETHING NEW. AND FAST.
OR I'LL NEED TO LOOK FOR A NEW JOB.
I'M SORRY, SWEETIE.
WHAT AM I GOING TO DO IF I CAN'T CREATE A SUCCESSFUL COMIC?
YOU CAN GO BACK TO DESIGNING ADS FOR THE FUNERAL HOME.
ANYTHING BUT THAT.
WELL, THERE'S ALWAYS THE "FAMILY BUSINESS."
YOU KNOW, VILLAINY?
I TAKE IT THAT'S A NO?

CHAPTER 3
McEvil, a History

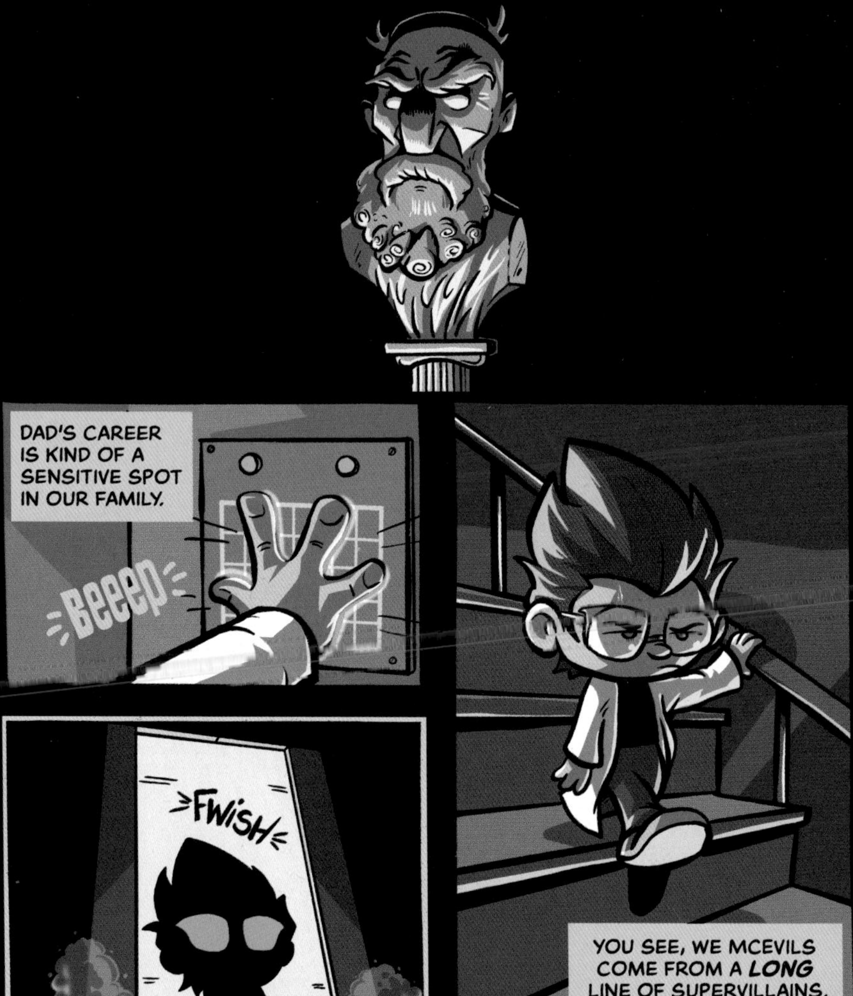
DAD'S CAREER IS KIND OF A SENSITIVE SPOT IN OUR FAMILY.
BEEEP
FWISH
YOU SEE, WE MCEVILS COME FROM A LONG LINE OF SUPERVILLAINS.

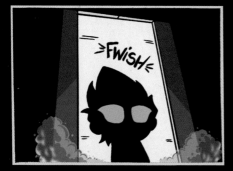

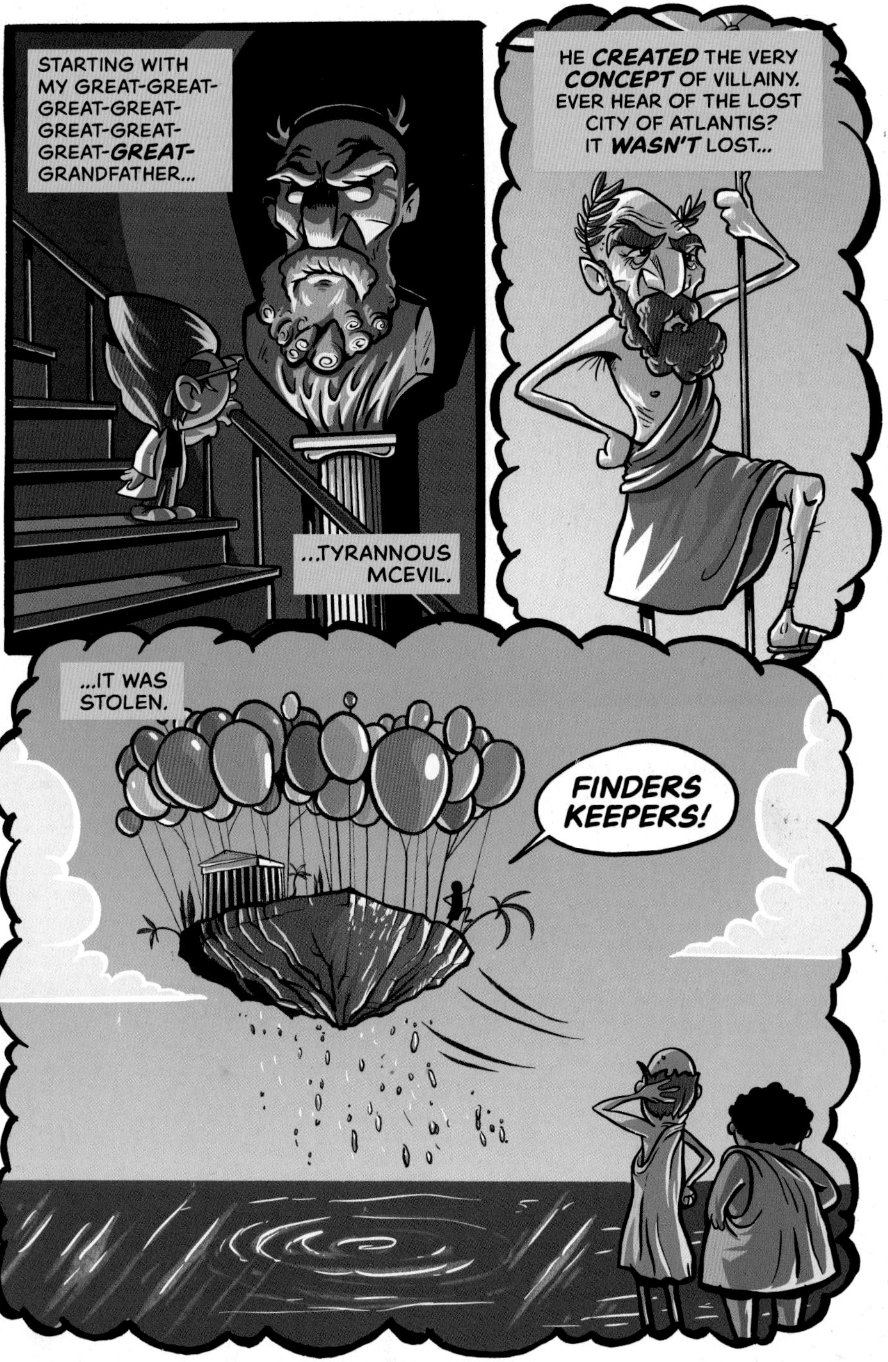
STARTING WITH MY GREAT-GREAT-GREAT-GREAT-GREAT-GREAT-GREAT-GREAT-GRANDFATHER...
...TYRANNOUS MCEVIL.
HE CREATED THE VERY CONCEPT OF VILLAINY. EVER HEAR OF THE LOST CITY OF ATLANTIS? IT WASN'T LOST...
...IT WAS STOLEN.
FINDERS KEEPERS!

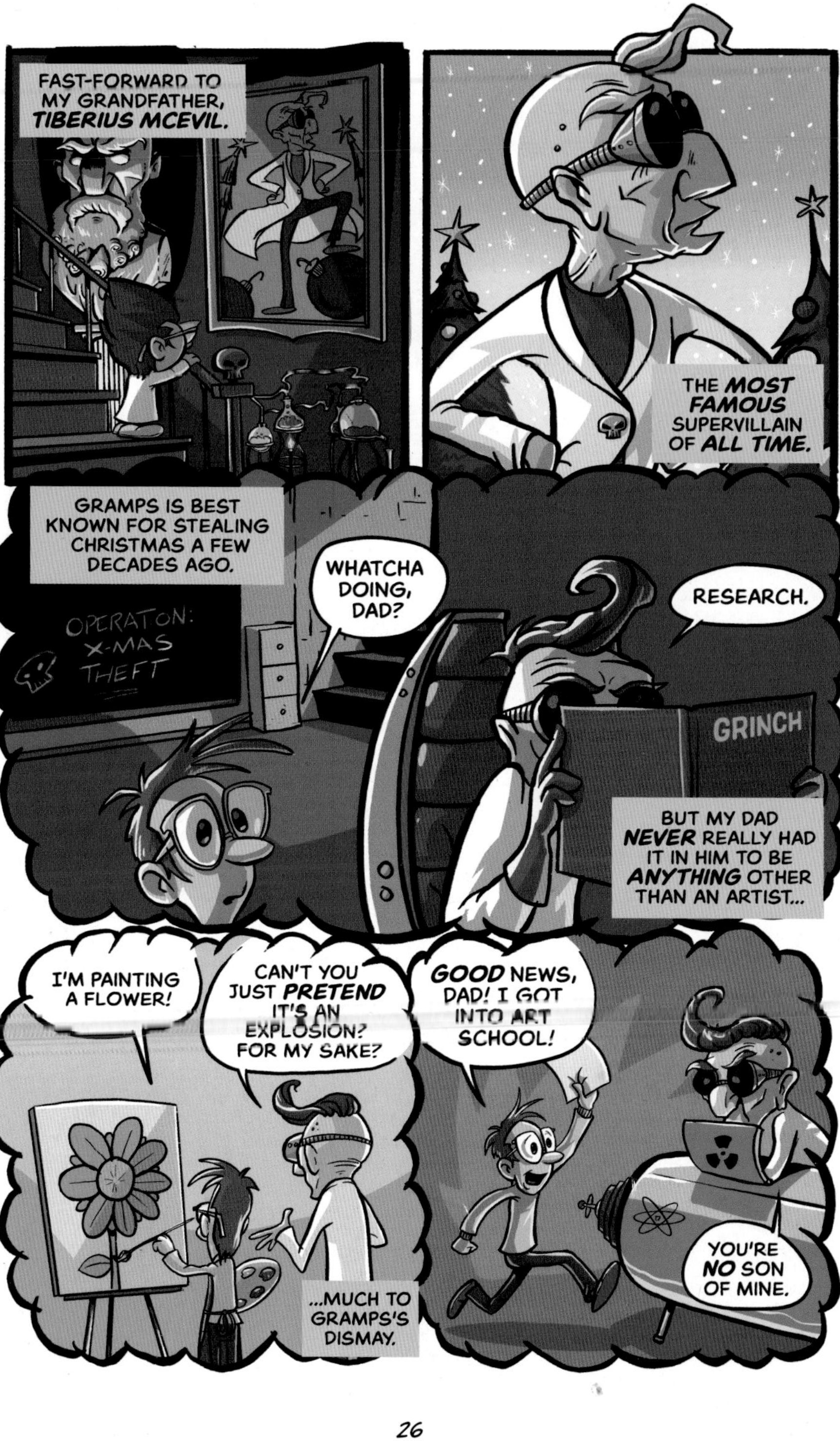
FAST-FORWARD TO MY GRANDFATHER, TIBERIUS MCEVIL.
THE MOST FAMOUS SUPERVILLAIN OF ALL TIME.
GRAMPS IS BEST KNOWN FOR STEALING CHRISTMAS A FEW DECADES AGO.
OPERATON: X-MAS THEFT
WHATCHA DOING, DAD?
RESEARCH.
GRINCH
BUT MY DAD NEVER REALLY HAD IT IN HIM TO BE ANYTHING OTHER THAN AN ARTIST...
I'M PAINTING A FLOWER!
CAN'T YOU JUST PRETEND IT'S AN EXPLOSION? FOR MY SAKE?
...MUCH TO GRAMPS'S DISMAY.
GOOD NEWS, DAD! I GOT INTO ART SCHOOL!
YOU'RE NO SON OF MINE.

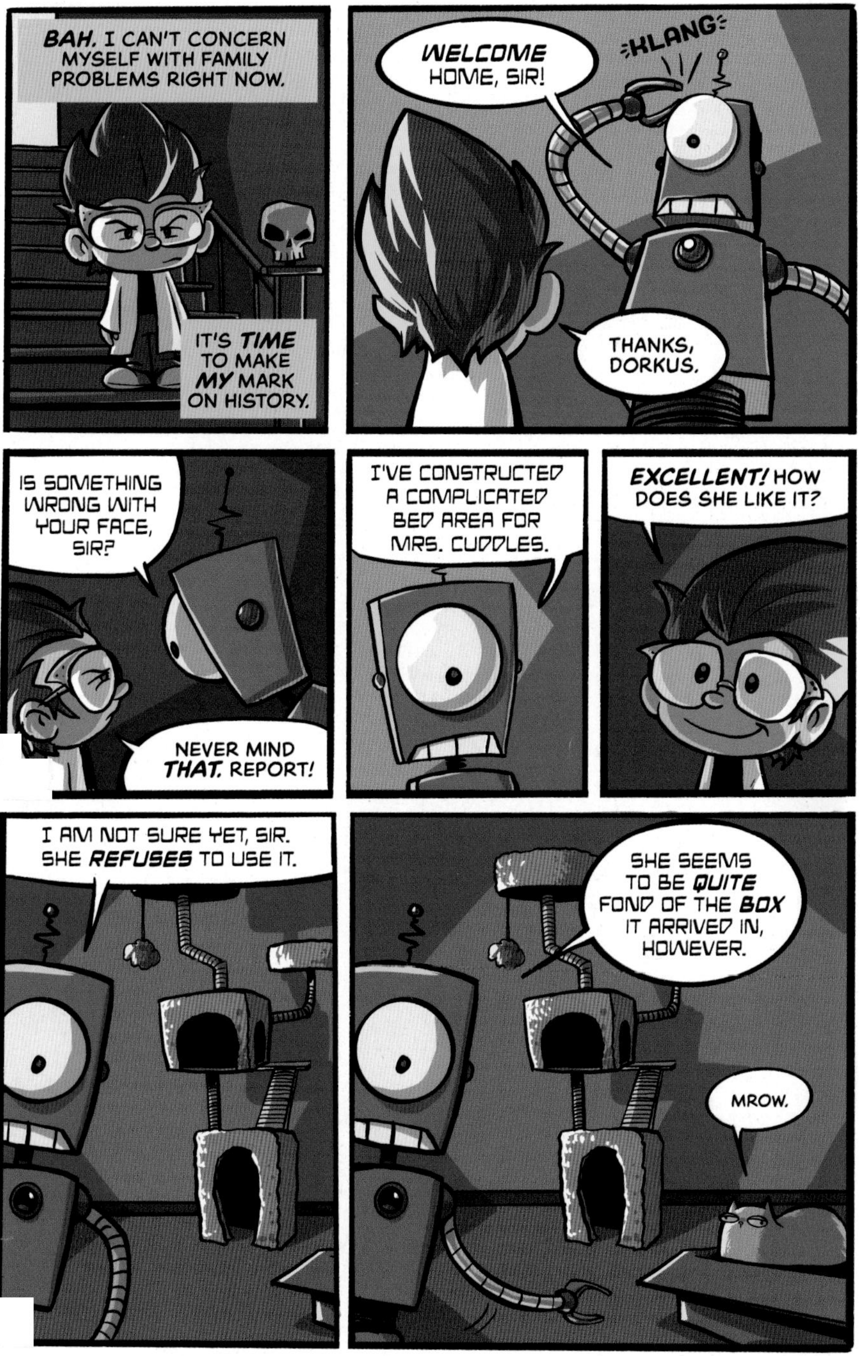
BAH. I CAN'T CONCERN MYSELF WITH FAMILY PROBLEMS RIGHT NOW.
IT'S TIME TO MAKE MY MARK ON HISTORY.
WELCOME HOME, SIR!
KLANG
THANKS, DORKUS.
IS SOMETHING WRONG WITH YOUR FACE, SIR?
NEVER MIND THAT. REPORT!
I'VE CONSTRUCTED A COMPLICATED BED AREA FOR MRS. CUDDLES.
EXCELLENT! HOW DOES SHE LIKE IT?
I AM NOT SURE YET, SIR. SHE REFUSES TO USE IT.
SHE SEEMS TO BE QUITE FOND OF THE BOX IT ARRIVED IN, HOWEVER.
MROW.

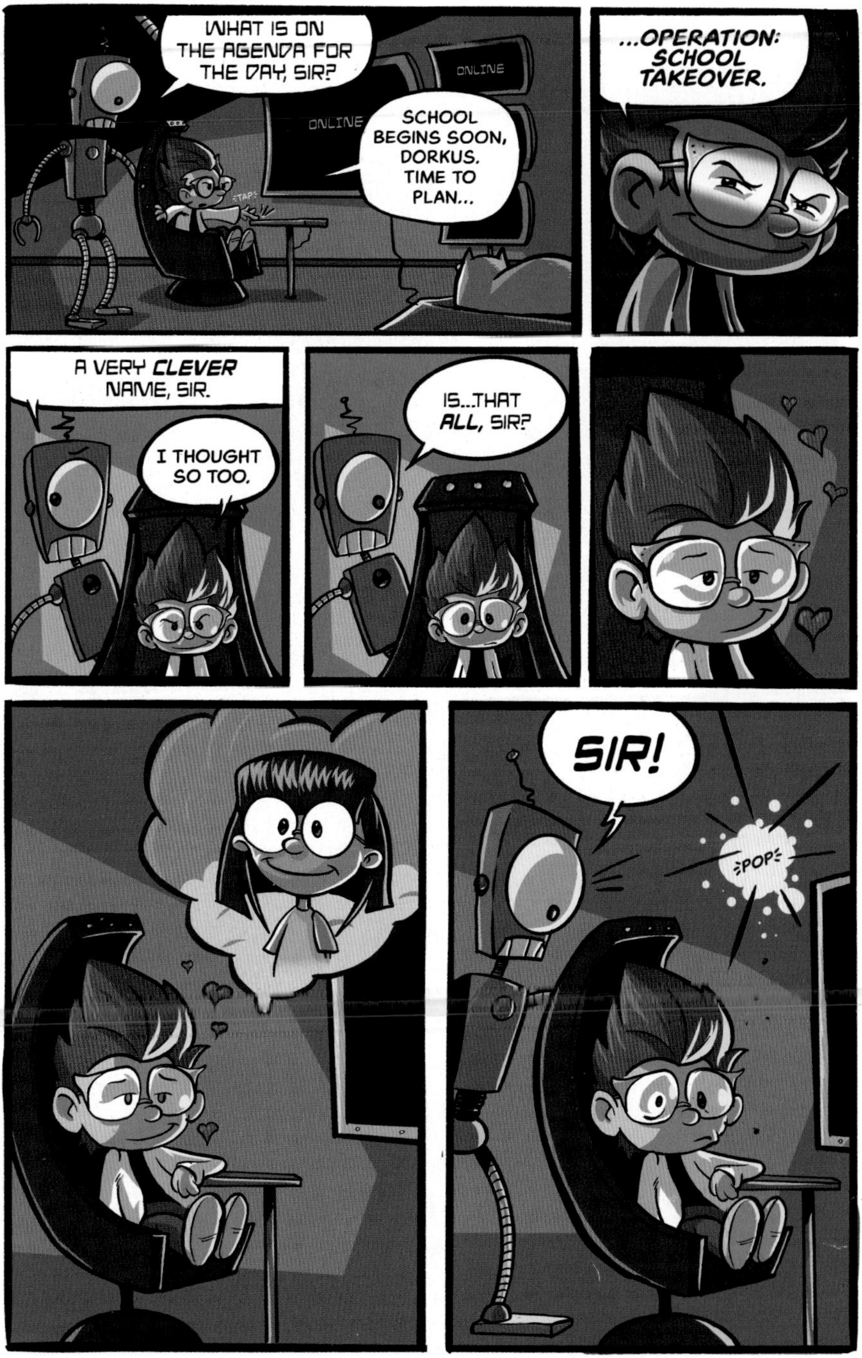
WHAT IS ON THE AGENDA FOR THE DAY, SIR?
ONLINE
ONLINE
SCHOOL BEGINS SOON, DORKUS. TIME TO PLAN...
TAP
...OPERATION: SCHOOL TAKEOVER.
A VERY CLEVER NAME, SIR.
I THOUGHT SO TOO.
IS...THAT ALL, SIR?
SIR!
POP

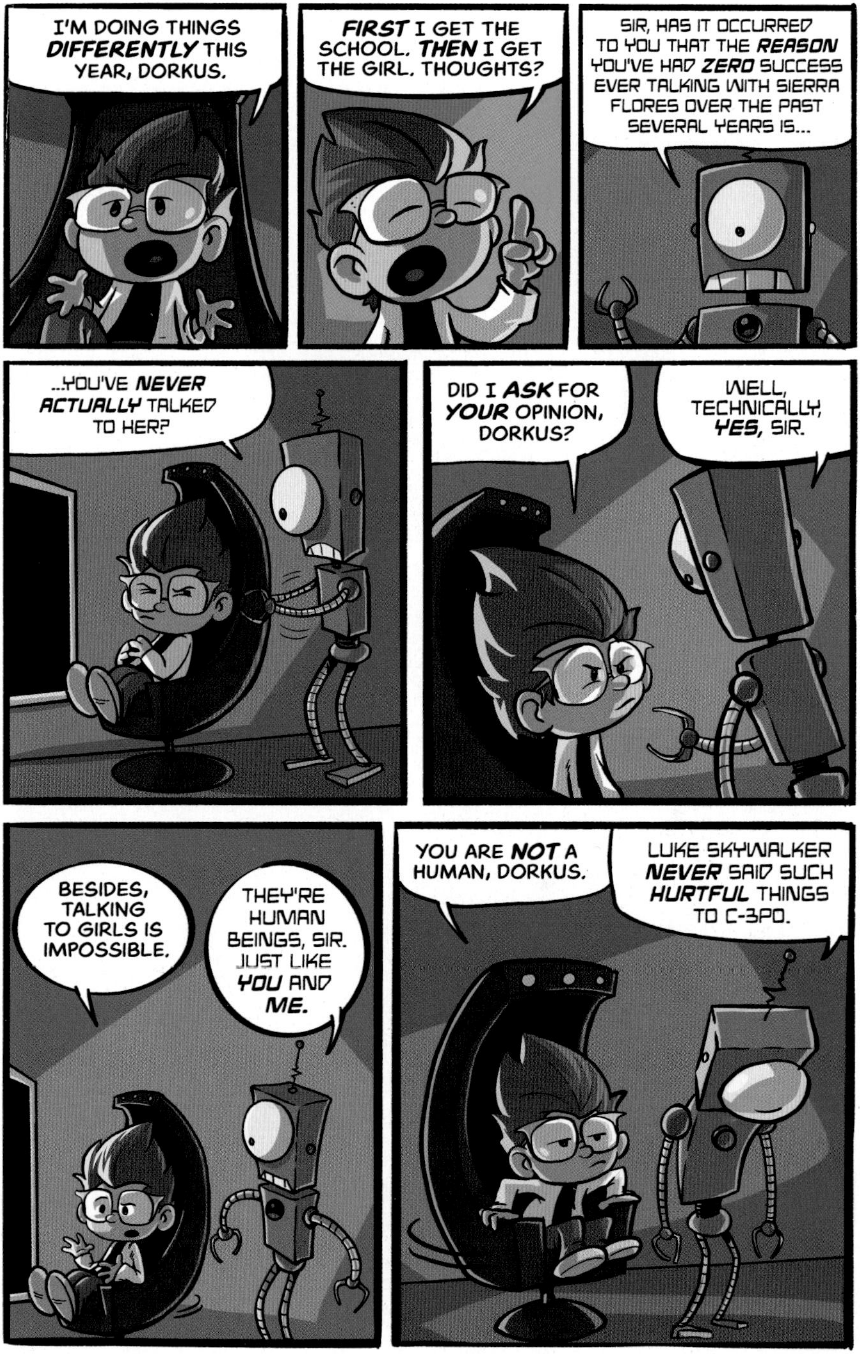
I'M DOING THINGS DIFFERENTLY THIS YEAR, DORKUS.
FIRST I GET THE SCHOOL. THEN I GET THE GIRL. THOUGHTS?
SIR, HAS IT OCCURRED TO YOU THAT THE REASON YOU'VE HAD ZERO SUCCESS EVER TALKING WITH SIERRA FLORES OVER THE PAST SEVERAL YEARS IS...
...YOU'VE NEVER ACTUALLY TALKED TO HER?
DID I ASK FOR YOUR OPINION, DORKUS?
WELL, TECHNICALLY, YES, SIR.
BESIDES, TALKING TO GIRLS IS IMPOSSIBLE.
THEY'RE HUMAN BEINGS, SIR. JUST LIKE YOU AND ME.
YOU ARE NOT A HUMAN, DORKUS.
LUKE SKYWALKER NEVER SAID SUCH HURTFUL THINGS TO C-3PO.

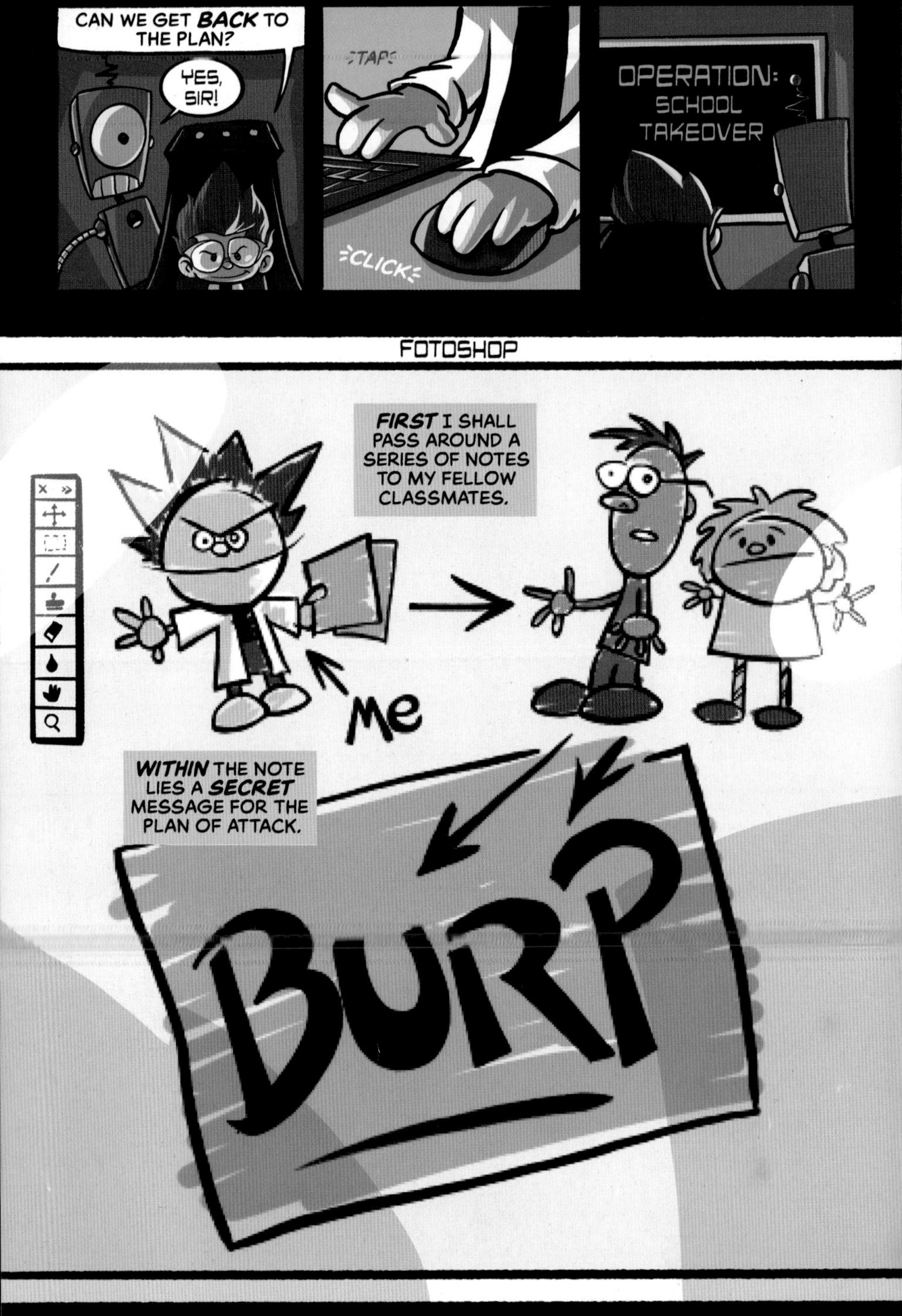
CAN WE GET BACK TO THE PLAN?
YES, SIR!
TAP
CLICK
OPERATION: SCHOOL TAKEOVER
FOTOSHOP
FIRST I SHALL PASS AROUND A SERIES OF NOTES TO MY FELLOW CLASSMATES.
ME
WITHIN THE NOTE LIES A SECRET MESSAGE FOR THE PLAN OF ATTACK.
BURP

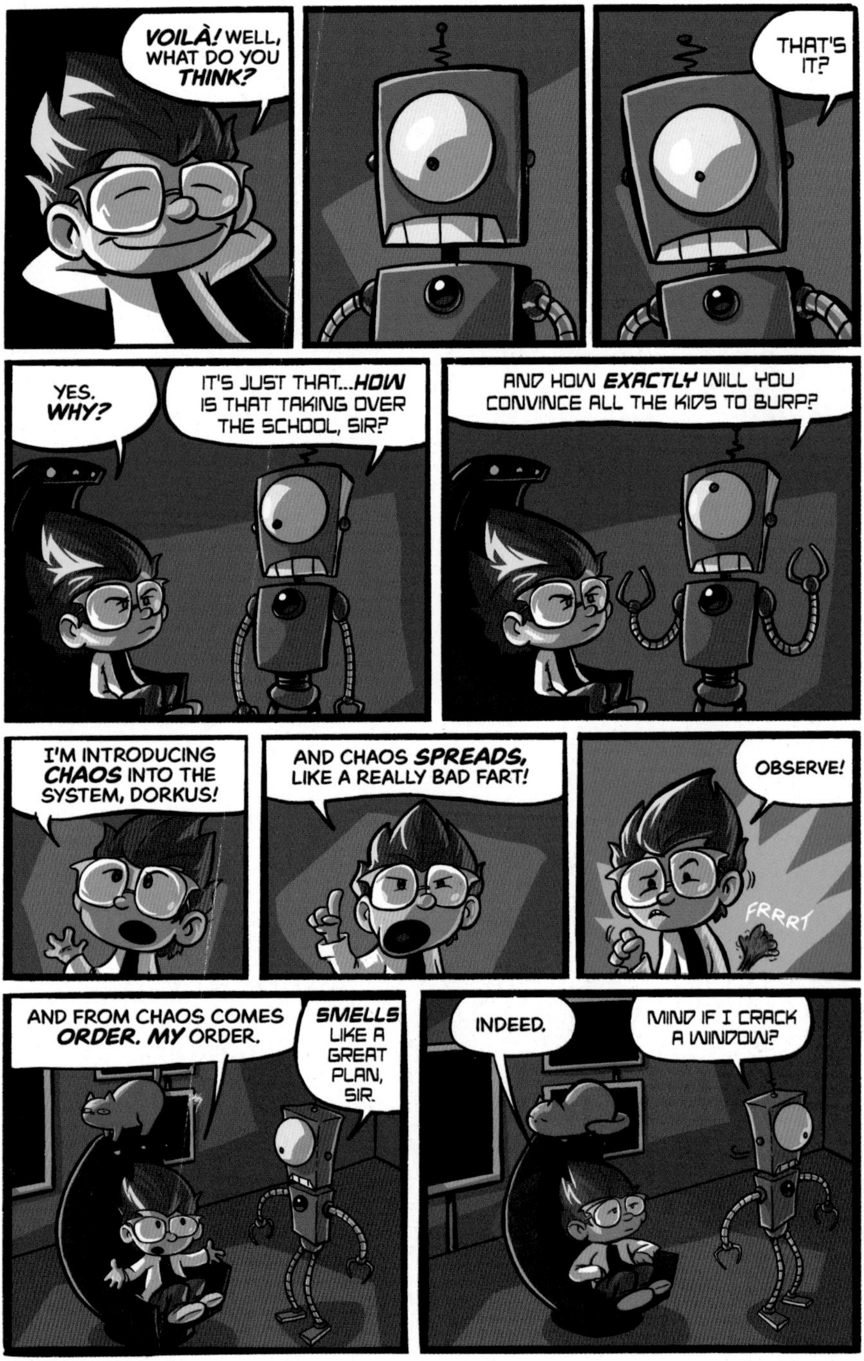
VOILÀ! WELL, WHAT DO YOU THINK?
THAT'S IT?
YES. WHY?
IT'S JUST THAT...HOW IS THAT TAKING OVER THE SCHOOL, SIR?
AND HOW EXACTLY WILL YOU CONVINCE ALL THE KIDS TO BURP?
I'M INTRODUCING CHAOS INTO THE SYSTEM, DORKUS!
AND CHAOS SPREADS, LIKE A REALLY BAD FART!
OBSERVE!
FRRRT
AND FROM CHAOS COMES ORDER. MY ORDER.
SMELLS LIKE A GREAT PLAN, SIR.
INDEED.
MIND IF I CRACK A WINDOW?

CHaPTeR 4
There Can Be Only One

THE NeXT MORNING...

HURRY UP! I'M OLD, AND TIME'S A-WASTIN'!

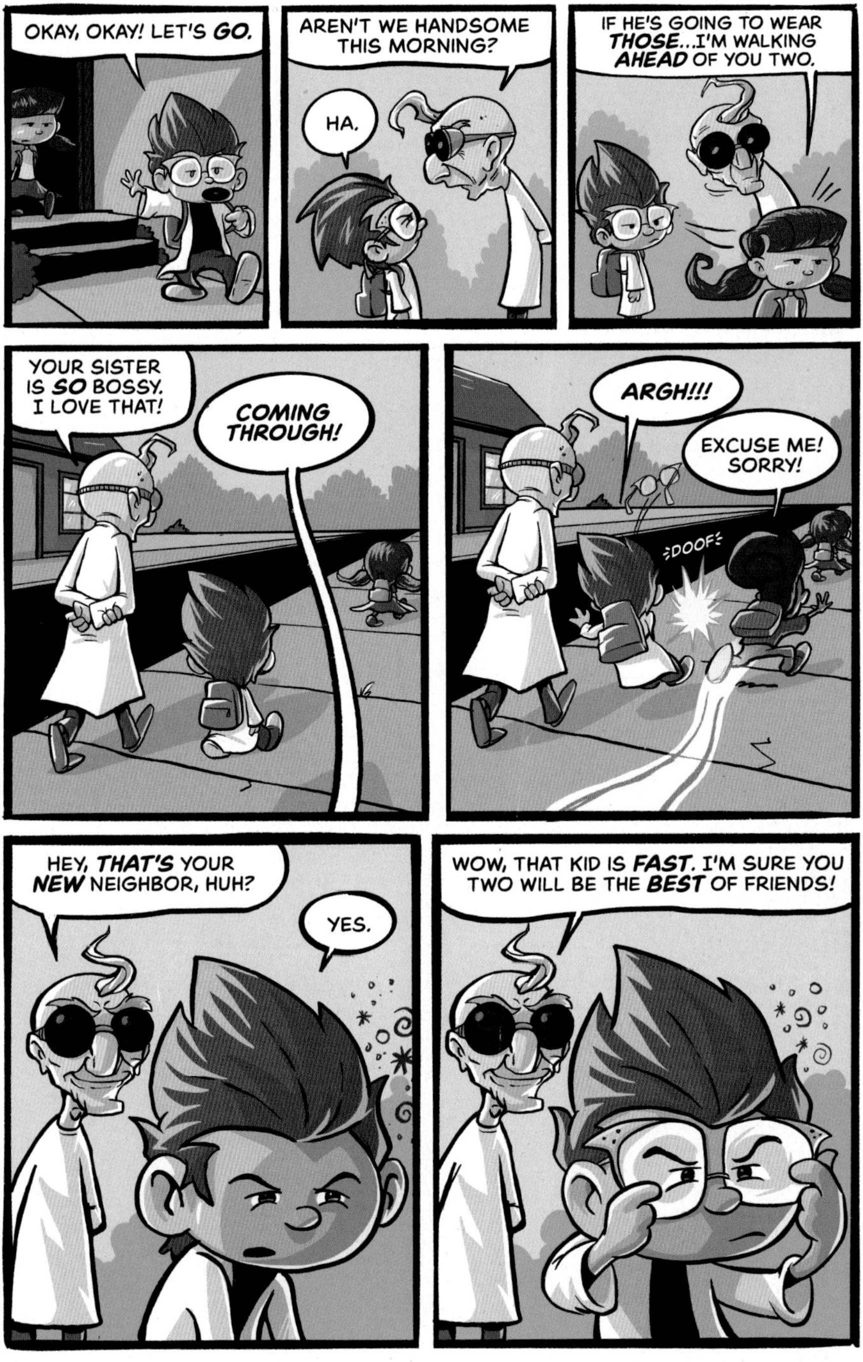
OKAY, OKAY! LET'S GO.
AREN'T WE HANDSOME THIS MORNING?
HA.
IF HE'S GOING TO WEAR THOSE...I'M WALKING AHEAD OF YOU TWO.
YOUR SISTER IS SO BOSSY. I LOVE THAT!
COMING THROUGH!
ARGH!!!
EXCUSE ME! SORRY!
DOOF
HEY, THAT'S YOUR NEW NEIGHBOR, HUH?
YES.
WOW, THAT KID IS FAST. I'M SURE YOU TWO WILL BE THE BEST OF FRIENDS!

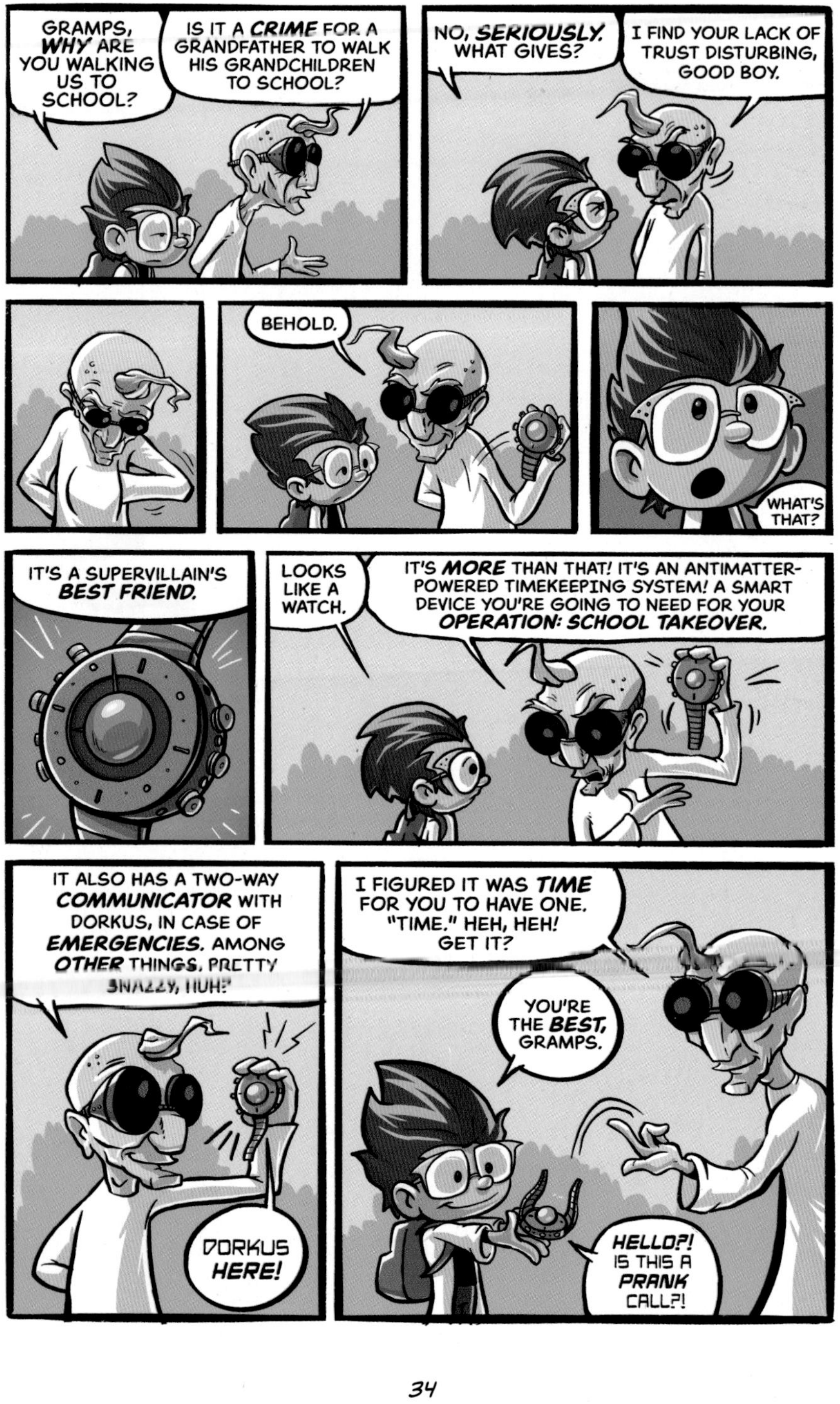
GRAMPS, WHY ARE YOU WALKING US TO SCHOOL?
IS IT A CRIME FOR A GRANDFATHER TO WALK HIS GRANDCHILDREN TO SCHOOL?
NO, SERIOUSLY. WHAT GIVES?
I FIND YOUR LACK OF TRUST DISTURBING, GOOD BOY.
BEHOLD.
WHAT'S THAT?
IT'S A SUPERVILLAIN'S BEST FRIEND.
LOOKS LIKE A WATCH.
IT'S MORE THAN THAT! IT'S AN ANTIMATTER-POWERED TIMEKEEPING SYSTEM! A SMART DEVICE YOU'RE GOING TO NEED FOR YOUR OPERATION: SCHOOL TAKEOVER.
IT ALSO HAS A TWO-WAY COMMUNICATOR WITH DORKUS, IN CASE OF EMERGENCIES. AMONG OTHER THINGS. PRETTY SNAZZY, HUH?
DORKUS HERE!
I FIGURED IT WAS TIME FOR YOU TO HAVE ONE. "TIME." HEH, HEH! GET IT?
YOU'RE THE BEST, GRAMPS.
HELLO?! IS THIS A PRANK CALL?!

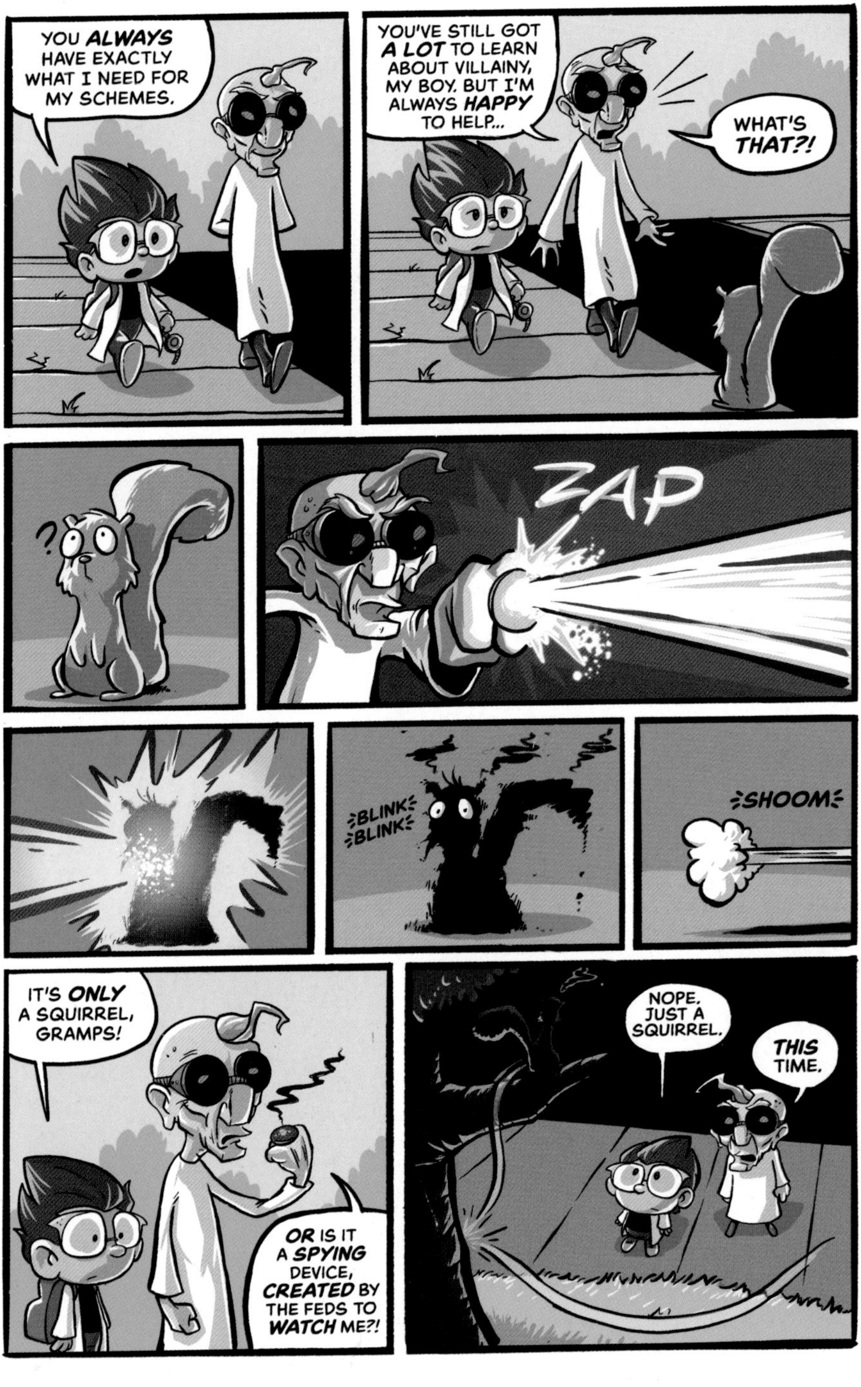
YOU ALWAYS HAVE EXACTLY WHAT I NEED FOR MY SCHEMES.
YOU'VE STILL GOT A LOT TO LEARN ABOUT VILLAINY, MY BOY. BUT I'M ALWAYS HAPPY TO HELP...
WHAT'S THAT?!
?
ZAP
BLINK BLINK
SHOOM
IT'S ONLY A SQUIRREL, GRAMPS!
OR IS IT A SPYING DEVICE, CREATED BY THE FEDS TO WATCH ME?!
NOPE. JUST A SQUIRREL.
THIS TIME.

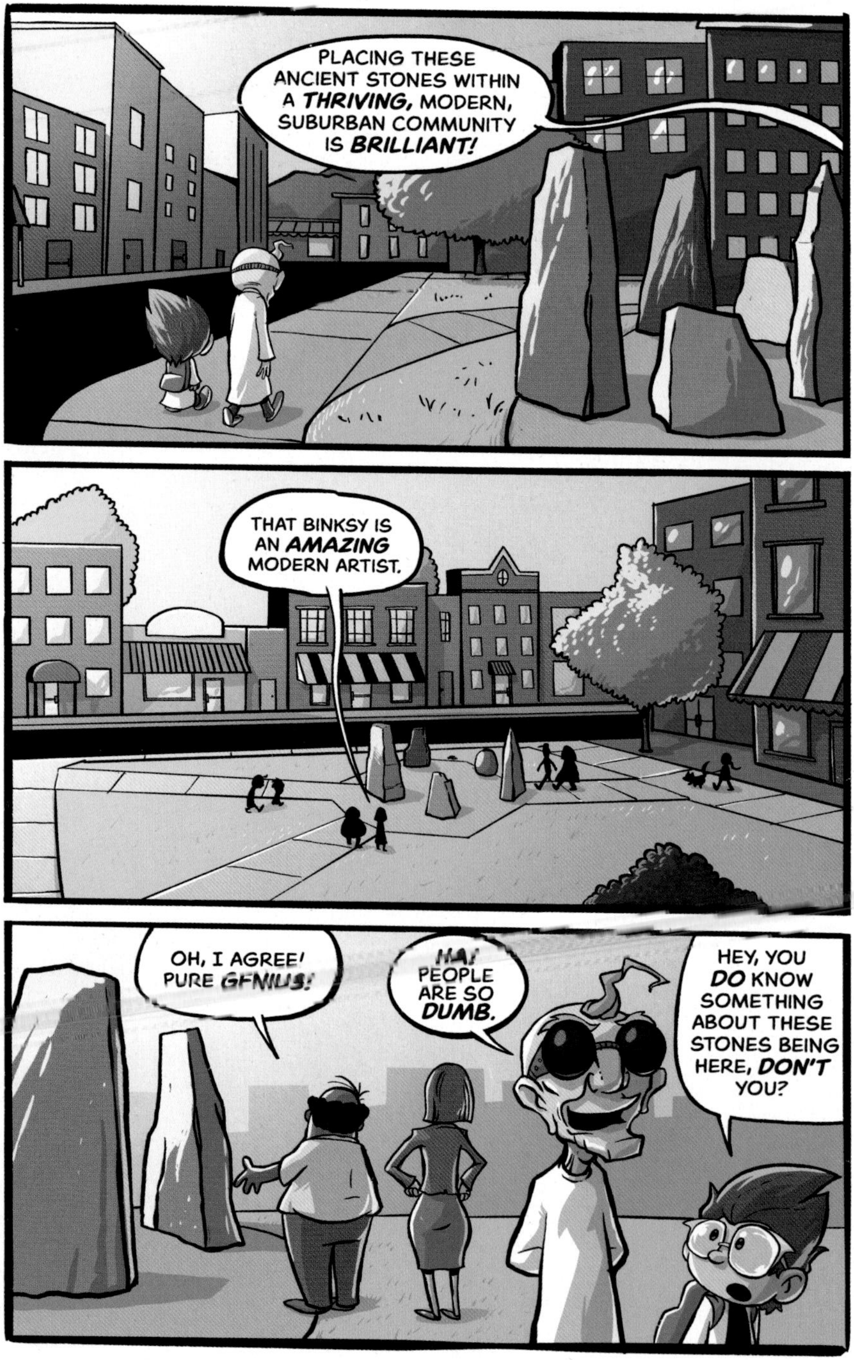
PLACING THESE ANCIENT STONES WITHIN A **THRIVING,** MODERN, SUBURBAN COMMUNITY IS **BRILLIANT!**
THAT BINKSY IS AN **AMAZING** MODERN ARTIST.
OH, I AGREE! PURE **GENIUS!**
HA! PEOPLE ARE SO **DUMB.**
HEY, YOU **DO** KNOW SOMETHING ABOUT THESE STONES BEING HERE, **DON'T** YOU?

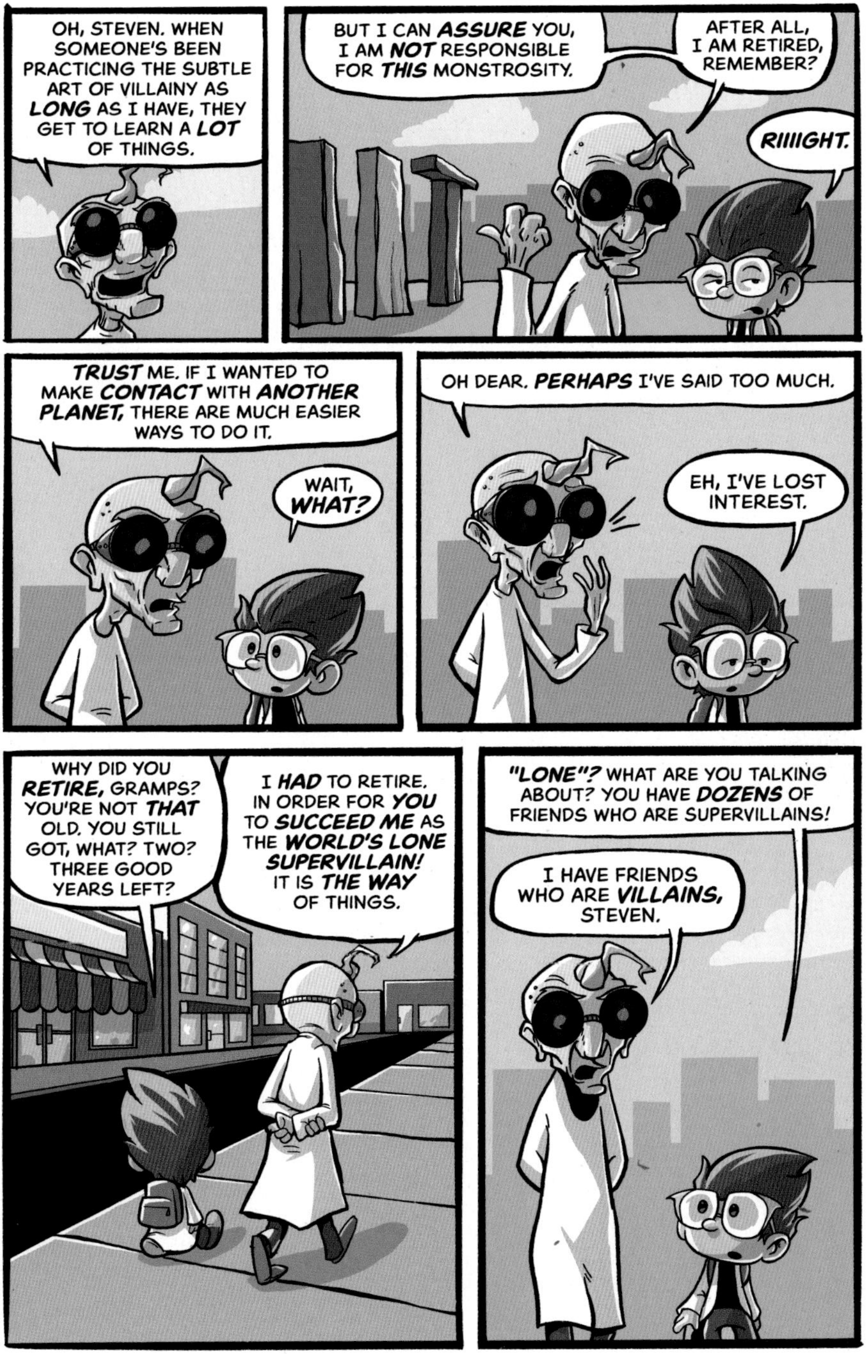
OH, STEVEN. WHEN SOMEONE'S BEEN PRACTICING THE SUBTLE ART OF VILLAINY AS LONG AS I HAVE, THEY GET TO LEARN A LOT OF THINGS.
BUT I CAN ASSURE YOU, I AM NOT RESPONSIBLE FOR THIS MONSTROSITY.
AFTER ALL, I AM RETIRED, REMEMBER?
RIIIIGHT.
TRUST ME. IF I WANTED TO MAKE CONTACT WITH ANOTHER PLANET, THERE ARE MUCH EASIER WAYS TO DO IT.
WAIT, WHAT?
OH DEAR. PERHAPS I'VE SAID TOO MUCH.
EH, I'VE LOST INTEREST.
WHY DID YOU RETIRE, GRAMPS? YOU'RE NOT THAT OLD. YOU STILL GOT, WHAT? TWO? THREE GOOD YEARS LEFT?
I HAD TO RETIRE. IN ORDER FOR YOU TO SUCCEED ME AS THE WORLD'S LONE SUPERVILLAIN! IT IS THE WAY OF THINGS.
"LONE"? WHAT ARE YOU TALKING ABOUT? YOU HAVE DOZENS OF FRIENDS WHO ARE SUPERVILLAINS!
I HAVE FRIENDS WHO ARE VILLAINS, STEVEN.

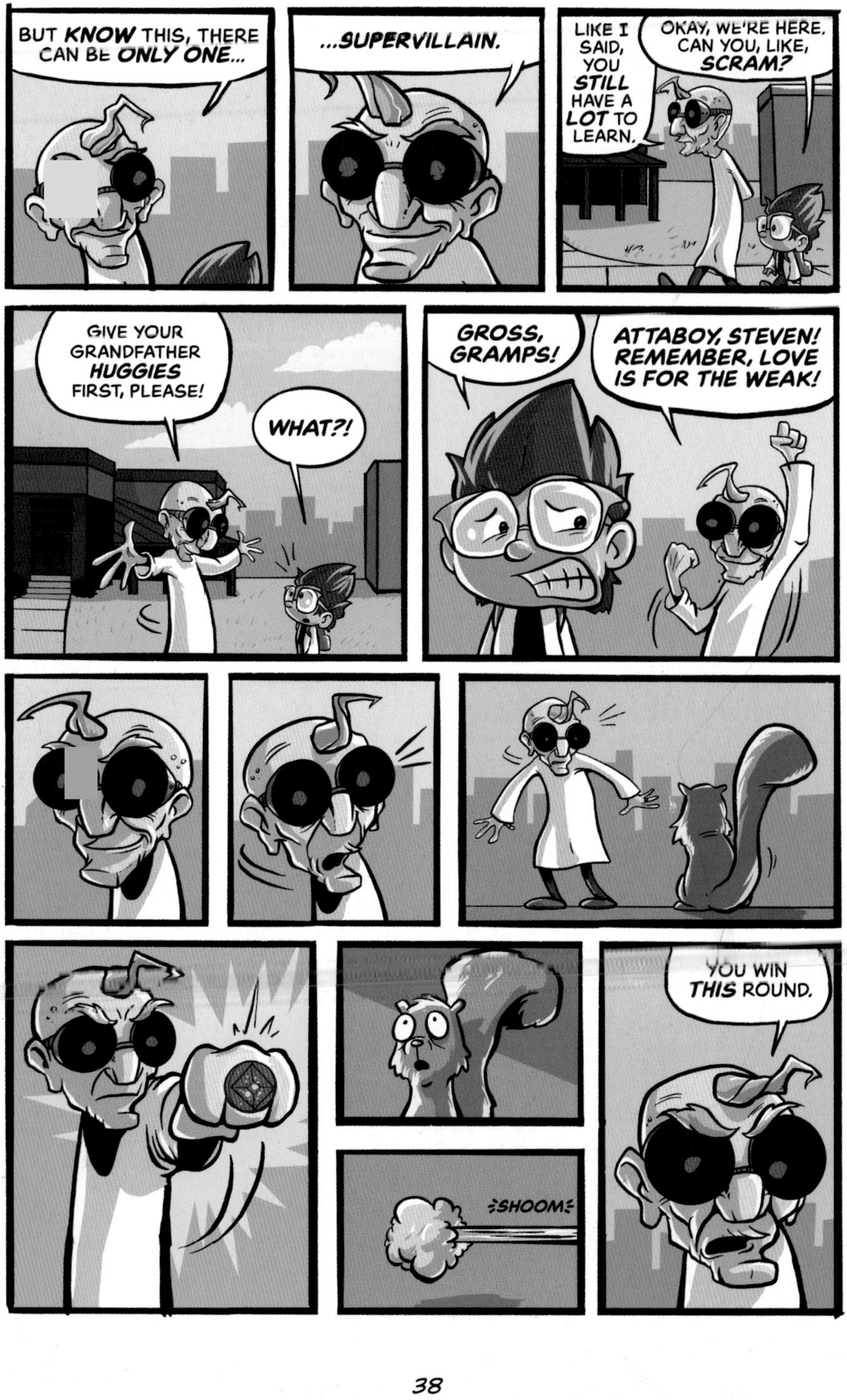
BUT KNOW THIS, THERE CAN BE ONLY ONE...
...SUPERVILLAIN.
LIKE I SAID, YOU STILL HAVE A LOT TO LEARN.
OKAY, WE'RE HERE. CAN YOU, LIKE, SCRAM?
GIVE YOUR GRANDFATHER HUGGIES FIRST, PLEASE!
WHAT?!
GROSS, GRAMPS!
ATTABOY, STEVEN! REMEMBER, LOVE IS FOR THE WEAK!
SHOOM
YOU WIN THIS ROUND.

CHAPTER 5

The New Kid

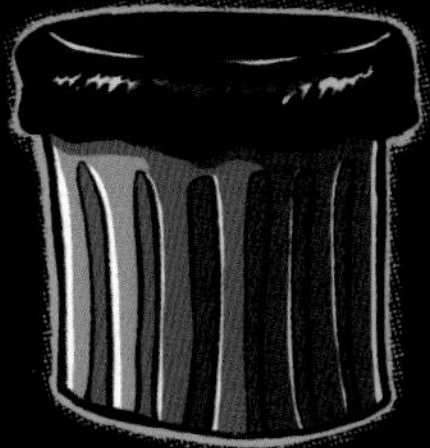

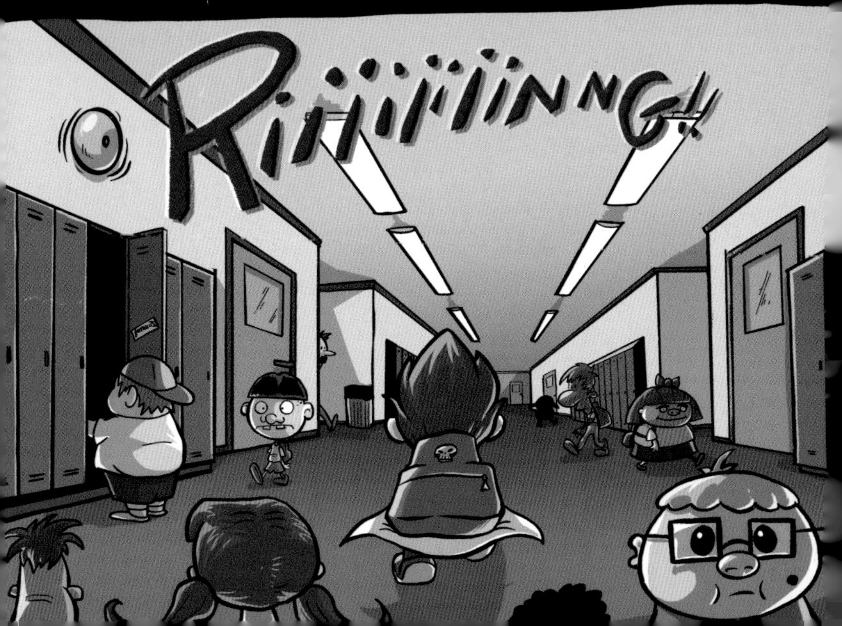
Riiiiiiiinng!!

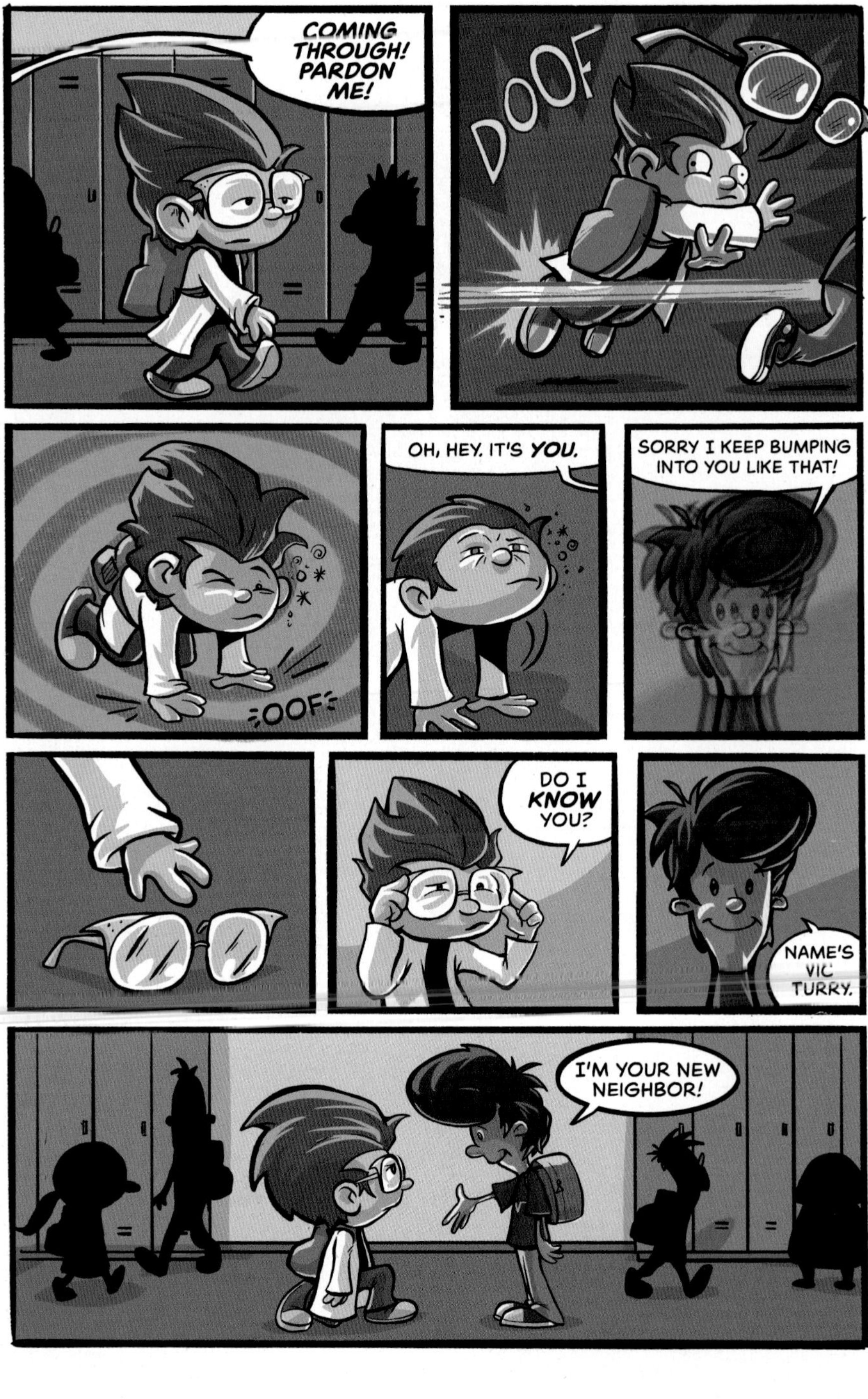
COMING THROUGH! PARDON ME!
DOOF
OOF
OH, HEY. IT'S YOU.
SORRY I KEEP BUMPING INTO YOU LIKE THAT!
DO I KNOW YOU?
NAME'S VIC TURRY.
I'M YOUR NEW NEIGHBOR!

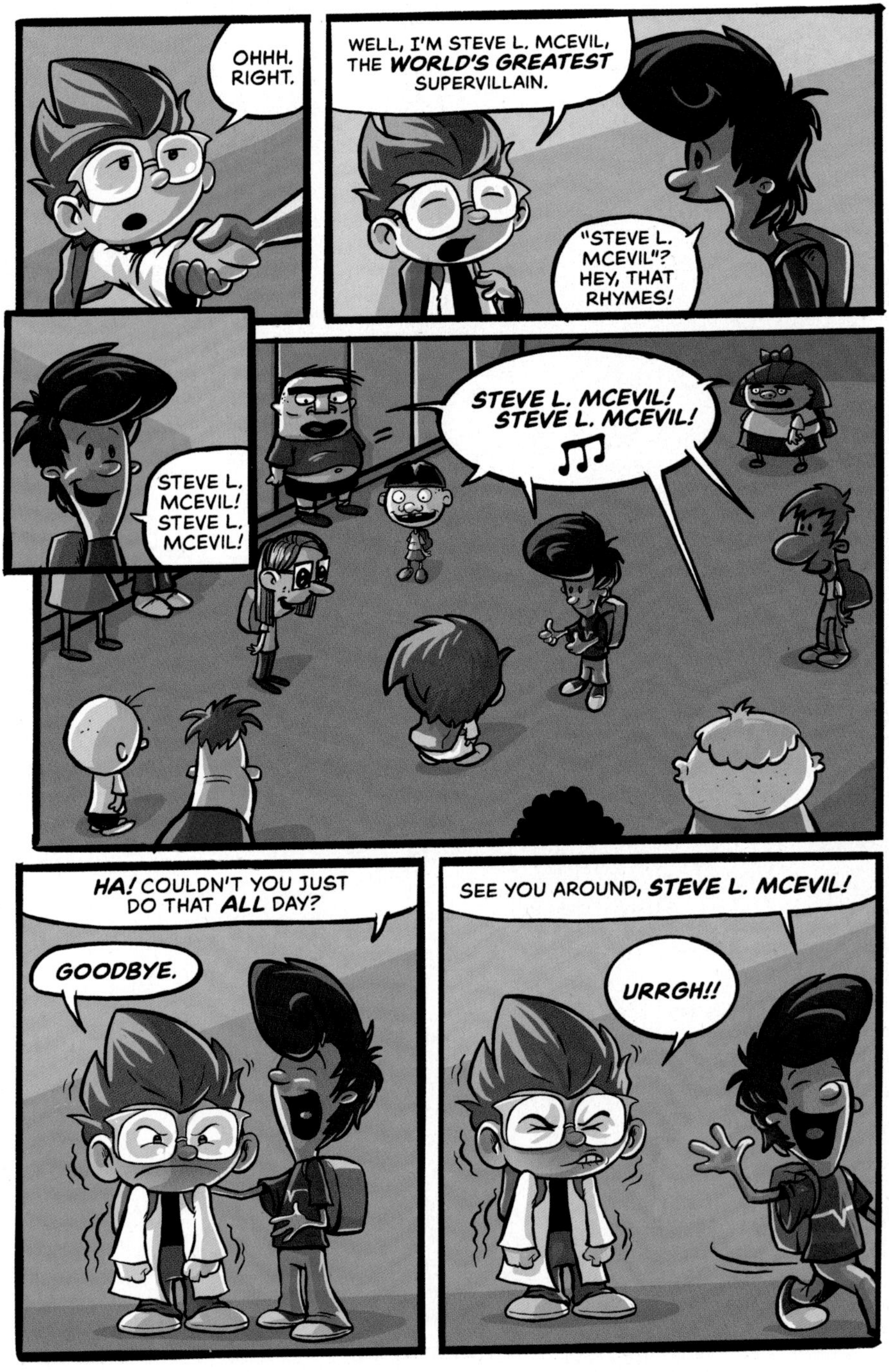
OHHH. RIGHT.
WELL, I'M STEVE L. MCEVIL, THE WORLD'S GREATEST SUPERVILLAIN.
"STEVE L. MCEVIL"? HEY, THAT RHYMES!
STEVE L. MCEVIL! STEVE L. MCEVIL!
STEVE L. MCEVIL! STEVE L. MCEVIL!
HA! COULDN'T YOU JUST DO THAT ALL DAY?
GOODBYE.
SEE YOU AROUND, STEVE L. MCEVIL!
URRGH!!

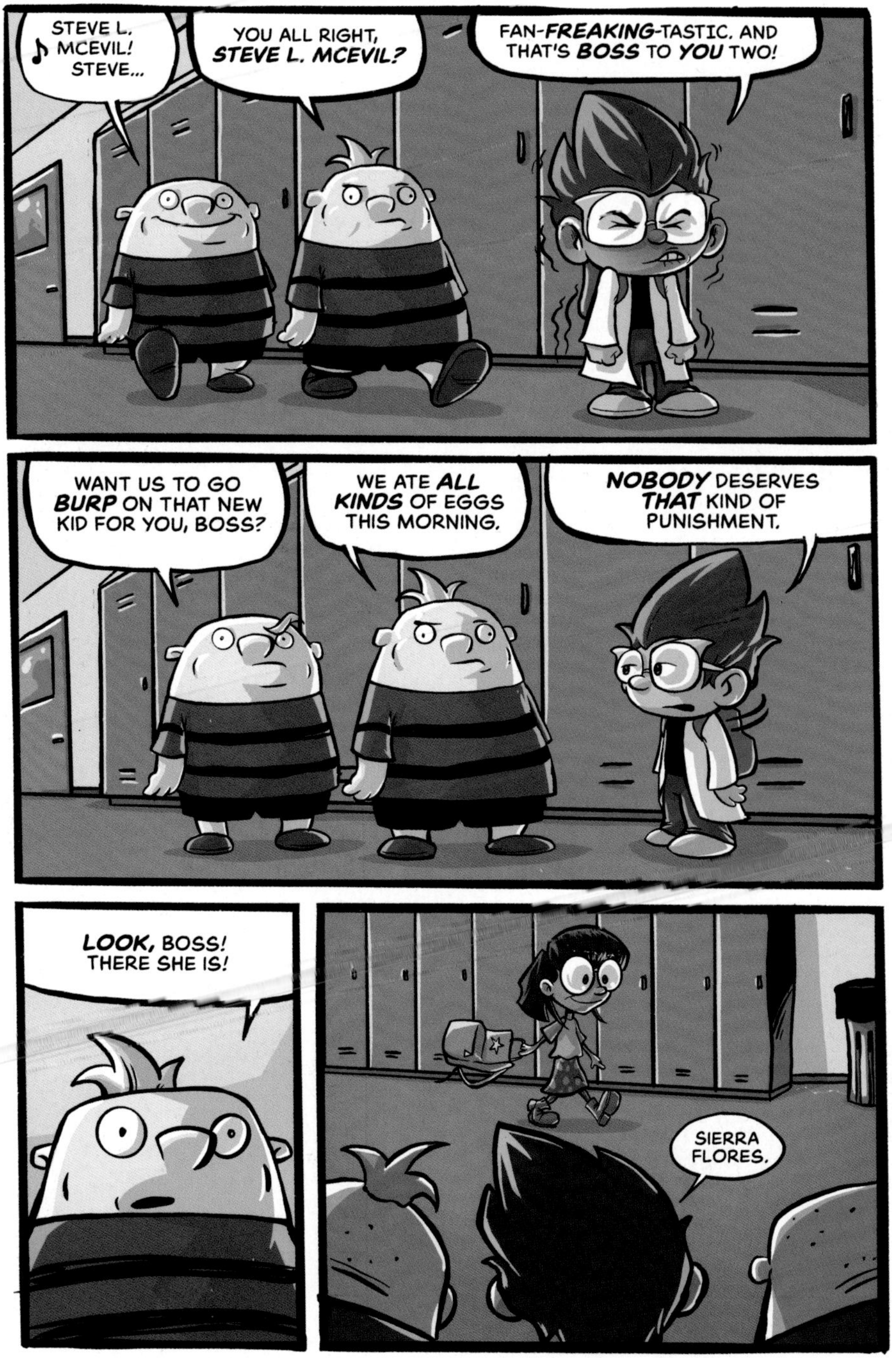
STEVE L. ♪ MCEVIL! STEVE...
YOU ALL RIGHT, STEVE L. MCEVIL?
FAN-FREAKING-TASTIC. AND THAT'S BOSS TO YOU TWO!
WANT US TO GO BURP ON THAT NEW KID FOR YOU, BOSS?
WE ATE ALL KINDS OF EGGS THIS MORNING.
NOBODY DESERVES THAT KIND OF PUNISHMENT.
LOOK, BOSS! THERE SHE IS!
SIERRA FLORES.

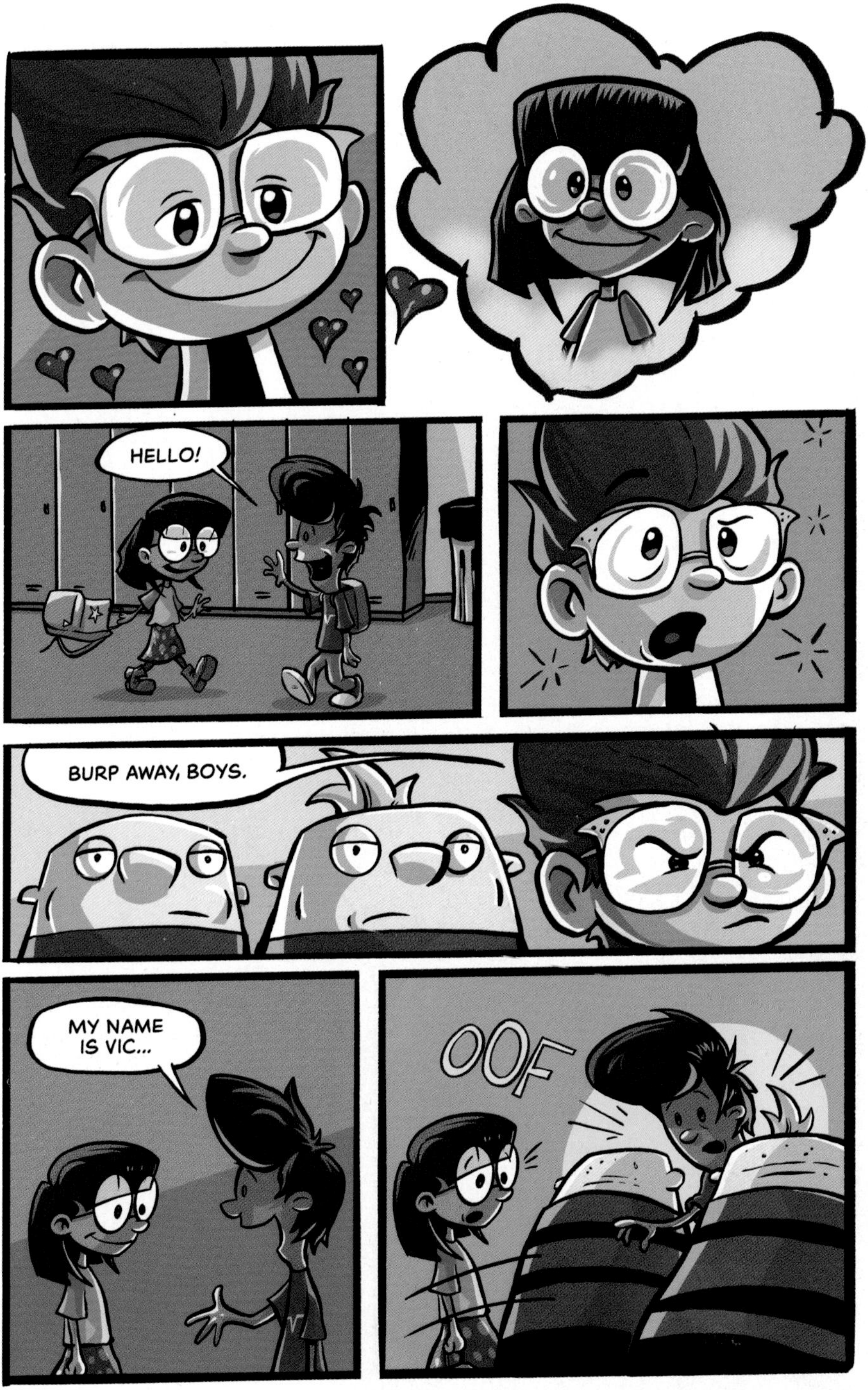
HELLO!
BURP AWAY, BOYS.
MY NAME IS VIC...
OOF

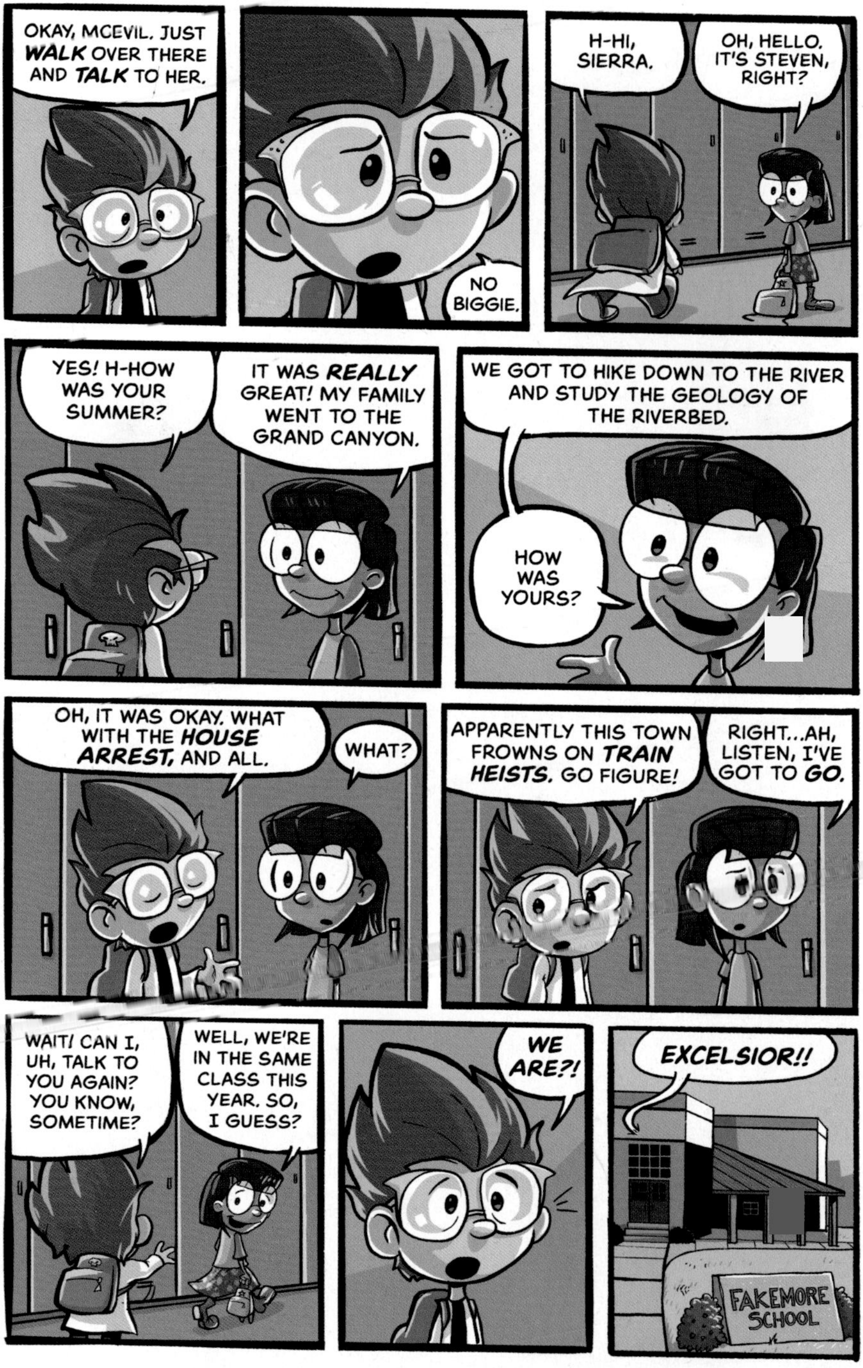
OKAY, MCEVIL. JUST WALK OVER THERE AND TALK TO HER.
NO BIGGIE.
H-HI, SIERRA.
OH, HELLO. IT'S STEVEN, RIGHT?
YES! H-HOW WAS YOUR SUMMER?
IT WAS REALLY GREAT! MY FAMILY WENT TO THE GRAND CANYON.
WE GOT TO HIKE DOWN TO THE RIVER AND STUDY THE GEOLOGY OF THE RIVERBED.
HOW WAS YOURS?
OH, IT WAS OKAY. WHAT WITH THE HOUSE ARREST, AND ALL.
WHAT?
APPARENTLY THIS TOWN FROWNS ON TRAIN HEISTS. GO FIGURE!
RIGHT...AH, LISTEN, I'VE GOT TO GO.
WAIT! CAN I, UH, TALK TO YOU AGAIN? YOU KNOW, SOMETIME?
WELL, WE'RE IN THE SAME CLASS THIS YEAR. SO, I GUESS?
WE ARE?!
EXCELSIOR!!
FAKEMORE SCHOOL

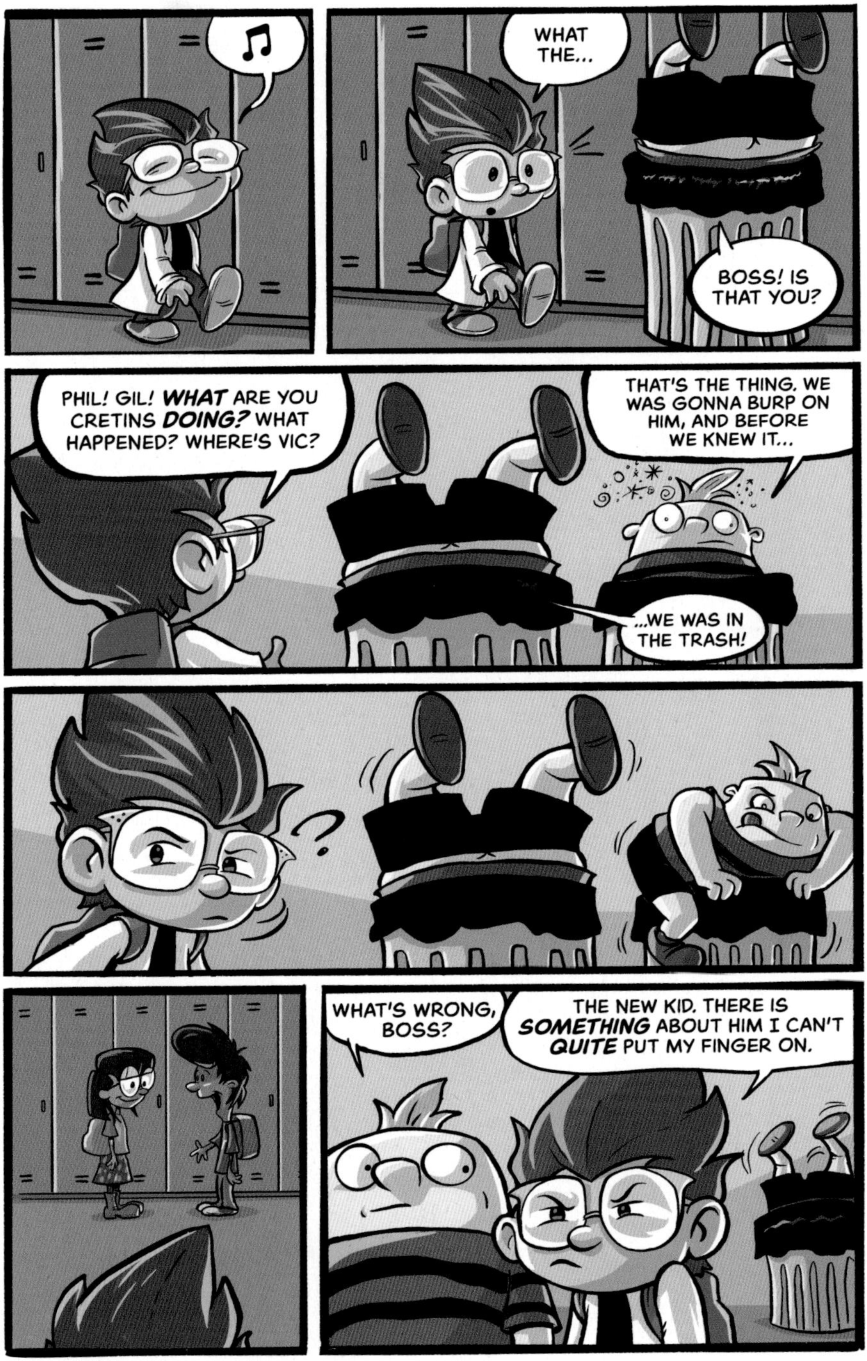
♫
WHAT THE...
BOSS! IS THAT YOU?
PHIL! GIL! **WHAT** ARE YOU CRETINS **DOING?** WHAT HAPPENED? WHERE'S VIC?
THAT'S THE THING. WE WAS GONNA BURP ON HIM, AND BEFORE WE KNEW IT...
...WE WAS IN THE TRASH!
WHAT'S WRONG, BOSS?
THE NEW KID. THERE IS **SOMETHING** ABOUT HIM I CAN'T **QUITE** PUT MY FINGER ON.

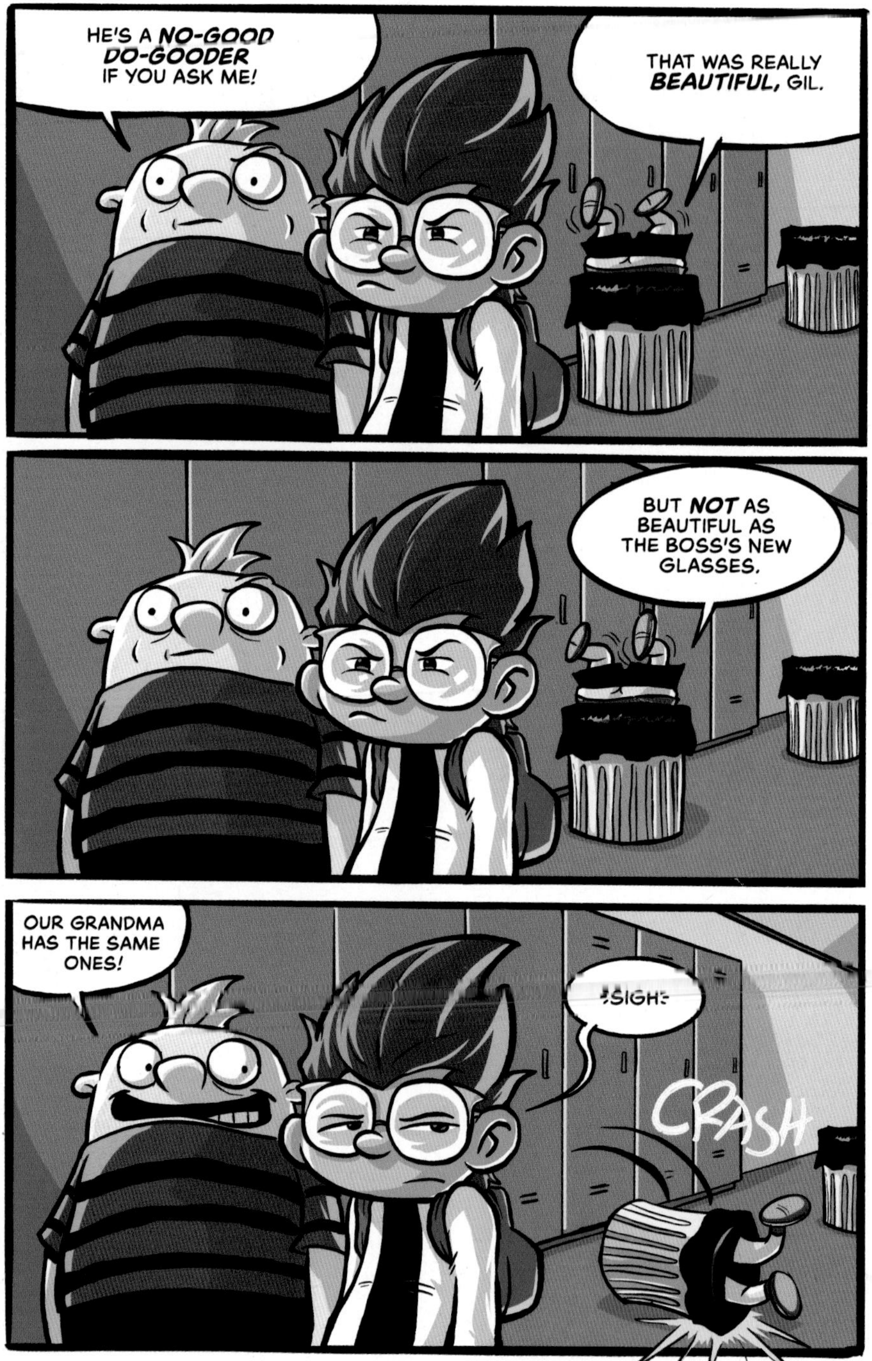
HE'S A **NO-GOOD DO-GOODER** IF YOU ASK ME!
THAT WAS REALLY **BEAUTIFUL,** GIL.
BUT **NOT** AS BEAUTIFUL AS THE BOSS'S NEW GLASSES.
OUR GRANDMA HAS THE SAME ONES!
SIGH
CRASH

CHAPTER 6

The Stinger

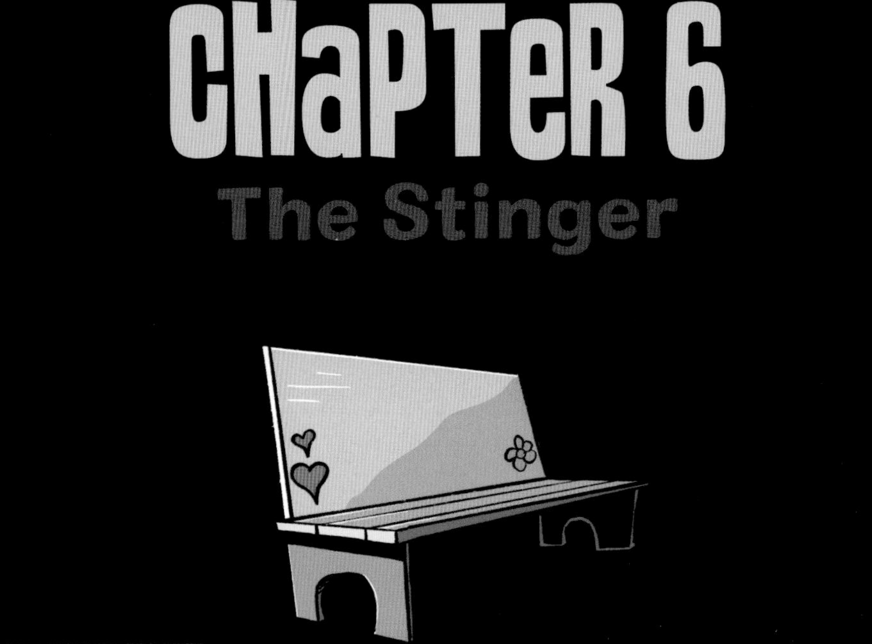

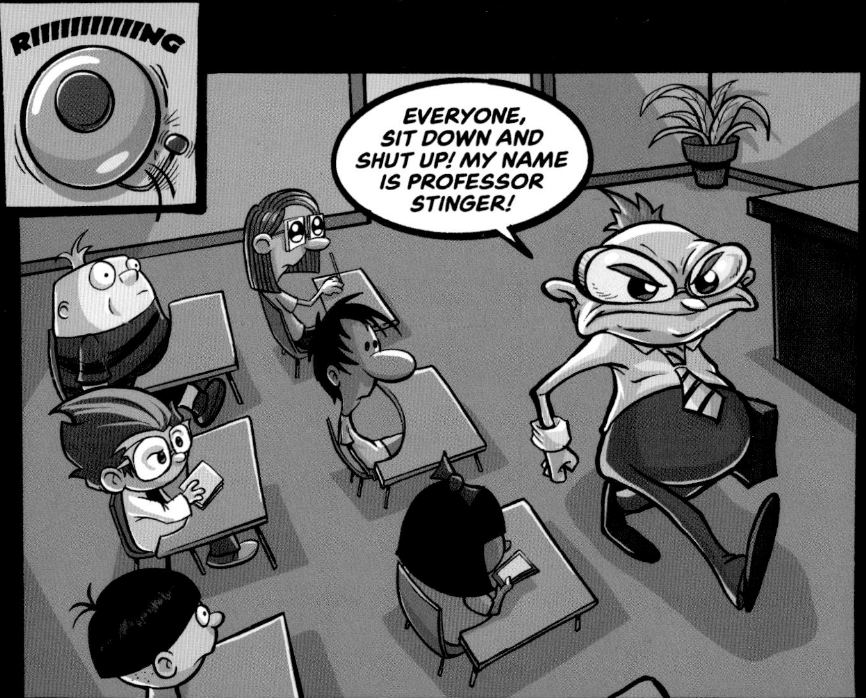
RIIIIIIIIIIING
EVERYONE, SIT DOWN AND SHUT UP! MY NAME IS PROFESSOR STINGER!

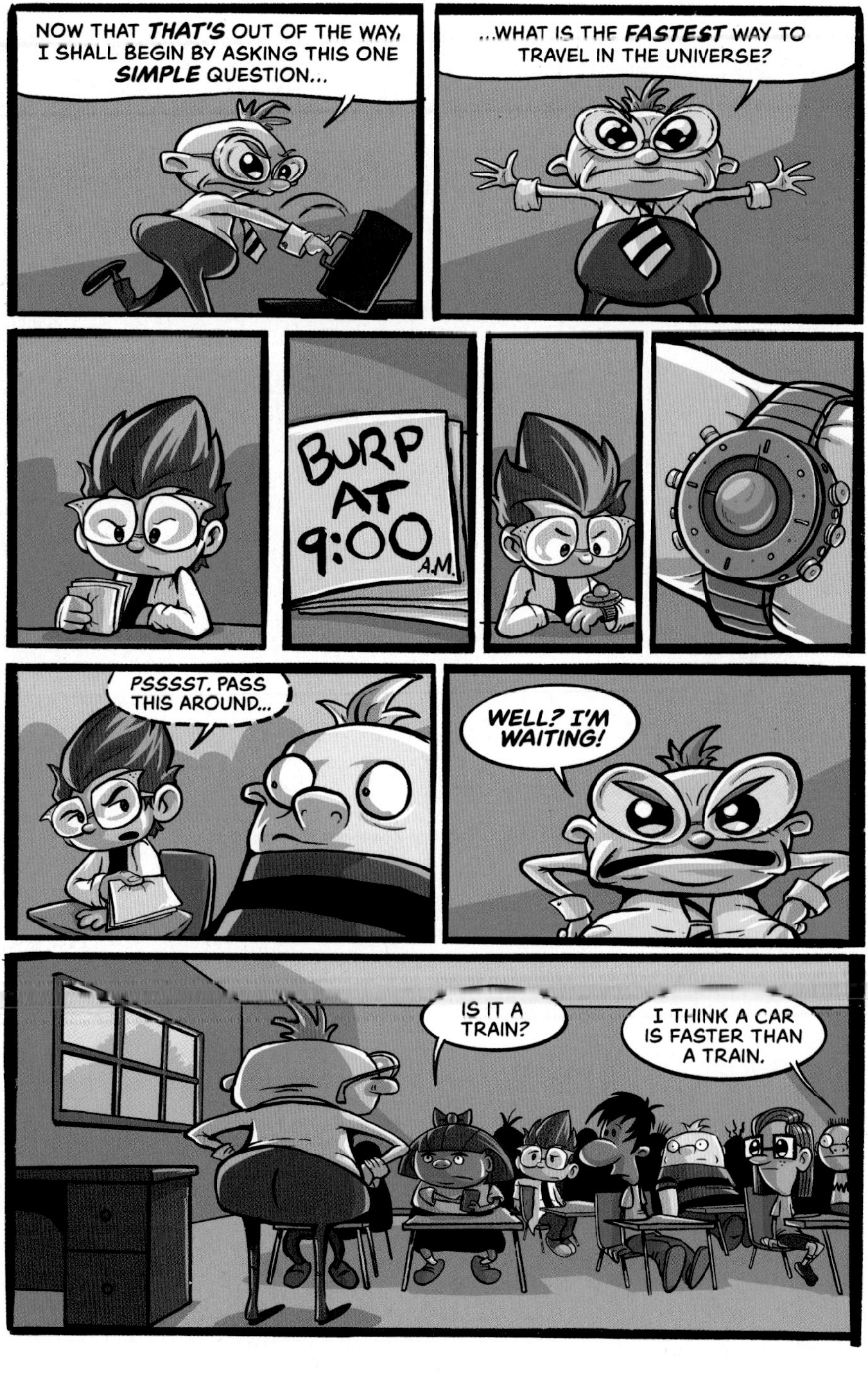
NOW THAT THAT'S OUT OF THE WAY, I SHALL BEGIN BY ASKING THIS ONE SIMPLE QUESTION...
...WHAT IS THE FASTEST WAY TO TRAVEL IN THE UNIVERSE?
BURP AT 9:00 A.M.
PSSSST. PASS THIS AROUND...
WELL? I'M WAITING!
IS IT A TRAIN?
I THINK A CAR IS FASTER THAN A TRAIN.

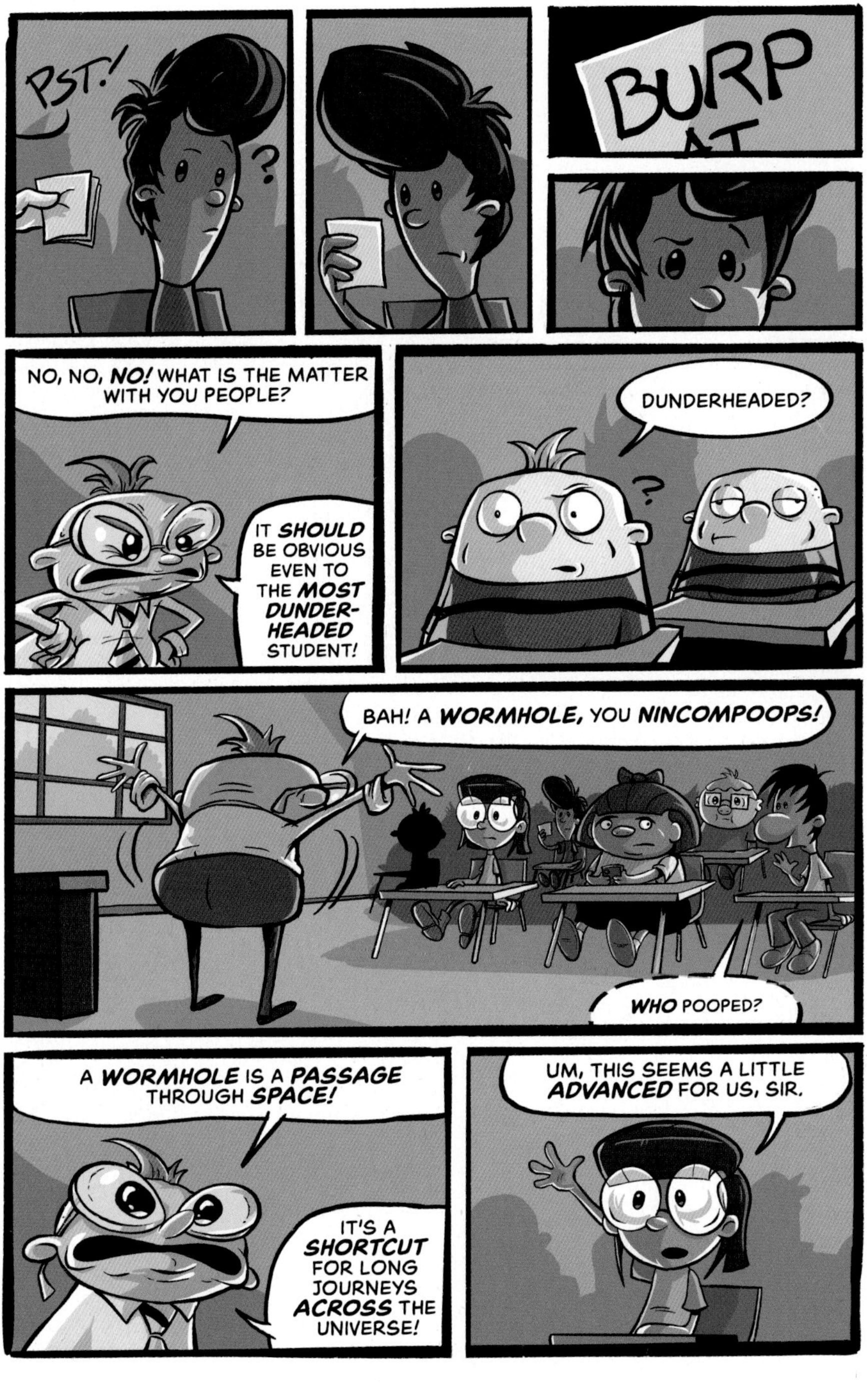
PST!
?
BURP
NO, NO, NO! WHAT IS THE MATTER WITH YOU PEOPLE?
IT SHOULD BE OBVIOUS EVEN TO THE MOST DUNDER-HEADED STUDENT!
DUNDERHEADED?
?
BAH! A WORMHOLE, YOU NINCOMPOOPS!
WHO POOPED?
A WORMHOLE IS A PASSAGE THROUGH SPACE!
IT'S A SHORTCUT FOR LONG JOURNEYS ACROSS THE UNIVERSE!
UM, THIS SEEMS A LITTLE ADVANCED FOR US, SIR.

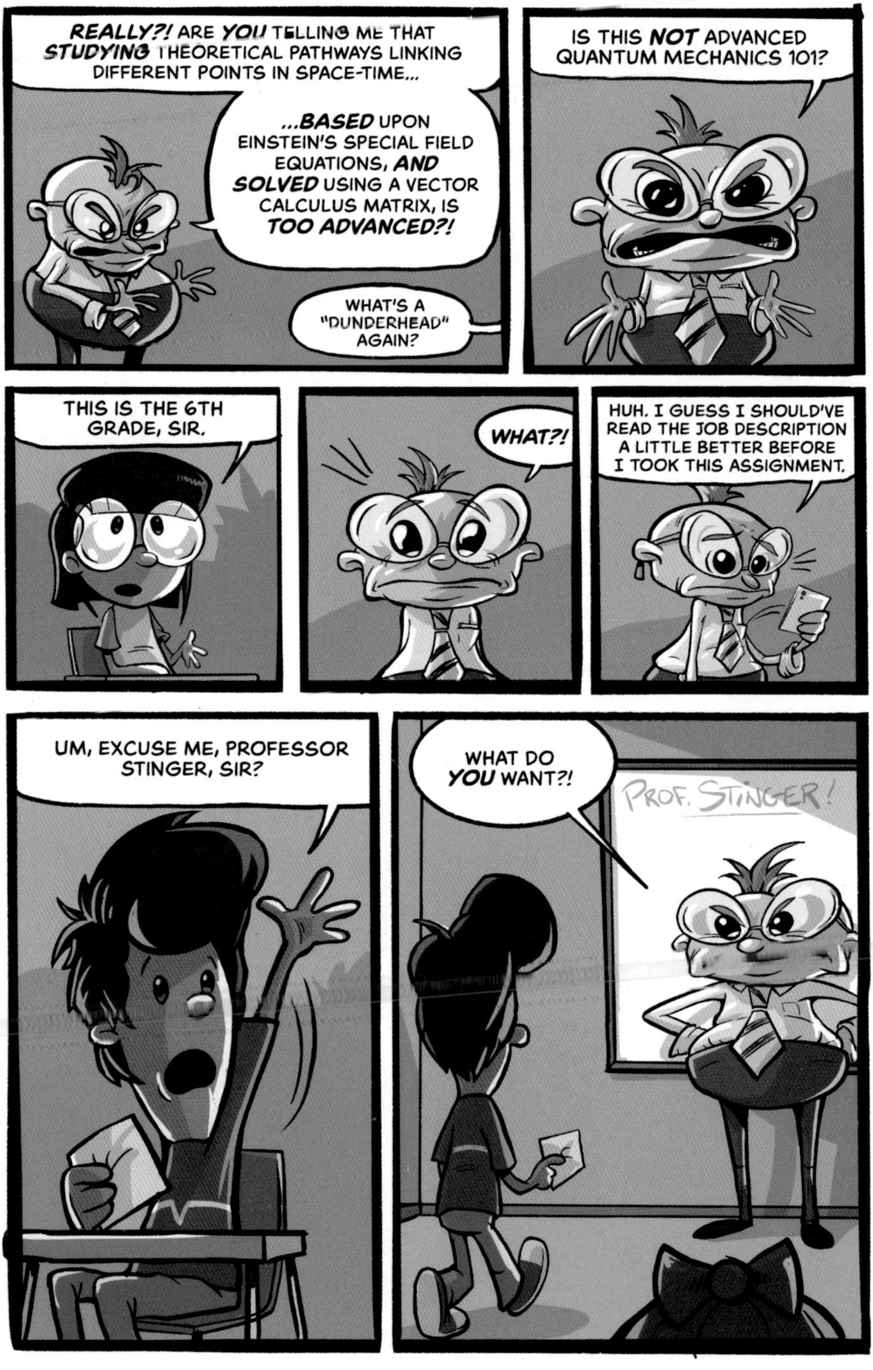
REALLY?! ARE YOU TELLING ME THAT STUDYING THEORETICAL PATHWAYS LINKING DIFFERENT POINTS IN SPACE-TIME...
...BASED UPON EINSTEIN'S SPECIAL FIELD EQUATIONS, AND SOLVED USING A VECTOR CALCULUS MATRIX, IS TOO ADVANCED?!
WHAT'S A "DUNDERHEAD" AGAIN?
IS THIS NOT ADVANCED QUANTUM MECHANICS 101?
THIS IS THE 6TH GRADE, SIR.
WHAT?!
HUH. I GUESS I SHOULD'VE READ THE JOB DESCRIPTION A LITTLE BETTER BEFORE I TOOK THIS ASSIGNMENT.
UM, EXCUSE ME, PROFESSOR STINGER, SIR?
WHAT DO YOU WANT?!
PROF. STINGER!

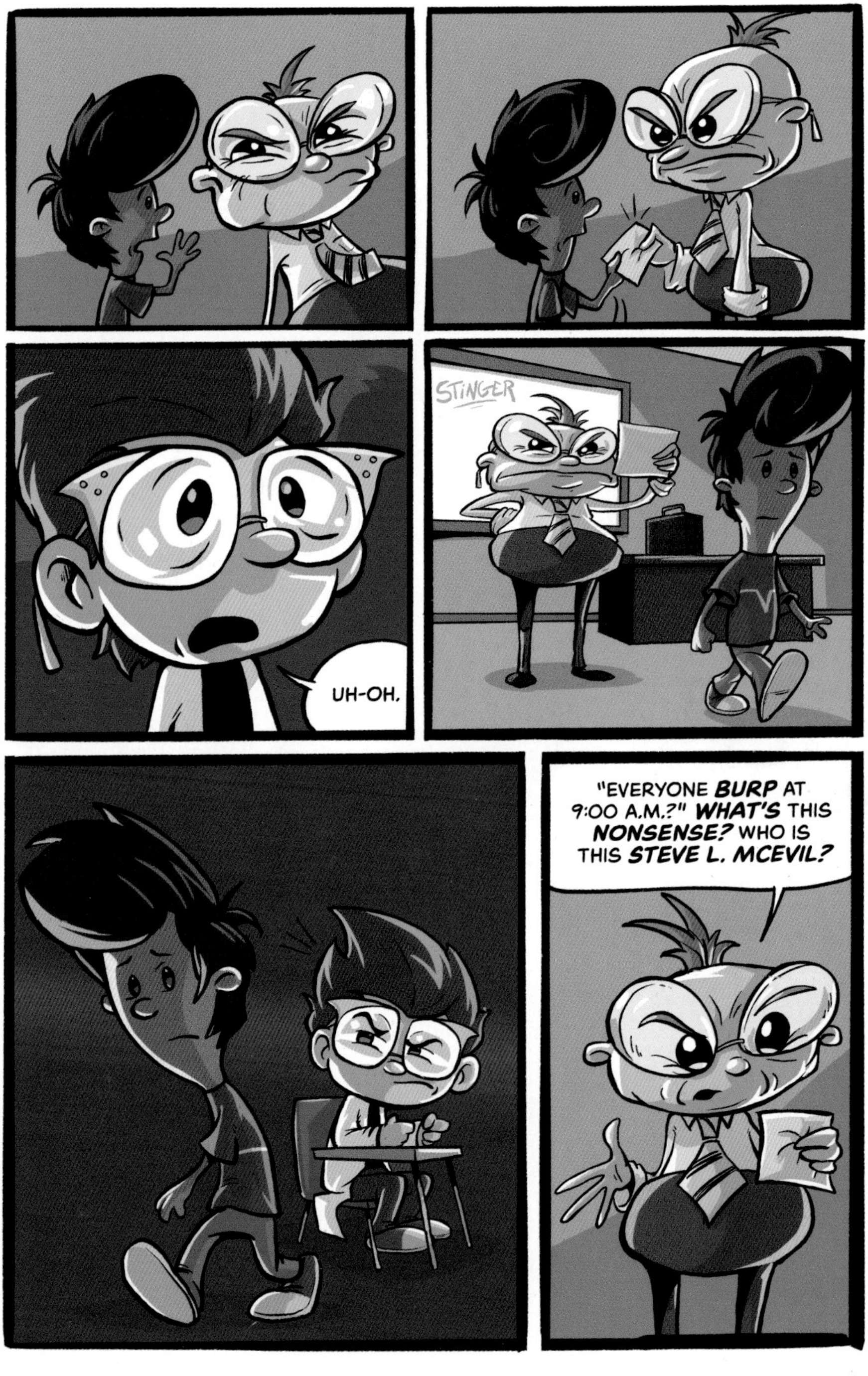
STINGER
UH-OH.
"EVERYONE BURP AT 9:00 A.M.?" WHAT'S THIS NONSENSE? WHO IS THIS STEVE L. MCEVIL?

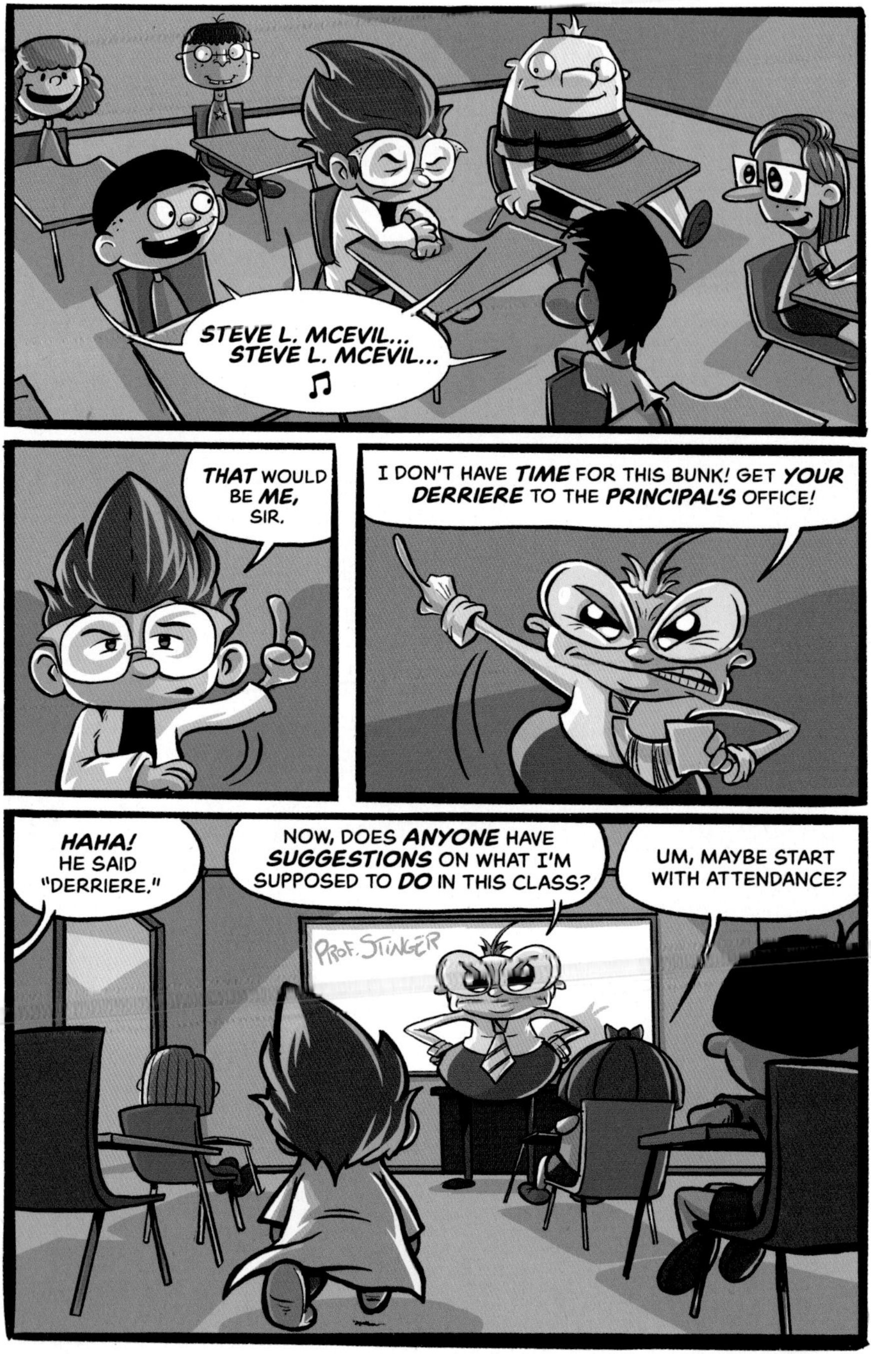
STEVE L. MCEVIL... STEVE L. MCEVIL... ♫
THAT WOULD BE ME, SIR.
I DON'T HAVE TIME FOR THIS BUNK! GET YOUR DERRIERE TO THE PRINCIPAL'S OFFICE!
HAHA! HE SAID "DERRIERE."
NOW, DOES ANYONE HAVE SUGGESTIONS ON WHAT I'M SUPPOSED TO DO IN THIS CLASS?
UM, MAYBE START WITH ATTENDANCE?
PROF. STINGER

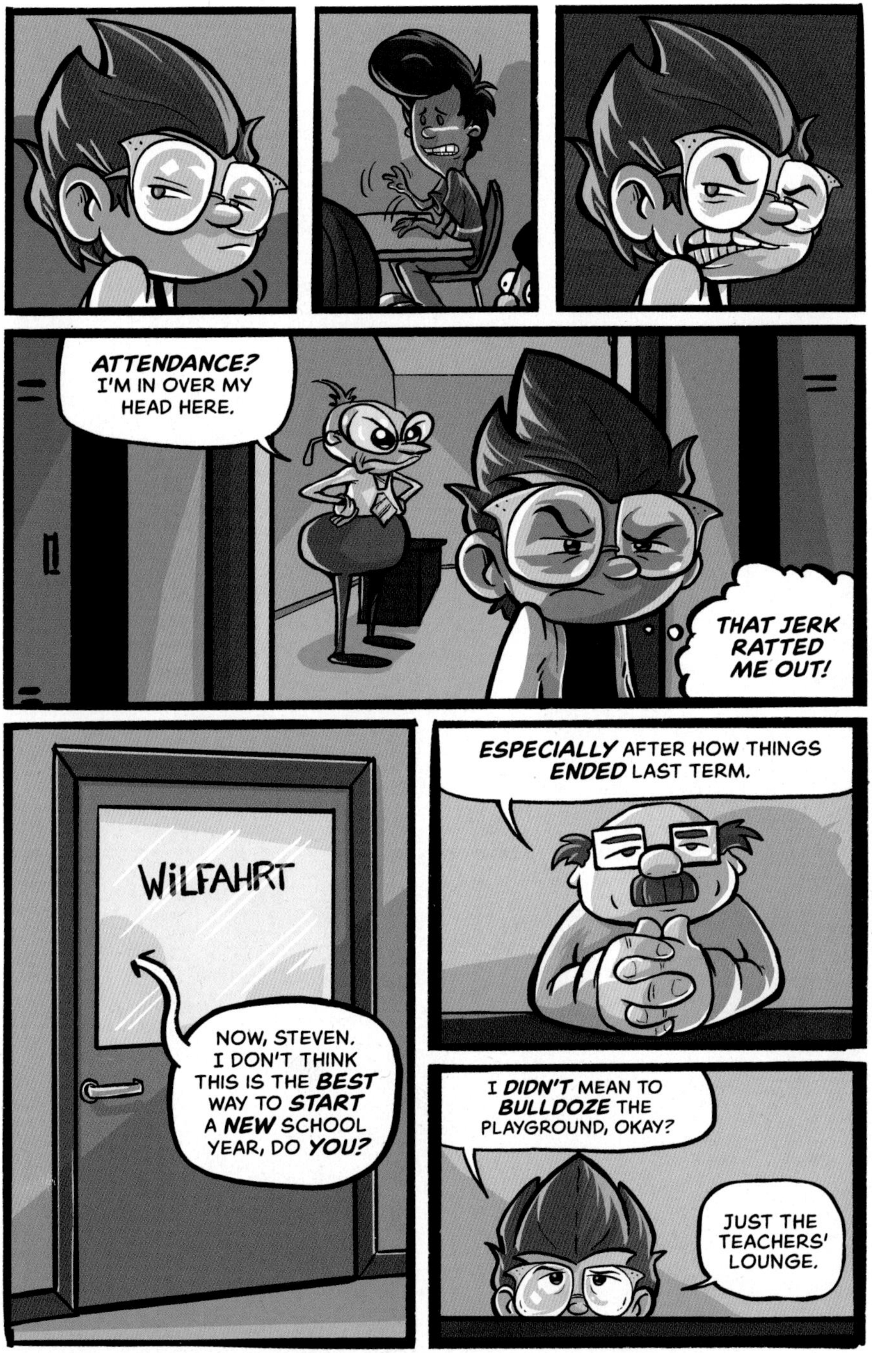
ATTENDANCE? I'M IN OVER MY HEAD HERE.
THAT JERK RATTED ME OUT!
WILFAHRT
NOW, STEVEN. I DON'T THINK THIS IS THE BEST WAY TO START A NEW SCHOOL YEAR, DO YOU?
ESPECIALLY AFTER HOW THINGS ENDED LAST TERM.
I DIDN'T MEAN TO BULLDOZE THE PLAYGROUND, OKAY?
JUST THE TEACHERS' LOUNGE.

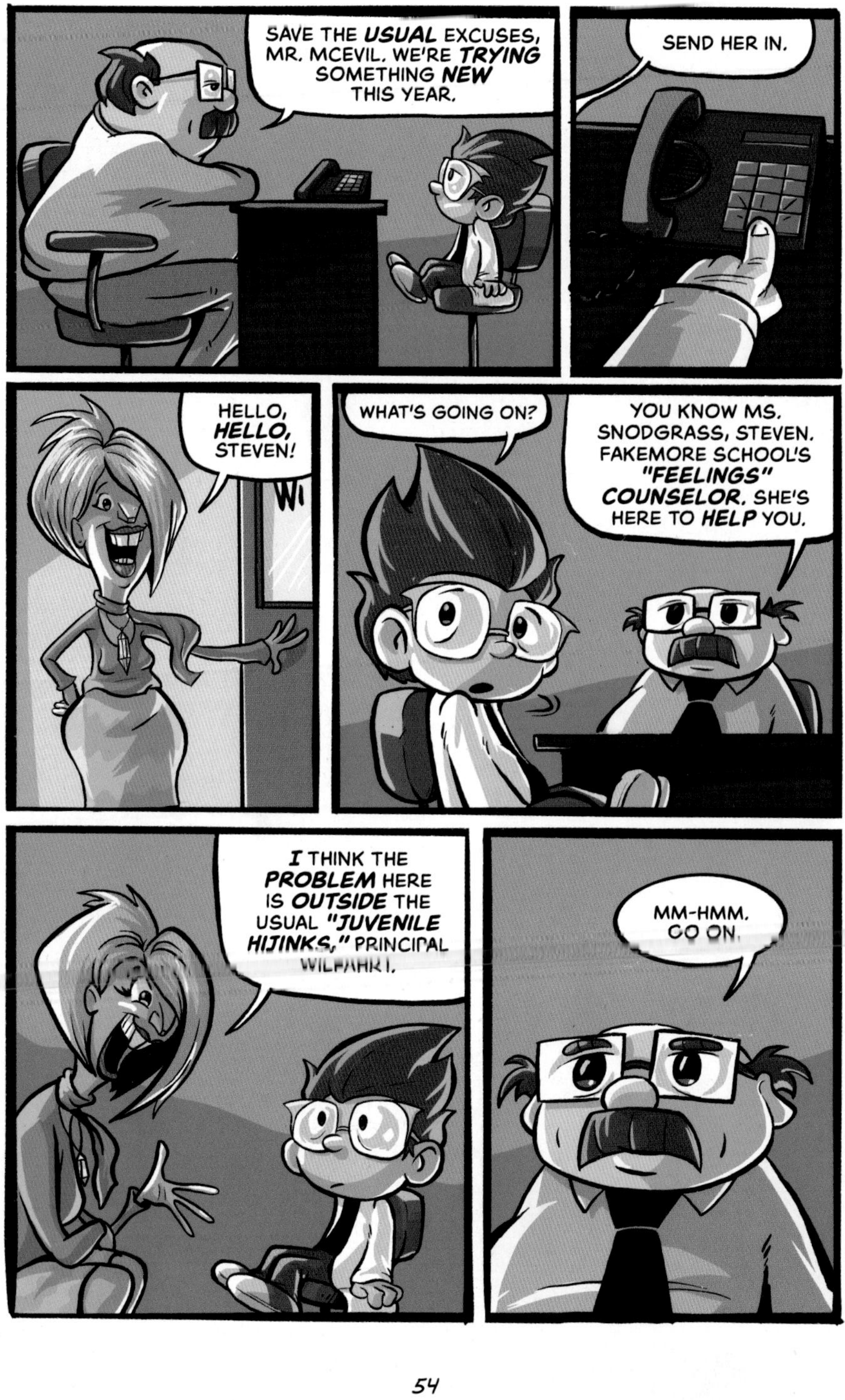
SAVE THE USUAL EXCUSES, MR. MCEVIL. WE'RE TRYING SOMETHING NEW THIS YEAR.
SEND HER IN.
HELLO, HELLO, STEVEN!
WHAT'S GOING ON?
YOU KNOW MS. SNODGRASS, STEVEN. FAKEMORE SCHOOL'S "FEELINGS" COUNSELOR. SHE'S HERE TO HELP YOU.
I THINK THE PROBLEM HERE IS OUTSIDE THE USUAL "JUVENILE HIJINKS," PRINCIPAL WILFAHRT.
MM-HMM. GO ON.

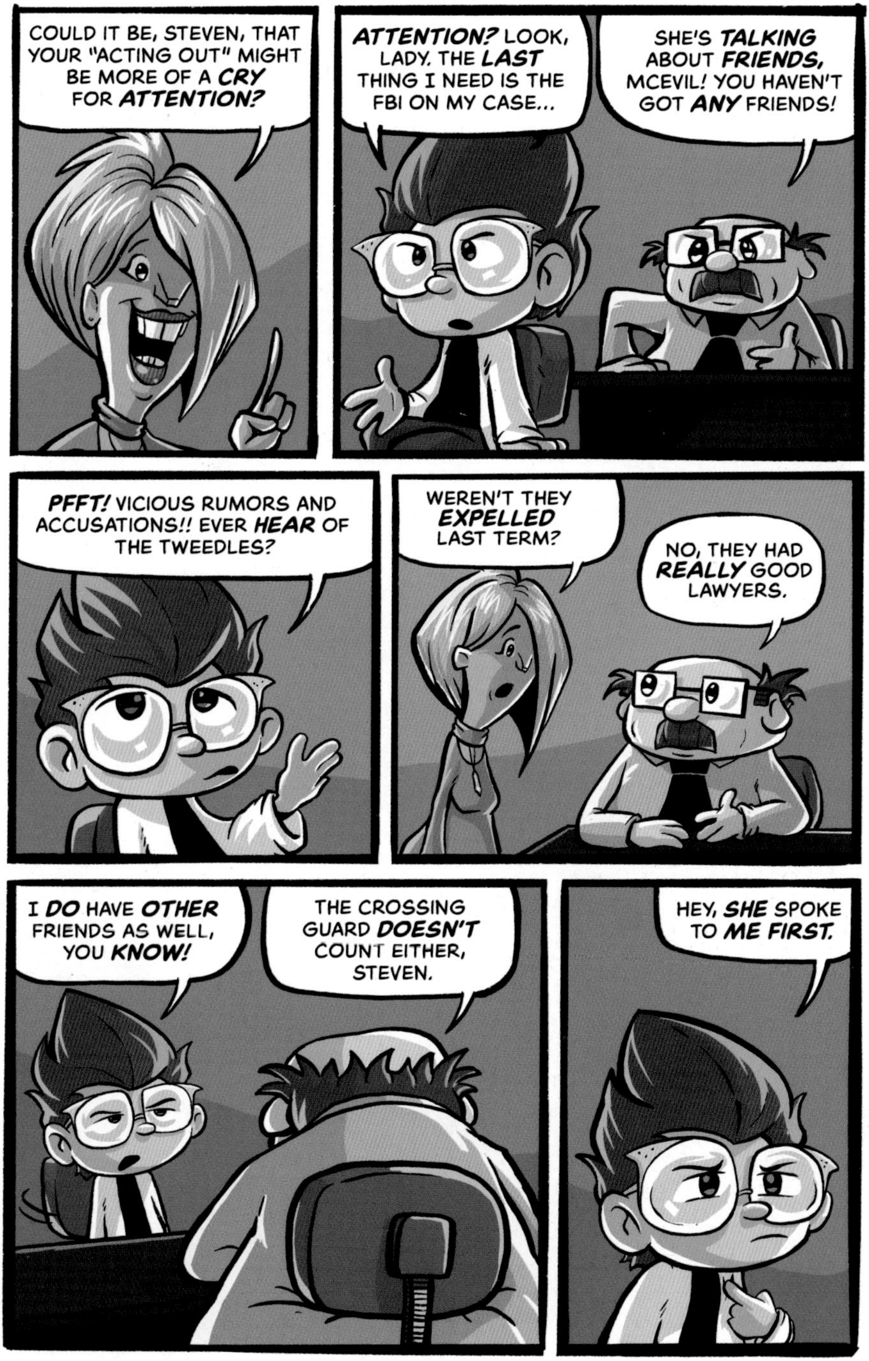
COULD IT BE, STEVEN, THAT YOUR "ACTING OUT" MIGHT BE MORE OF A CRY FOR ATTENTION?
ATTENTION? LOOK, LADY. THE LAST THING I NEED IS THE FBI ON MY CASE...
SHE'S TALKING ABOUT FRIENDS, MCEVIL! YOU HAVEN'T GOT ANY FRIENDS!
PFFT! VICIOUS RUMORS AND ACCUSATIONS!! EVER HEAR OF THE TWEEDLES?
WEREN'T THEY EXPELLED LAST TERM?
NO, THEY HAD REALLY GOOD LAWYERS.
I DO HAVE OTHER FRIENDS AS WELL, YOU KNOW!
THE CROSSING GUARD DOESN'T COUNT EITHER, STEVEN.
HEY, SHE SPOKE TO ME FIRST.

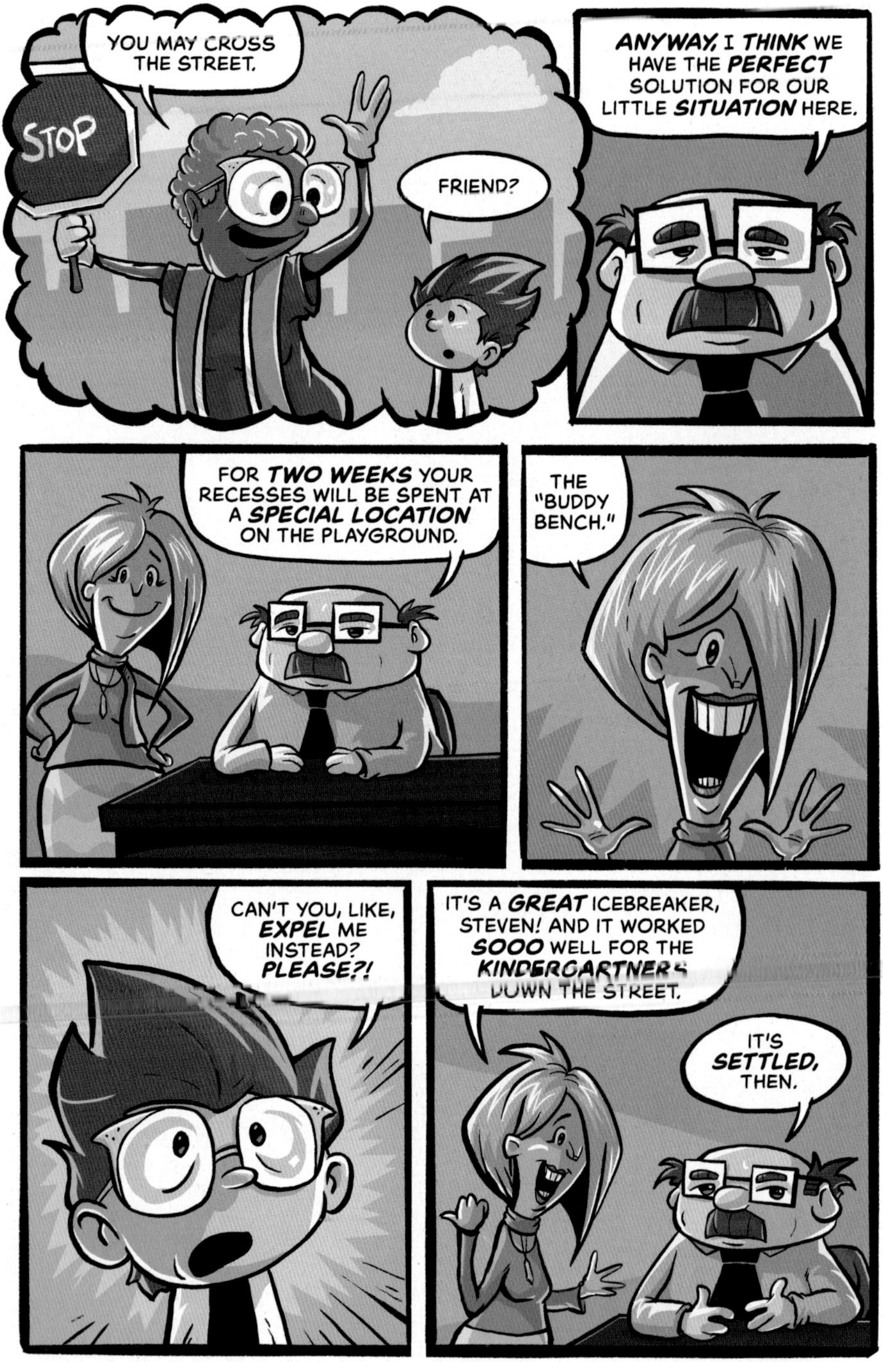
YOU MAY CROSS THE STREET.
STOP
FRIEND?
ANYWAY, I THINK WE HAVE THE PERFECT SOLUTION FOR OUR LITTLE SITUATION HERE.
FOR TWO WEEKS YOUR RECESSES WILL BE SPENT AT A SPECIAL LOCATION ON THE PLAYGROUND.
THE "BUDDY BENCH."
CAN'T YOU, LIKE, EXPEL ME INSTEAD? PLEASE?!
IT'S A GREAT ICEBREAKER, STEVEN! AND IT WORKED SOOO WELL FOR THE KINDERGARTNERS DOWN THE STREET.
IT'S SETTLED, THEN.

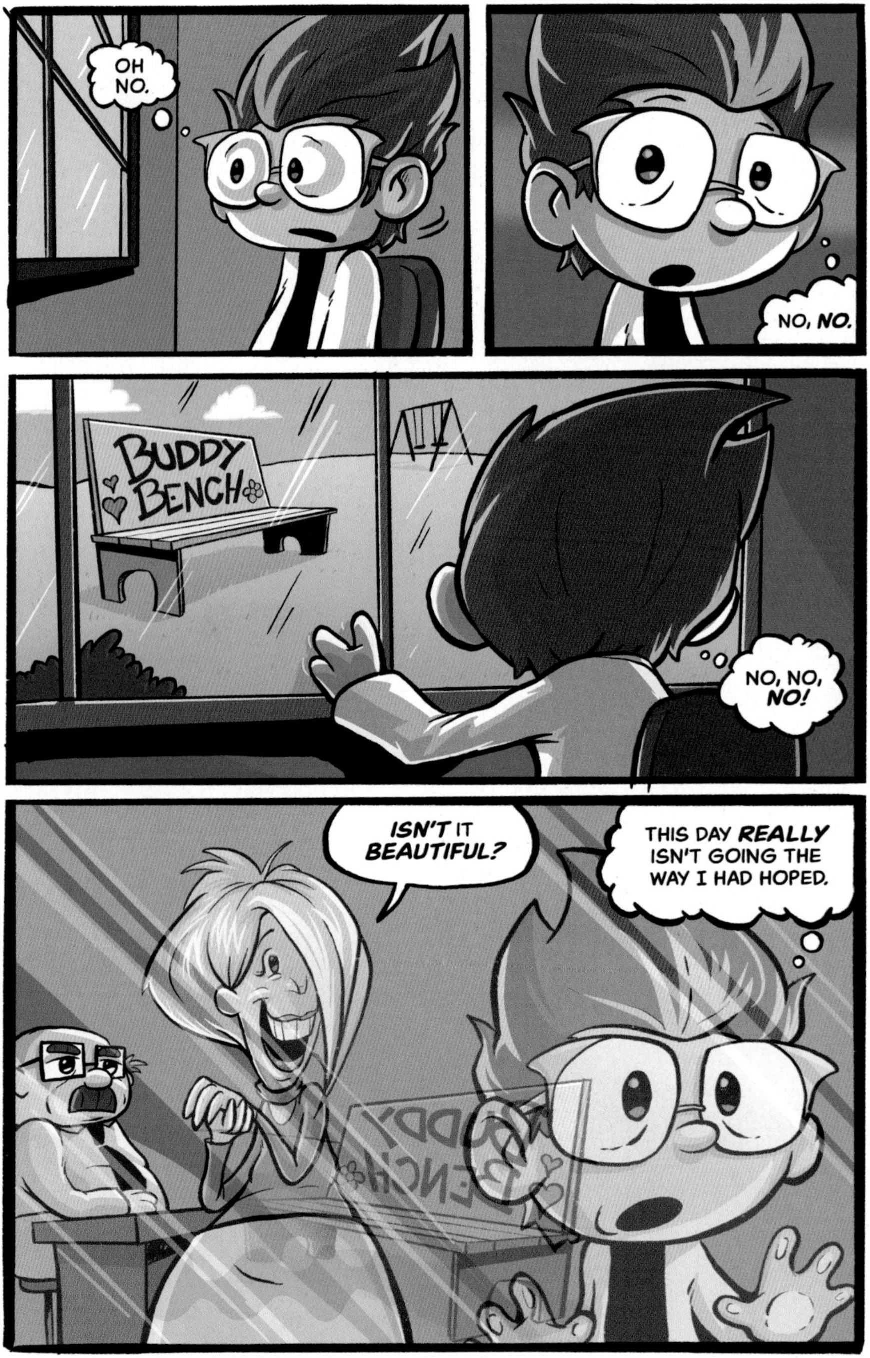
OH NO.
NO, NO.
BUDDY BENCH
NO, NO, NO!
ISN'T IT BEAUTIFUL?
THIS DAY REALLY ISN'T GOING THE WAY I HAD HOPED.

CHAPTER 7

A Different Perspective

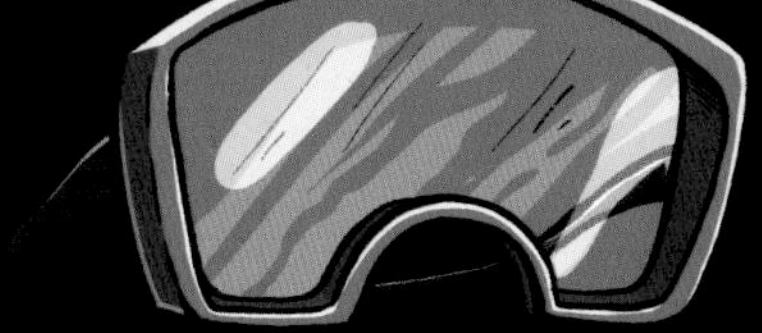

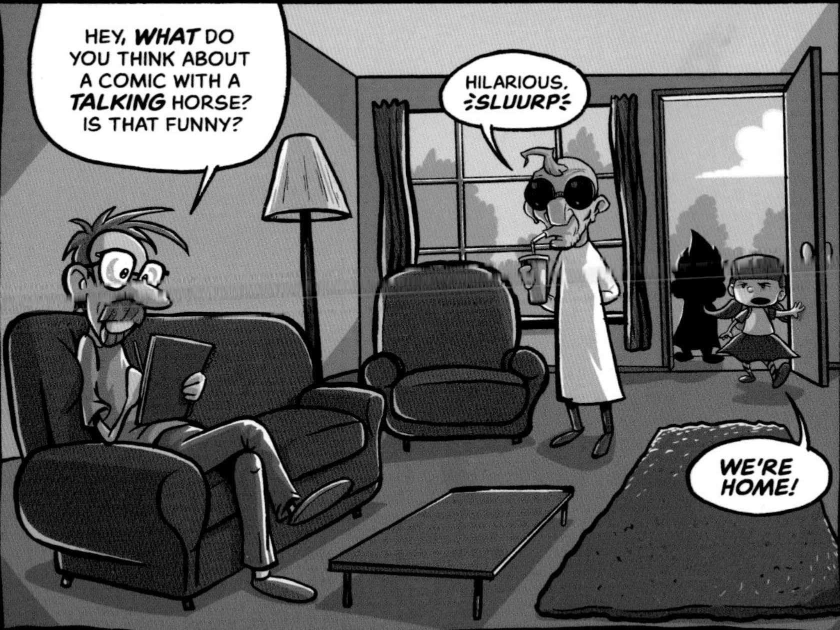
HEY, **WHAT** DO YOU THINK ABOUT A COMIC WITH A **TALKING** HORSE? IS THAT FUNNY?
HILARIOUS. *SLUURP*
WE'RE HOME!

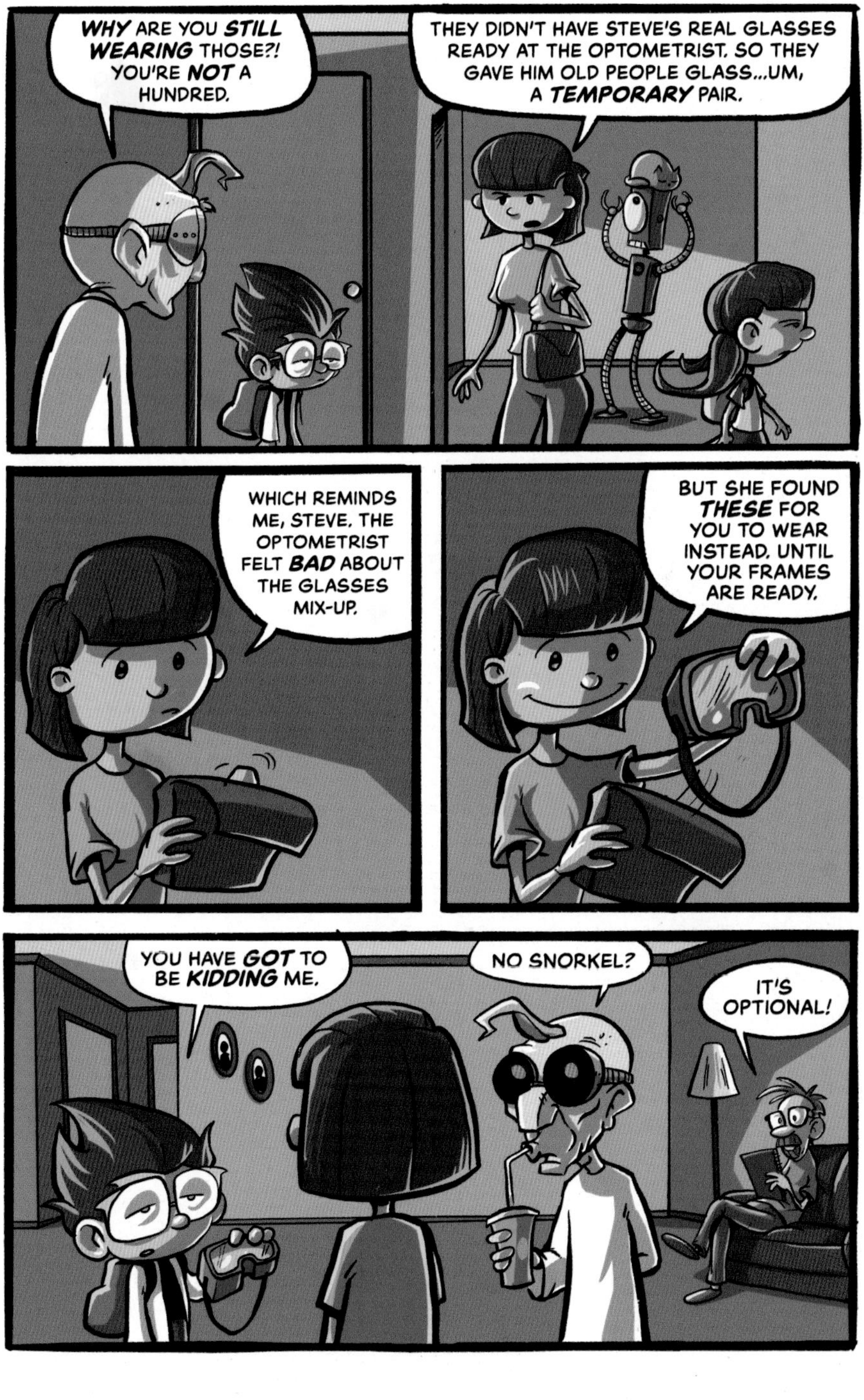
WHY ARE YOU STILL WEARING THOSE?! YOU'RE NOT A HUNDRED.
THEY DIDN'T HAVE STEVE'S REAL GLASSES READY AT THE OPTOMETRIST, SO THEY GAVE HIM OLD PEOPLE GLASS...UM, A TEMPORARY PAIR.
WHICH REMINDS ME, STEVE, THE OPTOMETRIST FELT BAD ABOUT THE GLASSES MIX-UP.
BUT SHE FOUND THESE FOR YOU TO WEAR INSTEAD, UNTIL YOUR FRAMES ARE READY.
YOU HAVE GOT TO BE KIDDING ME.
NO SNORKEL?
IT'S OPTIONAL!

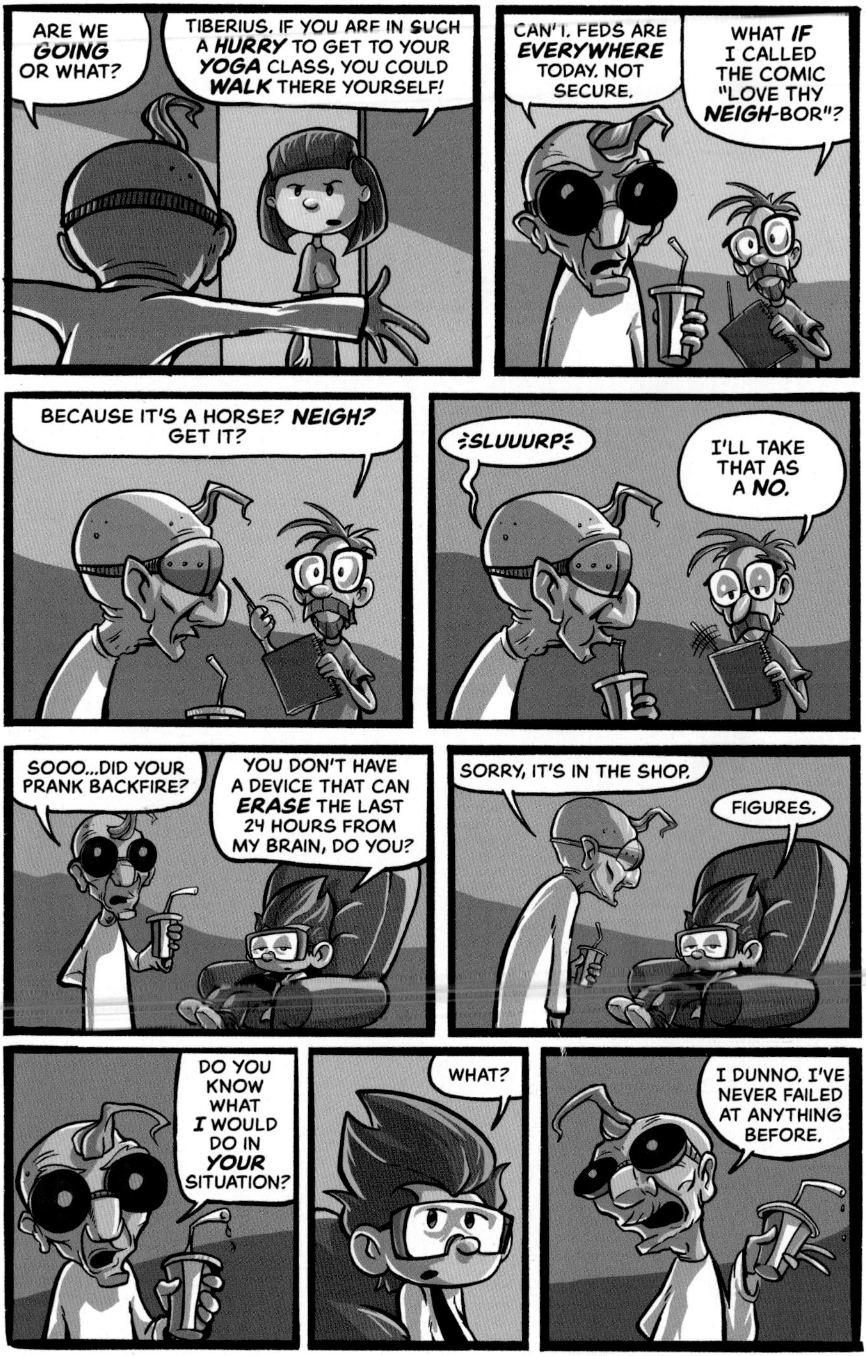

ARE WE GOING OR WHAT?
TIBERIUS, IF YOU ARE IN SUCH A HURRY TO GET TO YOUR YOGA CLASS, YOU COULD WALK THERE YOURSELF!
CAN'T. FEDS ARE EVERYWHERE TODAY. NOT SECURE.
WHAT IF I CALLED THE COMIC "LOVE THY NEIGH-BOR"?
BECAUSE IT'S A HORSE? NEIGH? GET IT?
SLUUURP
I'LL TAKE THAT AS A NO.
SOOO...DID YOUR PRANK BACKFIRE?
YOU DON'T HAVE A DEVICE THAT CAN ERASE THE LAST 24 HOURS FROM MY BRAIN, DO YOU?
SORRY, IT'S IN THE SHOP.
FIGURES.
DO YOU KNOW WHAT I WOULD DO IN YOUR SITUATION?
WHAT?
I DUNNO. I'VE NEVER FAILED AT ANYTHING BEFORE.

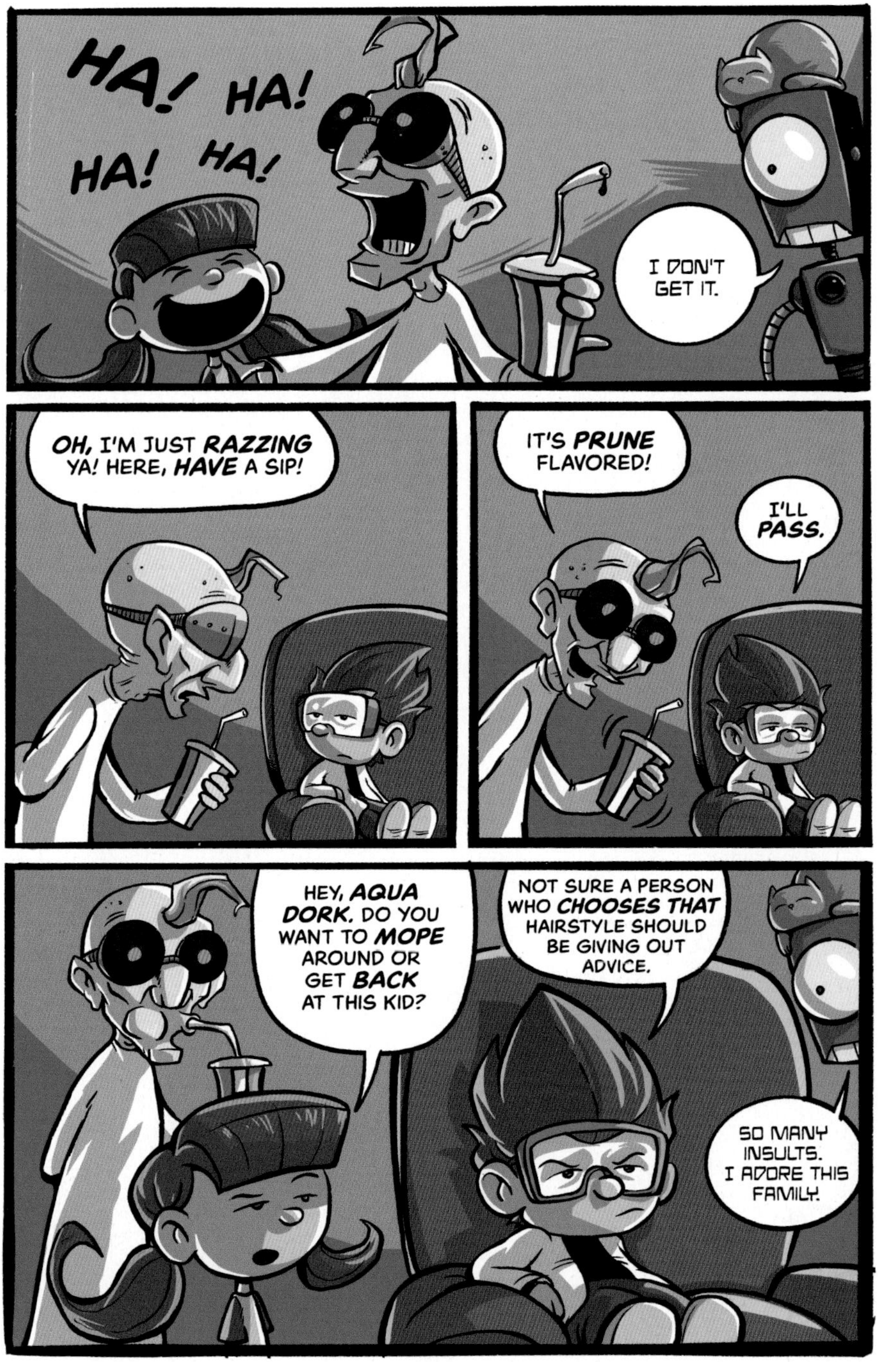
HA! HA!
HA! HA!
I DON'T GET IT.
OH, I'M JUST RAZZING YA! HERE, HAVE A SIP!
IT'S PRUNE FLAVORED!
I'LL PASS.
HEY, AQUA DORK. DO YOU WANT TO MOPE AROUND OR GET BACK AT THIS KID?
NOT SURE A PERSON WHO CHOOSES THAT HAIRSTYLE SHOULD BE GIVING OUT ADVICE.
SO MANY INSULTS. I ADORE THIS FAMILY.

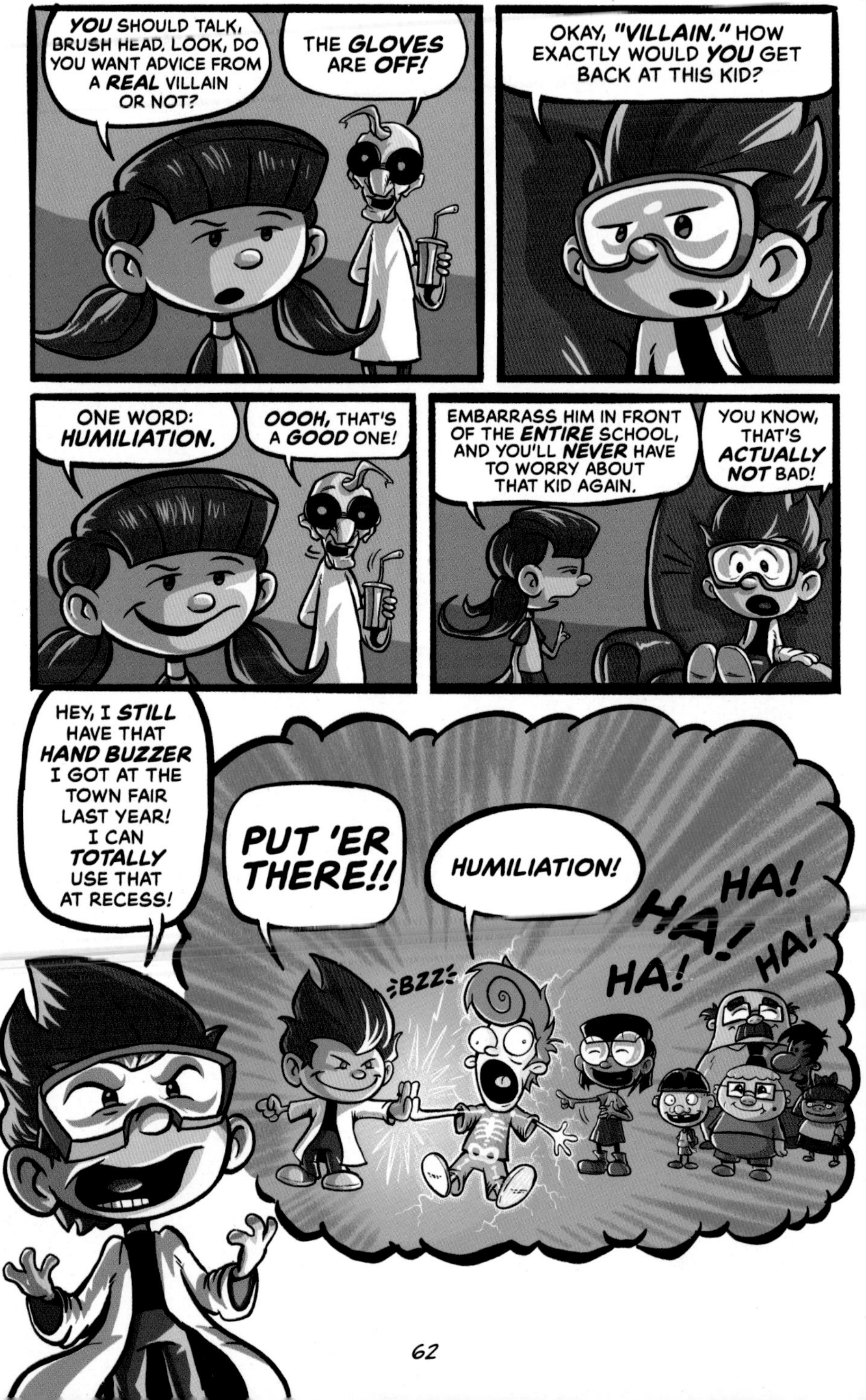
YOU SHOULD TALK, BRUSH HEAD. LOOK, DO YOU WANT ADVICE FROM A REAL VILLAIN OR NOT?
THE GLOVES ARE OFF!
OKAY, "VILLAIN." HOW EXACTLY WOULD YOU GET BACK AT THIS KID?
ONE WORD: HUMILIATION.
OOOH, THAT'S A GOOD ONE!
EMBARRASS HIM IN FRONT OF THE ENTIRE SCHOOL, AND YOU'LL NEVER HAVE TO WORRY ABOUT THAT KID AGAIN.
YOU KNOW, THAT'S ACTUALLY NOT BAD!
HEY, I STILL HAVE THAT HAND BUZZER I GOT AT THE TOWN FAIR LAST YEAR! I CAN TOTALLY USE THAT AT RECESS!
PUT 'ER THERE!!
HUMILIATION!
HA! HA! HA! HA! HA!
BZZ

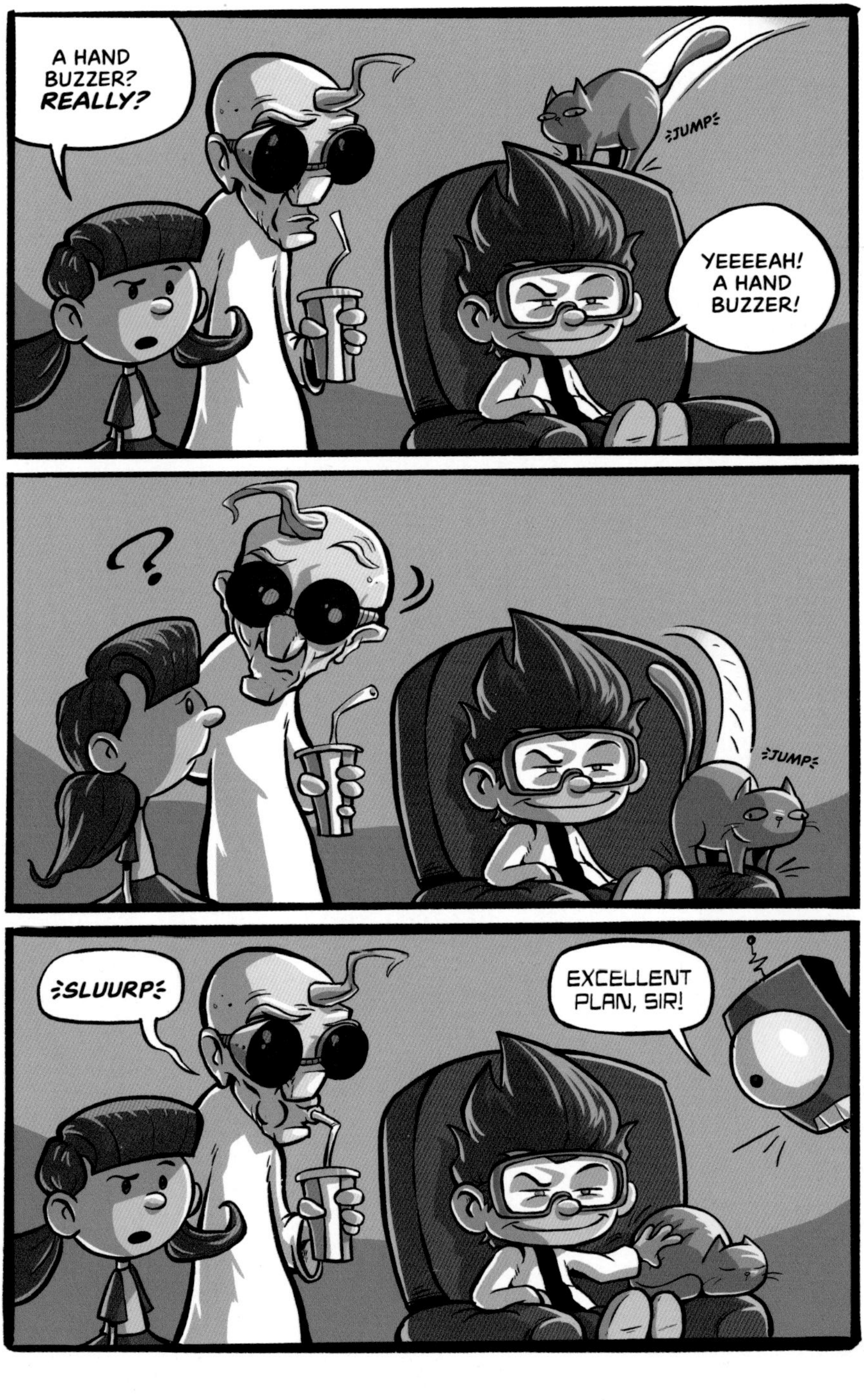
A HAND BUZZER? REALLY?
JUMP
YEEEEAH! A HAND BUZZER!
?
JUMP
SLUURP
EXCELLENT PLAN, SIR!

CHAPTER 8
Archenemy

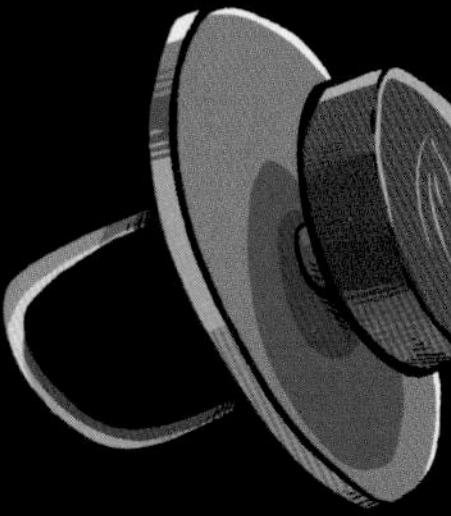

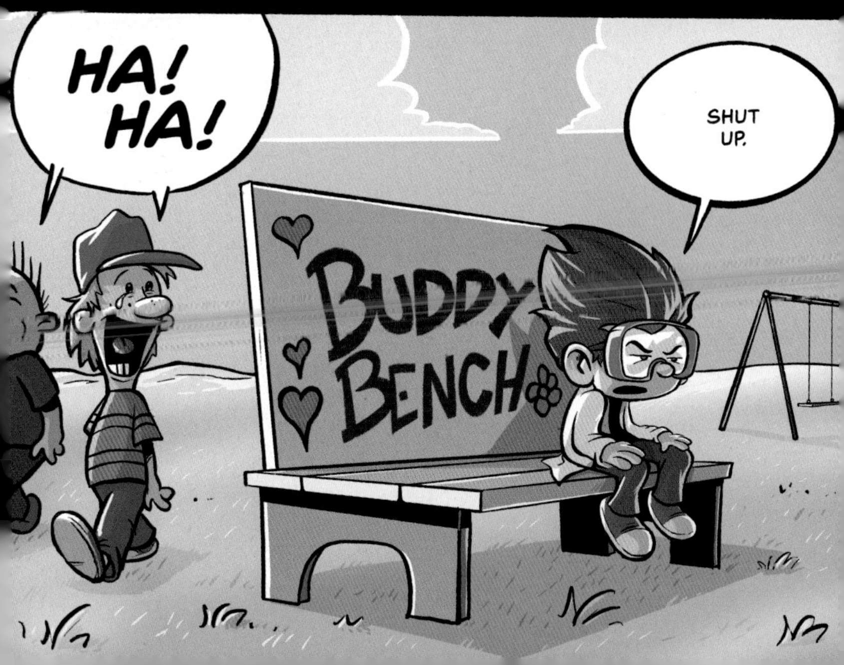
HA! HA!
SHUT UP.
BUDDY BENCH

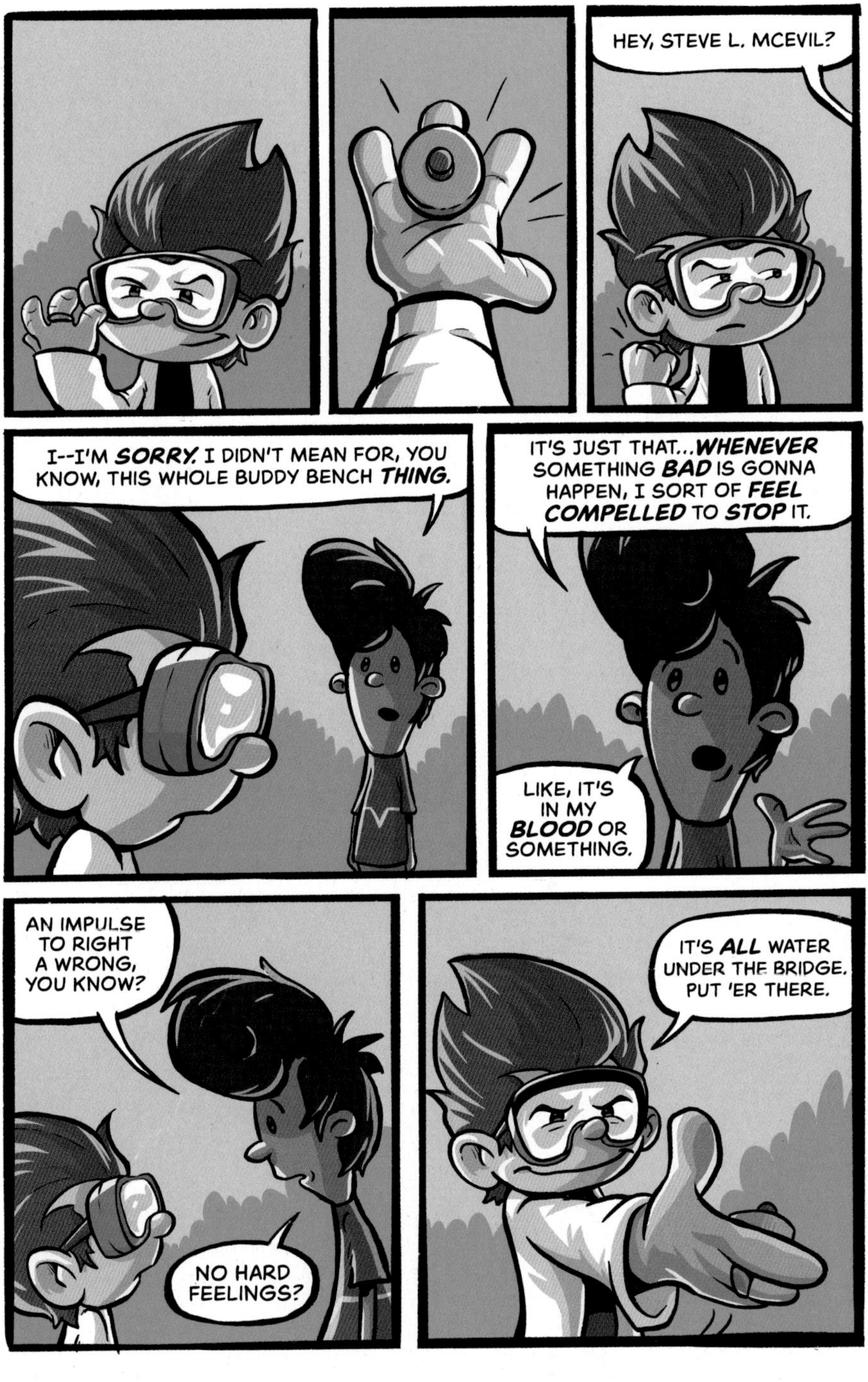
HEY, STEVE L. MCEVIL?
I--I'M SORRY. I DIDN'T MEAN FOR, YOU KNOW, THIS WHOLE BUDDY BENCH THING.
IT'S JUST THAT...WHENEVER SOMETHING BAD IS GONNA HAPPEN, I SORT OF FEEL COMPELLED TO STOP IT.
LIKE, IT'S IN MY BLOOD OR SOMETHING.
AN IMPULSE TO RIGHT A WRONG, YOU KNOW?
NO HARD FEELINGS?
IT'S ALL WATER UNDER THE BRIDGE. PUT 'ER THERE.

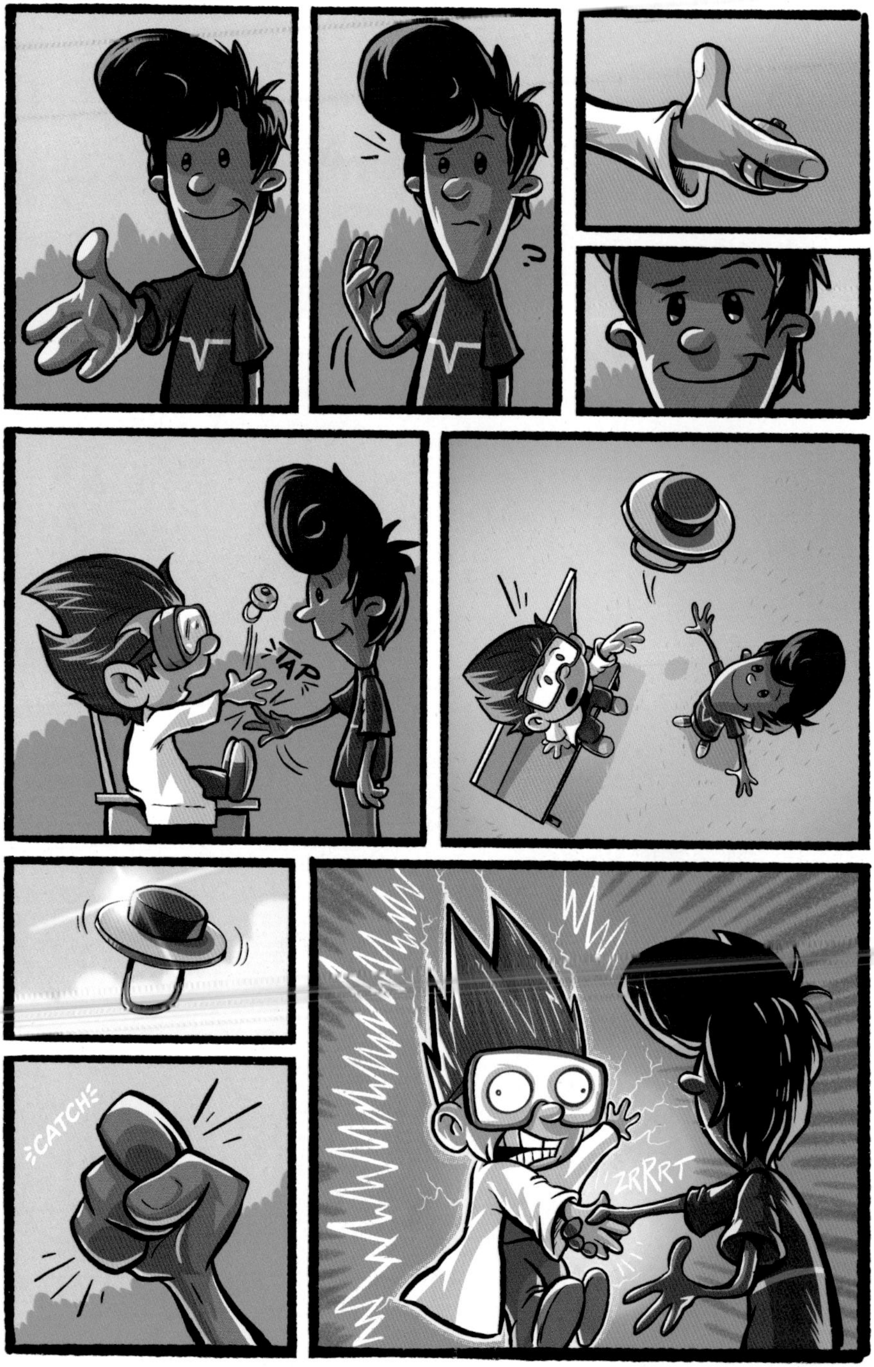
TAP
CATCH
ZRRRT

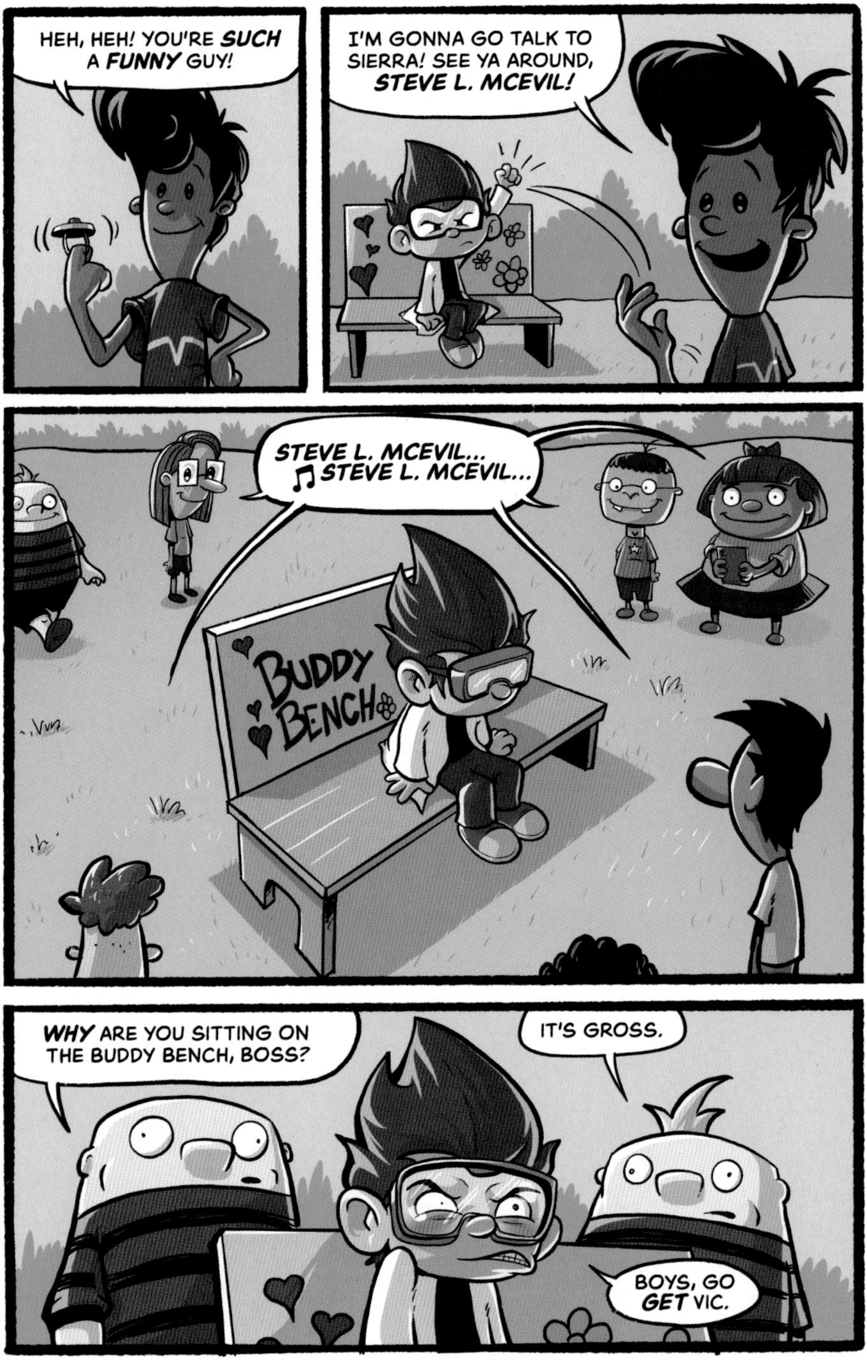
HEH, HEH! YOU'RE **SUCH** A **FUNNY** GUY!
I'M GONNA GO TALK TO SIERRA! SEE YA AROUND, **STEVE L. MCEVIL!**
STEVE L. MCEVIL... ♫ *STEVE L. MCEVIL...*
BUDDY BENCH
WHY ARE YOU SITTING ON THE BUDDY BENCH, BOSS?
IT'S GROSS.
BOYS, GO ***GET*** VIC.

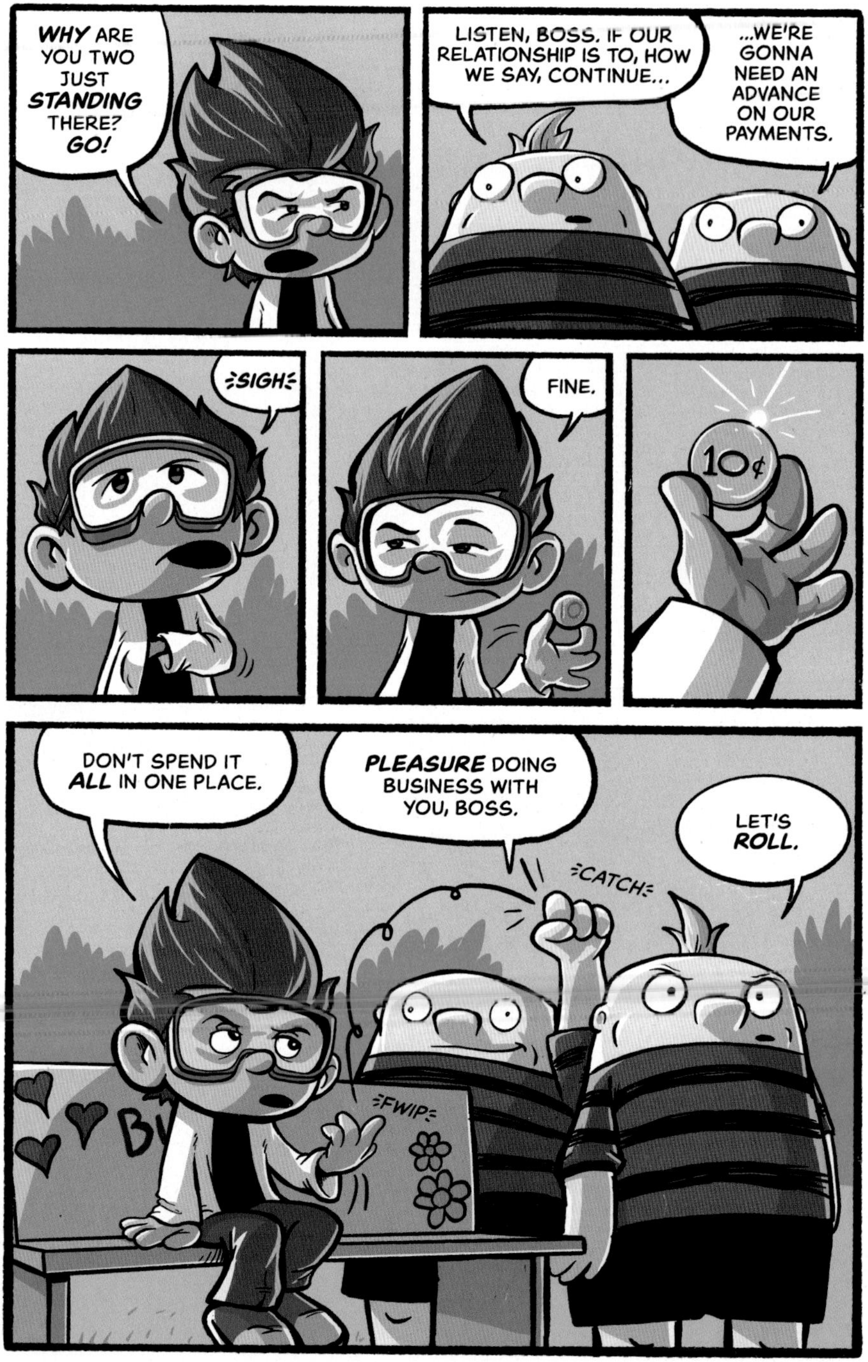
WHY ARE YOU TWO JUST STANDING THERE? GO!
LISTEN, BOSS. IF OUR RELATIONSHIP IS TO, HOW WE SAY, CONTINUE...
...WE'RE GONNA NEED AN ADVANCE ON OUR PAYMENTS.
SIGH
FINE.
10¢
DON'T SPEND IT ALL IN ONE PLACE.
PLEASURE DOING BUSINESS WITH YOU, BOSS.
LET'S ROLL.
CATCH
FWIP

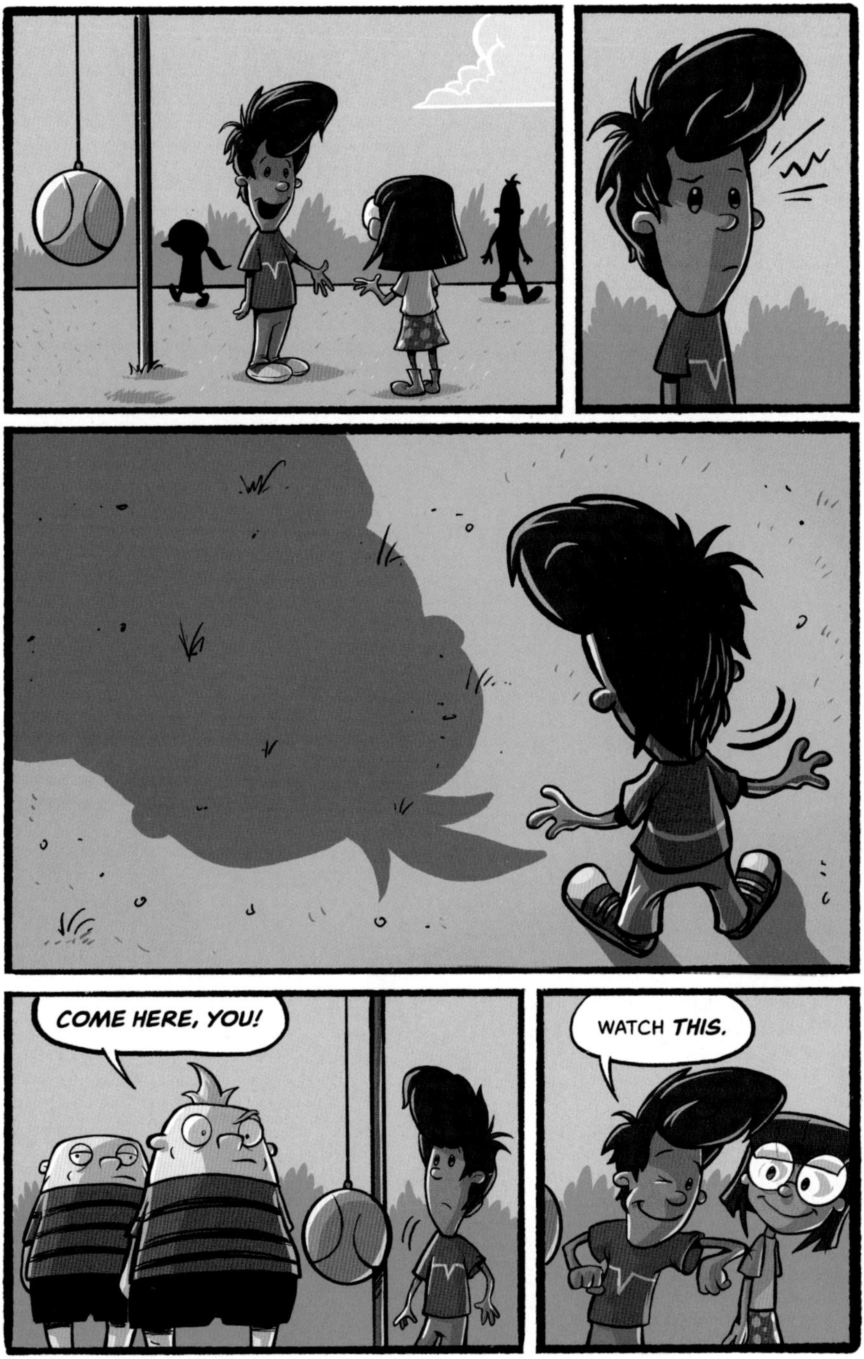
COME HERE, YOU!
WATCH THIS.

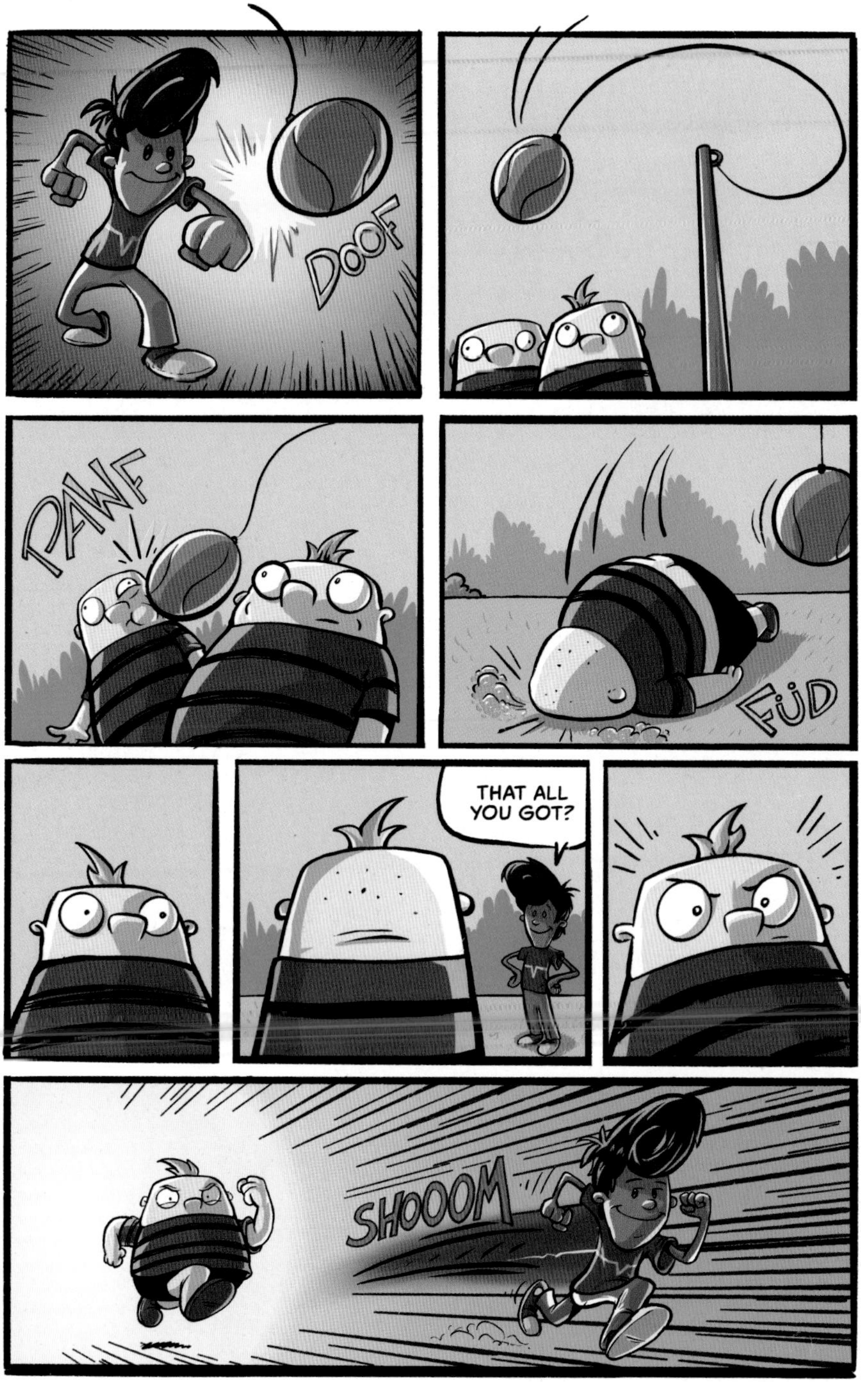
DOOF
PAWF
FÜD
THAT ALL YOU GOT?
SHOOOM

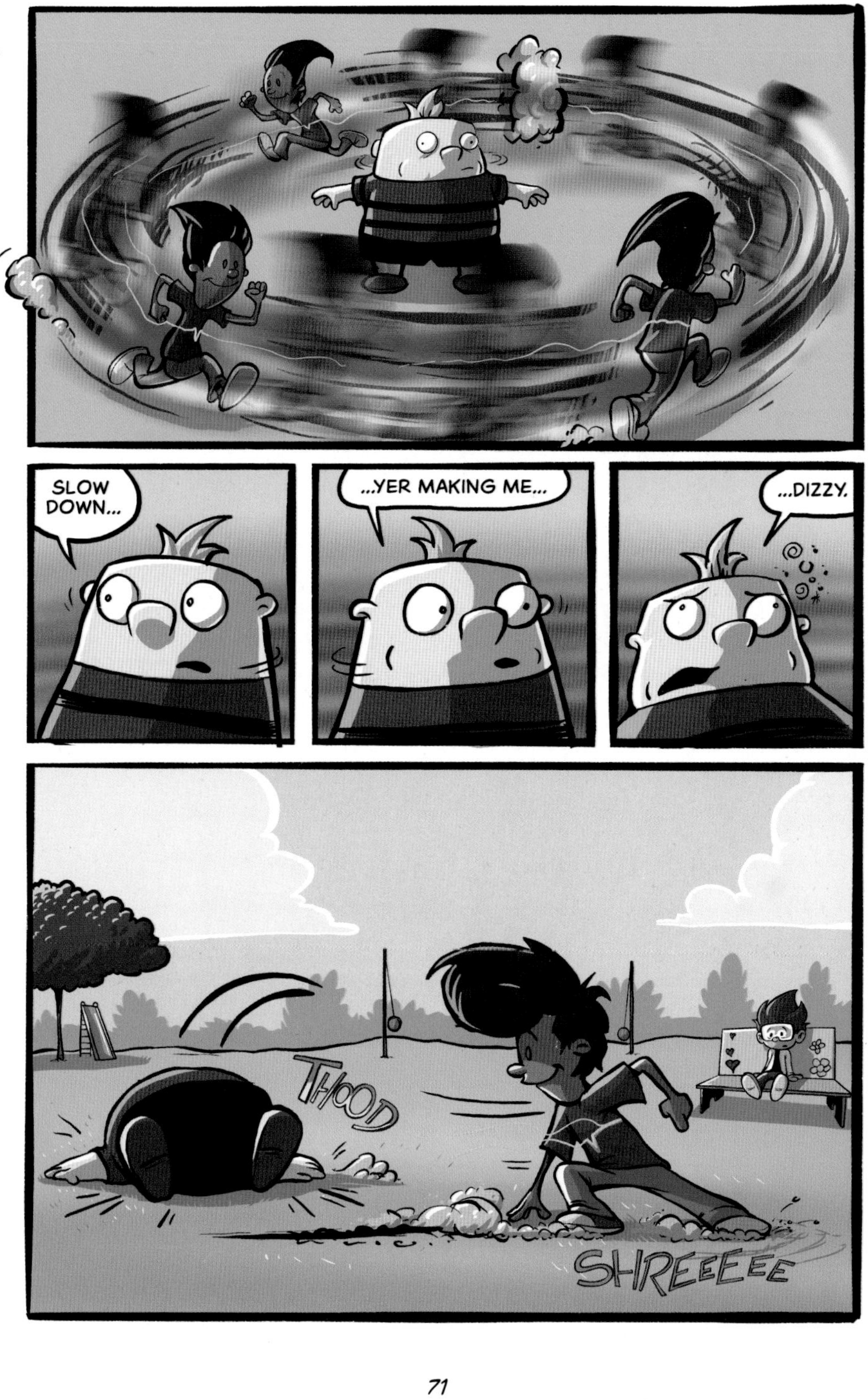
SLOW DOWN...
...YER MAKING ME...
...DIZZY.
THOOD
SHREEEEEE

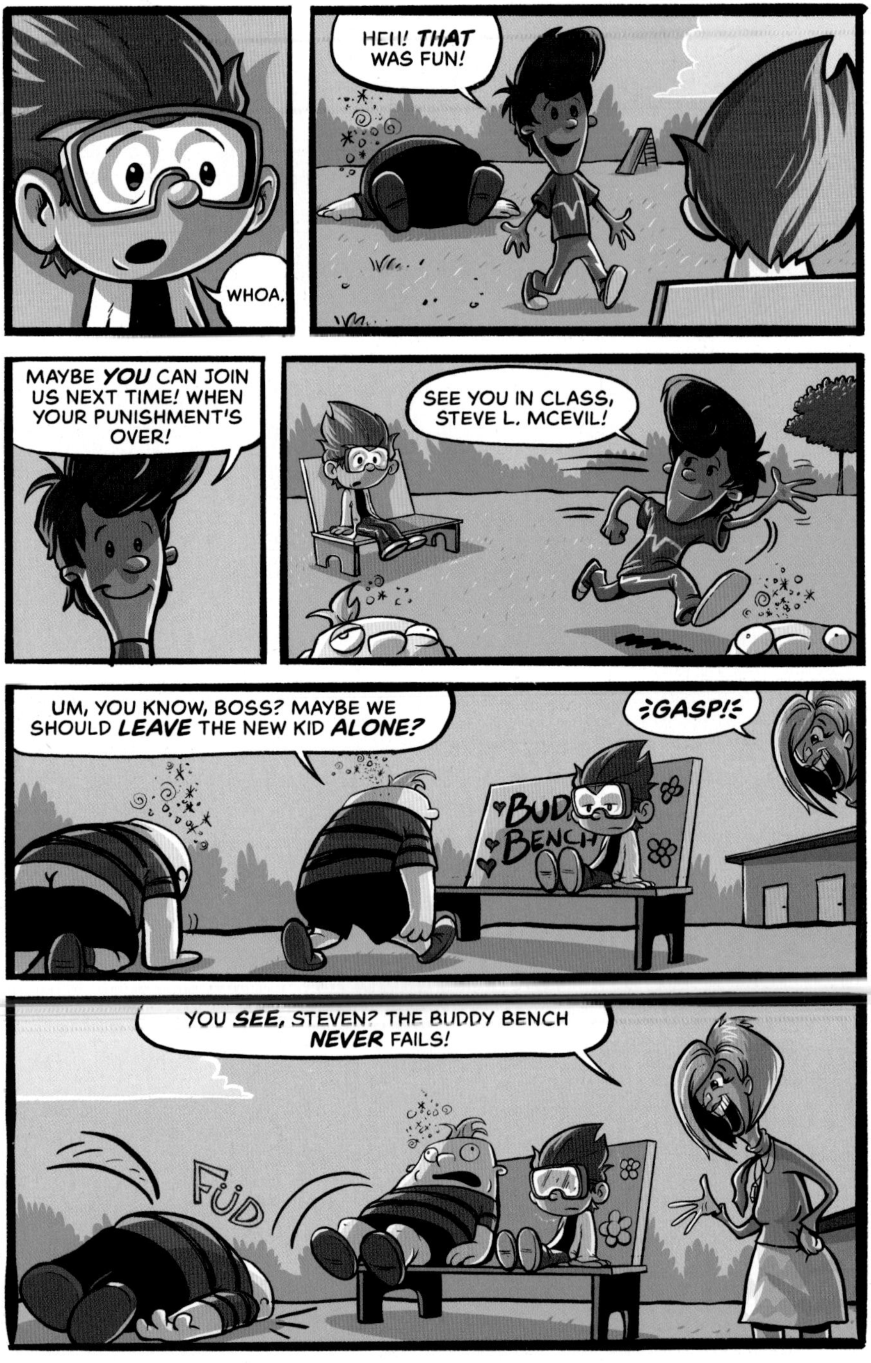
WHOA.
HEH! THAT WAS FUN!
MAYBE YOU CAN JOIN US NEXT TIME! WHEN YOUR PUNISHMENT'S OVER!
SEE YOU IN CLASS, STEVE L. MCEVIL!
UM, YOU KNOW, BOSS? MAYBE WE SHOULD LEAVE THE NEW KID ALONE?
GASP!
BUDDY BENCH
YOU SEE, STEVEN? THE BUDDY BENCH NEVER FAILS!
FUD

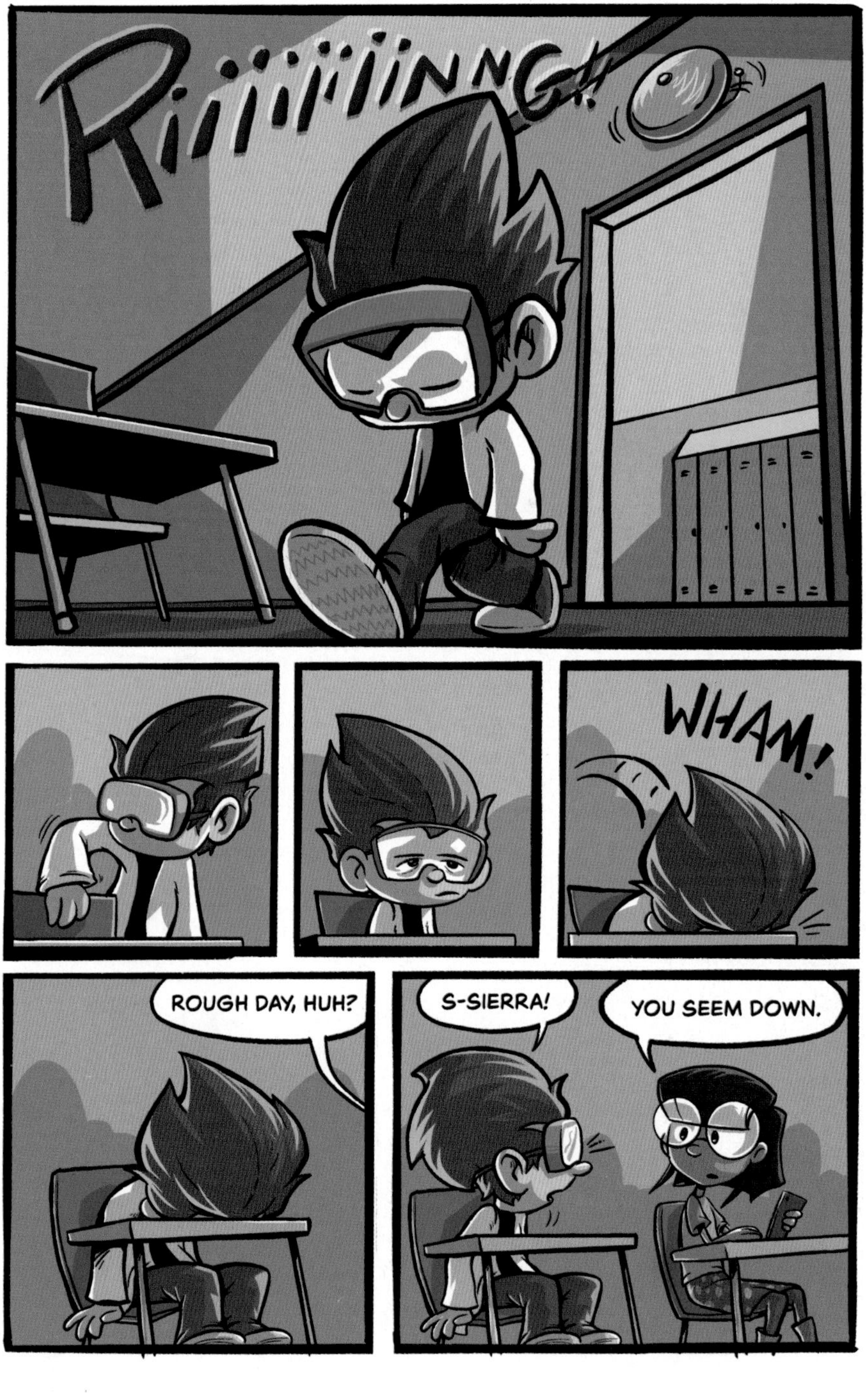
Riiiiiiinng!!
WHAM!
ROUGH DAY, HUH?
S-SIERRA!
YOU SEEM DOWN.

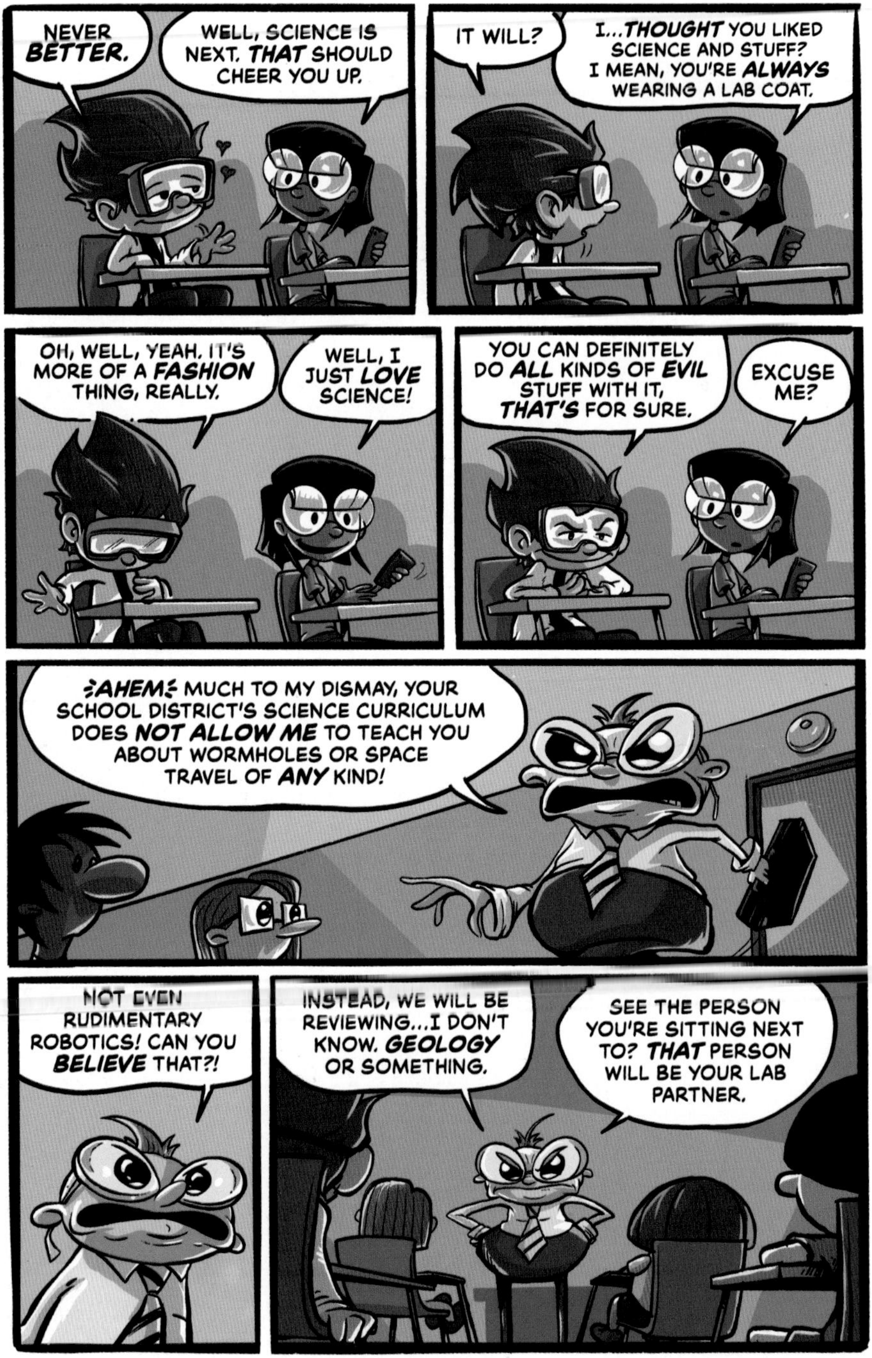
NEVER BETTER.
WELL, SCIENCE IS NEXT. THAT SHOULD CHEER YOU UP.
IT WILL?
I...THOUGHT YOU LIKED SCIENCE AND STUFF? I MEAN, YOU'RE ALWAYS WEARING A LAB COAT.
OH, WELL, YEAH. IT'S MORE OF A FASHION THING, REALLY.
WELL, I JUST LOVE SCIENCE!
YOU CAN DEFINITELY DO ALL KINDS OF EVIL STUFF WITH IT, THAT'S FOR SURE.
EXCUSE ME?
AHEM MUCH TO MY DISMAY, YOUR SCHOOL DISTRICT'S SCIENCE CURRICULUM DOES NOT ALLOW ME TO TEACH YOU ABOUT WORMHOLES OR SPACE TRAVEL OF ANY KIND!
NOT EVEN RUDIMENTARY ROBOTICS! CAN YOU BELIEVE THAT?!
INSTEAD, WE WILL BE REVIEWING...I DON'T KNOW. GEOLOGY OR SOMETHING.
SEE THE PERSON YOU'RE SITTING NEXT TO? THAT PERSON WILL BE YOUR LAB PARTNER.

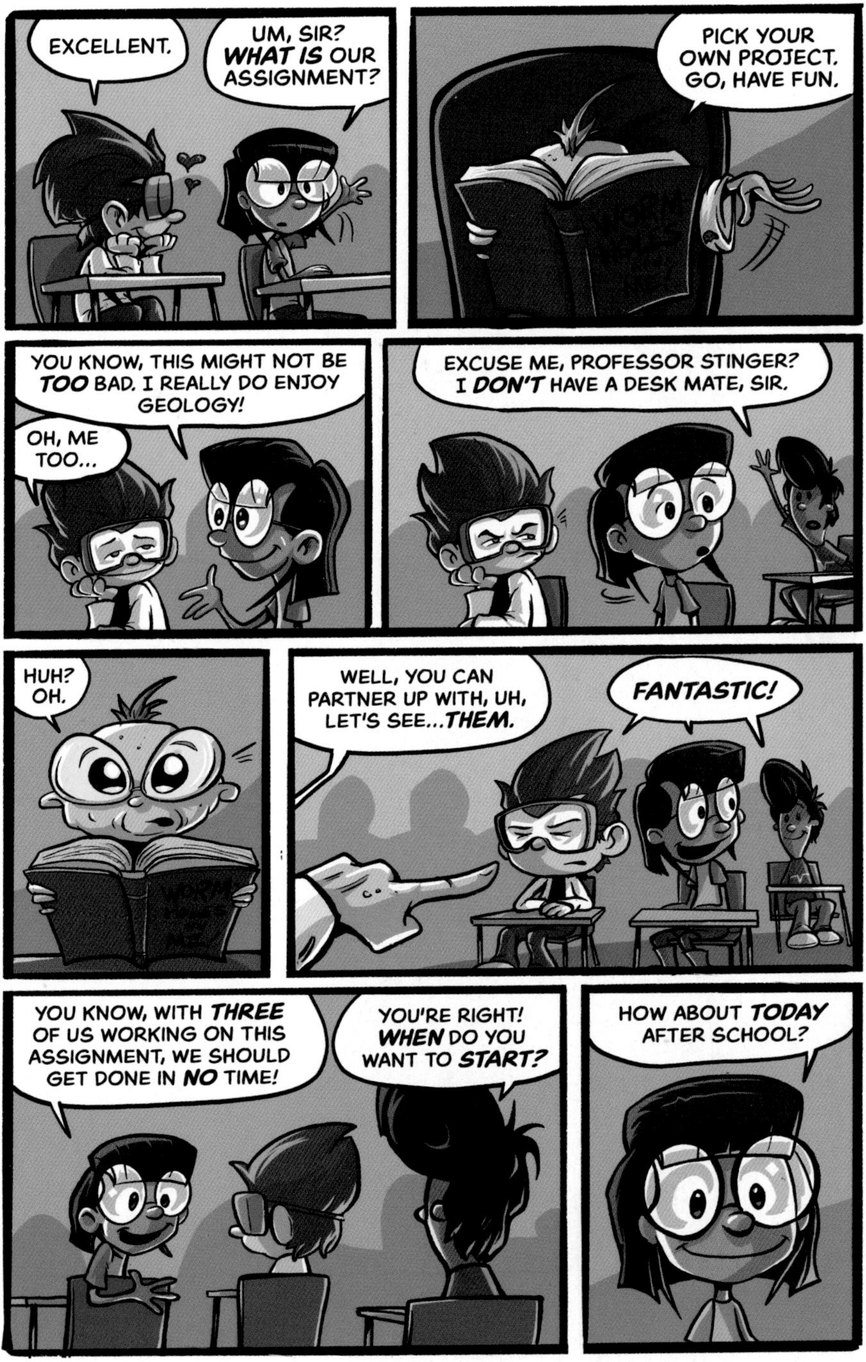
EXCELLENT.
UM, SIR? WHAT IS OUR ASSIGNMENT?
PICK YOUR OWN PROJECT. GO, HAVE FUN.
YOU KNOW, THIS MIGHT NOT BE TOO BAD. I REALLY DO ENJOY GEOLOGY!
OH, ME TOO...
EXCUSE ME, PROFESSOR STINGER? I DON'T HAVE A DESK MATE, SIR.
HUH? OH.
WELL, YOU CAN PARTNER UP WITH, UH, LET'S SEE...THEM.
FANTASTIC!
YOU KNOW, WITH THREE OF US WORKING ON THIS ASSIGNMENT, WE SHOULD GET DONE IN NO TIME!
YOU'RE RIGHT! WHEN DO YOU WANT TO START?
HOW ABOUT TODAY AFTER SCHOOL?

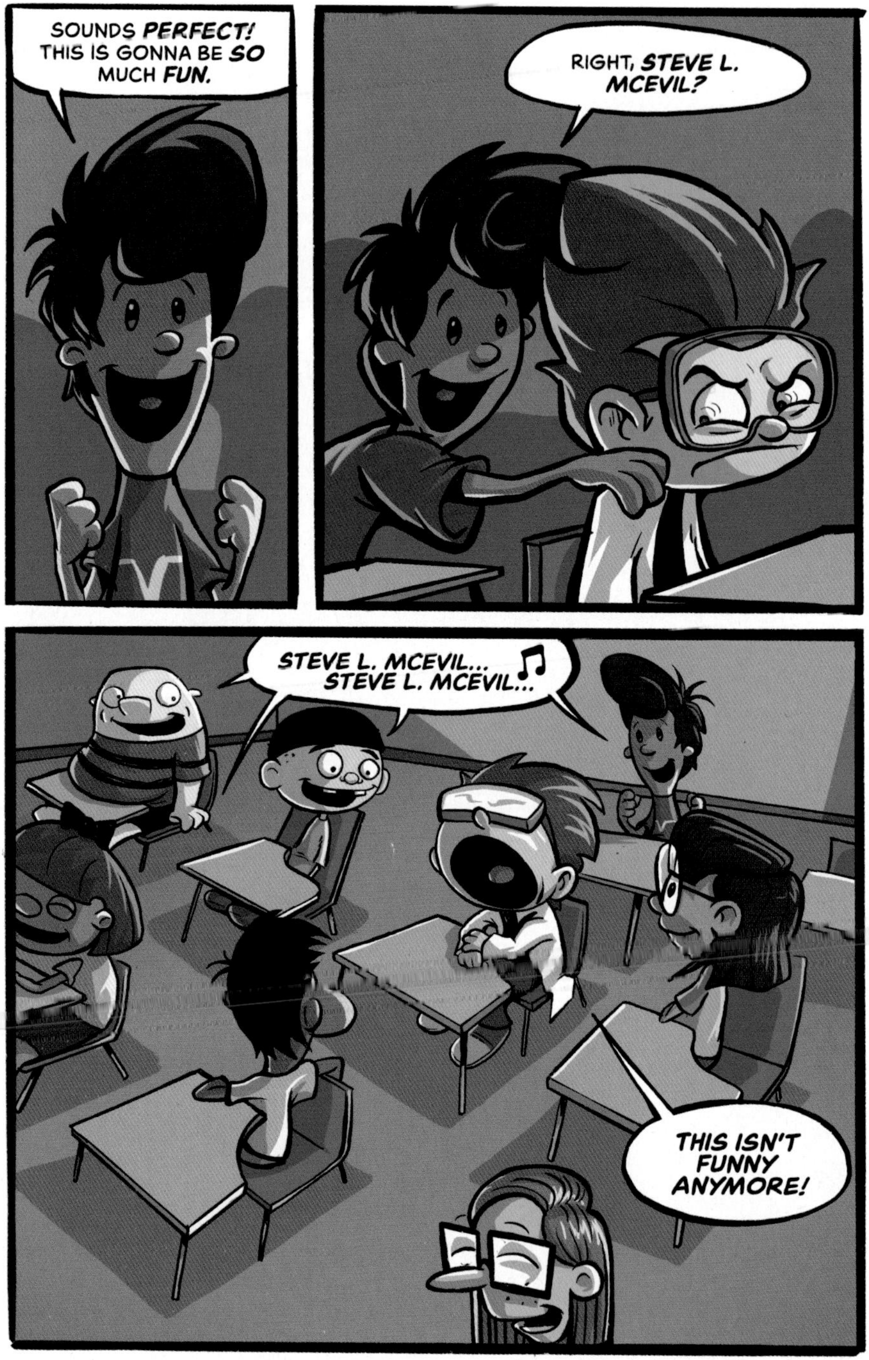
SOUNDS PERFECT! THIS IS GONNA BE SO MUCH FUN.
RIGHT, STEVE L. MCEVIL?
STEVE L. MCEVIL... STEVE L. MCEVIL...
THIS ISN'T FUNNY ANYMORE!

CHaPTeR 9
Rock On

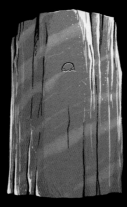

LATER...

DO EITHER OF YOU UNDERSTAND WHAT EXACTLY IT IS WE'RE **SUPPOSED** TO BE DOING?

I'M SORT OF LOST.

STUDYING ROCKS, OF COURSE!

VERY GOOD, VIC.

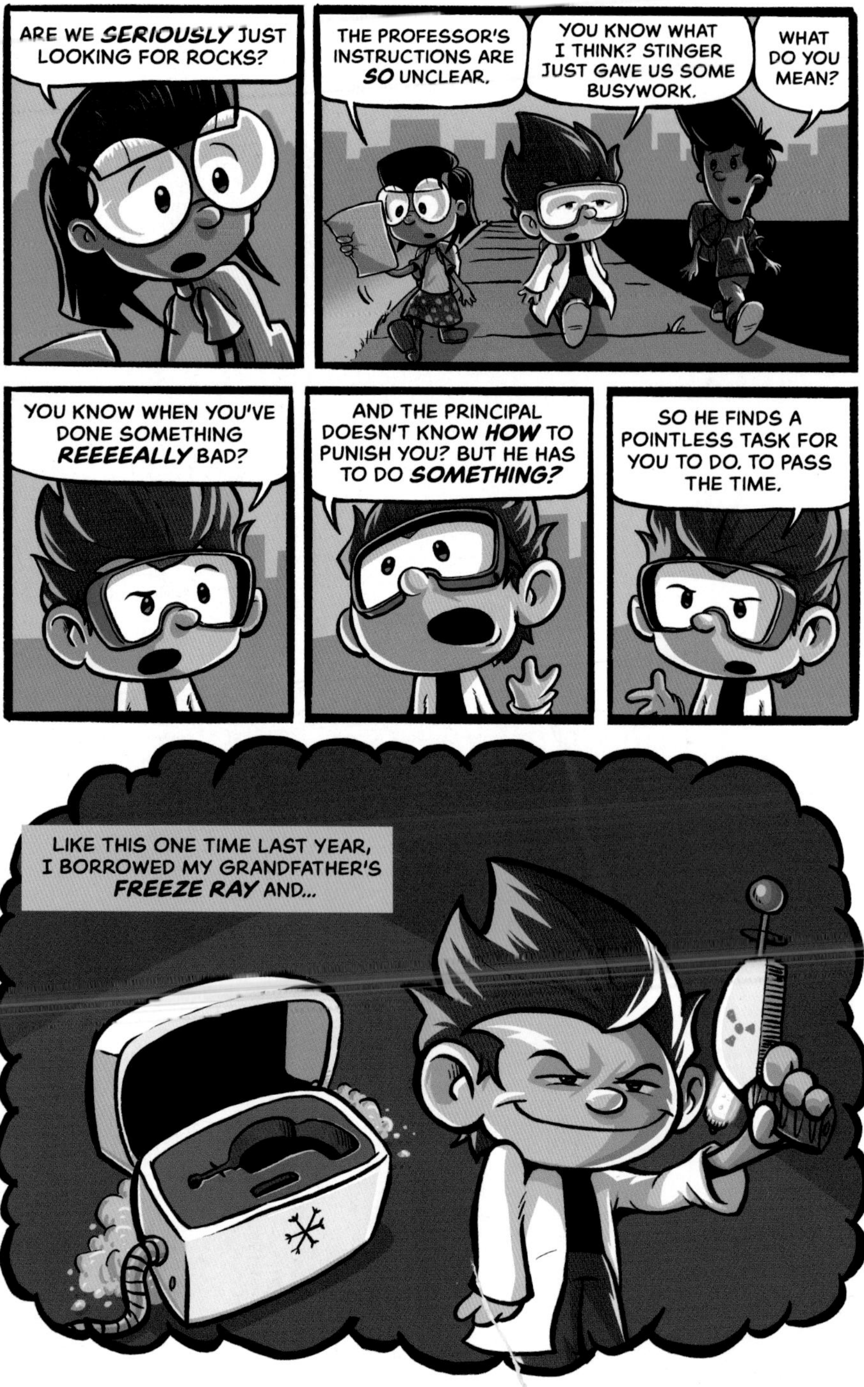
ARE WE SERIOUSLY JUST LOOKING FOR ROCKS?
THE PROFESSOR'S INSTRUCTIONS ARE SO UNCLEAR.
YOU KNOW WHAT I THINK? STINGER JUST GAVE US SOME BUSYWORK.
WHAT DO YOU MEAN?
YOU KNOW WHEN YOU'VE DONE SOMETHING REEEEALLY BAD?
AND THE PRINCIPAL DOESN'T KNOW HOW TO PUNISH YOU? BUT HE HAS TO DO SOMETHING?
SO HE FINDS A POINTLESS TASK FOR YOU TO DO, TO PASS THE TIME.
LIKE THIS ONE TIME LAST YEAR, I BORROWED MY GRANDFATHER'S FREEZE RAY AND...

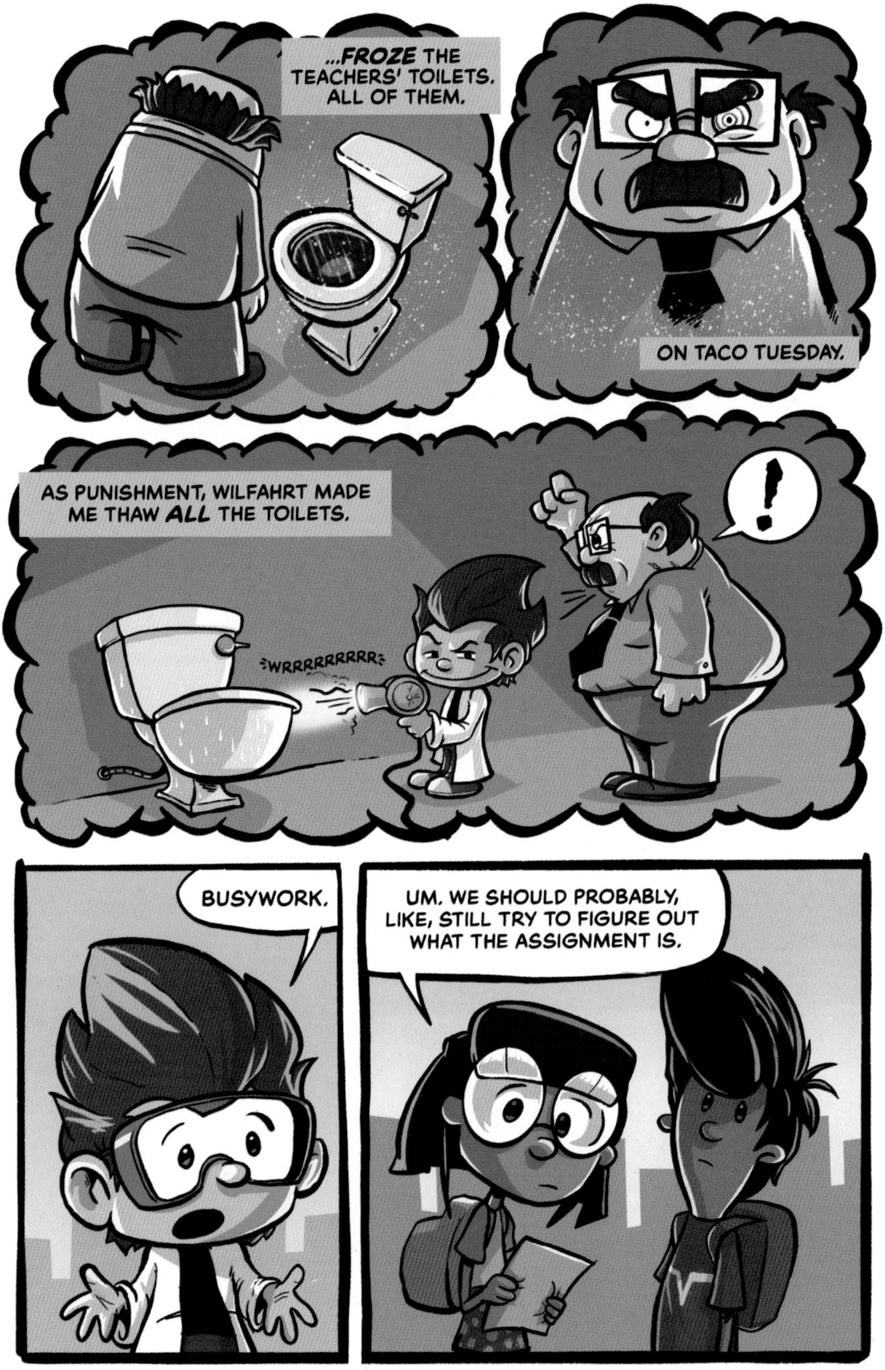
...FROZE THE TEACHERS' TOILETS. ALL OF THEM.
ON TACO TUESDAY.
AS PUNISHMENT, WILFAHRT MADE ME THAW ALL THE TOILETS.
!
WRRRRRRRRR
BUSYWORK.
UM. WE SHOULD PROBABLY, LIKE, STILL TRY TO FIGURE OUT WHAT THE ASSIGNMENT IS.

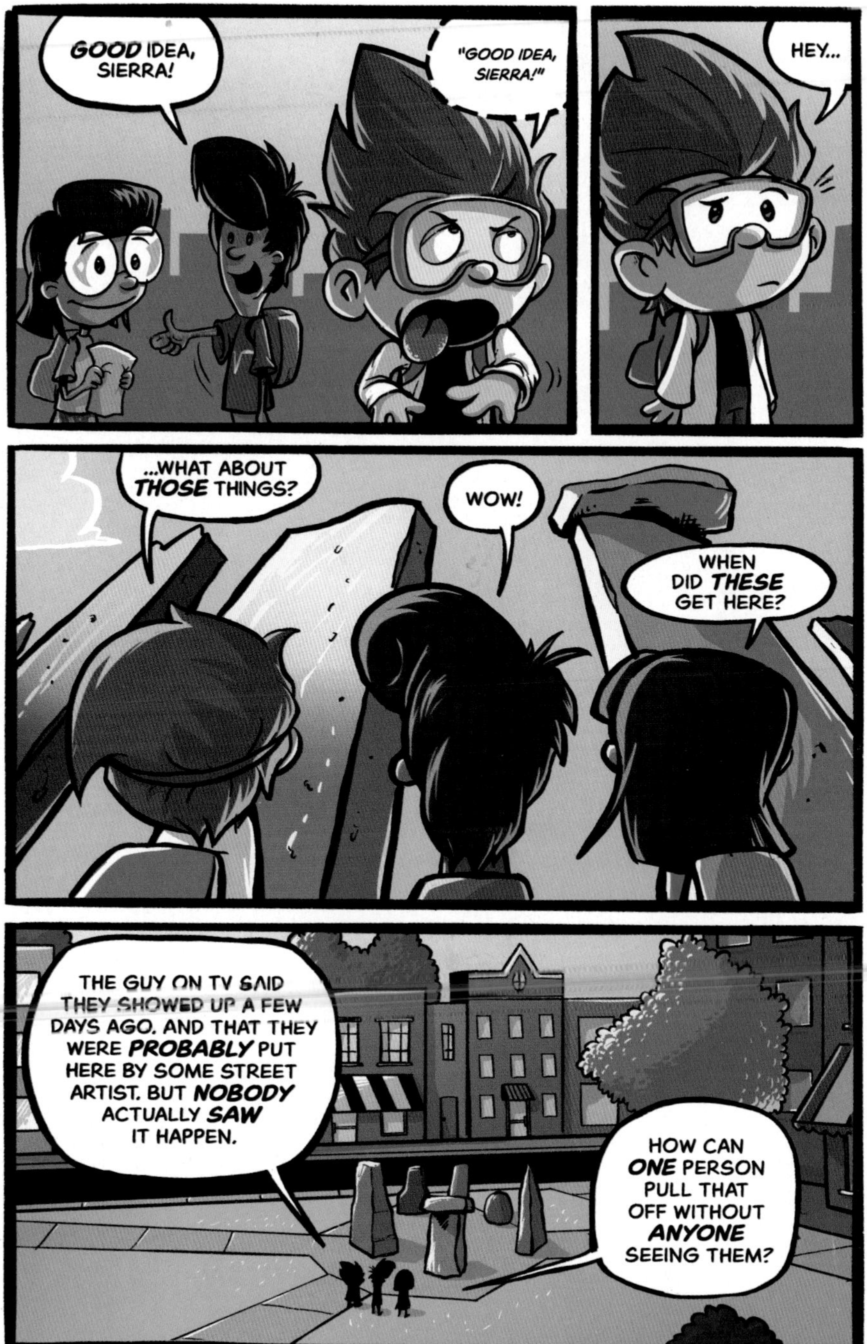
GOOD IDEA, SIERRA!
"GOOD IDEA, SIERRA!"
HEY...
...WHAT ABOUT THOSE THINGS?
WOW!
WHEN DID THESE GET HERE?
THE GUY ON TV SAID THEY SHOWED UP A FEW DAYS AGO. AND THAT THEY WERE PROBABLY PUT HERE BY SOME STREET ARTIST. BUT NOBODY ACTUALLY SAW IT HAPPEN.
HOW CAN ONE PERSON PULL THAT OFF WITHOUT ANYONE SEEING THEM?

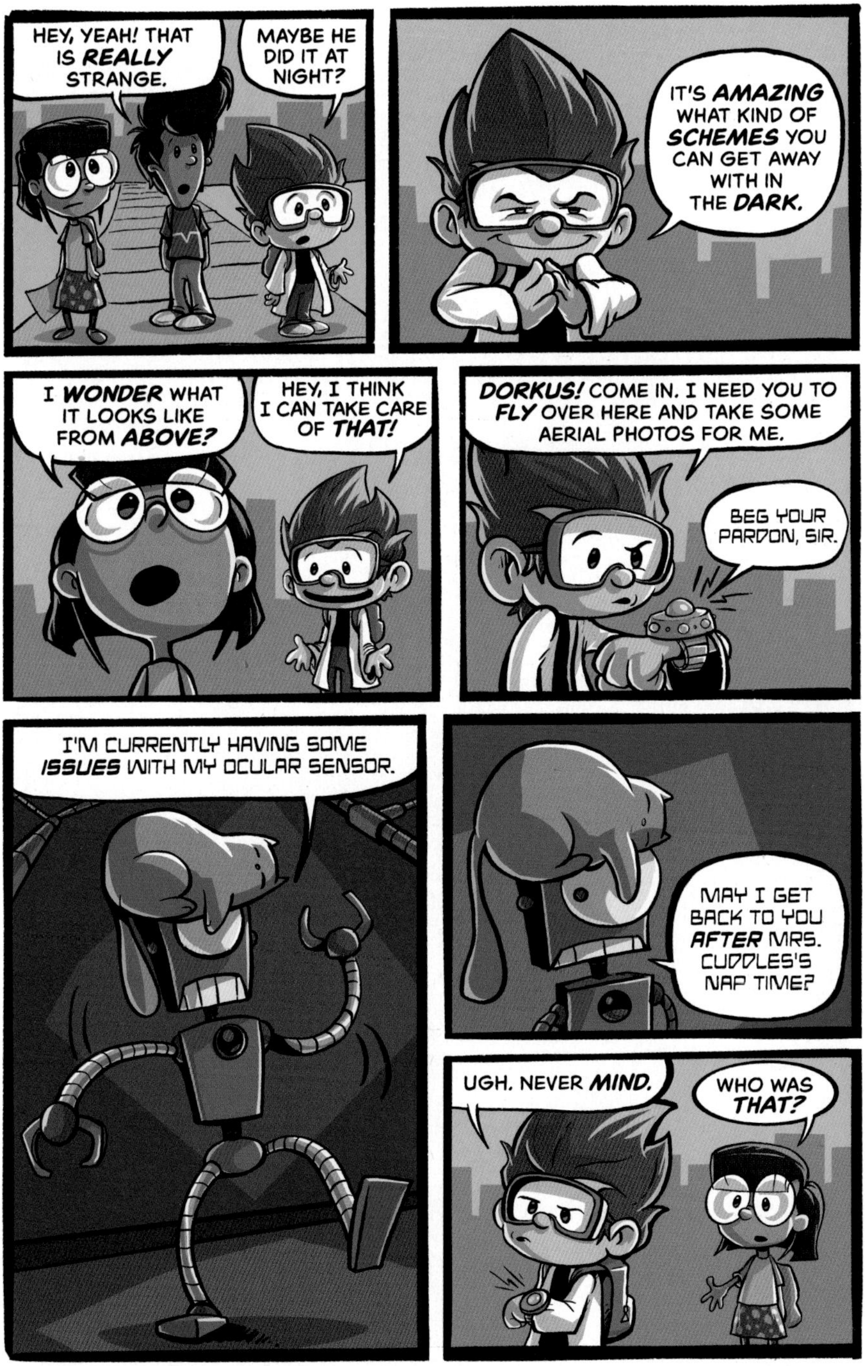

HEY, YEAH! THAT IS REALLY STRANGE.
MAYBE HE DID IT AT NIGHT?
IT'S AMAZING WHAT KIND OF SCHEMES YOU CAN GET AWAY WITH IN THE DARK.
I WONDER WHAT IT LOOKS LIKE FROM ABOVE?
HEY, I THINK I CAN TAKE CARE OF THAT!
DORKUS! COME IN. I NEED YOU TO FLY OVER HERE AND TAKE SOME AERIAL PHOTOS FOR ME.
BEG YOUR PARDON, SIR.
I'M CURRENTLY HAVING SOME ISSUES WITH MY OCULAR SENSOR.
MAY I GET BACK TO YOU AFTER MRS. CUDDLES'S NAP TIME?
UGH. NEVER MIND.
WHO WAS THAT?

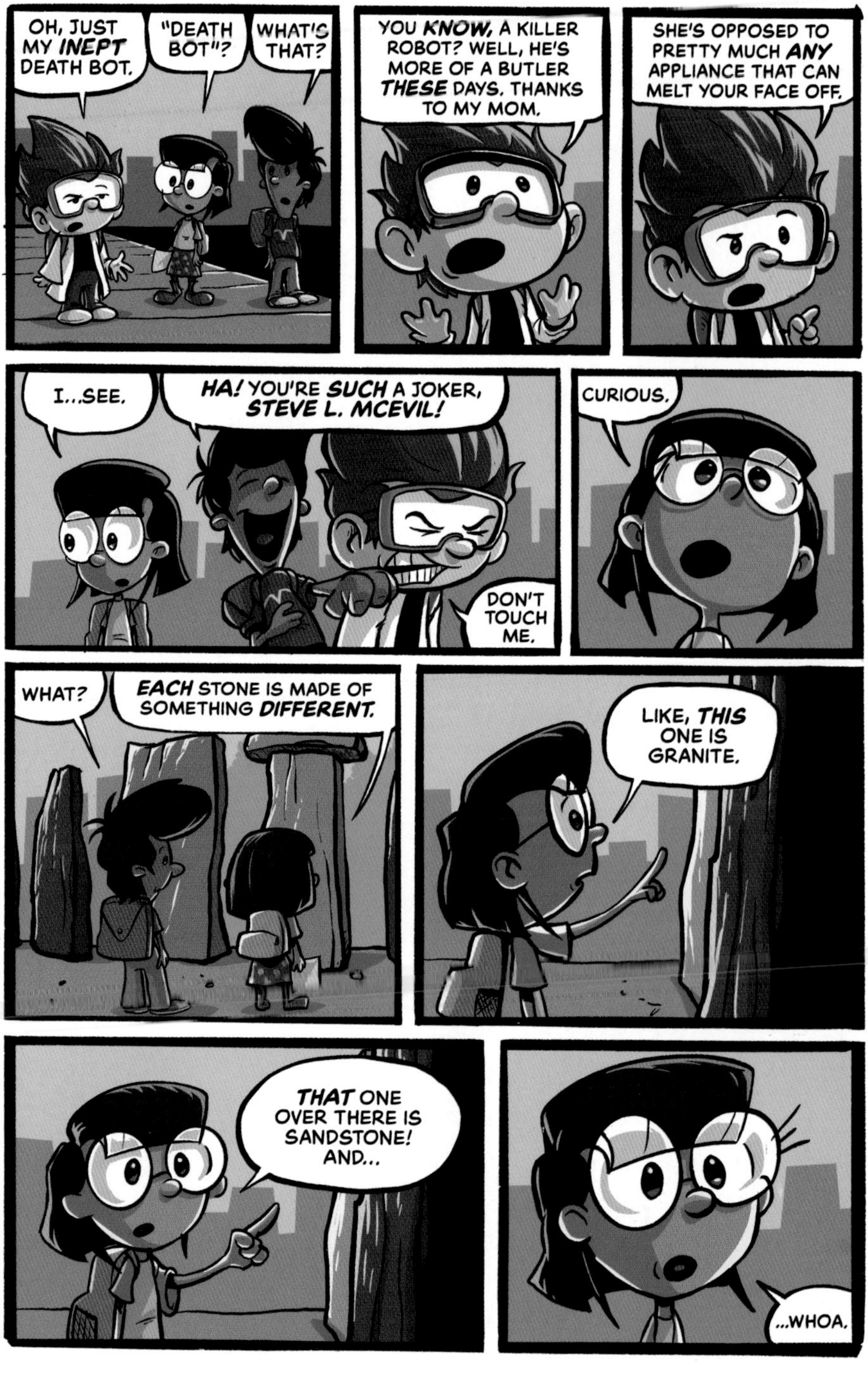
OH, JUST MY INEPT DEATH BOT.
"DEATH BOT"?
WHAT'S THAT?
YOU KNOW, A KILLER ROBOT? WELL, HE'S MORE OF A BUTLER THESE DAYS. THANKS TO MY MOM.
SHE'S OPPOSED TO PRETTY MUCH ANY APPLIANCE THAT CAN MELT YOUR FACE OFF.
I...SEE.
HA! YOU'RE SUCH A JOKER, STEVE L. MCEVIL!
DON'T TOUCH ME.
CURIOUS.
WHAT?
EACH STONE IS MADE OF SOMETHING DIFFERENT.
LIKE, THIS ONE IS GRANITE.
THAT ONE OVER THERE IS SANDSTONE! AND...
...WHOA.

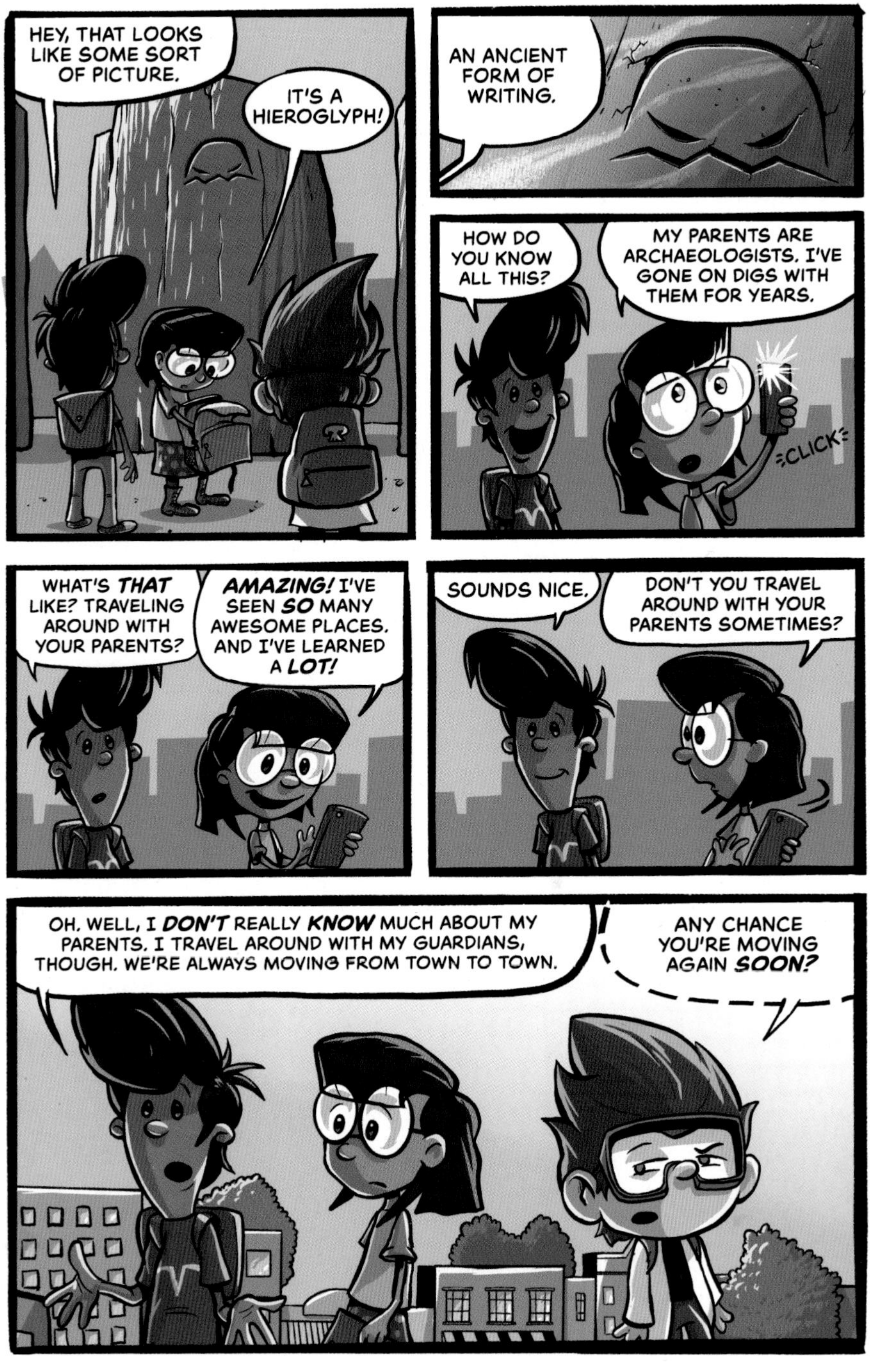
HEY, THAT LOOKS LIKE SOME SORT OF PICTURE.
IT'S A HIEROGLYPH!
AN ANCIENT FORM OF WRITING.
HOW DO YOU KNOW ALL THIS?
MY PARENTS ARE ARCHAEOLOGISTS. I'VE GONE ON DIGS WITH THEM FOR YEARS.
CLICK
WHAT'S THAT LIKE? TRAVELING AROUND WITH YOUR PARENTS?
AMAZING! I'VE SEEN SO MANY AWESOME PLACES, AND I'VE LEARNED A LOT!
SOUNDS NICE.
DON'T YOU TRAVEL AROUND WITH YOUR PARENTS SOMETIMES?
OH, WELL, I DON'T REALLY KNOW MUCH ABOUT MY PARENTS. I TRAVEL AROUND WITH MY GUARDIANS, THOUGH. WE'RE ALWAYS MOVING FROM TOWN TO TOWN.
ANY CHANCE YOU'RE MOVING AGAIN SOON?

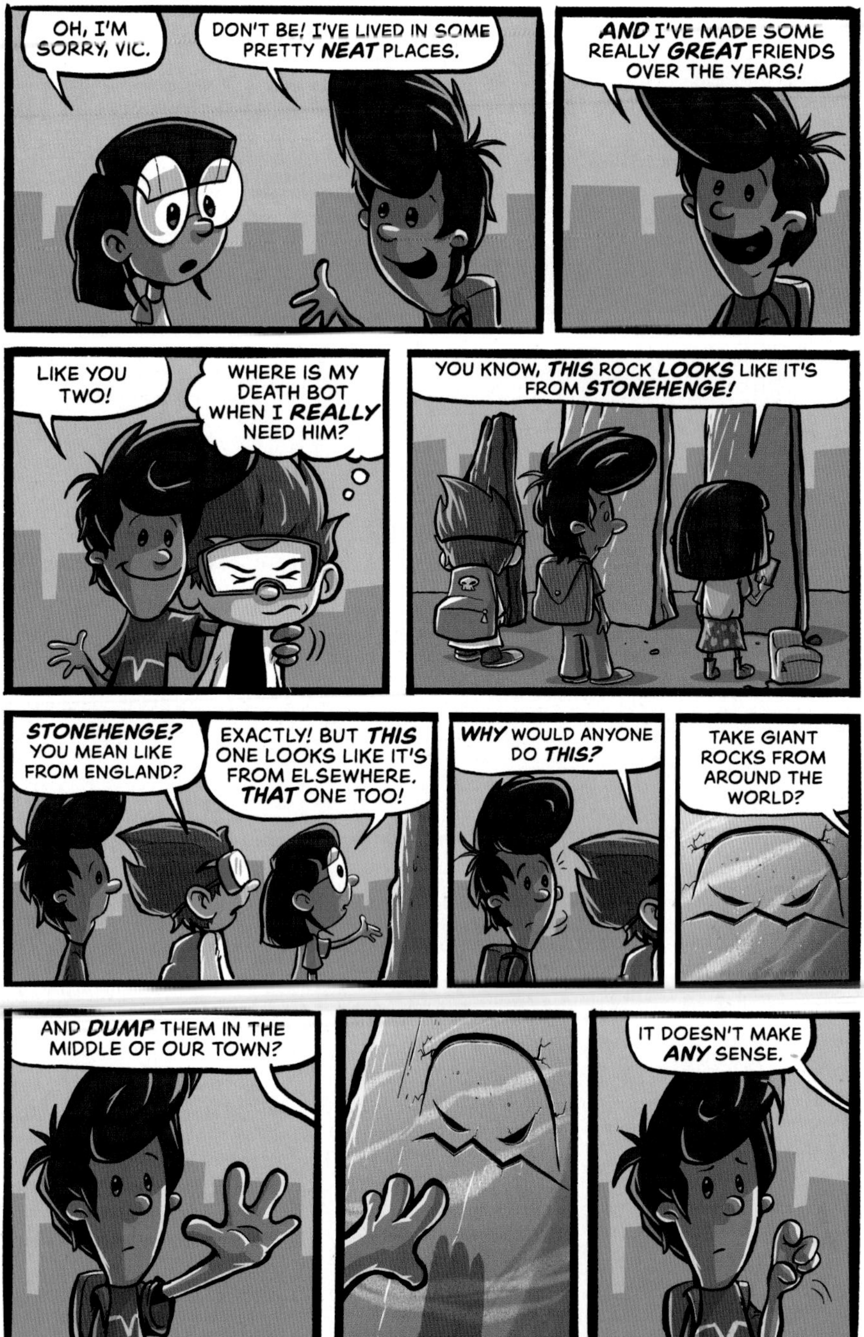
OH, I'M SORRY, VIC.
DON'T BE! I'VE LIVED IN SOME PRETTY **NEAT** PLACES.
AND I'VE MADE SOME REALLY **GREAT** FRIENDS OVER THE YEARS!
LIKE YOU TWO!
WHERE IS MY DEATH BOT WHEN I **REALLY** NEED HIM?
YOU KNOW, **THIS** ROCK **LOOKS** LIKE IT'S FROM **STONEHENGE!**
STONEHENGE? YOU MEAN LIKE FROM ENGLAND?
EXACTLY! BUT **THIS** ONE LOOKS LIKE IT'S FROM ELSEWHERE. **THAT** ONE TOO!
WHY WOULD ANYONE DO **THIS?**
TAKE GIANT ROCKS FROM AROUND THE WORLD?
AND **DUMP** THEM IN THE MIDDLE OF OUR TOWN?
IT DOESN'T MAKE **ANY** SENSE.

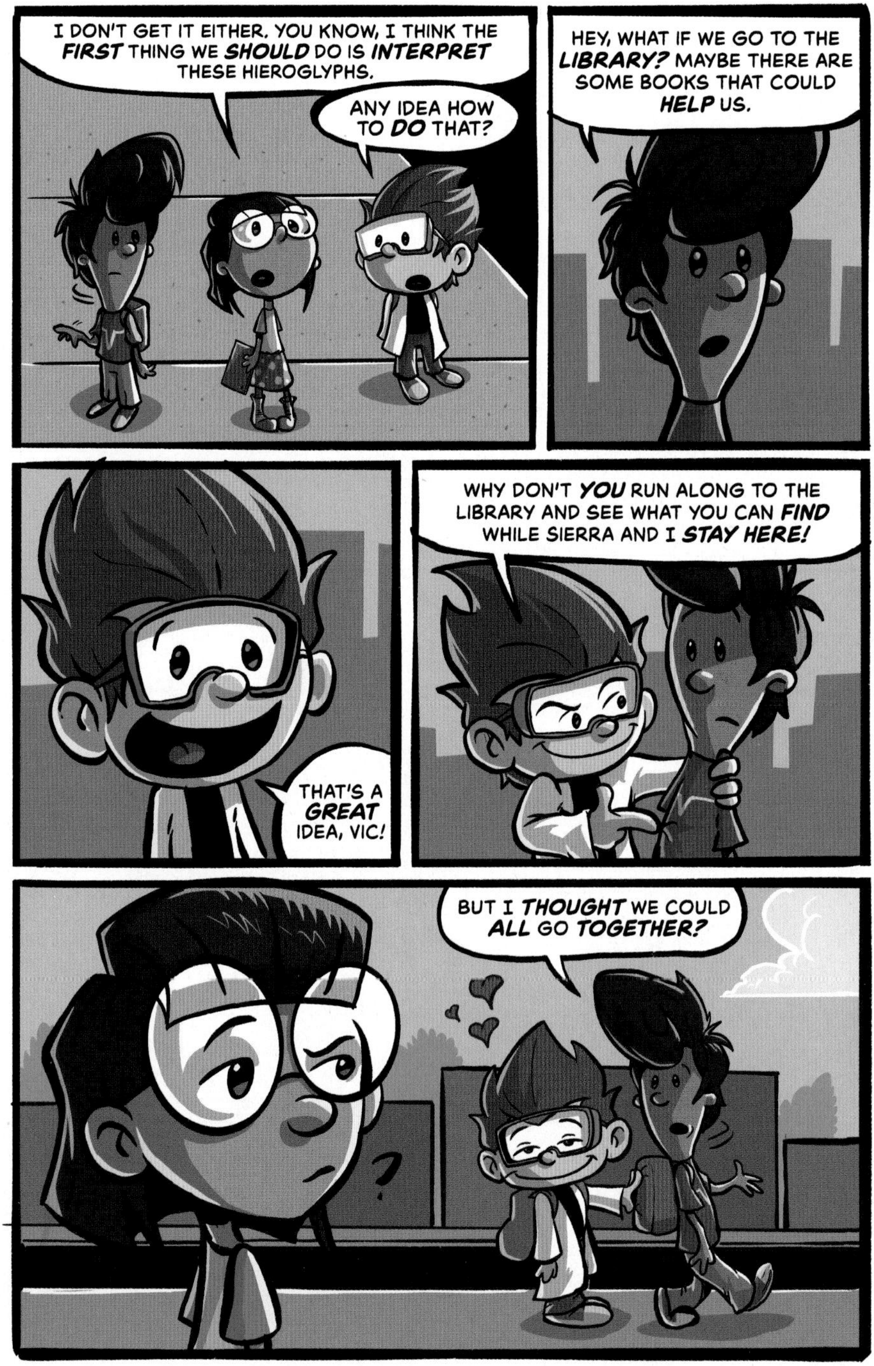
I DON'T GET IT EITHER. YOU KNOW, I THINK THE FIRST THING WE SHOULD DO IS INTERPRET THESE HIEROGLYPHS.
ANY IDEA HOW TO DO THAT?
HEY, WHAT IF WE GO TO THE LIBRARY? MAYBE THERE ARE SOME BOOKS THAT COULD HELP US.
THAT'S A GREAT IDEA, VIC!
WHY DON'T YOU RUN ALONG TO THE LIBRARY AND SEE WHAT YOU CAN FIND WHILE SIERRA AND I STAY HERE!
BUT I THOUGHT WE COULD ALL GO TOGETHER?
?

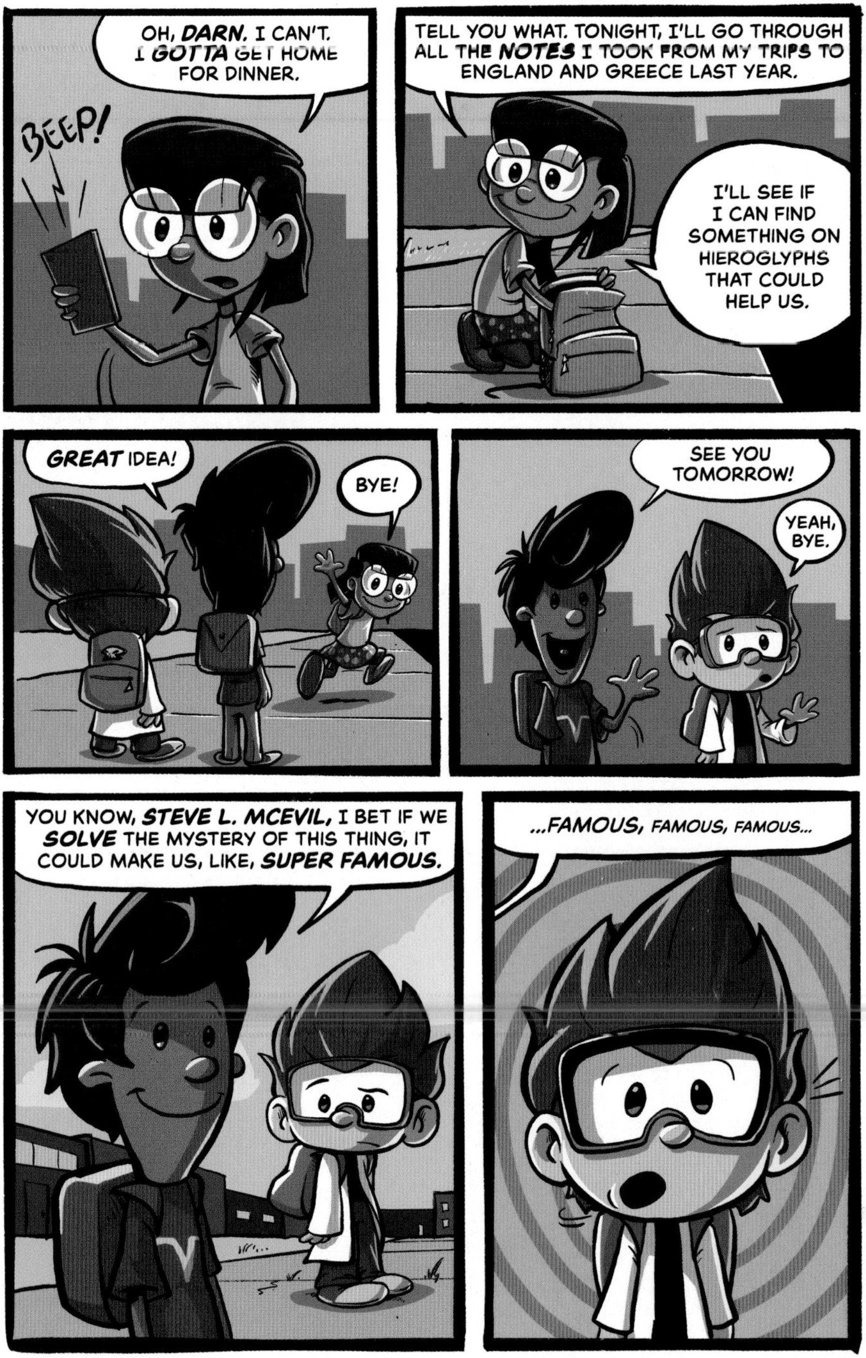
OH, DARN. I CAN'T. I GOTTA GET HOME FOR DINNER.
BEEP!
TELL YOU WHAT. TONIGHT, I'LL GO THROUGH ALL THE NOTES I TOOK FROM MY TRIPS TO ENGLAND AND GREECE LAST YEAR.
I'LL SEE IF I CAN FIND SOMETHING ON HIEROGLYPHS THAT COULD HELP US.
GREAT IDEA!
BYE!
SEE YOU TOMORROW!
YEAH, BYE.
YOU KNOW, STEVE L. MCEVIL, I BET IF WE SOLVE THE MYSTERY OF THIS THING, IT COULD MAKE US, LIKE, SUPER FAMOUS.
...FAMOUS, FAMOUS, FAMOUS...

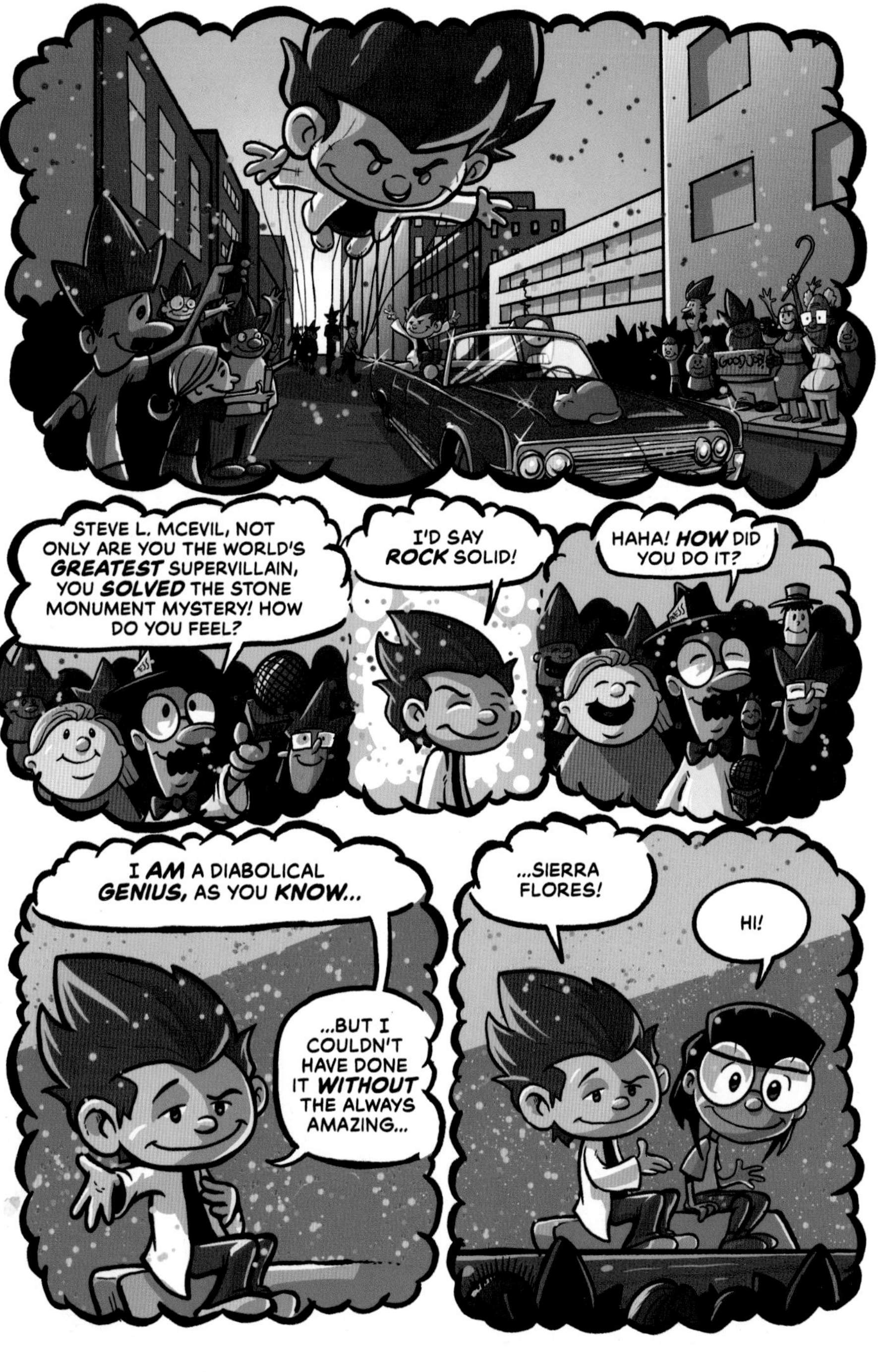
STEVE L. MCEVIL, NOT ONLY ARE YOU THE WORLD'S GREATEST SUPERVILLAIN, YOU SOLVED THE STONE MONUMENT MYSTERY! HOW DO YOU FEEL?
I'D SAY ROCK SOLID!
HAHA! HOW DID YOU DO IT?
I AM A DIABOLICAL GENIUS, AS YOU KNOW...
...BUT I COULDN'T HAVE DONE IT WITHOUT THE ALWAYS AMAZING...
...SIERRA FLORES!
HI!

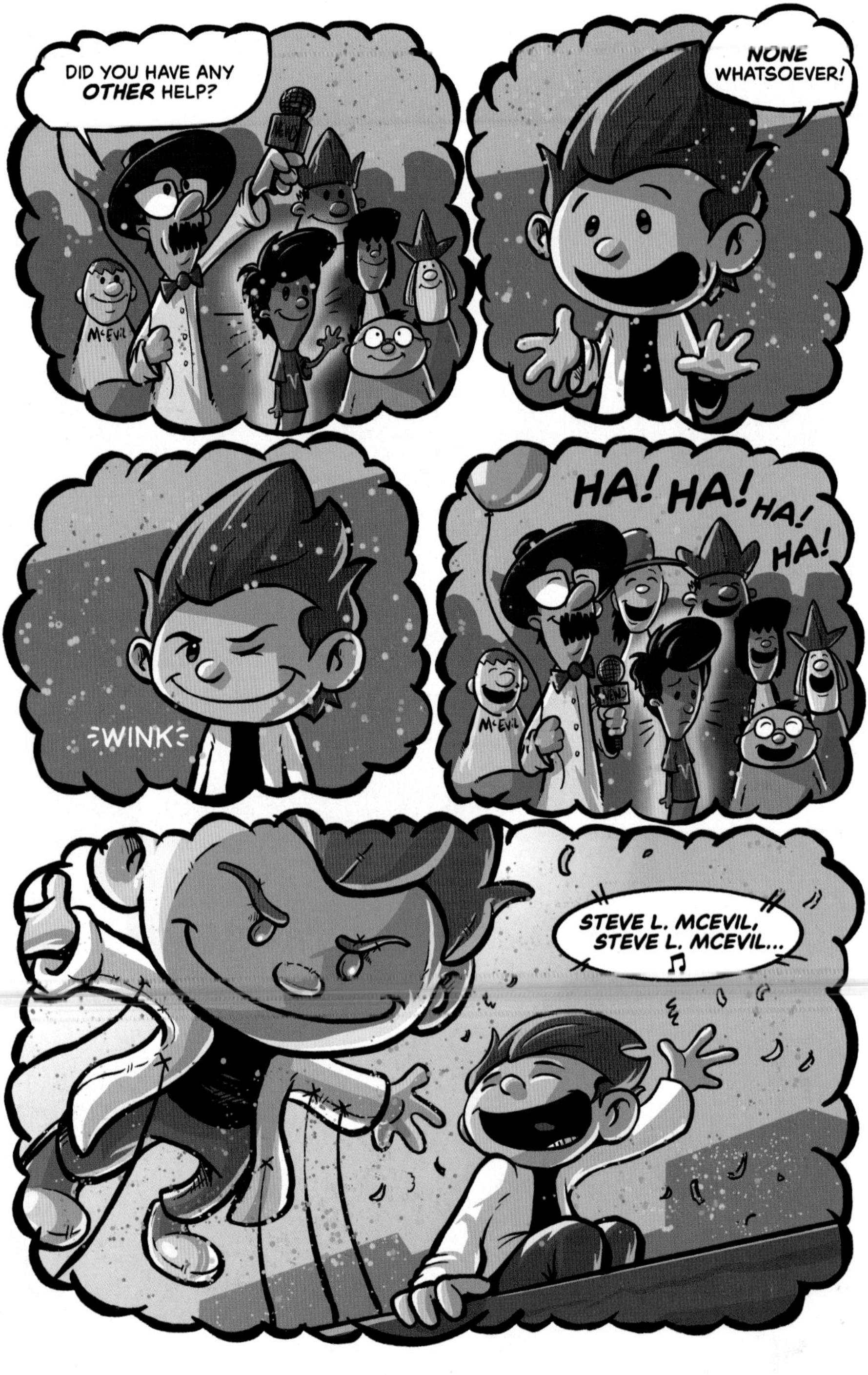
DID YOU HAVE ANY OTHER HELP?
NEWS
NONE WHATSOEVER!
WINK
HA! HA! HA! HA!
NEWS
STEVE L. MCEVIL, STEVE L. MCEVIL...

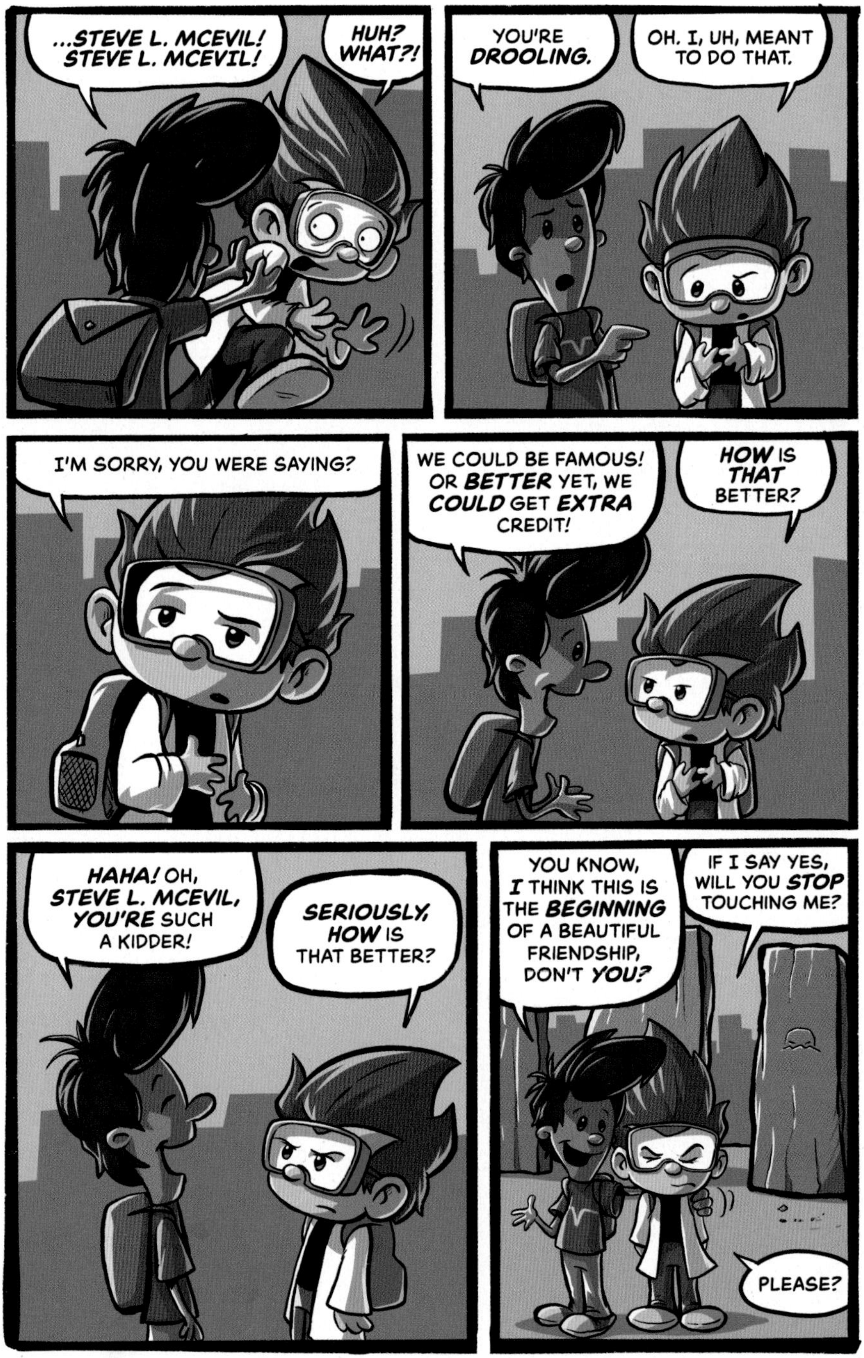
...STEVE L. MCEVIL! STEVE L. MCEVIL!
HUH? WHAT?!
YOU'RE DROOLING.
OH. I, UH, MEANT TO DO THAT.
I'M SORRY, YOU WERE SAYING?
WE COULD BE FAMOUS! OR BETTER YET, WE COULD GET EXTRA CREDIT!
HOW IS THAT BETTER?
HAHA! OH, STEVE L. MCEVIL, YOU'RE SUCH A KIDDER!
SERIOUSLY, HOW IS THAT BETTER?
YOU KNOW, I THINK THIS IS THE BEGINNING OF A BEAUTIFUL FRIENDSHIP, DON'T YOU?
IF I SAY YES, WILL YOU STOP TOUCHING ME?
PLEASE?

CHAPTER 10

Use Your Confusion

WHAT IS YOUR PROBLEM, DORKUS?
IT'S NOT THAT I DON'T ENJOY HAVING RANDOM ELECTRODES ATTACHED TO MY HEAD, SIR. BUT WOULDN'T IT BE EASIER TO USE YOUR SUPERVILLAIN COMPUTER?

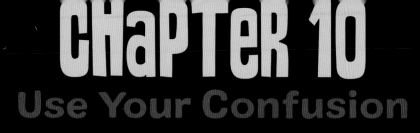

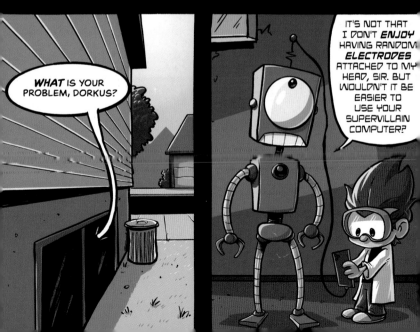

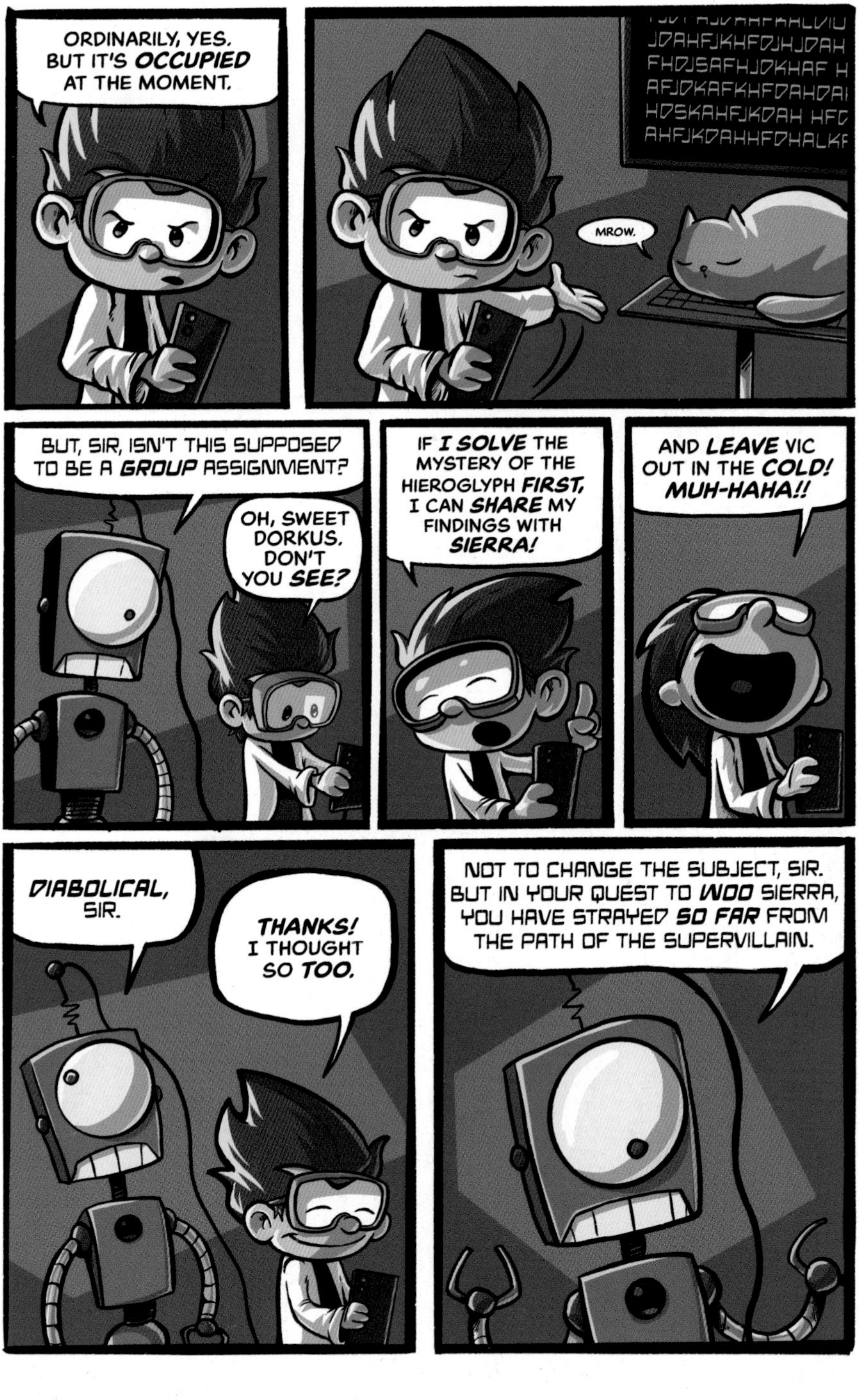
ORDINARILY, YES. BUT IT'S OCCUPIED AT THE MOMENT.
MROW.
BUT, SIR, ISN'T THIS SUPPOSED TO BE A GROUP ASSIGNMENT?
OH, SWEET DORKUS. DON'T YOU SEE?
IF I SOLVE THE MYSTERY OF THE HIEROGLYPH FIRST, I CAN SHARE MY FINDINGS WITH SIERRA!
AND LEAVE VIC OUT IN THE COLD! MUH-HAHA!!
DIABOLICAL, SIR.
THANKS! I THOUGHT SO TOO.
NOT TO CHANGE THE SUBJECT, SIR. BUT IN YOUR QUEST TO WOO SIERRA, YOU HAVE STRAYED SO FAR FROM THE PATH OF THE SUPERVILLAIN.

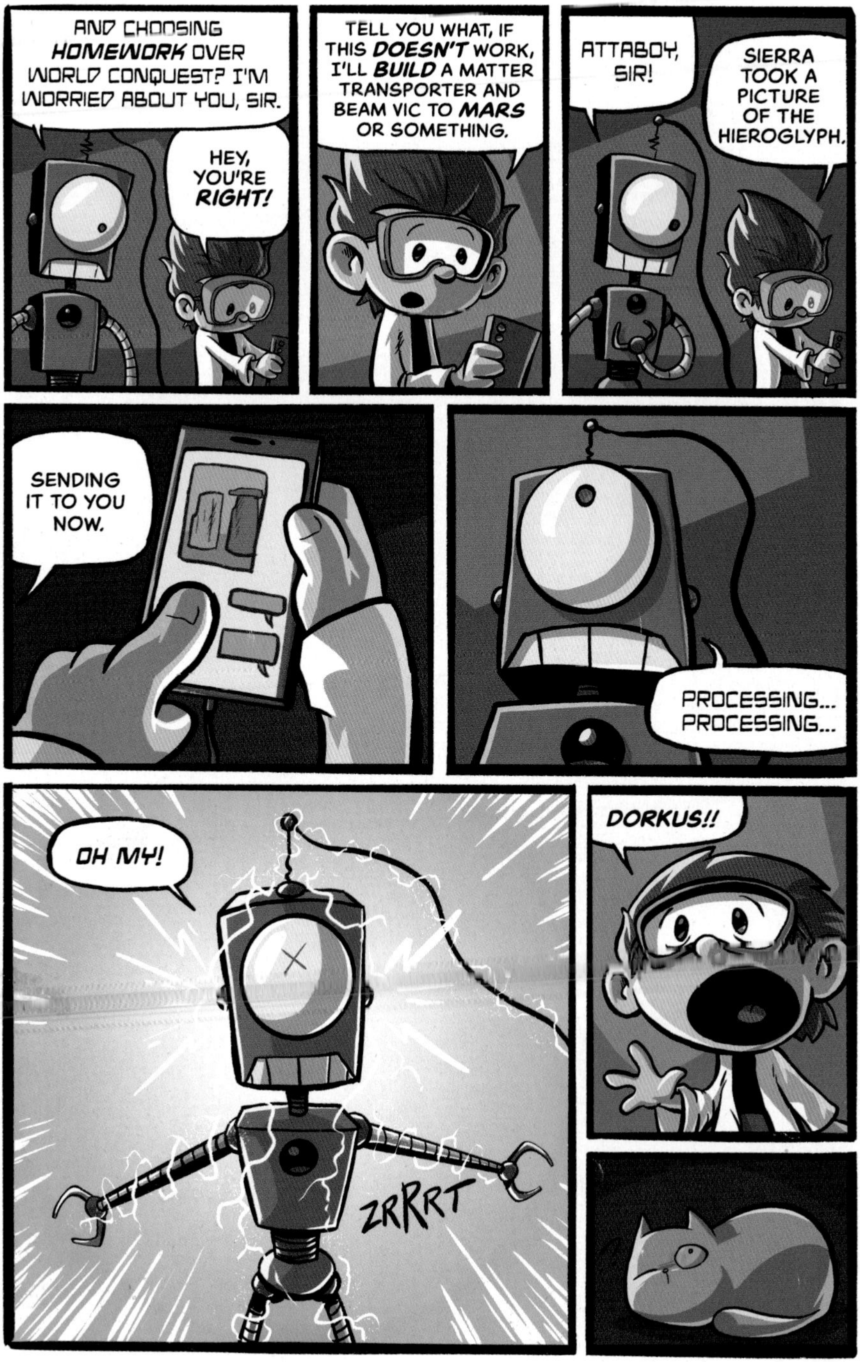
AND CHOOSING HOMEWORK OVER WORLD CONQUEST? I'M WORRIED ABOUT YOU, SIR.
HEY, YOU'RE RIGHT!
TELL YOU WHAT, IF THIS DOESN'T WORK, I'LL BUILD A MATTER TRANSPORTER AND BEAM VIC TO MARS OR SOMETHING.
ATTABOY, SIR!
SIERRA TOOK A PICTURE OF THE HIEROGLYPH.
SENDING IT TO YOU NOW.
PROCESSING... PROCESSING...
OH MY!
ZRRRT
DORKUS!!

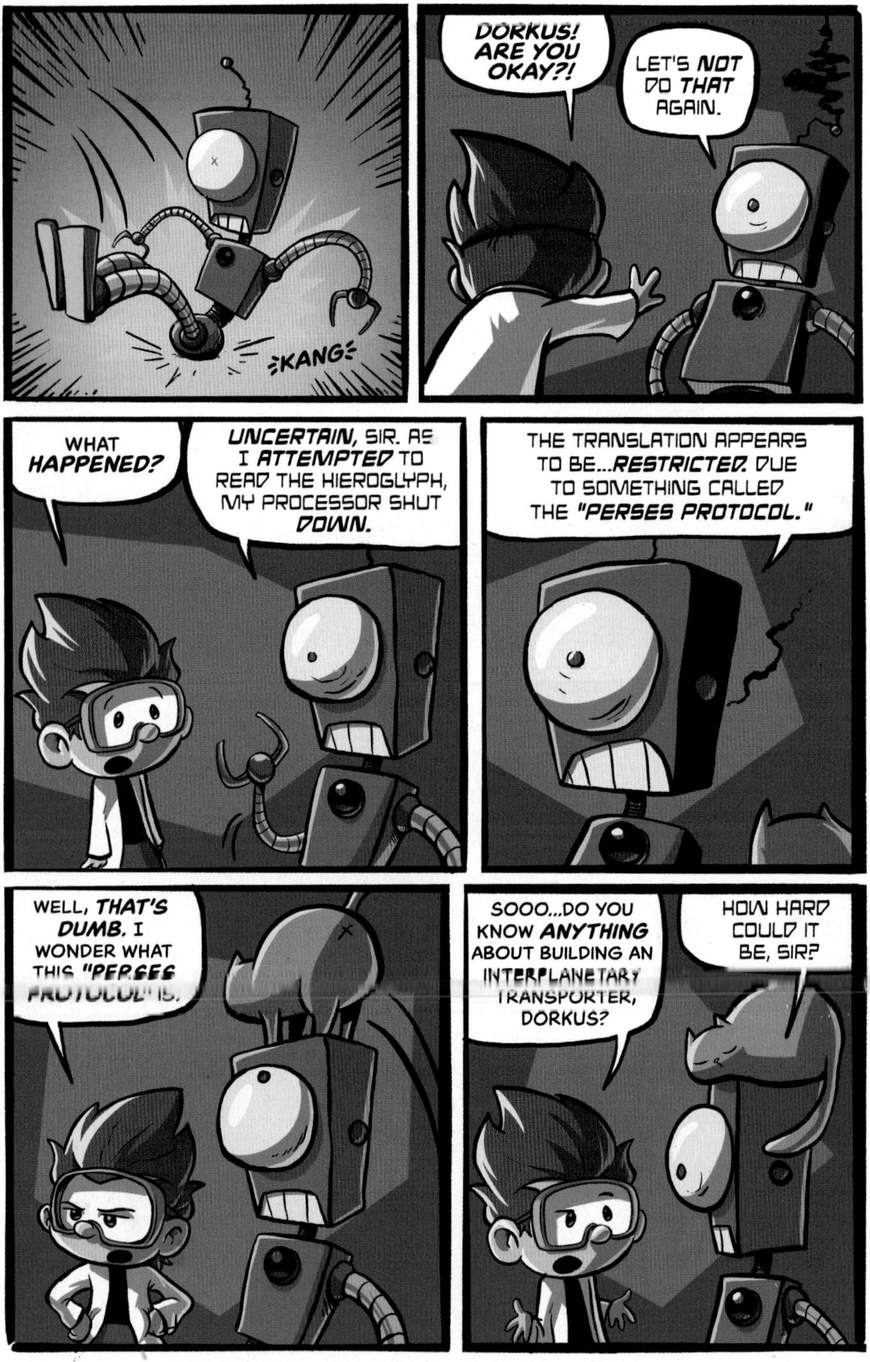
KANG
DORKUS! ARE YOU OKAY?!
LET'S NOT DO THAT AGAIN.
WHAT HAPPENED?
UNCERTAIN, SIR. AS I ATTEMPTED TO READ THE HIEROGLYPH, MY PROCESSOR SHUT DOWN.
THE TRANSLATION APPEARS TO BE...RESTRICTED. DUE TO SOMETHING CALLED THE "PERSES PROTOCOL."
WELL, THAT'S DUMB. I WONDER WHAT THIS "PERSES PROTOCOL" IS.
SOOO...DO YOU KNOW ANYTHING ABOUT BUILDING AN INTERPLANETARY TRANSPORTER, DORKUS?
HOW HARD COULD IT BE, SIR?

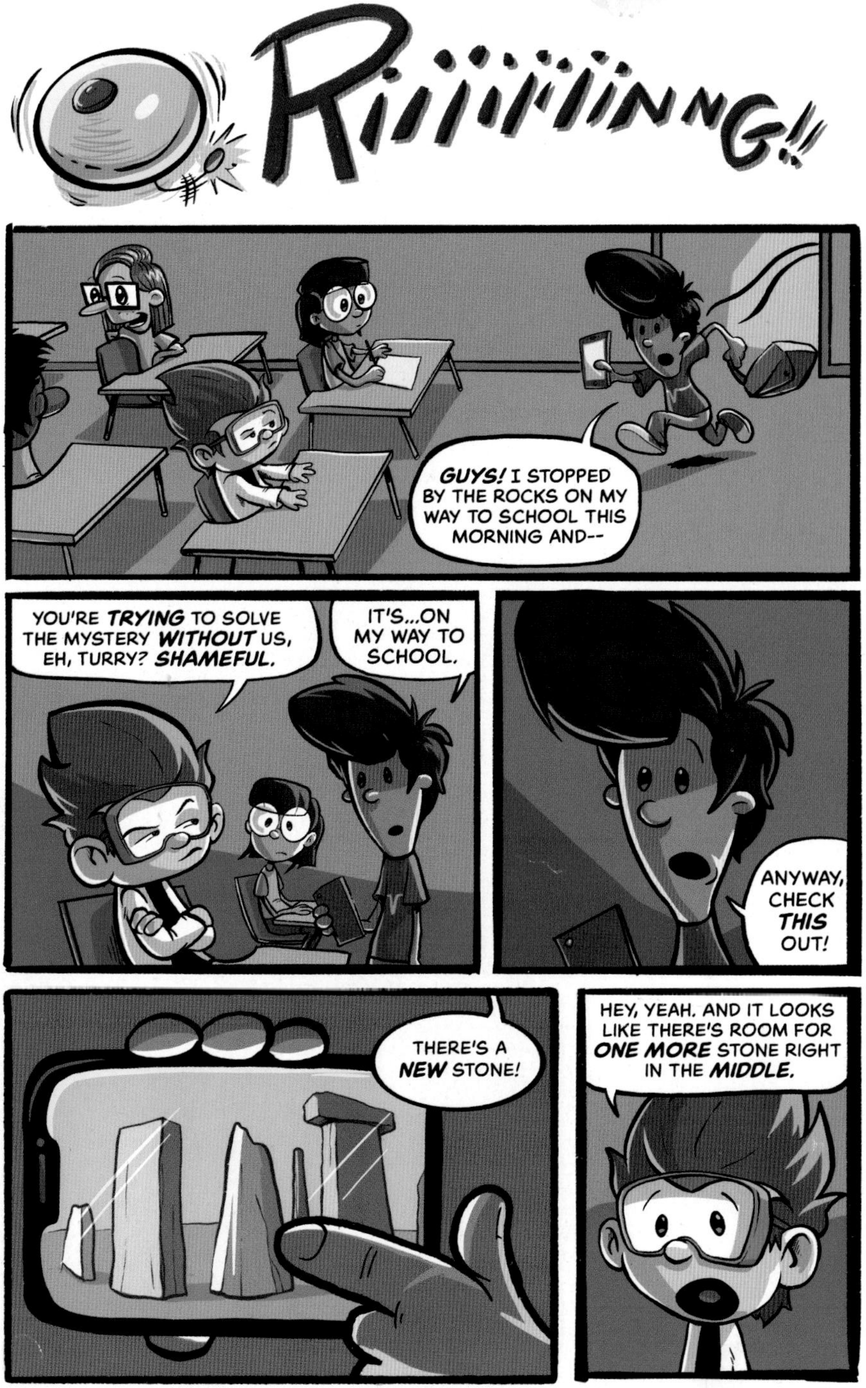
RIIIIIIINNNG!!
GUYS! I STOPPED BY THE ROCKS ON MY WAY TO SCHOOL THIS MORNING AND--
YOU'RE TRYING TO SOLVE THE MYSTERY WITHOUT US, EH, TURRY? SHAMEFUL.
IT'S...ON MY WAY TO SCHOOL.
ANYWAY, CHECK THIS OUT!
THERE'S A NEW STONE!
HEY, YEAH. AND IT LOOKS LIKE THERE'S ROOM FOR ONE MORE STONE RIGHT IN THE MIDDLE.

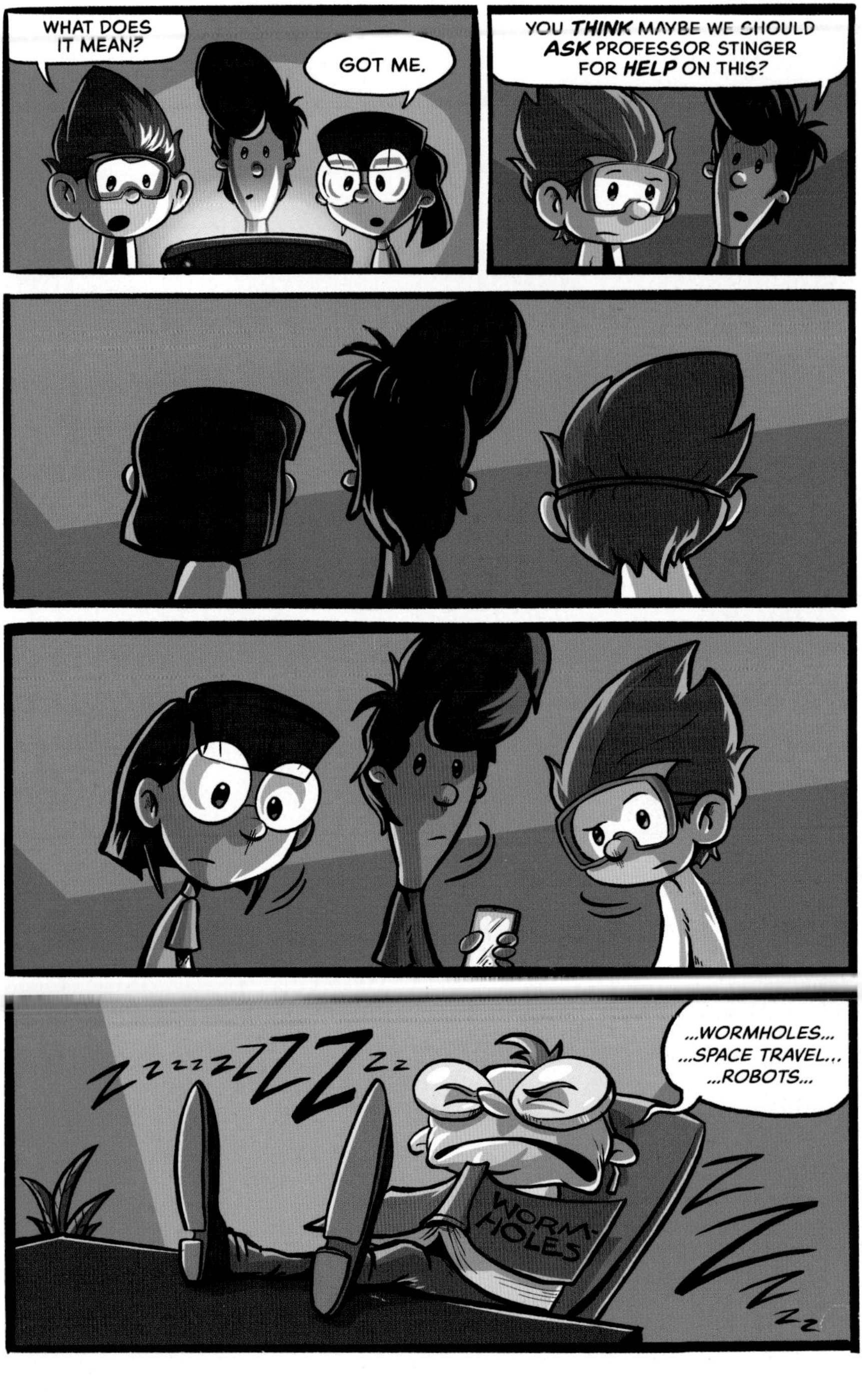

WHAT DOES IT MEAN?
GOT ME.
YOU THINK MAYBE WE SHOULD ASK PROFESSOR STINGER FOR HELP ON THIS?
ZZZZZZZZZZZ
...WORMHOLES... ...SPACE TRAVEL... ...ROBOTS...
WORM-HOLES

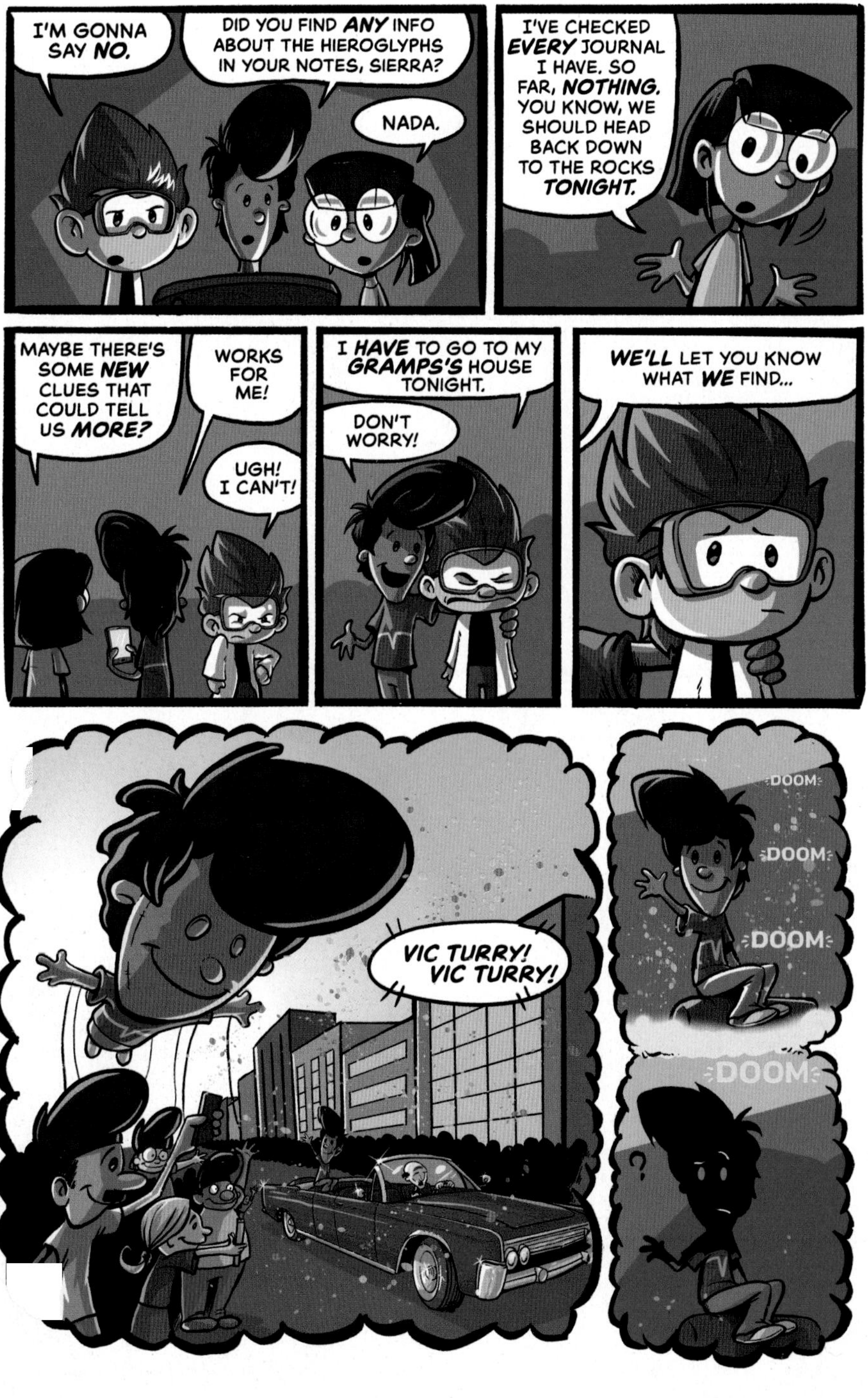
I'M GONNA SAY NO.
DID YOU FIND ANY INFO ABOUT THE HIEROGLYPHS IN YOUR NOTES, SIERRA?
NADA.
I'VE CHECKED EVERY JOURNAL I HAVE. SO FAR, NOTHING. YOU KNOW, WE SHOULD HEAD BACK DOWN TO THE ROCKS TONIGHT.
MAYBE THERE'S SOME NEW CLUES THAT COULD TELL US MORE?
WORKS FOR ME!
UGH! I CAN'T!
I HAVE TO GO TO MY GRAMPS'S HOUSE TONIGHT.
DON'T WORRY!
WE'LL LET YOU KNOW WHAT WE FIND...
VIC TURRY! VIC TURRY!
DOOM
DOOM
DOOM
DOOM
?

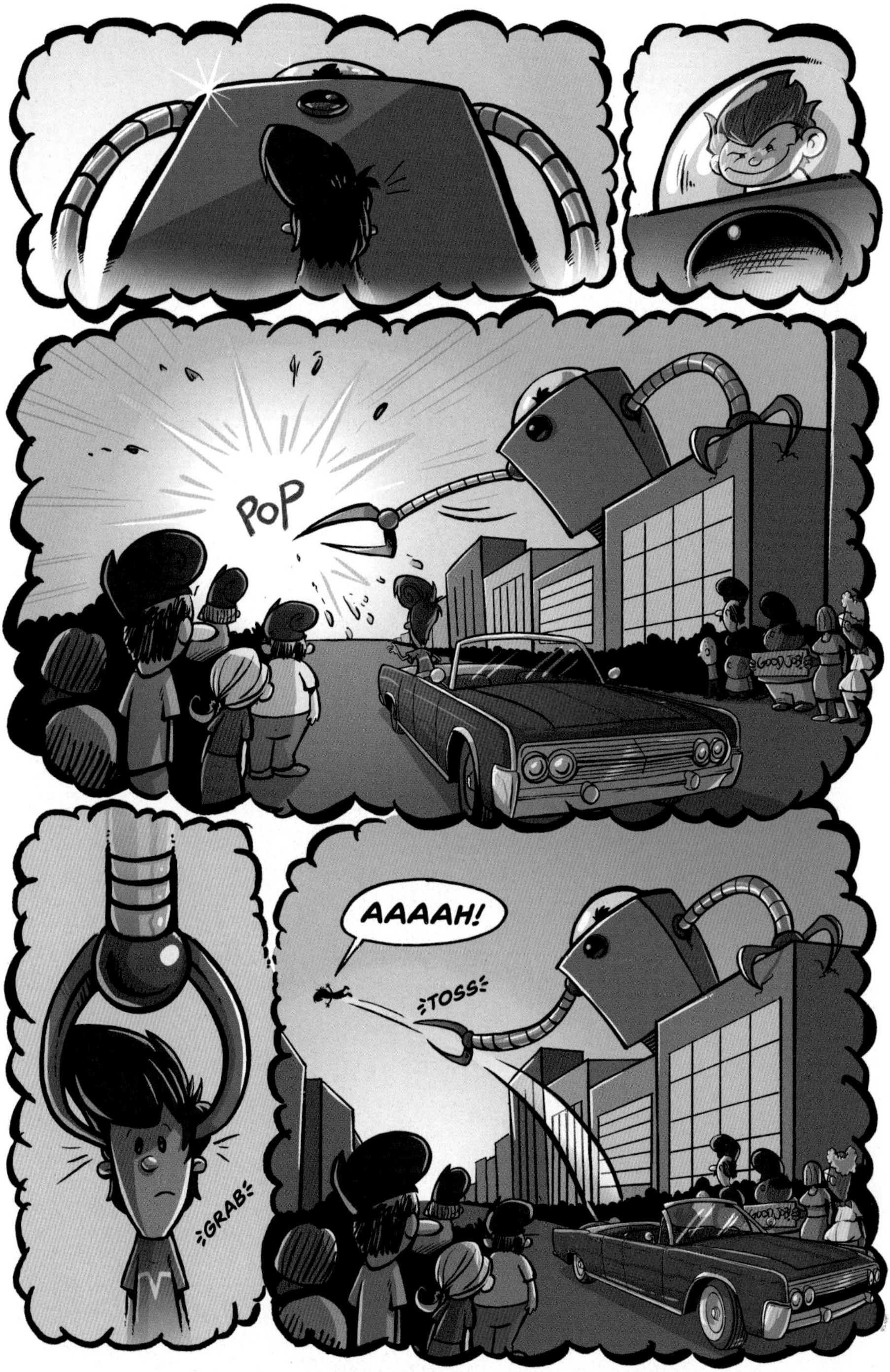
POP
GOOD JOB!
GRAB
AAAAH!
TOSS

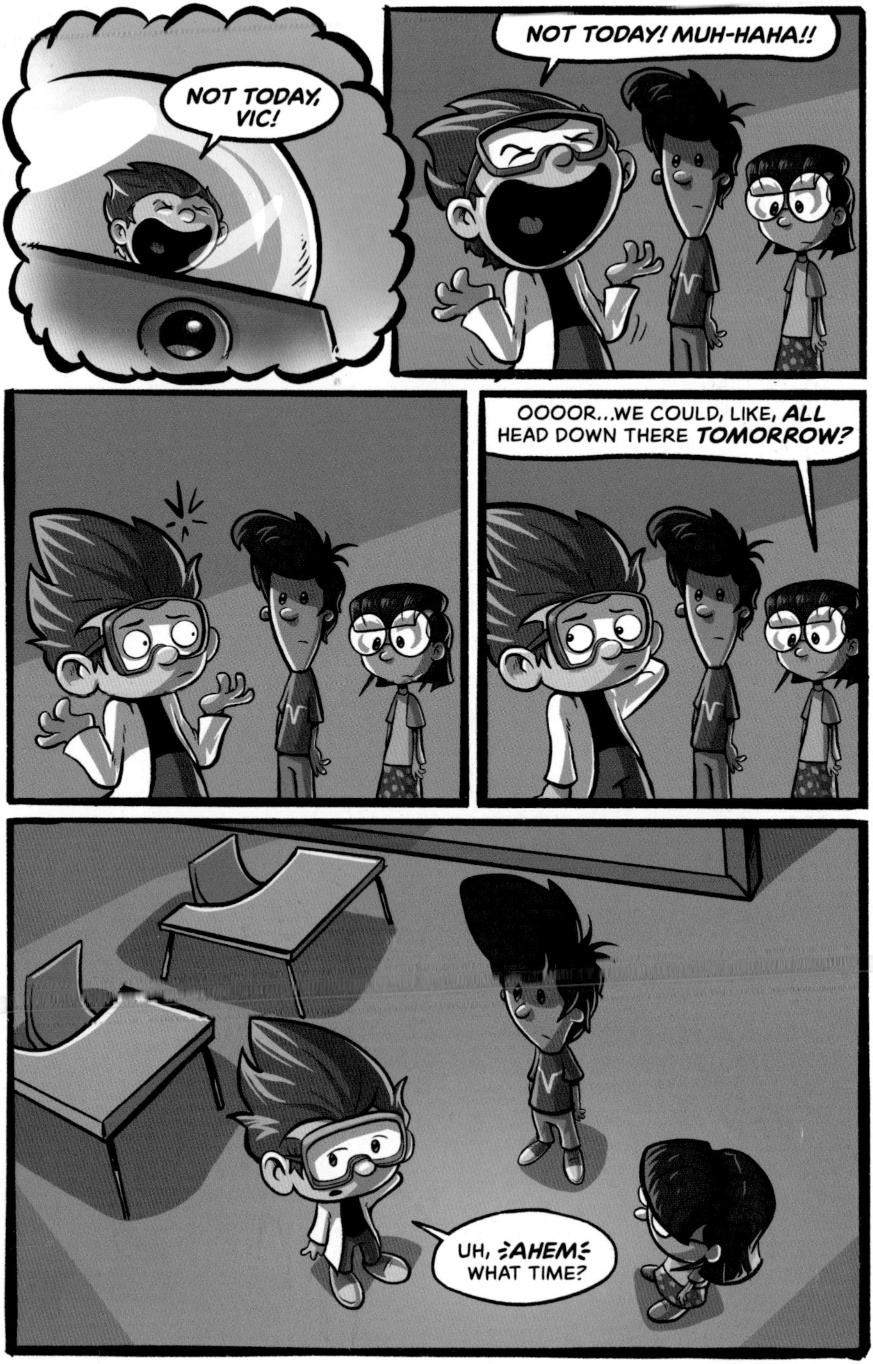
NOT TODAY, VIC!
NOT TODAY! MUH-HAHA!!
OOOOR...WE COULD, LIKE, ALL HEAD DOWN THERE TOMORROW?
UH, AHEM WHAT TIME?

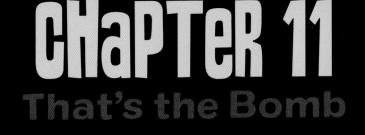

CHAPTER 11
That's the Bomb

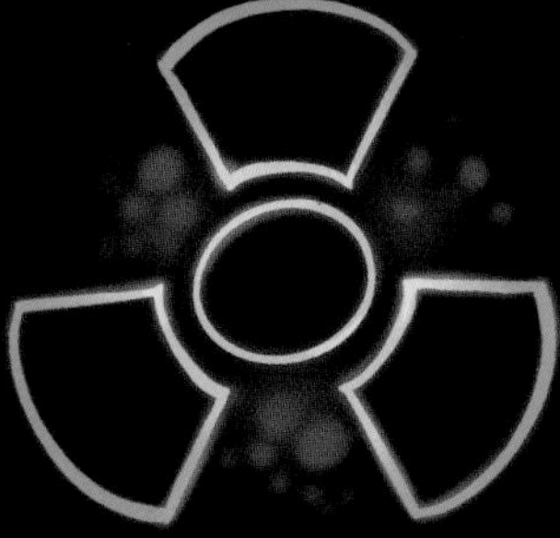

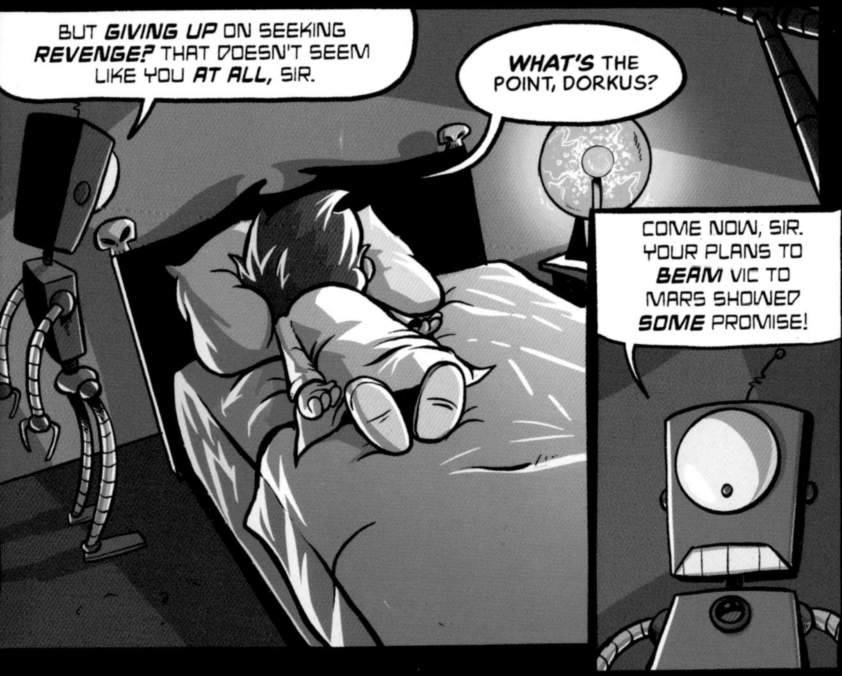
BUT GIVING UP ON SEEKING REVENGE? THAT DOESN'T SEEM LIKE YOU AT ALL, SIR.
WHAT'S THE POINT, DORKUS?
COME NOW, SIR. YOUR PLANS TO BEAM VIC TO MARS SHOWED SOME PROMISE!

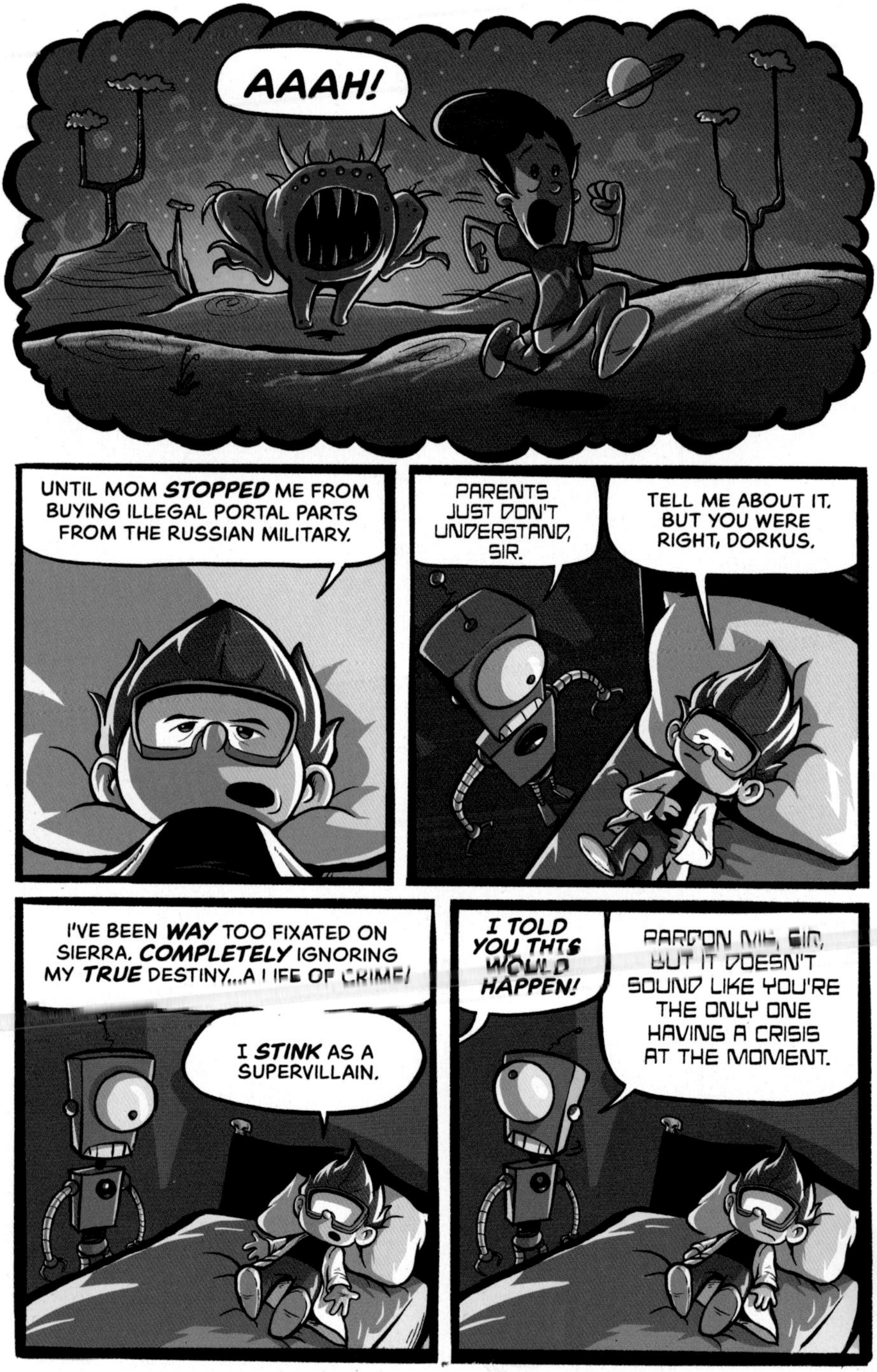
AAAH!
UNTIL MOM STOPPED ME FROM BUYING ILLEGAL PORTAL PARTS FROM THE RUSSIAN MILITARY.
PARENTS JUST DON'T UNDERSTAND, SIR.
TELL ME ABOUT IT. BUT YOU WERE RIGHT, DORKUS.
I'VE BEEN WAY TOO FIXATED ON SIERRA. COMPLETELY IGNORING MY TRUE DESTINY...A LIFE OF CRIME!
I STINK AS A SUPERVILLAIN.
I TOLD YOU THIS WOULD HAPPEN!
PARDON ME, SIR, BUT IT DOESN'T SOUND LIKE YOU'RE THE ONLY ONE HAVING A CRISIS AT THE MOMENT.

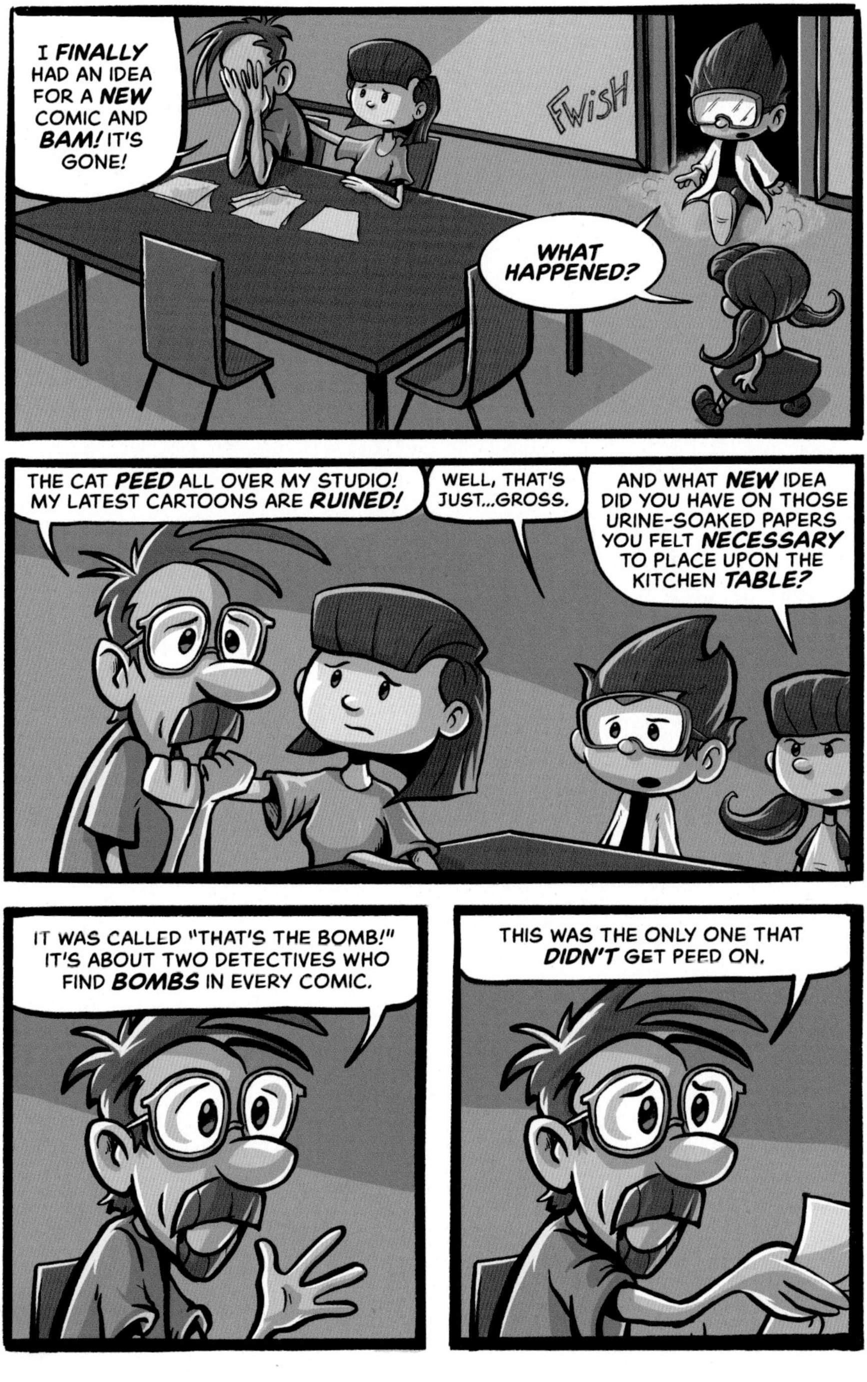
I FINALLY HAD AN IDEA FOR A NEW COMIC AND BAM! IT'S GONE!
FWISH
WHAT HAPPENED?
THE CAT PEED ALL OVER MY STUDIO! MY LATEST CARTOONS ARE RUINED!
WELL, THAT'S JUST...GROSS.
AND WHAT NEW IDEA DID YOU HAVE ON THOSE URINE-SOAKED PAPERS YOU FELT NECESSARY TO PLACE UPON THE KITCHEN TABLE?
IT WAS CALLED "THAT'S THE BOMB!" IT'S ABOUT TWO DETECTIVES WHO FIND BOMBS IN EVERY COMIC.
THIS WAS THE ONLY ONE THAT DIDN'T GET PEED ON.

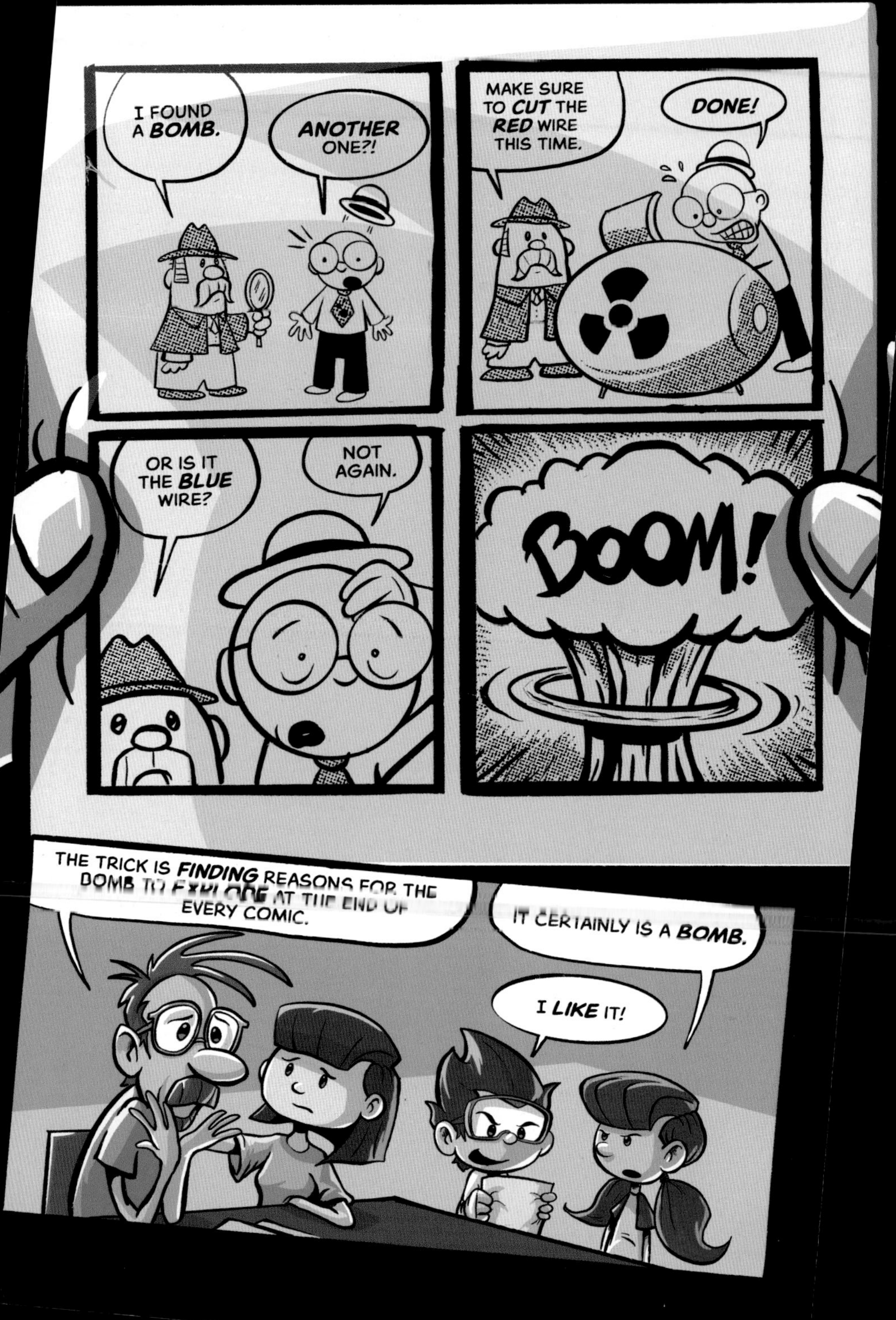
I FOUND A BOMB.
ANOTHER ONE?!
MAKE SURE TO CUT THE RED WIRE THIS TIME.
DONE!
OR IS IT THE BLUE WIRE?
NOT AGAIN.
BOOM!
THE TRICK IS FINDING REASONS FOR THE BOMB TO EXPLODE AT THE END OF EVERY COMIC.
IT CERTAINLY IS A BOMB.
I LIKE IT!

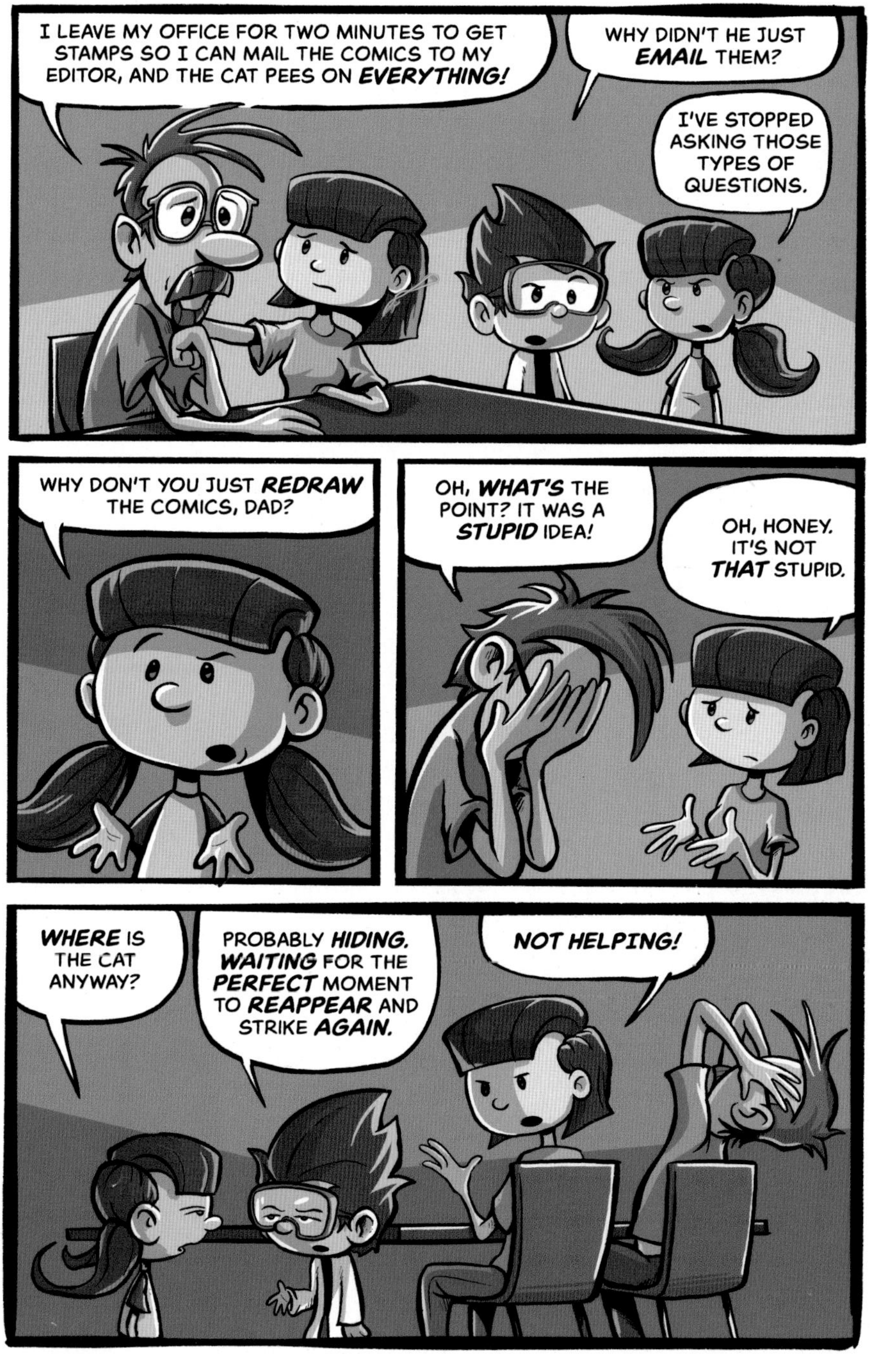
I LEAVE MY OFFICE FOR TWO MINUTES TO GET STAMPS SO I CAN MAIL THE COMICS TO MY EDITOR, AND THE CAT PEES ON *EVERYTHING!*
WHY DIDN'T HE JUST *EMAIL* THEM?
I'VE STOPPED ASKING THOSE TYPES OF QUESTIONS.
WHY DON'T YOU JUST *REDRAW* THE COMICS, DAD?
OH, *WHAT'S* THE POINT? IT WAS A *STUPID* IDEA!
OH, HONEY. IT'S NOT *THAT* STUPID.
WHERE IS THE CAT ANYWAY?
PROBABLY *HIDING. WAITING* FOR THE *PERFECT* MOMENT TO *REAPPEAR* AND STRIKE *AGAIN.*
NOT HELPING!

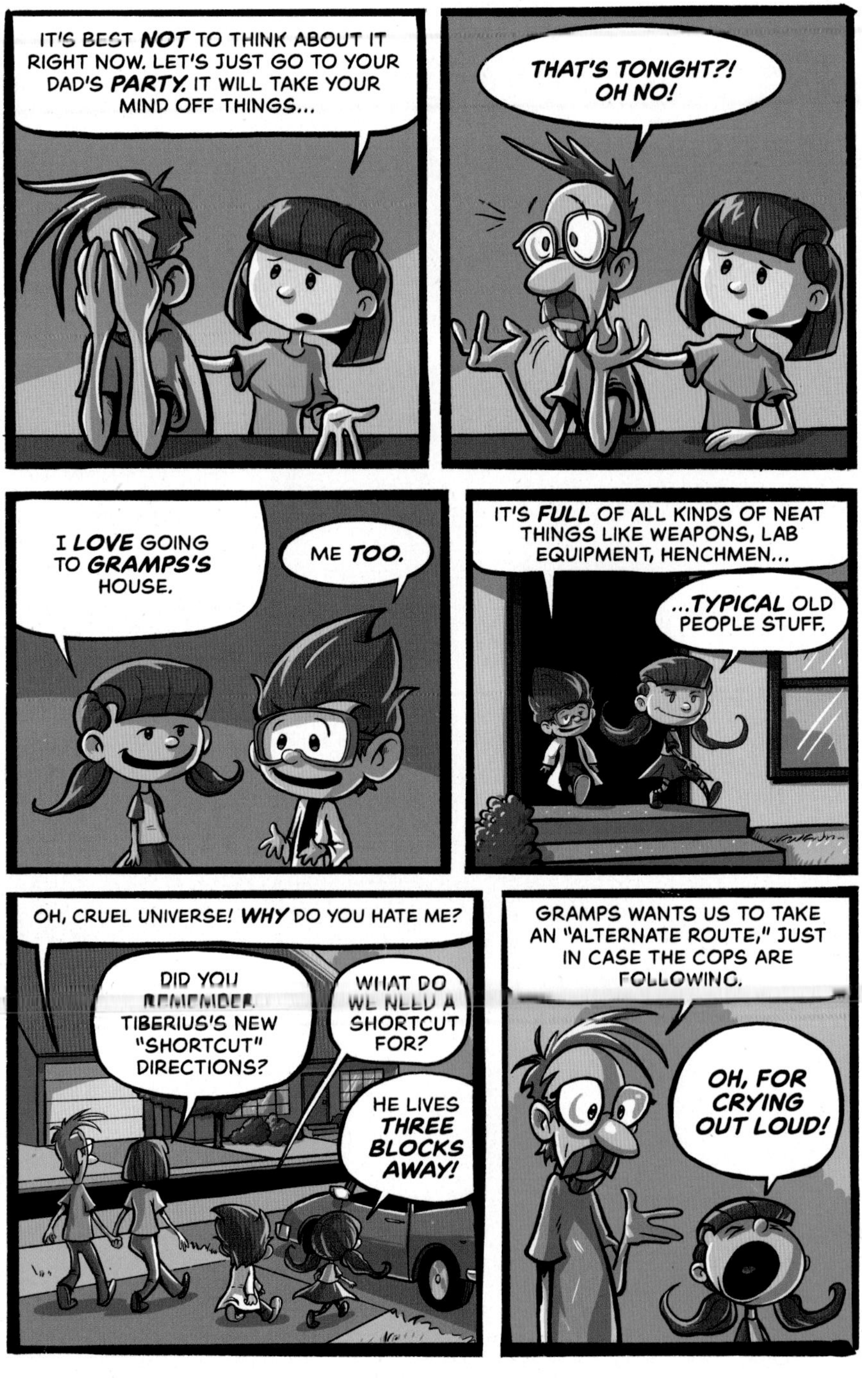
IT'S BEST NOT TO THINK ABOUT IT RIGHT NOW. LET'S JUST GO TO YOUR DAD'S PARTY. IT WILL TAKE YOUR MIND OFF THINGS...
THAT'S TONIGHT?! OH NO!
I LOVE GOING TO GRAMPS'S HOUSE.
ME TOO.
IT'S FULL OF ALL KINDS OF NEAT THINGS LIKE WEAPONS, LAB EQUIPMENT, HENCHMEN...
...TYPICAL OLD PEOPLE STUFF.
OH, CRUEL UNIVERSE! WHY DO YOU HATE ME?
DID YOU REMEMBER TIBERIUS'S NEW "SHORTCUT" DIRECTIONS?
WHAT DO WE NEED A SHORTCUT FOR?
HE LIVES THREE BLOCKS AWAY!
GRAMPS WANTS US TO TAKE AN "ALTERNATE ROUTE," JUST IN CASE THE COPS ARE FOLLOWING.
OH, FOR CRYING OUT LOUD!

LATER...

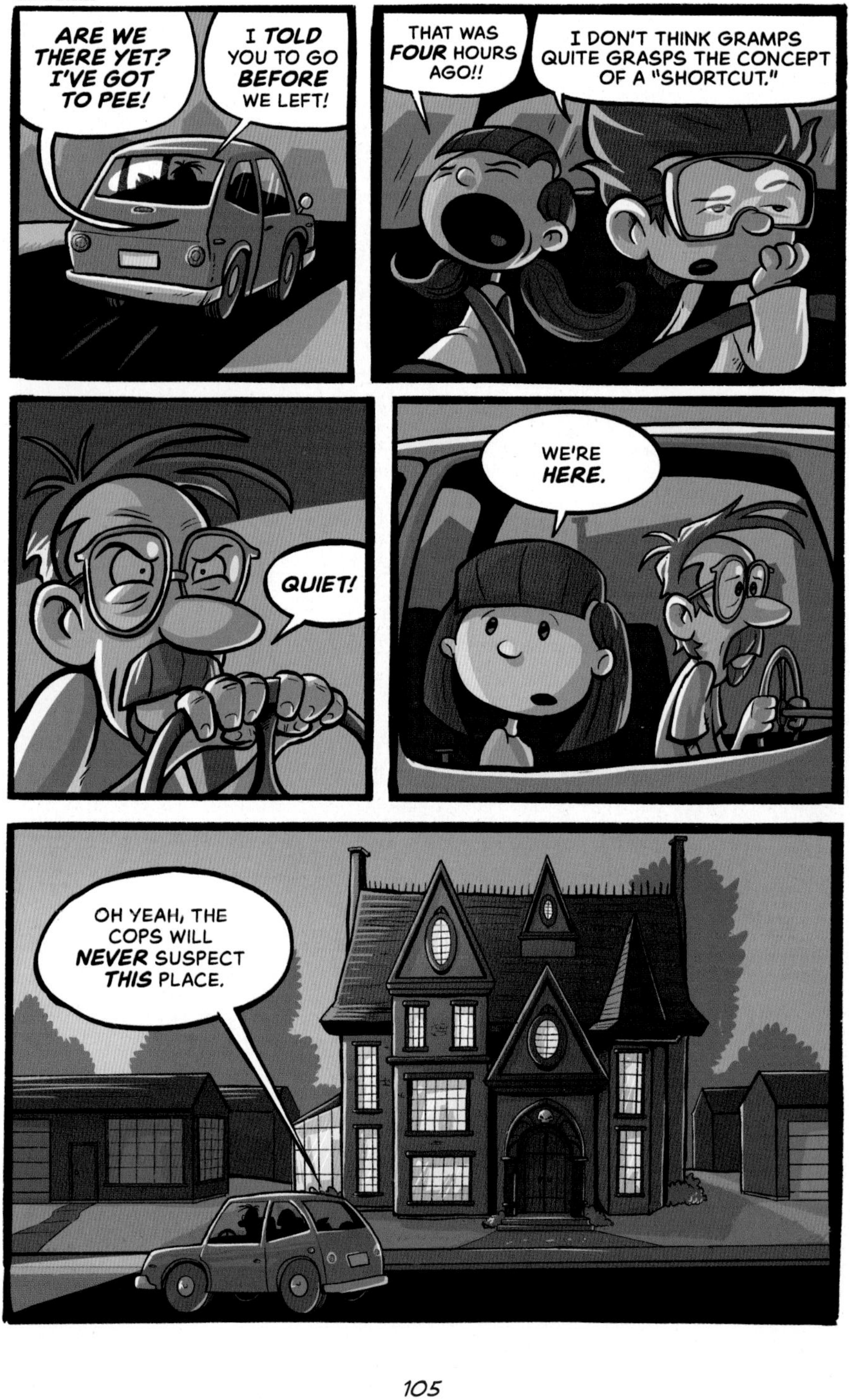
ARE WE THERE YET? I'VE GOT TO PEE!
I TOLD YOU TO GO BEFORE WE LEFT!
THAT WAS FOUR HOURS AGO!!
I DON'T THINK GRAMPS QUITE GRASPS THE CONCEPT OF A "SHORTCUT."
QUIET!
WE'RE HERE.
OH YEAH, THE COPS WILL NEVER SUSPECT THIS PLACE.

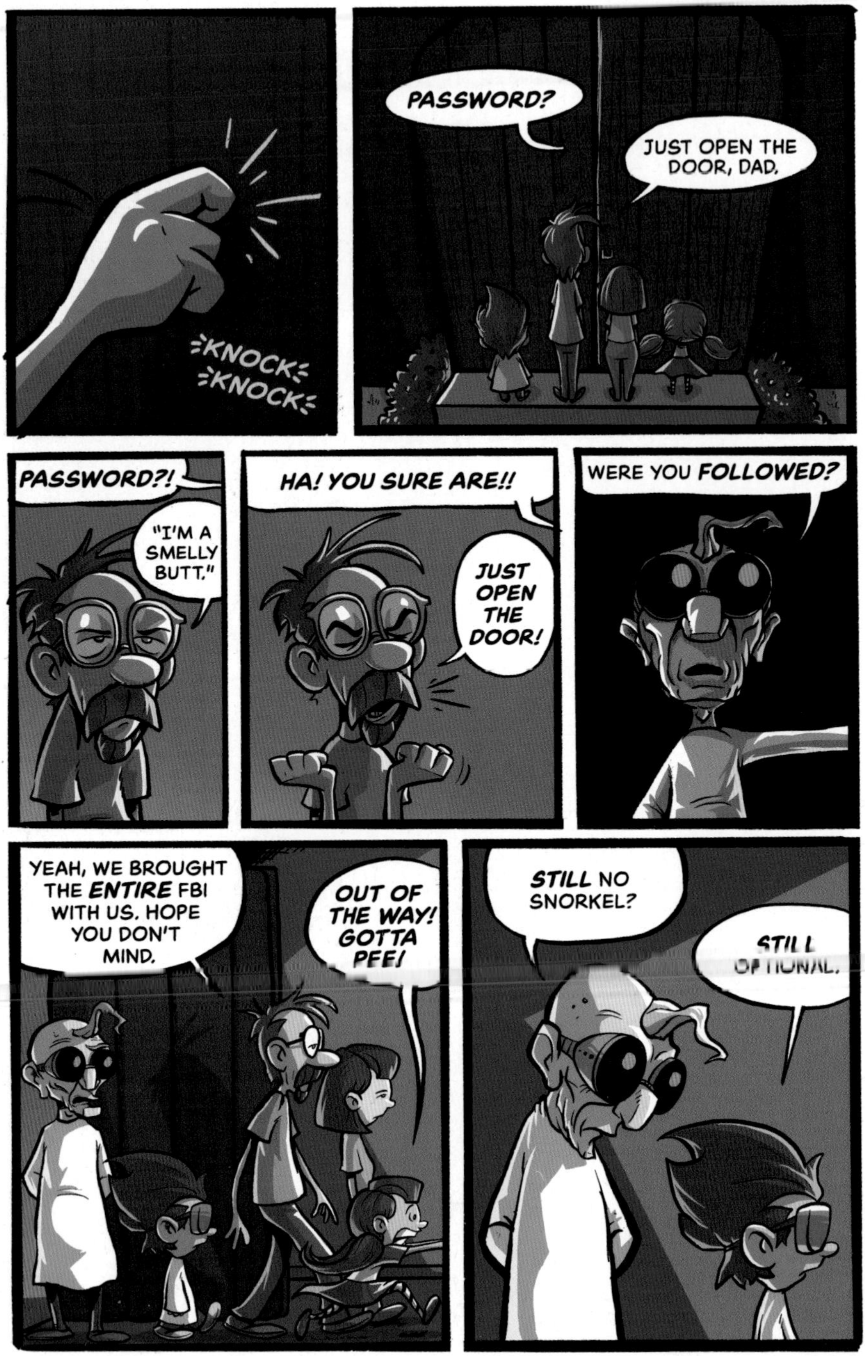
KNOCK KNOCK
PASSWORD?
JUST OPEN THE DOOR, DAD.
PASSWORD?!
"I'M A SMELLY BUTT."
HA! YOU SURE ARE!!
JUST OPEN THE DOOR!
WERE YOU FOLLOWED?
YEAH, WE BROUGHT THE ENTIRE FBI WITH US. HOPE YOU DON'T MIND.
OUT OF THE WAY! GOTTA PEE!
STILL NO SNORKEL?
STILL OPTIONAL.

CHAPTER 12
Dread Man's Party

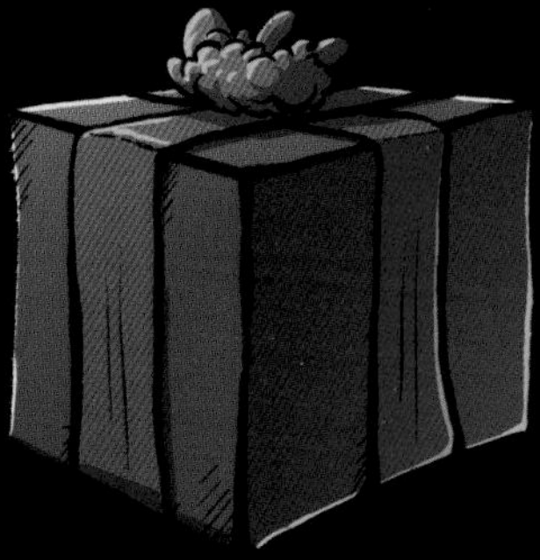

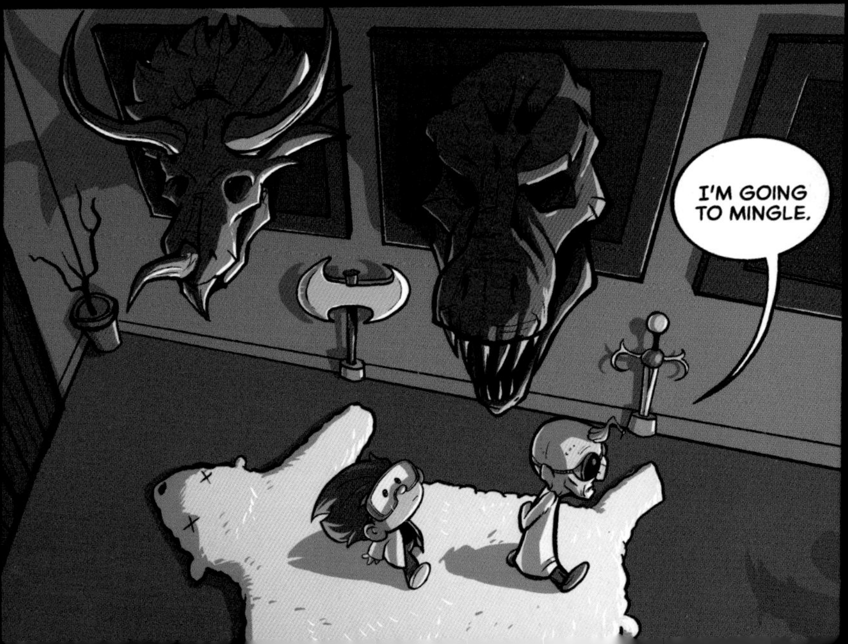
I'M GOING TO MINGLE.

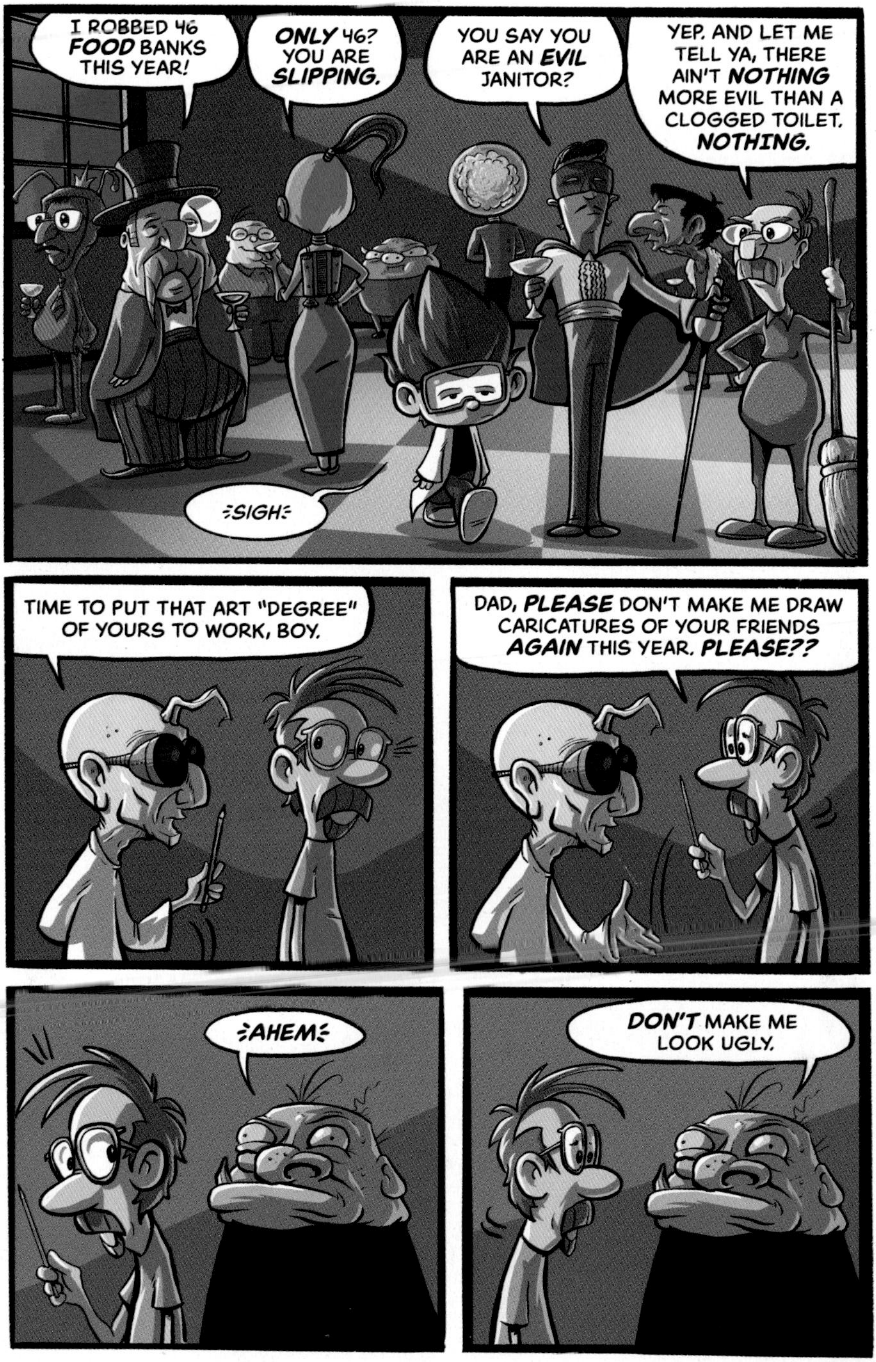
I ROBBED 46 FOOD BANKS THIS YEAR!
ONLY 46? YOU ARE SLIPPING.
YOU SAY YOU ARE AN EVIL JANITOR?
YEP. AND LET ME TELL YA, THERE AIN'T NOTHING MORE EVIL THAN A CLOGGED TOILET. NOTHING.
SIGH
TIME TO PUT THAT ART "DEGREE" OF YOURS TO WORK, BOY.
DAD, PLEASE DON'T MAKE ME DRAW CARICATURES OF YOUR FRIENDS AGAIN THIS YEAR. PLEASE??
AHEM
DON'T MAKE ME LOOK UGLY.

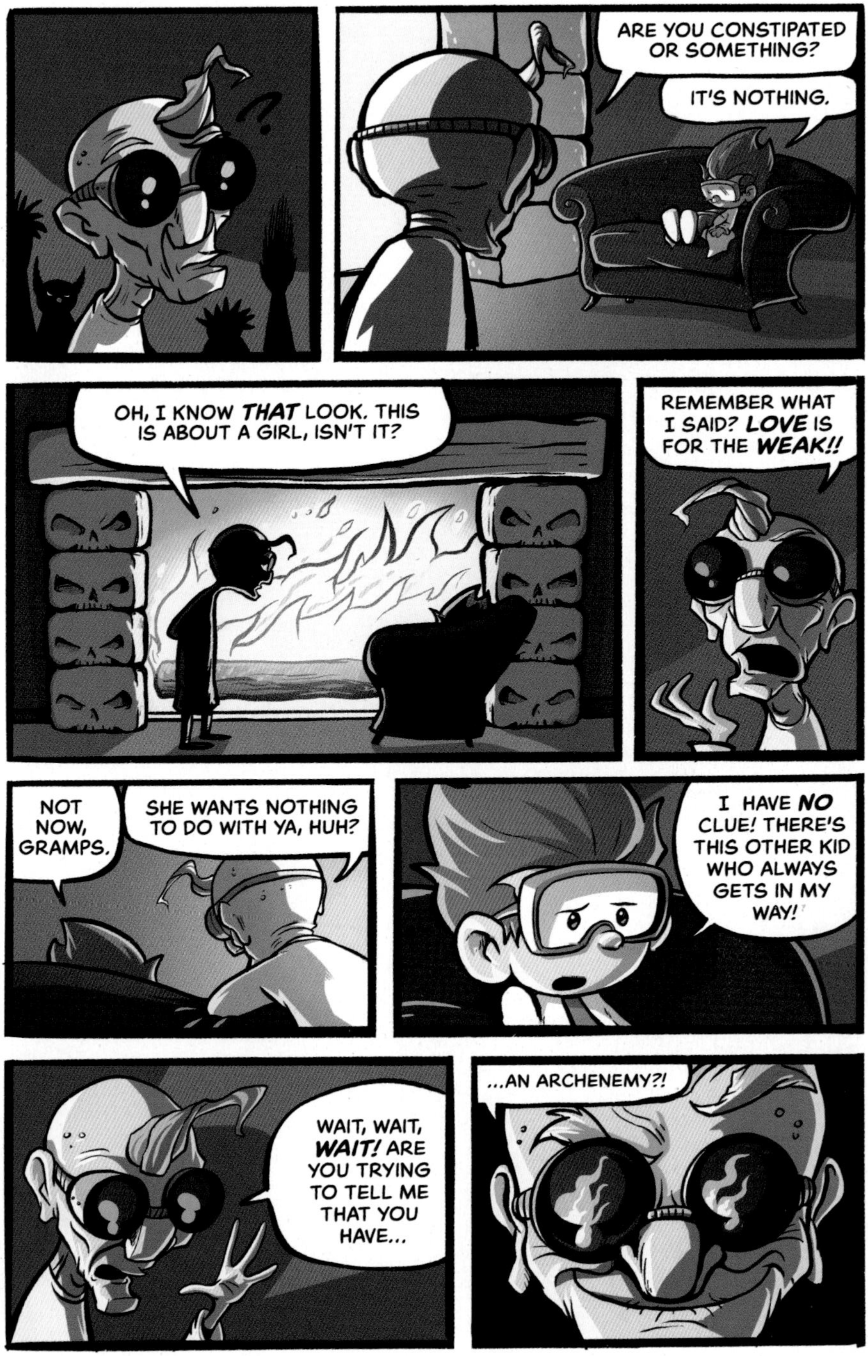
?
ARE YOU CONSTIPATED OR SOMETHING?
IT'S NOTHING.
OH, I KNOW THAT LOOK. THIS IS ABOUT A GIRL, ISN'T IT?
REMEMBER WHAT I SAID? LOVE IS FOR THE WEAK!!
NOT NOW, GRAMPS.
SHE WANTS NOTHING TO DO WITH YA, HUH?
I HAVE NO CLUE! THERE'S THIS OTHER KID WHO ALWAYS GETS IN MY WAY!
WAIT, WAIT, WAIT! ARE YOU TRYING TO TELL ME THAT YOU HAVE...
...AN ARCHENEMY?!

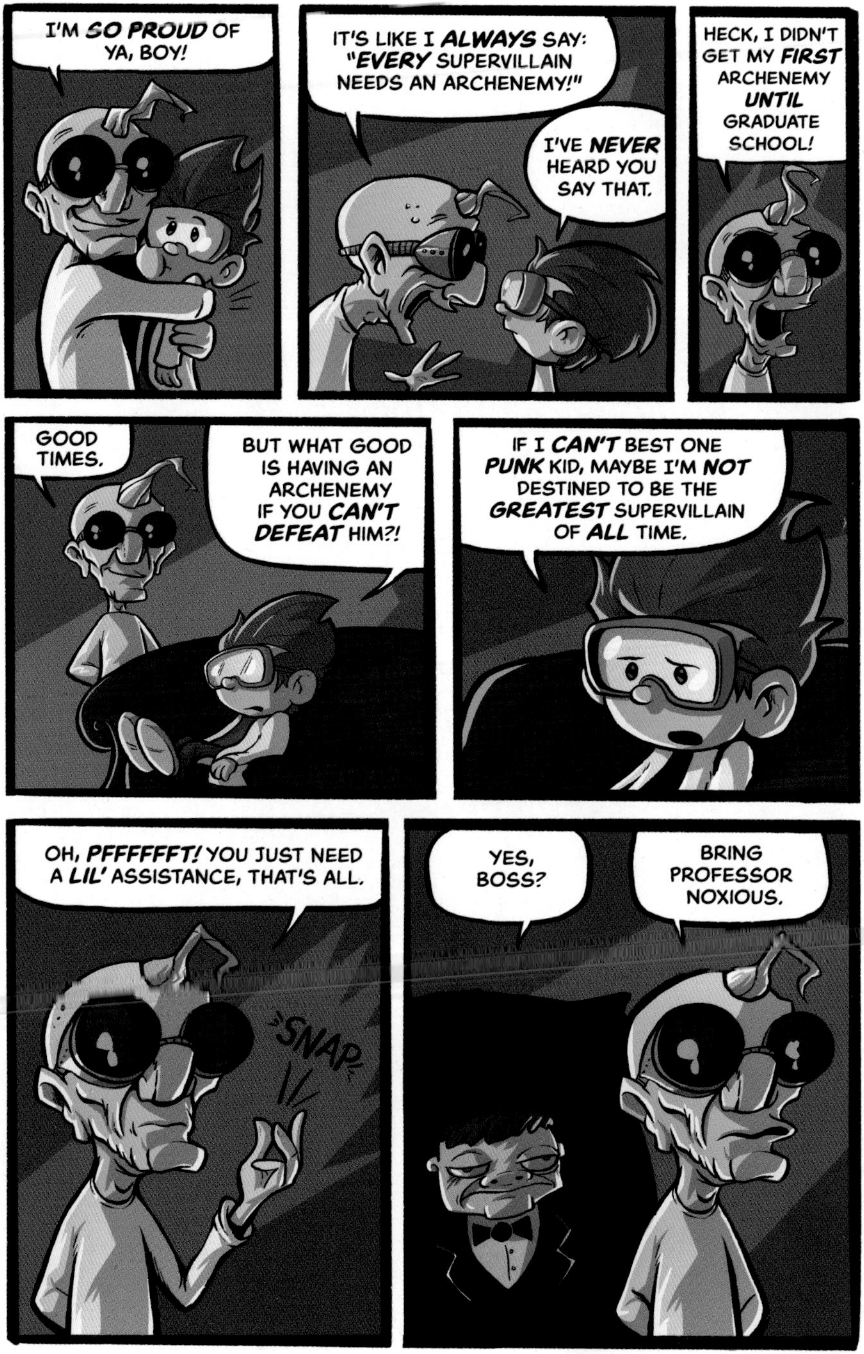

I'M SO PROUD OF YA, BOY!
IT'S LIKE I ALWAYS SAY: "EVERY SUPERVILLAIN NEEDS AN ARCHENEMY!"
I'VE NEVER HEARD YOU SAY THAT.
HECK, I DIDN'T GET MY FIRST ARCHENEMY UNTIL GRADUATE SCHOOL!
GOOD TIMES.
BUT WHAT GOOD IS HAVING AN ARCHENEMY IF YOU CAN'T DEFEAT HIM?!
IF I CAN'T BEST ONE PUNK KID, MAYBE I'M NOT DESTINED TO BE THE GREATEST SUPERVILLAIN OF ALL TIME.
OH, PFFFFFFT! YOU JUST NEED A LIL' ASSISTANCE, THAT'S ALL.
SNAP
YES, BOSS?
BRING PROFESSOR NOXIOUS.

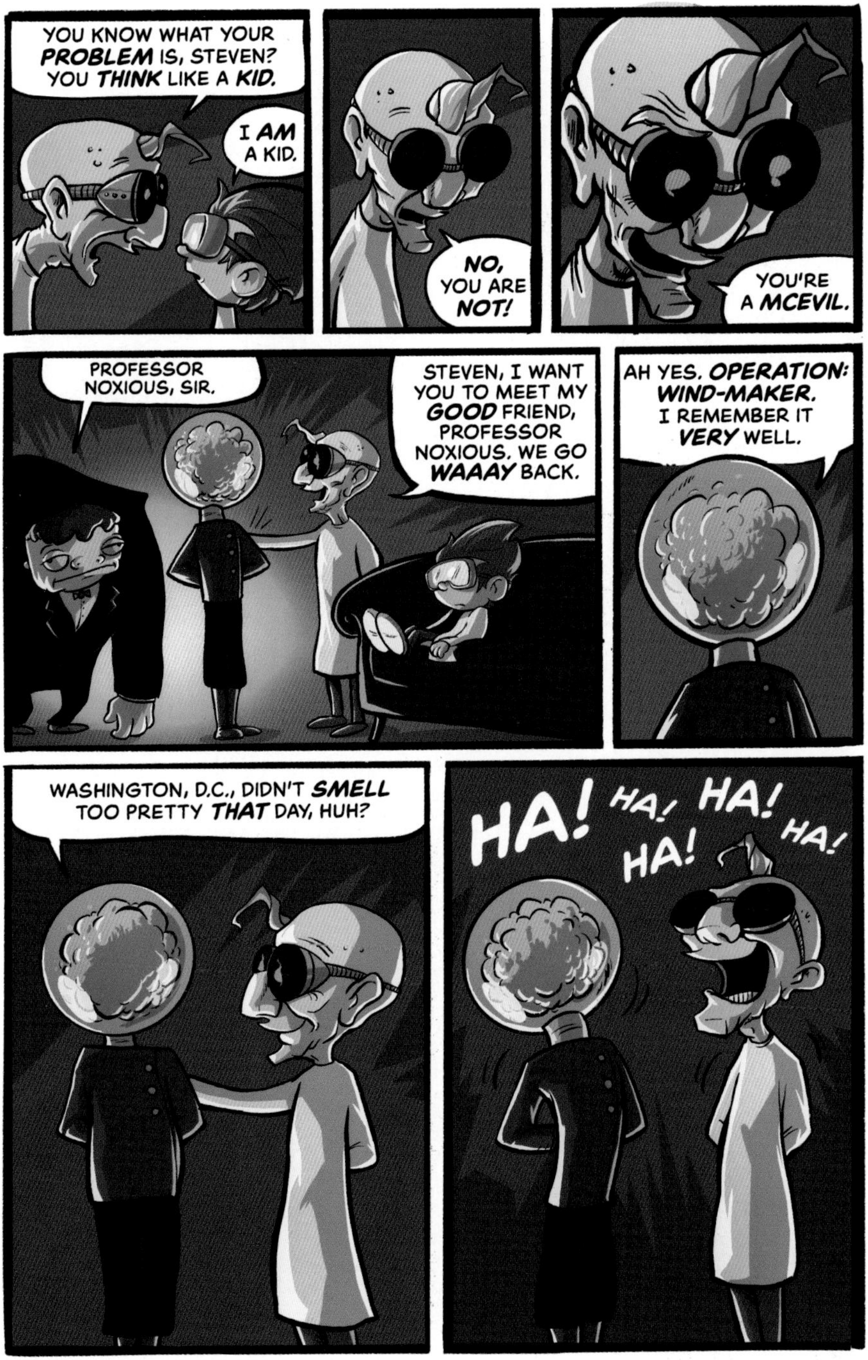
YOU KNOW WHAT YOUR PROBLEM IS, STEVEN? YOU THINK LIKE A KID.
I AM A KID.
NO, YOU ARE NOT!
YOU'RE A MCEVIL.
PROFESSOR NOXIOUS, SIR.
STEVEN, I WANT YOU TO MEET MY GOOD FRIEND, PROFESSOR NOXIOUS. WE GO WAAAY BACK.
AH YES. OPERATION: WIND-MAKER. I REMEMBER IT VERY WELL.
WASHINGTON, D.C., DIDN'T SMELL TOO PRETTY THAT DAY, HUH?
HA! HA! HA! HA! HA!

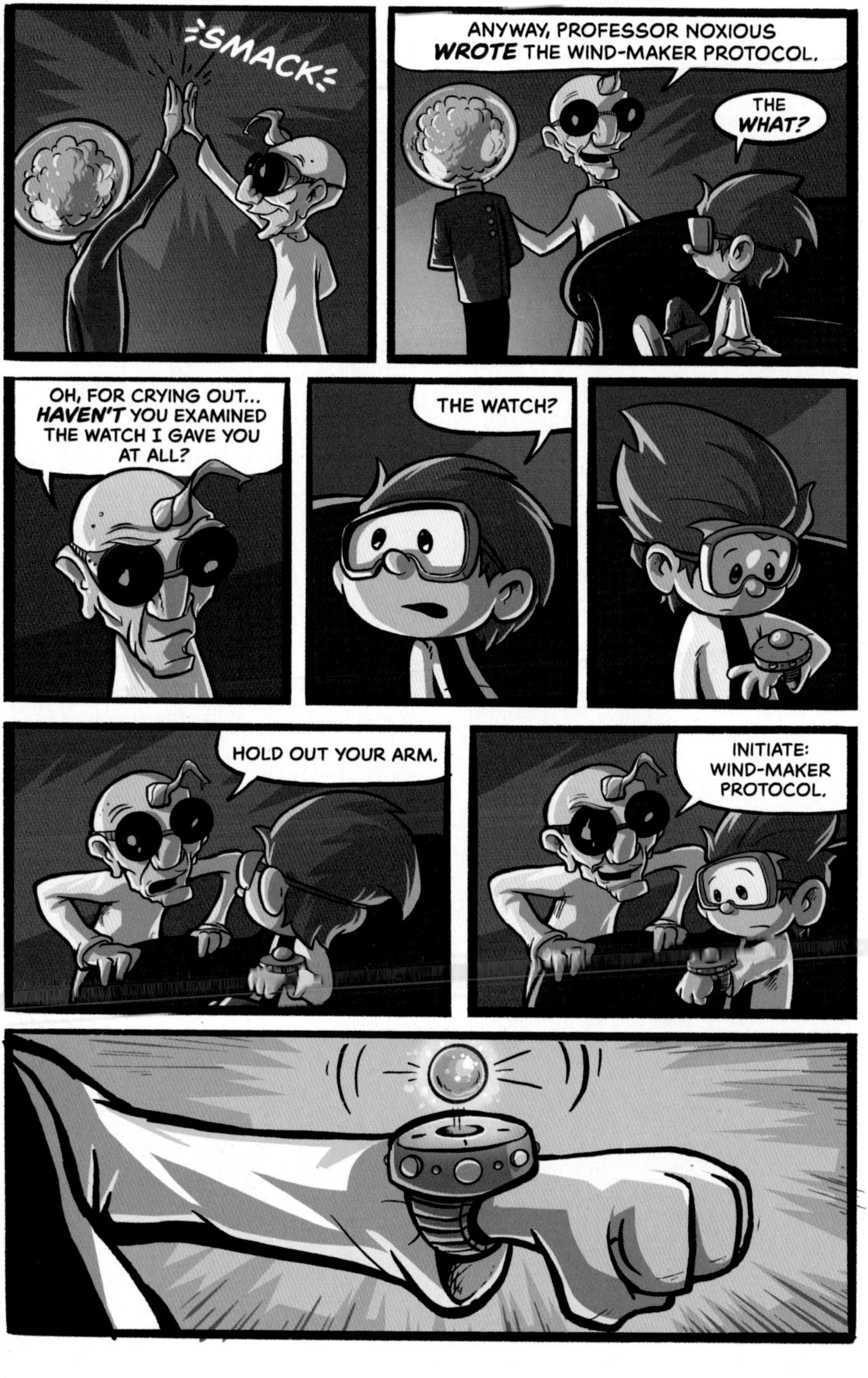
SMACK
ANYWAY, PROFESSOR NOXIOUS **WROTE** THE WIND-MAKER PROTOCOL.
THE **WHAT?**
OH, FOR CRYING OUT... **HAVEN'T** YOU EXAMINED THE WATCH I GAVE YOU AT ALL?
THE WATCH?
HOLD OUT YOUR ARM.
INITIATE: WIND-MAKER PROTOCOL.

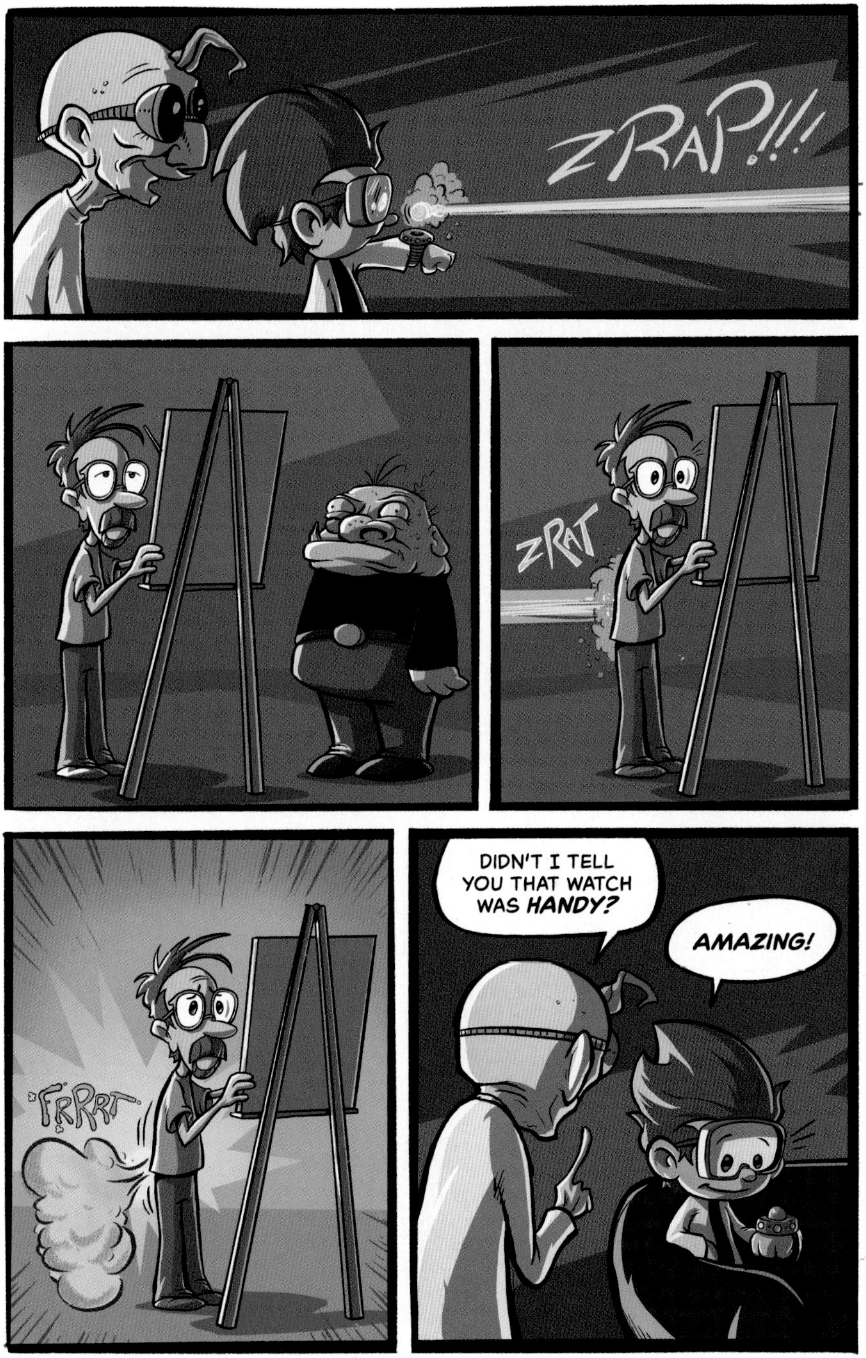
ZRAP!!!
ZRAT
FRRRT
DIDN'T I TELL YOU THAT WATCH WAS HANDY?
AMAZING!

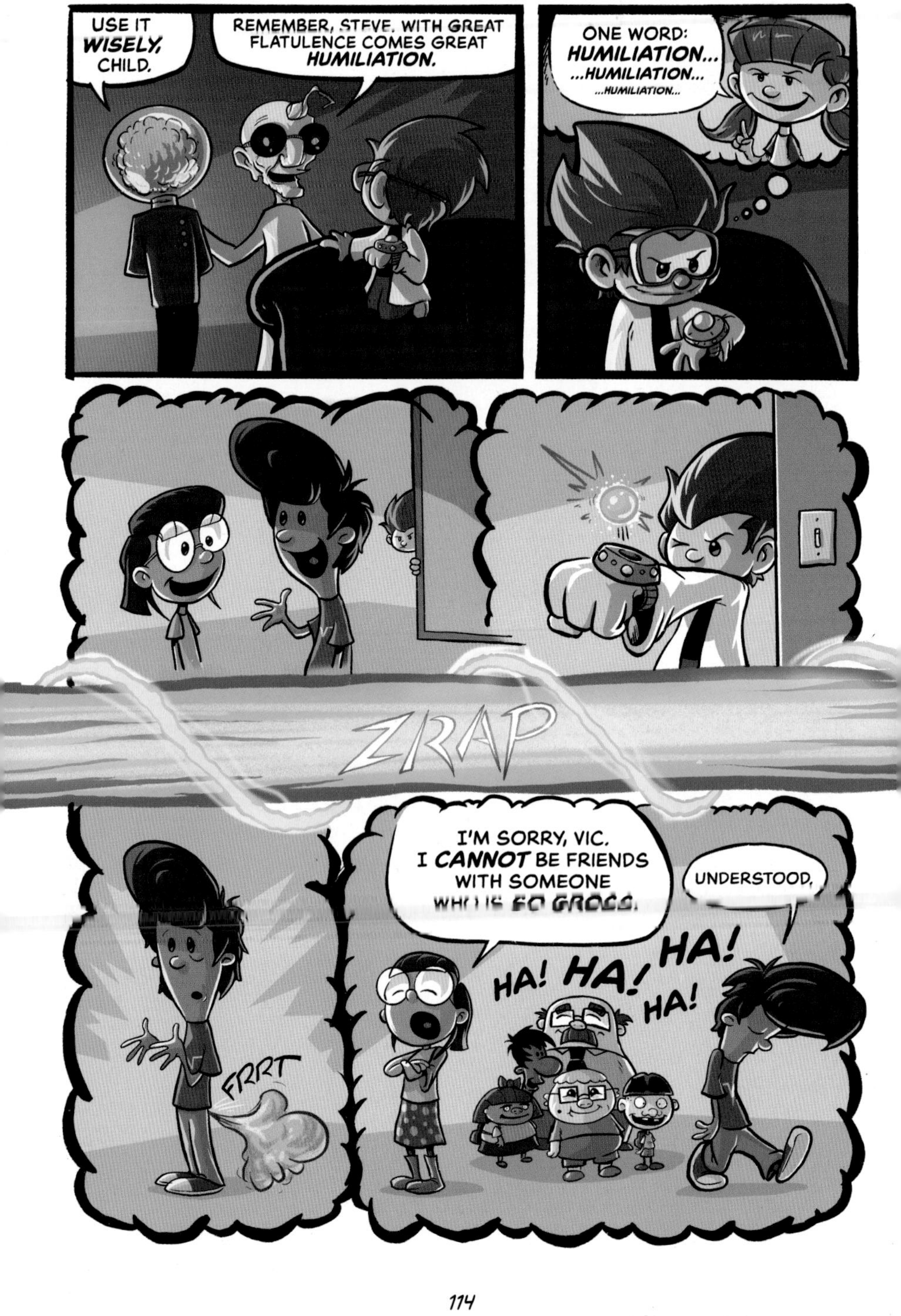
USE IT **WISELY,** CHILD.
REMEMBER, STEVE. WITH GREAT FLATULENCE COMES GREAT **HUMILIATION.**
ONE WORD: **HUMILIATION...** **...HUMILIATION...** ...HUMILIATION...
ZRAP
FRRT
I'M SORRY, VIC. I **CANNOT** BE FRIENDS WITH SOMEONE
UNDERSTOOD.
HA! HA! HA! HA!

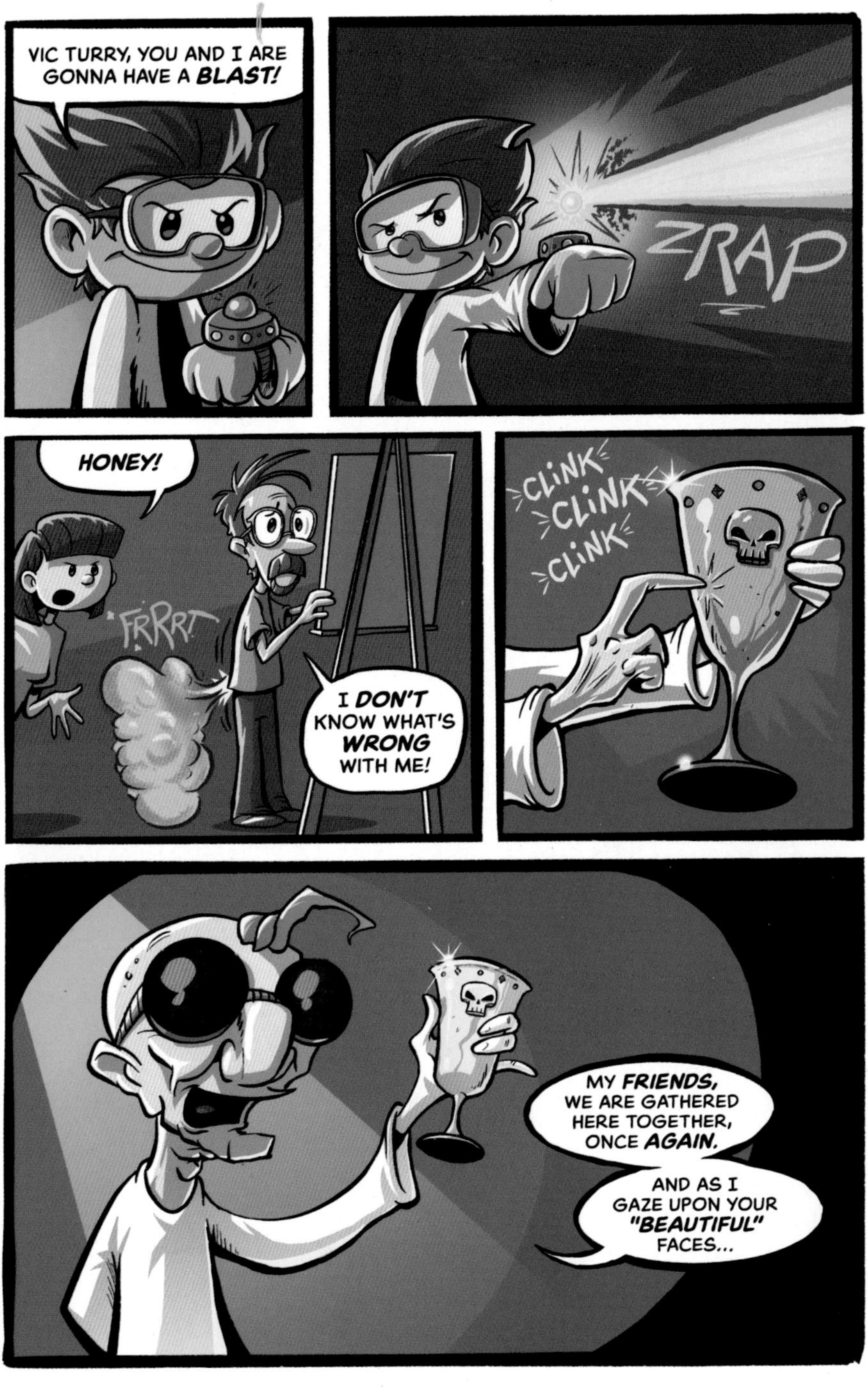
VIC TURRY, YOU AND I ARE GONNA HAVE A **BLAST!**
ZRAP
HONEY!
FRRRT
I **DON'T** KNOW WHAT'S **WRONG** WITH ME!
CLINK
CLINK
CLINK
MY **FRIENDS,** WE ARE GATHERED HERE TOGETHER, ONCE **AGAIN.**
AND AS I GAZE UPON YOUR **"BEAUTIFUL"** FACES...

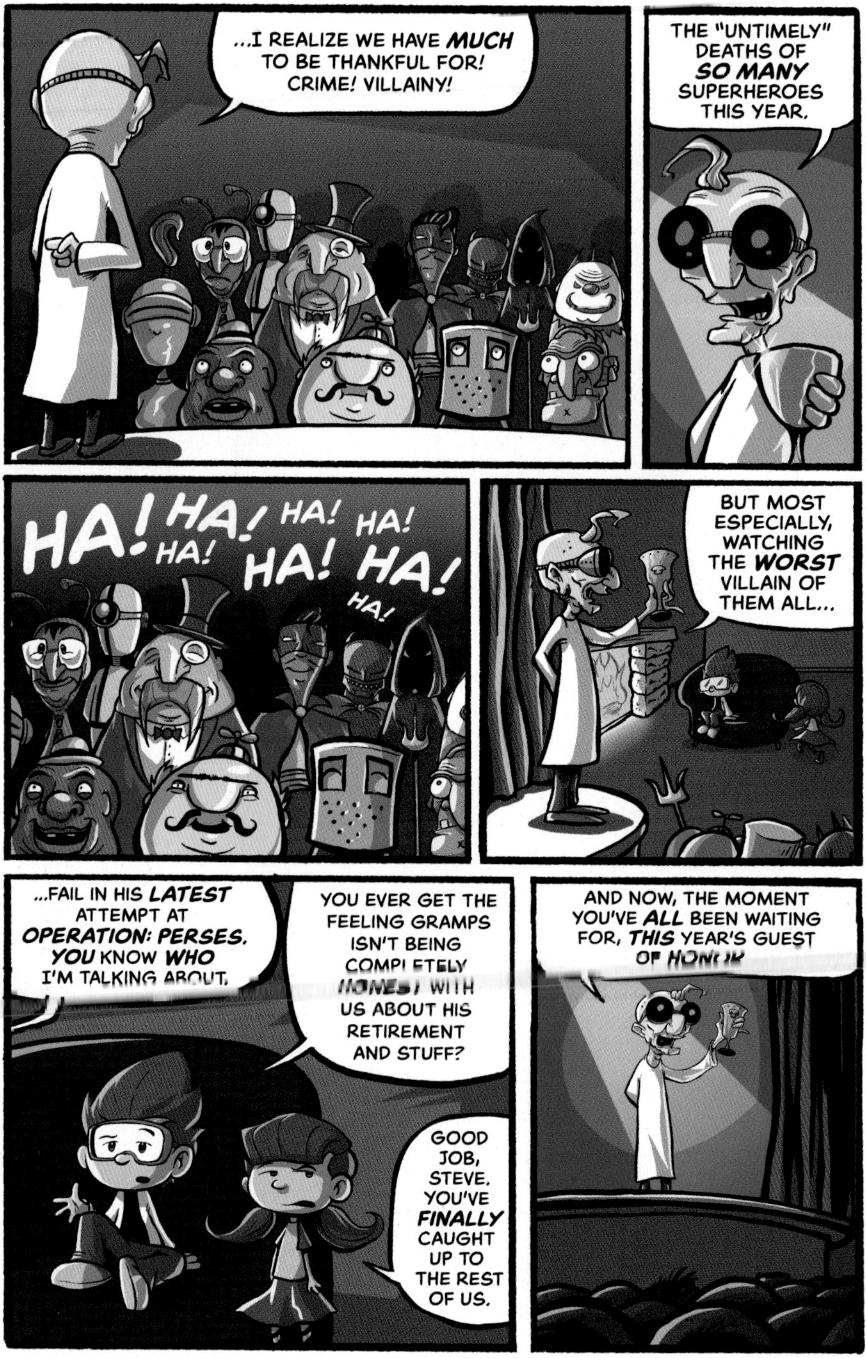
...I REALIZE WE HAVE MUCH TO BE THANKFUL FOR! CRIME! VILLAINY!
THE "UNTIMELY" DEATHS OF SO MANY SUPERHEROES THIS YEAR.
HA! HA! HA! HA! HA! HA! HA! HA!
BUT MOST ESPECIALLY, WATCHING THE WORST VILLAIN OF THEM ALL...
...FAIL IN HIS LATEST ATTEMPT AT OPERATION: PERSES. YOU KNOW WHO I'M TALKING ABOUT.
YOU EVER GET THE FEELING GRAMPS ISN'T BEING COMPLETELY HONEST WITH US ABOUT HIS RETIREMENT AND STUFF?
GOOD JOB, STEVE. YOU'VE FINALLY CAUGHT UP TO THE REST OF US.
AND NOW, THE MOMENT YOU'VE ALL BEEN WAITING FOR, THIS YEAR'S GUEST OF HONOR

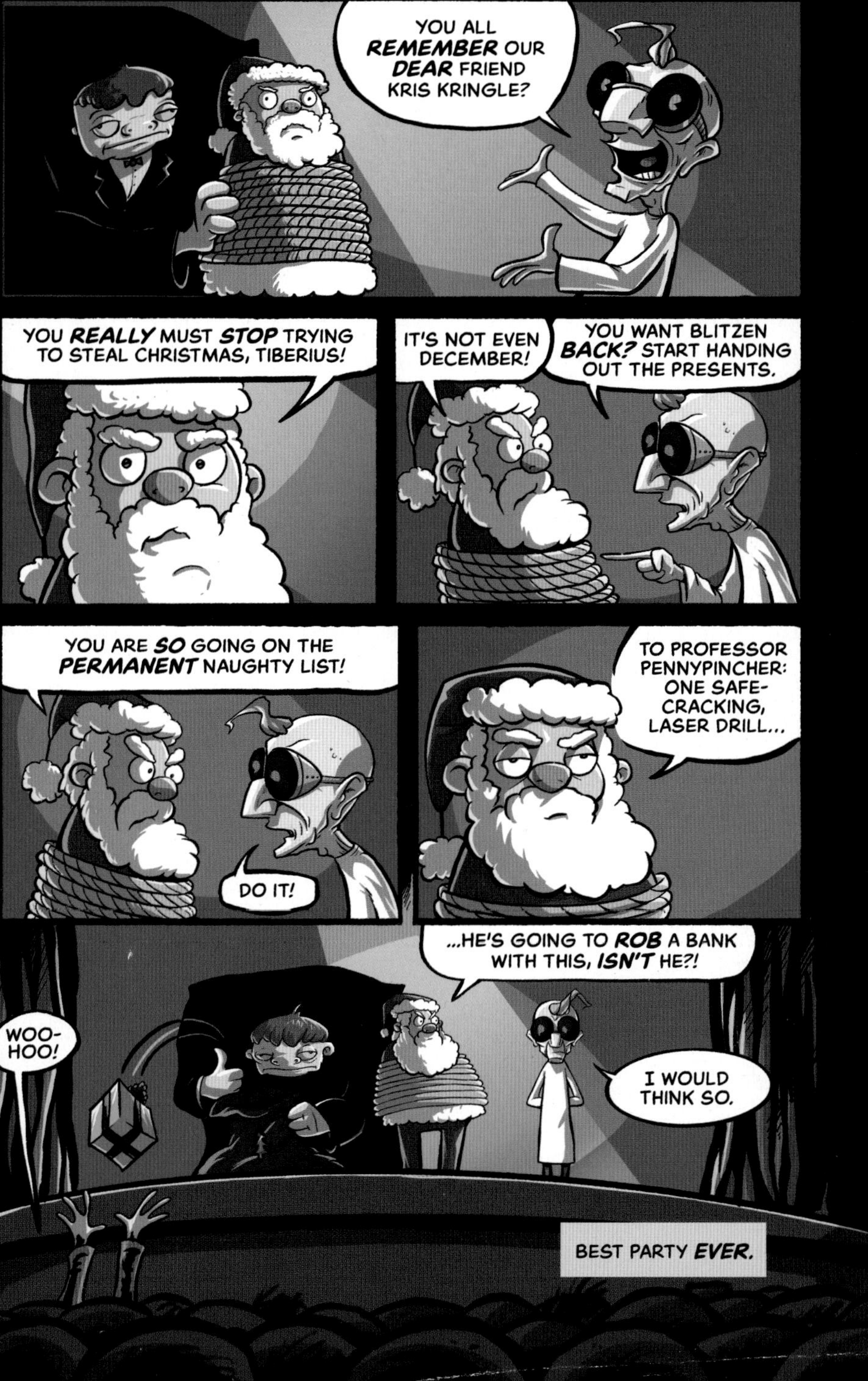
YOU ALL REMEMBER OUR DEAR FRIEND KRIS KRINGLE?
YOU REALLY MUST STOP TRYING TO STEAL CHRISTMAS, TIBERIUS!
IT'S NOT EVEN DECEMBER!
YOU WANT BLITZEN BACK? START HANDING OUT THE PRESENTS.
YOU ARE SO GOING ON THE PERMANENT NAUGHTY LIST!
DO IT!
TO PROFESSOR PENNYPINCHER: ONE SAFE-CRACKING, LASER DRILL...
...HE'S GOING TO ROB A BANK WITH THIS, ISN'T HE?!
WOO-HOO!
I WOULD THINK SO.
BEST PARTY EVER.

CHAPTER 13
Destroyer of Worlds

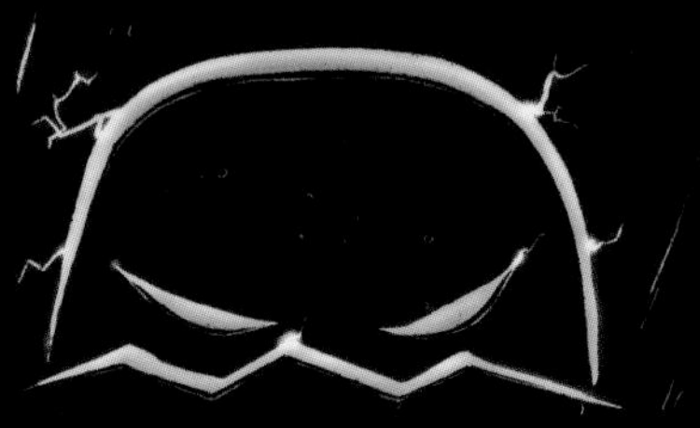

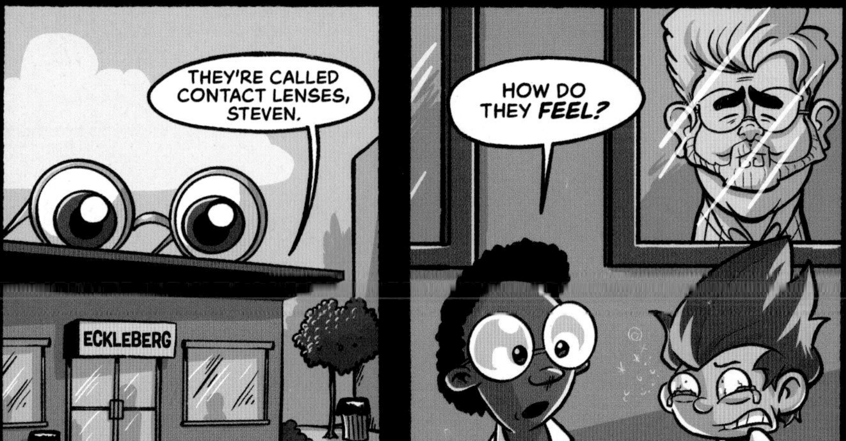

THEY'RE CALLED CONTACT LENSES, STEVEN.
ECKLEBERG
HOW DO THEY *FEEL?*

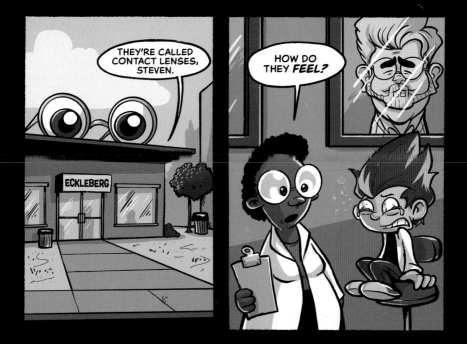

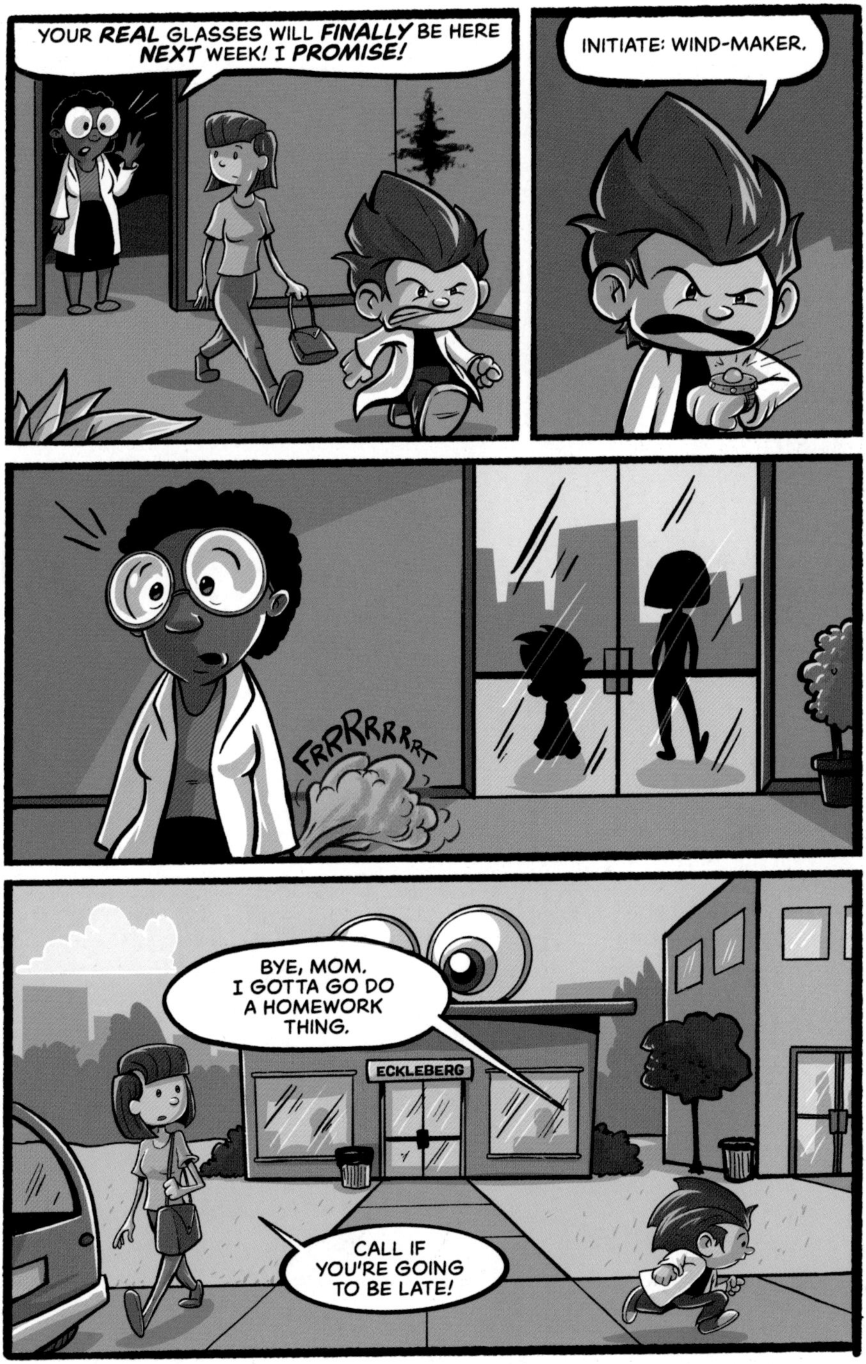
YOUR REAL GLASSES WILL FINALLY BE HERE NEXT WEEK! I PROMISE!
INITIATE: WIND-MAKER.
FRRRRRRRT
BYE, MOM. I GOTTA GO DO A HOMEWORK THING.
ECKLEBERG
CALL IF YOU'RE GOING TO BE LATE!

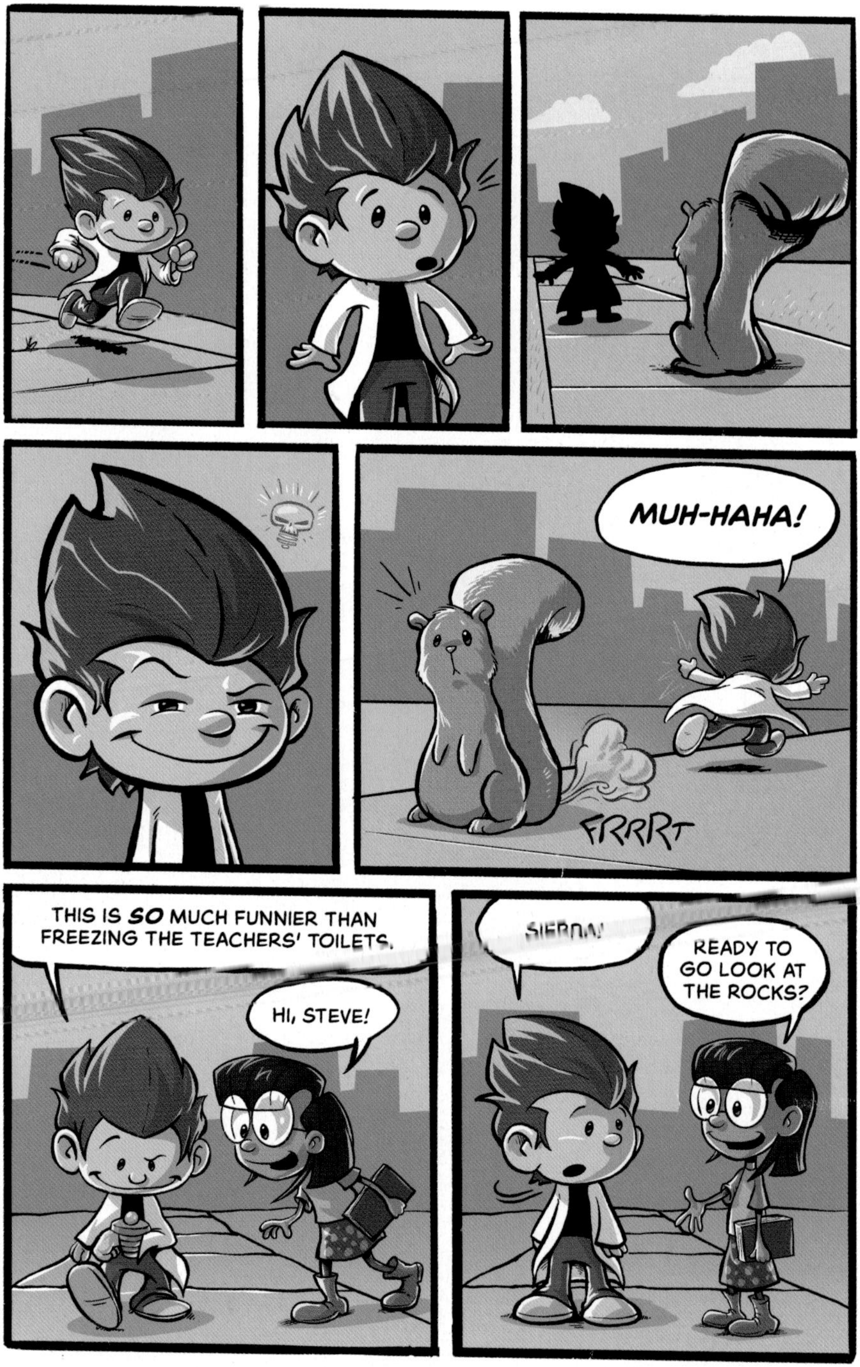
MUH-HAHA!
FRRRT
THIS IS SO MUCH FUNNIER THAN FREEZING THE TEACHERS' TOILETS.
HI, STEVE!
SIERRA!
READY TO GO LOOK AT THE ROCKS?

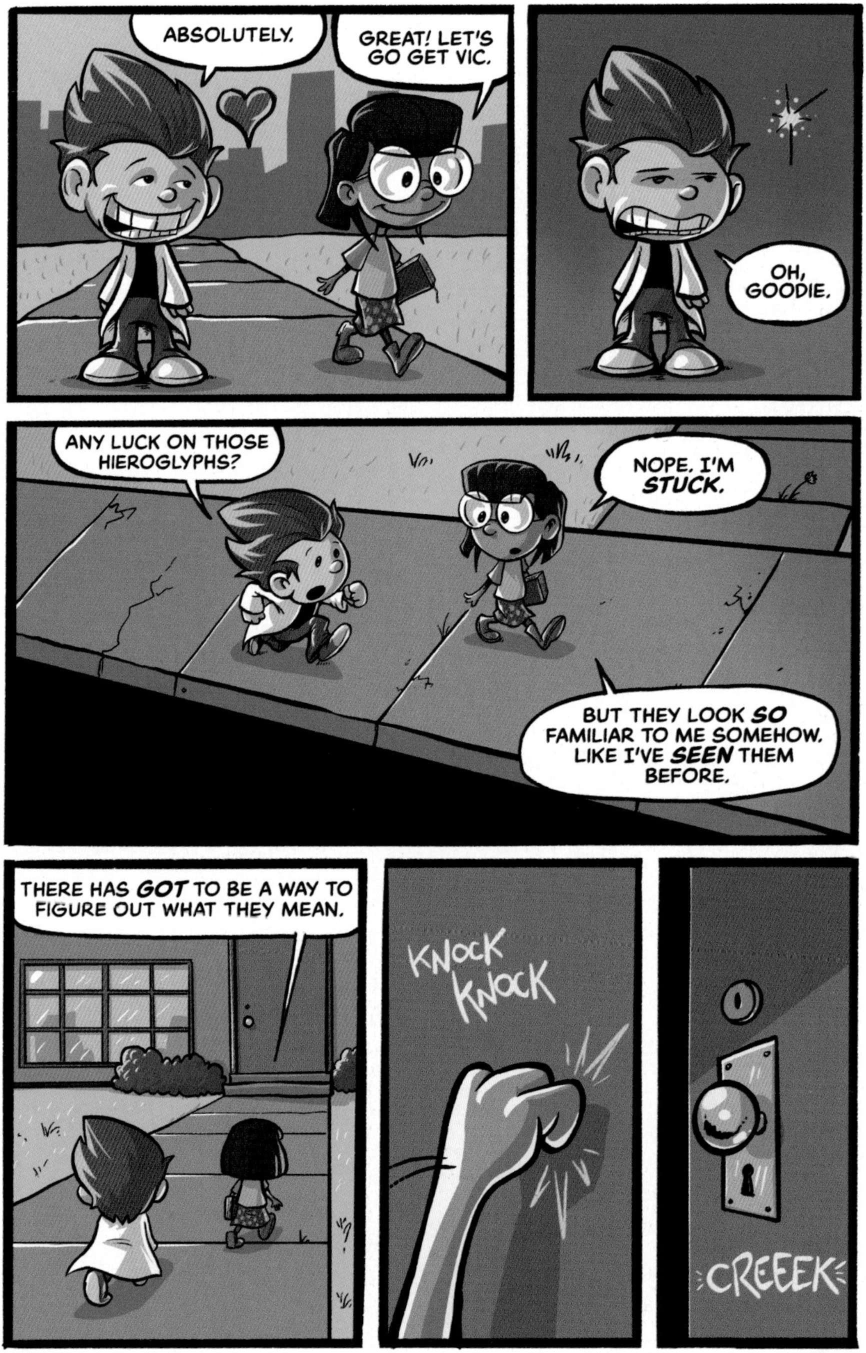
ABSOLUTELY.
GREAT! LET'S GO GET VIC.
OH, GOODIE.
ANY LUCK ON THOSE HIEROGLYPHS?
NOPE. I'M STUCK.
BUT THEY LOOK SO FAMILIAR TO ME SOMEHOW. LIKE I'VE SEEN THEM BEFORE.
THERE HAS GOT TO BE A WAY TO FIGURE OUT WHAT THEY MEAN.
KNOCK KNOCK
CREEEK

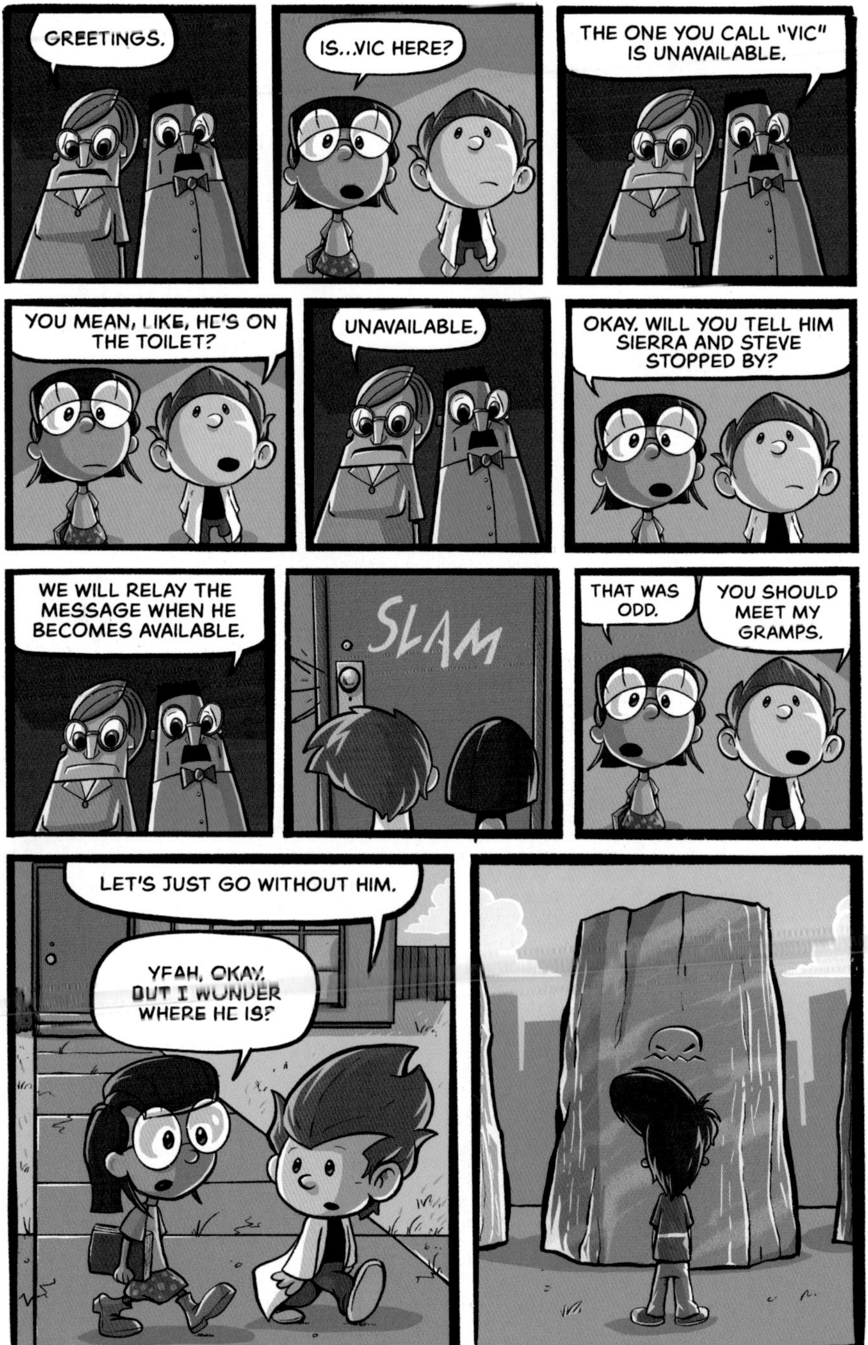
GREETINGS.
IS...VIC HERE?
THE ONE YOU CALL "VIC" IS UNAVAILABLE.
YOU MEAN, LIKE, HE'S ON THE TOILET?
UNAVAILABLE.
OKAY. WILL YOU TELL HIM SIERRA AND STEVE STOPPED BY?
WE WILL RELAY THE MESSAGE WHEN HE BECOMES AVAILABLE.
SLAM
THAT WAS ODD.
YOU SHOULD MEET MY GRAMPS.
LET'S JUST GO WITHOUT HIM.
YEAH, OKAY. BUT I WONDER WHERE HE IS?

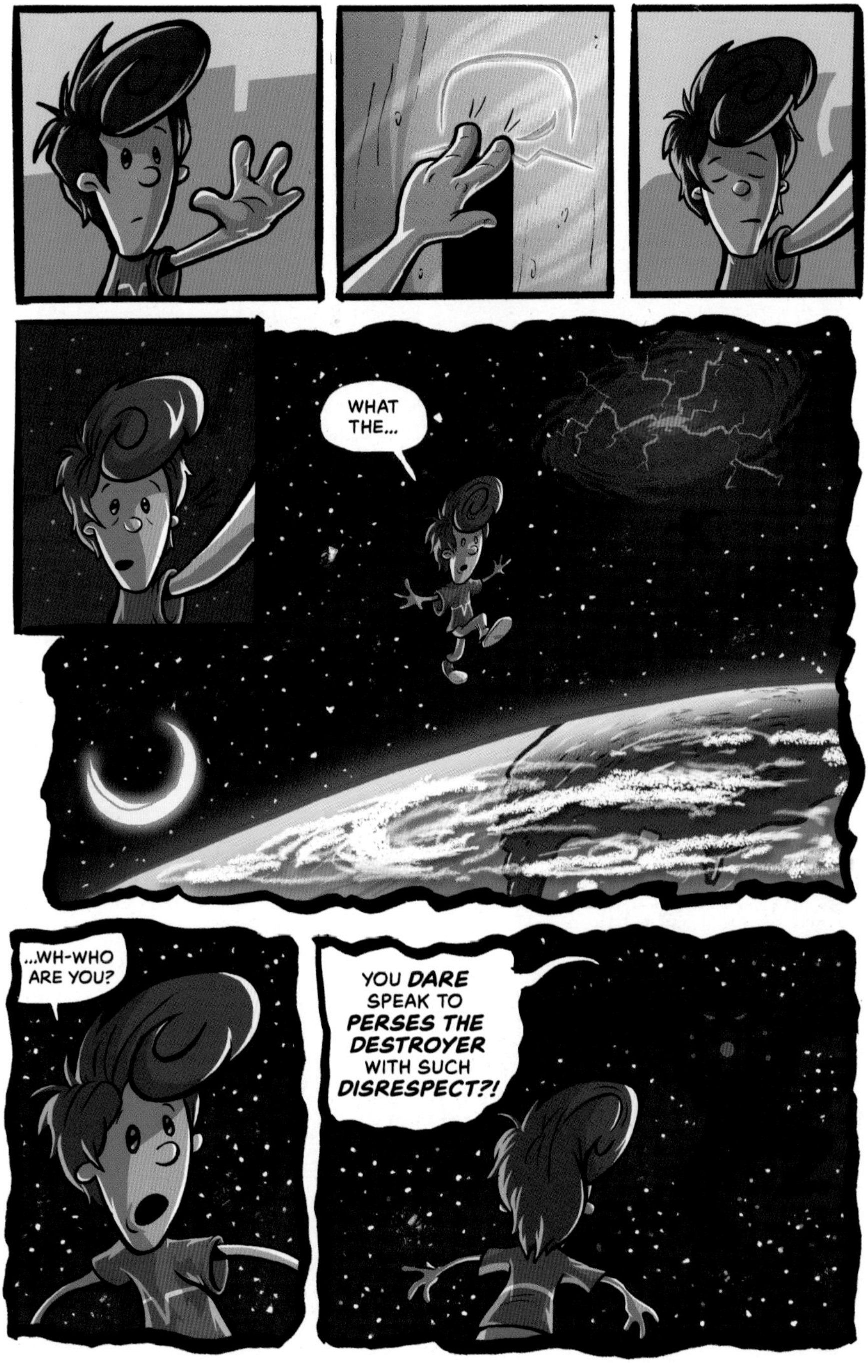
WHAT THE...
...WH-WHO ARE YOU?
YOU **DARE** SPEAK TO **PERSES THE DESTROYER** WITH SUCH **DISRESPECT?!**

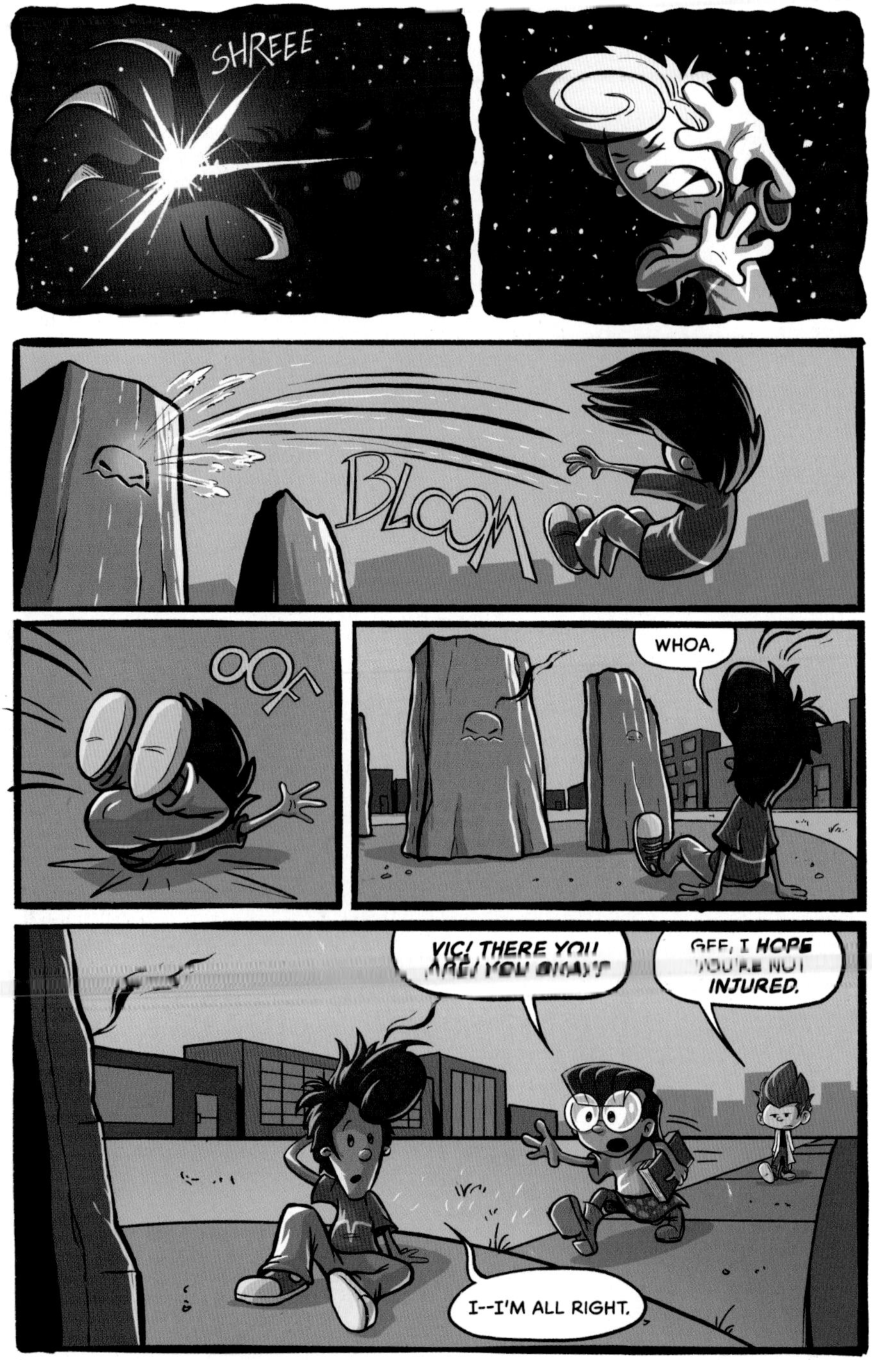
SHREEE
BLOOM
OOF
WHOA.
VIC! THERE YOU
GEE, I HOPE YOU'RE NOT INJURED.
I--I'M ALL RIGHT.

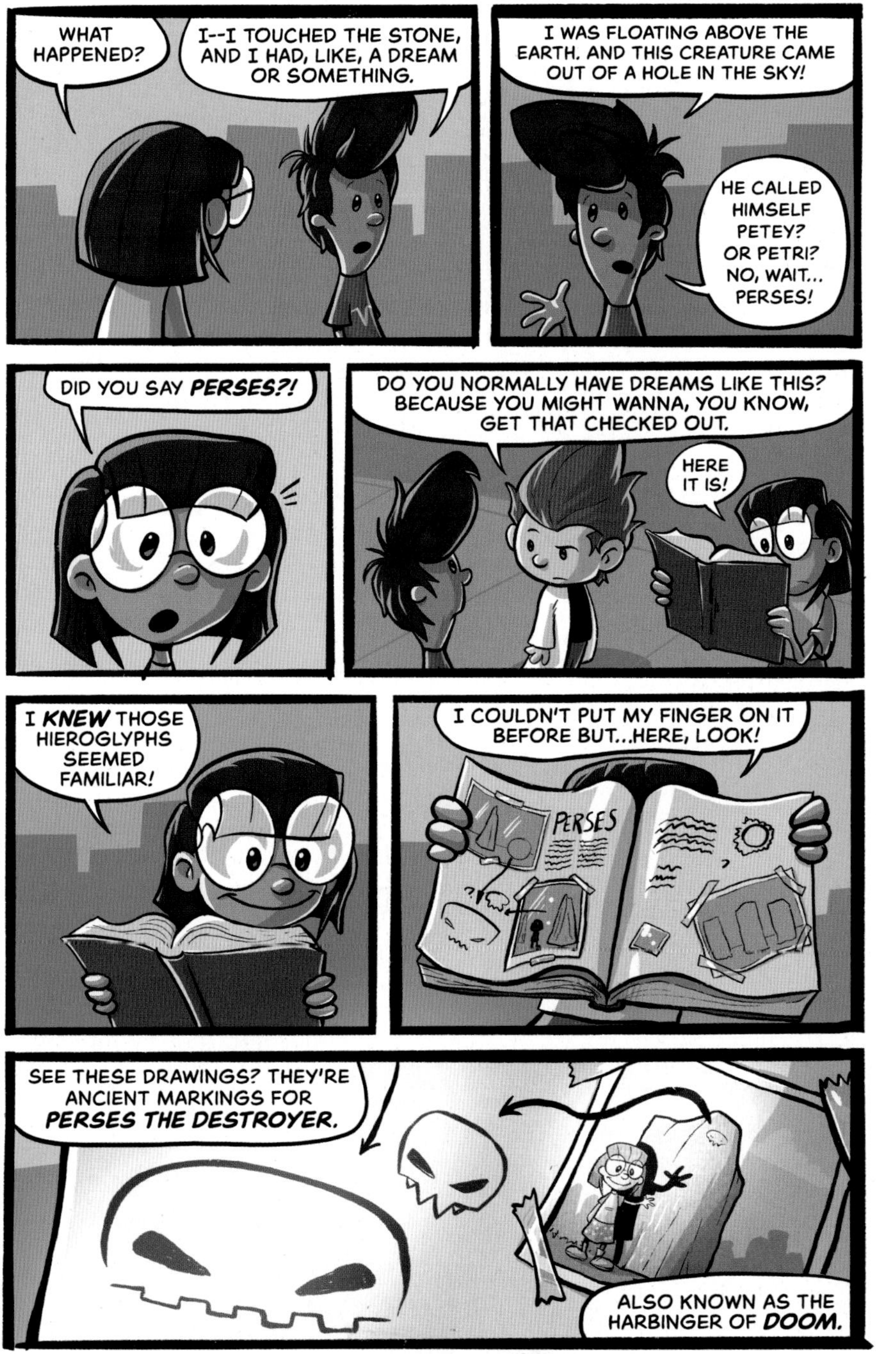
WHAT HAPPENED?
I--I TOUCHED THE STONE, AND I HAD, LIKE, A DREAM OR SOMETHING.
I WAS FLOATING ABOVE THE EARTH. AND THIS CREATURE CAME OUT OF A HOLE IN THE SKY!
HE CALLED HIMSELF PETEY? OR PETRI? NO, WAIT... PERSES!
DID YOU SAY ***PERSES?!***
DO YOU NORMALLY HAVE DREAMS LIKE THIS? BECAUSE YOU MIGHT WANNA, YOU KNOW, GET THAT CHECKED OUT.
HERE IT IS!
I ***KNEW*** THOSE HIEROGLYPHS SEEMED FAMILIAR!
I COULDN'T PUT MY FINGER ON IT BEFORE BUT...HERE, LOOK!
PERSES
SEE THESE DRAWINGS? THEY'RE ANCIENT MARKINGS FOR ***PERSES THE DESTROYER.***
ALSO KNOWN AS THE HARBINGER OF ***DOOM.***

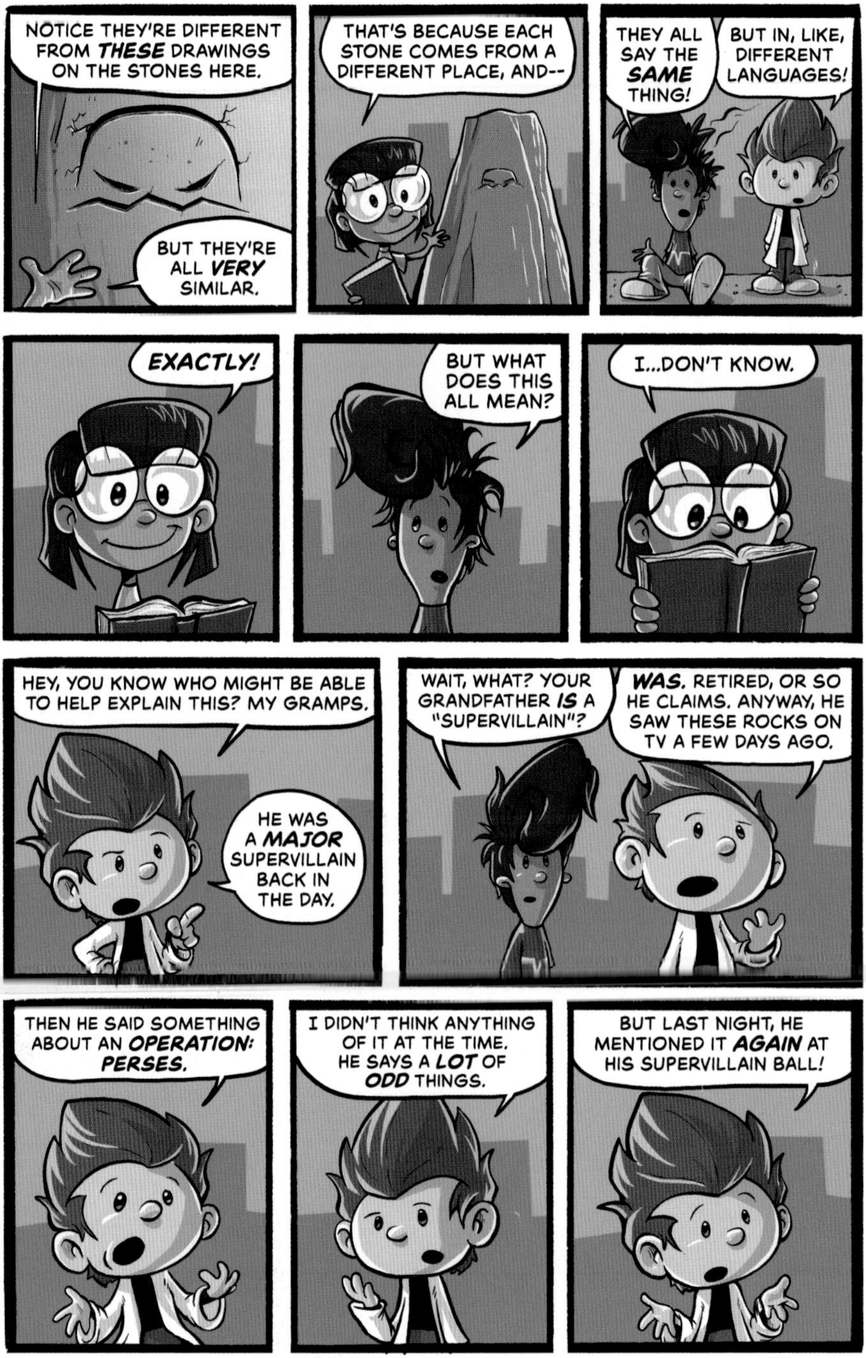
NOTICE THEY'RE DIFFERENT FROM THESE DRAWINGS ON THE STONES HERE.
BUT THEY'RE ALL VERY SIMILAR.
THAT'S BECAUSE EACH STONE COMES FROM A DIFFERENT PLACE, AND--
THEY ALL SAY THE SAME THING!
BUT IN, LIKE, DIFFERENT LANGUAGES!
EXACTLY!
BUT WHAT DOES THIS ALL MEAN?
I...DON'T KNOW.
HEY, YOU KNOW WHO MIGHT BE ABLE TO HELP EXPLAIN THIS? MY GRAMPS.
HE WAS A MAJOR SUPERVILLAIN BACK IN THE DAY.
WAIT, WHAT? YOUR GRANDFATHER IS A "SUPERVILLAIN"?
WAS. RETIRED, OR SO HE CLAIMS. ANYWAY, HE SAW THESE ROCKS ON TV A FEW DAYS AGO.
THEN HE SAID SOMETHING ABOUT AN OPERATION: PERSES.
I DIDN'T THINK ANYTHING OF IT AT THE TIME. HE SAYS A LOT OF ODD THINGS.
BUT LAST NIGHT, HE MENTIONED IT AGAIN AT HIS SUPERVILLAIN BALL!

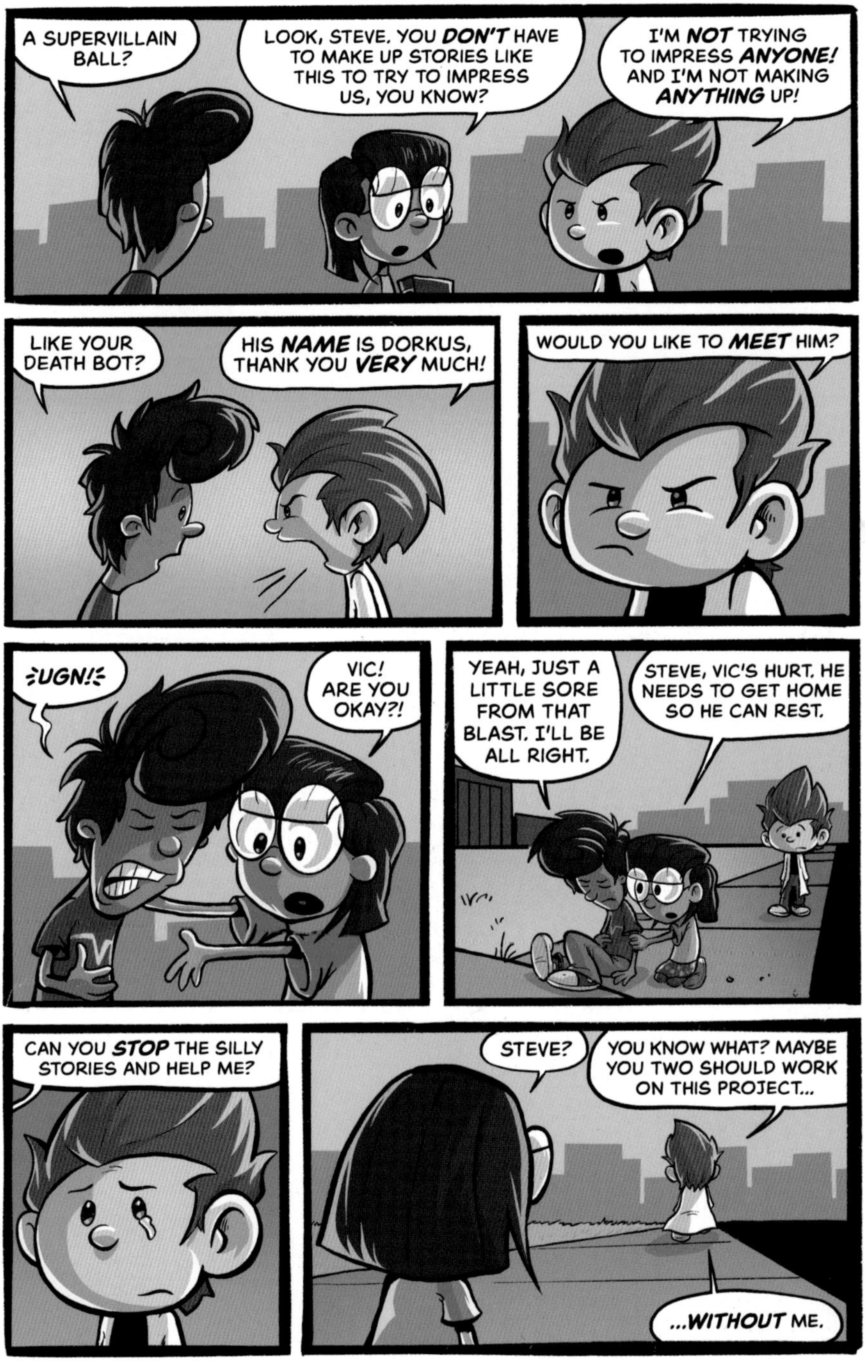
A SUPERVILLAIN BALL?
LOOK, STEVE. YOU DON'T HAVE TO MAKE UP STORIES LIKE THIS TO TRY TO IMPRESS US, YOU KNOW?
I'M NOT TRYING TO IMPRESS ANYONE! AND I'M NOT MAKING ANYTHING UP!
LIKE YOUR DEATH BOT?
HIS NAME IS DORKUS, THANK YOU VERY MUCH!
WOULD YOU LIKE TO MEET HIM?
UGN!
VIC! ARE YOU OKAY?!
YEAH, JUST A LITTLE SORE FROM THAT BLAST. I'LL BE ALL RIGHT.
STEVE, VIC'S HURT. HE NEEDS TO GET HOME SO HE CAN REST.
CAN YOU STOP THE SILLY STORIES AND HELP ME?
STEVE?
YOU KNOW WHAT? MAYBE YOU TWO SHOULD WORK ON THIS PROJECT...
...WITHOUT ME.

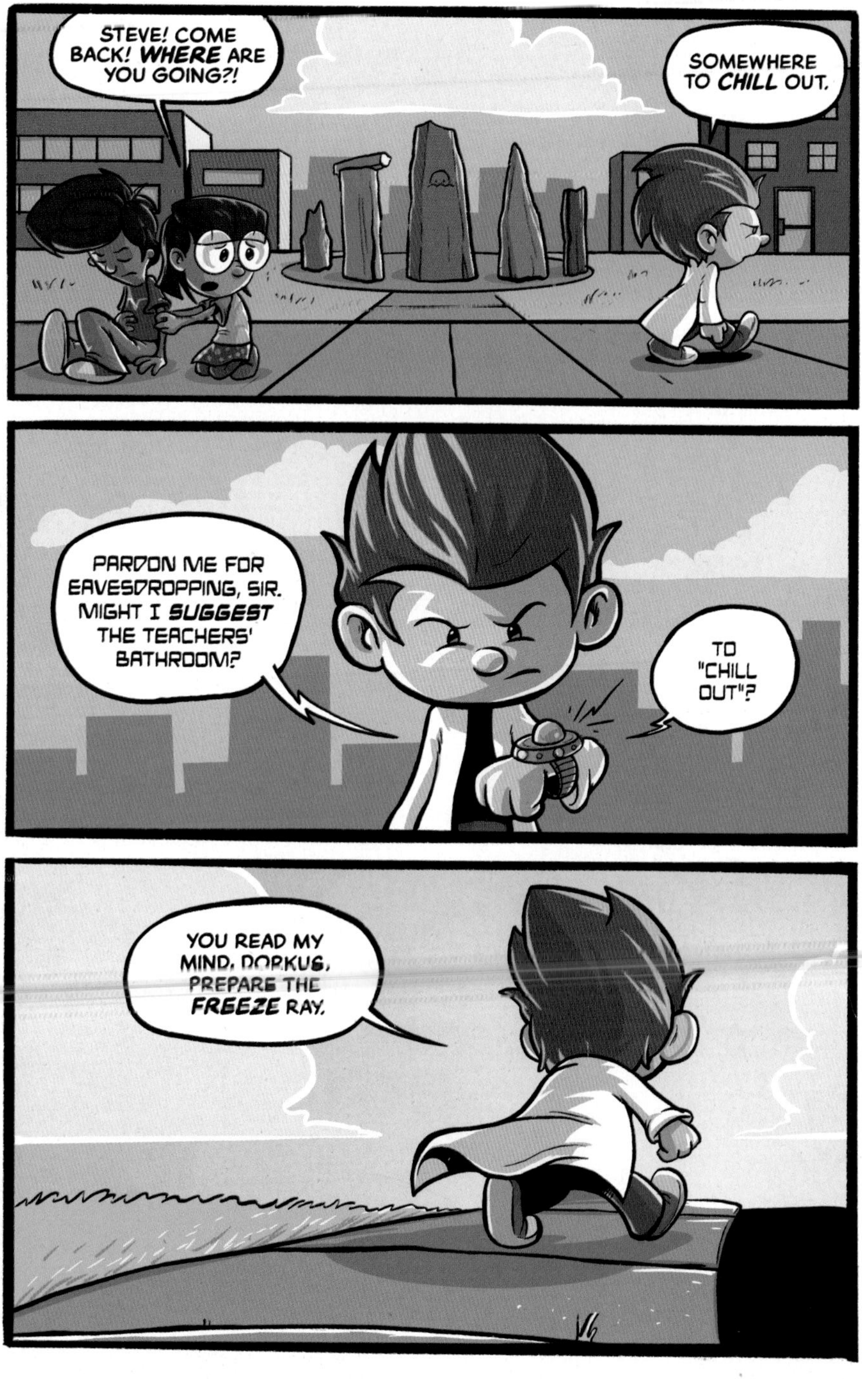
STEVE! COME BACK! **WHERE** ARE YOU GOING?!
SOMEWHERE TO **CHILL** OUT.
PARDON ME FOR EAVESDROPPING, SIR. MIGHT I **SUGGEST** THE TEACHERS' BATHROOM?
TO "CHILL OUT"?
YOU READ MY MIND, DORKUS. PREPARE THE **FREEZE** RAY.

CHAPTER 14
If the Shoe Hits

MONDAY MORNING...

=SIGH= **WHY** DOES YOUR BACKPACK ALWAYS FEEL **HEAVIER** WHEN YOU **DON'T** WANT TO BE AT SCHOOL, DORKUS?

EXCUSE ME, SIR. BUT I HAVE **NOT** BEEN ABLE TO LOCATE MRS. CUDDLES FOR HER MIDMORNING TUMMY RUBS.

DID YOU LOOK IN THE NEIGHBOR'S BIRDBATH? IT'S BREAKFAST TIME.

I DID, SIR. BUT ALL THE BIRDS ARE STILL...FINE.

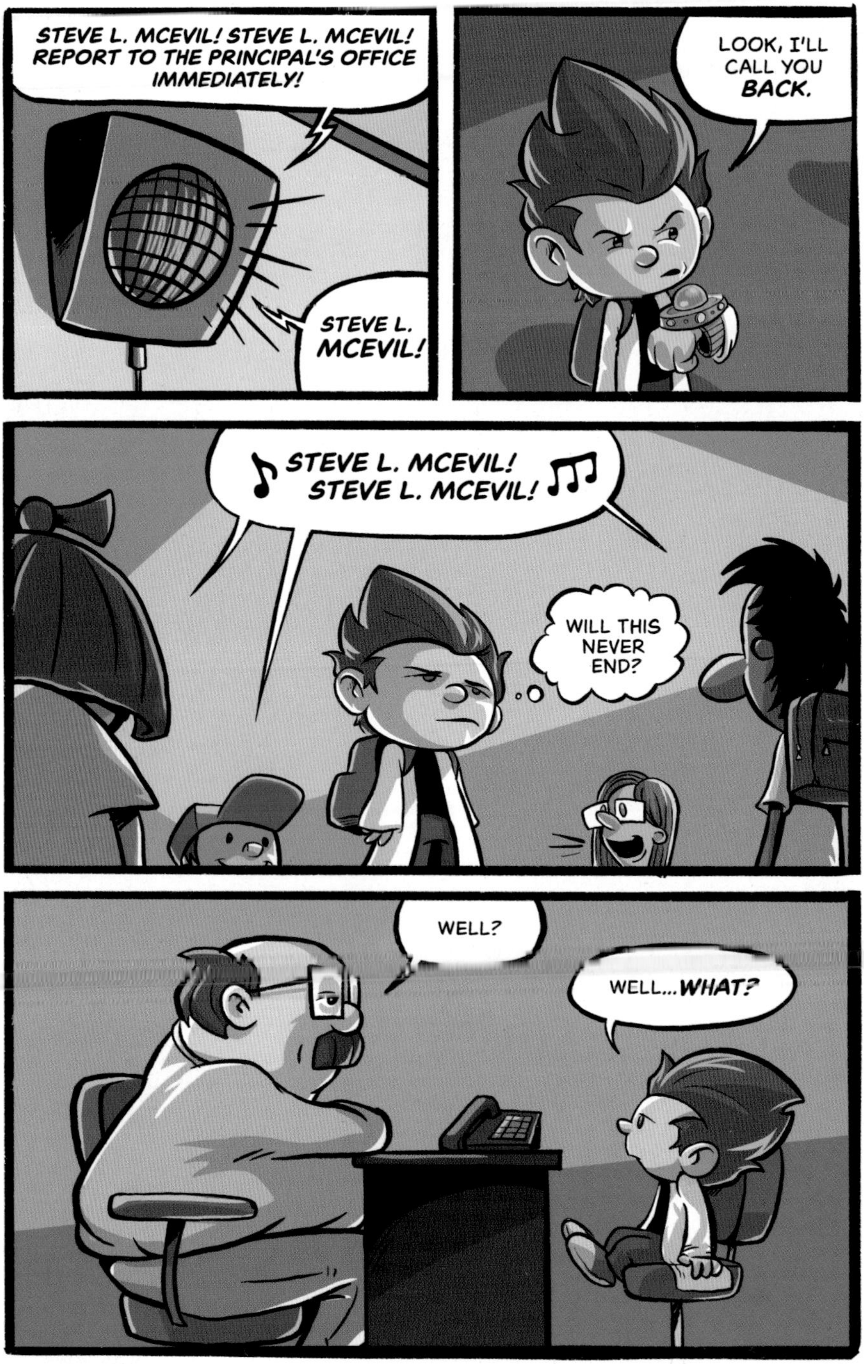
STEVE L. MCEVIL! STEVE L. MCEVIL! REPORT TO THE PRINCIPAL'S OFFICE IMMEDIATELY!
STEVE L. MCEVIL!
LOOK, I'LL CALL YOU BACK.
STEVE L. MCEVIL! STEVE L. MCEVIL!
WILL THIS NEVER END?
WELL?
WELL...WHAT?

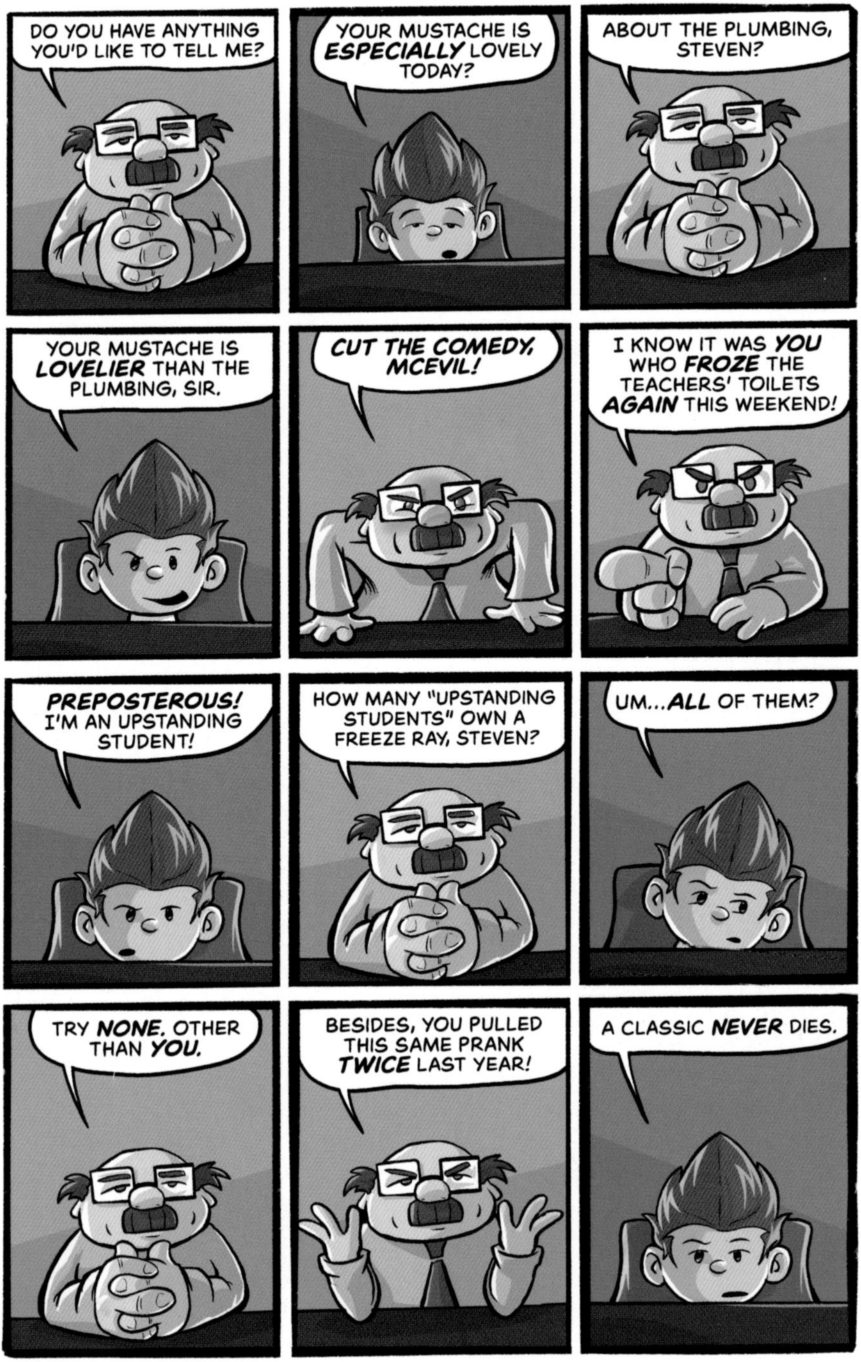
DO YOU HAVE ANYTHING YOU'D LIKE TO TELL ME?
YOUR MUSTACHE IS ESPECIALLY LOVELY TODAY?
ABOUT THE PLUMBING, STEVEN?
YOUR MUSTACHE IS LOVELIER THAN THE PLUMBING, SIR.
CUT THE COMEDY, MCEVIL!
I KNOW IT WAS YOU WHO FROZE THE TEACHERS' TOILETS AGAIN THIS WEEKEND!
PREPOSTEROUS! I'M AN UPSTANDING STUDENT!
HOW MANY "UPSTANDING STUDENTS" OWN A FREEZE RAY, STEVEN?
UM...ALL OF THEM?
TRY NONE. OTHER THAN YOU.
BESIDES, YOU PULLED THIS SAME PRANK TWICE LAST YEAR!
A CLASSIC NEVER DIES.

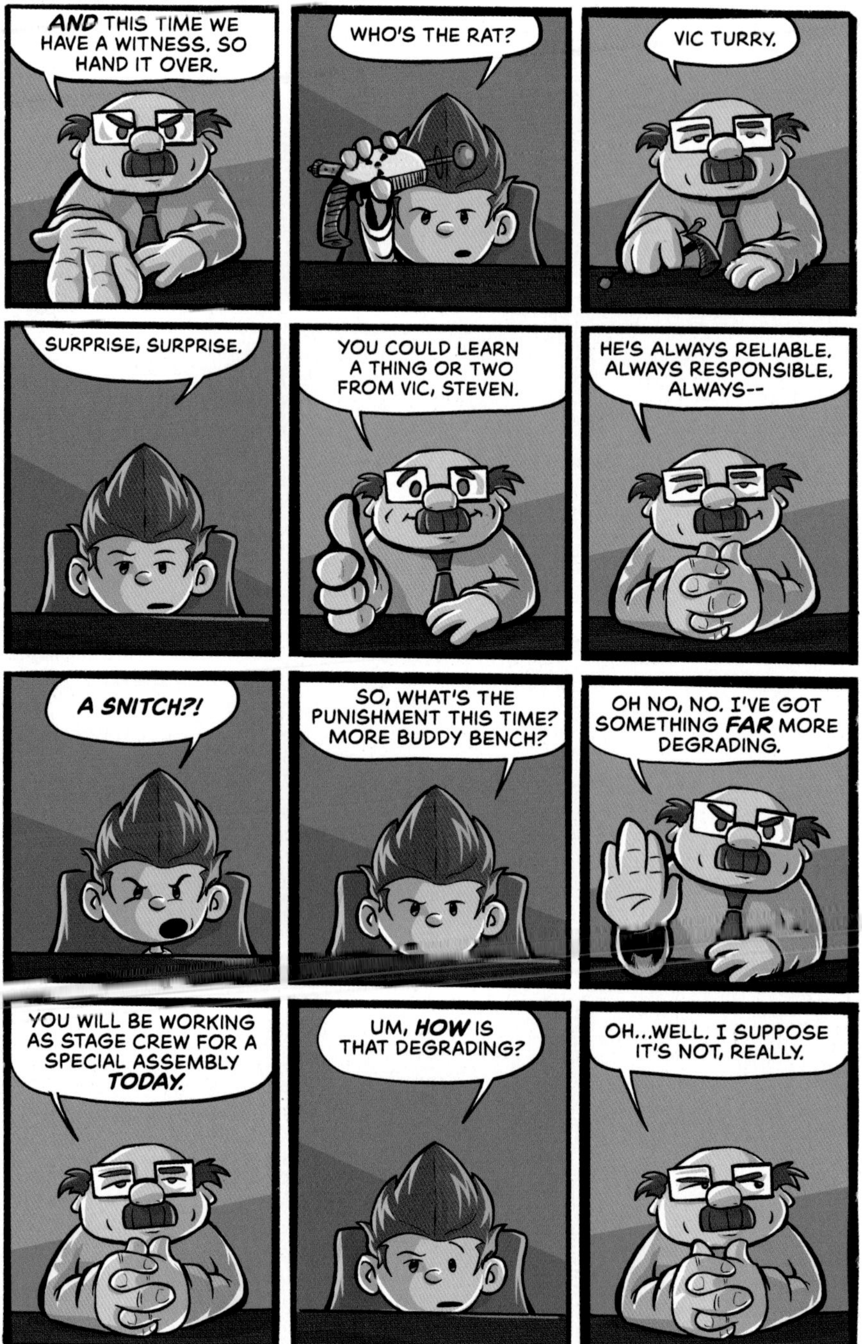
AND THIS TIME WE HAVE A WITNESS. SO HAND IT OVER.
WHO'S THE RAT?
VIC TURRY.
SURPRISE, SURPRISE.
YOU COULD LEARN A THING OR TWO FROM VIC, STEVEN.
HE'S ALWAYS RELIABLE. ALWAYS RESPONSIBLE. ALWAYS--
A SNITCH?!
SO, WHAT'S THE PUNISHMENT THIS TIME? MORE BUDDY BENCH?
OH NO, NO. I'VE GOT SOMETHING FAR MORE DEGRADING.
YOU WILL BE WORKING AS STAGE CREW FOR A SPECIAL ASSEMBLY TODAY.
UM, HOW IS THAT DEGRADING?
OH...WELL. I SUPPOSE IT'S NOT, REALLY.

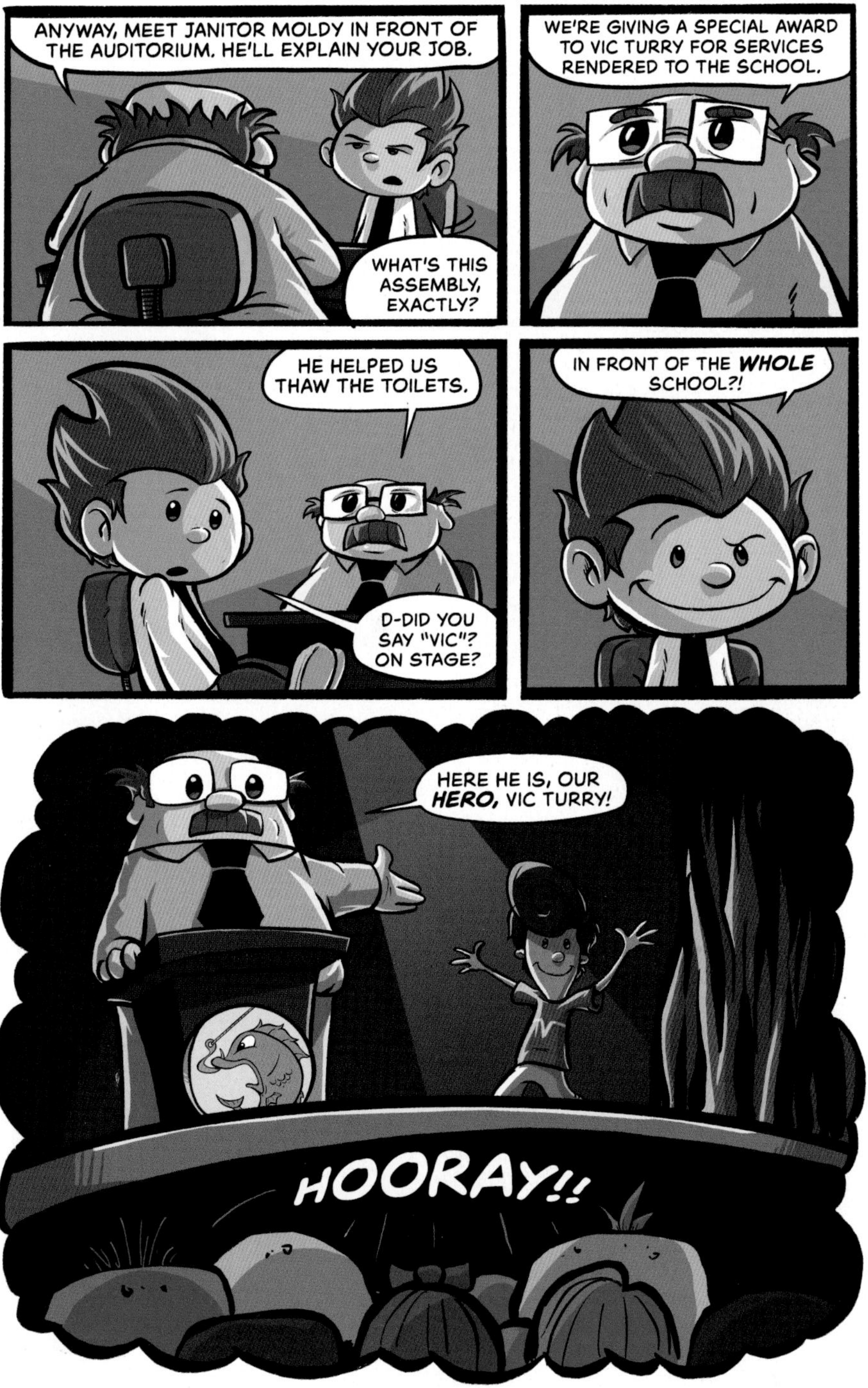
ANYWAY, MEET JANITOR MOLDY IN FRONT OF THE AUDITORIUM. HE'LL EXPLAIN YOUR JOB.
WHAT'S THIS ASSEMBLY, EXACTLY?
WE'RE GIVING A SPECIAL AWARD TO VIC TURRY FOR SERVICES RENDERED TO THE SCHOOL.
HE HELPED US THAW THE TOILETS.
D-DID YOU SAY "VIC"? ON STAGE?
IN FRONT OF THE WHOLE SCHOOL?!
HERE HE IS, OUR HERO, VIC TURRY!
HOORAY!!

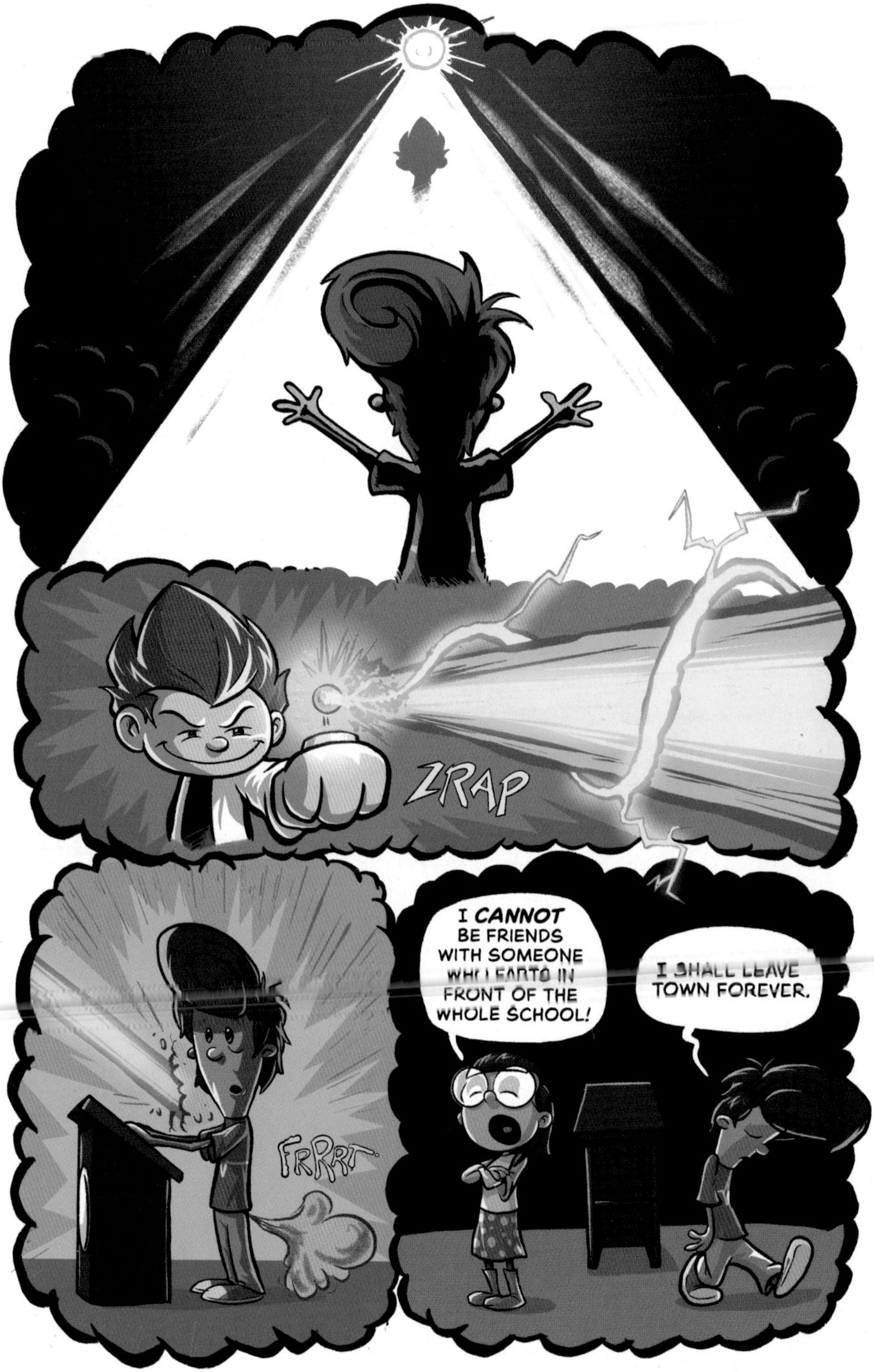
ZRAP
FRRRT
I *CANNOT* BE FRIENDS WITH SOMEONE WHO FARTS IN FRONT OF THE WHOLE SCHOOL!
I SHALL LEAVE TOWN FOREVER.

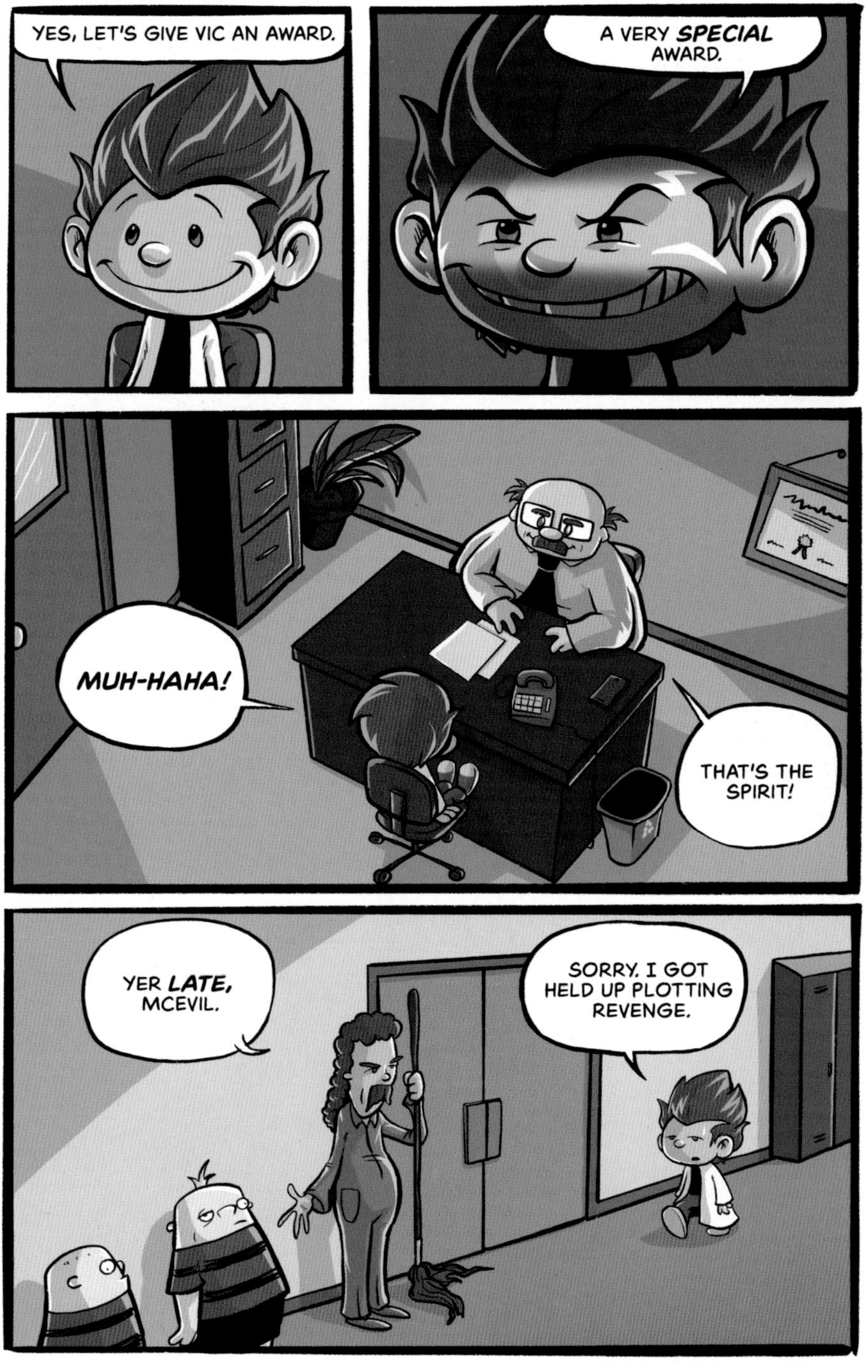
YES, LET'S GIVE VIC AN AWARD.
A VERY SPECIAL AWARD.
MUH-HAHA!
THAT'S THE SPIRIT!
YER LATE, MCEVIL.
SORRY. I GOT HELD UP PLOTTING REVENGE.

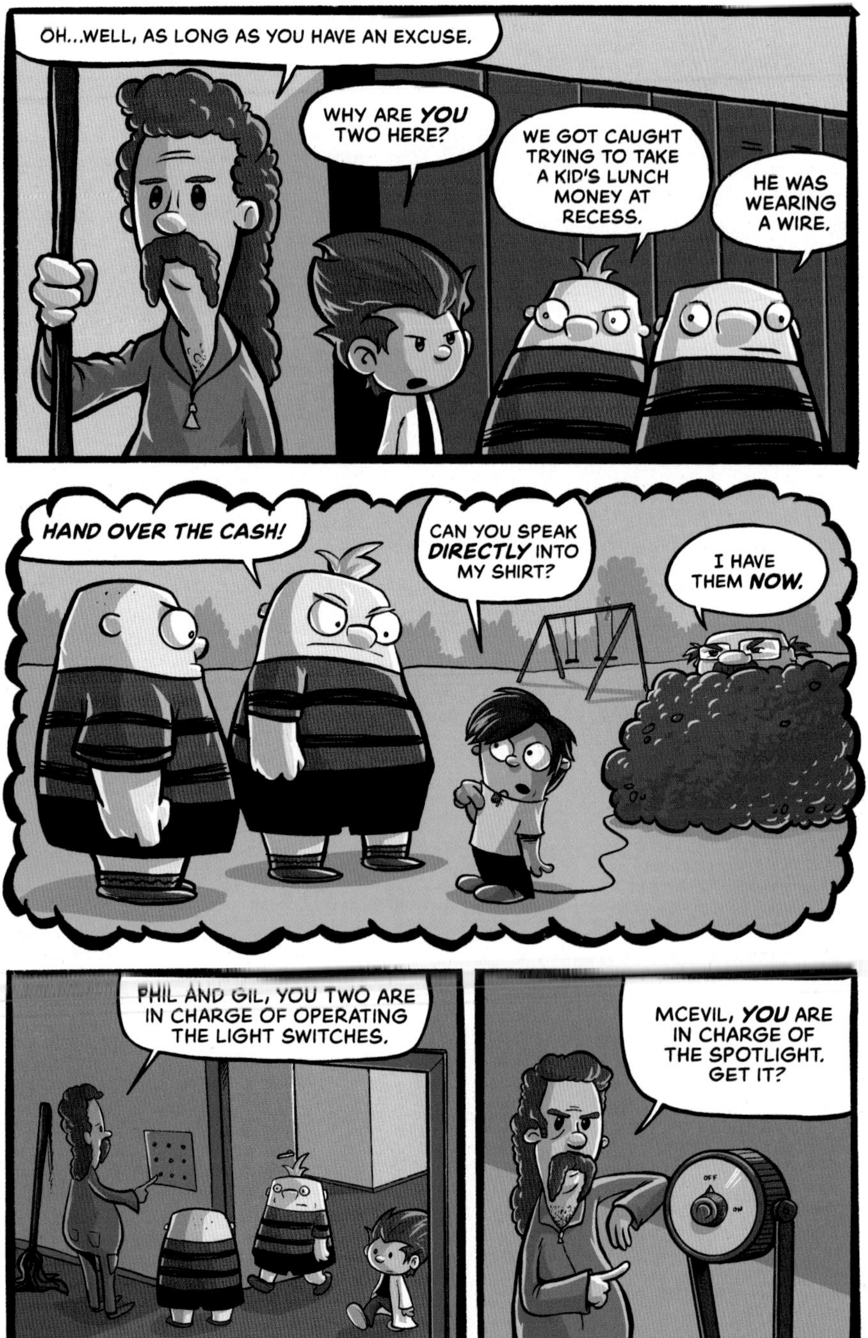
OH...WELL, AS LONG AS YOU HAVE AN EXCUSE.
WHY ARE *YOU* TWO HERE?
WE GOT CAUGHT TRYING TO TAKE A KID'S LUNCH MONEY AT RECESS.
HE WAS WEARING A WIRE.
HAND OVER THE CASH!
CAN YOU SPEAK *DIRECTLY* INTO MY SHIRT?
I HAVE THEM *NOW.*
PHIL AND GIL, YOU TWO ARE IN CHARGE OF OPERATING THE LIGHT SWITCHES.
MCEVIL, *YOU* ARE IN CHARGE OF THE SPOTLIGHT. GET IT?
OFF
ON

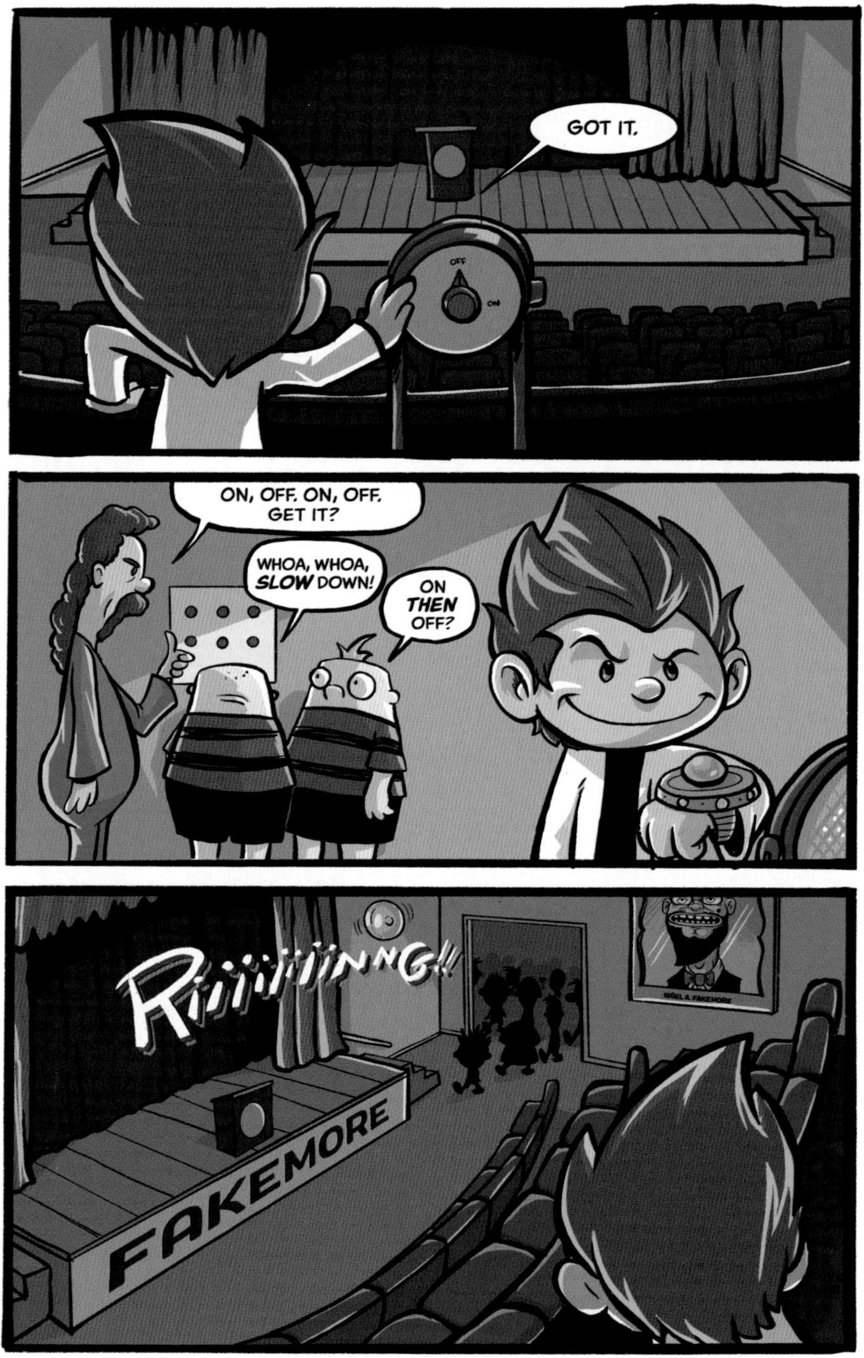
GOT IT.
OFF
ON
ON, OFF. ON, OFF. GET IT?
WHOA, WHOA, SLOW DOWN!
ON THEN OFF?
RIIIIIIIINNG!!
FAKEMORE

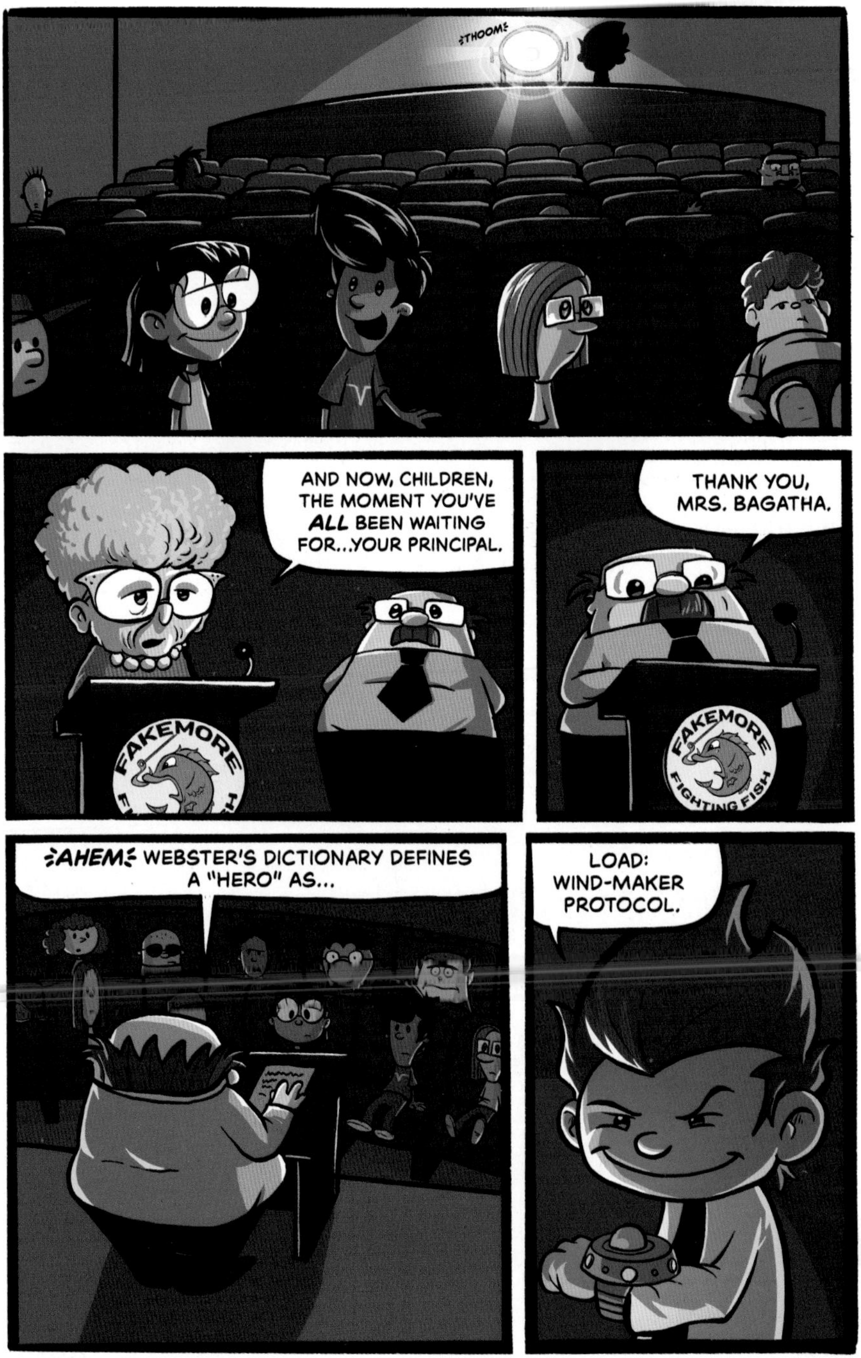
THOOM
AND NOW, CHILDREN, THE MOMENT YOU'VE ALL BEEN WAITING FOR...YOUR PRINCIPAL.
FAKEMORE
THANK YOU, MRS. BAGATHA.
FAKEMORE FIGHTING FISH
AHEM WEBSTER'S DICTIONARY DEFINES A "HERO" AS...
LOAD: WIND-MAKER PROTOCOL.

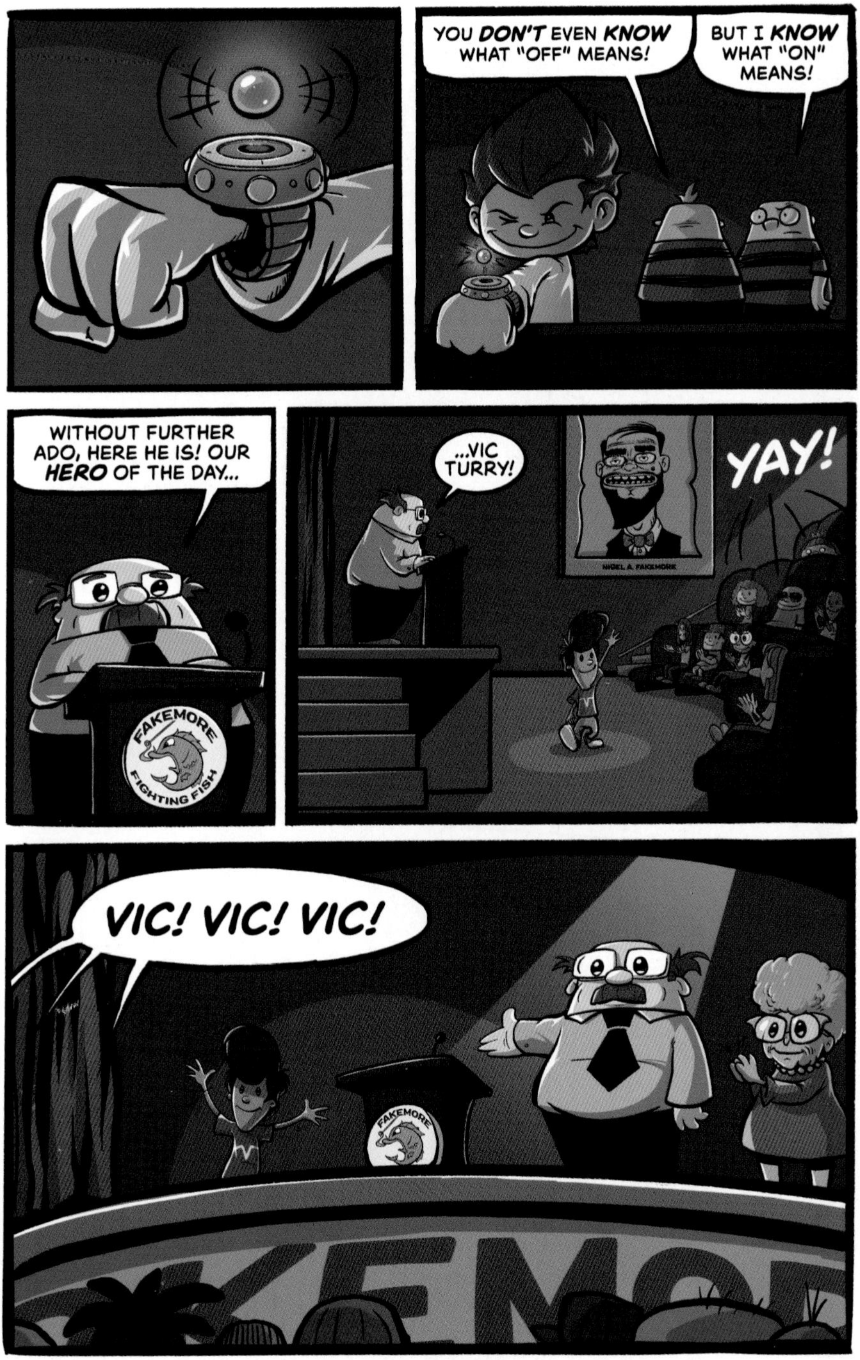
YOU DON'T EVEN KNOW WHAT "OFF" MEANS!
BUT I KNOW WHAT "ON" MEANS!
WITHOUT FURTHER ADO, HERE HE IS! OUR HERO OF THE DAY...
...VIC TURRY!
NIGEL A. FAKEMORE
YAY!
FAKEMORE FIGHTING FISH
VIC! VIC! VIC!
FAKEMORE

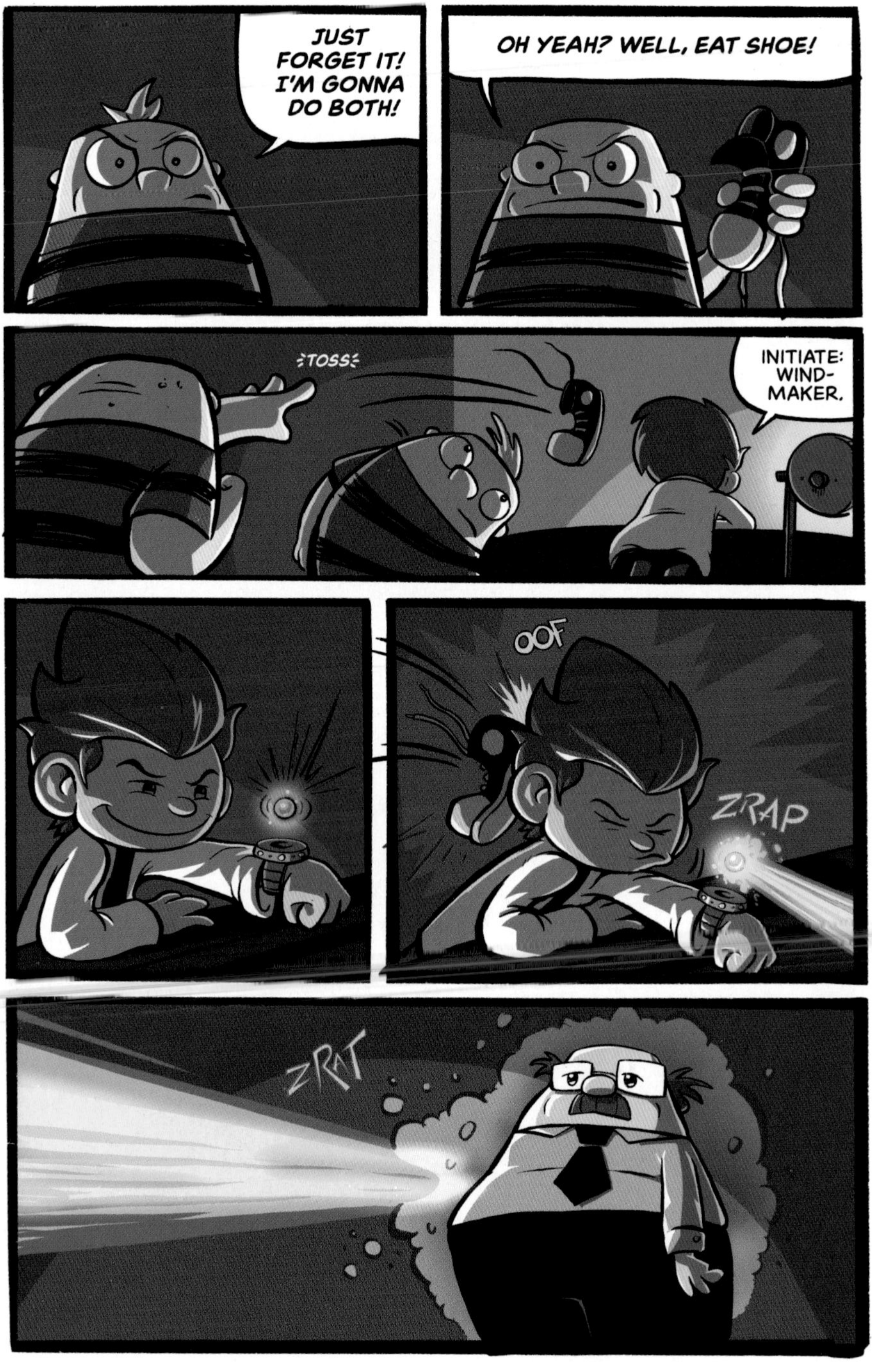
JUST FORGET IT! I'M GONNA DO BOTH!
OH YEAH? WELL, EAT SHOE!
TOSS
INITIATE: WIND-MAKER.
OOF
ZRAP
ZRAT

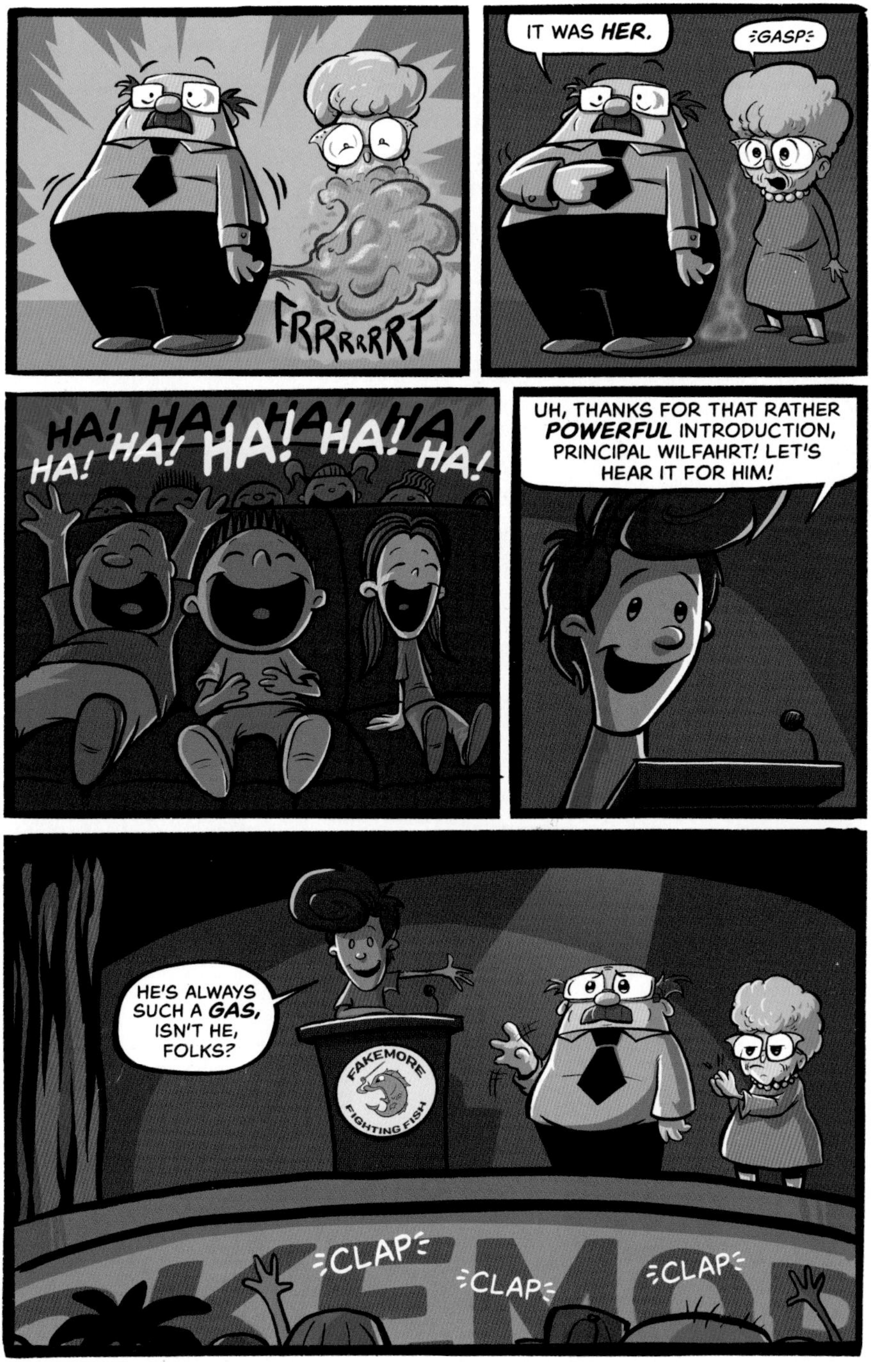
FRRRRRRT
IT WAS HER.
GASP
HA! HA! HA! HA! HA! HA! HA! HA! HA!
UH, THANKS FOR THAT RATHER POWERFUL INTRODUCTION, PRINCIPAL WILFAHRT! LET'S HEAR IT FOR HIM!
HE'S ALWAYS SUCH A GAS, ISN'T HE, FOLKS?
FAKEMORE FIGHTING FISH
CLAP
CLAP
CLAP

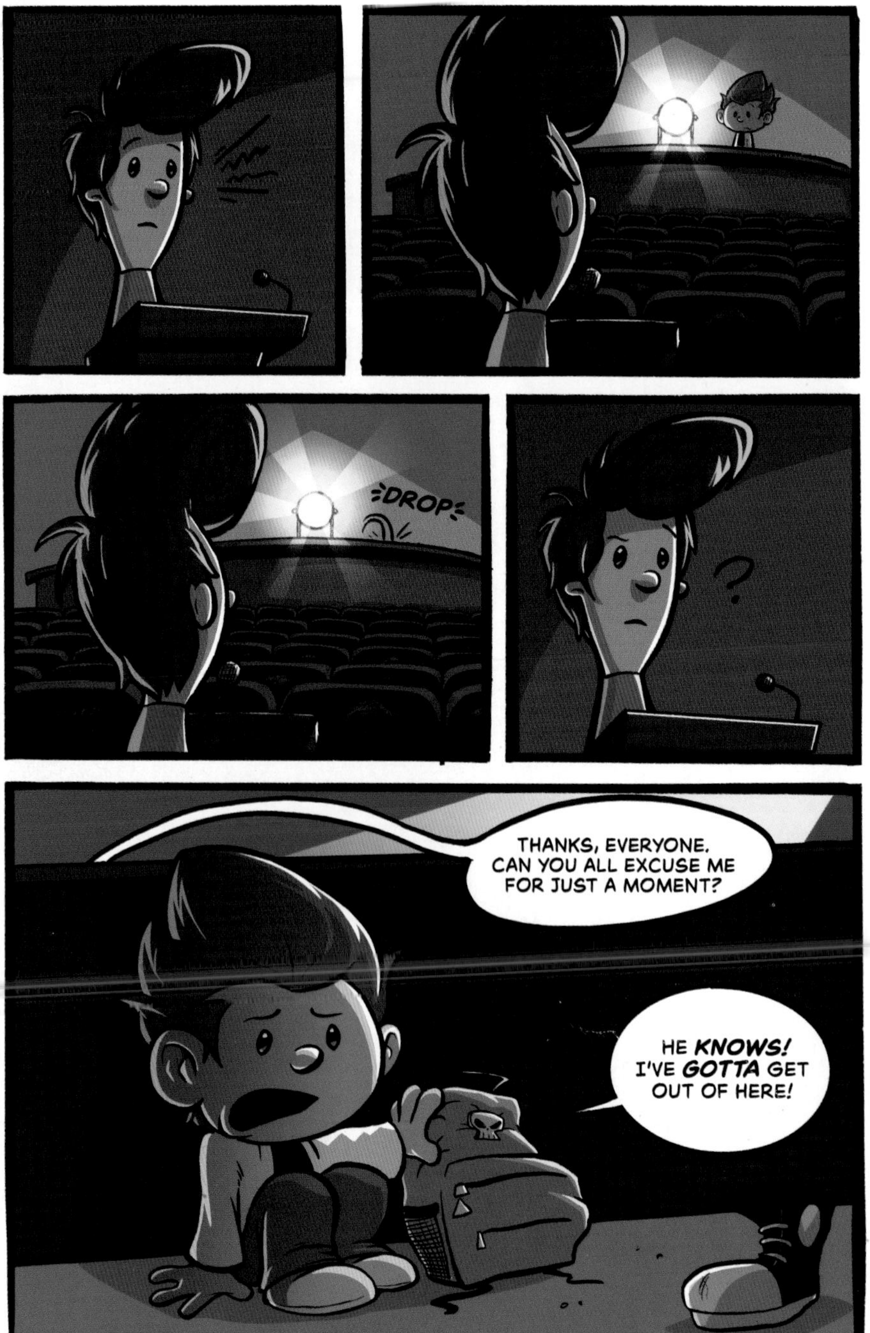
DROP
THANKS, EVERYONE. CAN YOU ALL EXCUSE ME FOR JUST A MOMENT?
HE **KNOWS!** I'VE **GOTTA** GET OUT OF HERE!

CHAPTER 15
Out of the Bag

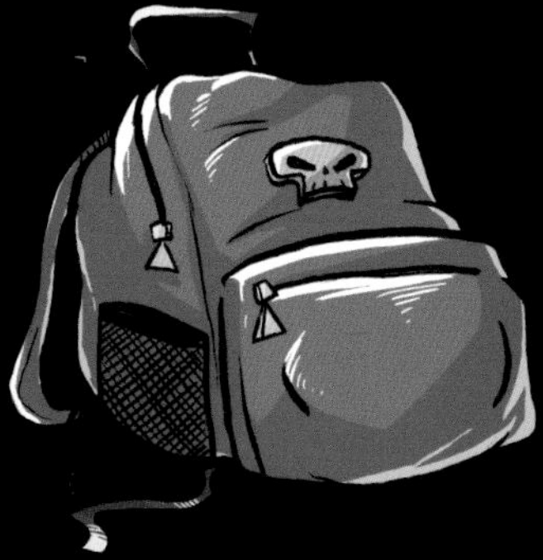

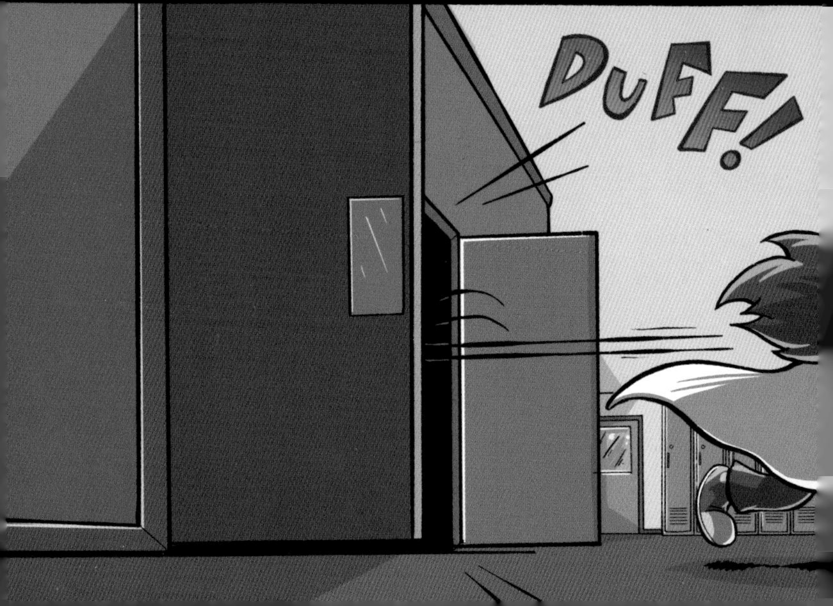
DUFF!

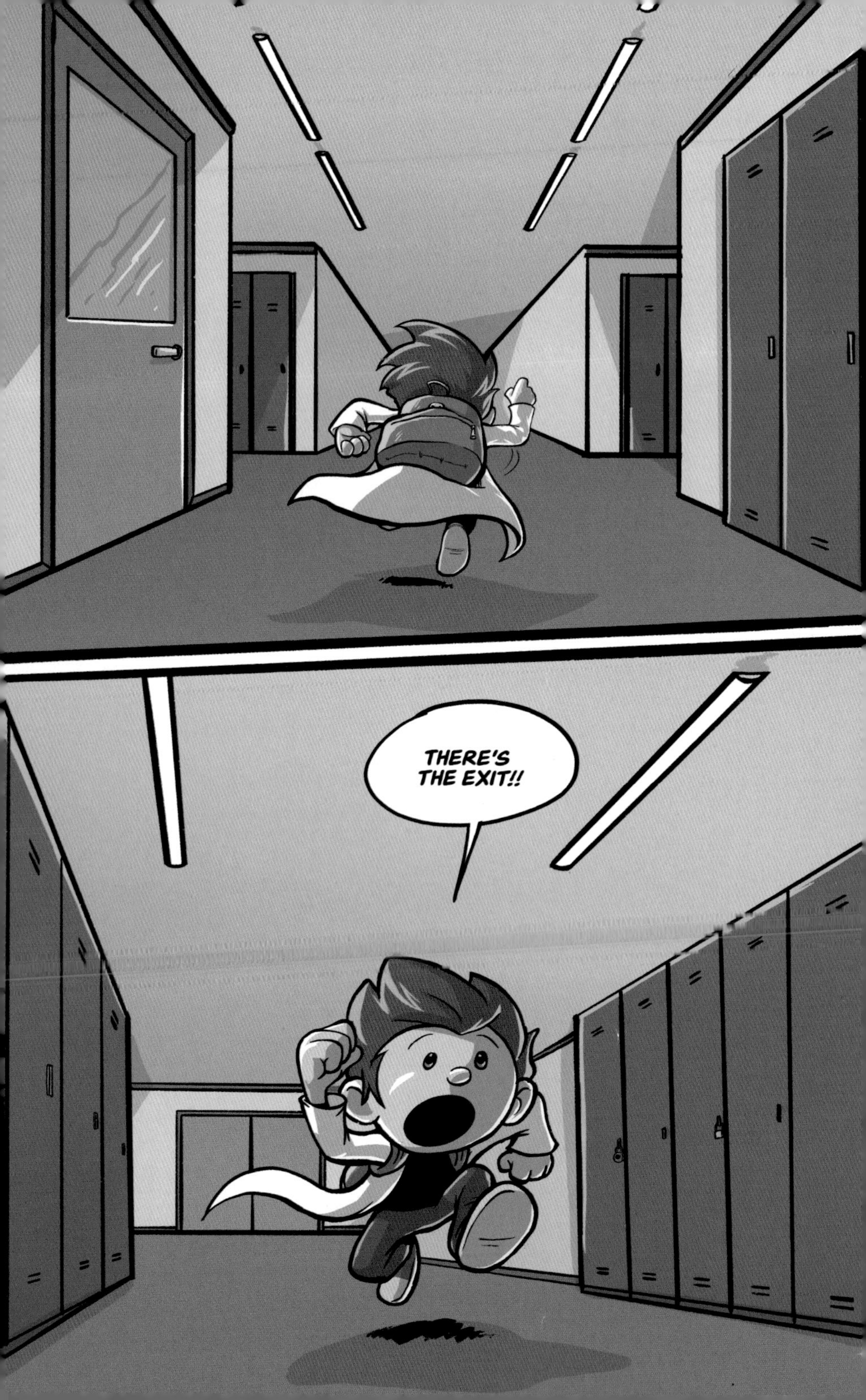
THERE'S THE EXIT!!

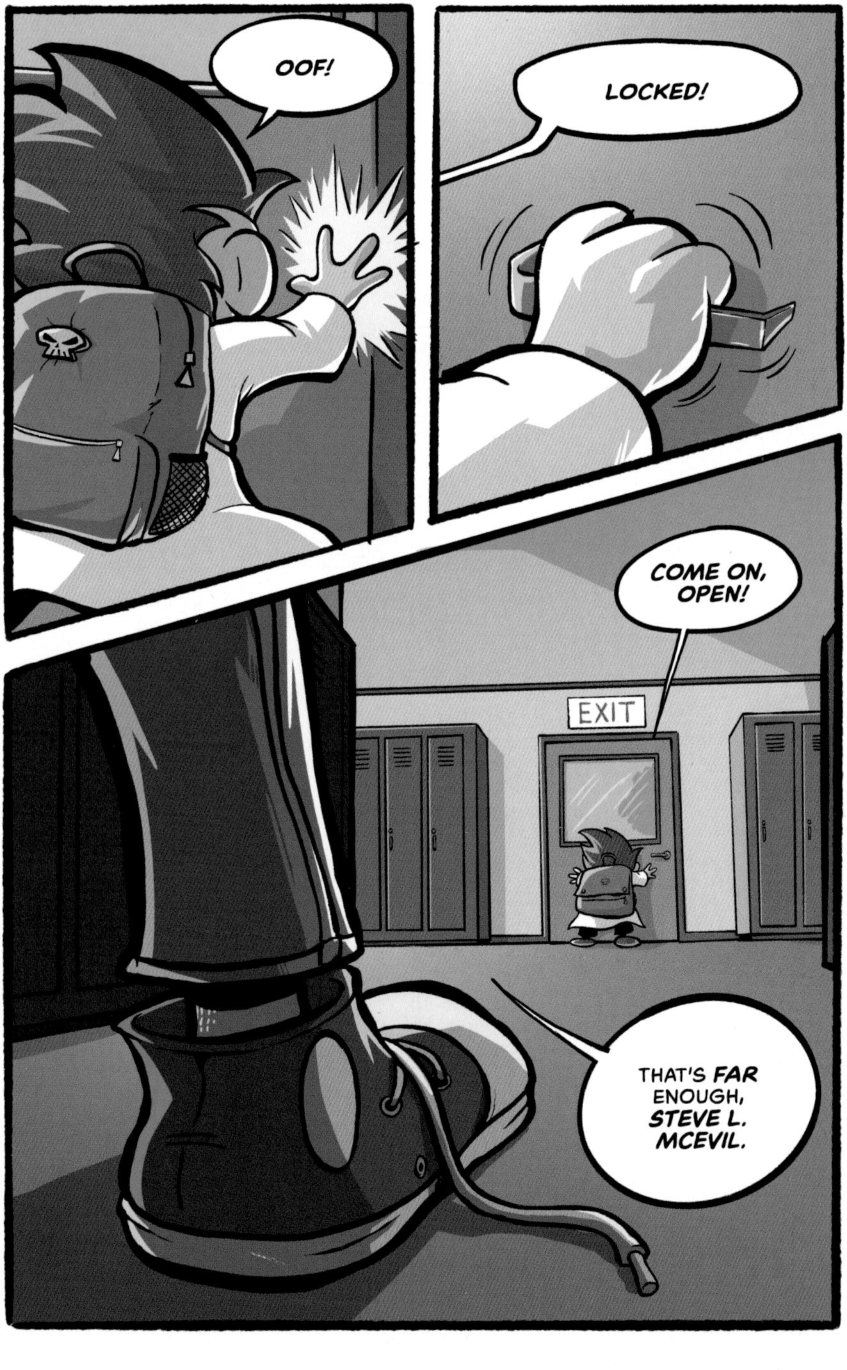
OOF!
LOCKED!
COME ON, OPEN!
EXIT
THAT'S FAR ENOUGH, STEVE L. MCEVIL.

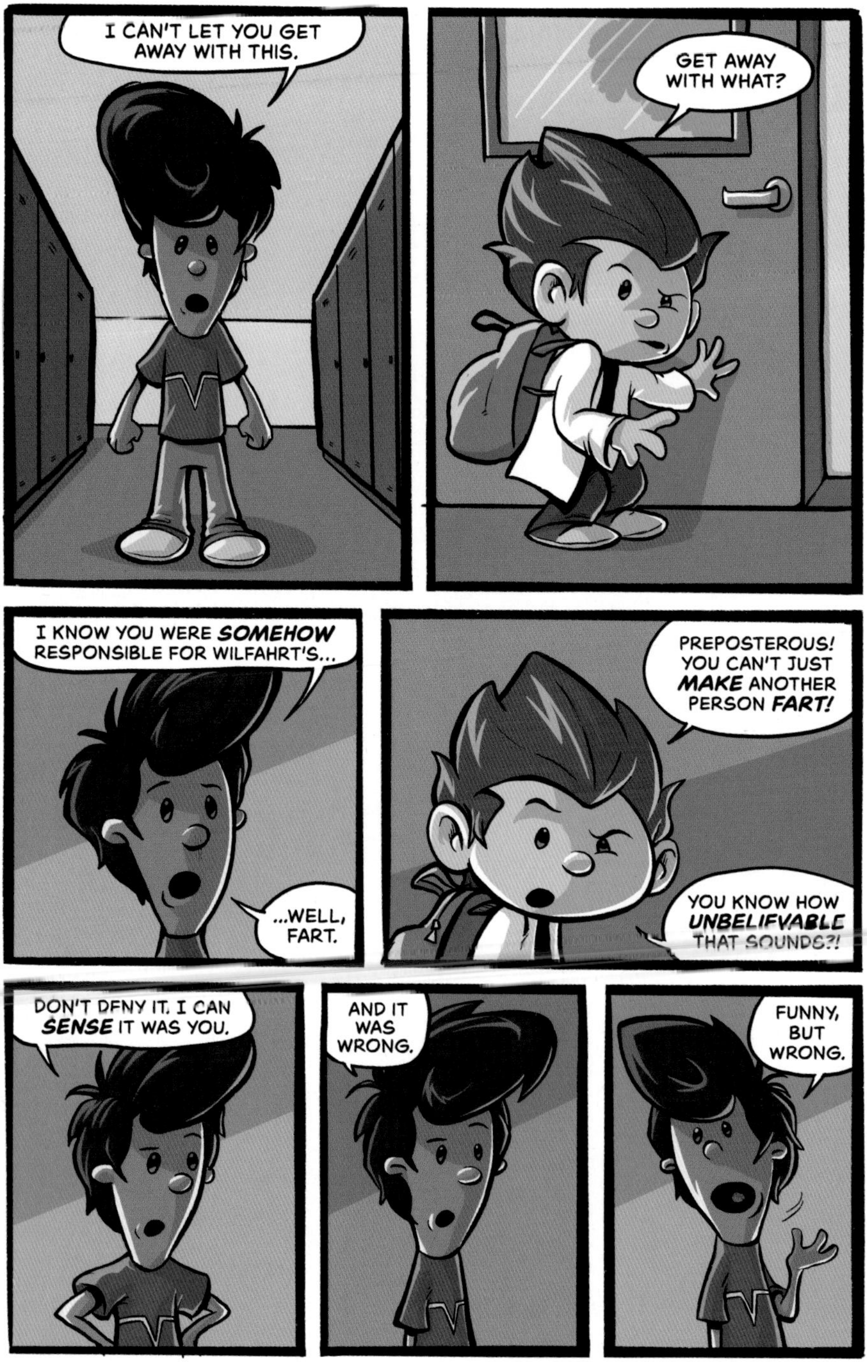
I CAN'T LET YOU GET AWAY WITH THIS.
GET AWAY WITH WHAT?
I KNOW YOU WERE **SOMEHOW** RESPONSIBLE FOR WILFAHRT'S...
...WELL, FART.
PREPOSTEROUS! YOU CAN'T JUST **MAKE** ANOTHER PERSON **FART!**
YOU KNOW HOW **UNBELIEVABLE** THAT SOUNDS?!
DON'T DENY IT. I CAN **SENSE** IT WAS YOU.
AND IT WAS WRONG.
FUNNY, BUT WRONG.

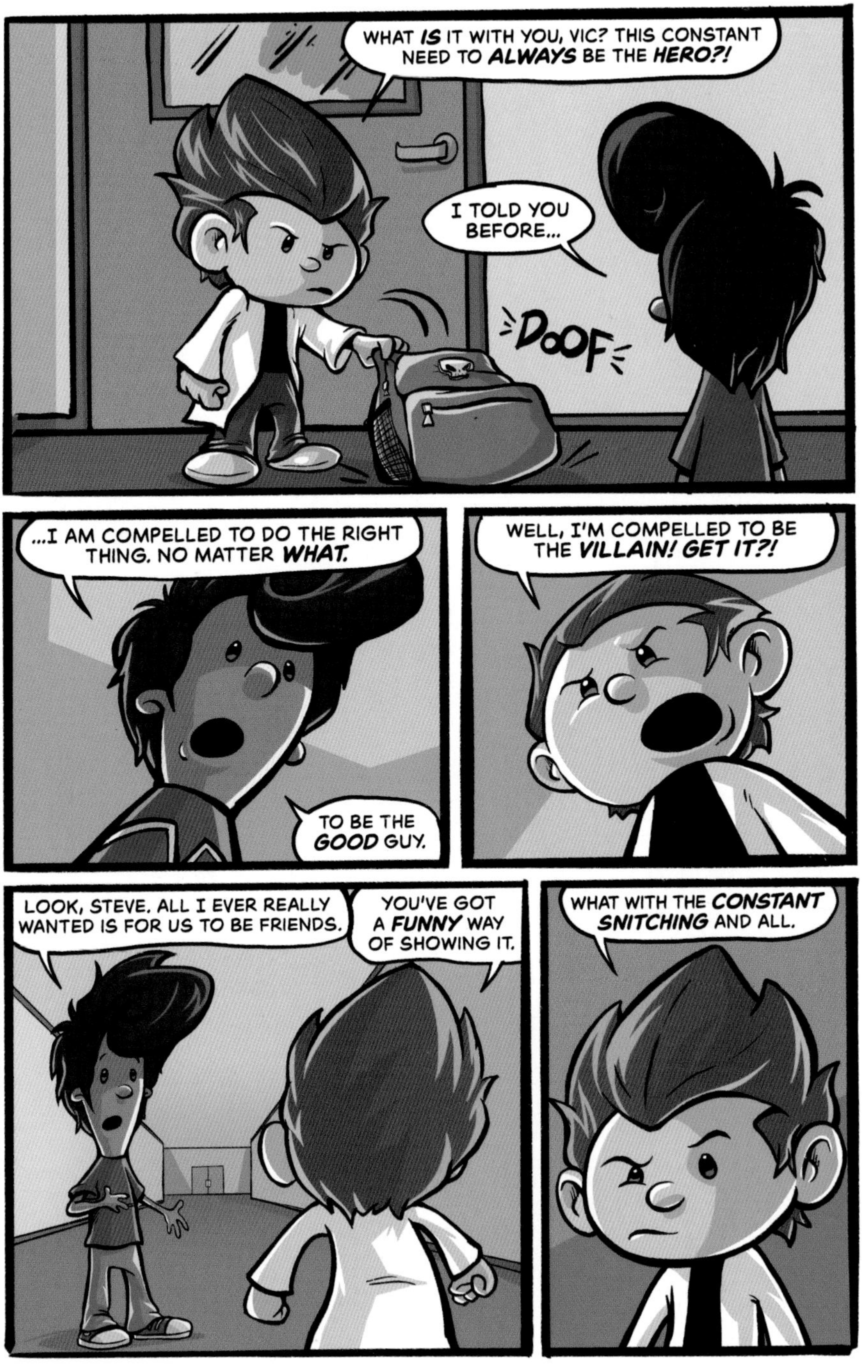
WHAT *IS* IT WITH YOU, VIC? THIS CONSTANT NEED TO *ALWAYS* BE THE *HERO?!*
I TOLD YOU BEFORE...
DOOF
...I AM COMPELLED TO DO THE RIGHT THING. NO MATTER *WHAT.*
TO BE THE *GOOD* GUY.
WELL, I'M COMPELLED TO BE THE *VILLAIN! GET IT?!*
LOOK, STEVE. ALL I EVER REALLY WANTED IS FOR US TO BE FRIENDS.
YOU'VE GOT A *FUNNY* WAY OF SHOWING IT.
WHAT WITH THE *CONSTANT SNITCHING* AND ALL.

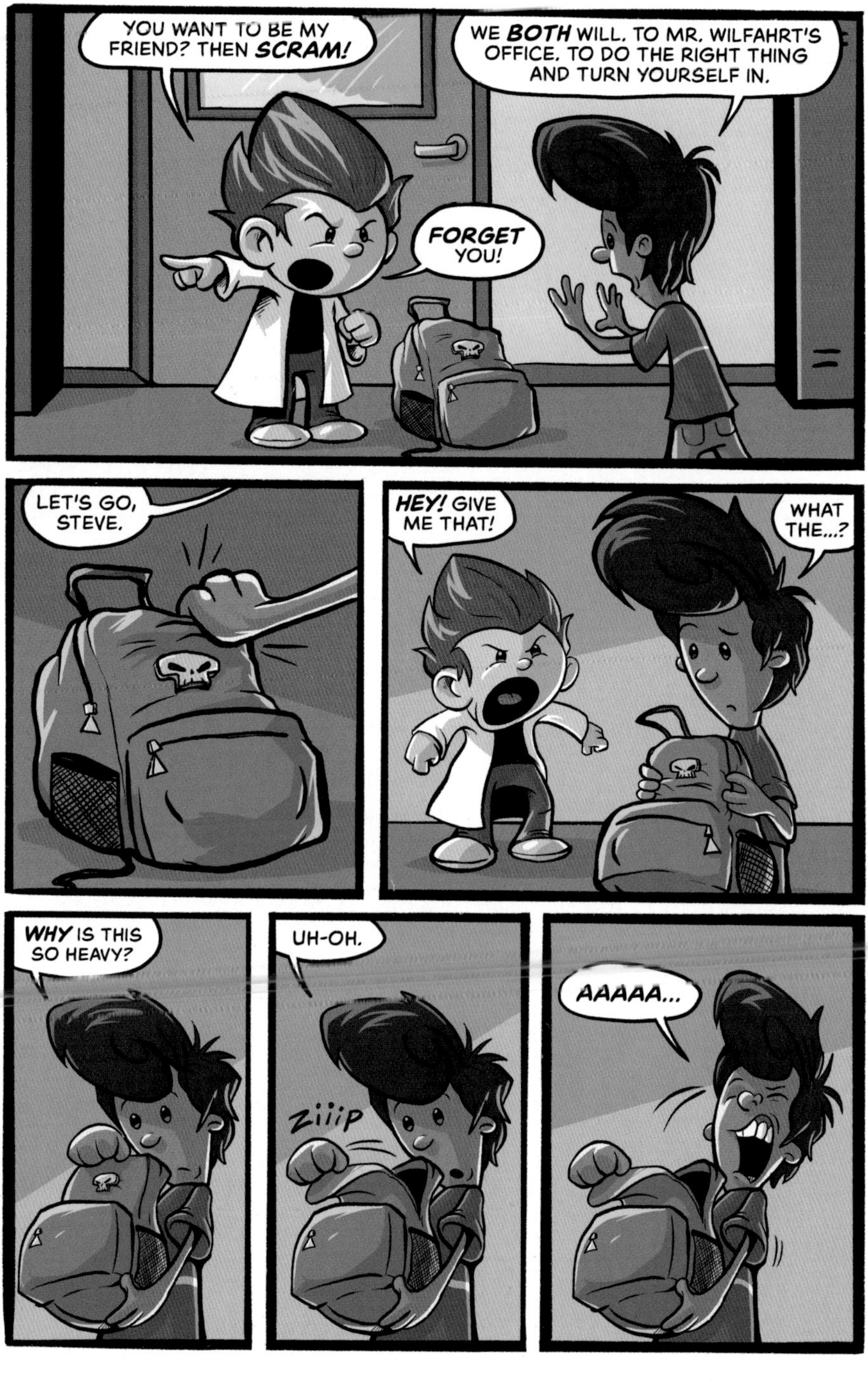
YOU WANT TO BE MY FRIEND? THEN SCRAM!
WE BOTH WILL. TO MR. WILFAHRT'S OFFICE. TO DO THE RIGHT THING AND TURN YOURSELF IN.
FORGET YOU!
LET'S GO, STEVE.
HEY! GIVE ME THAT!
WHAT THE...?
WHY IS THIS SO HEAVY?
UH-OH.
ZIIIP
AAAAA...

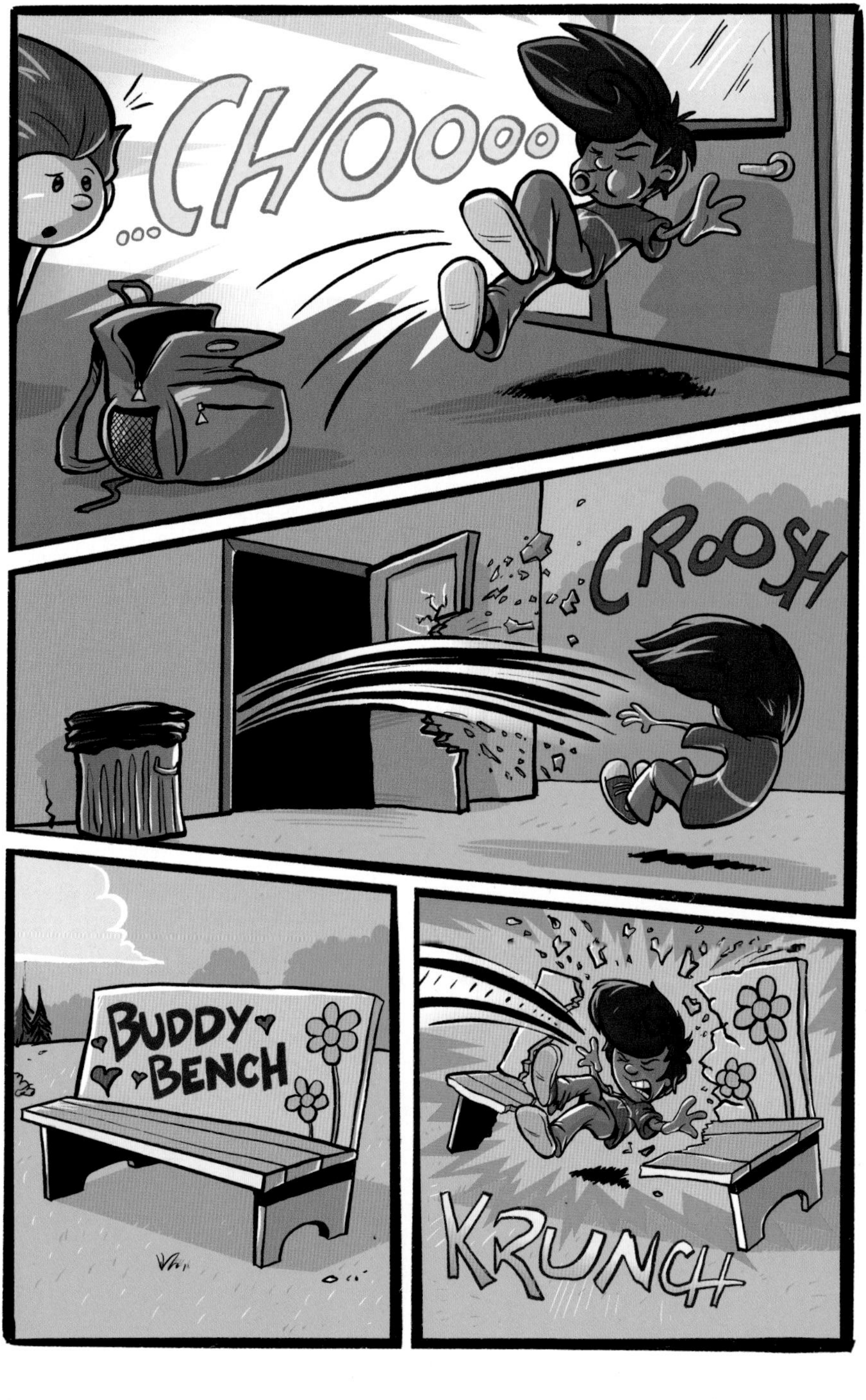
...CHOOOO
CROOSH
BUDDY BENCH
KRUNCH

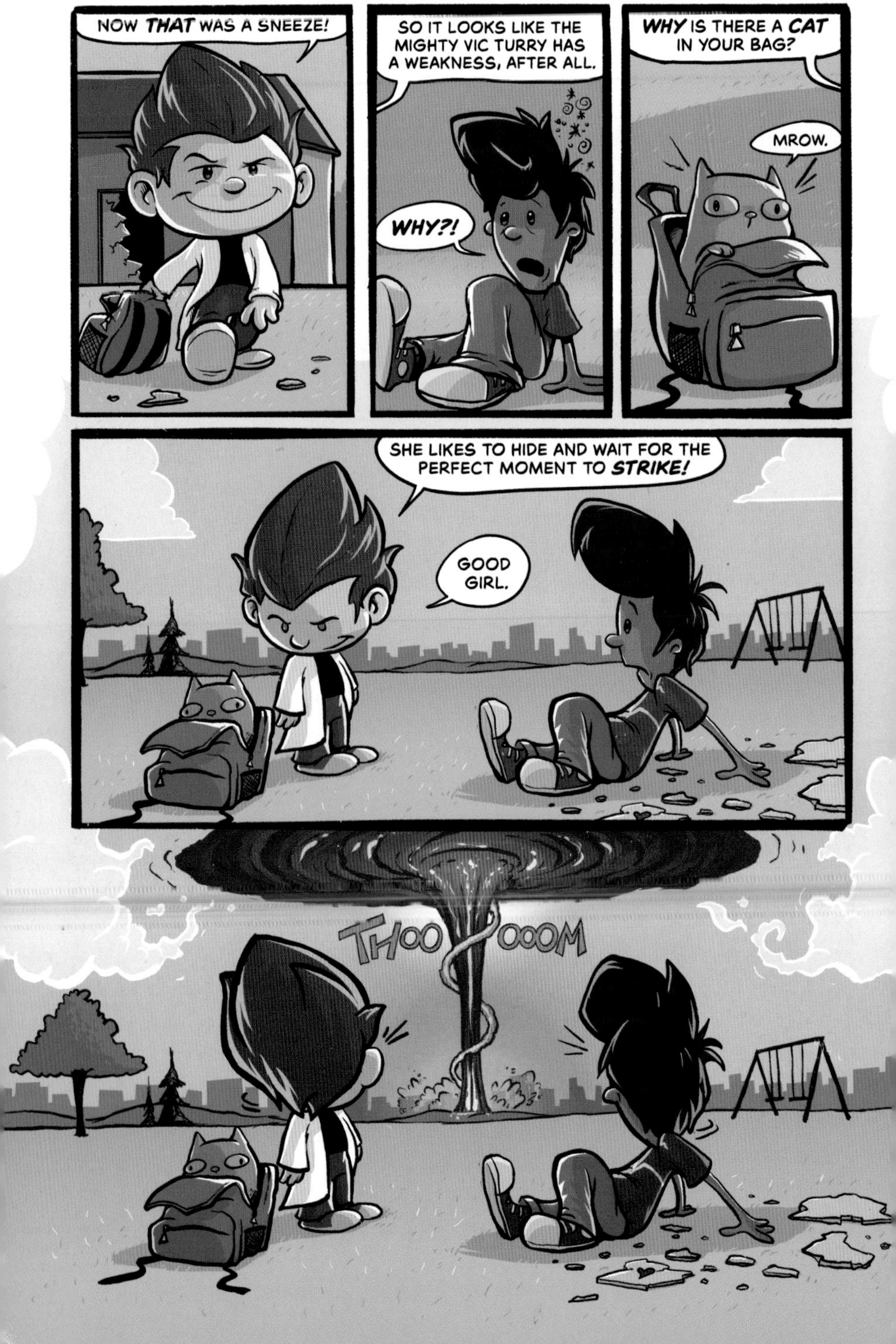
NOW THAT WAS A SNEEZE!
SO IT LOOKS LIKE THE MIGHTY VIC TURRY HAS A WEAKNESS, AFTER ALL.
WHY?!
WHY IS THERE A CAT IN YOUR BAG?
MROW.
SHE LIKES TO HIDE AND WAIT FOR THE PERFECT MOMENT TO STRIKE!
GOOD GIRL.
THOOOOOM

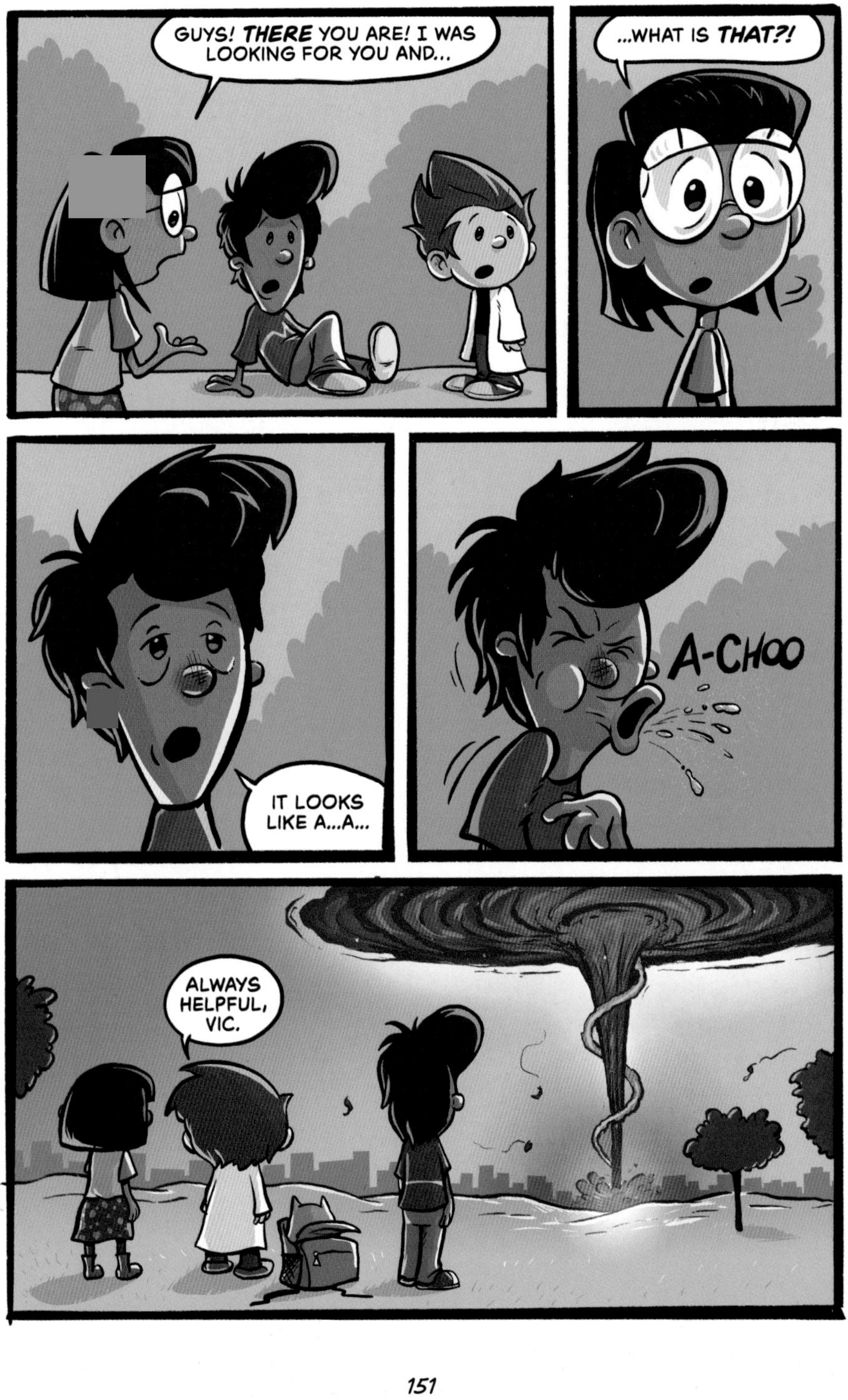
GUYS! THERE YOU ARE! I WAS LOOKING FOR YOU AND...
...WHAT IS THAT?!
IT LOOKS LIKE A...A...
A-CHOO
ALWAYS HELPFUL, VIC.

CHAPTER 16

Come Fly with Me

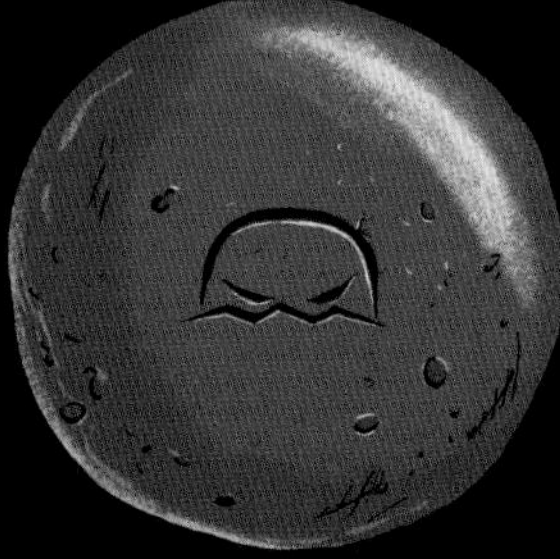

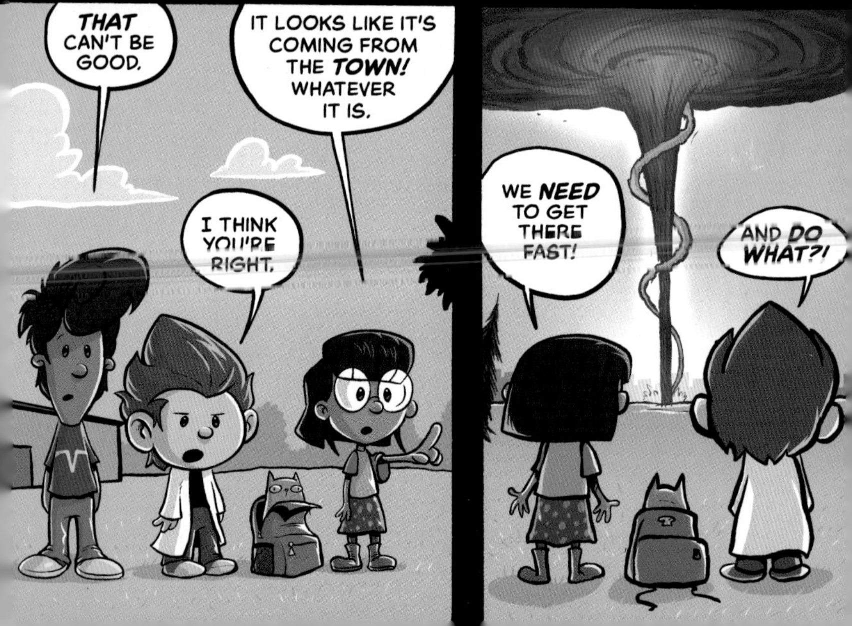

THAT CAN'T BE GOOD.
IT LOOKS LIKE IT'S COMING FROM THE TOWN! WHATEVER IT IS.
I THINK YOU'RE RIGHT.
WE NEED TO GET THERE FAST!
AND DO WHAT?!

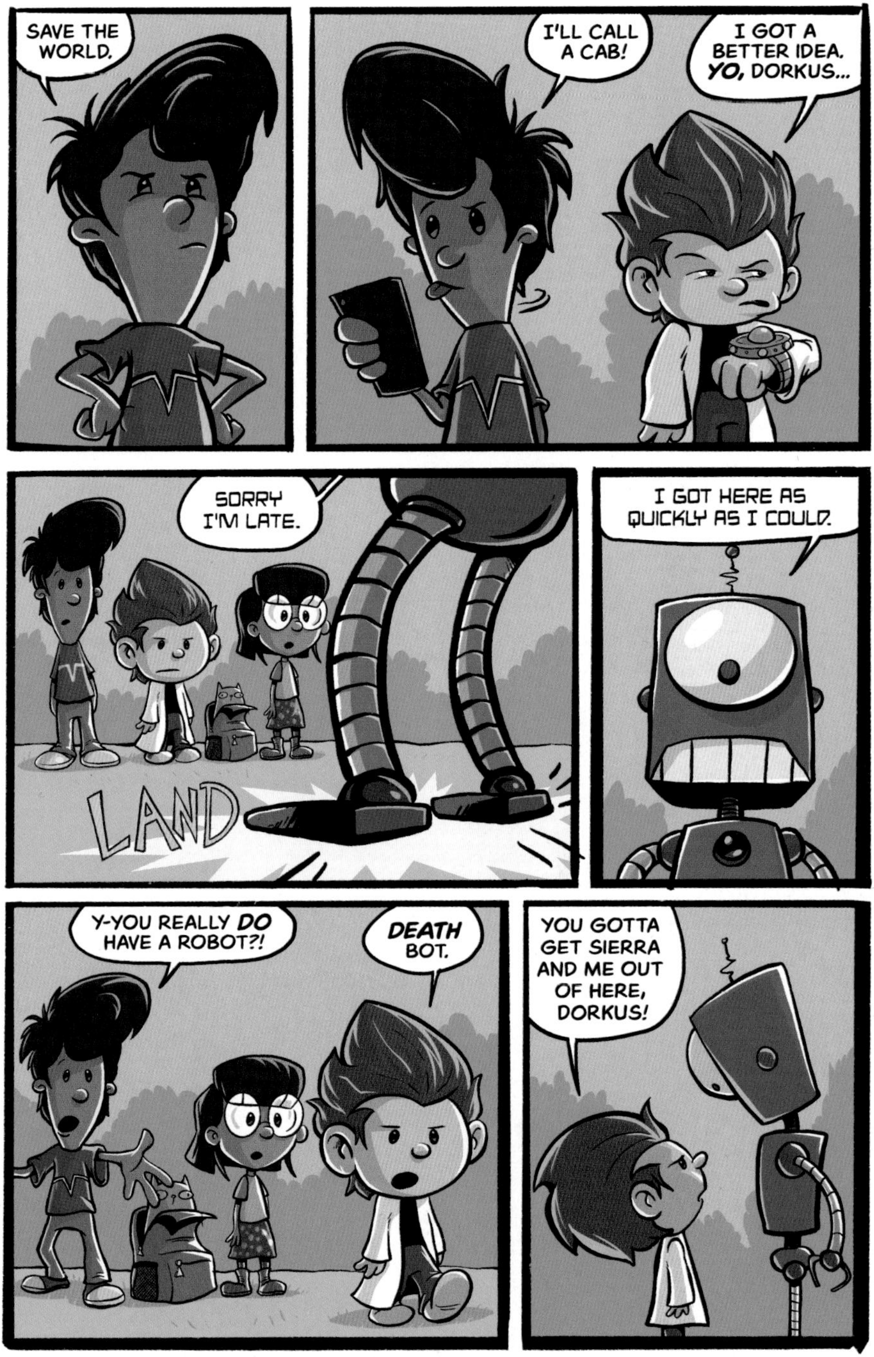
SAVE THE WORLD.
I'LL CALL A CAB!
I GOT A BETTER IDEA. *YO,* DORKUS...
SORRY I'M LATE.
LAND
I GOT HERE AS QUICKLY AS I COULD.
Y-YOU REALLY *DO* HAVE A ROBOT?!
DEATH BOT.
YOU GOTTA GET SIERRA AND ME OUT OF HERE, DORKUS!

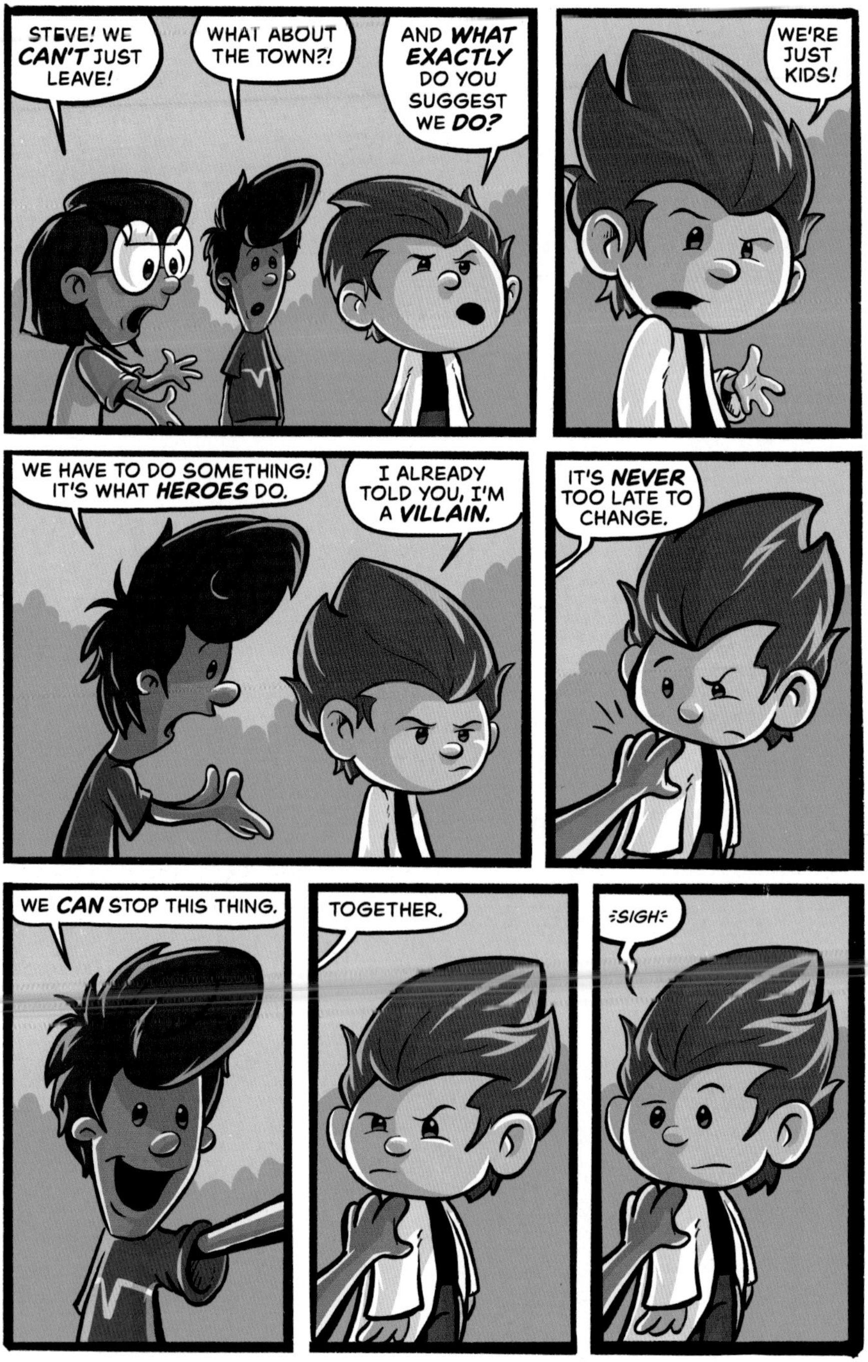
STEVE! WE CAN'T JUST LEAVE!
WHAT ABOUT THE TOWN?!
AND WHAT EXACTLY DO YOU SUGGEST WE DO?
WE'RE JUST KIDS!
WE HAVE TO DO SOMETHING! IT'S WHAT HEROES DO.
I ALREADY TOLD YOU, I'M A VILLAIN.
IT'S NEVER TOO LATE TO CHANGE.
WE CAN STOP THIS THING.
TOGETHER.
SIGH

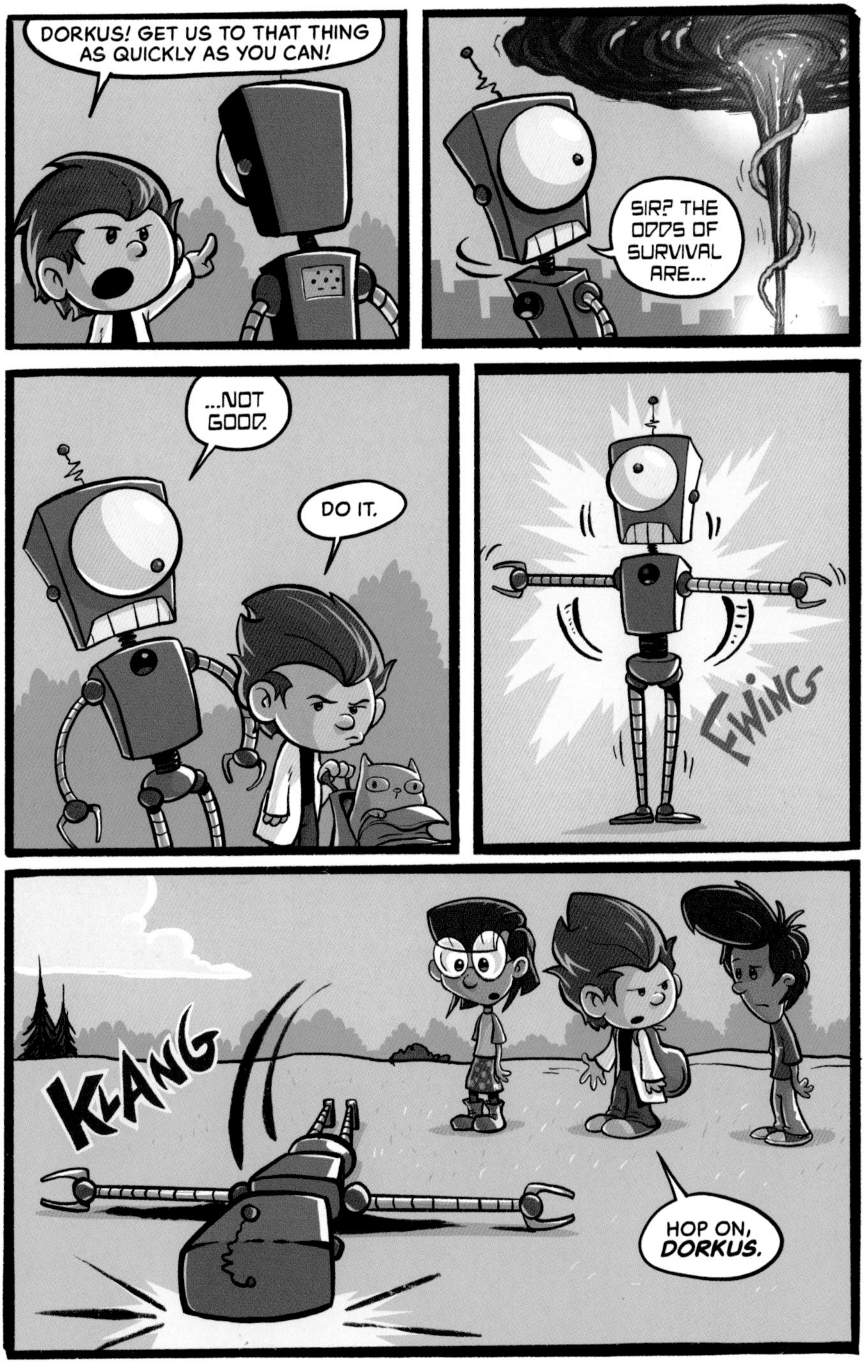
DORKUS! GET US TO THAT THING AS QUICKLY AS YOU CAN!
SIR? THE ODDS OF SURVIVAL ARE...
...NOT GOOD.
DO IT.
FWING
KLANG
HOP ON, **DORKUS.**

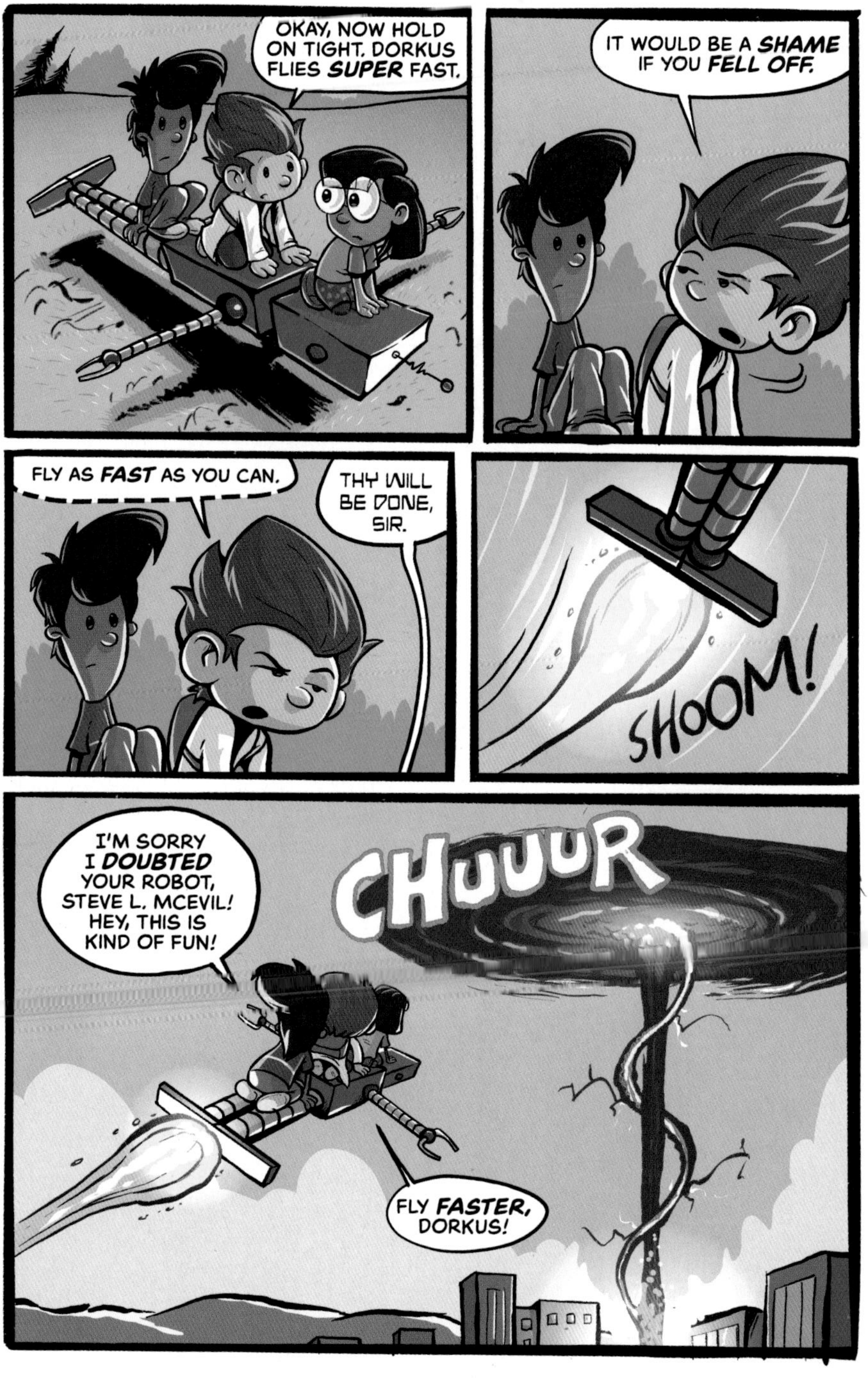
OKAY, NOW HOLD ON TIGHT. DORKUS FLIES SUPER FAST.
IT WOULD BE A SHAME IF YOU FELL OFF.
FLY AS FAST AS YOU CAN.
THY WILL BE DONE, SIR.
SHOOM!
I'M SORRY I DOUBTED YOUR ROBOT, STEVE L. MCEVIL! HEY, THIS IS KIND OF FUN!
CHUUUR
FLY FASTER, DORKUS!

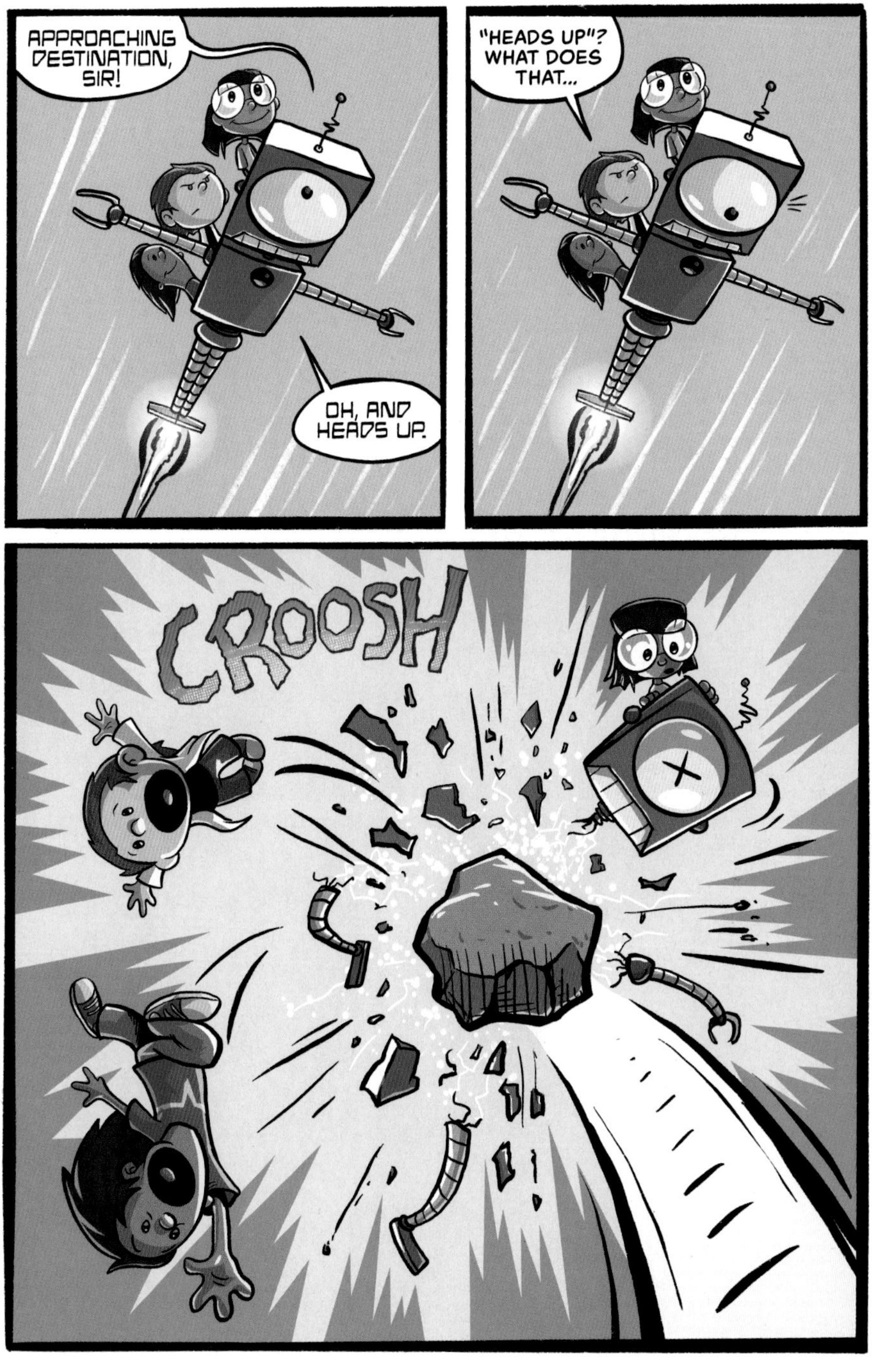
APPROACHING DESTINATION, SIR!
OH, AND HEADS UP.
"HEADS UP"? WHAT DOES THAT...
CROOSH

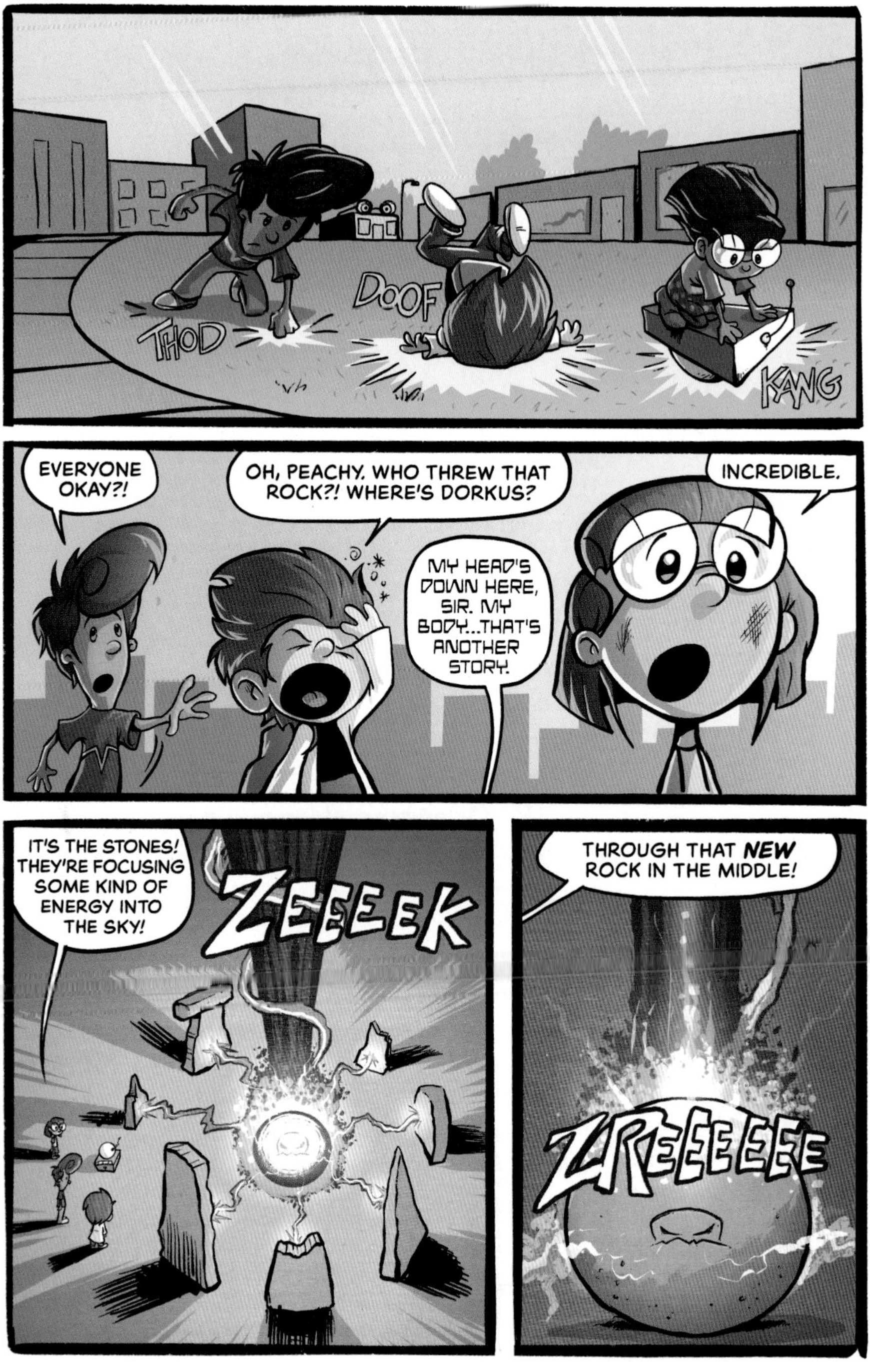
THOD
DOOF
KANG
EVERYONE OKAY?!
OH, PEACHY. WHO THREW THAT ROCK?! WHERE'S DORKUS?
MY HEAD'S DOWN HERE, SIR. MY BODY...THAT'S ANOTHER STORY.
INCREDIBLE.
IT'S THE STONES! THEY'RE FOCUSING SOME KIND OF ENERGY INTO THE SKY!
ZEEEEK
THROUGH THAT **NEW** ROCK IN THE MIDDLE!
ZREEEEEEE

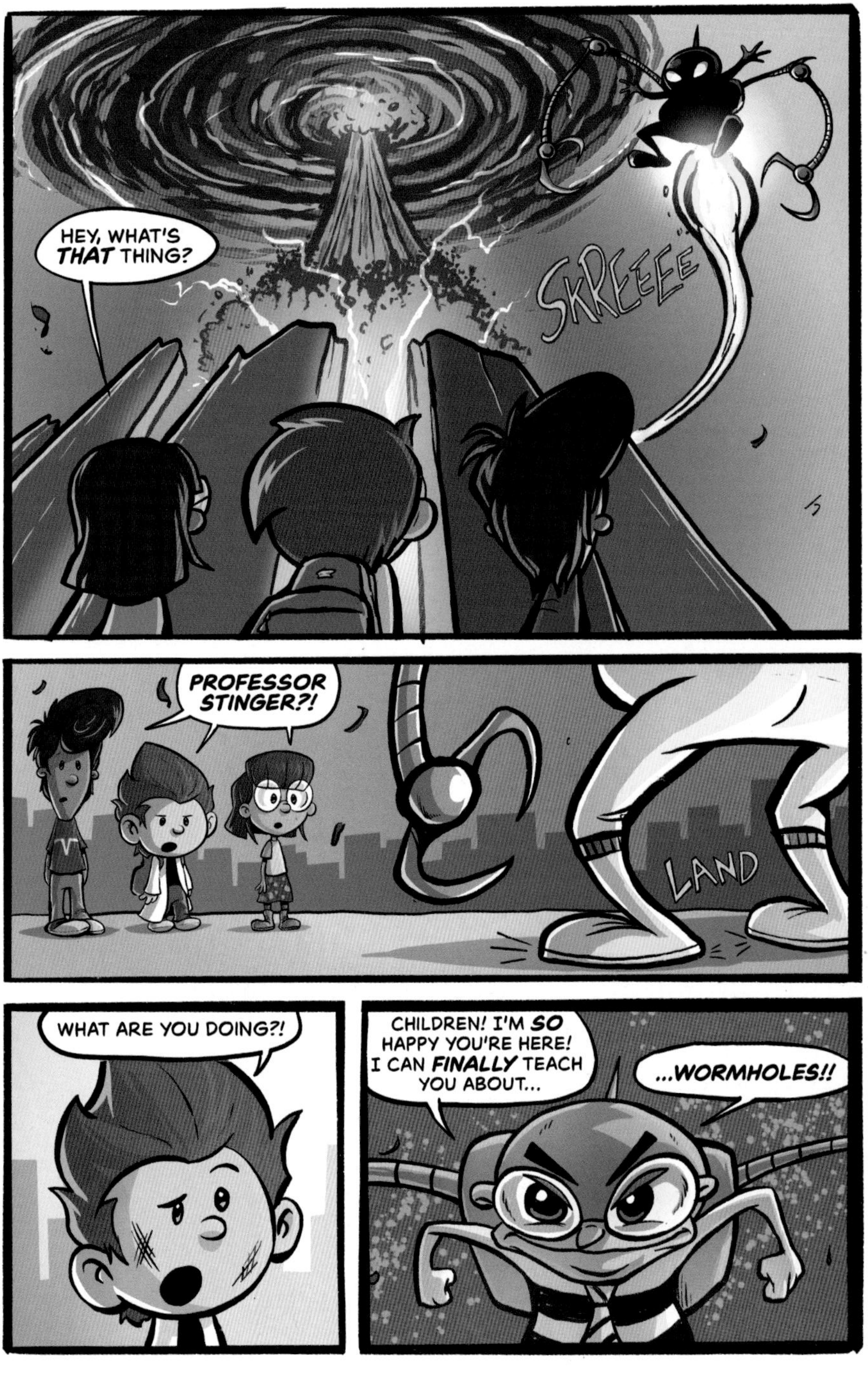
HEY, WHAT'S **THAT** THING?
SKREEEE
PROFESSOR STINGER?!
LAND
WHAT ARE YOU DOING?!
CHILDREN! I'M **SO** HAPPY YOU'RE HERE! I CAN **FINALLY** TEACH YOU ABOUT...
...WORMHOLES!!

CHAPTER 17
Stung

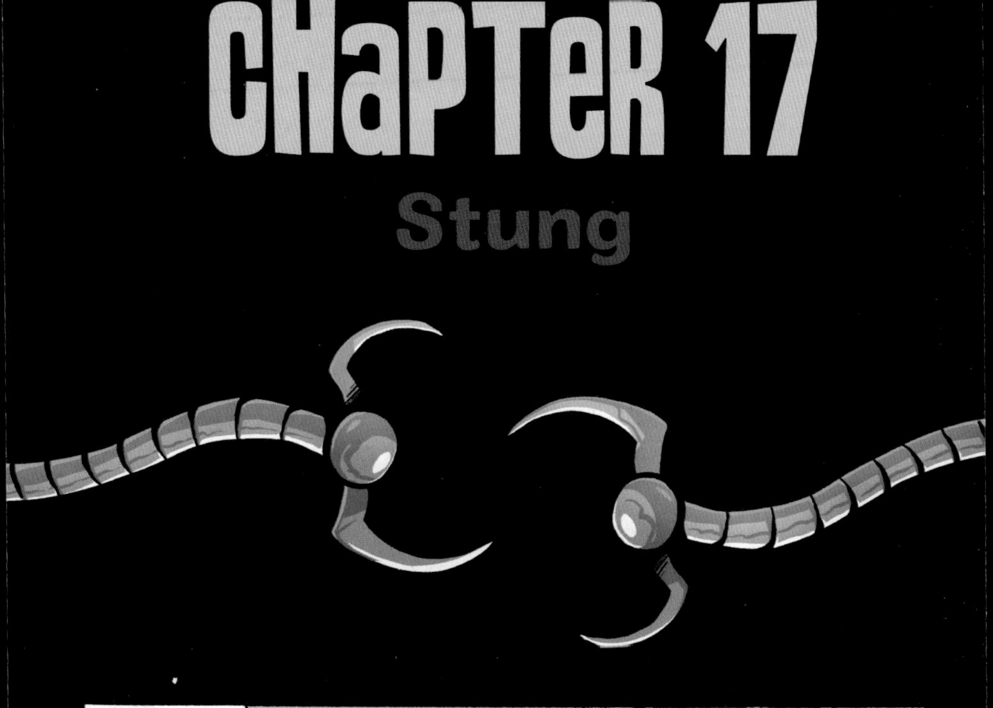

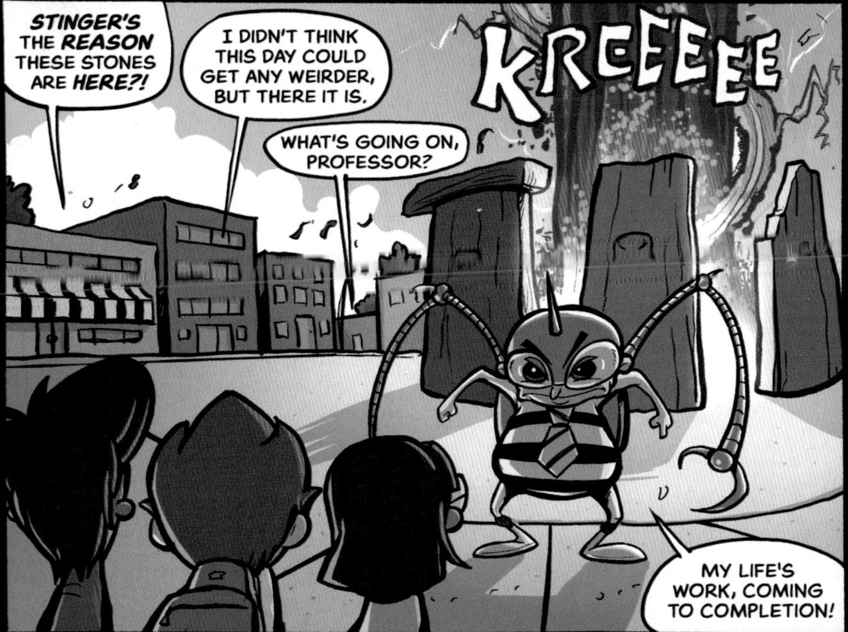

STINGER'S THE REASON THESE STONES ARE HERE?!
I DIDN'T THINK THIS DAY COULD GET ANY WEIRDER, BUT THERE IT IS.
WHAT'S GOING ON, PROFESSOR?
KREEEEE
MY LIFE'S WORK, COMING TO COMPLETION!

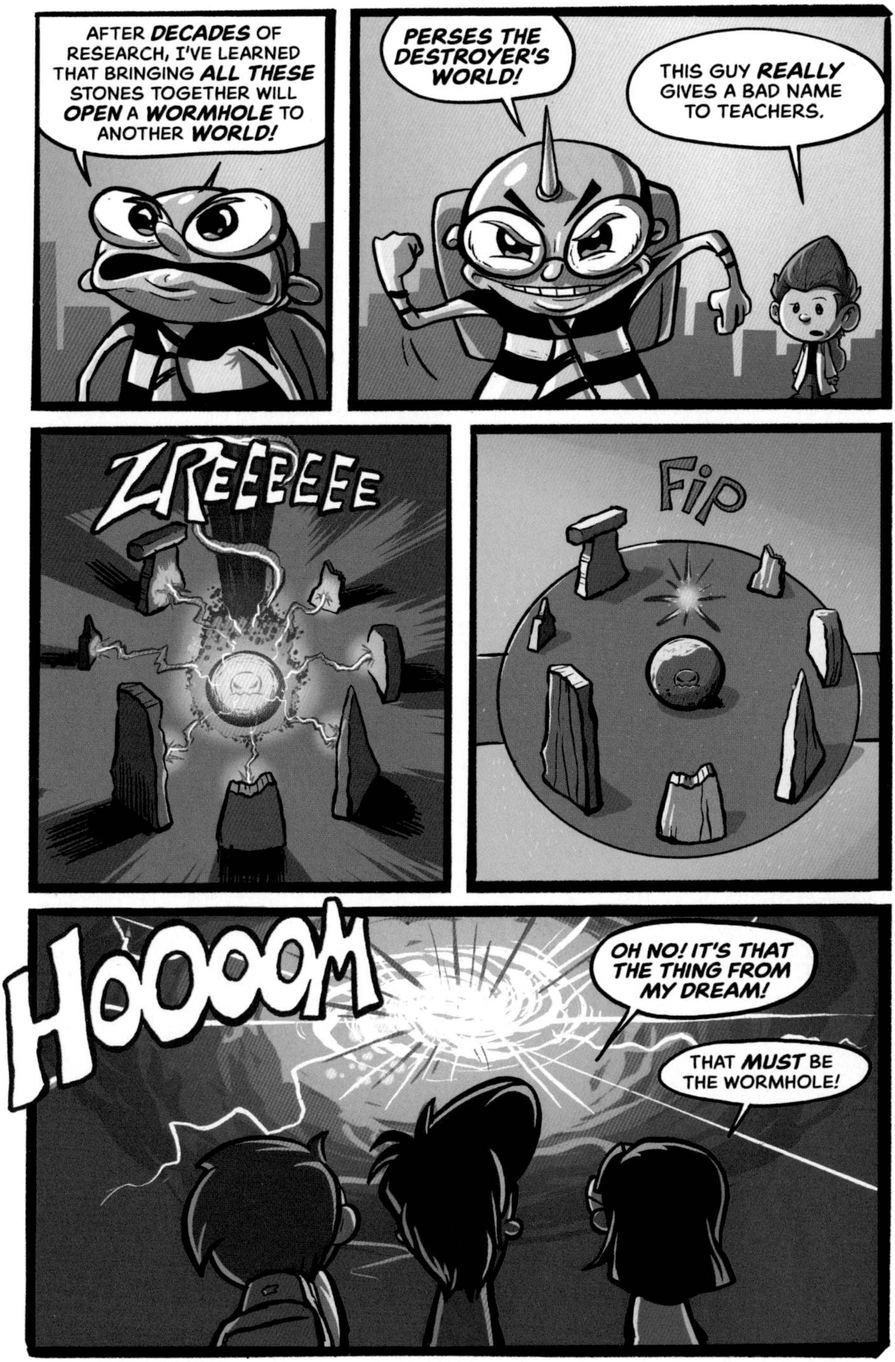
AFTER DECADES OF RESEARCH, I'VE LEARNED THAT BRINGING ALL THESE STONES TOGETHER WILL OPEN A WORMHOLE TO ANOTHER WORLD!
PERSES THE DESTROYER'S WORLD!
THIS GUY REALLY GIVES A BAD NAME TO TEACHERS.
ZREEEEEE
FIP
HOOOOM
OH NO! IT'S THAT THE THING FROM MY DREAM!
THAT MUST BE THE WORMHOLE!

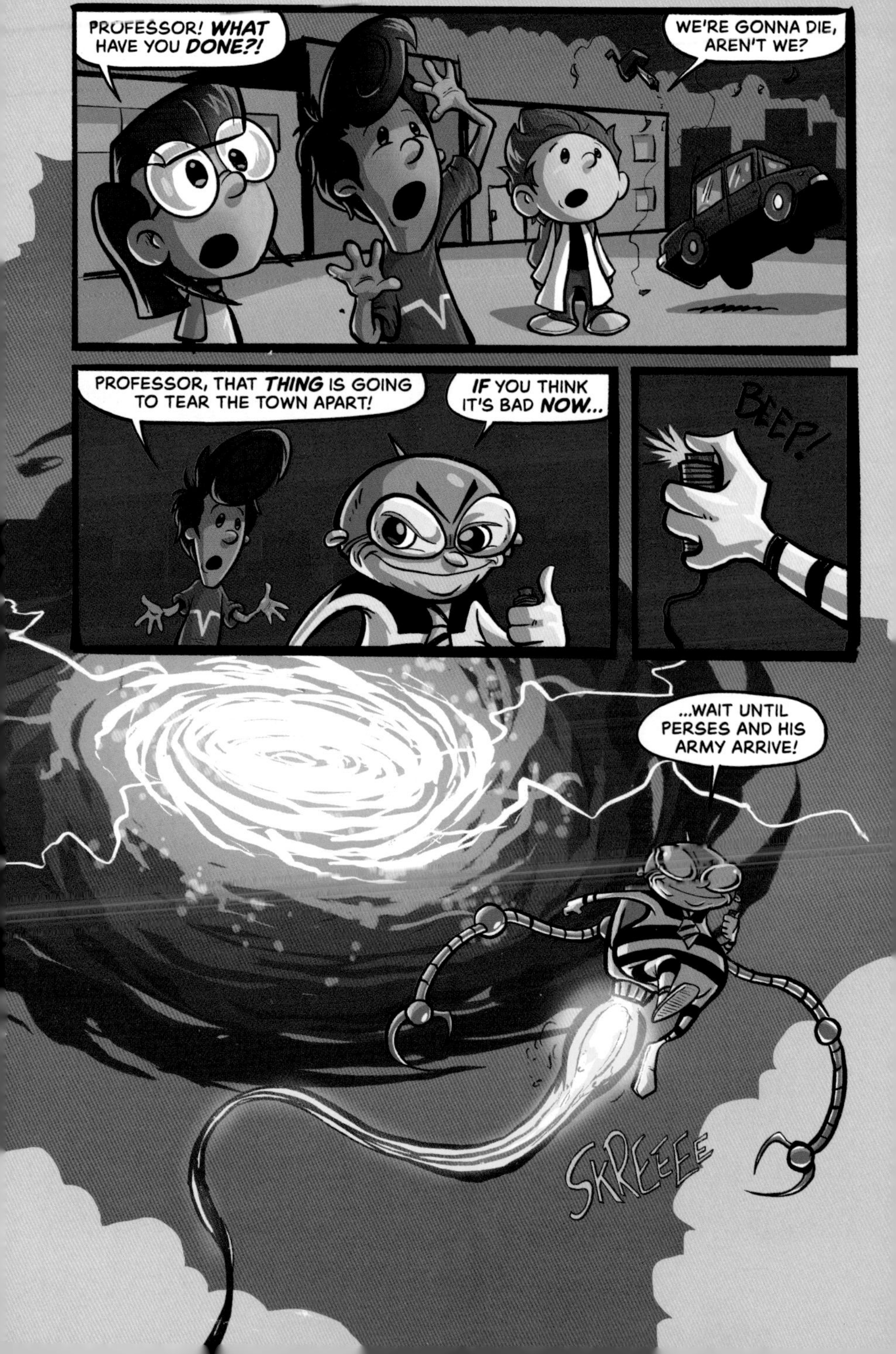
PROFESSOR! WHAT HAVE YOU DONE?!
WE'RE GONNA DIE, AREN'T WE?
PROFESSOR, THAT THING IS GOING TO TEAR THE TOWN APART!
IF YOU THINK IT'S BAD NOW...
BEEP!
...WAIT UNTIL PERSES AND HIS ARMY ARRIVE!
SKREEEEE

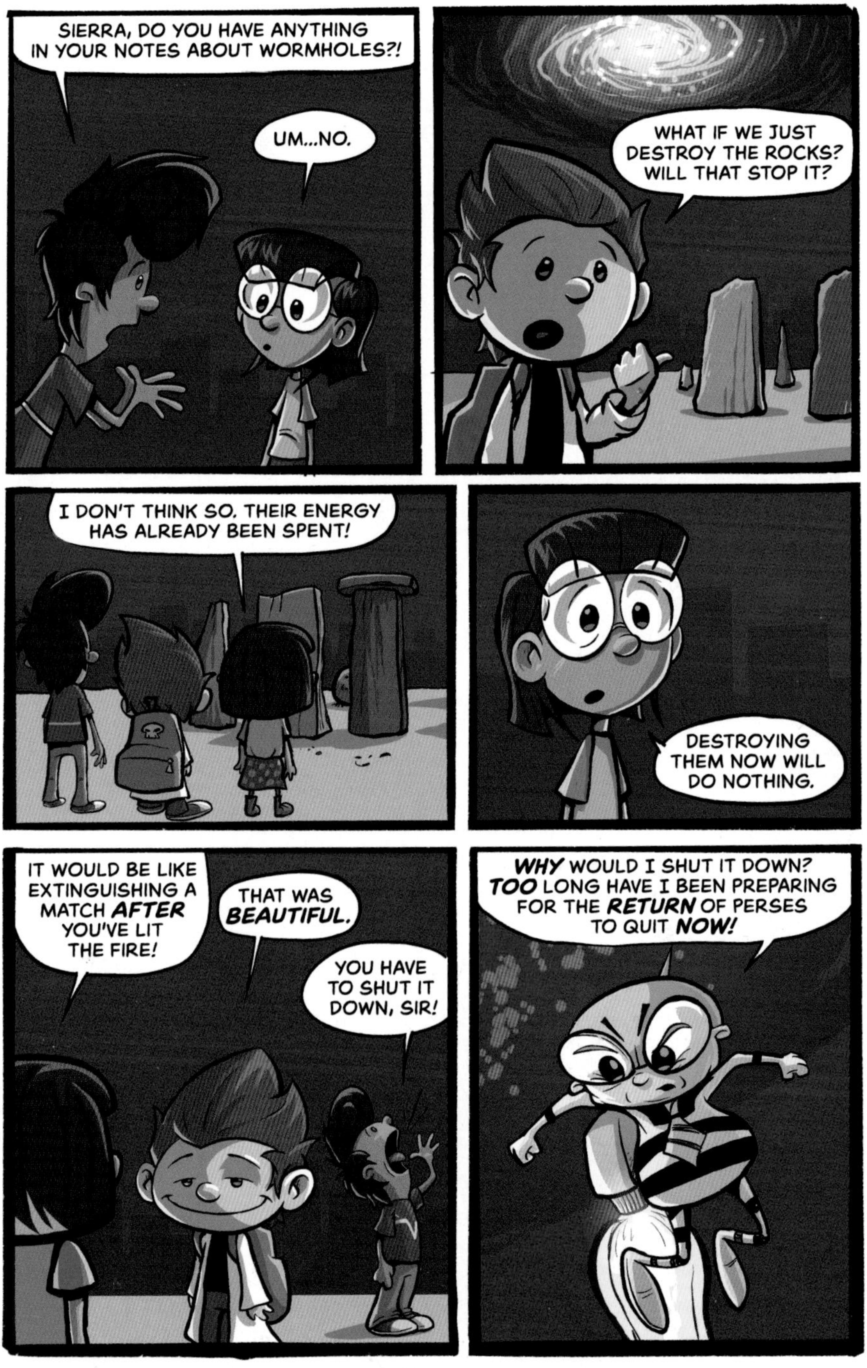
SIERRA, DO YOU HAVE ANYTHING IN YOUR NOTES ABOUT WORMHOLES?!
UM...NO.
WHAT IF WE JUST DESTROY THE ROCKS? WILL THAT STOP IT?
I DON'T THINK SO. THEIR ENERGY HAS ALREADY BEEN SPENT!
DESTROYING THEM NOW WILL DO NOTHING.
IT WOULD BE LIKE EXTINGUISHING A MATCH ***AFTER*** YOU'VE LIT THE FIRE!
THAT WAS ***BEAUTIFUL.***
YOU HAVE TO SHUT IT DOWN, SIR!
WHY WOULD I SHUT IT DOWN? ***TOO*** LONG HAVE I BEEN PREPARING FOR THE ***RETURN*** OF PERSES TO QUIT ***NOW!***

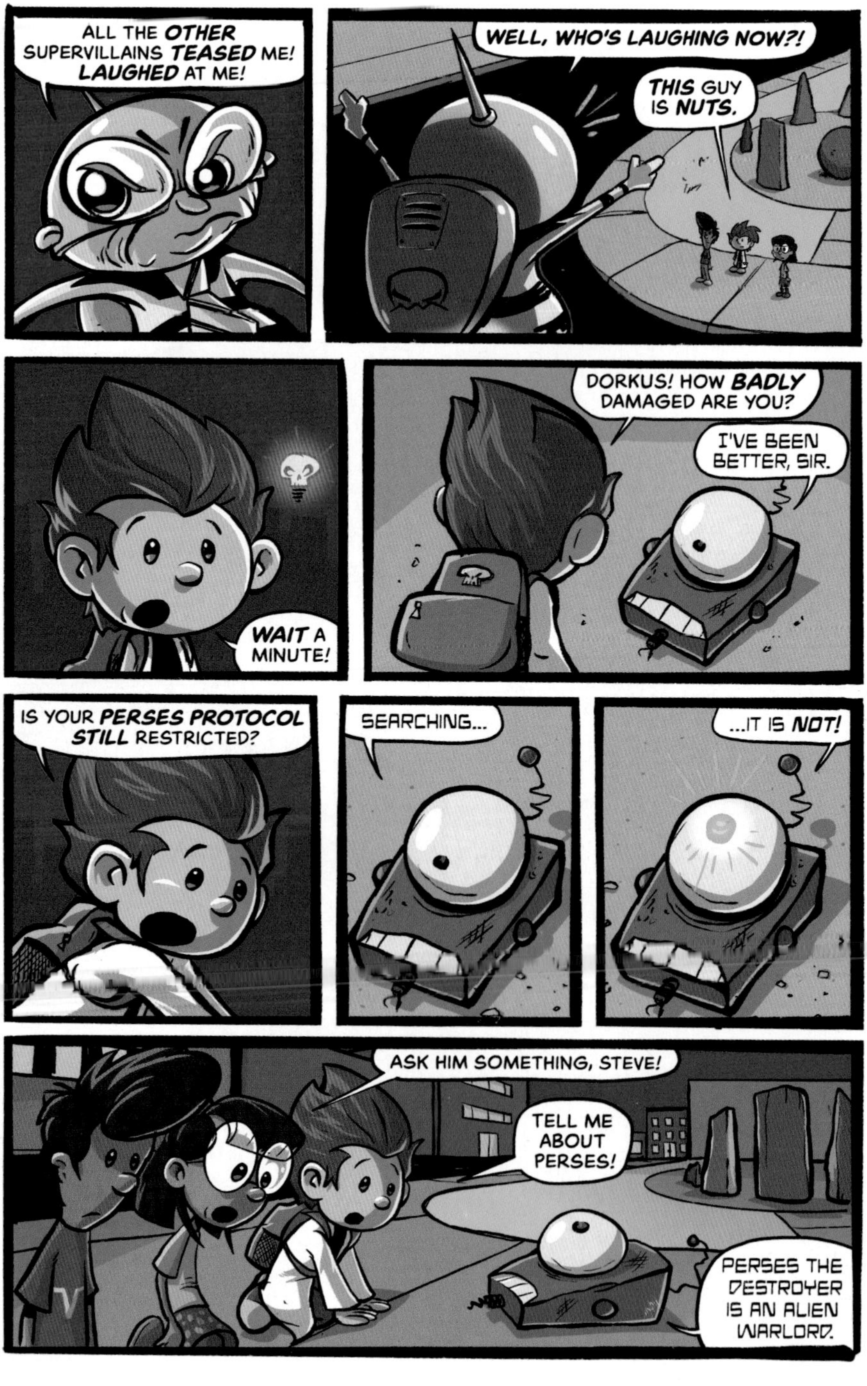
ALL THE OTHER SUPERVILLAINS TEASED ME! LAUGHED AT ME!
WELL, WHO'S LAUGHING NOW?!
THIS GUY IS NUTS.
WAIT A MINUTE!
DORKUS! HOW BADLY DAMAGED ARE YOU?
I'VE BEEN BETTER, SIR.
IS YOUR PERSES PROTOCOL STILL RESTRICTED?
SEARCHING...
...IT IS NOT!
ASK HIM SOMETHING, STEVE!
TELL ME ABOUT PERSES!
PERSES THE DESTROYER IS AN ALIEN WARLORD.

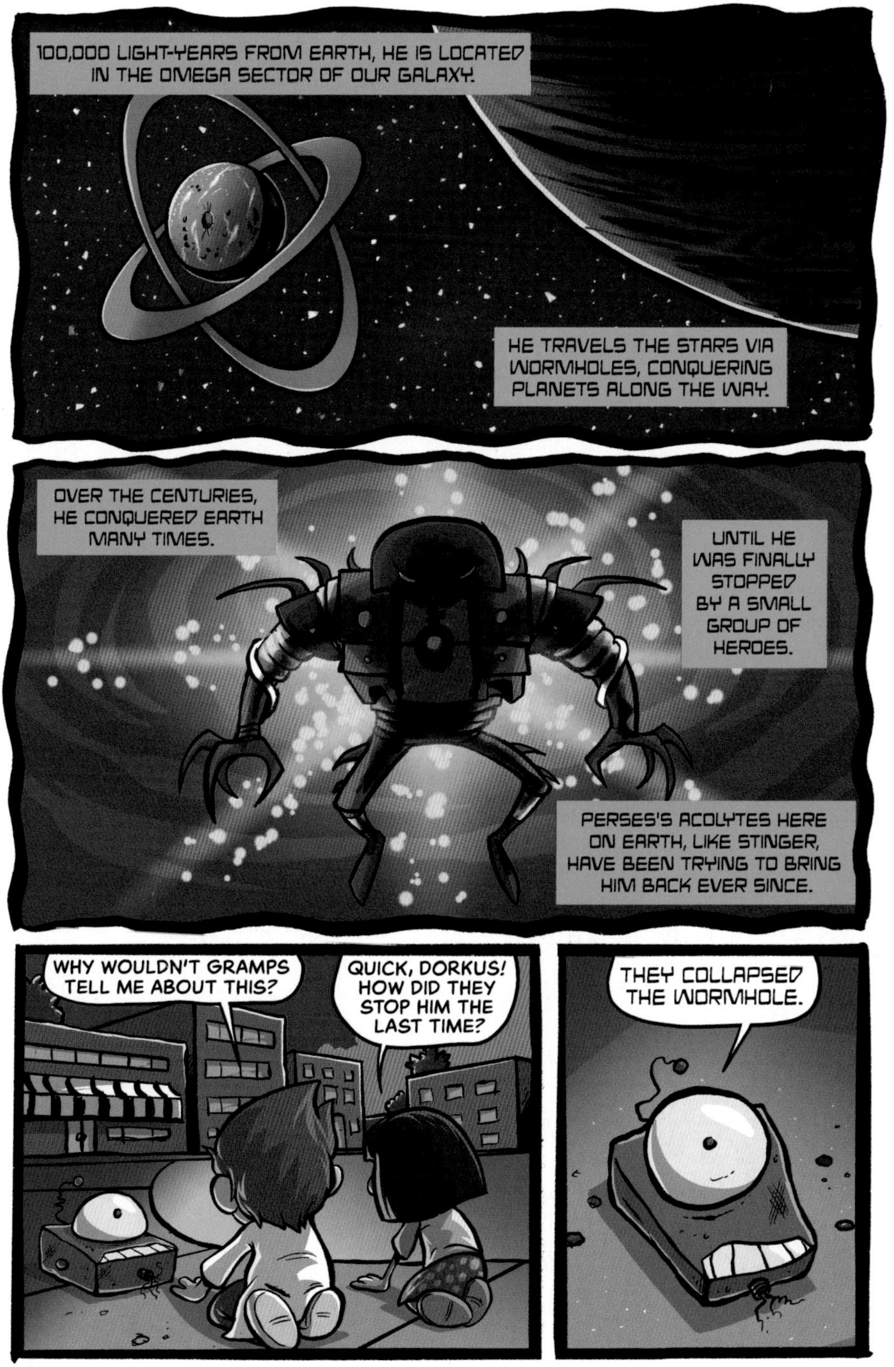
100,000 LIGHT-YEARS FROM EARTH, HE IS LOCATED IN THE OMEGA SECTOR OF OUR GALAXY.
HE TRAVELS THE STARS VIA WORMHOLES, CONQUERING PLANETS ALONG THE WAY.
OVER THE CENTURIES, HE CONQUERED EARTH MANY TIMES.
UNTIL HE WAS FINALLY STOPPED BY A SMALL GROUP OF HEROES.
PERSES'S ACOLYTES HERE ON EARTH, LIKE STINGER, HAVE BEEN TRYING TO BRING HIM BACK EVER SINCE.
WHY WOULDN'T GRAMPS TELL ME ABOUT THIS?
QUICK, DORKUS! HOW DID THEY STOP HIM THE LAST TIME?
THEY COLLAPSED THE WORMHOLE.

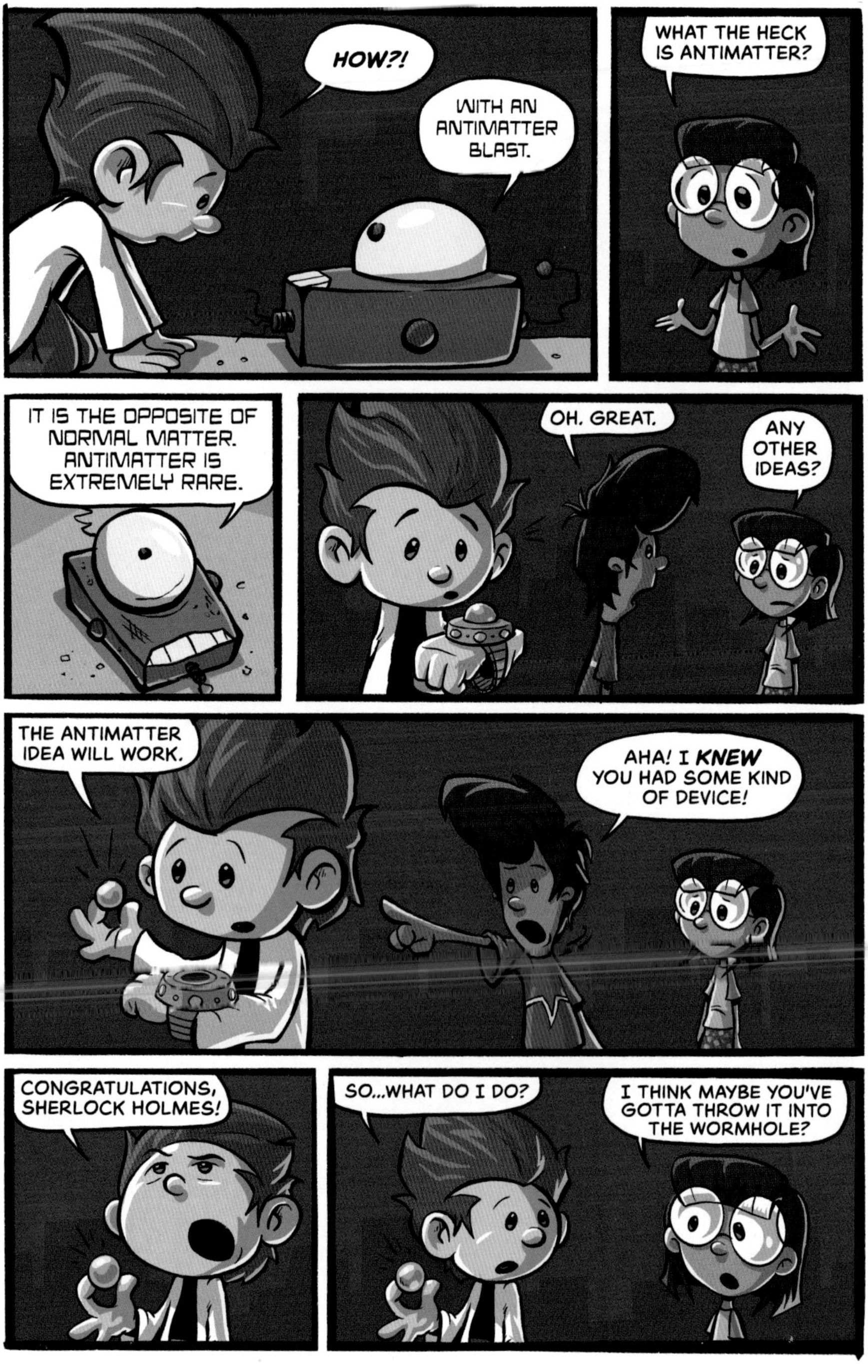
HOW?!
WITH AN ANTIMATTER BLAST.
WHAT THE HECK IS ANTIMATTER?
IT IS THE OPPOSITE OF NORMAL MATTER. ANTIMATTER IS EXTREMELY RARE.
OH. GREAT.
ANY OTHER IDEAS?
THE ANTIMATTER IDEA WILL WORK.
AHA! I KNEW YOU HAD SOME KIND OF DEVICE!
CONGRATULATIONS, SHERLOCK HOLMES!
SO...WHAT DO I DO?
I THINK MAYBE YOU'VE GOTTA THROW IT INTO THE WORMHOLE?

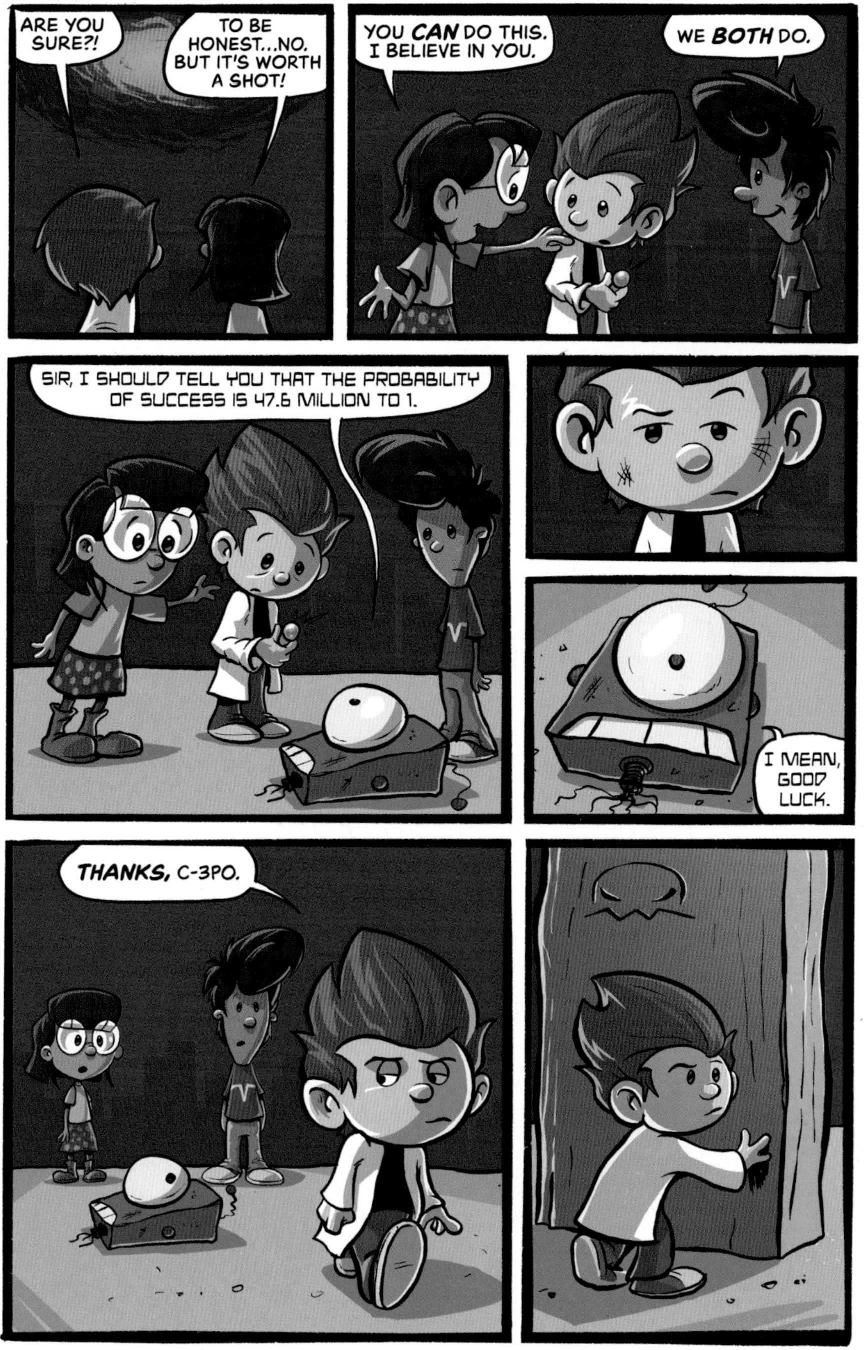
ARE YOU SURE?!
TO BE HONEST...NO. BUT IT'S WORTH A SHOT!
YOU **CAN** DO THIS. I BELIEVE IN YOU.
WE **BOTH** DO.
SIR, I SHOULD TELL YOU THAT THE PROBABILITY OF SUCCESS IS 47.6 MILLION TO 1.
I MEAN, GOOD LUCK.
THANKS, C-3PO.

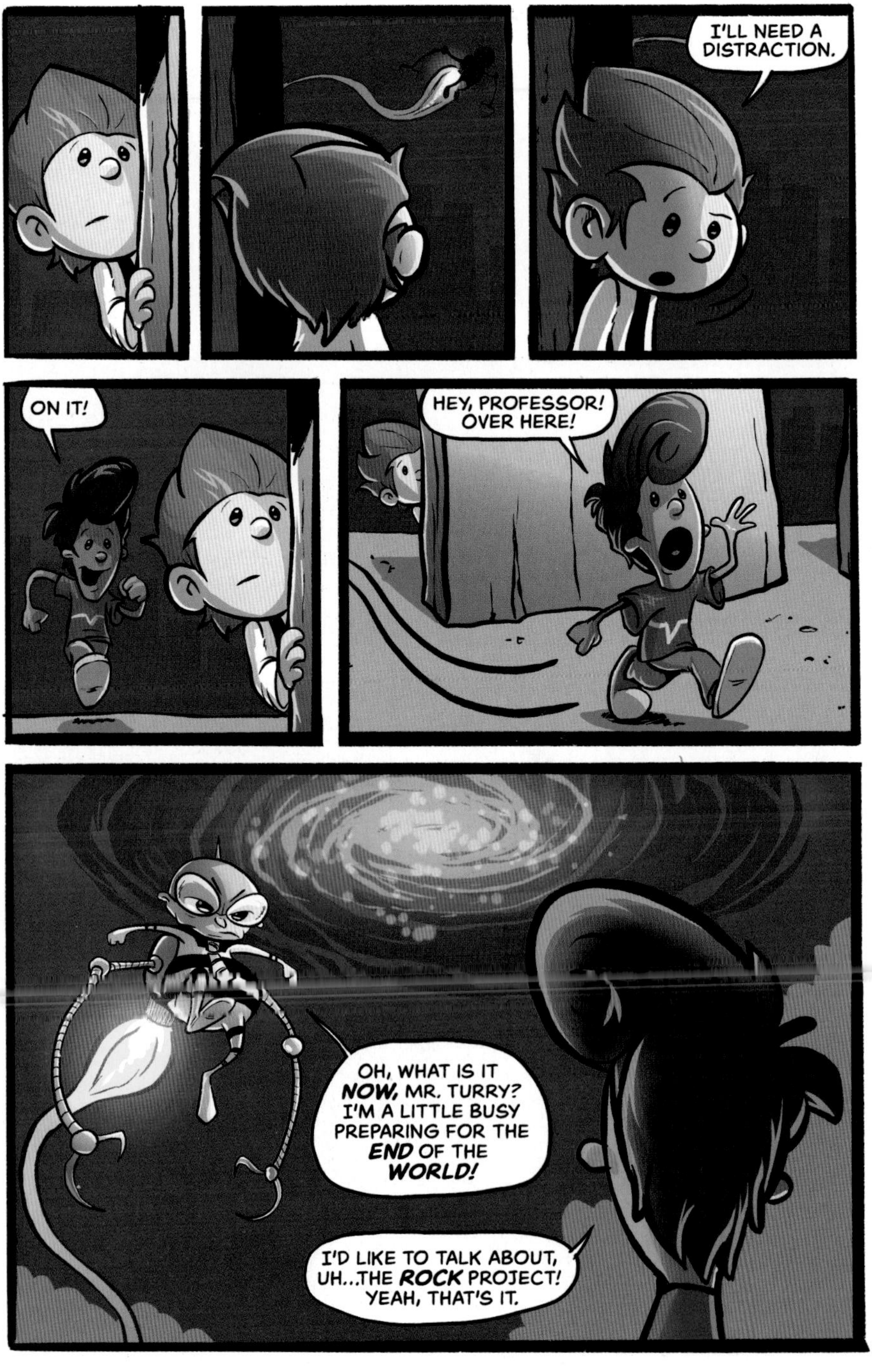
I'LL NEED A DISTRACTION.
ON IT!
HEY, PROFESSOR! OVER HERE!
OH, WHAT IS IT NOW, MR. TURRY? I'M A LITTLE BUSY PREPARING FOR THE END OF THE WORLD!
I'D LIKE TO TALK ABOUT, UH...THE ROCK PROJECT! YEAH, THAT'S IT.

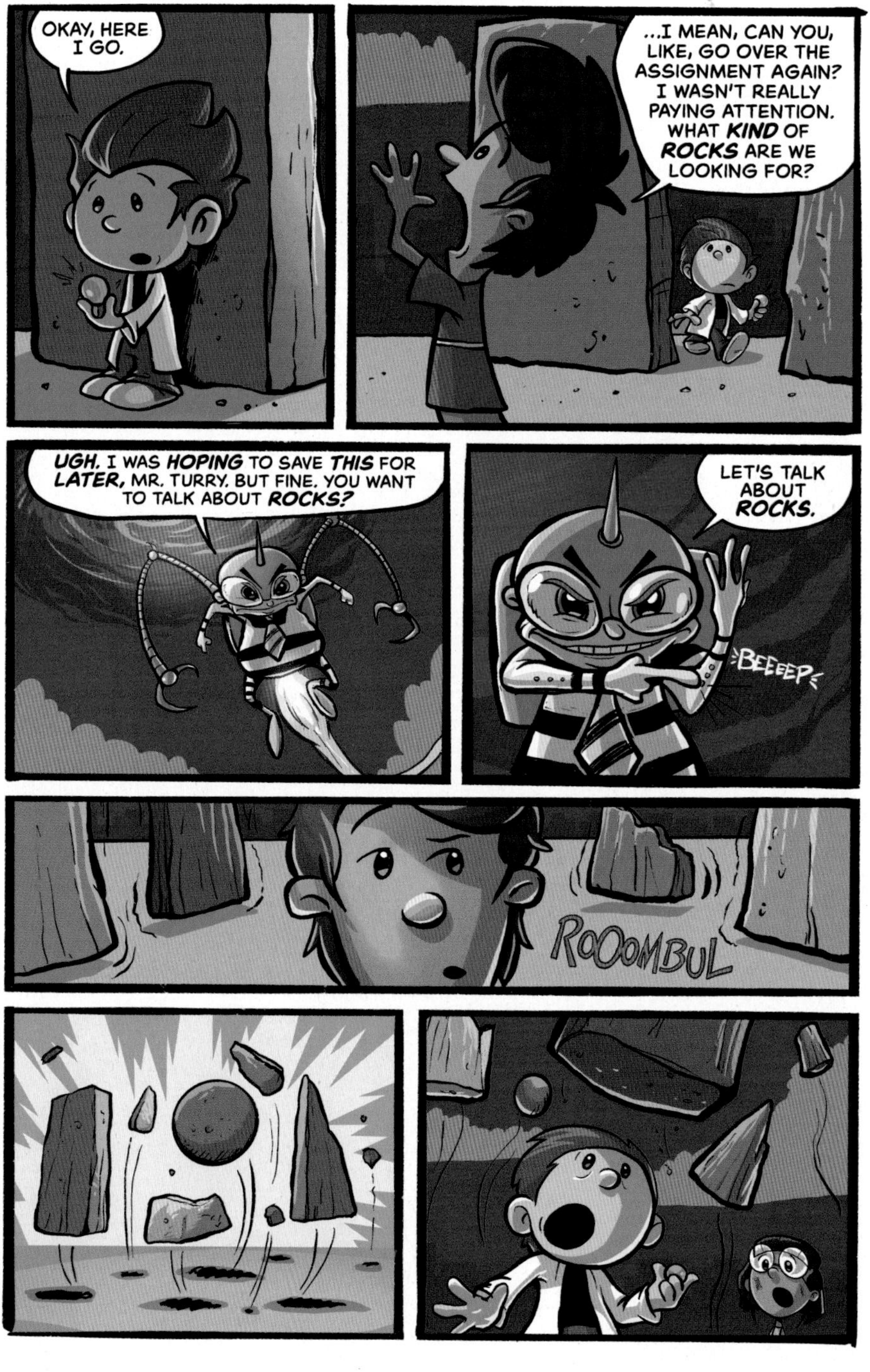
OKAY, HERE I GO.
...I MEAN, CAN YOU, LIKE, GO OVER THE ASSIGNMENT AGAIN? I WASN'T REALLY PAYING ATTENTION. WHAT KIND OF ROCKS ARE WE LOOKING FOR?
UGH. I WAS HOPING TO SAVE THIS FOR LATER, MR. TURRY. BUT FINE. YOU WANT TO TALK ABOUT ROCKS?
LET'S TALK ABOUT ROCKS.
BEEEEP
ROOOMBUL

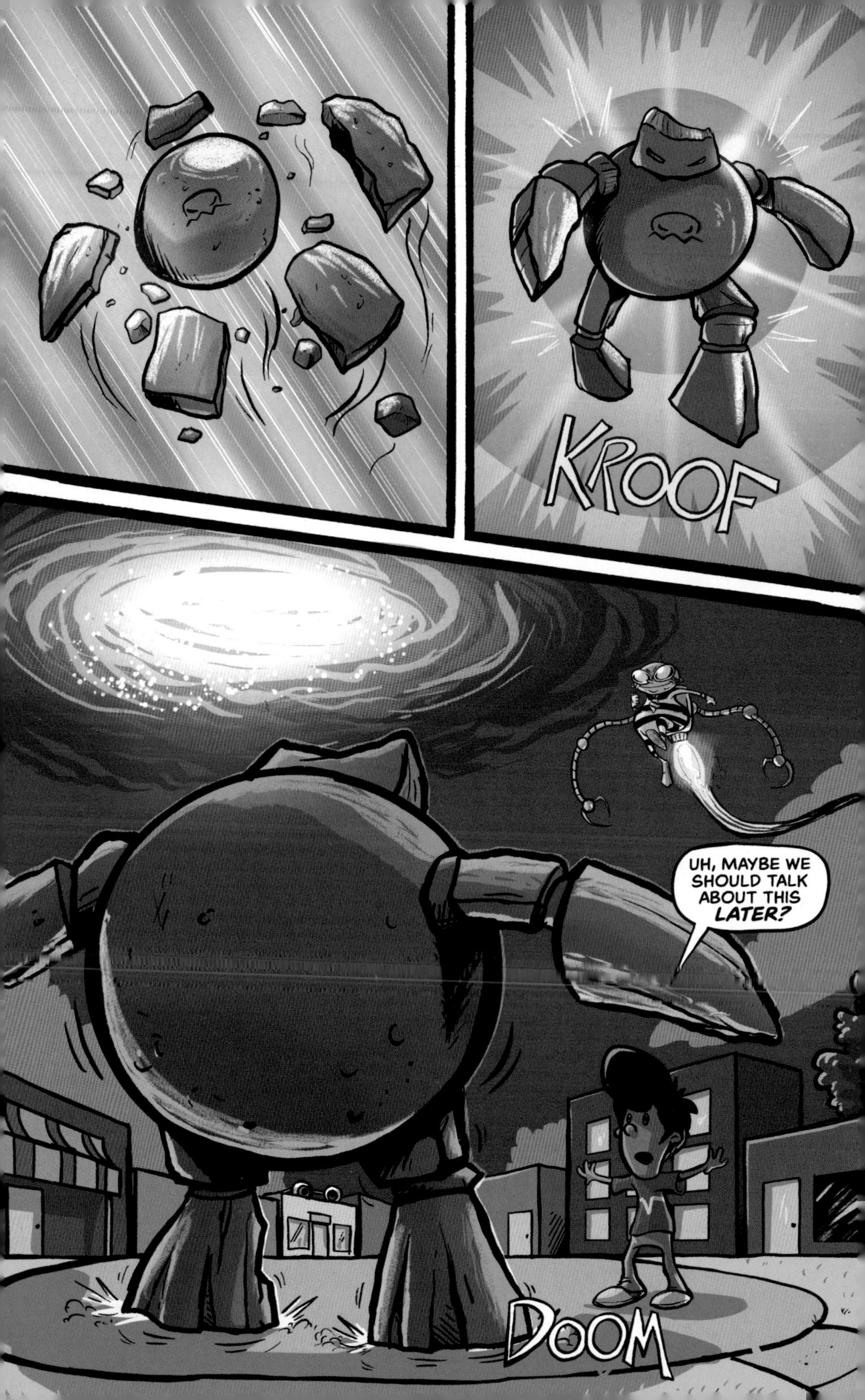
KROOF
UH, MAYBE WE SHOULD TALK ABOUT THIS *LATER?*
DOOM

CHAPTER 18

We Will Rock You

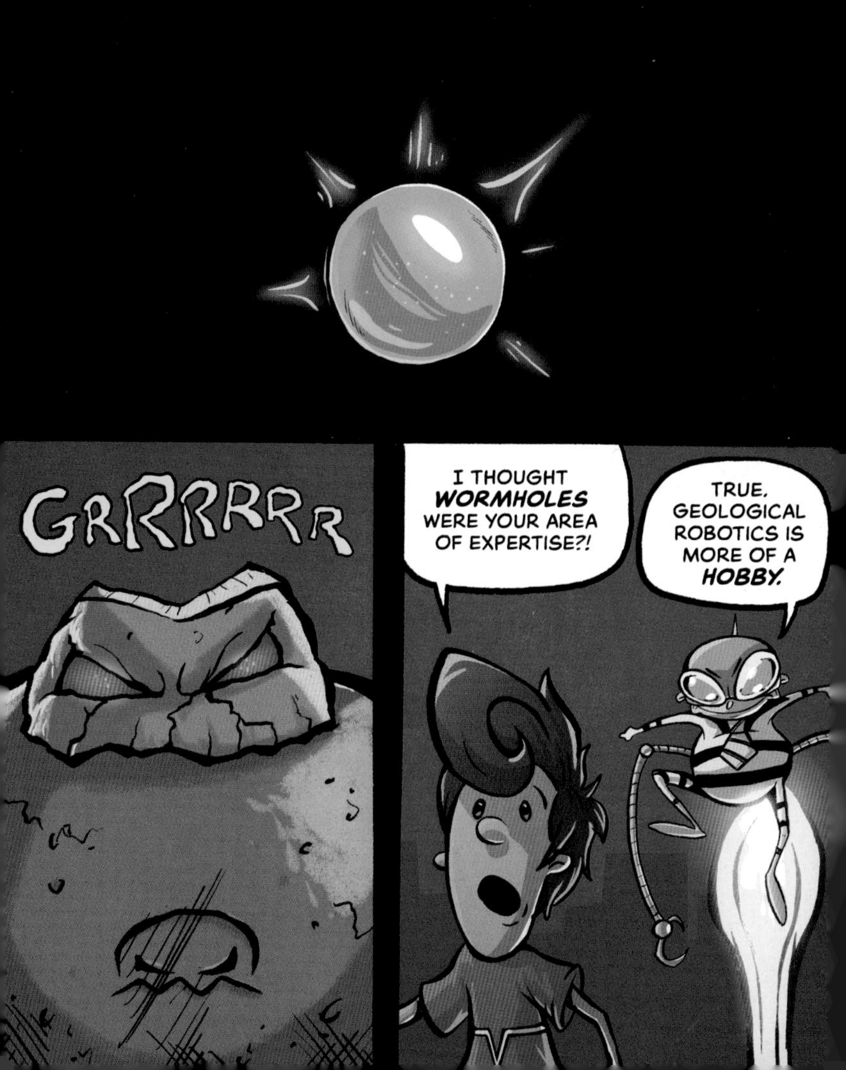
GRRRRRR
I THOUGHT WORMHOLES WERE YOUR AREA OF EXPERTISE?!
TRUE. GEOLOGICAL ROBOTICS IS MORE OF A HOBBY.

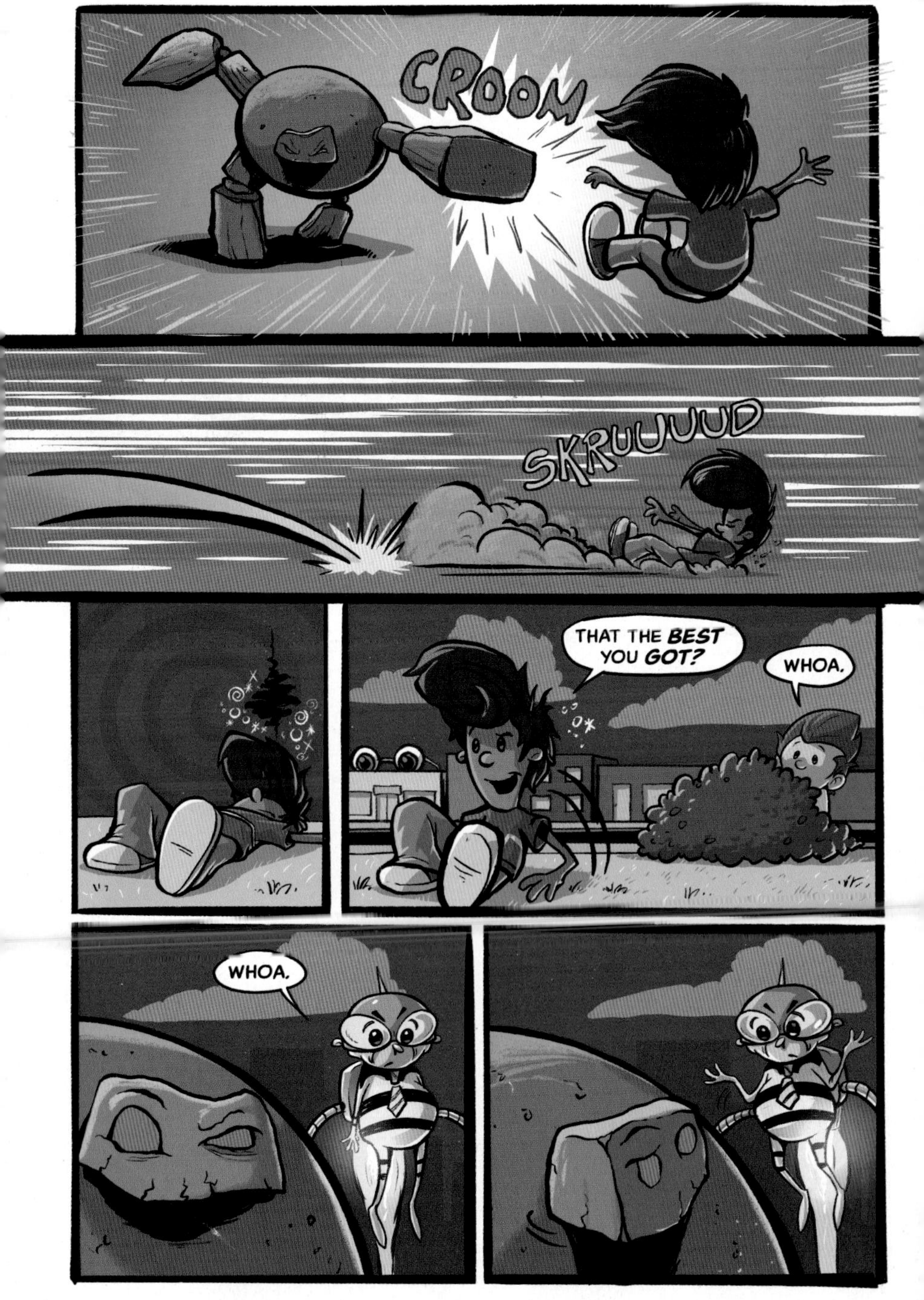
CROOM
SKRUUUUD
THAT THE BEST YOU GOT?
WHOA.
WHOA.

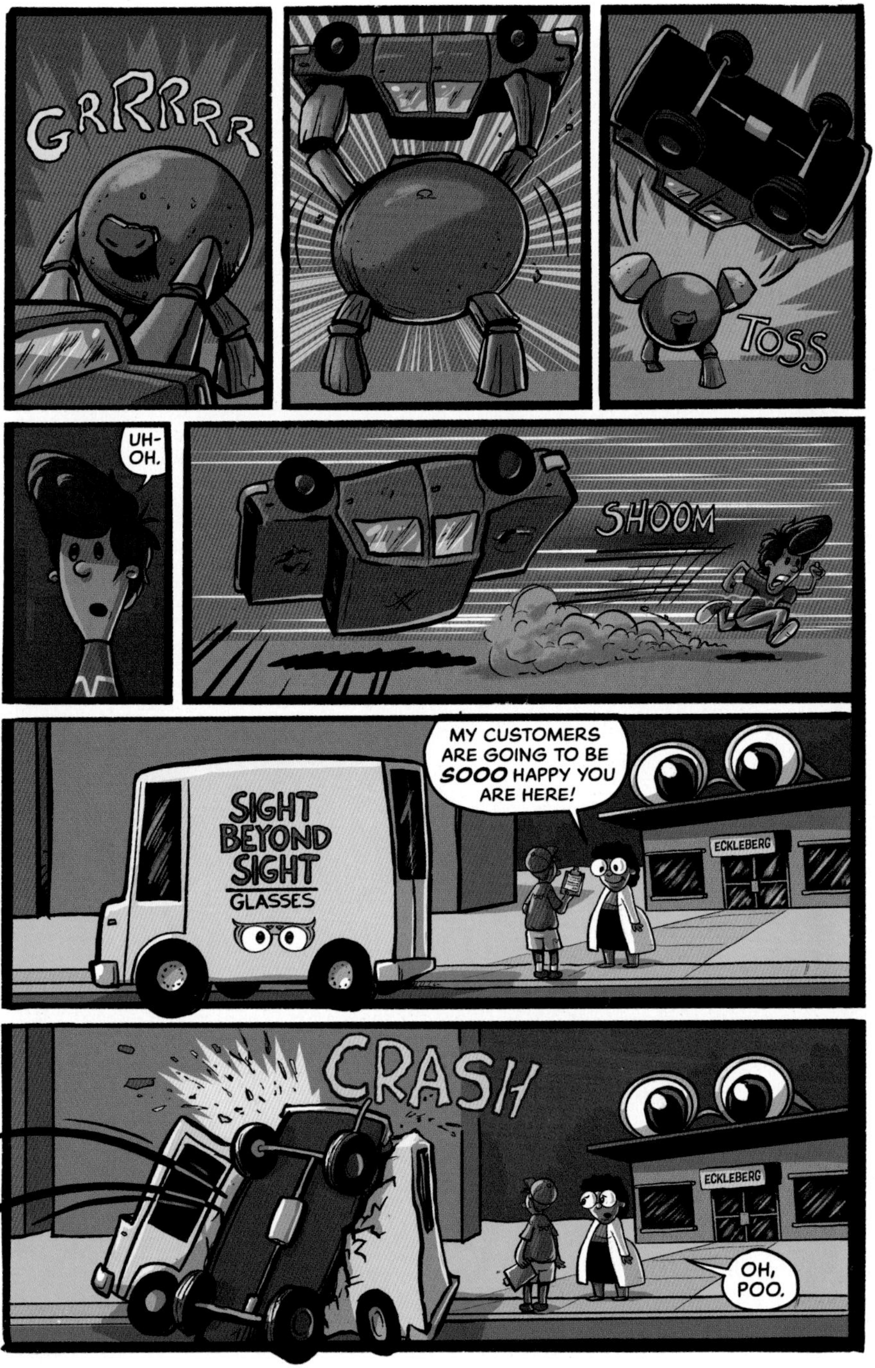
GRRRRRR
TOSS
UH-OH.
SHOOM
SIGHT BEYOND SIGHT
GLASSES
MY CUSTOMERS ARE GOING TO BE SOOO HAPPY YOU ARE HERE!
ECKLEBERG
CRASH
ECKLEBERG
OH, POO.

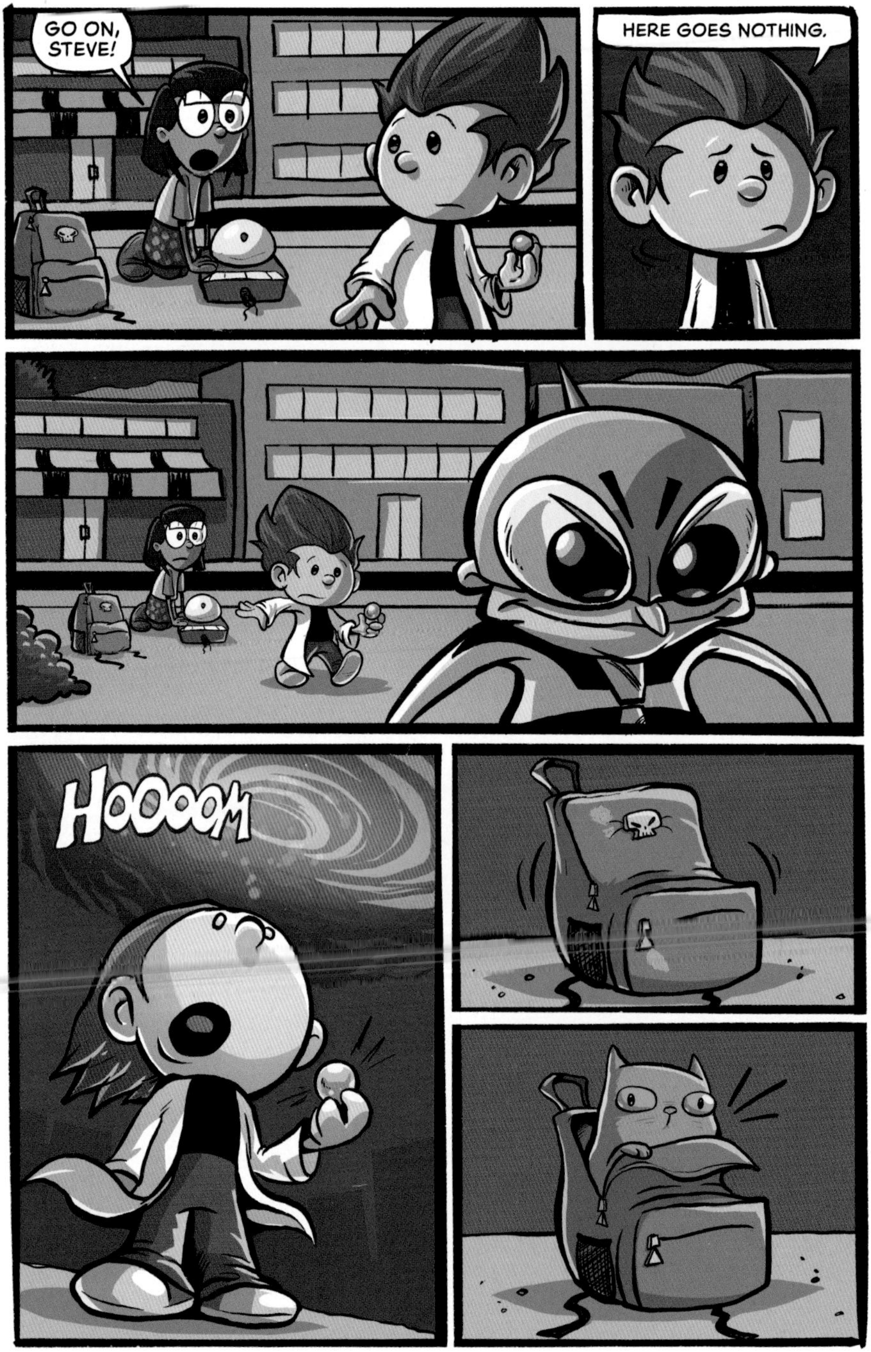
GO ON, STEVE!
HERE GOES NOTHING.
HOOOOM

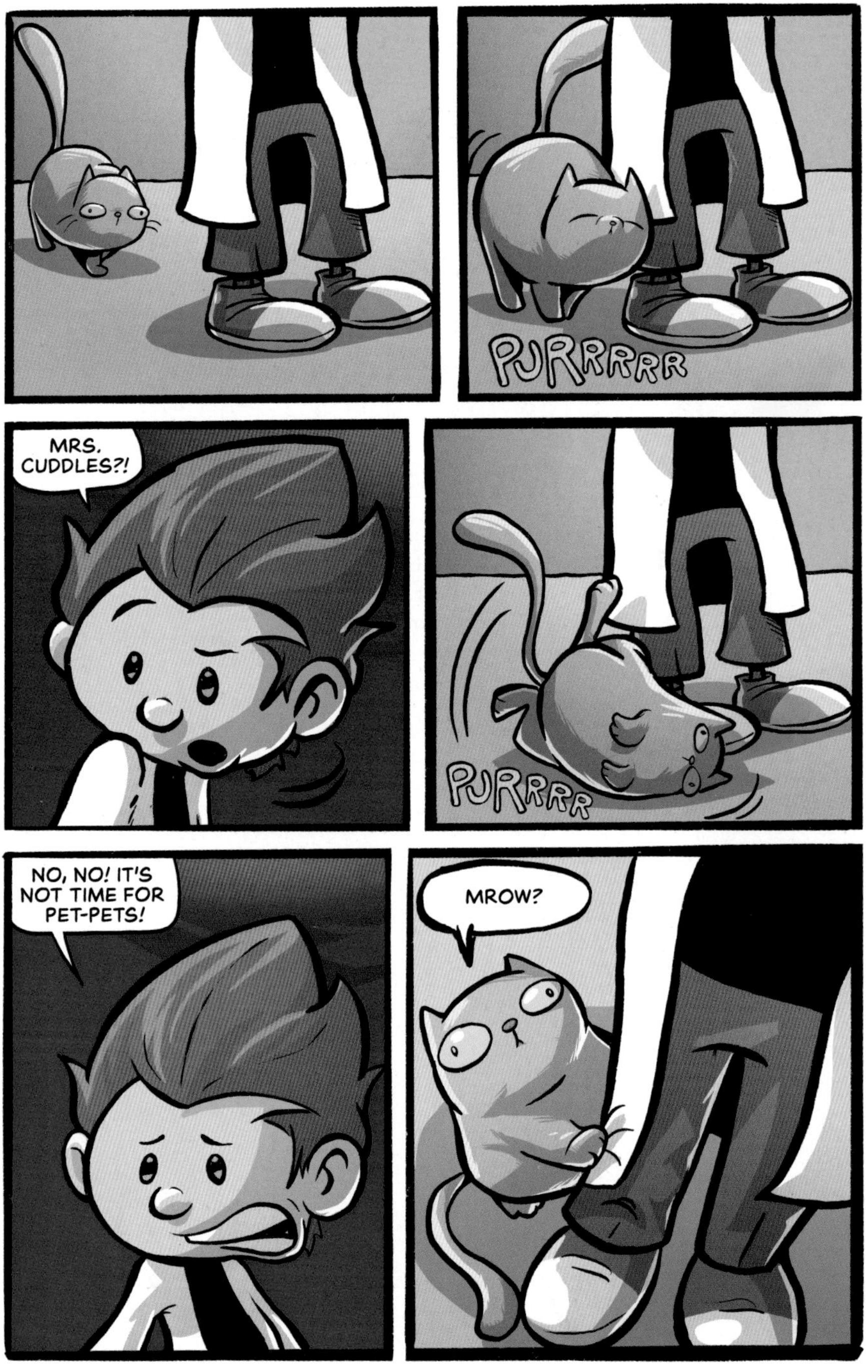
PURRRRRR
MRS. CUDDLES?!
PURRRRR
NO, NO! IT'S NOT TIME FOR PET-PETS!
MROW?

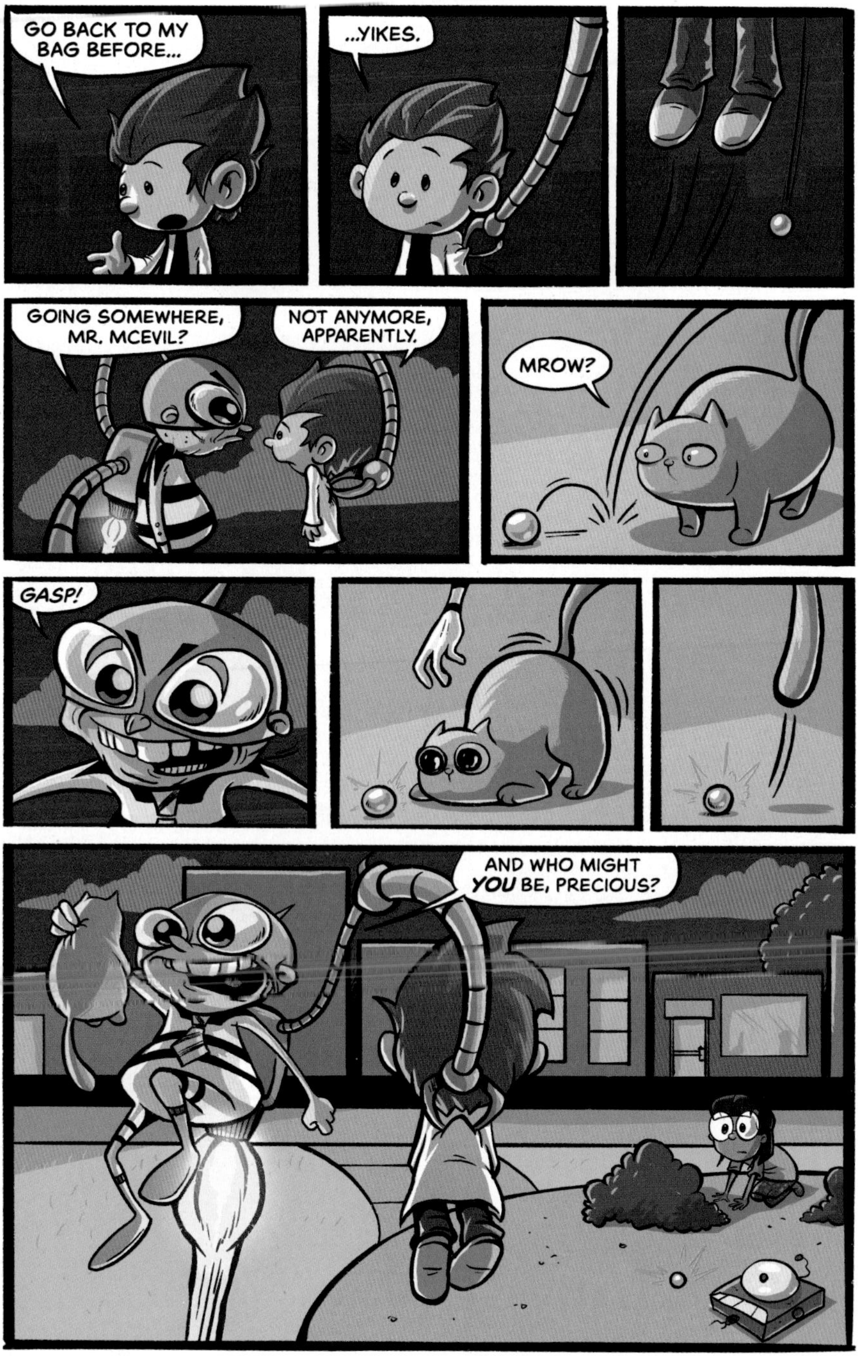
GO BACK TO MY BAG BEFORE...
...YIKES.
GOING SOMEWHERE, MR. MCEVIL?
NOT ANYMORE, APPARENTLY.
MROW?
GASP!
AND WHO MIGHT *YOU* BE, PRECIOUS?

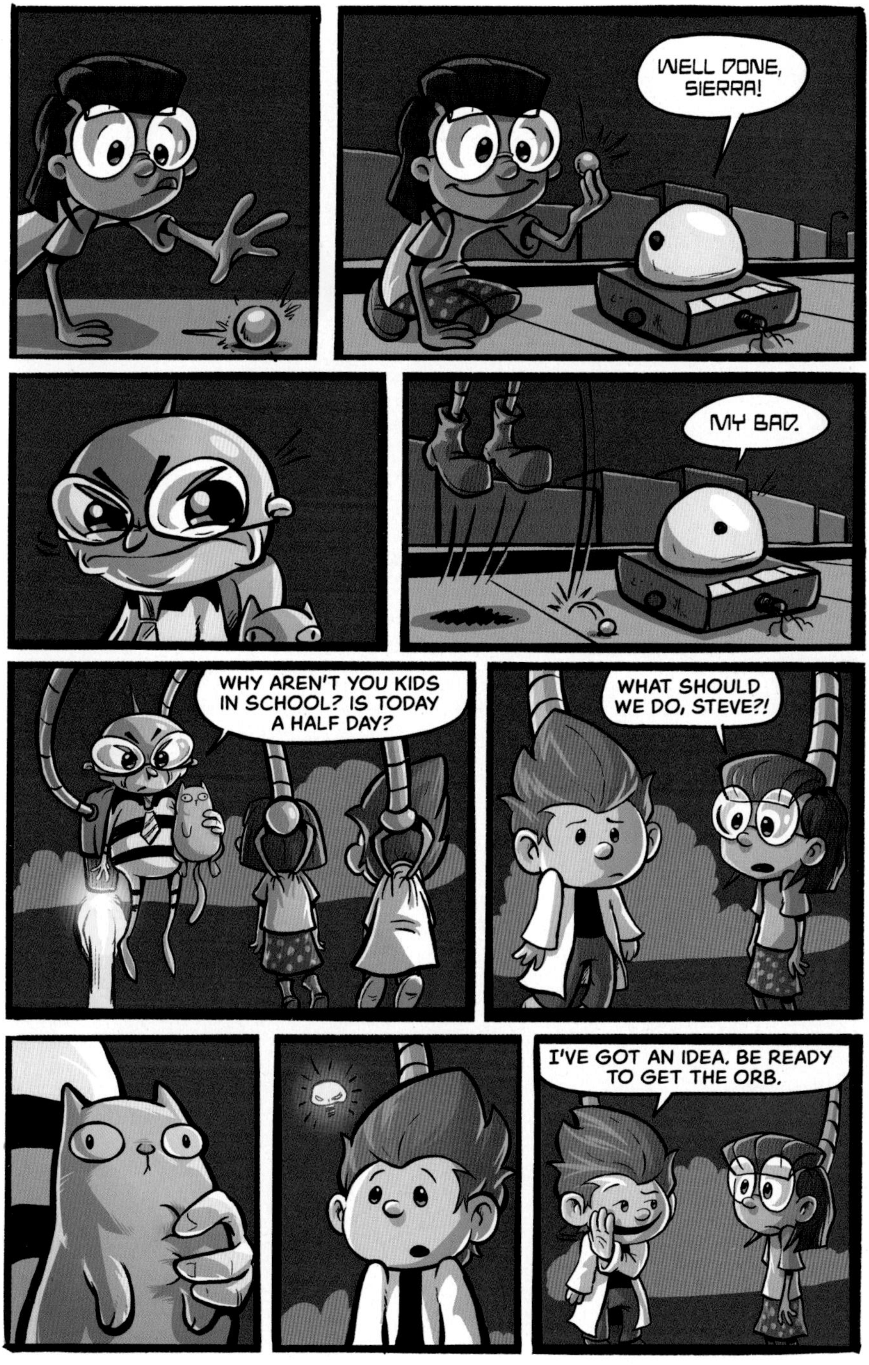
WELL DONE, SIERRA!
MY BAD.
WHY AREN'T YOU KIDS IN SCHOOL? IS TODAY A HALF DAY?
WHAT SHOULD WE DO, STEVE?!
I'VE GOT AN IDEA. BE READY TO GET THE ORB.

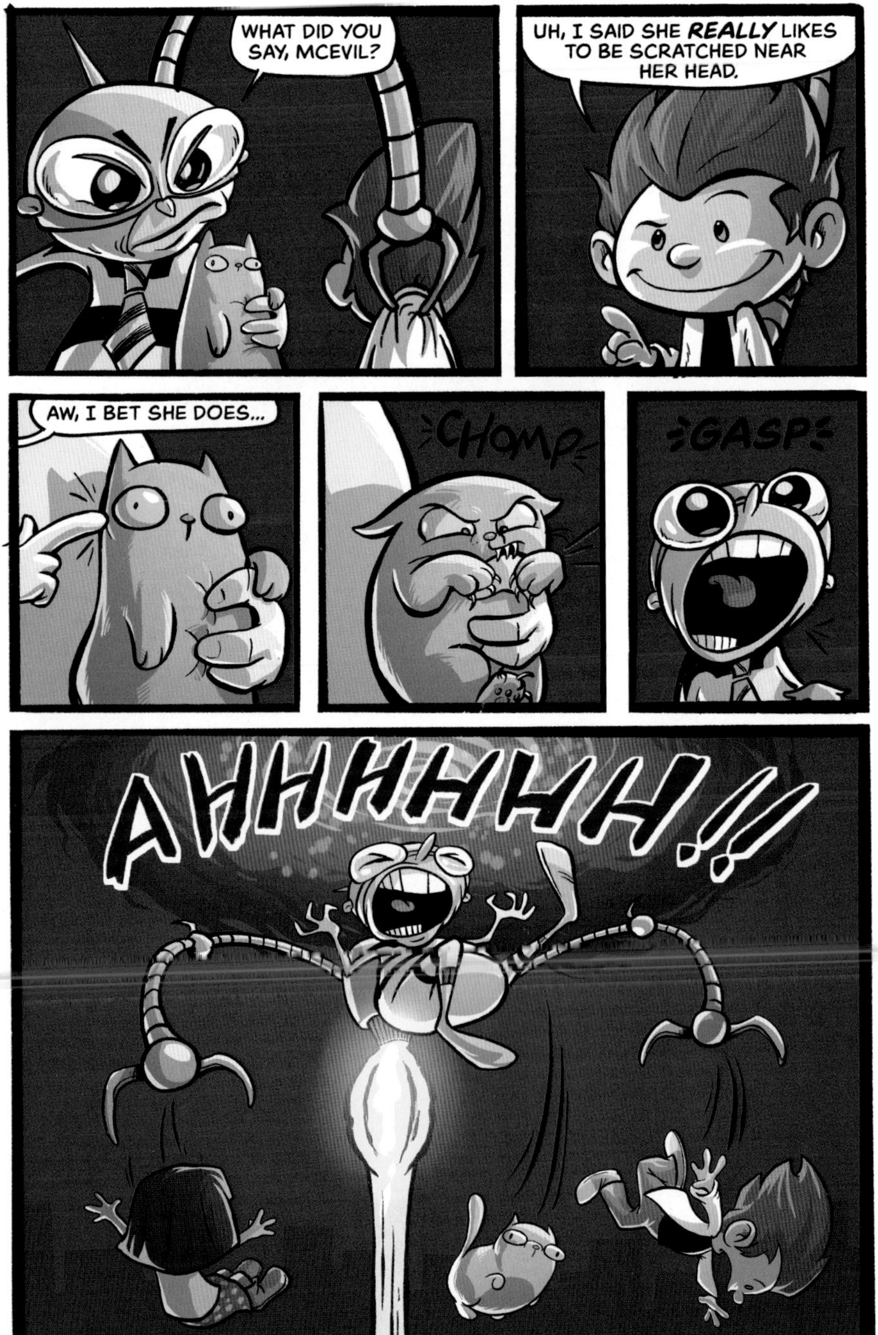
WHAT DID YOU SAY, MCEVIL?
UH, I SAID SHE **REALLY** LIKES TO BE SCRATCHED NEAR HER HEAD.
AW, I BET SHE DOES...
CHOMP
GASP
AHHHHHH!!

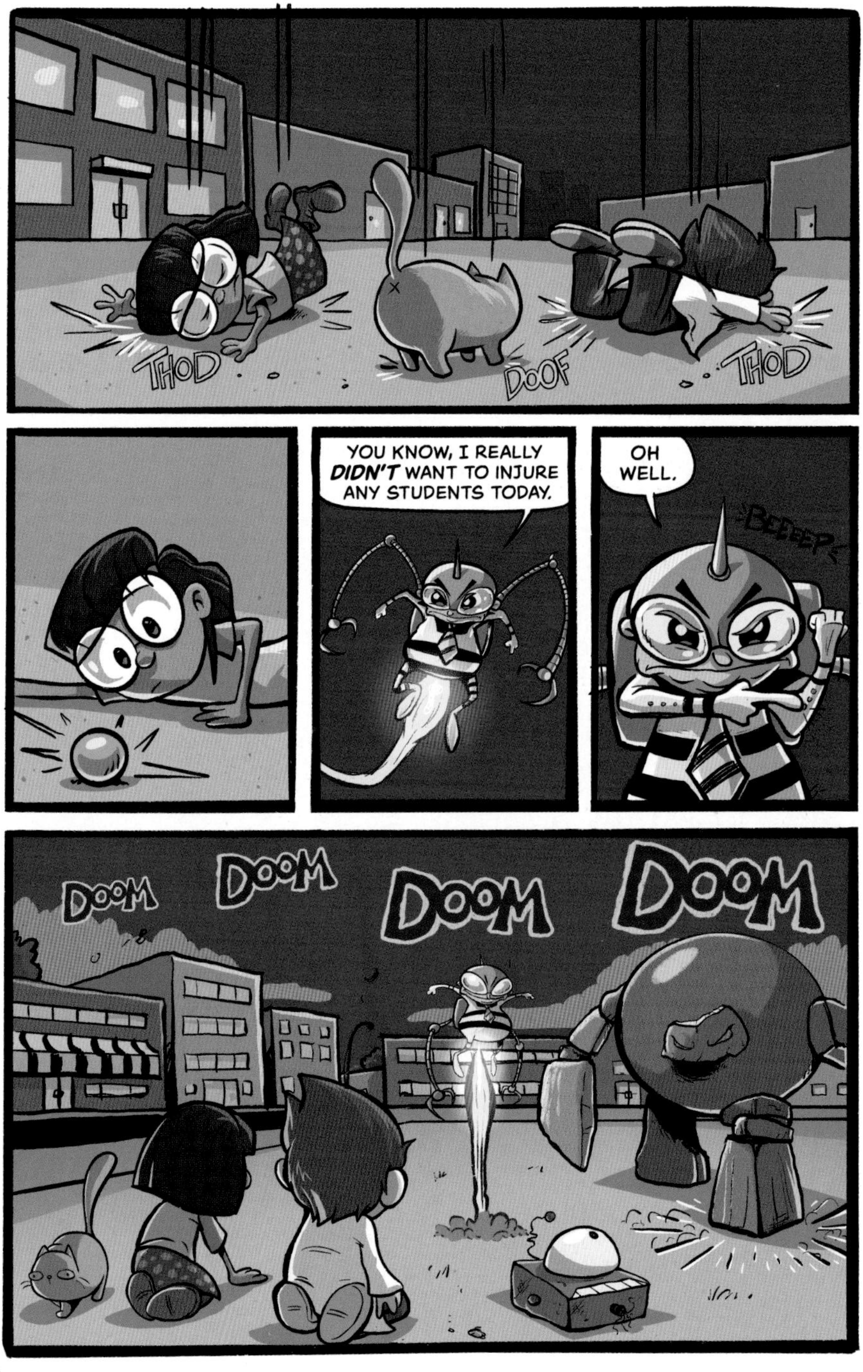
THOD
DOOF
THOD
YOU KNOW, I REALLY DIDN'T WANT TO INJURE ANY STUDENTS TODAY.
OH WELL.
BEEEEP
DOOM
DOOM
DOOM
DOOM

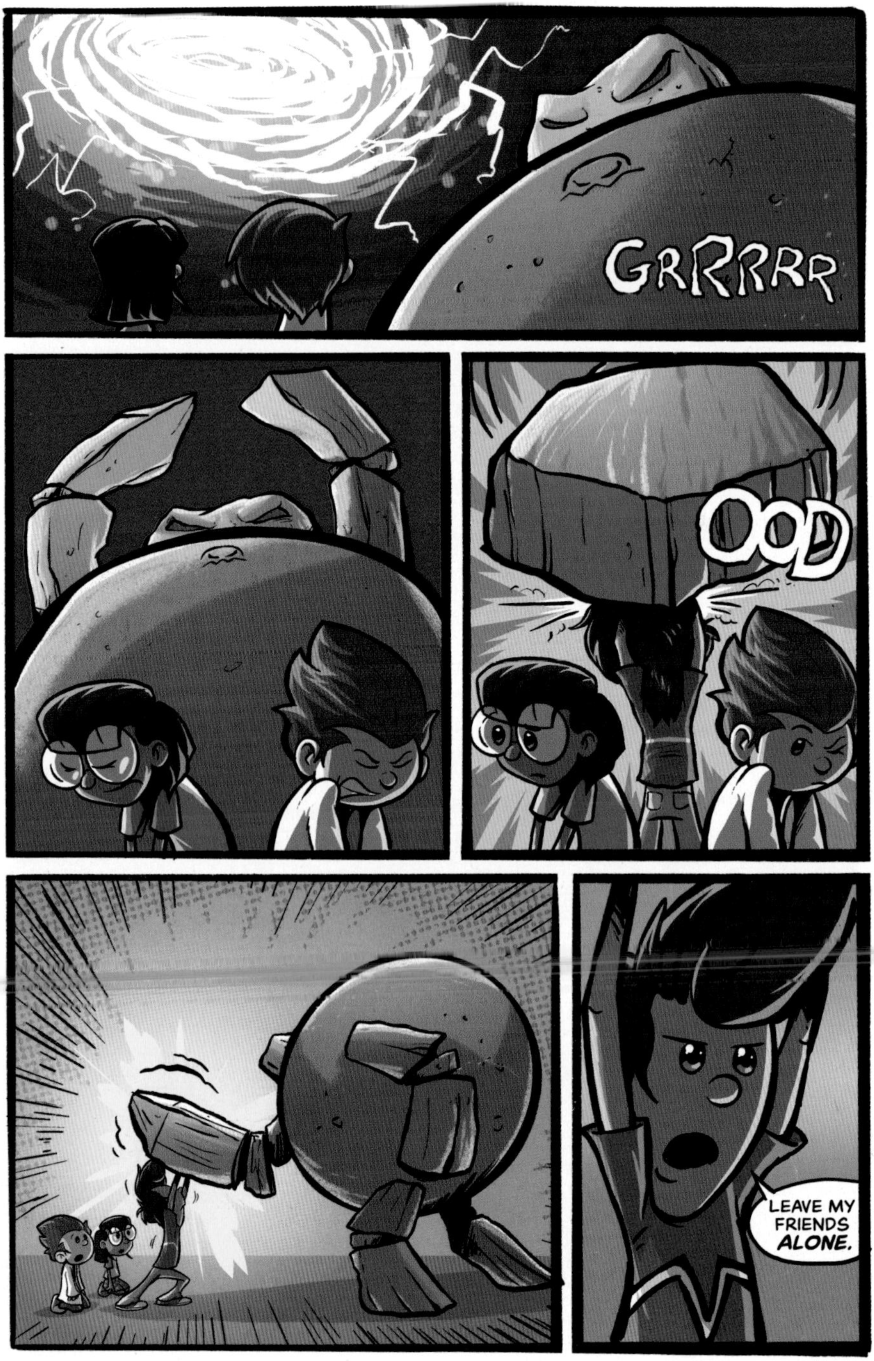
GRRRRR
OOD
LEAVE MY FRIENDS ALONE.

We Are the Champions

V

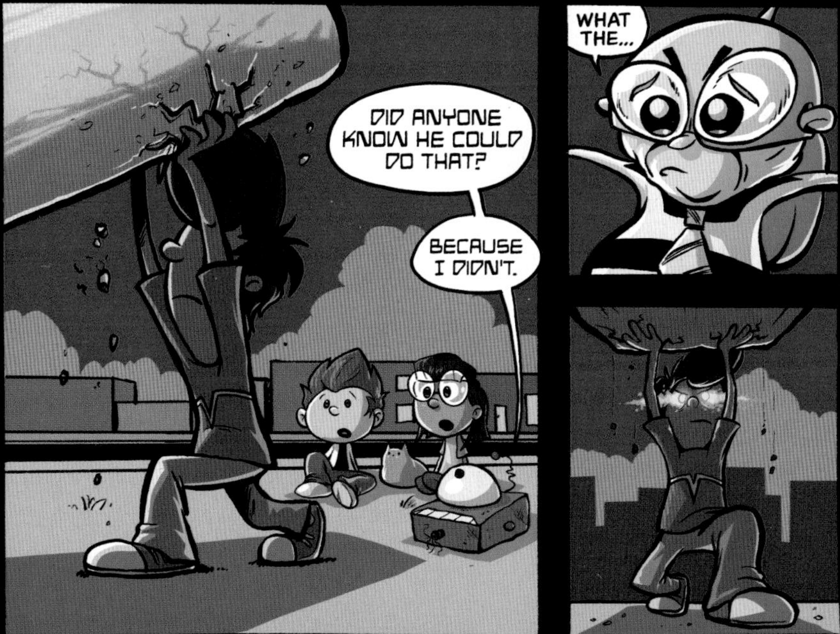
DID ANYONE KNOW HE COULD DO THAT?
BECAUSE I DIDN'T.
WHAT THE...

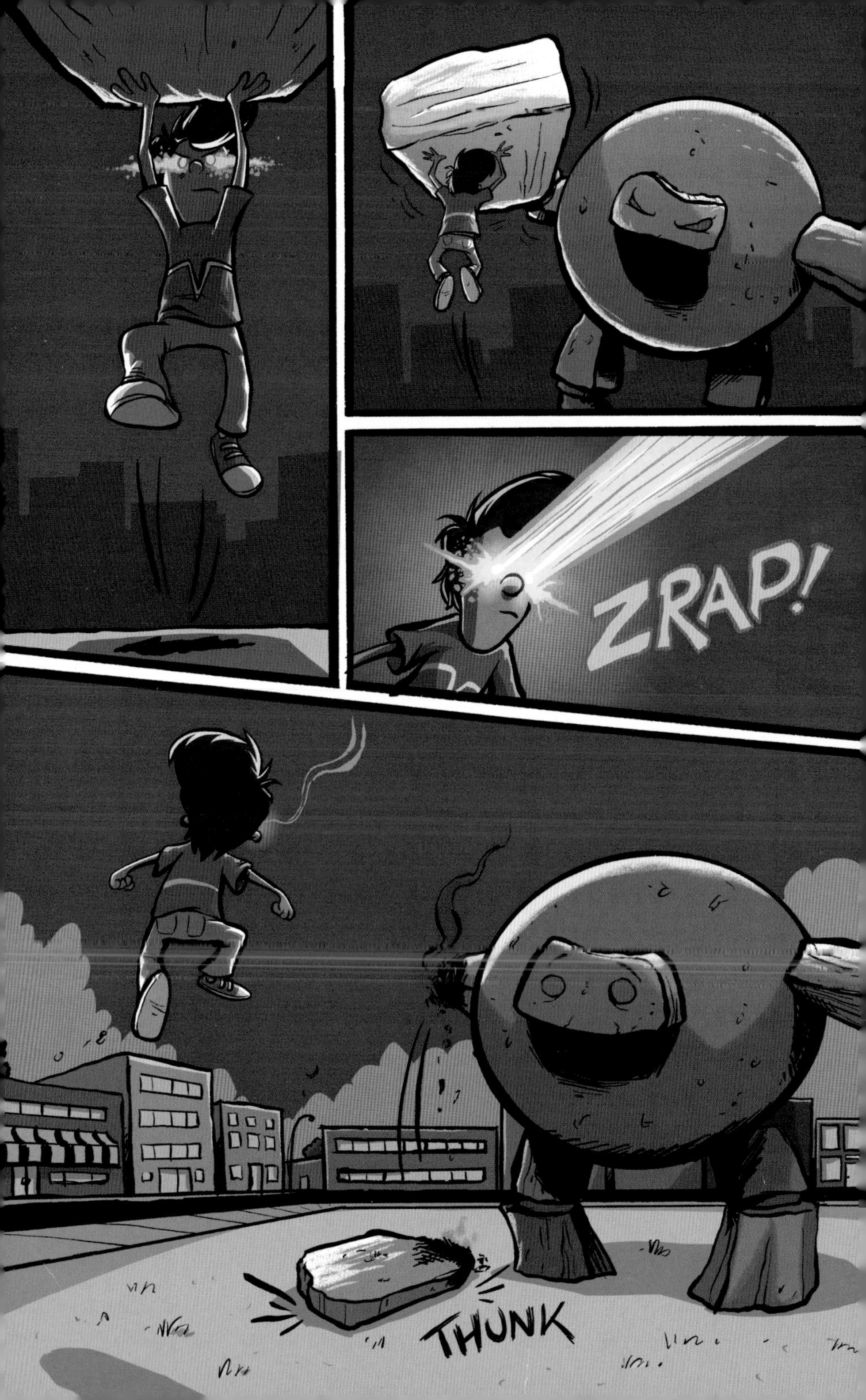
ZRAP!
THUNK

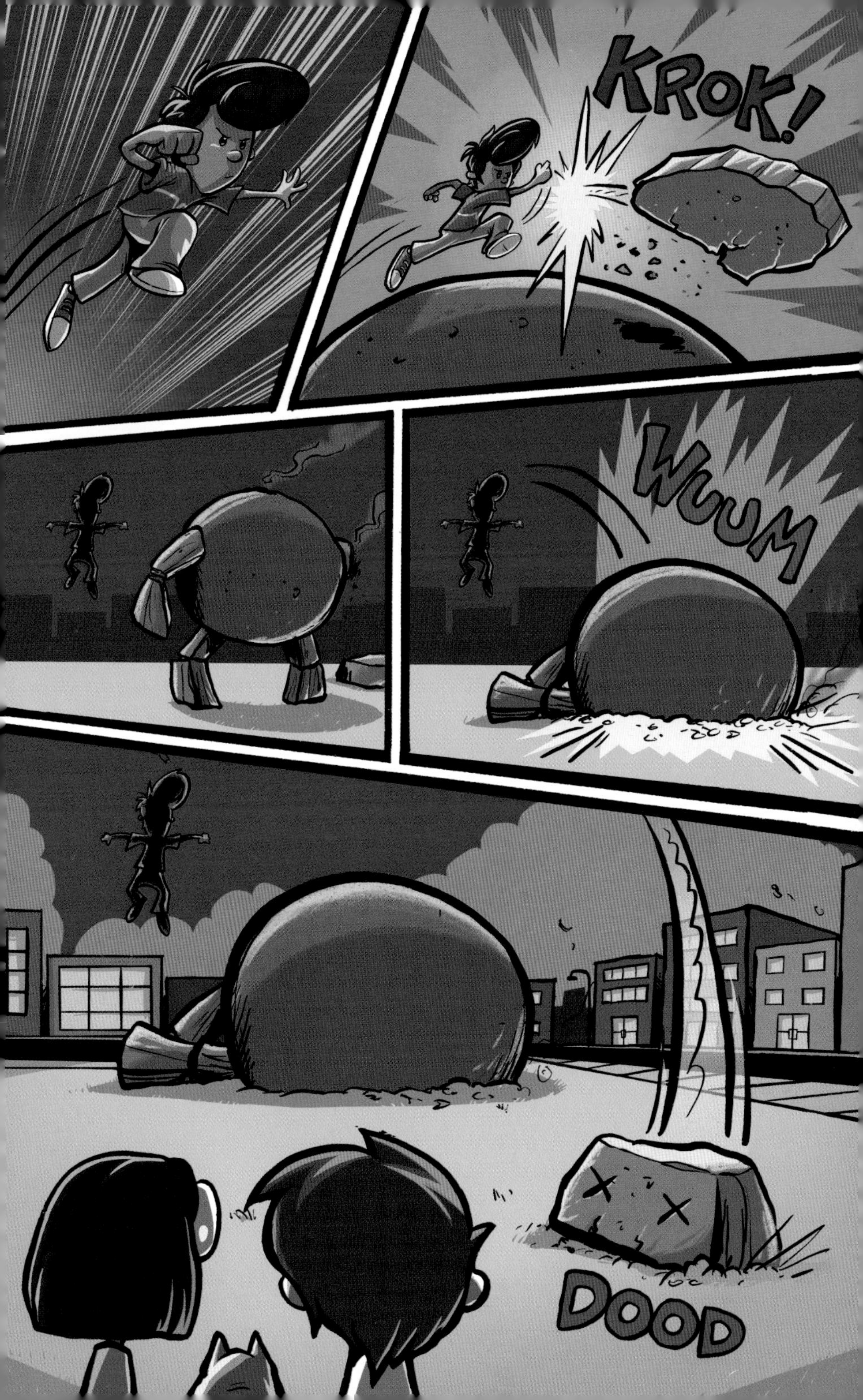
KROK!
WUUM
DOOD

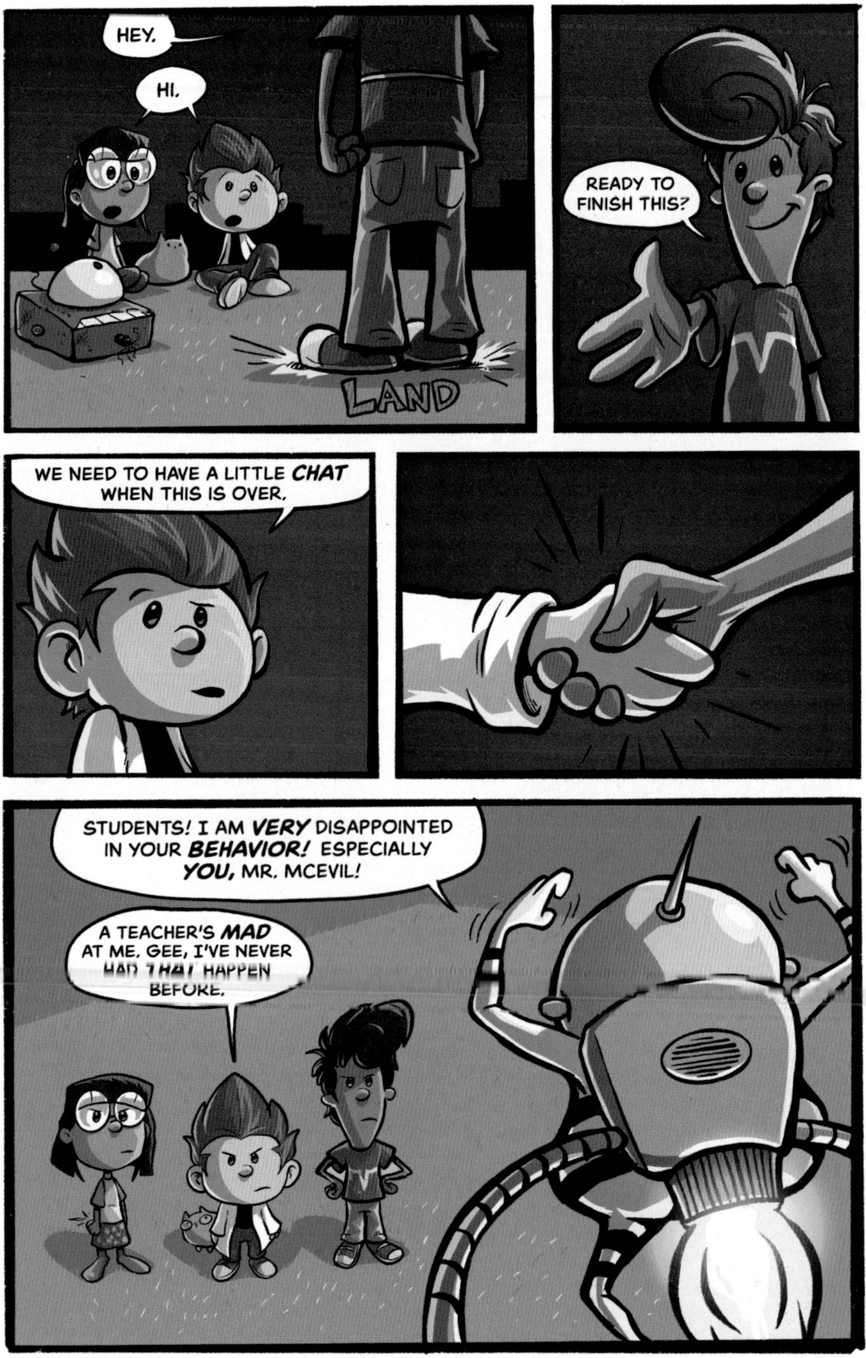
HEY.
HI.
LAND
READY TO FINISH THIS?
WE NEED TO HAVE A LITTLE *CHAT* WHEN THIS IS OVER.
STUDENTS! I AM *VERY* DISAPPOINTED IN YOUR *BEHAVIOR!* ESPECIALLY *YOU,* MR. MCEVIL!
A TEACHER'S *MAD* AT ME. GEE, I'VE NEVER HAD *THAT* HAPPEN BEFORE.

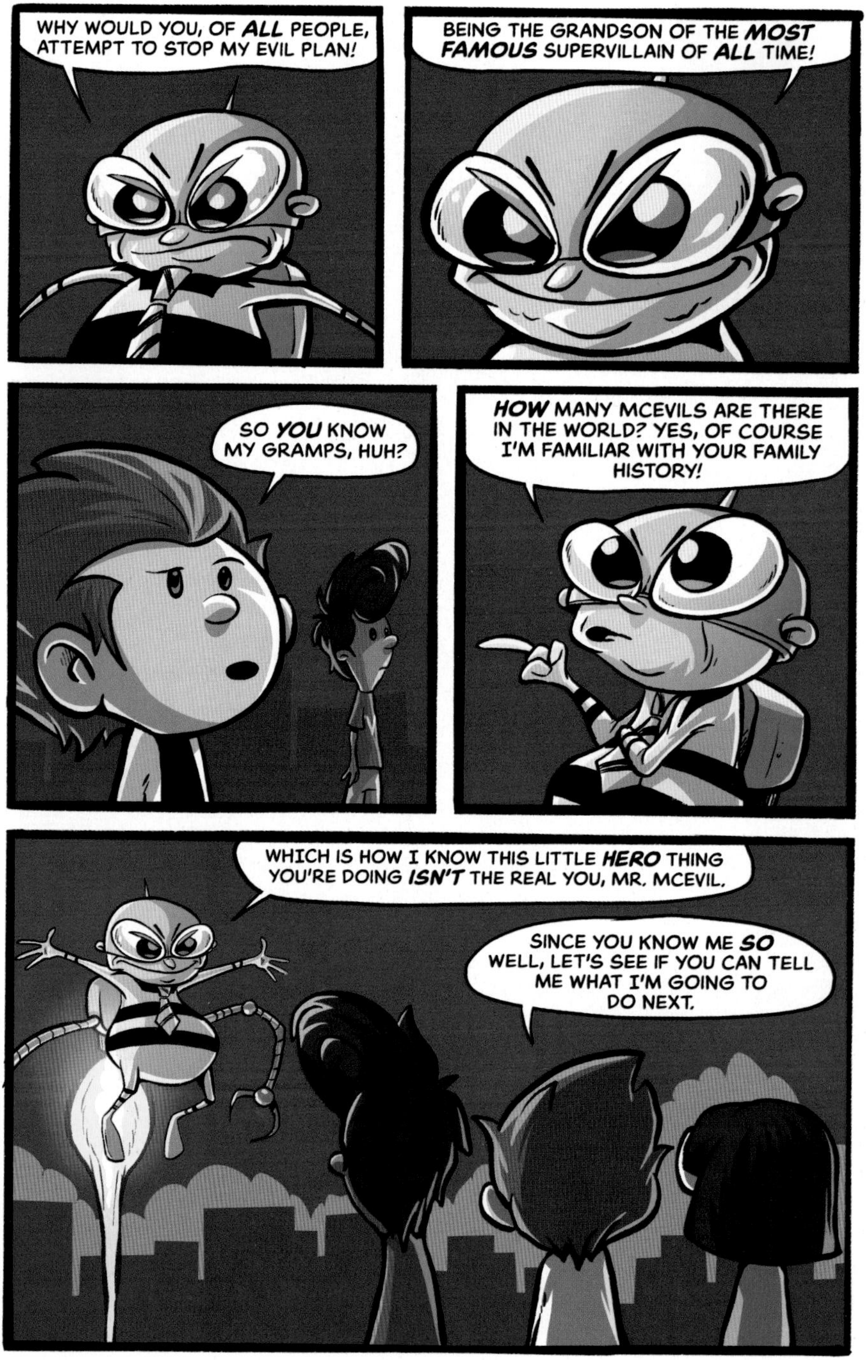
WHY WOULD YOU, OF ALL PEOPLE, ATTEMPT TO STOP MY EVIL PLAN!
BEING THE GRANDSON OF THE MOST FAMOUS SUPERVILLAIN OF ALL TIME!
SO YOU KNOW MY GRAMPS, HUH?
HOW MANY MCEVILS ARE THERE IN THE WORLD? YES, OF COURSE I'M FAMILIAR WITH YOUR FAMILY HISTORY!
WHICH IS HOW I KNOW THIS LITTLE HERO THING YOU'RE DOING ISN'T THE REAL YOU, MR. MCEVIL.
SINCE YOU KNOW ME SO WELL, LET'S SEE IF YOU CAN TELL ME WHAT I'M GOING TO DO NEXT.

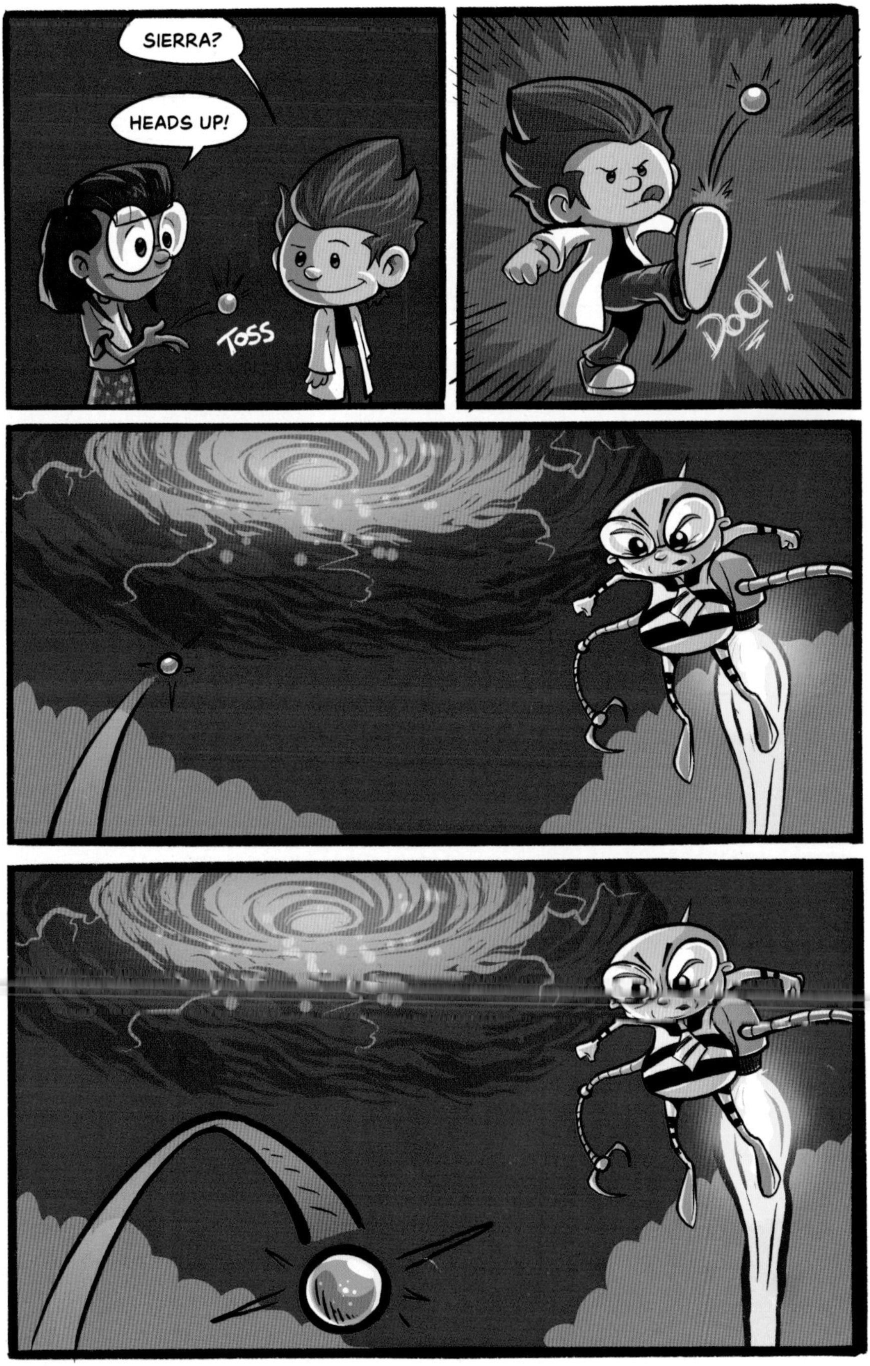
SIERRA?
HEADS UP!
TOSS
DOOF!

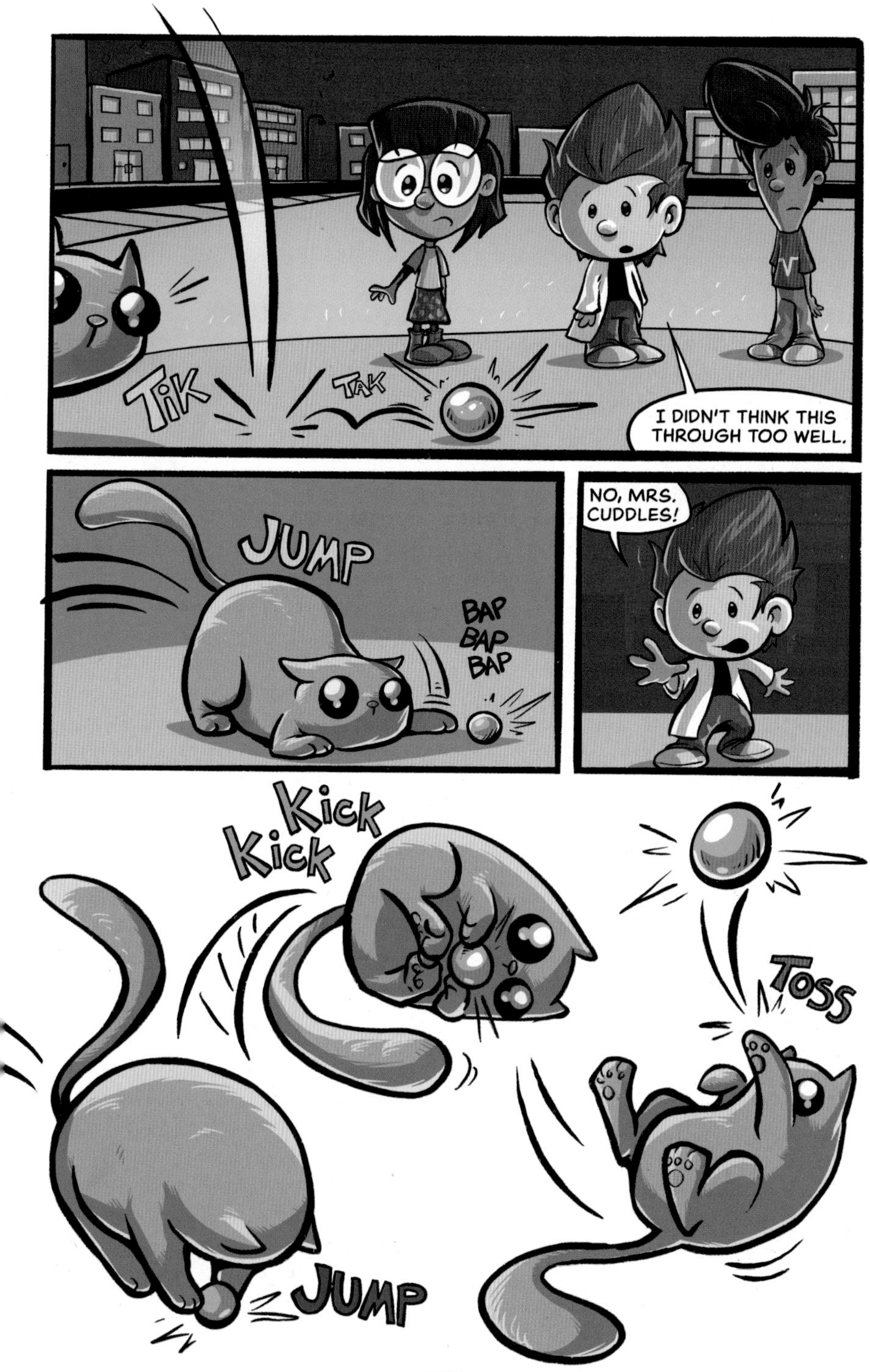
TIK
TAK
I DIDN'T THINK THIS THROUGH TOO WELL.
JUMP
BAP BAP BAP
NO, MRS. CUDDLES!
Kick
Kick
TOSS
JUMP

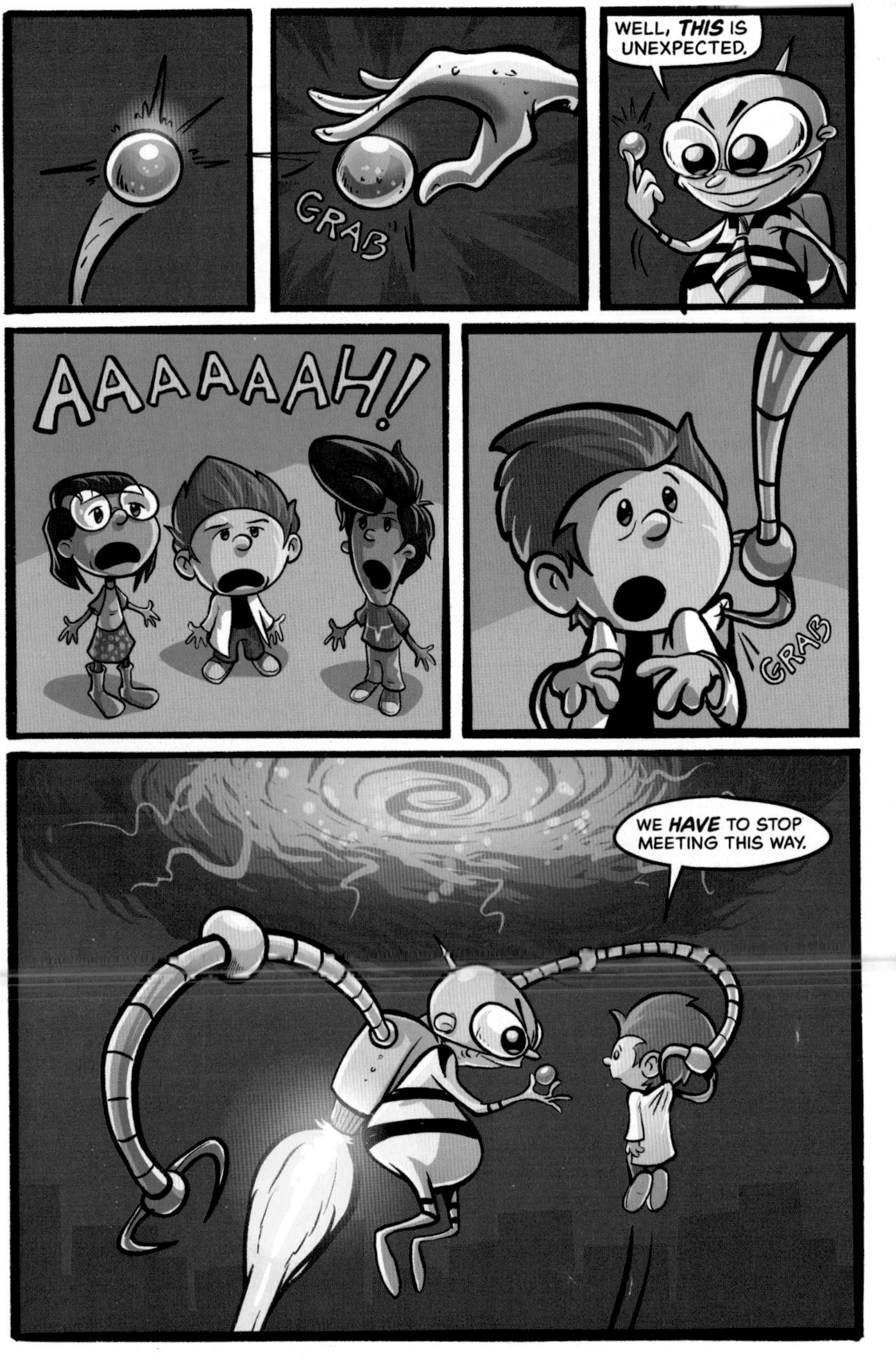
GRAB
WELL, THIS IS UNEXPECTED.
AAAAAAH!
GRAB
WE HAVE TO STOP MEETING THIS WAY.

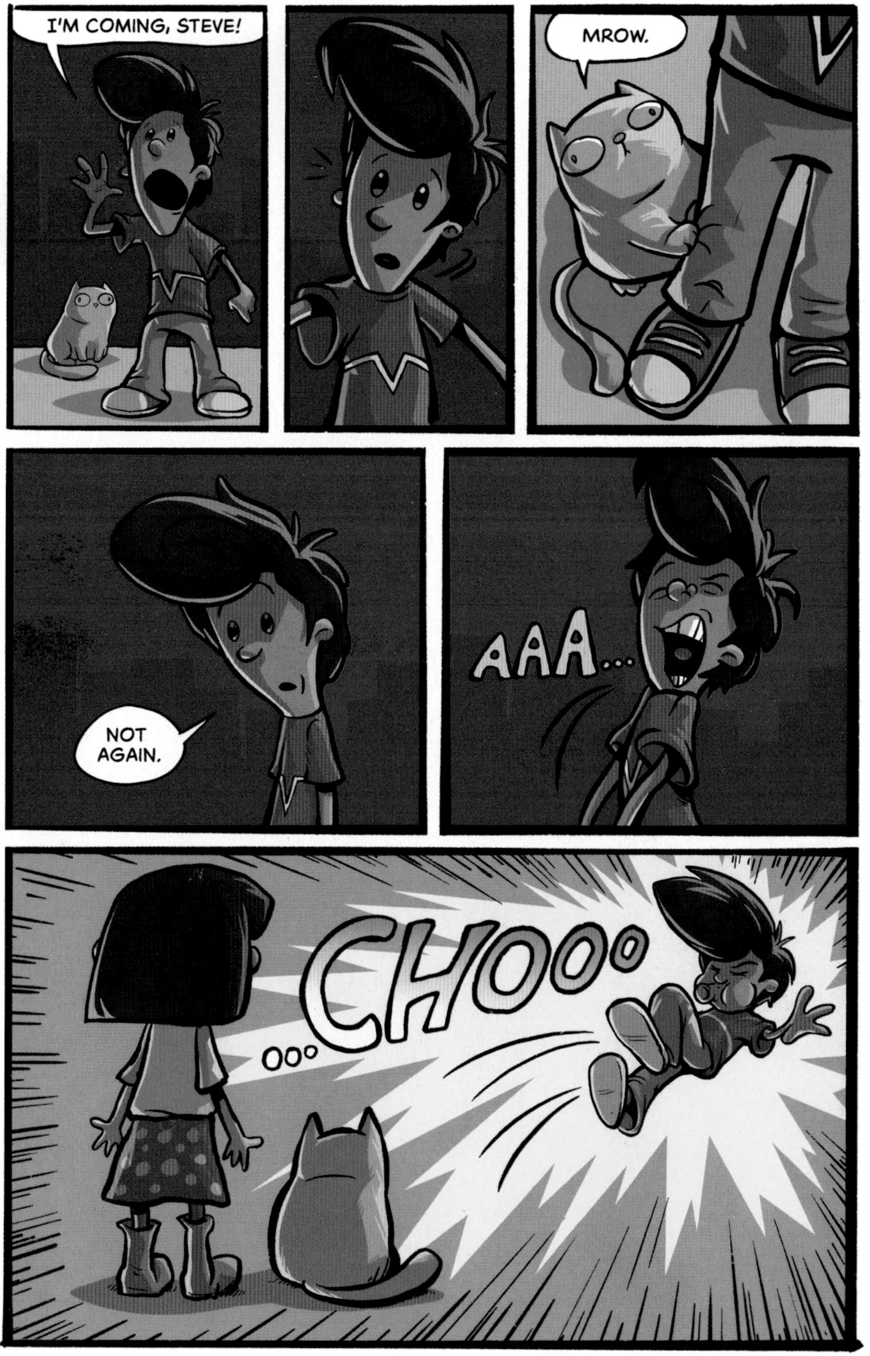
I'M COMING, STEVE!
MROW.
NOT AGAIN.
AAA...
CHOOO
ooo

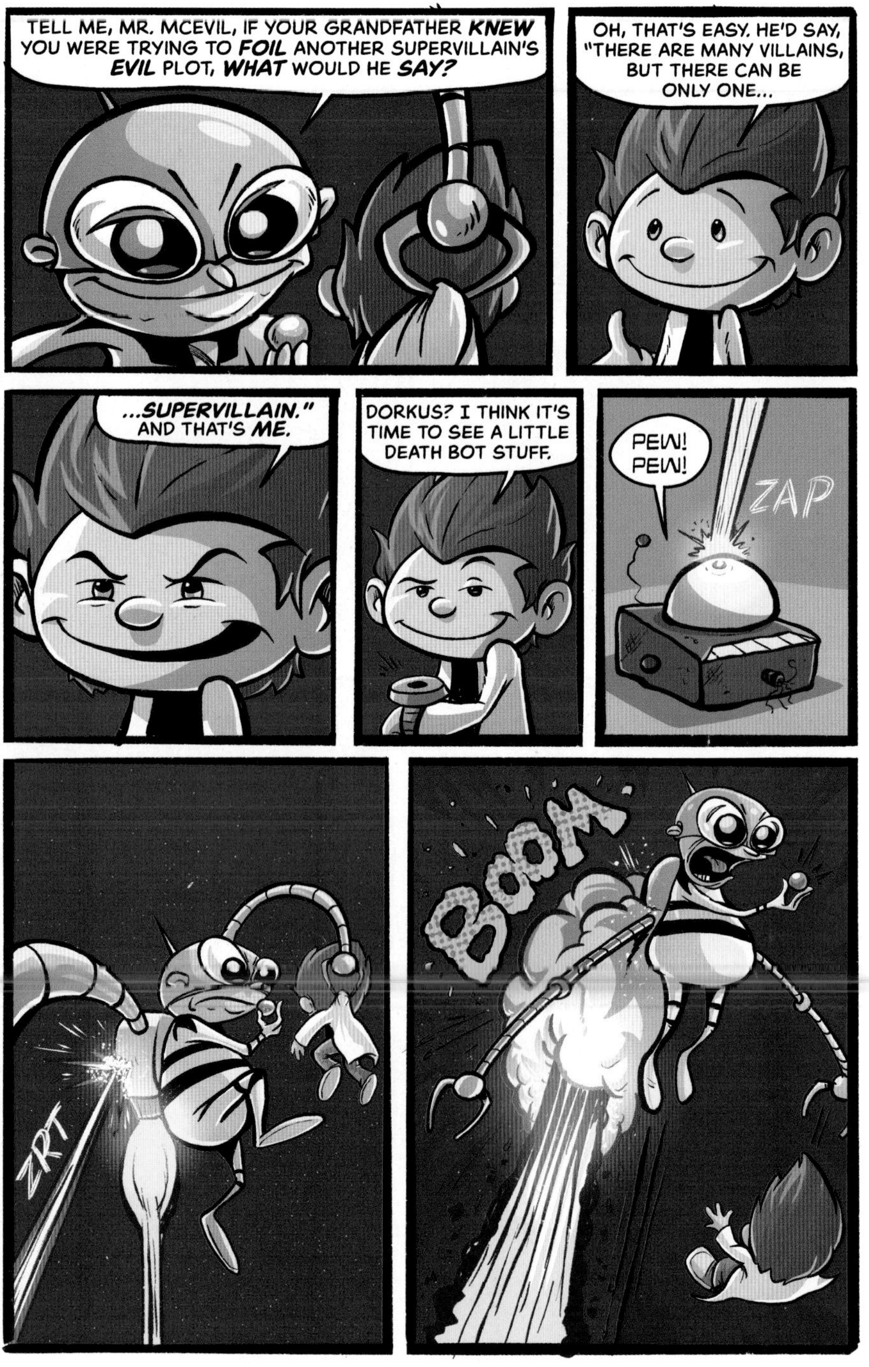
TELL ME, MR. MCEVIL, IF YOUR GRANDFATHER KNEW YOU WERE TRYING TO FOIL ANOTHER SUPERVILLAIN'S EVIL PLOT, WHAT WOULD HE SAY?
OH, THAT'S EASY. HE'D SAY, "THERE ARE MANY VILLAINS, BUT THERE CAN BE ONLY ONE...
...SUPERVILLAIN." AND THAT'S ME.
DORKUS? I THINK IT'S TIME TO SEE A LITTLE DEATH BOT STUFF.
PEW! PEW!
ZAP
ZRT
BOOM

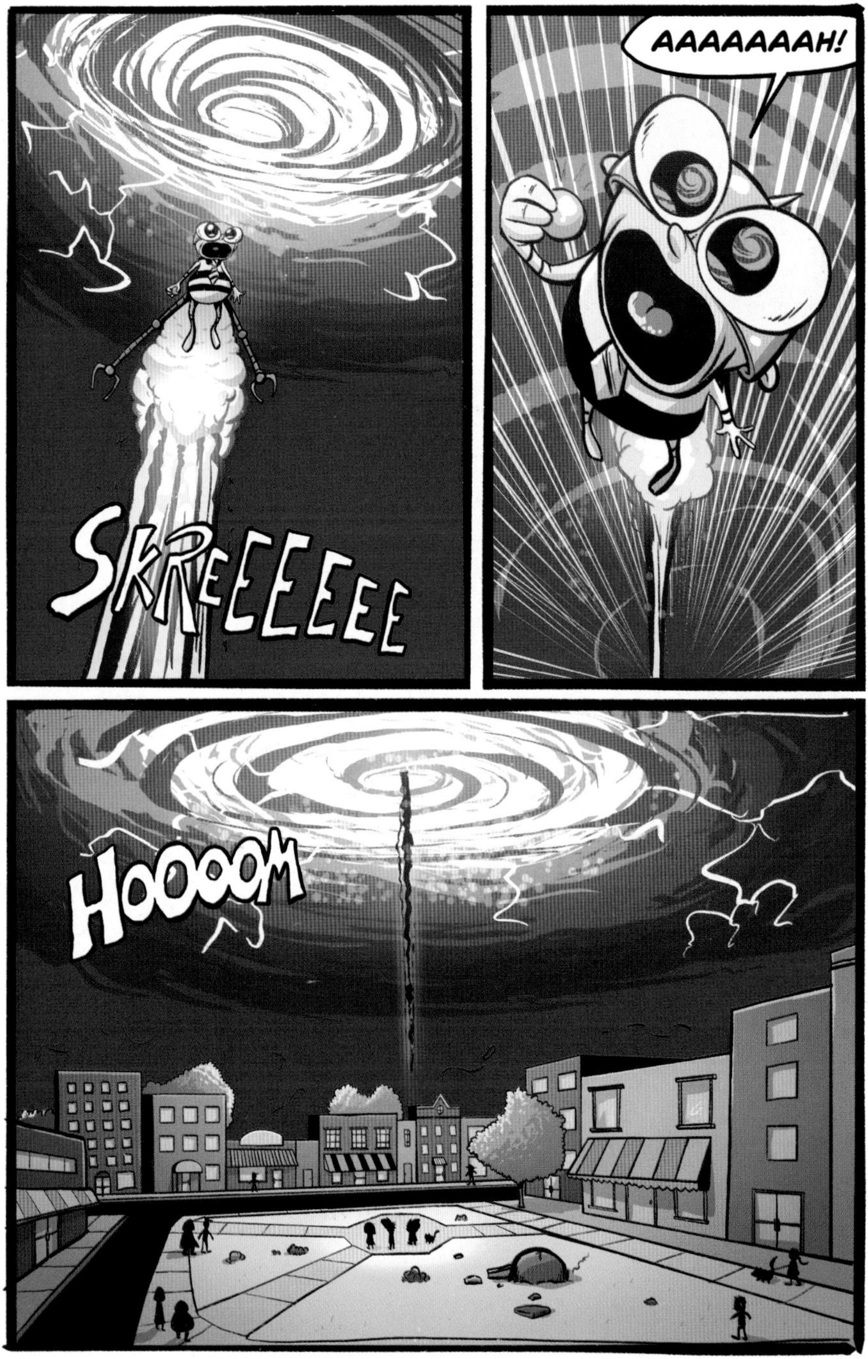
SKREEEEEE
AAAAAAAH!
HOOOOM

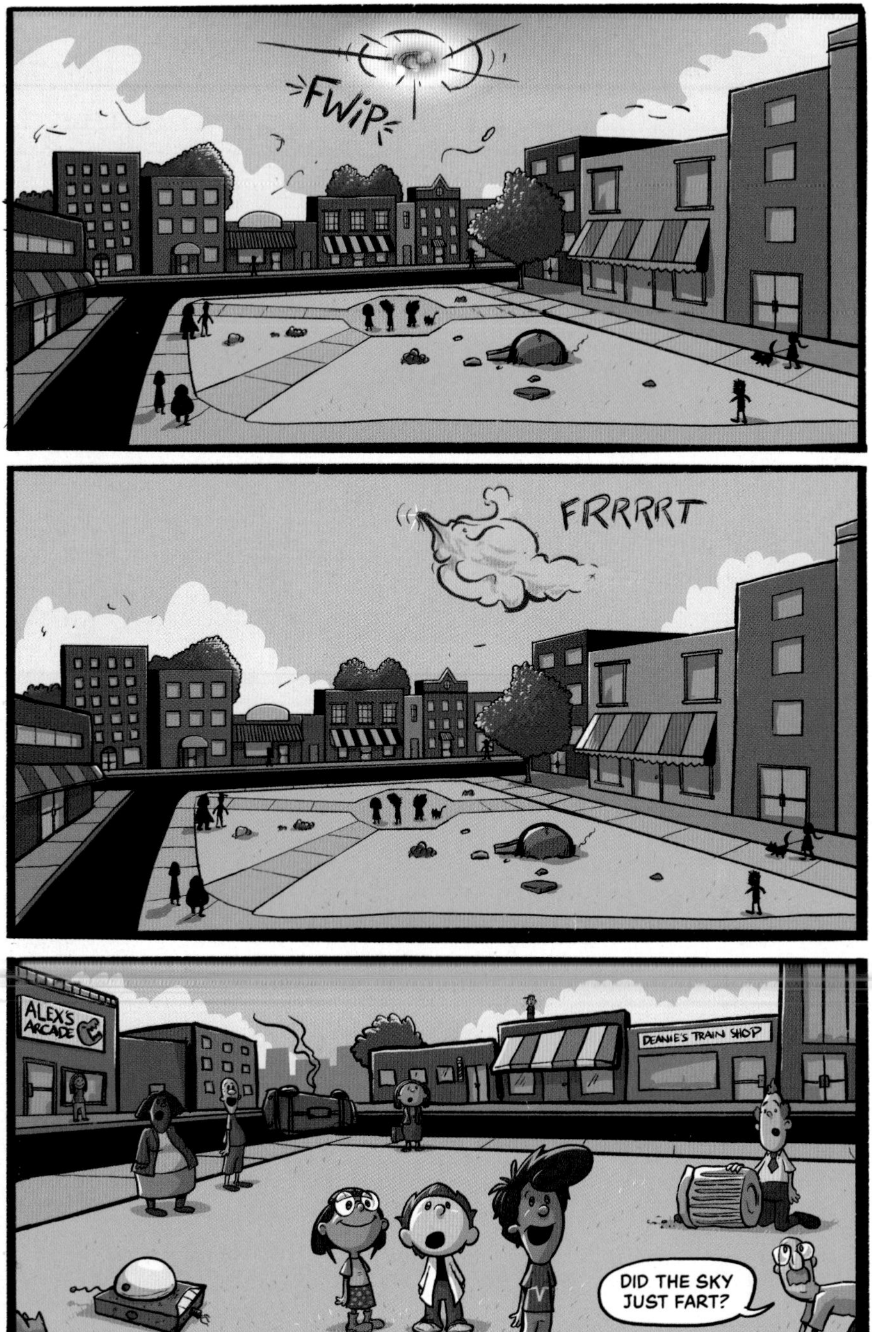
FWIP
FRRRRT
ALEX'S ARCADE
DEANIE'S TRAIN SHOP
DID THE SKY JUST FART?

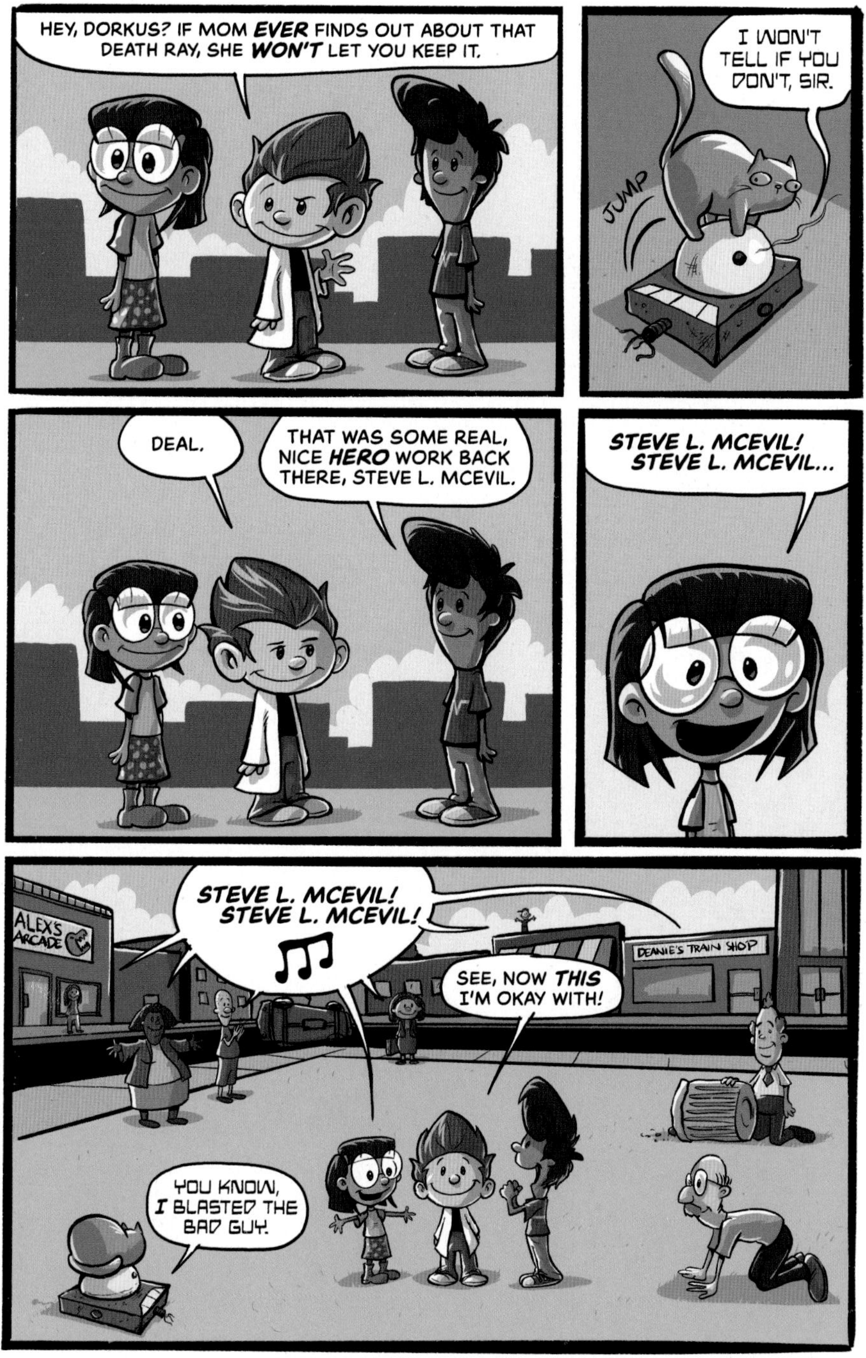
HEY, DORKUS? IF MOM EVER FINDS OUT ABOUT THAT DEATH RAY, SHE WON'T LET YOU KEEP IT.
I WON'T TELL IF YOU DON'T, SIR.
JUMP
DEAL.
THAT WAS SOME REAL, NICE HERO WORK BACK THERE, STEVE L. MCEVIL.
STEVE L. MCEVIL! STEVE L. MCEVIL...
ALEX'S ARCADE
STEVE L. MCEVIL! STEVE L. MCEVIL!
DEANIE'S TRAIN SHOP
SEE, NOW THIS I'M OKAY WITH!
YOU KNOW, I BLASTED THE BAD GUY.

CHAPTER 20

Thank You for Being a Fiend

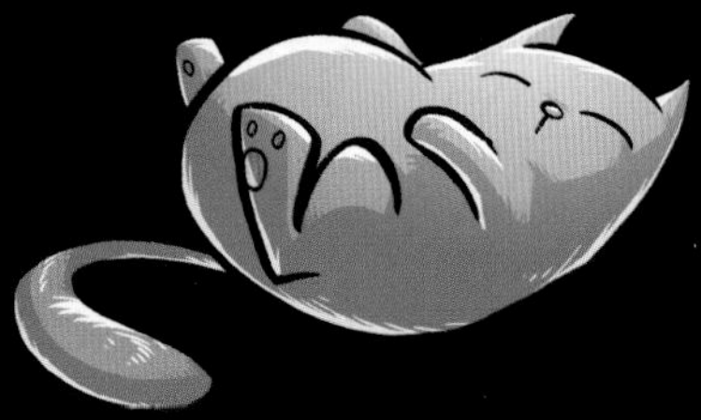

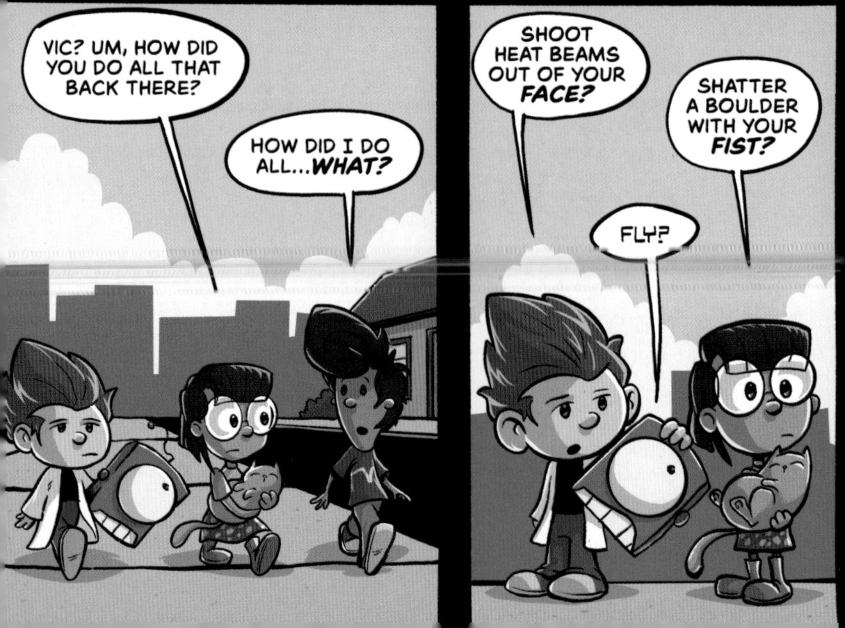
VIC? UM, HOW DID YOU DO ALL THAT BACK THERE?
HOW DID I DO ALL...WHAT?
SHOOT HEAT BEAMS OUT OF YOUR FACE?
SHATTER A BOULDER WITH YOUR FIST?
FLY?

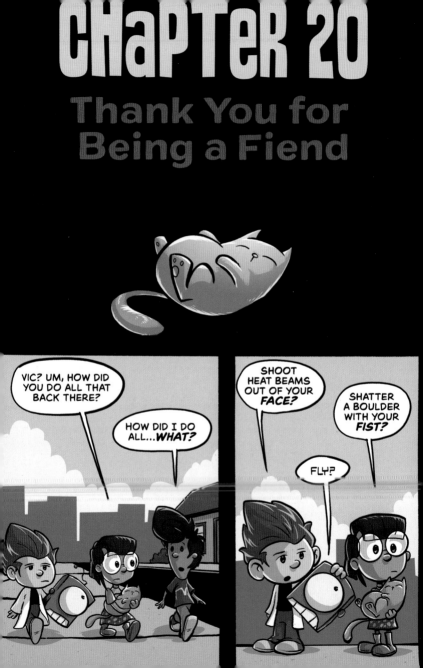

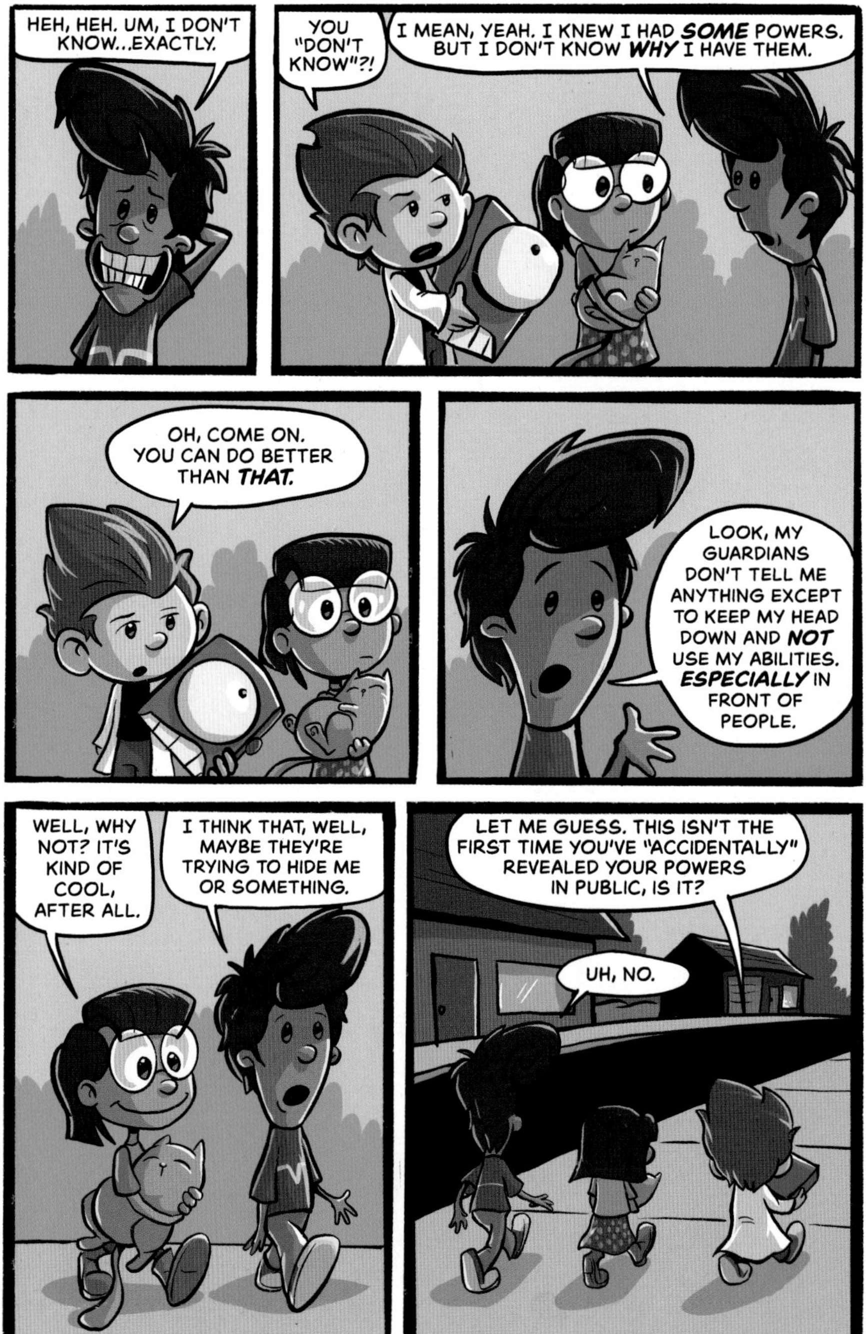
HEH, HEH. UM, I DON'T KNOW...EXACTLY.
YOU "DON'T KNOW"?!
I MEAN, YEAH. I KNEW I HAD SOME POWERS. BUT I DON'T KNOW WHY I HAVE THEM.
OH, COME ON. YOU CAN DO BETTER THAN THAT.
LOOK, MY GUARDIANS DON'T TELL ME ANYTHING EXCEPT TO KEEP MY HEAD DOWN AND NOT USE MY ABILITIES. ESPECIALLY IN FRONT OF PEOPLE.
WELL, WHY NOT? IT'S KIND OF COOL, AFTER ALL.
I THINK THAT, WELL, MAYBE THEY'RE TRYING TO HIDE ME OR SOMETHING.
LET ME GUESS. THIS ISN'T THE FIRST TIME YOU'VE "ACCIDENTALLY" REVEALED YOUR POWERS IN PUBLIC, IS IT?
UH, NO.

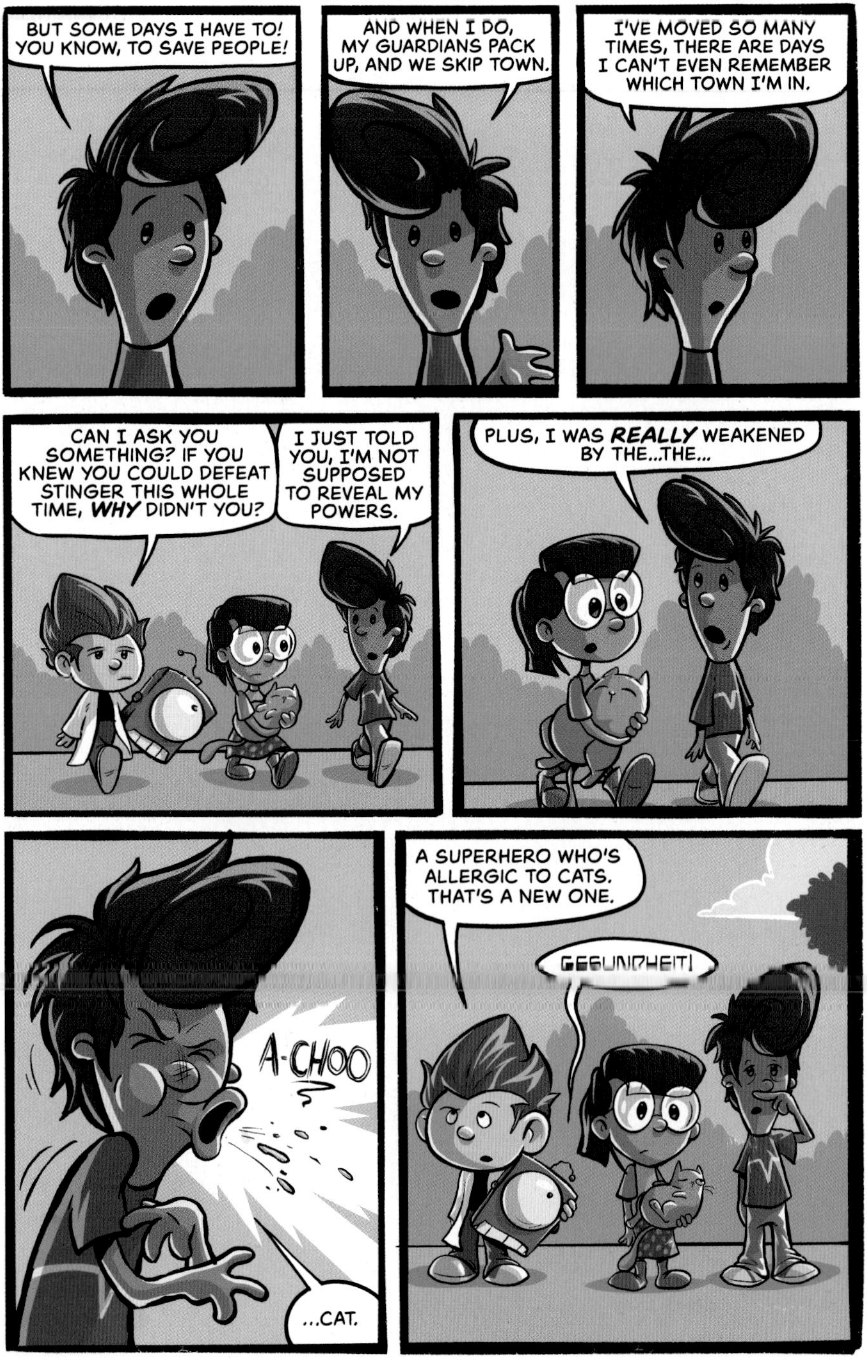
BUT SOME DAYS I HAVE TO! YOU KNOW, TO SAVE PEOPLE!
AND WHEN I DO, MY GUARDIANS PACK UP, AND WE SKIP TOWN.
I'VE MOVED SO MANY TIMES, THERE ARE DAYS I CAN'T EVEN REMEMBER WHICH TOWN I'M IN.
CAN I ASK YOU SOMETHING? IF YOU KNEW YOU COULD DEFEAT STINGER THIS WHOLE TIME, WHY DIDN'T YOU?
I JUST TOLD YOU, I'M NOT SUPPOSED TO REVEAL MY POWERS.
PLUS, I WAS REALLY WEAKENED BY THE...THE...
A-CHOO
...CAT.
A SUPERHERO WHO'S ALLERGIC TO CATS. THAT'S A NEW ONE.
GESUNDHEIT!

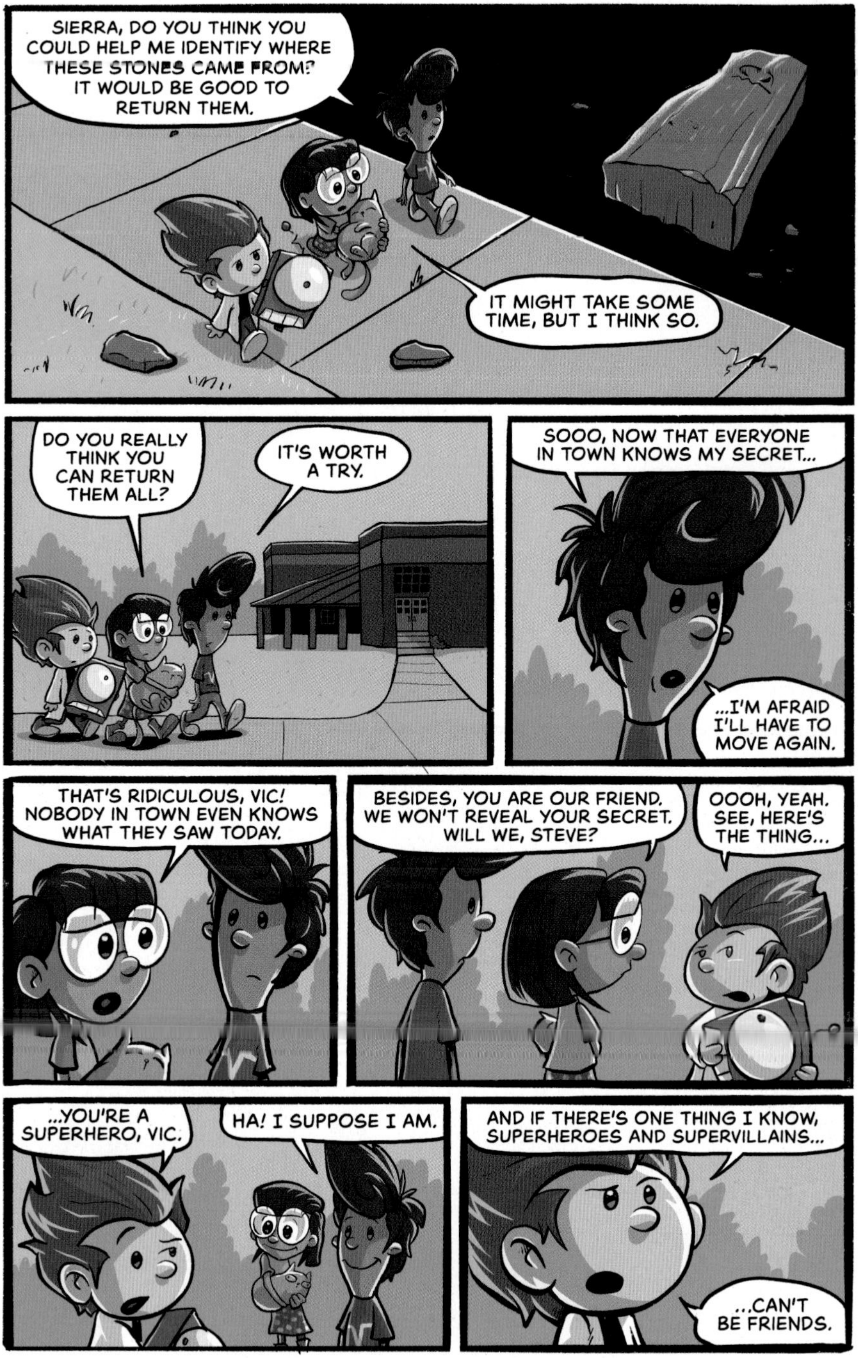
SIERRA, DO YOU THINK YOU COULD HELP ME IDENTIFY WHERE THESE STONES CAME FROM? IT WOULD BE GOOD TO RETURN THEM.
IT MIGHT TAKE SOME TIME, BUT I THINK SO.
DO YOU REALLY THINK YOU CAN RETURN THEM ALL?
IT'S WORTH A TRY.
SOOO, NOW THAT EVERYONE IN TOWN KNOWS MY SECRET...
...I'M AFRAID I'LL HAVE TO MOVE AGAIN.
THAT'S RIDICULOUS, VIC! NOBODY IN TOWN EVEN KNOWS WHAT THEY SAW TODAY.
BESIDES, YOU ARE OUR FRIEND. WE WON'T REVEAL YOUR SECRET. WILL WE, STEVE?
OOOH, YEAH. SEE, HERE'S THE THING...
...YOU'RE A SUPERHERO, VIC.
HA! I SUPPOSE I AM.
AND IF THERE'S ONE THING I KNOW, SUPERHEROES AND SUPERVILLAINS...
...CAN'T BE FRIENDS.

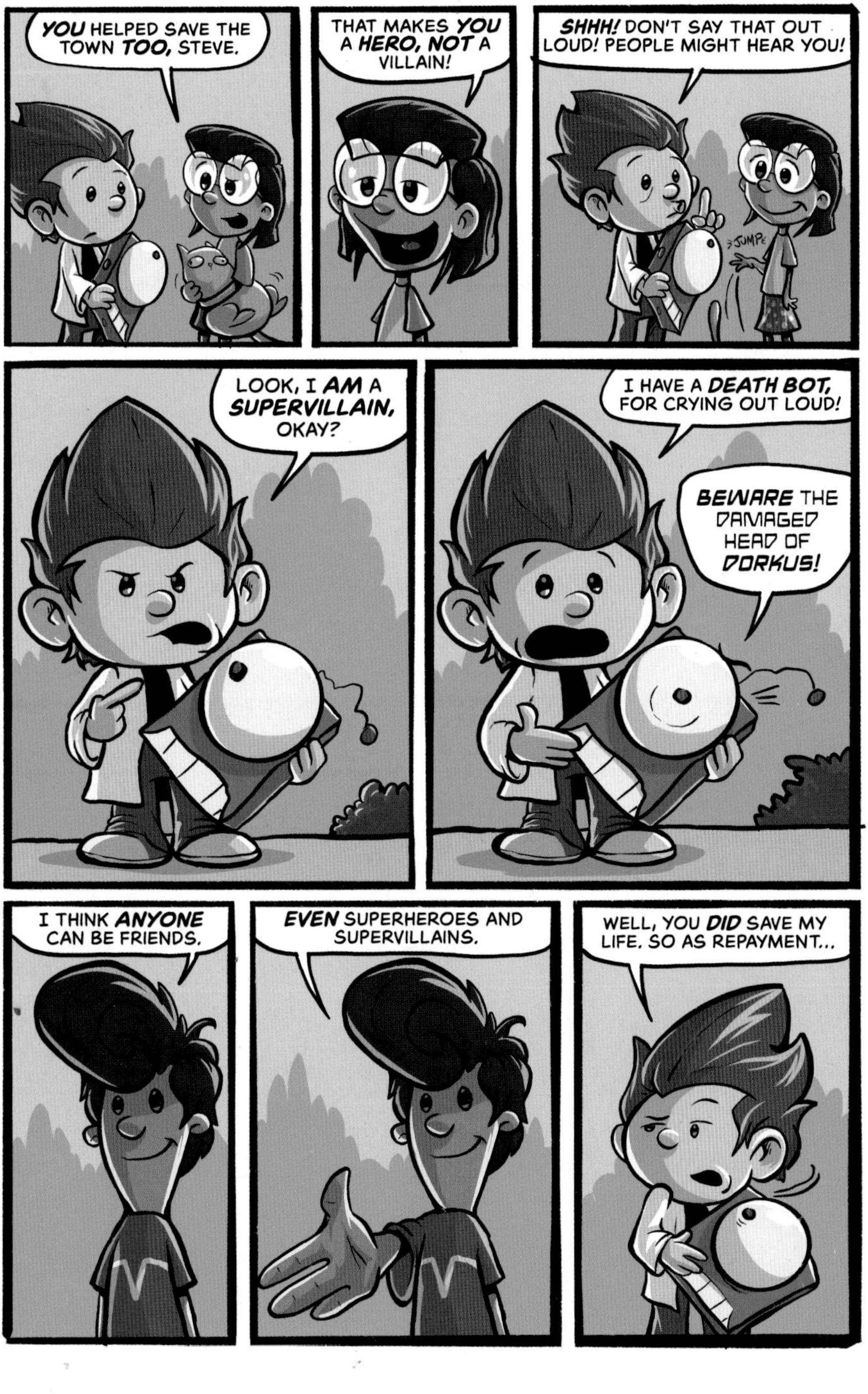

YOU HELPED SAVE THE TOWN TOO, STEVE.
THAT MAKES YOU A HERO, NOT A VILLAIN!
SHHH! DON'T SAY THAT OUT LOUD! PEOPLE MIGHT HEAR YOU!
JUMP
LOOK, I AM A SUPERVILLAIN, OKAY?
I HAVE A DEATH BOT, FOR CRYING OUT LOUD!
BEWARE THE DAMAGED HEAD OF DORKUS!
I THINK ANYONE CAN BE FRIENDS.
EVEN SUPERHEROES AND SUPERVILLAINS.
WELL, YOU DID SAVE MY LIFE. SO AS REPAYMENT...

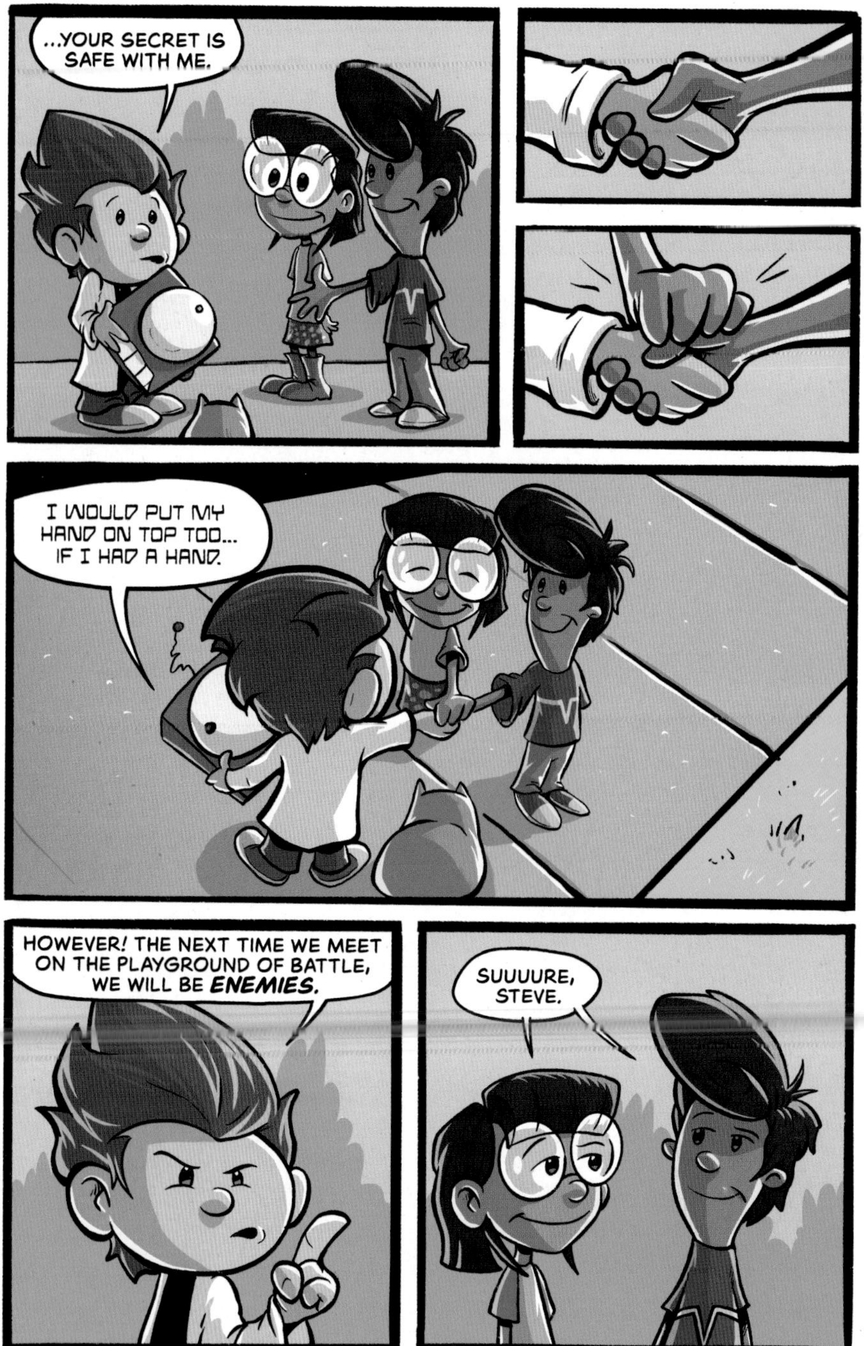
...YOUR SECRET IS SAFE WITH ME.
I WOULD PUT MY HAND ON TOP TOO... IF I HAD A HAND.
HOWEVER! THE NEXT TIME WE MEET ON THE PLAYGROUND OF BATTLE, WE WILL BE ENEMIES.
SUUUURE, STEVE.

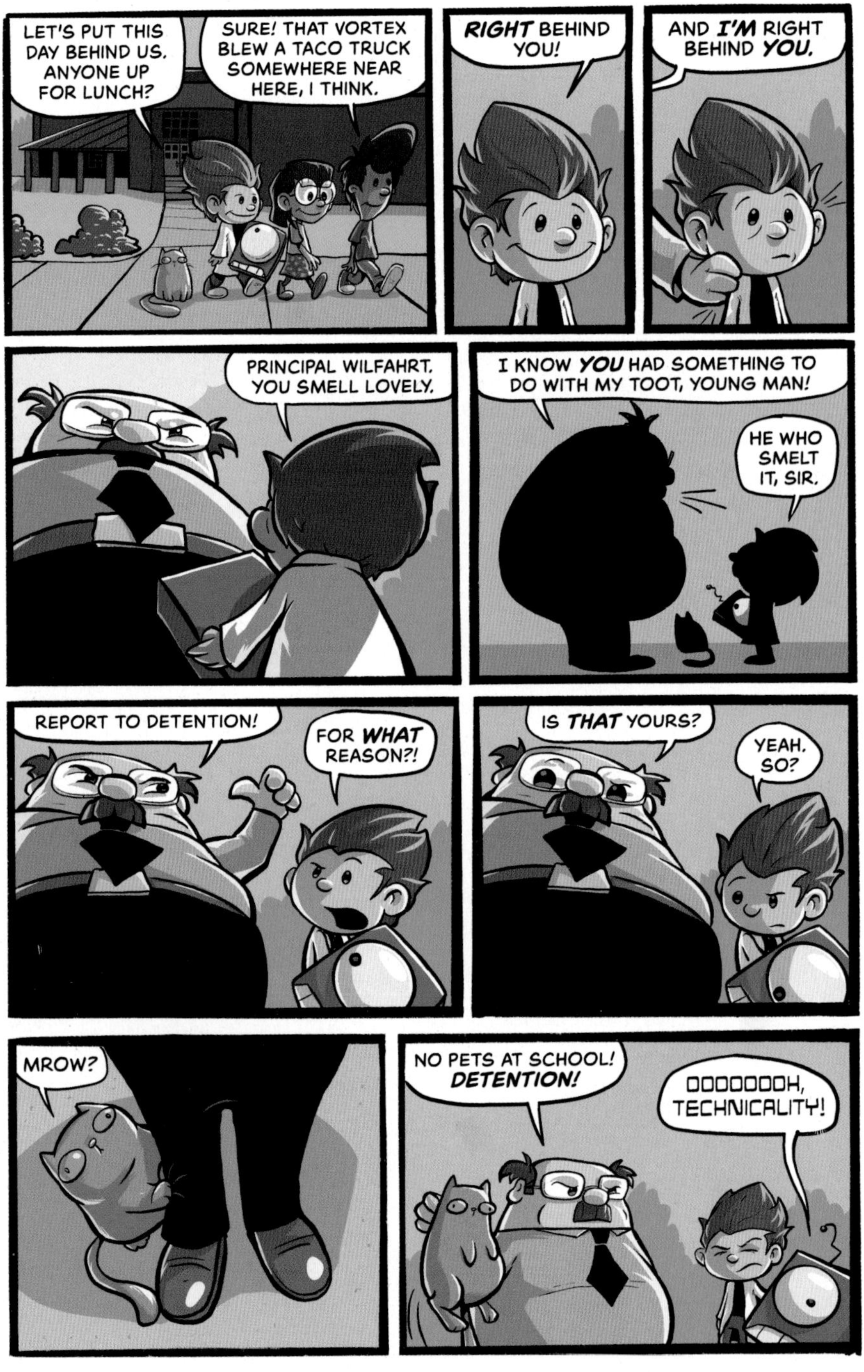
LET'S PUT THIS DAY BEHIND US. ANYONE UP FOR LUNCH?
SURE! THAT VORTEX BLEW A TACO TRUCK SOMEWHERE NEAR HERE, I THINK.
RIGHT BEHIND YOU!
AND I'M RIGHT BEHIND YOU.
PRINCIPAL WILFAHRT. YOU SMELL LOVELY.
I KNOW YOU HAD SOMETHING TO DO WITH MY TOOT, YOUNG MAN!
HE WHO SMELT IT, SIR.
REPORT TO DETENTION!
FOR WHAT REASON?!
IS THAT YOURS?
YEAH. SO?
MROW?
NO PETS AT SCHOOL! DETENTION!
OOOOOOOH, TECHNICALITY!

CHAPTER 21
To See, or Not to See

Many Days Later...

HURRY UP AND EAT YOUR BREAKFAST, KIDS, WE *DON'T* WANT TO BE *LATE* FOR SCHOOL!

OH, I'M WALKING WITH VIC AND SIERRA TODAY!

OH, THAT'S *GREAT*, HONEY. *REALLY* GREAT!

HUZZAH! I DID IT!

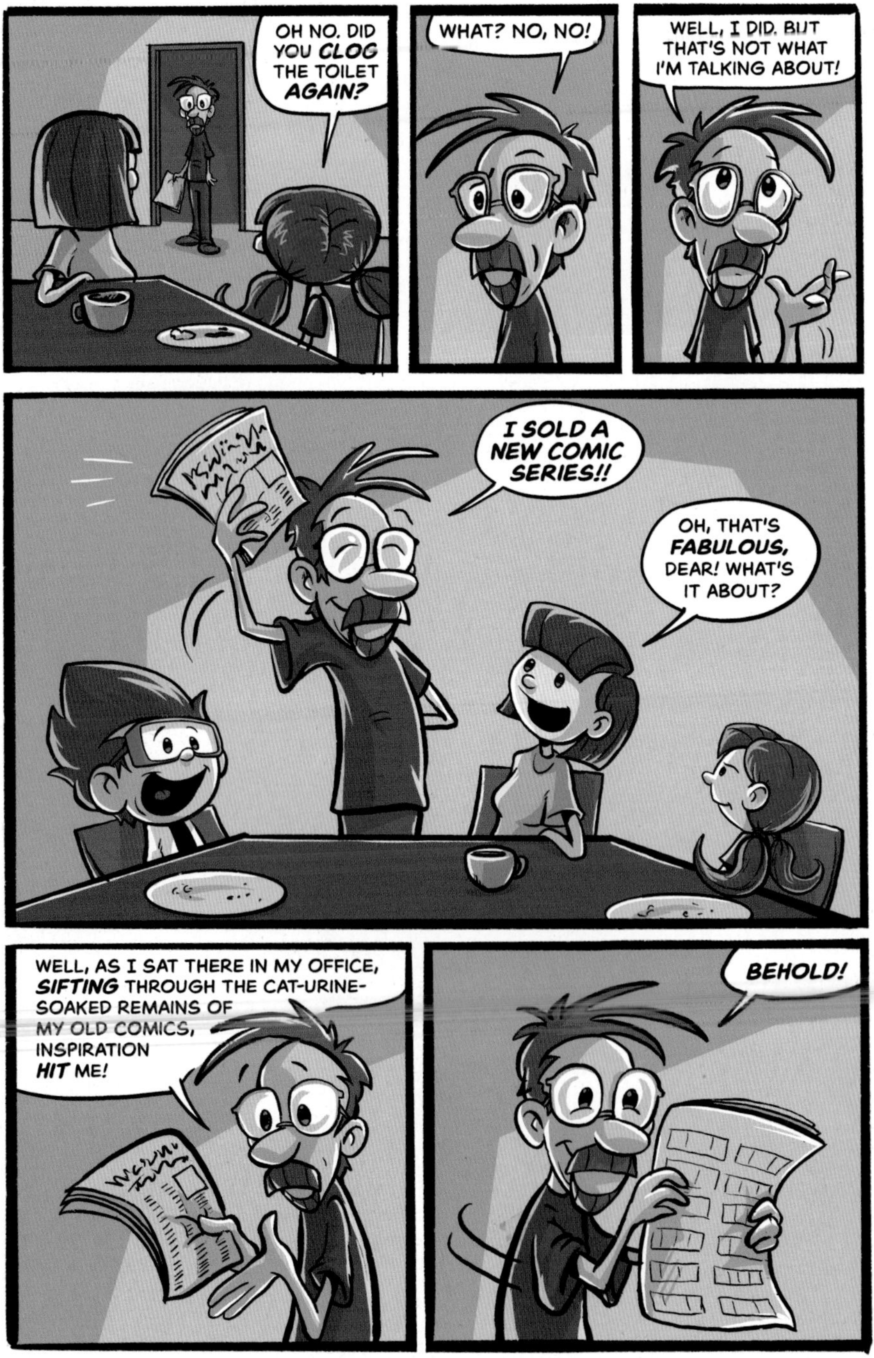
OH NO. DID YOU CLOG THE TOILET AGAIN?
WHAT? NO, NO!
WELL, I DID. BUT THAT'S NOT WHAT I'M TALKING ABOUT!
I SOLD A NEW COMIC SERIES!!
OH, THAT'S FABULOUS, DEAR! WHAT'S IT ABOUT?
WELL, AS I SAT THERE IN MY OFFICE, SIFTING THROUGH THE CAT-URINE-SOAKED REMAINS OF MY OLD COMICS, INSPIRATION HIT ME!
BEHOLD!

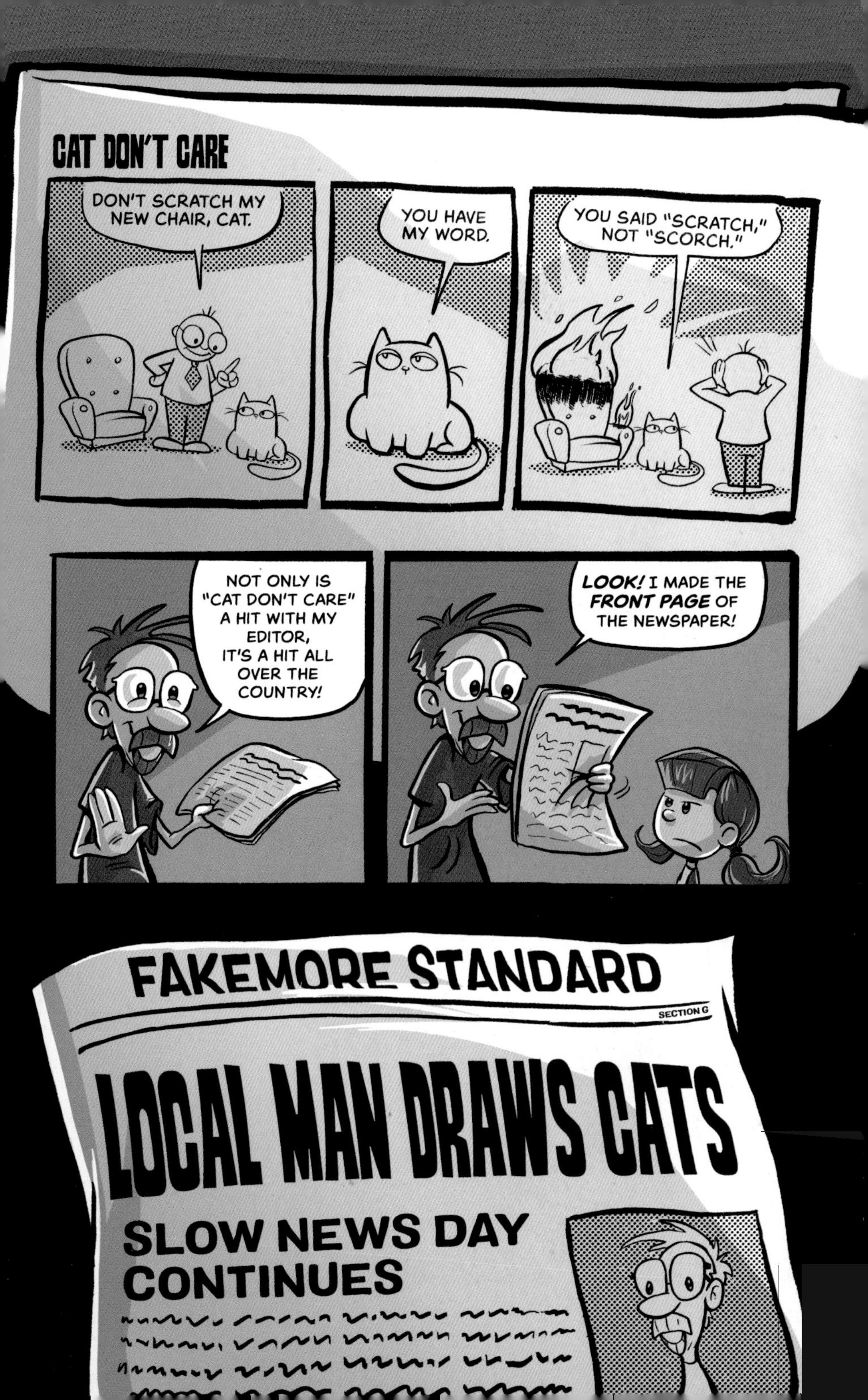
CAT DON'T CARE
DON'T SCRATCH MY NEW CHAIR, CAT.
YOU HAVE MY WORD.
YOU SAID "SCRATCH," NOT "SCORCH."
NOT ONLY IS "CAT DON'T CARE" A HIT WITH MY EDITOR, IT'S A HIT ALL OVER THE COUNTRY!
LOOK! I MADE THE FRONT PAGE OF THE NEWSPAPER!
FAKEMORE STANDARD
SECTION G
LOCAL MAN DRAWS CATS
SLOW NEWS DAY CONTINUES

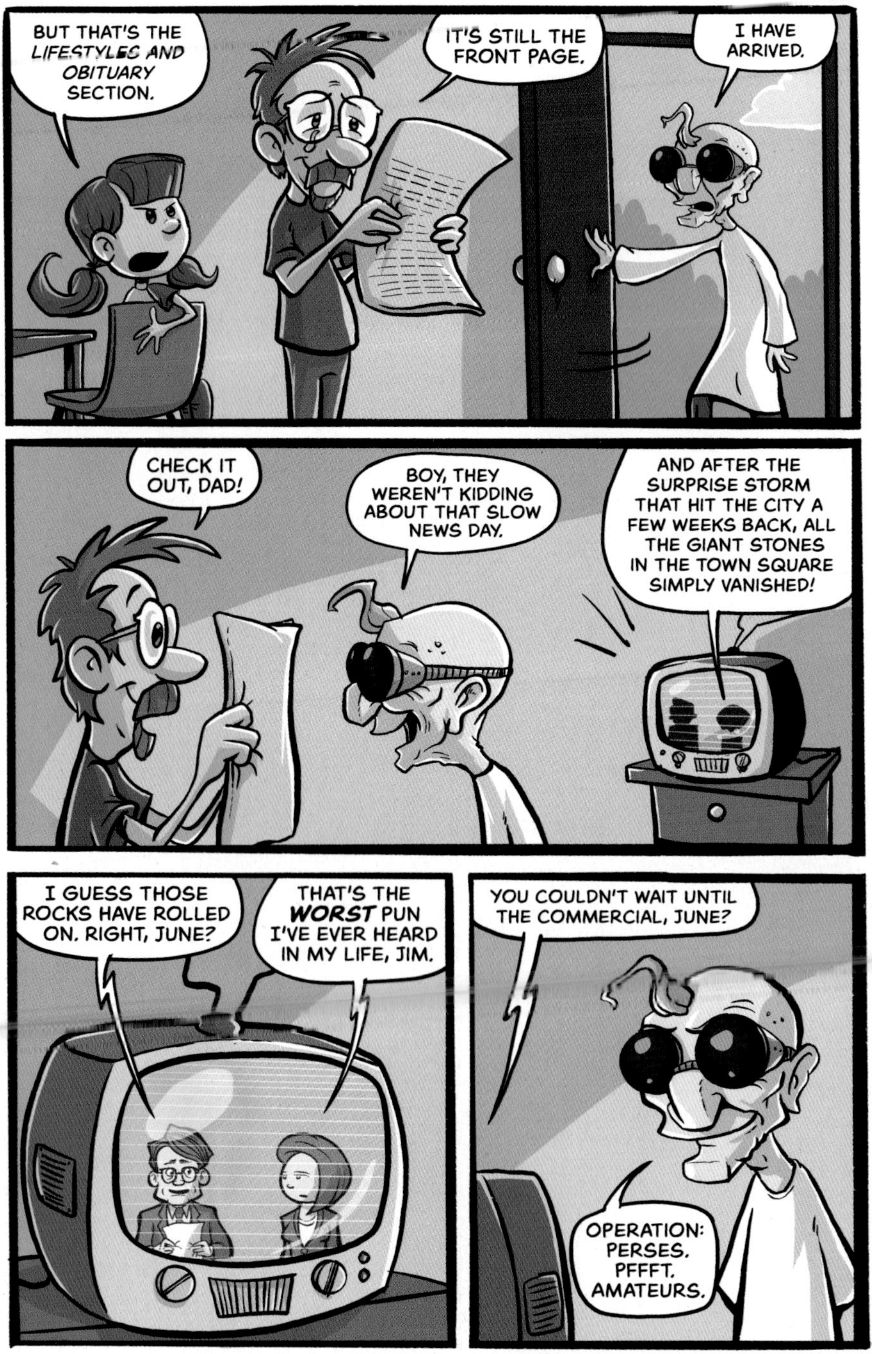
BUT THAT'S THE *LIFESTYLES AND OBITUARY* SECTION.
IT'S STILL THE FRONT PAGE.
I HAVE ARRIVED.
CHECK IT OUT, DAD!
BOY, THEY WEREN'T KIDDING ABOUT THAT SLOW NEWS DAY.
AND AFTER THE SURPRISE STORM THAT HIT THE CITY A FEW WEEKS BACK, ALL THE GIANT STONES IN THE TOWN SQUARE SIMPLY VANISHED!
I GUESS THOSE ROCKS HAVE ROLLED ON. RIGHT, JUNE?
THAT'S THE ***WORST*** PUN I'VE EVER HEARD IN MY LIFE, JIM.
YOU COULDN'T WAIT UNTIL THE COMMERCIAL, JUNE?
OPERATION: PERSES. PFFFT. AMATEURS.

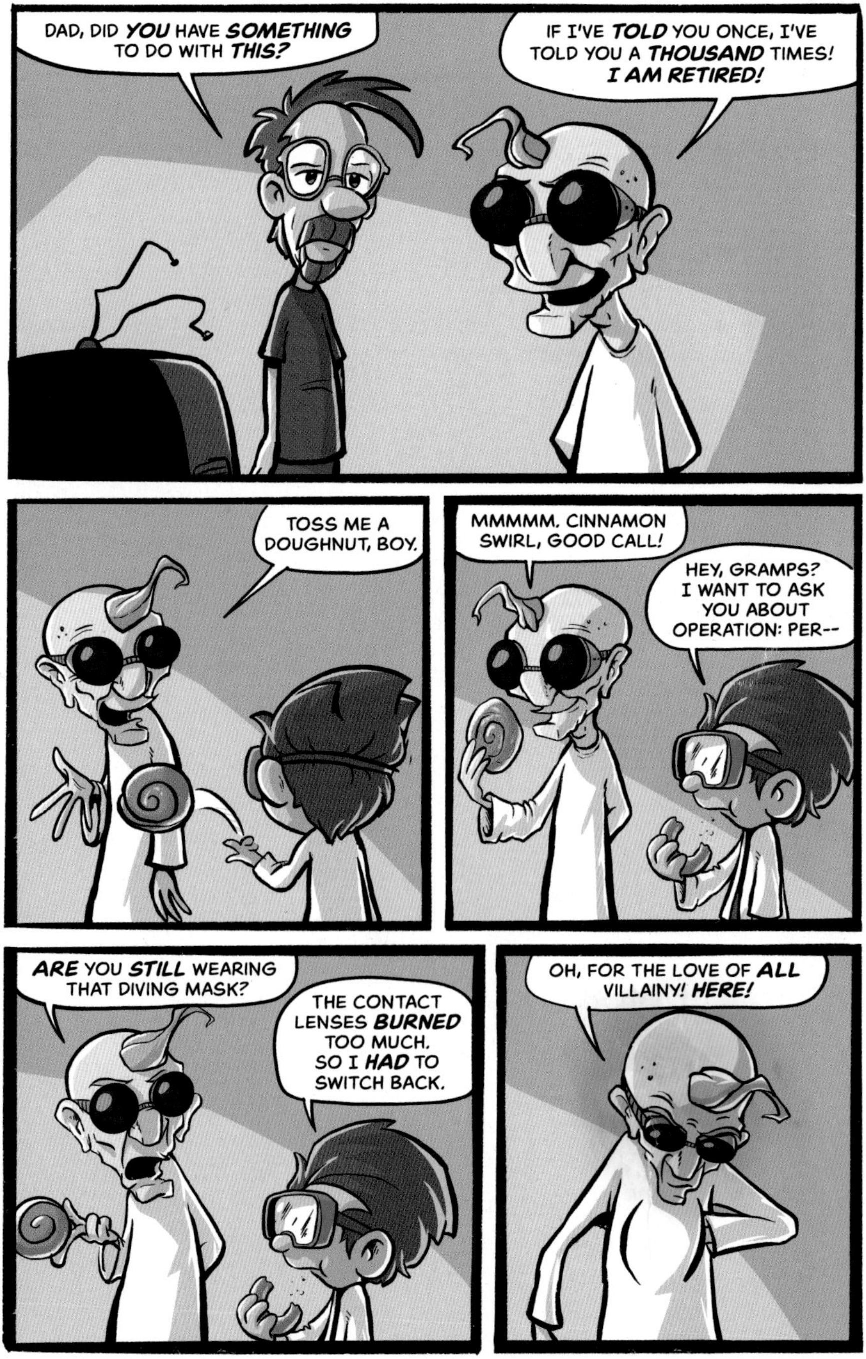
DAD, DID YOU HAVE SOMETHING TO DO WITH THIS?
IF I'VE TOLD YOU ONCE, I'VE TOLD YOU A THOUSAND TIMES! I AM RETIRED!
TOSS ME A DOUGHNUT, BOY.
MMMMM. CINNAMON SWIRL, GOOD CALL!
HEY, GRAMPS? I WANT TO ASK YOU ABOUT OPERATION: PER--
ARE YOU STILL WEARING THAT DIVING MASK?
THE CONTACT LENSES BURNED TOO MUCH, SO I HAD TO SWITCH BACK.
OH, FOR THE LOVE OF ALL VILLAINY! HERE!

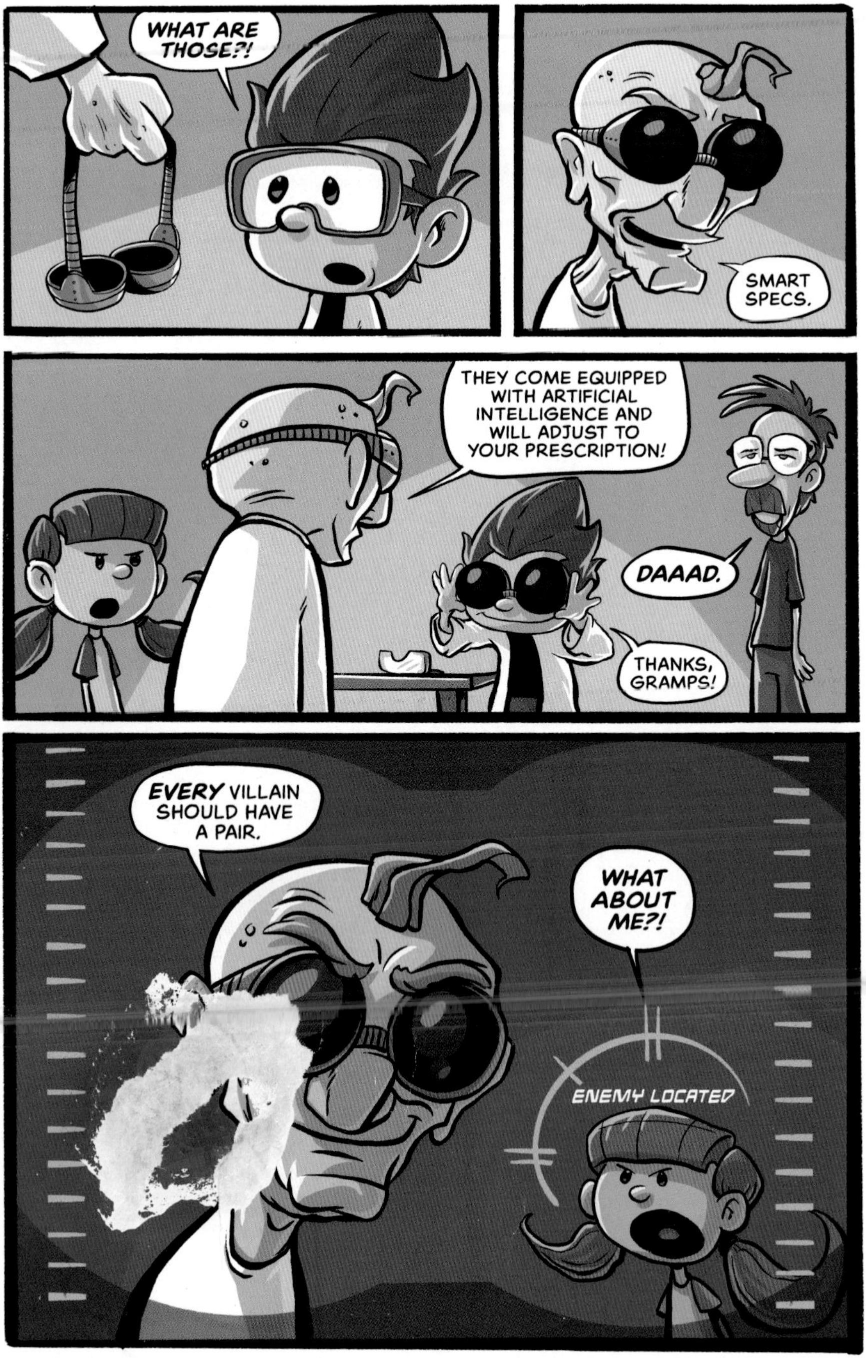
WHAT ARE THOSE?!
SMART SPECS.
THEY COME EQUIPPED WITH ARTIFICIAL INTELLIGENCE AND WILL ADJUST TO YOUR PRESCRIPTION!
DAAAD.
THANKS, GRAMPS!
EVERY VILLAIN SHOULD HAVE A PAIR.
WHAT ABOUT ME?!
ENEMY LOCATED

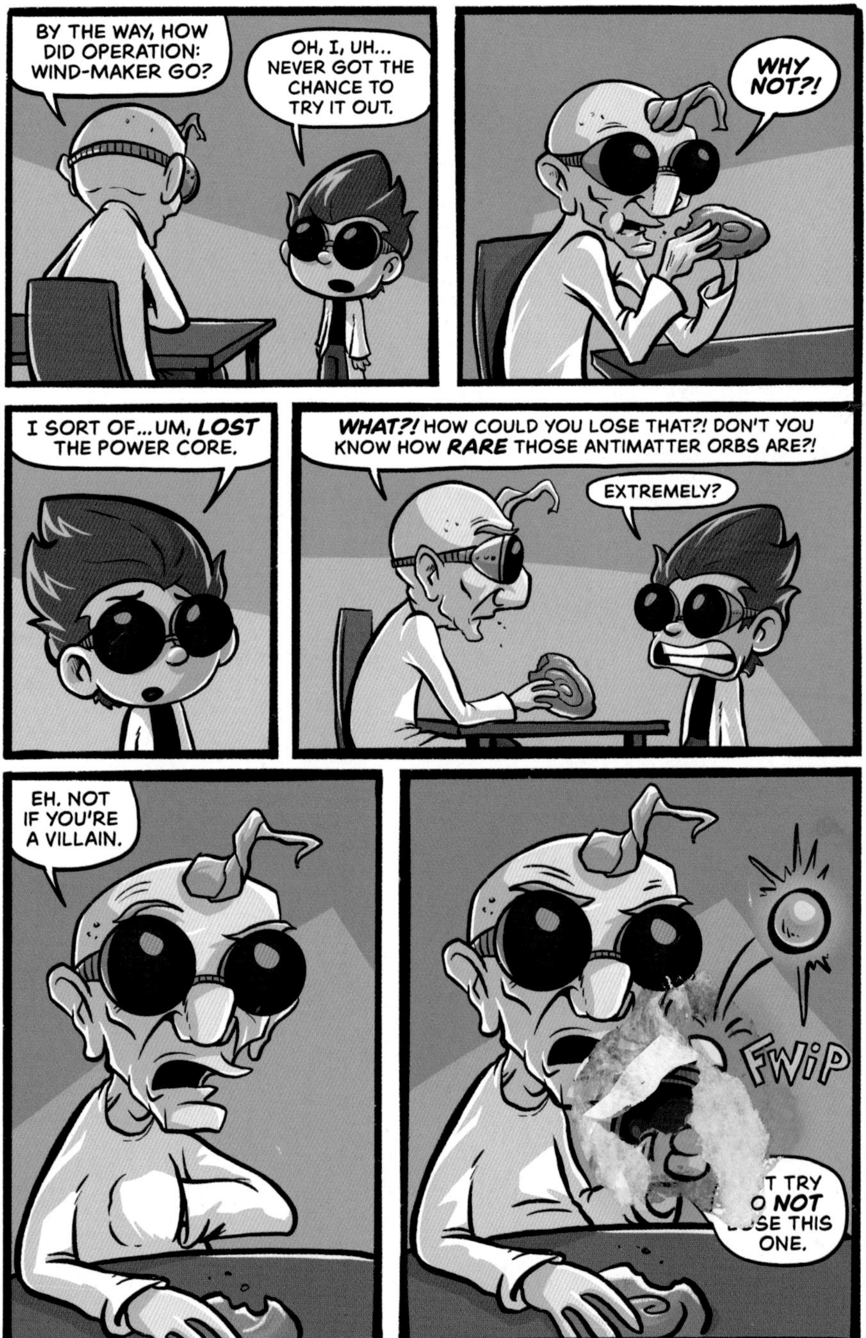
BY THE WAY, HOW DID OPERATION: WIND-MAKER GO?
OH, I, UH... NEVER GOT THE CHANCE TO TRY IT OUT.
WHY NOT?!
I SORT OF...UM, LOST THE POWER CORE.
WHAT?! HOW COULD YOU LOSE THAT?! DON'T YOU KNOW HOW RARE THOSE ANTIMATTER ORBS ARE?!
EXTREMELY?
EH. NOT IF YOU'RE A VILLAIN.
FWIP
T TRY O NOT SE THIS ONE.

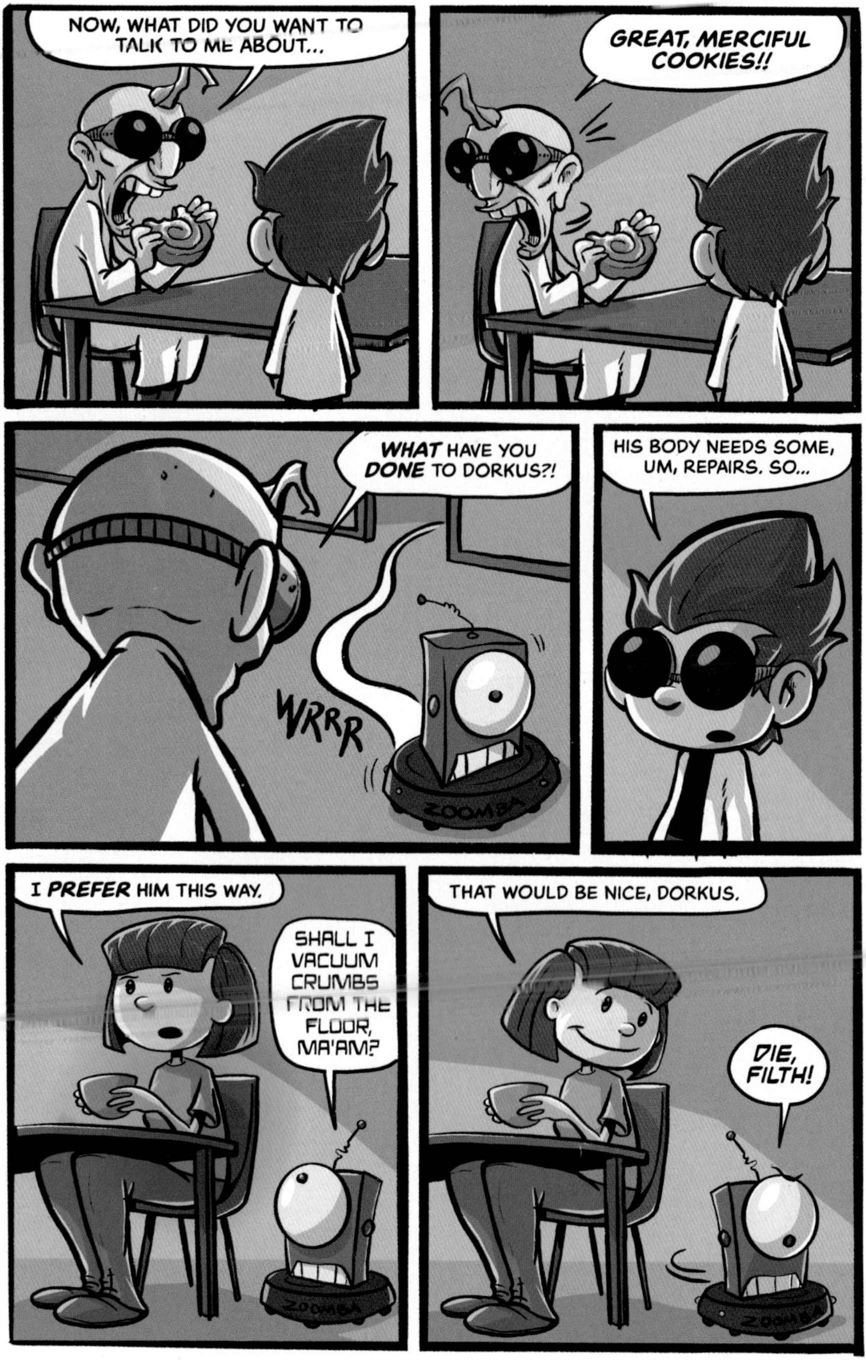
NOW, WHAT DID YOU WANT TO TALK TO ME ABOUT...
GREAT, MERCIFUL COOKIES!!
WHAT HAVE YOU DONE TO DORKUS?!
WRRR
ZOOMBA
HIS BODY NEEDS SOME, UM, REPAIRS. SO...
I PREFER HIM THIS WAY.
SHALL I VACUUM CRUMBS FROM THE FLOOR, MA'AM?
ZOOMBA
THAT WOULD BE NICE, DORKUS.
DIE, FILTH!
ZOOMBA

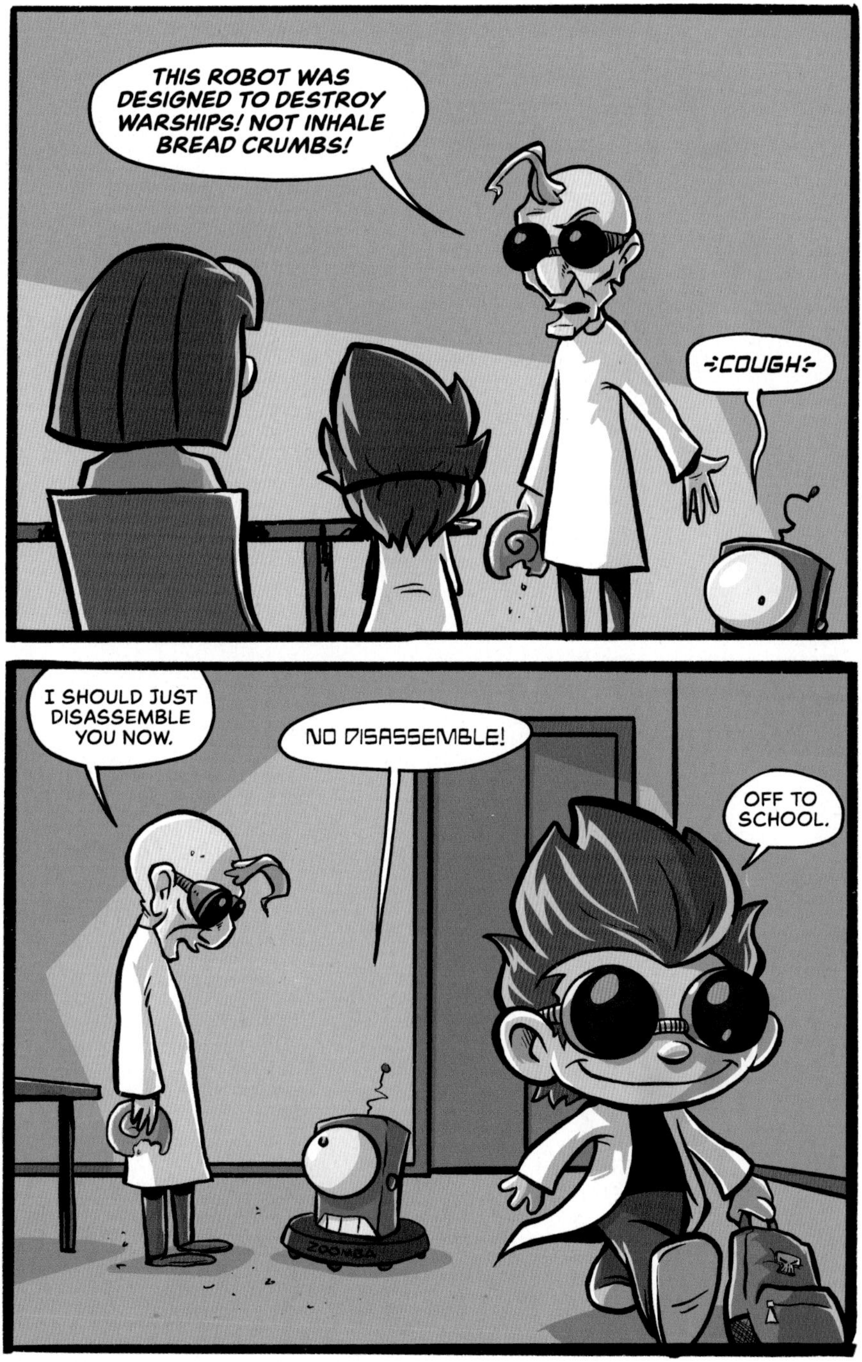
THIS ROBOT WAS DESIGNED TO DESTROY WARSHIPS! NOT INHALE BREAD CRUMBS!
COUGH
I SHOULD JUST DISASSEMBLE YOU NOW.
NO DISASSEMBLE!
OFF TO SCHOOL.

CHAPTER 22

Far, Far Away...

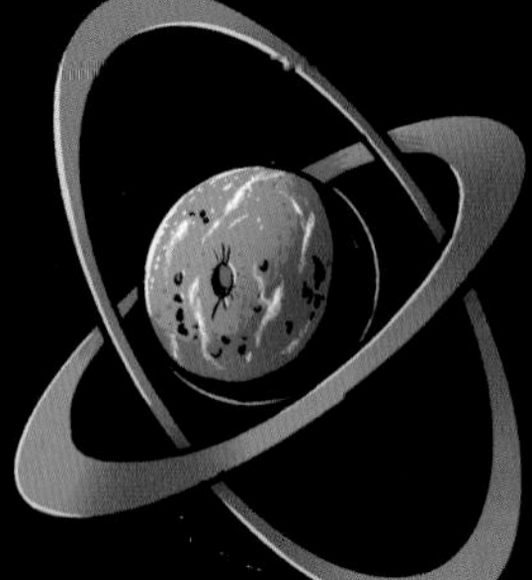

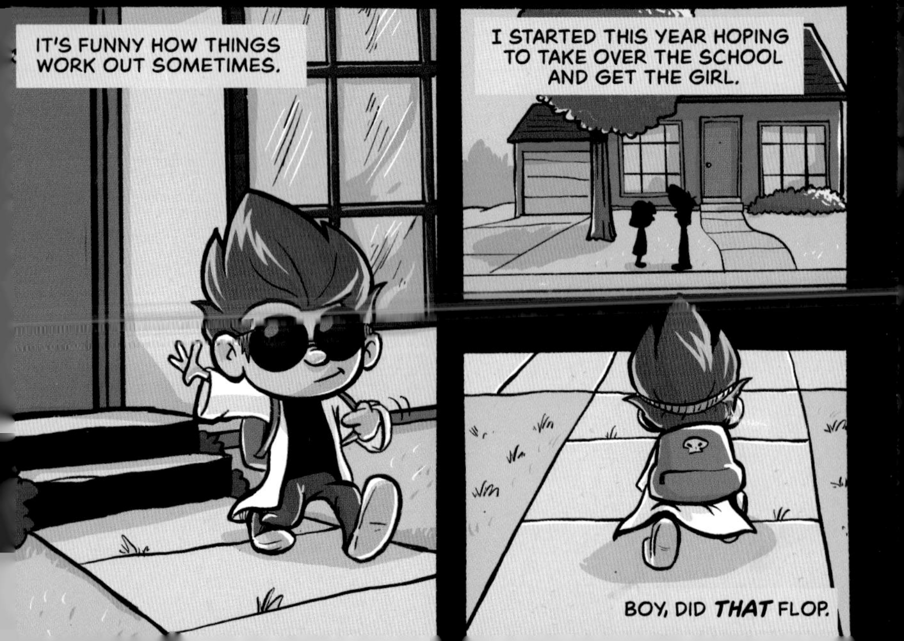
IT'S FUNNY HOW THINGS WORK OUT SOMETIMES.
I STARTED THIS YEAR HOPING TO TAKE OVER THE SCHOOL AND GET THE GIRL.
BOY, DID *THAT* FLOP.

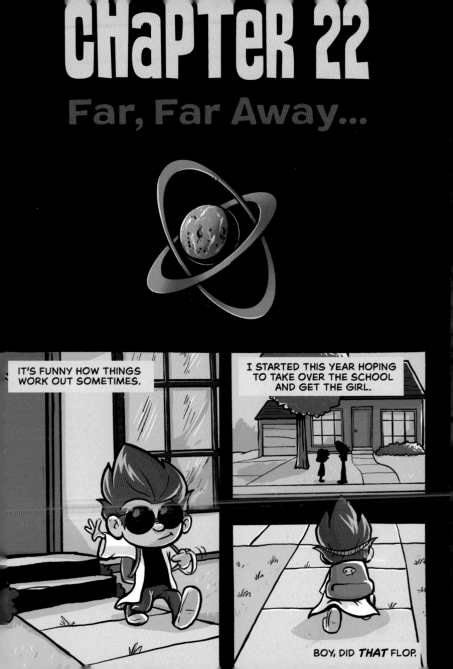

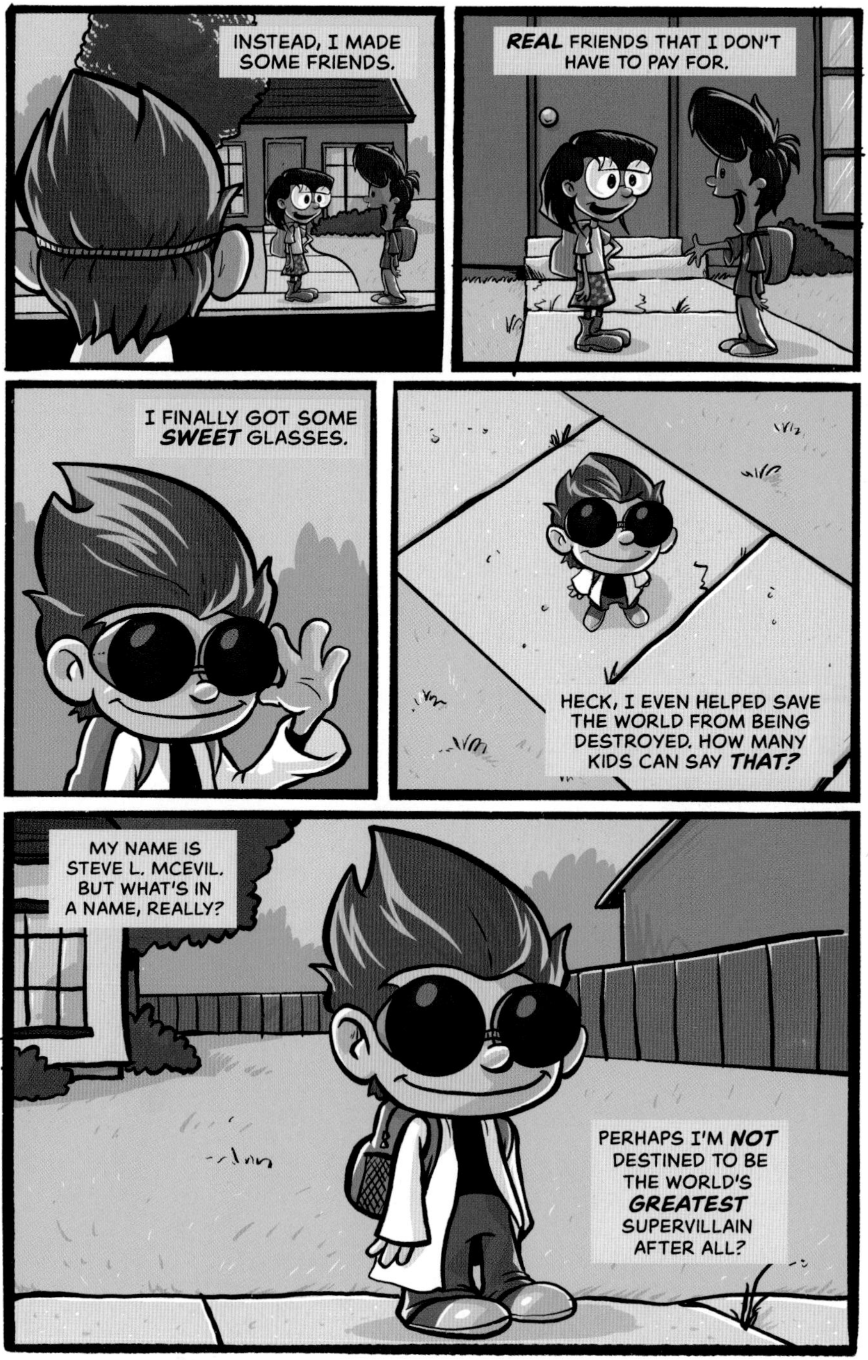
INSTEAD, I MADE SOME FRIENDS.
REAL FRIENDS THAT I DON'T HAVE TO PAY FOR.
I FINALLY GOT SOME SWEET GLASSES.
HECK, I EVEN HELPED SAVE THE WORLD FROM BEING DESTROYED. HOW MANY KIDS CAN SAY THAT?
MY NAME IS STEVE L. MCEVIL. BUT WHAT'S IN A NAME, REALLY?
PERHAPS I'M NOT DESTINED TO BE THE WORLD'S GREATEST SUPERVILLAIN AFTER ALL?

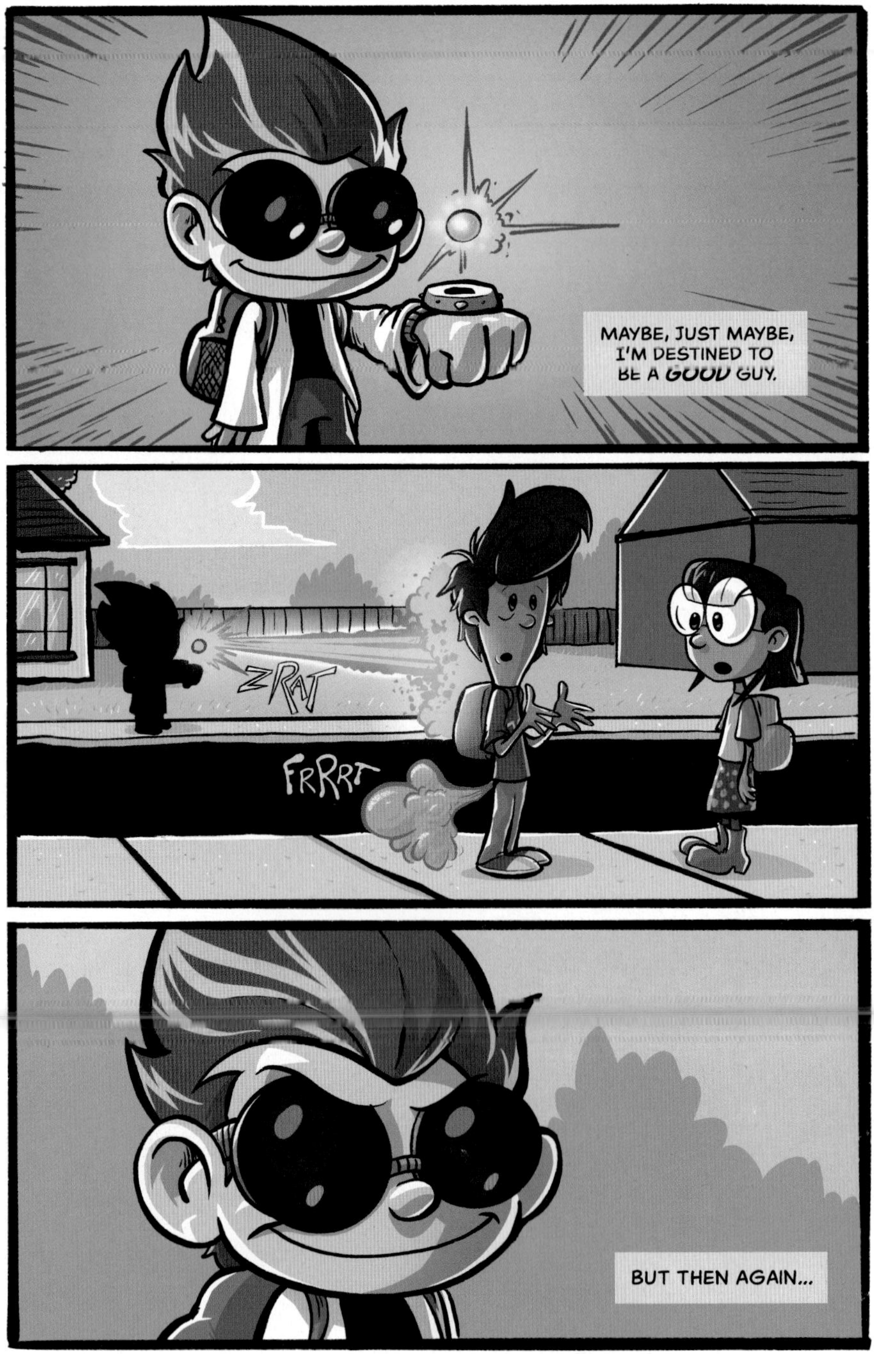
MAYBE, JUST MAYBE, I'M DESTINED TO BE A GOOD GUY.
ZRAT
FRRRT
BUT THEN AGAIN...

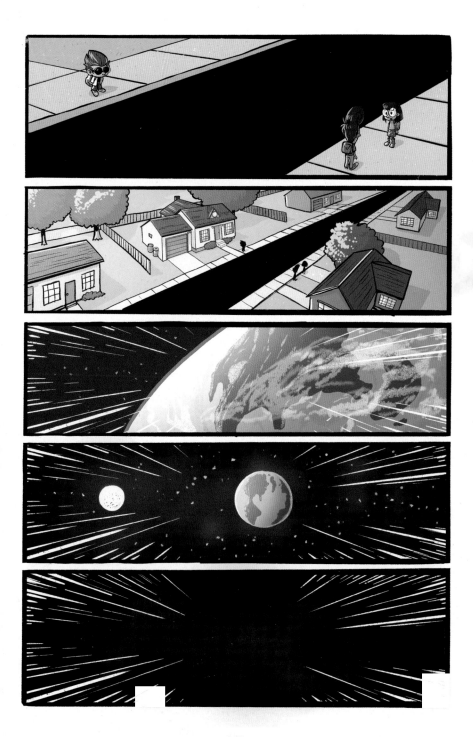

213

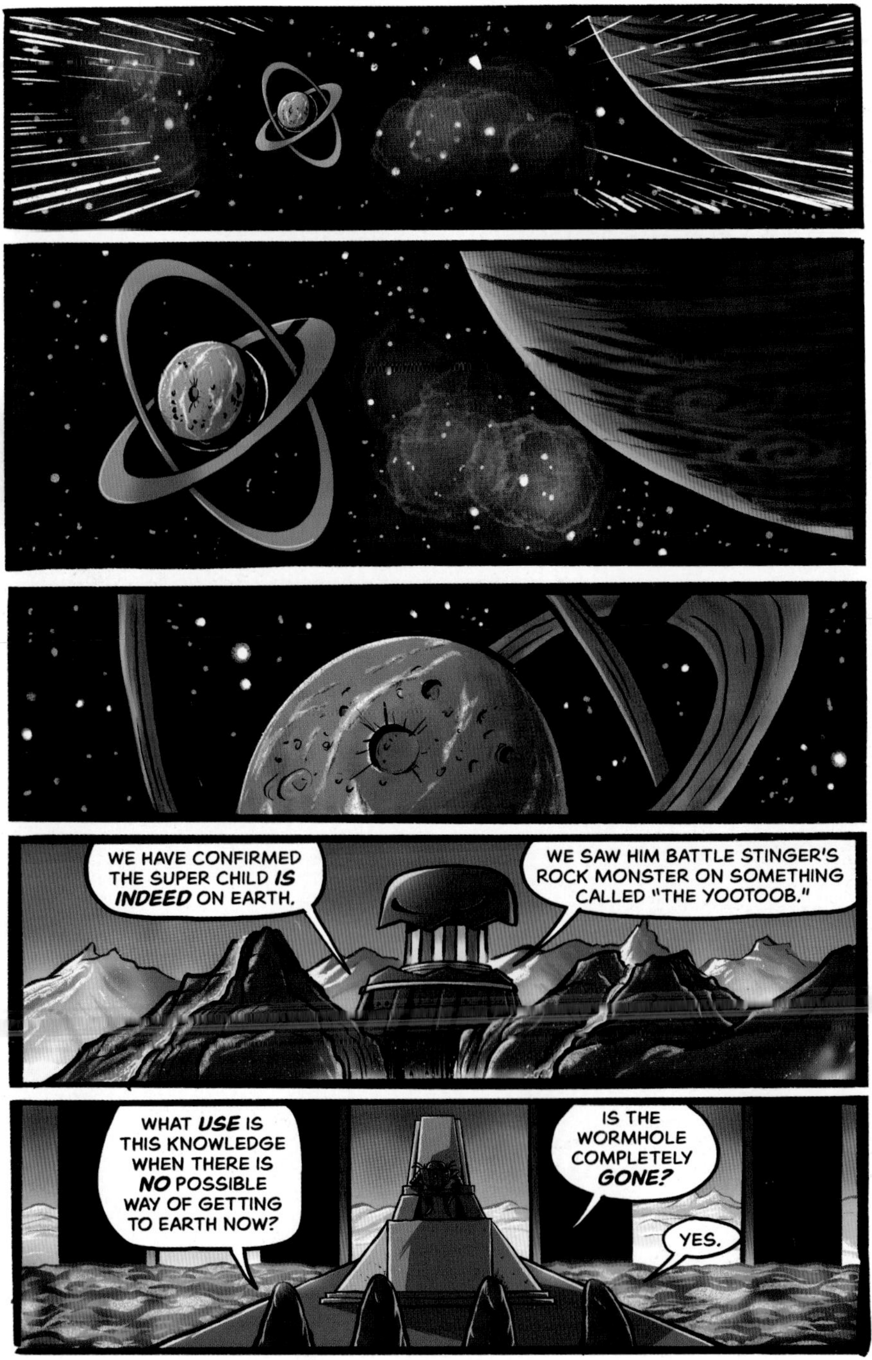
WE HAVE CONFIRMED THE SUPER CHILD IS INDEED ON EARTH.
WE SAW HIM BATTLE STINGER'S ROCK MONSTER ON SOMETHING CALLED "THE YOOTOOB."
WHAT USE IS THIS KNOWLEDGE WHEN THERE IS NO POSSIBLE WAY OF GETTING TO EARTH NOW?
IS THE WORMHOLE COMPLETELY GONE?
YES.

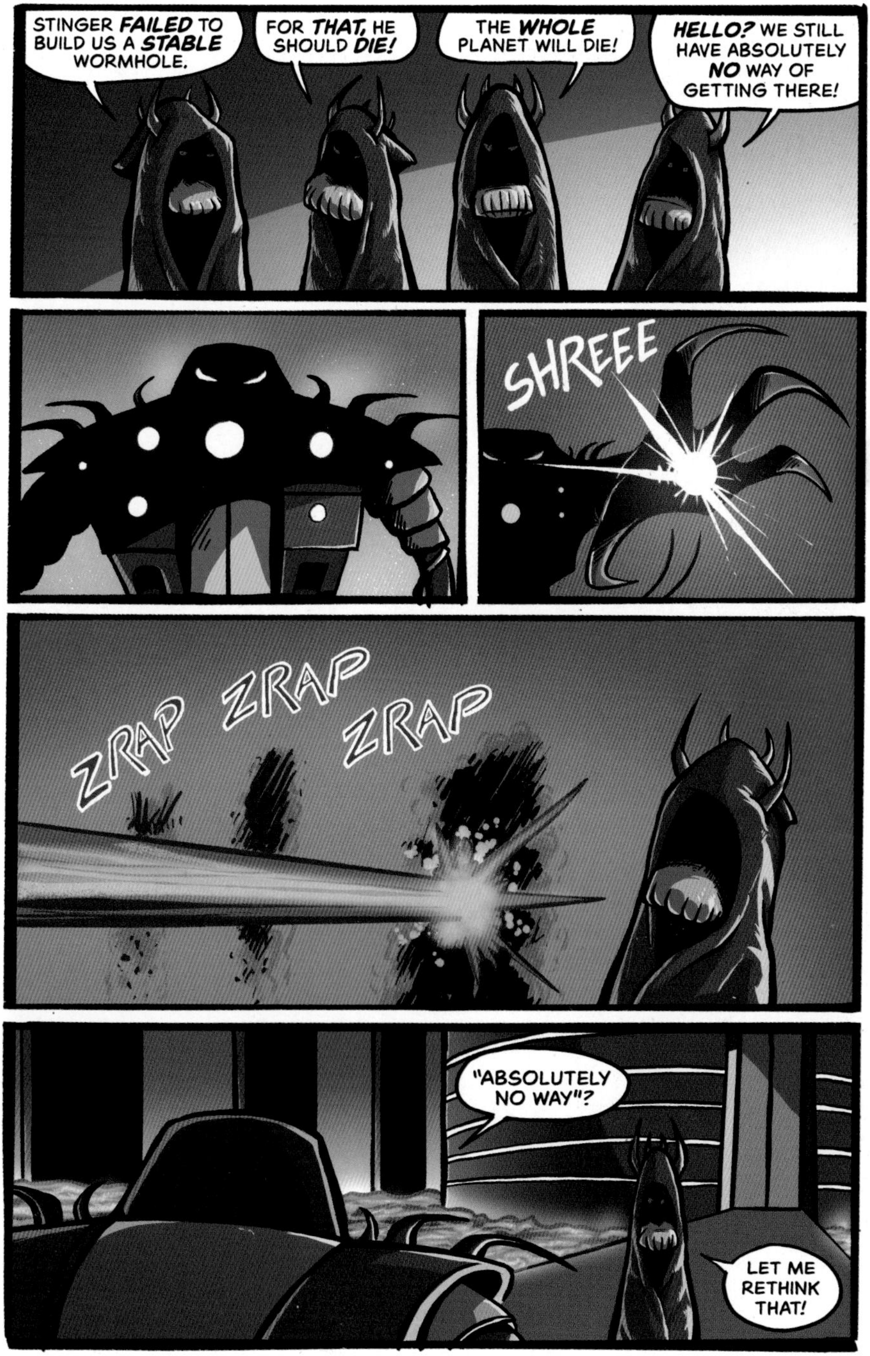
STINGER FAILED TO BUILD US A STABLE WORMHOLE.
FOR THAT, HE SHOULD DIE!
THE WHOLE PLANET WILL DIE!
HELLO? WE STILL HAVE ABSOLUTELY NO WAY OF GETTING THERE!
SHREEE
ZRAP ZRAP ZRAP
"ABSOLUTELY NO WAY"?
LET ME RETHINK THAT!

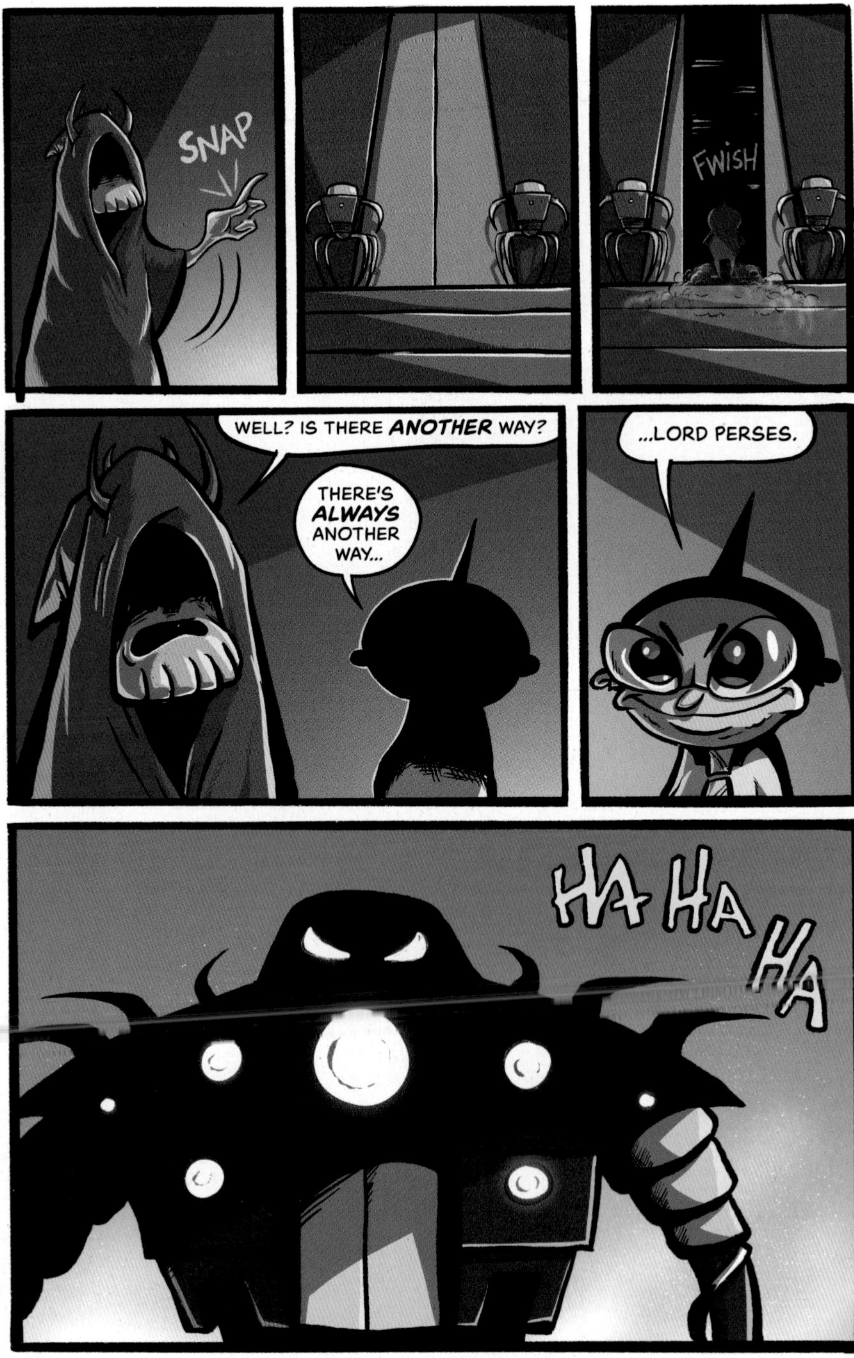
SNAP
FWISH
WELL? IS THERE ANOTHER WAY?
THERE'S ALWAYS ANOTHER WAY...
...LORD PERSES.
HA HA HA HA

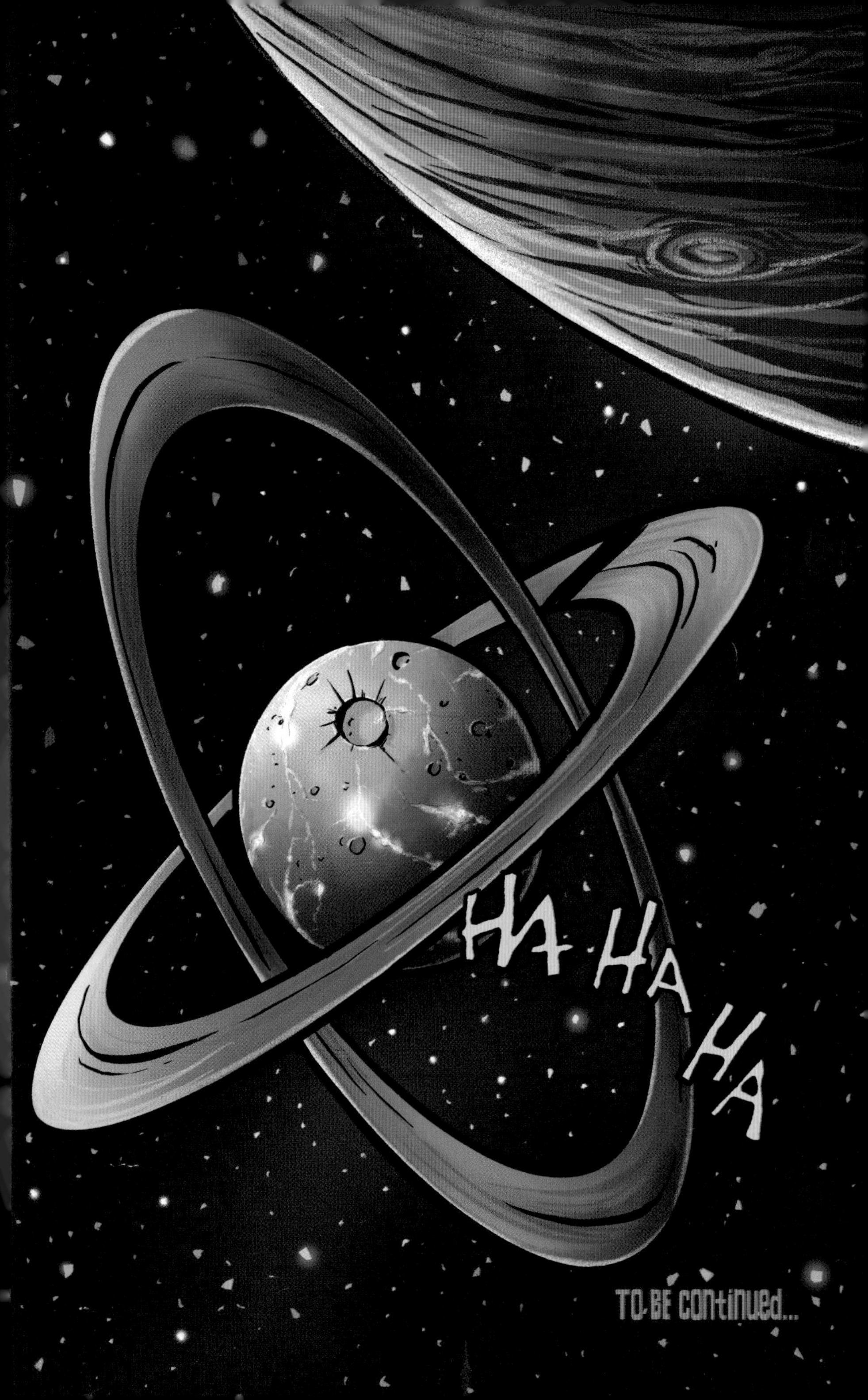
HA HA HA HA
TO BE CONTINUED...

You would think a person like me, who grew up on the shores of Hawaii, would spend all of their time at the beach. Well, I did, but not to swim. All day long, I would create and draw wacky stories about my favorite cartoon and movie characters, with their vehicles and gadgets, getting involved in zany adventures. Shark surfing, for example, was one of my favorites.

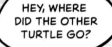

HEY, WHERE DID THE OTHER TURTLE GO?

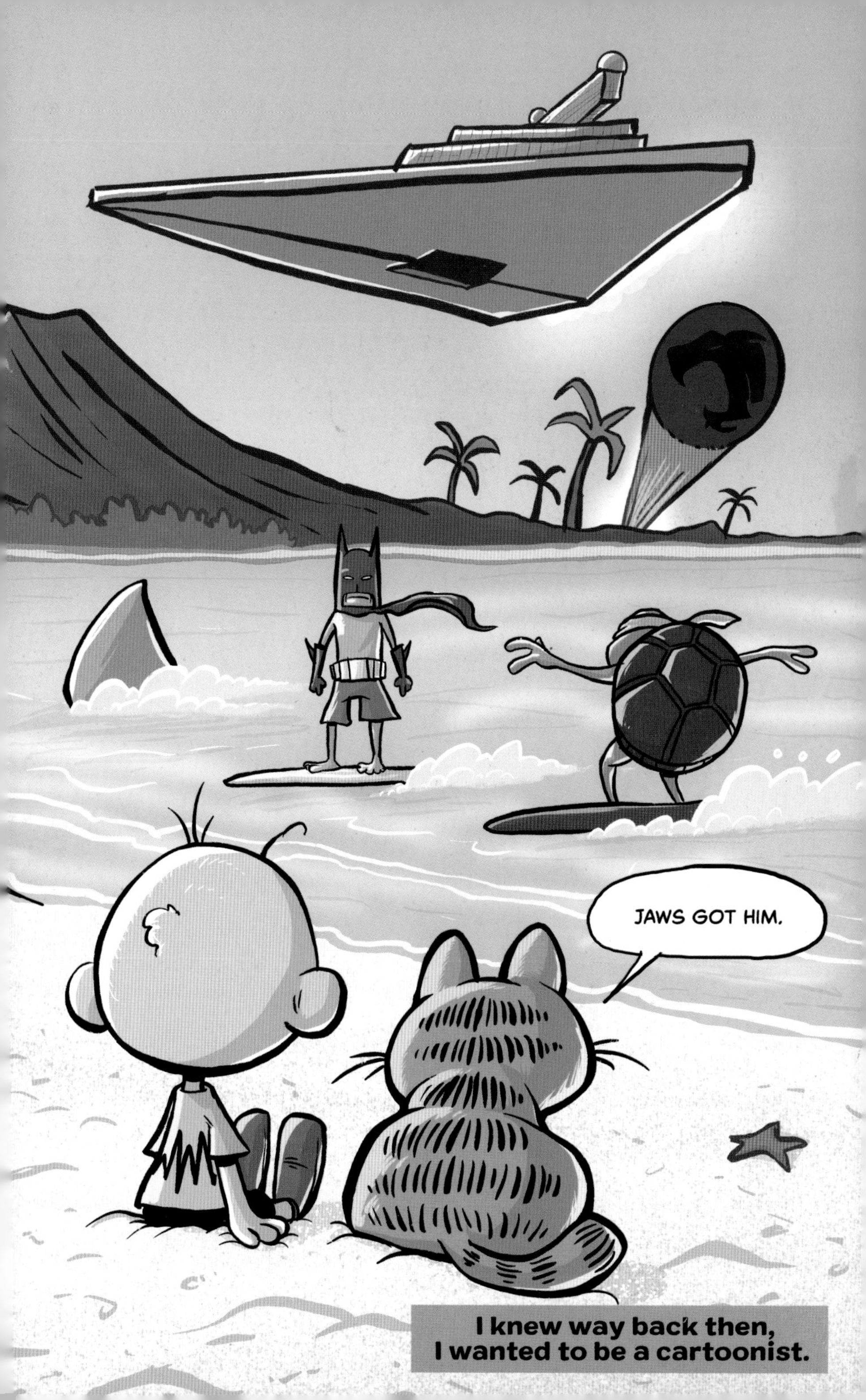
JAWS GOT HIM.
I knew way back then, I wanted to be a cartoonist.

So I practiced drawing and writing every day for YEARS, and now...I'm a cartoonist! These days, I create zany adventures, but with my OWN characters like STEVE L. McEVIL, DORKUS, and many others in my art studio.
IT'S ***NOT*** AS MUCH FUN AS DRAWING ON THE BEACH, THOUGH.

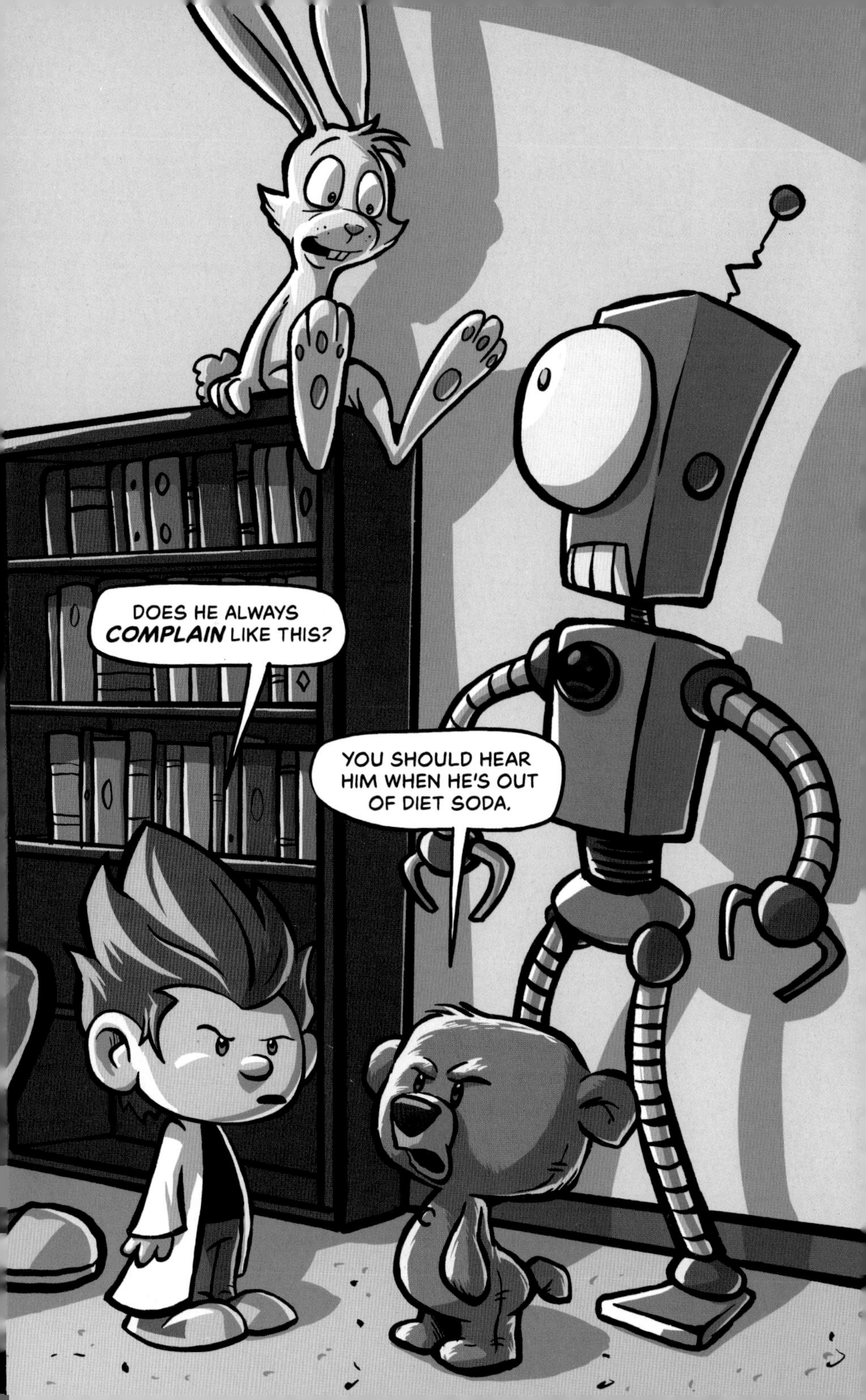
DOES HE ALWAYS COMPLAIN LIKE THIS?
YOU SHOULD HEAR HIM WHEN HE'S OUT OF DIET SODA.

HOW TO CREATE A THREE-PANEL COMIC STRIP!

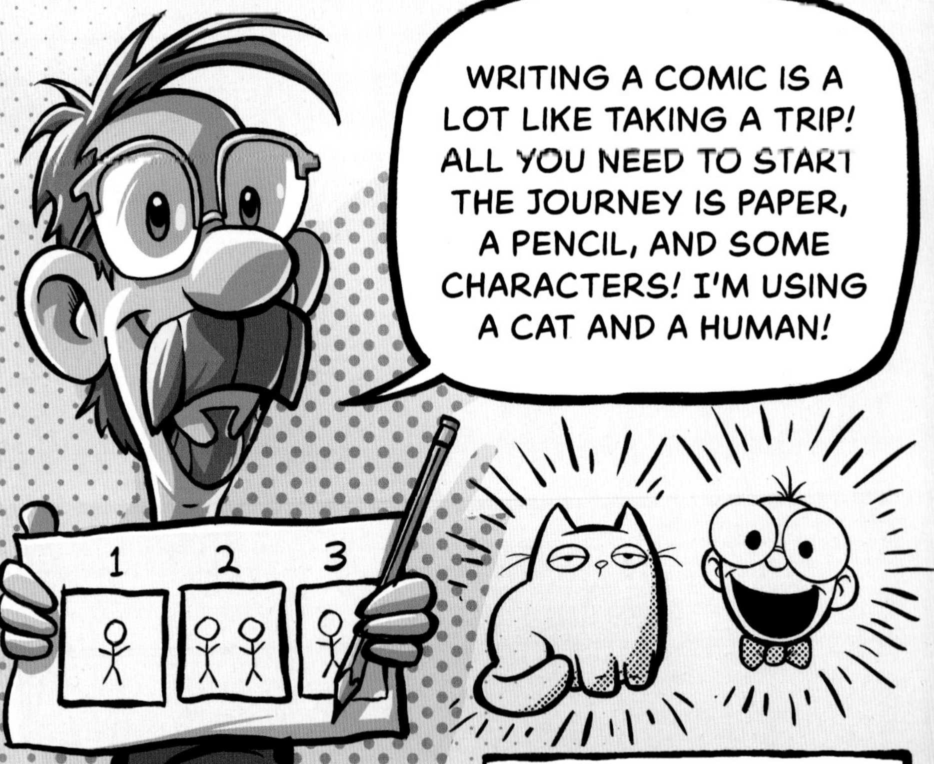
WRITING A COMIC IS A LOT LIKE TAKING A TRIP! ALL YOU NEED TO START THE JOURNEY IS PAPER, A PENCIL, AND SOME CHARACTERS! I'M USING A CAT AND A HUMAN!
1
2
3

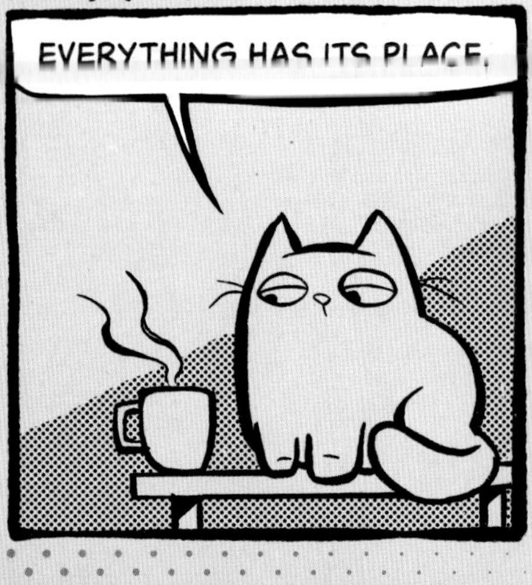
EVERYTHING HAS ITS PLACE.

PANEL 1:
Beginning (setup)

Think of this place as your starting point. Here, you will use a character to set up your gag or joke.

PANEL 2:
Middle (buildup)

Are we there yet?! Almost! But not quite. Here, you'll boost, or reinforce, the setup from panel 1. Sometimes by adding a twist!

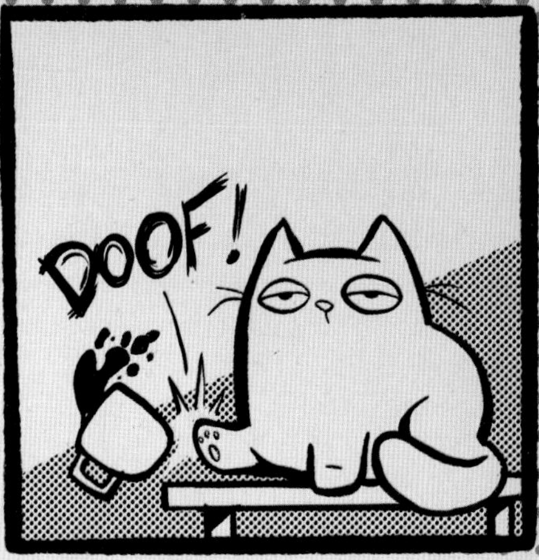
DOOF!

PANEL 3:
End (punch line)

You've arrived at your final destination: THE PUNCH LINE! This is where your setup resolves itself and the joke pays off!

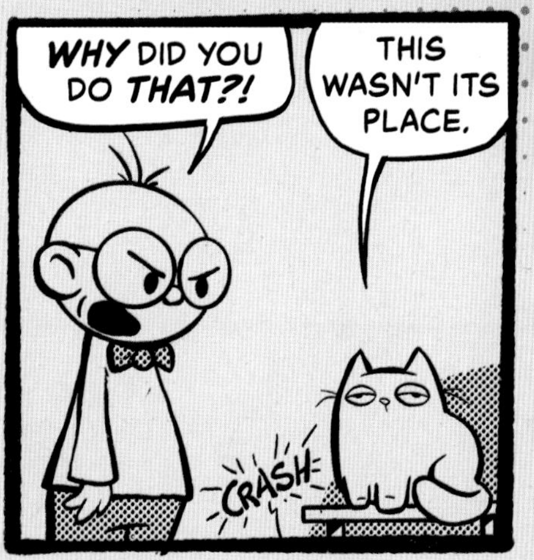
WHY DID YOU DO THAT?!
THIS WASN'T ITS PLACE.
CRASH

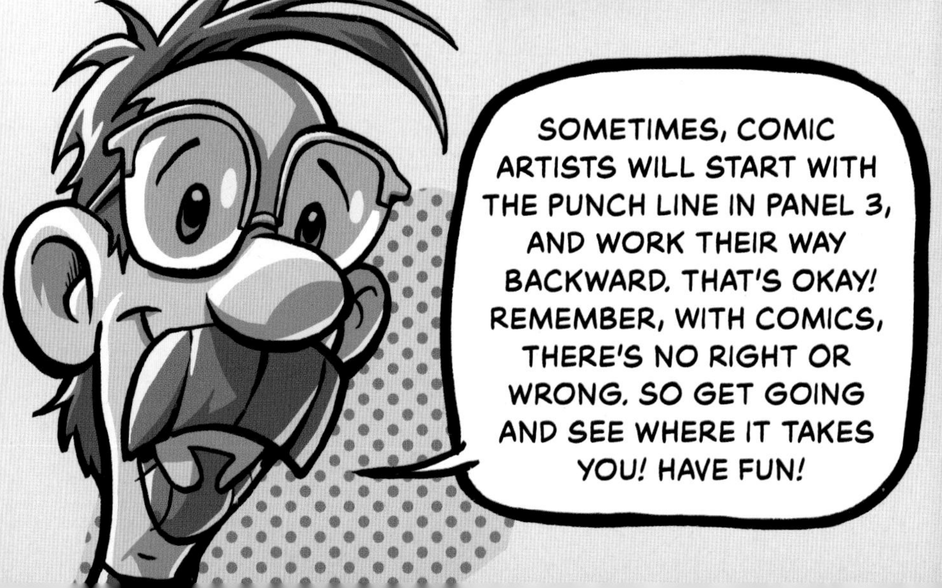
SOMETIMES, COMIC ARTISTS WILL START WITH THE PUNCH LINE IN PANEL 3, AND WORK THEIR WAY BACKWARD. THAT'S OKAY! REMEMBER, WITH COMICS, THERE'S NO RIGHT OR WRONG. SO GET GOING AND SEE WHERE IT TAKES YOU! HAVE FUN!

HOW TO DRAW STEVE L. McEVIL

Grab your pencil and let's draw!

TIPS: A) Follow the steps in order; B) Don't press your pencil down on the paper too hard; C) Make lots of little lines to complete your shapes.

1. Lightly sketch oval.

2. Add two ovals for ears.

3. Begin sketches for hair.

4. Finish hair on top.

5. Add hair line and sideburns.

6. Draw Steve's eyes, nose, mouth, ears, and hair lines.

7. Sketch rectangle for shirt.

8. Add jacket and hands.

9. Draw pants and shoes.

10. Grab a pen and trace over your pencil lines. Once finished, erase the light pencil lines.

HOW TO DRAW DORKUS

Grab your pencil and let's draw!

TIPS: A) Follow the steps in order; B) Don't press your pencil down on the paper too hard; C) Make lots of little lines to complete your shapes.

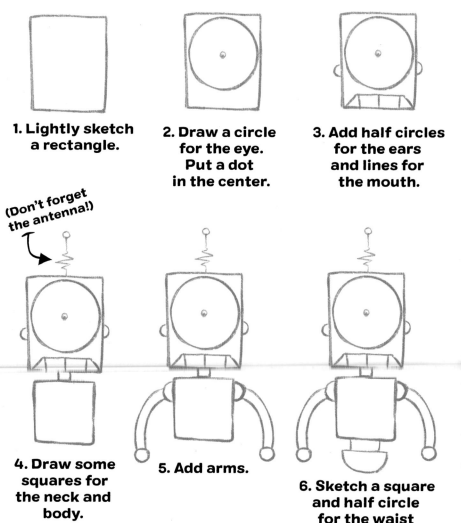

1. Lightly sketch a rectangle.

2. Draw a circle for the eye. Put a dot in the center.

3. Add half circles for the ears and lines for the mouth.

(Don't forget the antenna!)

4. Draw some squares for the neck and body.

5. Add arms.

6. Sketch a square and half circle for the waist and hips.

7. Draw legs.

8. Add claws and feet.

9. Sketch circles on the chest. Add lines on the arms and legs.

10. Trace over your sketch with a pen. Erase the light pencil lines.

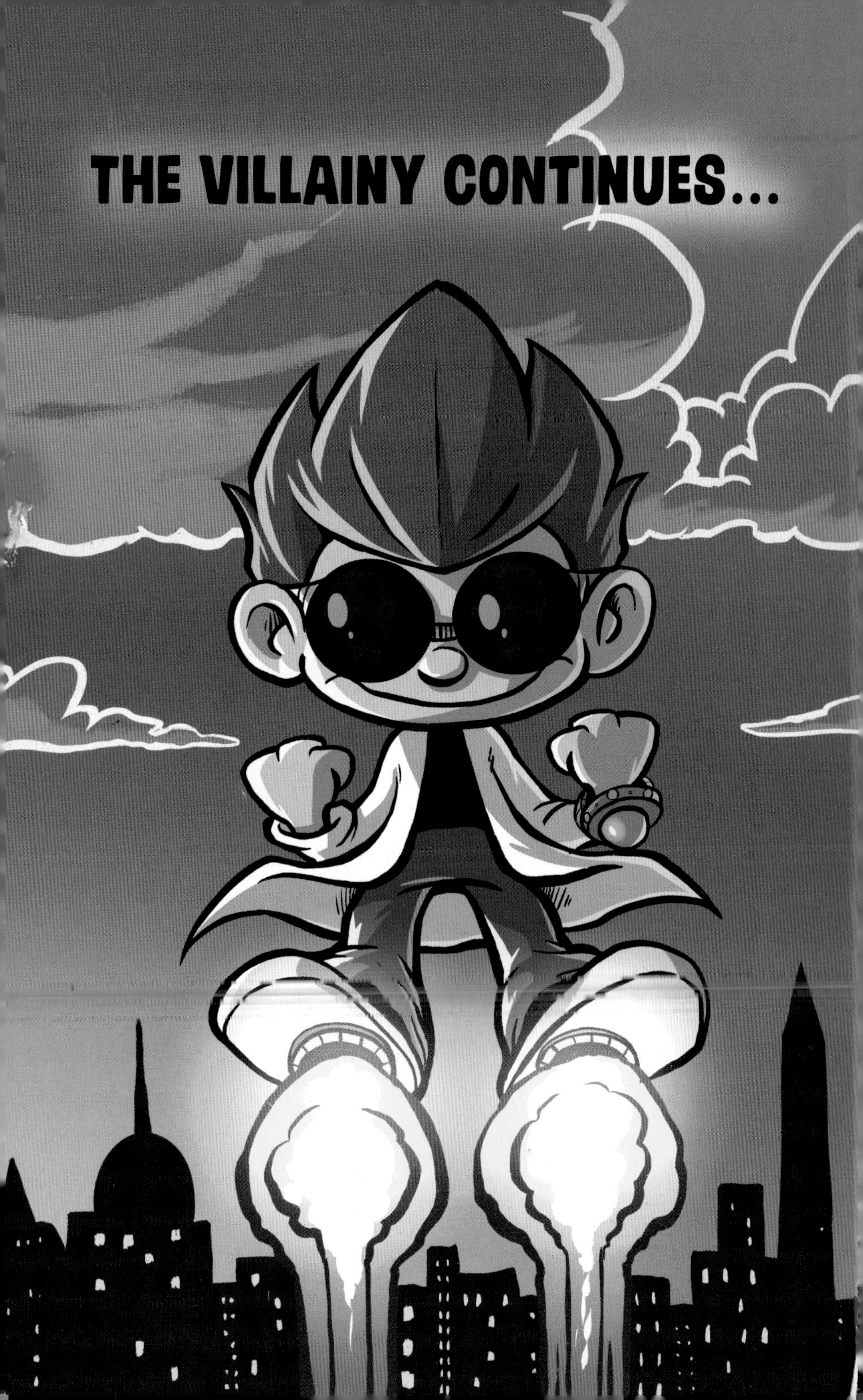
THE VILLAINY CONTINUES...

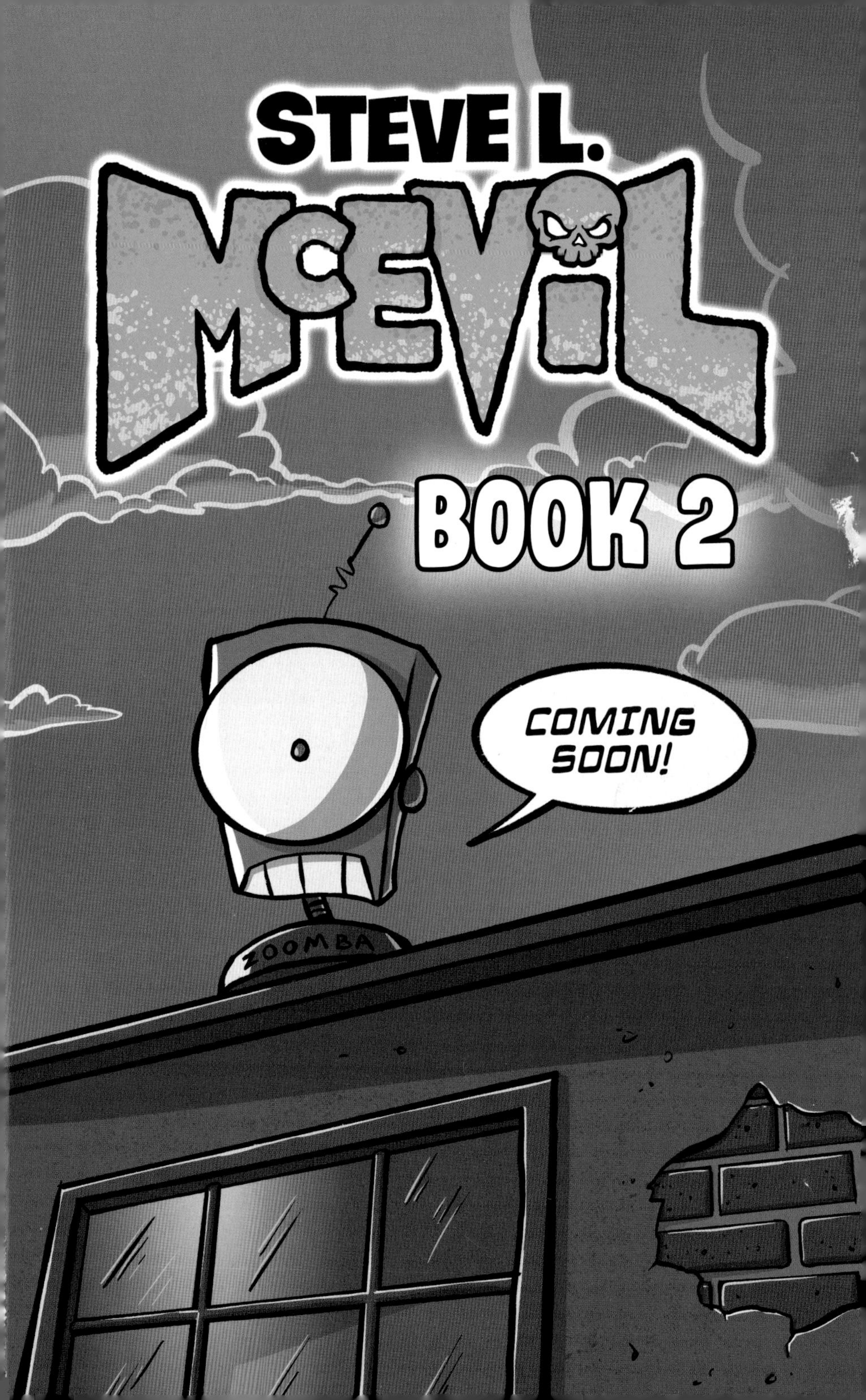
STEVE L.
McEVIL
BOOK 2
COMING SOON!
ZOOMBA

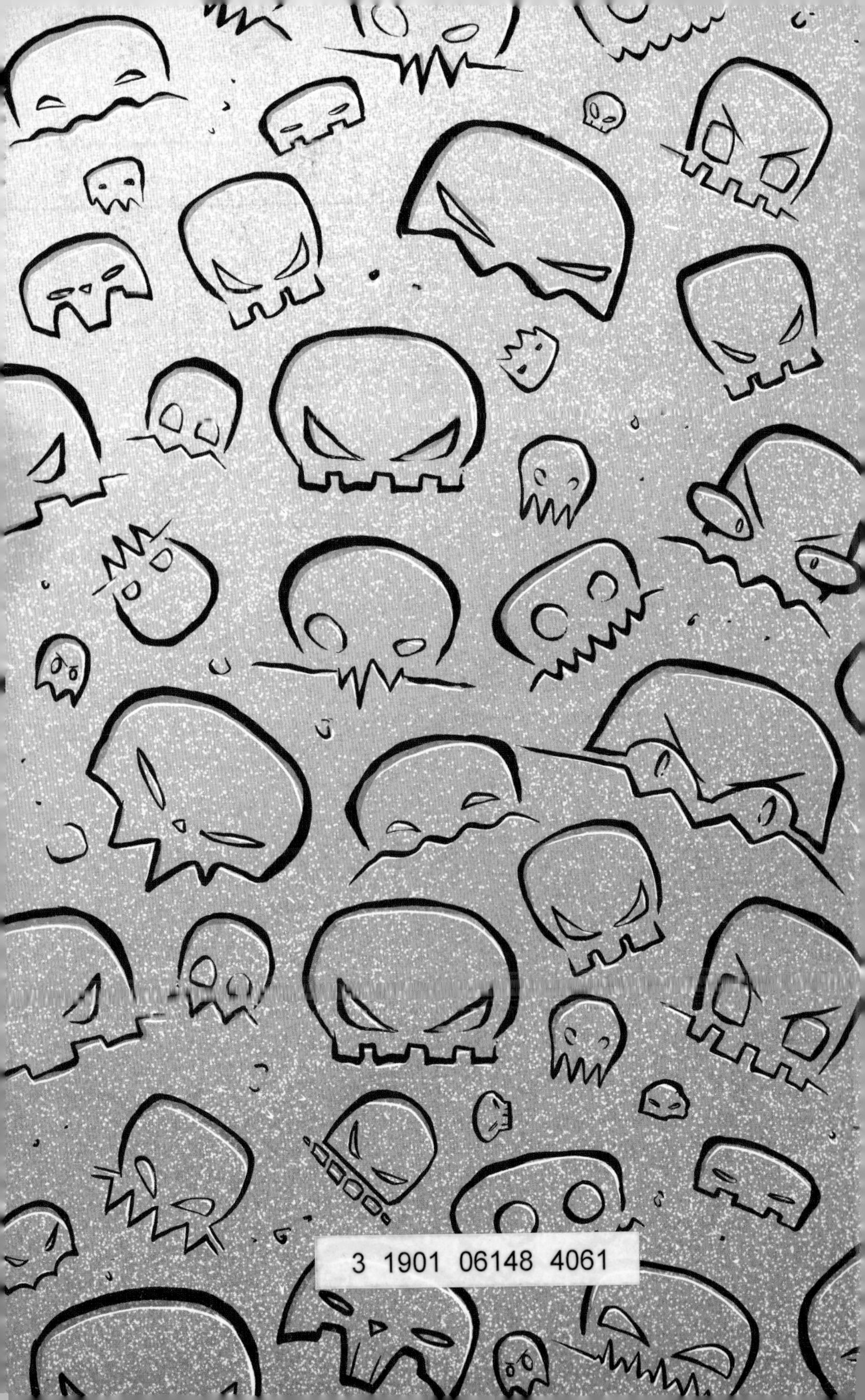